Shadows Of Medusa

Brian Enke

PublishAmerica
Baltimore

© 2004 by Brian Enke
All rights reserved. No part of this book may be reproduced, stored in a retrieval system or transmitted in any form or by any means without the prior written permission of the publishers, except by a reviewer who may quote brief passages in a review to be printed in a newspaper, magazine or journal.

First printing

ISBN: 1-4137-3582-7
PUBLISHED BY PUBLISHAMERICA, LLLP
www.publishamerica.com
Baltimore

Printed in the United States of America

This book is dedicated to the countless legions of brave men and women who have sacrificed their lives throughout history to advance the noble cause of human exploration.
Recently added to this honored list are:
Gus Grissom, Edward White II, and Roger Chaffee (*Apollo 1*)
Dick Scobee, Michael Smith, Judith Resnik, Ellison Onizuka (*Challenger*)
Ronald McNair, Gregory Jarvis, S. Christa McAuliff (*Challenger*)
Rick Husband, William McCool, Michael Anderson (*Columbia*)
Kalpana Chawla, Ilan Ramon, Laurel Clark, David Brown (*Columbia*)
Your dreams will live forever.

AND

To the millions of active volunteers in the
Mars Society,
National Space Society,
Planetary Society,
Red Colony,
Space Frontier Foundation,
Artemis Society International,
…and hundreds of other space advocacy groups around the world.
Your enthusiastic optimism will shape the future.

AND

To my beloved wife Sandy, our family, and our friends.
I couldn't have persevered without your love, patience, and understanding.
How did everyone put up with me during the past two years?

AND

To you, dear reader, as you embark upon your own bold journeys to distant places.

ACKNOWLEDGMENTS

Writing this novel has been a 28-month marathon. So many incredible people have contributed their support and ideas that I hardly know where to begin my most grateful acknowledgments. If you contributed to the novel and I haven't mentioned your name below, please accept my humblest apologies, and let me know so I can update the website!

The website for this novel is http://www.shadowsofmedusa.com. Check that site for the latest, best list of acknowledgments, along with other information about the novel or space exploration in general.

The plot had some rough edges to be smoothed, and my closest ally in this initial process was my good friend Dewey Anderson. Dewey is an excellent engineer with an amazing eye for critical detail. He joyfully punched holes in the plot. When he stopped finding new holes, I knew the plot was ready for prime time.

Next came a daunting list of technical details to be investigated. The following people graciously lent their immense expertise in the various scientific or engineering aspects of a Mars mission: Tony Muscatello (*in situ* benzene production), Bill Clancey (crew psych, tele-robotics, *Mobile Agents*), Gary Fisher (Greenhab), Dennis Creamer (biology), Paul Graham (drilling, mining, geology, Greenhab), Julie Edwards (biology), Jennifer Heldmann (subsurface ice, geology), Scot Rafkin (weather models), Tim Michaels (weather models), Keith Harrison (geology), Bob Grimm (geology), Ron Greeley (geology), Bill Hartmann (geology), Dominic Mazzoni (Pasadena info), Wayne White (laws, treaties), Dan Durda (asteroid missions), David Grinspoon (life, atmosphere, comparative planetology), Gwynne Gurevich (SpaceX BFR-V specs and time frame), Anna Paulson (rovers), Chris McKay (contamination), Bob Zubrin (launch vehicles, *Mars*

Direct, Case for Mars info), Mark Bullock (crops, contamination), Meredith Wills-Davey (solar physics, caller in chapter 29), and Diana Mann (youth motivation, risk tolerance). These are some of the people who can make it all happen, for real!

As the writing proceeded, many wonderful friends emerged and offered their time and support as reviewers. This lengthy list includes Dewey Anderson; Lorraine Bell; Bob Bloomer; Bill Clancey; Frank Crossman; Alisdair Davey; Pat and Carole Dust; Julie Edwards; Dave, Laura, and Sean Enke; Sandy Enke; Alisha Hackerson; Richard Hogen; Shannon Rupert-Robles; Andrea Schweitzer; Karin and Jeff Strong; and Meredith Wills-Davey. These people endured my frequent changes and helped me to forge my extremely rough drafts into something publishable. Sorry about all the lost sleep, Bill!

In addition to everyone mentioned above, the following people helped to inspire and encourage me during the long journey toward a finished novel: David Hicks (writing coach), Bill Hartmann (published sci-fi author), Gary White and Elyn Aviva (Pilgrims Process, published mystery authors), Mark Cohen (Muddy Gap Press, published mystery author), Bob Zubrin (published science/sci-fi author), David Grinspoon (published science author), all my work friends at the Southwest Research Institute (SwRI), and Katie Hartlove (my hard-working editor) and the other helpful publishing experts at PublishAmerica.

Special thanks are accorded to Bill Merline, Clark Chapman, and Alan Stern at SwRI for enabling a challenging work environment with enough stability that I could focus some part-time energy toward writing this novel.

Finally, I would like to acknowledge Paul Davies, a renowned physicist, writer, and broadcaster. Chapter 35 is for you, Paul! The courage in your ideas is an inspiration.

PREFACE

Dear Reader,

For most Americans, September of 2001 conjures images of the 9/11 terrorist attacks. The world was a very different place. The *Columbia* was one of four active space shuttles. Enron and MCI were seldom-noticed corporations. Martha Stewart was the queen of inside (interior décor) information. The SEA was just a vague body of water.

For me, September of 2001 invokes happier images of personal transformation. In a major career change, I began to swim in the turbulent waters of space science research at the Southwest Research Institute in Boulder, Colorado. Following your dreams is often scary, but it can also be exhilarating, enlightening, and liberating. In my case, it was all those things and so much more. After leaving my nice corporate fiefdom at Bell Labs, where I had worked for 17 years as a software/systems expert, I suddenly had a whole new universe to explore—and a whole new lease on life.

Without this career move, I wouldn't have been in the right frame of mind to *receive* the plot of this mystery/sci-fi novel when it whacked me atop the head four months later in January of 2002. I had always been an active volunteer for several non-profit space advocacy groups, including the Mars Society, the National Space Society, and the Planetary Society. I worked on various projects for these groups and assisted however I could, but I wanted to do more, learn more, and make more of a difference. Now my fundamental interest in space exploration had a new, creative outlet.

But where did the plot come from? The seed was germinated much earlier, in the fall of the year 2000, when I volunteered to give a talk about Mars to an engineering club at the University of Colorado. I've given similar talks many times, to all ages of students from first-grade through college, but that night was special. As I was dazzling the graduate students with insightful details about Mars transfer orbits, free-return trajectories, and other egghead technobabble, one of the students asked a question. It was a very simple question, really, but I fumbled for a good answer. The seed had been planted. Over a year later, it bloomed into the plot of a novel and whacked me atop the head, as I mentioned before.

The plot wouldn't let me sleep at night until I wrapped some characters around it and started writing. I took some helpful writing classes and cautiously began to slug through the preparations. Immediately, I encountered a serious credibility problem. I wanted the novel to appeal to a wider "mystery" audience, not just to hardcore sci-fi fans. However, the general public had endured 30 years of not-much-excitement-in-space. I needed to find a way to bridge this apathy. Even worse, I realized that most people would view certain critical plot elements as pure, wild fantasy.

Fortunately, reality came to the rescue. One by one, the more unbelievable aspects of my plot ended up on the front pages of the New York Times. The *Columbia* tragedy smashed the public apathy issue, at least temporarily. Major scandals at Enron and MCI reestablished the precedent of powerful entities maneuvering in secret. China became the third space-faring nation—with possible ambitions of lunar settlement. For the first time in 15 years, an American president proposed an initiative to do something bold in space. Europe and Russia announced Mars mission plans. The SEA (Space Exploration Alliance) was formed, promising some much-needed, long-term political clout for space advocates.

As I hand the manuscript to my publisher in May of 2004, 28 months later, I now realize there's very little hardcore sci-fi left in this novel. Most of it has already become reality, or is at least realistic. So much for my being a great visionary. Oh well.

"But wait!" you might say. "What about the very premise of sending human explorers to Mars? Isn't that the purest of fantasy, too?"

Various scenarios for sending human explorers to Mars have been hashed and rehashed since at least the 1960s. Details have trickled out to the public through Hollywood, sometimes with embarrassing results. I'll summarize the conclusions of at least 40 years of often-heated debate:

"We can do it."

It's possible to send human explorers to Mars using 1970s technology and a 1990s strategy. Most of the respectable debate now centers on issues like cost, risk, and capability. In other words, how much is a government or private entity willing to pay to lower the risk of a mission while still doing something they deem to be useful.

My contribution to this heated debate is merely to suggest that a reasonable mission with highly-focused objectives would be risky, but it would also be extremely cheap...*if wise objectives are chosen!* Do you remember the plot that kept me awake? It sprang from this premise and led to this book.

"But what about that *risk* part?" you ask.

Risk is a four-letter word, at least for most adults today. A human exploration mission to Mars will certainly be risky. But is risk a good thing or a bad thing? And what about that other four-letter word, revealed in Chapter 35—is it far worse?

I should add a standard disclaimer that none of the characters in the novel are based upon real people, living or otherwise. However, oddly enough, the converse of that statement is no longer true. Several real-world people, including AP writer Paul Recer and New Republic editor Gregg Easterbrook, have recently attempted to base themselves upon a character in my novel. In doing so, they've removed another barrier to the plot's believability. I won't go into specifics, but before you've reached Chapter 10, you'll know what I mean. I've included a quotation from Paul Recer below to help you draw the connection. I could say a lot more on this subject, but I had better not.

During your reading, if you encounter any *holes* in the plot, my advice is to think *clues*. Challenge your assumptions. Remember that this is a mystery novel, first and foremost. I wish I could guarantee that all discrepancies are clues, but that's hard to do. However, I have confidence in my reviewers and in the overall simplicity of the plot.

By the way, that last statement was a *clue* too...don't get caught up in the complexity of events in the novel. Search for simple solutions. Skim past the bits of technical detail, if you aren't into that—most aren't needed to solve the various mysteries.

I apologize for leaving the final chapter a bit open-ended. To resolve everything, a sequel will be needed...for reasons that will become obvious when you reach the end. It could have been worse—I was strongly tempted to end the novel after Chapter 34, but kinder thoughts prevailed.

Several people have asked me about references to *time*. I tried to avoid any direct references, since it's possible that a simple mission will be perpetually "five years away" for quite some time to come. Whenever you're reading this, add five years to the current year, and that's when the story takes place.

Of course, it's also possible that a human exploration mission to Mars will happen soon! Many people are working hard to make this incredible dream a reality. By reading this book and opening your mind to new possibilities, you've already helped as well. Thank you! I encourage you to take the next step. Become a member of one of the organizations in the SEA. Several are listed on the Dedications page, or you can check the novel's website for more details (http://www.shadowsofmedusa.com).

Someday, I hope to be quite mortified when my representation of Mars becomes naïvely antiquated. Our knowledge of the vast resources in our solar system is expanding every day, and the revelations should continue for some time to come. A similar fate has befallen several sci-fi classics over the years. Reality always has the last word, and our preconceived notions must continue to adapt. It's all part of the learning process, as humanity grows up. A bit of personal mortification is a small price that I'm most willing to pay to be involved.

I hope you enjoy reading the novel as much as I've enjoyed writing it! Don't forget to check the website for reader forums and links to information about human space exploration.

I'll leave you with some relevant quotations on the next page. Most of these quotations are timeless. If you take nothing else away from this novel, please try to recall some of these words whenever you need a shot of inspiration.

Sincerely,
Brian Enke, Author

"The optimist sees opportunity in every danger;
the pessimist sees danger in every opportunity."
- Sir Winston Churchill

"Death is nothing, but to live defeated and inglorious is to die daily."
- Napoleon Bonaparte

"Your goals, minus your doubts, equal your reality."
- Ralph Marston

"There are those who look at things the way they are,
and ask why…I dream of things that never were,
and ask why not?"
- Robert Kennedy

"Give me a fast ship, for I intend to sail into harm's way."
- John Paul Jones (common paraphrase)

"No firm cost estimates have been developed,
but informal discussions have put the cost of a
Mars expedition at nearly $1 trillion."
- Paul Recer, *Associated Press*, January 9, 2004

"Recer's unnamed sources had completely misinterpreted
the history…When informed of this, Recer paused for several seconds
and finally answered, 'oh well.'"
- Dwayne A. Day, *The Space Review*, March 22, 2004

"If you're going through hell, keep going."
- Sir Winston Churchill

"That's one small step for a man, one giant leap for mankind."
- Neil Armstrong

CHAPTER 1
SPIN

MarsDay 1, 3:50 a.m.
(November 21, 12:16 p.m.)

    As Anna floated through the cloudless blue sky, time lost all meaning. Warm updrafts helped her soar to new heights. All that existed was the warmth above, the lush landscape below, and the gentle breezes between.
    With a sudden rush, she swooped down to the garden, where other bees were playing little games. Anna joined them as they hid behind bushes and chased each other through groves of spindly trees. Bathed in tranquil sunlight, she enjoyed the lazy summer day to its fullest.
    Becoming aware of the fragrant flowers in her dream, she quickly lost interest in the other bees. Tantalizing scents drew her ever closer to the ground. Drunk with heady aromas, she landed on a particularly large sunflower and was surprised when it collapsed under her weight. She fell.
    As she touched the soil beneath, she regained her human form. Her delicate wings were gone. She immediately mourned her loss and longed to soar, dance, and play with her friends in the sky. But she could never return. She was human now—heavy, naked, and alone.
    The other bees noticed her transformation. Their peaceful droning turned deeper and more menacing. An outsider had infiltrated them, and they weren't happy to see her true form revealed.
    With frenzied movements, the swarm grouped and held council. Anna's fate was being decided, and she was powerless to affect the outcome. Fearing

a guilty verdict, she slowly backed away. After a few steps, she turned and ran as fast as her human legs could carry her. Now more than ever, she longed for the freedom her wings had given her.

The bees pursued.

The tranquil sunlight was blotted out by ominous storm clouds. Day instantly morphed into twilight, and bitter cold replaced warmth. Stiff winds bent the trees all about her, yet Anna could feel nothing, and the trailing bees were unhindered.

A dark chasm loomed ahead. From her vantage point, she couldn't tell if it was a five-foot gully or a five hundred foot cliff. The swarm behind left little choice. Her best hope of survival was to proceed onward.

Buzzing filled her ears, but she resisted the urge to look back. Her leg muscles burned as she sprinted the final yards and launched herself into the abyss.

Fortunately, the gully turned out to be of the shallow, five-foot variety, so her flight was a short one. She hit the bottom and rolled in the mud, coming back onto her feet in a graceful, effortless maneuver, never breaking stride. Her human reflexes had returned. Years of gymnastic training during her childhood had allowed her to accomplish this acrobatic maneuver by instinct.

The swarm was not impressed, nor was it inconvenienced by the gully. It closed in on her from behind.

The other side was a gentle, muddy incline. Ooze clamped around her ankles, sucking her feet down and causing her to lose precious seconds as she clambered to reach the top.

She felt a sharp pain in her left shoulder as the first bee reached its objective. More would surely follow.

Beyond the gully was a barren plain. A shiny, modern trailer was parked a few steps to her right. Its open door invited her to rest inside. At last, she had found a place of refuge.

Now that her desperate dash had a goal, the final yards seemed like miles. Jagged rocks hindered her progress, tearing at her vulnerable feet. As she reached the trailer, she felt three more bee stings on her back. Driven by the pain, she leaped inside and slammed the door shut.

The sturdy trailer had no windows or cracks to let in sunlight or bees. The interior was pitch black, but Anna didn't care. A solid, impenetrable shell protected her. That was all that mattered.

Buzzing filled the air outside, louder than ever. Bees began to pound the trailer like hailstones, but they couldn't reach her now. She turned her back upon the sturdy door. As she slumped to the floor against it, her sigh of relief was long and luxurious. She was safe.

After a few moments of rest, she became aware of new dangers. Her bee stings had already swollen into throbbing masses of agony, and she could feel their venom in her blood.

Where is my portable medical kit?

Of course it wasn't here.

She tried rising to her feet, but nausea forced her back onto the icy floor. She shivered, cold, so cold.

The bees continued their assault on the trailer. They pounded at the sides, the roof, even the underside of the floor. An eternity passed, and the pounding became infrequent. The swarm hypnotized her with its buzzing, and she became aware of another sound, a barely audible, wheezing noise. Repeating steadily, it slowly gained in volume, as if it was moving closer.

She recognized the sound as shallow, raspy breathing. A new stab of fear pierced her chest. She knew with dead certainty that she was not alone in the trailer.

Was this newcomer a human or an animal? A friend or a foe?

She had no friends here.

From the darkness, a voice whispered, "You should not be here."

The voice sounded familiar, but she couldn't place it. Her perception of raw danger was heightened. She desperately wanted to escape, but she couldn't move. Her whole body was paralyzed by fear. She couldn't even close her eyes.

The buzzing of the bees grew louder, intermittent, and more demanding. They were calling to her. They were almost inside her head.

Mercifully, a tenuous thread of consciousness wrapped itself around her and began to pull her up from the depths of her nightmare. Anna slowly realized her terrors were only minions of the subconscious world.

Then the thread broke, leaving her trapped in that soft place between dreams and reality. Cold darkness continued to smother her. In an effort to protect herself from the perceived threats around her, she curled herself into a tight ball of fragile humanity.

Her mind continued its upward struggle toward greater levels of consciousness, assisted by the buzzing of an alarm in her ear. She had never been a bee, but she was flying faster than any bee could ever imagine, soaring higher than the warmest draft of air.

The trailer was also an illusion. In reality, her refuge was a tiny space capsule, traveling five kilometers farther away from the Earth every second. She was a human bullet, speeding through a vast void toward an impossibly distant target.

The planet Mars.

She began to wonder about other things.

Why was I sleeping on the floor?

Pondering this simple question provided her with another lifeline, a faster escape from her unpleasant dream world. She recalled yesterday's exciting launch activities, multiple rocket boosts, and breathtaking views of the receding Earth. Later, she had retired to her cabin, hindered by near weightlessness. That was all she could remember.

She must have fallen asleep before hooking the zero-G safety netting around her. At least, the blanket on her bed was slightly crumpled. Hopefully, she had slept under it for part of the evening. Like most of the clothing in her wardrobe closet, the blanket was infused with Demron-4, a material that partially blocked several types of low energy radiation. She reached over, grabbed the blanket, and pulled it tightly around herself.

Gravity now anchored her firmly to the floor. Gravity was a comfort. It was good, it was normal, and it was her best friend. But wait! It wasn't normal at all. Something was wrong—its grip was far too weak.

Ah, yes. Mars gravity: 38 percent of Earth-normal gravity.

The presence of simulated Mars gravity reassured her struggling mind that the next steps of their flight plan were complete. The ship had probably reached its peak velocity of five kilometers per second, relative to Earth, over four hours ago. At that time, the mission plan called for separating the third stage of the rocket from the *Perseus* habitat, her comfortable, pressurized home where she would live for the next six months of spaceflight. A spider's web of strong tethers, hundreds of meters in length, maintained a firm connection between the *Perseus* and the empty fuel tanks of the third stage. Spinning the configuration created artificial gravity.

The last few hours must have been tense ones for her fellow travelers, even though both were skilled engineers who had practiced the spin-up procedures thoroughly ahead of time. In reality, those maneuvers had been performed only once before—on an unmanned test vehicle.

She had slept while the others worked. Since Anna was a biologist, EMT, and a hastily trained doctor, she would have been worse than useless to the engineers during the spin-up procedure. She probably would have gotten in their way and increased their stress level by worrying over every little sound and vibration. In the unlikely event that they had needed a doctor, they would have awakened her.

So all was well in her new world...except her sleeping quarters had an overpowering new car smell, and she kept hearing a light buzzing noise in her ear.

The alarm...they ARE trying to wake me up.

She lurched to her knees and reached for her cabin's computer console, with its adjustable plastic display and micro camera for two-way video communication. Just in time, she recalled her current state of disrobement and disarray. Video would be a bad thing right now.

Fortunately, the tiny receiver in her ear also contained an audio transmitter and microphone. Touching the device activated it, and the buzzing stopped immediately. With her finger in her ear, she whispered, "I'm here."

The microphone should amplify her voice adequately. By whispering, she hoped to avoid waking up Evelyn Day, the commander. If Evelyn was following her schedule to the letter, she should now be asleep in her cabin on the deck below.

Waking up the commander on the first night of their voyage would not be a very smart thing to do. Though the floor of Anna's cabin was a lightweight plastic composite that didn't conduct sound very well, she still didn't want to take any chances.

Anna's mattress was located near the floor, and the mattress in Evelyn's cabin on the deck below was close to the ceiling. This arrangement created some acoustical problems, but it minimized the crew's exposure to radiation while they slept. The volume of the two sleeping areas was surrounded on five sides by several feet of radiation-blocking food and water supplies.

If Evelyn was asleep as planned, her caller had to be Doctor Oliver Sainsbury, the primary geologist and backup engineer. Sure enough, Ollie responded immediately. His thin English accent was diluted by 30 years of living and working with Americans.

"Good morning, Anna!"

Startled, she realized his voice had been in her dream. It was the menacing voice from the darkness.

Oh, great, my next psych session with Kahuna is going to last for 20 years. I'll be old and gray before she is through with me.

"Sorry to page you," continued Ollie, oblivious to Anna's distress. "It's time for your shift to begin. So get your cute bum up here. I need some sleep."

Though she wasn't feeling very social yet, Anna couldn't pass up the opportunity for an easy comeback. "Why Ollie, was that a compliment I just heard? I might start to think you really do notice my anatomy. You're ruining your reputation." Risqué jokes and innuendos had always been safe around Ollie, due to his sexual orientation.

"Oh, I notice many things," he said. "Like I notice Mission Support has sent you some wake-up music to hurry you along. It's a nice choice, too. Someone back on Earth must be proud of you."

"OK, please put it on my ear receiver. I'll be up in a minute. Cheers."

Trying to be as quiet as a mouse, yet also trying not to think about the dreadful possibility of mice living on spaceships, quiet or otherwise, she released the clasp on her wardrobe closet, removed a red t-shirt and shorts, and dressed to the muted sounds of regal music. Back in the 19th century, this beautiful German march had been reserved for the Kaiser. The music from her homeland didn't match her mood, however, so she turned the volume down further.

She wanted to look her best today because her schedule included several video sessions with the news media in America, Brazil, Australia, and Russia. Later, as daylight spread to that part of the Earth, she expected to talk to the media in her native country and elsewhere in the European Union.

Satisfied with her attire, she retrieved one of her two wigs from the closet and fretted over the shoulder-length blond locks. The hairpiece had the same look and texture of her natural hair, most of which had been sacrificed to the barber shears before their final quarantine period. Unfortunately, the wig ends tended to curl up in a familiar, but annoying, manner.

With a whimsical chuckle, she wondered what would happen if she showed up for the media sessions without wearing her hairpiece. Doing so would certainly cause quite a stir back on Earth. The love-struck teenage boys in her audience would probably never recover from the shock.

On the other hand, revealing her ultra-short haircut on television would certainly be more honest. It might also steer the discussion toward some important issues, like water conservation. At some point in the dialogue, she could point out the limitations of their minimal water supply during the outward voyage. People might understand her needing to drink her water allocation rather than washing her hair with it.

In her mind, she started to rehearse her script.

Mention that we intend to find plenty of frozen groundwater a few meters beneath the surface of Mars.

On second thought, perhaps it's best not to say too much about our expectations and assumptions. Reality often has a way of interfering with the best of plans. Don't openly tempt Murphy's Law.

If the groundwater under the surface was unreachable or unusable for some reason, they would have to ration and recycle every drop throughout the entire mission. That was not a pleasant prospect.

While the playful side of Anna still toyed with the idea of going wigless, her practical side refused to even consider the possibility. She was a media personality now, and she had certain obligations. One of those obligations was to be careful about her physical appearance, as much as it might irritate her to do so. Her appearance was a powerful ally in promoting her message.

Minimizing her femininity had always seemed easier and more sensible to her than spending hours tediously painting, combing, and primping. She inspected her 26-year-old face, with its striking features and clear complexion. Her long-deceased mother had never used any makeup, so neither did Anna. Even the thought of being seen on television by a billion people wasn't enough to change her mind. Knowing ahead of time she might be tempted, she didn't bring any cosmetics.

But wait—did she see a wrinkle in the mirror? No, it was just a trick of the dim light. Someday, as her youthful appearance transitioned into middle age, her aversion to cosmetics might change...or perhaps she would die on Mars, wearing the face God gave her.

She looked around the cabin, checking to make sure everything was tidy and clean. Ollie was a neat-freak, and he would soon be sleeping here. Having her own personal quarters during the transit to Mars would have been a great comfort, but the *Perseus* was just too small. She mentally marked off one day, the first of 180 days of sharing the cabin, plus a few extra days once they reached Mars. They would need time to rearrange enough supplies so Ollie could occupy the third sleeping cabin.

With a sigh, she flipped down Ollie's foam sleep pad. At least they wouldn't be sharing the same mattress. She placed her hand beneath Ollie's pad and lovingly rubbed her own mattress, the one she had bought years ago during her freshman year at college and had insisted on bringing to Mars. The NASA-designed foam was ultra-light, ultra-durable, ultra-comfortable, and most important at the time she bought it, ultra-cheap.

Finally ready to interact with the world, she left her cabin and reached for the ladder connecting the three levels of the ship. She called, "Up ladder!" as loudly as she dared, while glancing above and below. Besides the commander's quarters, the lowest level contained an Extravehicular Activity room, or EVA room, where space suits were stored and suitports allowed access to the void outside their vehicle.

Ascending to the upper level brought her into an open crew lounge and kitchen. The rest of her day would probably be spent on this level because the crew lounge also served as their primary media and operations center.

The new car smell wasn't as strong on the upper level of the *Perseus*, and she quickly forgot about it. Light music was playing in the background, a delicate piano piece by Chopin, she reckoned.

She found Ollie sitting on an inflatable chair near the middle of the round room, with his back to the kitchen area. He greeted her again, easing her fears by adding, "All is well. We fixed a few problems last night, but nothing serious. I'm just finishing up my logbook entries now."

Then he returned his attention to the huge organic-diode computer display, which occupied most of the wall space in the lounge. The display contained nearly a billion organic diodes embedded in a flexible plastic polymer. It snugly fit the rounded contours of the outer wall.

During their early training, Anna was always a bit uncomfortable using the main computer. After some practice, however, she had learned to tolerate the powerful system, as well as the oddly curved geometry of the display in the lounge. Flat displays seemed strange now.

Gaining familiarity with the wireless keyboard and infrared pointer device had taken her even longer, but Ollie had always used them like they were extensions of his own body. She watched as he pointed and typed with reckless abandon.

She returned Ollie's greeting with warmth she didn't feel yet. Then she entered the small kitchen area, hoping a cup of strong tea would give her the extra jolt she needed this morning.

When he asked how she had slept, she waffled, replying that their cabin was quiet and comfortable. Ollie deserved the prospect of a good night's sleep. By now, he had been awake for nearly 30 hours. The crew's rigid duty schedule required someone to be awake at all times. Since too many critical engineering tasks were crammed into the first 30 hours of the mission, Ollie and the commander had both been working overtime.

She chose not to mention her nightmare, especially since his voice had played such an integral role. Under the ever-watchful eyes of the psych team, some things were best left unrevealed.

Ollie scowled. "Our overly compassionate commander has tweaked tomorrow's schedule to give me a few hours of extra sleep. How kind of her."

"She changed the schedule? What did Mission Support say?" Such an arbitrary change, on the first day of the mission, was surprising. Perhaps the commander was making a statement about crew autonomy.

Ollie waved his hand. "Who knows?"

During their two years of earnest training, Commander Day had often been strict and demanding, but was usually fair in her assignments and judgements. On this mission, it would be her way or the highway. Anna could tolerate that. If she had any serious issues with the commander's style, the support psychologists would have left Anna grounded back on Earth.

Still, she really did like Evelyn as a person, and Ollie's remark had sounded almost like an open criticism. It didn't sit right with her. She recalled a training course in basic human psychology emphasizing the importance of showing respect to the commander. Ollie had attended the same training, yet he continued to make subtle remarks about the commander behind her back. Anna didn't understand why the psychologists allowed this behavior, not that they could do much about it now. Perhaps they weren't even aware of it.

Though it would be challenging at times, they needed to make every effort to get along with each other. Avoiding either of her companions during their mission was simply not an option, even if it made sense to do so. The three decks of the *Perseus*, each with only a ten-foot radius, contained less than 1,000 square feet of total living space, the size of a small apartment on Earth. Almost half the floor space was currently taken up by equipment and supply storage. After a few months of being cooped up together, their meager living space would undoubtedly seem even smaller. That was a frightening prospect.

Since Evelyn was asleep, Ollie was her only subject of study. From where she stood in the kitchen, she noticed his posture was unusually slumped, as if the weight of the world was on his shoulders. Minor psych issues aside, he was usually very proper in his bearing and mannerisms, the living stereotype of an academic Englishman. His attitude was normally much more cheerful, too.

"Are you doing OK, Ollie?" she asked.

"Fine. Tired, is all. I haven't pulled an all-nighter since Libya in '04."

Ollie rarely talked about his personal background, except for occasional references to the exotic places he had visited. When Anna reached the age of 54, nearly 30 years from now, would she have similar tales to tell? Certainly, Mars would be the experience of a lifetime. Yet Ollie's 5'8" athletic body already emanated lifetimes of experience. He just seemed to have a natural way of doing things, of making difficult tasks seem trivial. Despite her own athletic prowess, she always felt clumsy and inept around him.

Putting some of her thoughts into words, she said, "Ollie, I'm really looking forward to seeing Mars through your eyes. I hope you'll be patient with my naïveté."

"Yes, well, nature reveals its secrets slowly, so a good geologist learns to be patient. As does a good engineer, though most of the blokes in that profession haven't figured that out yet."

Anna forgave his mild arrogance. She recalled an old quote from an egotistical baseball player: "It ain't braggin' if you can back it up." Ollie could certainly back up his confident words. His geology and engineering skills were top notch. He seemed equally adept with hardware and software engineering, as was the commander. The two of them appeared to get along well in their working relationship.

"I doubt whether Irena would have been very patient with me." Anna instantly regretted making this comment. Old wounds were better left closed.

Despite his mountains of experience in terrestrial geology, Ollie was a relative newcomer to the whole Mars exploration effort. During most of their lengthy training interval, he had been the backup geologist. A Russian woman named Irena Groskoya, a renowned expert in Martian geologic processes, had filled the top spot. Irena was also a capable engineer and a fully trained medical doctor.

Anna recalled her pre-Ollie days of training with some nostalgia, but mostly with regret, and ultimately, shame. She and Irena had not gotten along very well. Irena was an idealist with a major Messiah complex. She firmly believed exploring Mars would "help to save mankind from itself, while restoring the glory of Mother Russia."

During the various training exercises, Irena's attitude had been a constant source of stressful conflict. While Anna usually held her tongue, Evelyn often did not, which led to some fierce arguments. Since Anna's potential crewmates both had very strong personalities, perhaps conflict was inevitable. Anna sometimes tried to mediate, but more often, she just stayed out of the way. Drawing inward was her nature.

Six months ago, the situation changed abruptly. While scaling cliffs with the other geologist candidates at Zion National Park in Utah, Irena's line broke, and she plunged a thousand feet to the valley floor below. The dreadful accident was followed by a tear-filled funeral and the onslaught of Anna's own regrets.

She knew her own personality better than anyone. After losing most of her family at an early age, she tended to distance herself from others and avoid conflict. How much of her inability to bond with Irena had been her own fault? Now that Irena was dead, how could Anna ever resolve her own feelings of remorse?

Ollie said, "No, she wouldn't."

At first, Anna couldn't follow his comment. Lost in her painful memories, she couldn't recall her initial comment about patience. Then she remembered and felt a new wave of regret.

As if sensing her mood, Ollie added, "Irena probably wouldn't have made the final psychology cut, anyway. She would have been watching this mission from back on Earth. Forget about her, and what might have been. Focus on what is."

"I'll try."

Ollie's little tidbits of wisdom were often harshly pointed, but helpful. After Irena's accident, he had stepped onto the mission team like he had been there right from the start. As a geologist and an active environmentalist, he had gone through tougher training and lived in worse conditions quite often during his thirty-some years of active fieldwork. He described his journeys in vivid detail; trips to places Anna didn't even know existed.

Soon, they would have a whole planet to explore together.

Perhaps due to her irresolvable issues with Irena, Anna had made a stronger effort to befriend Ollie, superficially at least. Though Ollie acted like a loving uncle toward her, she could never be completely at ease with him. She could never be completely at ease with anyone. Her inner walls were too high and thick.

Refocusing her thoughts upon safer subjects, Anna unsealed an insulated porthole cover in the kitchen and gazed outside. Stargazing was one of her favorite activities, but the stars never looked like this back on Earth! Their multicolored brilliance overwhelmed her, and their crazy spinning motions, due to the movement of the *Perseus*, made her instantly nauseous. She closed the cover quickly.

Ugh. I'll have to work up to that more slowly. I'm not spending six months in space without enjoying the awesome view outside!

While her stomach was recovering, Ollie rose to his feet. He placed his keyboard and pointing device onto a small shelf near the video display. "All done," he announced with a sigh of relief. "I'll see you when I wake, love, in about 80 hours or so..."

Anna laughed. "Sleep loose, Ollie."

He moved to the ladder and methodically, rung by rung, descended toward the deck below. His movements didn't seem to benefit from the lighter gravity.

Just as his shoulders disappeared from sight, the lounge lights dimmed and a klaxon sounded. The ship's main computer spoke in a loud, monotone voice over the intercom: "Alert! Alert! Cabin pressure is dropping! Alert! Alert!"

Anna was frozen by surprise. She watched Ollie pivot on the ladder to face her. In a rare moment of sleep-deprived hesitation, his body seemed unsure of itself.

As the message repeated, leak-seeking balloons noisily inflated from the ceiling. The combination was a one-two punch felt deep in her gut. Something was terribly wrong, and she needed to act. Yet even the balloons hovered indecisively, mocking her inertia.

Recovering first, Ollie shouted, "To the EVA room! Now!" Then he turned and descended the ladder without waiting to see if she would follow.

Leaping in two strides across the small room, she reached the ladder and dropped rapidly, checking her speed by hitting every third rung with both feet. If the ship was losing air pressure, every moment was critical. They needed to reach the Extra-Vehicular Activity room on the lowest level, the place where the pressure suits were stored.

She imagined the hiss of their precious air supply as it escaped into the void, never to return. Indeed, the air pressure in the *Perseus* did seem to be dropping, slowly, but noticeably. Her ears popped.

This can't be happening, not on our very first day!

Reaching the EVA room, Ollie helped her close the pressurized hatch sealing the room from the rest of the ship. The hatch allowed the entire room to be used as an airlock, but the door closed inward, so the pressure seal was on the wrong side.

She prayed for the seal to hold. Even if the rest of the ship depressurized, they might be safe for the next few minutes…unless the air leak was in the EVA room, of course.

Unfortunately, most of the EVA room was being used as a storage area for supplies. They fumbled their way around some boxes to the pressure suit storage area along the inner wall. From a shelf labeled "Ollie," she grabbed the lower part of a Honeywell mechanical counter-pressure suit, a lightweight, elastic leotard with a dense polyurethane membrane.

Ollie hastily stripped down to his underwear, and Anna helped him put on the durable two-piece leotard. They had each practiced donning the counter-pressure suits alone, dozens of times, but it always seemed to work much faster with a second pair of hands to help. The zipper around the waist was especially tricky to seal alone. Since the suits were custom fitted for each wearer, putting them on was always a tight squeeze. This time, the process took longer than it should have. They both seemed to be all thumbs.

The elaborate "neck dam" component was stored on the same shelf. Anna reached for it, but paused.

"Where's Evelyn?" she asked.

"She's probably trying to locate the leak."

"But did you see her? If she had left her quarters, we should have come right past her!" Images flashed through her mind of the commander on the other side of the pressurized door, struggling to find the air leak, gasping for air, and finally collapsing to the floor.

She activated an intercom outlet near the doorway. "Commander Day, please respond. Evelyn!"

No response. They listened to silence for several moments.

"We've got to help her. I'm going back out there." She reached for the large, circular handle on the door, and Ollie roughly pulled her back.

"No! If you open that door, you'll depressurize the EVA room. We've got to put our suits on first."

Her head felt like it was floating above her body, unattached. After a few moments, the logic of his reasoning became obvious to her.

She grabbed the neck dam and clipped it over the neckline of Ollie's suit. Then she helped him lift an integrated bubble helmet, respiration unit over his head and shoulders. The bubble locked into the neck dam, providing an airtight seal.

The next step of the procedure was to connect an oxygen cylinder to the respiration unit. Suddenly weak, it took all her strength to lift a canister and snap it into place.

The final step was to verify the suit subsystems were working properly. A tiny computer in the neck dam would verify this, but she couldn't quite remember where the test button was located.

Why can't I concentrate? Of course! Not enough oxygen in the room!

Finally, she found the test button, and the neck dam displayed green lights for each major subsystem. She gave him a weak "thumbs-up" signal. Though the mechanical counter-pressure suits had never been intended for operation in a pure vacuum, Ollie should be protected for at least 30 minutes.

Now it was time to repeat the entire process, for Anna. The room was spinning madly about her, yet she felt happy and content as she slumped to the floor. All was well. Far off in the distance, someone was shouting at her, telling her to get up, trying to pull her shirt over her head.

Who is that rude person, and why is he yelling at me?

She didn't care. She was floating in a tranquil sky. Not even the distant sounds of thunder could disturb her peace. She vaguely remembered something important needing to be done. Whatever it was, she would sleep first and do it later.

CHAPTER 2
RELATIVITY

MarsDay 1, 4:47a.m.
(November 21, 1:15 p.m.)

    Brutally cold Colorado winds roared into downtown Boulder off the Flatirons mountain range. Winter was officially still a month away, and the frigid air knifed through many unprepared pedestrians on the outdoor Pearl Street mall, driving them indoors. The BookEnd Café, cozily attached to the Boulder Bookstore, was a warm haven for some.
    In addition to seeking warmth, David Debacco and his two out-of-town guests were inside the BookEnd because they had actually planned to meet there. His sister Cassie frequented the café, back when she lived in Boulder. Now that she had returned for a brief visit with her husband Ben, the BookEnd had seemed like the right place to meet for a quick coffee.
    They ordered warm drinks from the bar. By the time their order was filled, so too were all the indoor tables. Cassie gestured toward a small seating area outside, as if to prove that a year of married life in southern California hadn't thinned her blood.
    Her suggestion drew a skeptical look from Ben, but no objection. Ben was a California native who probably didn't even own a heavy coat. His trendy sweater and light jacket would be no match for the elements today.
    "Why don't we just take our drinks back to my place?" asked David, eyeing the plastic grocery bag that Ben held. His guests had insisted upon preparing him an Italian meal this afternoon, so they would be going back to

his apartment soon, anyway. On the way to meet him, they must have picked up some supplies at a local supermarket.

"I wanted to have a little *chat* with you here, first," replied Cassie. Her tone of voice implied the matter was not open to negotiation.

David sighed, and gave in to his sister's wishes, recalling too late that the BookEnd wasn't just an ordinary meeting place. It had also been their special place for airing weighty, difficult matters. Cassie seemed moody today, almost as if she was upset at him. She was always anxious or upset about something. Apparently, she would feel more comfortable talking about it, whatever it was, in these familiar surroundings.

He and his little sister had always been very close, and he could read her moods well. Now that she lived a thousand miles away, they talked less frequently, but he still felt the same emotional bonds. He still regarded her as one of his closest friends, confidantes, and supporters. In fact, she was the only member of his family he could really talk to.

Meeting her at the BookEnd brought back a lot of memories. Some were painful, while others were joyous, like the time she told him about her engagement to Ben. They were sitting at the square table against the faux-brick-over-real-brick wall, just over there. He would never forget the contented glow on her face as long as he lived.

As they maneuvered through the crowded tables toward the outside seating area, he noticed that his sister still possessed her graceful stride. She might have lost a few pounds since he had seen her last, not that she had much to lose. As a psychologist, Cassie was usually a pillar of strength and confidence for her clients and friends. However, her own self-esteem seemed to falter at times. She was always on some fad diet or another.

Wincing at his own hypocrisy, David considered whether he should go on a diet, too. Since the passing of his 30th birthday two years ago, his body had started to slow down. He had gained ten pounds over the past three months alone, hardly a cause for alarm, yet an uncomfortable trend. Too much pizza was probably the main culprit, amplified by the inevitable approach of middle age. He still exercised strenuously when he could, but his regular sessions had dwindled down to once a week. His waistline had grown half an inch, and his weight now topped 230 pounds. Fortunately, most of his mass was still muscle, and his 6'3" frame gave him plenty of room to spread any flab around.

Once outside, he discovered the wind had died down a bit. Diffuse sunlight bathed the north side of Pearl Street, making the conditions almost pleasant. Icicles hung from awnings and from the trees in the middle of the mall, reflecting the dim light in complex, sparkling patterns.

Ben chose a table, placed the groceries beneath, and held a chair for his wife. David took a seat across from them. Made of a strong metallic mesh, the chairs and table were freezing cold to his touch. At least they were free of snow.

David studied the happy couple before him. Both were fit and energetic, but his six-foot tall sister towered over her husband by about six inches and fifty pounds. For some reason, they contrasted more than usual today, perhaps because Ben wasn't wearing a heavy coat.

Ben, an engineer at NASA, was a lanky, perpetual whirlwind of motion. His protruding nose, light complexion, and piercing blue eyes gave him an intense appearance, quite handsome in its uniqueness. Cassie's hair and features were darker, more like his own, though softer and rounded in all the right places. She couldn't match David's bulk, nor would she want to, but she shared his laughing green eyes and impish nature.

Cassie was silent, evidently still contemplating some deep matter, but Ben seemed quite cheerful today. He happily engaged David in some shop talk, while a group of shivering shoppers lurched by. They kept their voices lowered.

"So, David, it must be quite a challenge to run Mission Support for the Mars mission. How do you like your new job as a terrorist?"

David laughed. Ben and Cassie both knew about his position within the ultra-secretive Mars movement. He had only held the job for six months, and as far as he was aware, no other outsiders even suspected his involvement.

"Me, a terrorist? Very funny."

Though he was sure that Ben was only teasing, David would be the first to agree that his team used methods pioneered by terrorists to keep their identities hidden. Maintaining a large, secret organization wasn't easy within this day and age, when individual liberties and personal rights to privacy were under attack from all directions. Yet ever-larger terrorist movements proliferated by using untraceable communications technology and carefully woven organizational cells to bypass the watchful eye of governments and the media. These techniques had worked for David's team, too. So far, they had eluded detection.

He looked around, making sure the shoppers had moved on. "The time commitment has definitely cut into my social life, not that there was very much to cut into."

Ignoring a grunt from Cassie, he continued. "It was even hard for me to get away and meet you this afternoon, though I do have some good helpers who watch the shop while I'm away. Still, despite the busy work schedule, this job is exactly what I need right now. It's a good, meaningful job. It even pays well for a change."

This was another old topic. David had often bemoaned the lack of jobs within his chosen fields of interest. Though he had earned dual PhDs in history and philosophy, his degrees were of marginal use outside the world of academia. Since completing his second degree, he had moved from one temporary contract position to the next without finding work he could feel passionate about. Until now.

"Not to mention, it's a very *responsible* job," commented Ben.

"Yeah, finally."

Ben seemed to be intentionally pushing all of David's hot buttons today. David often railed against the general lack of responsibility within society, while seething at his own inability to stand out from the crowd. People never took responsibility for anything. Yet these same people would look down upon him, perceiving his inability to find a nine-to-five job as a sign of irresponsibility. The world was upside down.

"Your parents would be happy to learn of your new job. Too bad you can't tell them about it."

With that comment, Ben had crossed the line. He knew all about David's stormy relationship with his parents, who constantly pressured him to give up his dreams and aspirations in order to conform to their own ideals of employment safety and security. David scowled at his brother-in-law across the table. He forced himself to relax by taking some deep, calming breaths.

"If my parents knew about my job, the local newspaper back in Northfield, Minnesota, would know all about it two minutes later."

"Would that be such a bad thing?"

"You know it would. All this job secrecy is a real pain, but it beats the alternatives. My new work requires constant attention, and quite often, I'm just totally swamped."

"So?" asked Ben, leading him on.

"So, the last thing I want right now is a bunch of reporters snooping around, doing their best to get in the way...not to mention wacko psychopaths, industrial spies, hackers, and whomever else is out there. Even the sympathy of well-wishers would probably smother me right now."

"But that's not the real reason for all the secrecy, is it?"

"No, probably not."

The conversation lapsed into silence. Thinking about his parents had really soured David's mood. To keep his self-esteem intact, he visited them rarely. Separation was best for everyone, in the short-term, though he hoped the relationship would improve over time. After all, he did have a good job now, one he thoroughly enjoyed, believed in, and alas, couldn't reveal.

Ben and Cassie were his family now. Despite living so far away, they filled a void in his life. They had even been the people who convinced him to apply for the Mars job, after Ben heard about it through the underground at NASA.

"You know, Ben," said David, "I'm not sure if I ever told you how surprised I was to receive the phone call from the SEA employment committee." SEA, the Space Exploration Alliance, was the public, non-profit organization "running" the current mission to Mars, as far as the public was concerned.

"Why so surprised? I told you right from the start that you had a lock on the job."

"You know I've always had a deep interest in space exploration, but I wasn't even a member of their society. I always intended to join, but I just kept putting it off, leaving it to other people to keep the dream alive. When I applied for the job, I just assumed they would choose one of their most loyal members. At least I followed the progress of their simulated missions over the Internet, whenever I had time. Maybe that counted for something."

"They made a good choice," growled Ben. "They couldn't ask for anyone more creative or energetic, and with your education to boot. If I were in their shoes, I'd pick someone with a fresh perspective and no baggage, too."

"That's hard for me to accept. The SEA people couldn't have known much about me ahead of time. My past job experience hasn't been stellar. Surely there were more qualified people available. So why was I chosen?"

"Is that a rhetorical question?" asked Ben.

"No. I would really like to know. This question keeps me awake at night."

Ben sipped his espresso and leaned back in his chair. After a few moments, he said, "As I see it, you do have some other qualifications. But I have nothing to do with SEA, so I'm completely guessing here."

"What other qualifications?"

"I hope you take this the right way."

David muttered, "Will you hurry up and spit it out? Why am I so qualified?"

"Because you're a faceless nobody."

David hesitated, surprised, and more than a little dismayed. That wasn't one of the answers he was expecting.

"I'm a faceless nobody? Don't mince words. What do you *really* think?"

Ben stifled a laugh. "I meant it in the best possible way. Look at yourself in the mirror, my friend. Socially, you're a loner. You have no spouse or steady girlfriend. Until six months ago, you had no job of consequence. Yet you're extremely intelligent, capable, and idealistic. You're a classic example of someone who would be recruited by a terrorist organization. They gave you a purpose, and then sent you off in the right direction, a direction of their own choosing. When you left normal society, nobody missed you."

"I'm not sure I like what I'm hearing. Are you really serious? What about my friends? Wouldn't they miss me?"

"You do have many friends," agreed Ben. "But casual friends are easy to fool. Don't you think that terrorists have friends?"

"I guess I never thought about it."

"Well, think about it! And compare your situation to that of other capable people, like me, for example. Maybe I could be a good Director of Mission Support, or maybe not. It doesn't matter. If I were to drop out of society suddenly, my colleagues at NASA would become suspicious. Word would get around. Cassie would be a 'loose end,' too. Also, my salary demands would be higher."

"You think salary has something to do with it?" David was starting to regret his insistence that Ben be so open about his thoughts.

Ben leaned forward and put his elbows on the table, staring David squarely in the eyes. "Look, I don't know how much you're being paid, but I guarantee it's a tiny fraction of what an experienced, senior management executive would demand. You're cheap, David. Cheap and expendable. Why would they pay someone ten times more when you can do the job just as well?"

David pondered Ben's analysis, searching for flaws. Usually, his job was fairly simple, though it took a lot of time and energy. He was a central point of contact, someone to make high-level decisions, interface with the SEA steering committee, and act swiftly if an emergency situation arose. Perhaps fanaticism, disguised as total personal commitment and availability, really was the most essential qualification he brought to the job.

Still, he desperately wanted to believe that he contributed a lot more to the mission. Mankind's first manned attempt to explore Mars had major historical and ethical ramifications. Wouldn't the SEA value someone with a strong background in history and philosophy? Sure, his technical knowledge was weak. But were his areas of strength merely a coincidence?

During the training process, he had quickly come to view his lack of technical experience as only a minor liability. The Director's position was not a technical job. He operated more like a shepherd, keeping watch over the flock of local support wizards. Others on his support team, real engineers, knew their systems intimately. The Director's main function was to address mundane, Earthly issues that the techies couldn't be bothered with.

"I'll need some time to think about what you've said, Ben. And I do appreciate your honesty. If you're right, and that's the main reason I was chosen, I'll be real disappointed. But in the end, their opinion is irrelevant to me. I'm still going to do the best job I can. Three lives are at stake, and history is hanging in the balance."

"That's my David!" Ben said, enthusiastically. "Nothing knocks you down for long. That's probably another good qualification you bring to the job."

"Yeah, it's hard to knock down a nobody. A faceless nobody."

"So now it's your turn to be open and honest, David." Ben took another sip of espresso. "After six months on the job, you must have heard some things on the inside. What's the real story? Why all the secrecy within your organization?"

"That's another question keeping me up at night, frequently." Even if David wanted to reveal the reasons for the shroud of secrecy surrounding his Mission Support team, the sponsors, and the planners of the Mars mission, he couldn't. He didn't know the reasons.

Ben was persistent, however. "You said earlier that you don't want any personal attention. I doubt the people who *really* hired you care much about that. The SEA is just a loose collection of dreamers and technomages with the expertise to put the Mars mission together. If they had any real money or power, they would have done it years ago. Who's calling the shots behind the scenes? Who's paying for the mission? Why don't they reveal themselves to the public?"

"I don't know. I don't even know who sends me my paycheck. It comes from some weird company in Colorado Springs that I've never even heard of."

"And I'll bet my next paycheck that the company doesn't even exist," said Ben. "Media hounds have been trying to track down the mission planners and financiers for months, without any luck. So you don't know who they are, either?"

"No clue. My support team is secretive, but the actual mission planners and financiers are downright paranoid! In fact, there's even a clause in my contract clearly stating that my job will be terminated if the media learns of my position. I believe that's true for most of my colleagues, too. Even the best technical experts."

"Amazing. You're right—that's downright paranoid."

"Totally. All I do know is that I'm going to be real careful. Like I said, I need this job, and I *want* this job. This is probably the first truly important thing I've done in my entire life!"

Realizing he had raised his voice a bit too far, David looked around. The street was still deserted.

"Careful, huh?" Ben seemed to be quite disappointed. "So you *can't* tell me anything? Or you *won't*?"

"Well, there is one little thing I've overheard," said David, after a moment of thought. "You have to promise not to spread it around, though."

"Of course," said Ben, eagerly.

"Most funding secrets are closely guarded, but on two separate occasions, I've overheard some SEA steering committee members talking about the cost of the mission. Both times, they referred to a billion dollar budget."

"That's all? No way!" Ben glanced around. Lowering his voice, he added, "Just building the rocket would cost more than that. Are you sure they weren't off by a digit or three?"

"You mean, a *trillion* dollars? Get real."

Ben lifted his eyes upward, toward the dreary sky, and smiled. "Yeah, only lazy AP reporters would be stupid enough to believe a number like that."

He was obviously referring to a scandal years ago when an Associated Press reporter had invented a fictitious trillion dollar cost estimate for a soon-to-be-proposed NASA plan to explore the Moon and Mars. The ridiculous figure acquired a life of its own, as it circulated widely throughout the media. Even to this day, media mega-networks like USNN still quoted the figure often.

"They said a *billion*. Again, I heard the same figure twice, from different people."

A strange look crossed Ben's face. It was quickly replaced by a soft laugh. "Look, trust me on this. Whoever's spreading that figure is as crazy as that AP reporter. Don't listen to them."

Cassie interrupted the conversation. "This is all interesting, but I would like a few words with my brother about another matter." As she spoke, a melodramatic gust of wind whipped through her hair. She blasted David with a frosty stare matching their surroundings.

Uh oh, here it comes, the real reason why we're sitting out here freezing our butts off.

David stirred his remaining coffee with a spoon, even though he always drank it black. He shifted his weight in his chair and looked out onto the frozen street again. None of these things made him invisible, however, which was what he needed the most. He slumped a bit in his seat, but that didn't work either.

If Cassie noticed his discomfort, she gave no indication. "You know, I really admire your dating technique, David. What did you say to my friend last night to send her home practically in tears?"

So that's what this was all about. The farcical events at the Mars launch party came flooding back to him. Since Boeing SeaLaunch ground controllers were subcontracted to perform the actual launch, David had taken a few hours off to enjoy a celebration on the University of Colorado campus as an anonymous member of the public.

Thinly disguising her attempt to set him up on a blind date, Cassie had invited Stacy Weaver, an old college classmate, to attend the party with them. At least 10,000 other people, mostly students, had shown up to celebrate the Mars launch, too. The place was a jungle of happy confusion. He and Stacy were soon separated from Ben and Cassie. They had found a quiet place to sit and talk, but after that, things went downhill quickly. Stacy left, and David enjoyed the rest of the evening, solo.

Perhaps he and Stacy weren't alone last night after all. Cassie always seemed to have an uncanny psychic ability to monitor relationships, especially when David's social life was involved. Her observational talents probably served her well in her blossoming psychology career.

David put on his best "I'm hurt" face. "Is that the only reason you wanted to meet this afternoon? Just to talk about her? What about the party last night? Wasn't it great?"

"Don't change the subject!"

Obviously, feeble attempts to distract his sister were not going to work. Cassie could also be extremely persistent—a focused, unstoppable force.

He didn't want to spend the last day of her visit arguing with her, but conflict appeared to be inevitable. The only way to halt an unstoppable force was to become an immovable object, something he was not very good at. He liked to consider himself to be a flexible tree, one that would bend with the wind, but would always remain firmly anchored to its roots.

Unfortunately, if a freight train were to jump its tracks and hit a tree, the tree would lose every time.

"Look, Cassie, I do appreciate your attempt to set me up on a date." David reached across the table to take her hand. "I know you did it because you care about me, and I'm touched. Really. But next time, please don't bother. I'm happy by myself, for now." He emphasized his statement with a squeeze of her hand, just before Cassie yanked it away.

"So you're content to just crawl into a hole and disappear. What kind of a life is that?"

As if to help make her point, David sank even lower in his seat. "Ben said it well, earlier. Relationships are loose ends. I can't let myself be distracted from my new job right now, especially by someone with no long-term vision."

He should have scored some points with this line of reasoning. His sister knew the importance of his job, and she fully supported the Mars mission. In fact, David had recently convinced her to volunteer her services on the mission's psychology subteam. He knew he should have left out the last part about "no long-term vision," but he couldn't resist. It was true, and he admired truth in all things.

Cassie frowned and looked down into her cup of hot chocolate. David could detect an almost physical transformation in her. She was shifting into her psychoanalytical persona.

This was bad. He would rather have faced her wrath directly. As a freight train, she would simply run over him. As a skilled psychologist, she had the ability to uproot him first and then run over him.

"David, just because someone doesn't share your view of the world doesn't mean you should shut them out of your life. Stacy has some qualities that would complement yours. Are you searching for a carbon copy of yourself?"

He shot up in his chair. Trying not to raise his voice again, he said, "Let me quote your friend. 'This whole Mars thing is a big waste of time and effort. These people should get out in the real world and do something useful with their lives.'" He injected as much sarcasm into his voice as he could. "She's trying to tell someone with PhDs in history and philosophy what the real world is like? Someone should buy her a vowel. She thinks the real world is where you work a nine-to-five job in the good ol' U. S. of A., sip coffee every morning at Starbucks, absorb the propaganda in the newspaper, and buy a whole bunch of things on credit that you don't need. What a good little western consumer! What a life! What perspective! What long-term vision!"

Having failed to keep his voice low, he slapped his palm on the metal table for added emphasis. Then he continued his tirade, a bit more muted. "Imagine Stacy Weaver as the first sea life to struggle up onto the land. She would have immediately turned back because life was easier in the water. And she wouldn't have been the only one!" He motioned to the nearly empty street with a sweep of his hand.

Much of his pontification was probably wasted on Cassie, who dealt with similar outbursts from her clients every day. "Calm down, will you? Look, I know you have better long-term vision than most people, but give others a chance! People can learn and change. You can't expect everyone to view things exactly like you do. Sharing different views, attitudes, and ideas are some of the things that can make a relationship between two special people so wonderful!"

"I don't have time for her. I have more important things to worry about. There's plenty of time for someone like her later."

"Later? When?" Cassie lowered her voice and flashed him an overly analytical stare. "David, why are you alone? You're the epitome of tall, dark, and handsome. You're also intelligent, sensitive, and fun to be around. You're a good person, and you have so much to offer. Compatible women flock to you, yet you always find some excuse to push them away. Why?"

"Why not?" David had tired of the conversation. If he wanted someone to control his life, he would go call his parents.

"Don't you want to give yourself to someone? Care for someone? Feel complete with someone?"

"Why should I care for only one other person? I care about everybody."

"But what do you want for yourself? Don't you want any personal meaning in your life?"

"Drop it, Cassie." This remark, coming from Ben, surprised both of them. They turned to stare at him, as if noticing his presence for the first time.

Ben and Cassie were an odd mixture of personalities. Though physically energetic, Ben was usually a very quiet, thoughtful person, almost to the point of introversion. In fact, their earlier discussion had been quite atypical. Ben often went out of his way to avoid conflict. His graduate degree from CalTech and career at NASA's Jet Propulsion Laboratory (JPL) supported the stereotype of a typical computer geek.

But David knew differently. Ben had a powerful personality, with many non-academic interests. He never seemed to argue with Cassie, probably by intent. Undoubtedly, he had learned to choose his battles wisely and hold a lot inside.

Ben shifted in his seat before continuing his interruption. "David has plenty of satisfaction in his life already. He doesn't need a steady relationship to give his life meaning."

"Everyone needs companionship," countered Cassie. "It's not healthy for him to live in denial!"

"I don't hear him denying anything. I hear him setting priorities. I hear him putting off relationships temporarily so he can focus on other things of more importance to him." He looked up at the cloudless sky, a wistful expression on his face. "And to be truthful, I really envy his ability to do that."

The effect of his words on Cassie was probably the same as if Ben had thrown his espresso into her face. With her hand quivering, she carefully placed her hot chocolate back on the table. "So…does that mean…you don't think our own relationship is very important, either?"

Cassie the victim was much worse than Cassie the inquisitor. Ben slapped his forehead with his right palm and held it there for a few moments, a portrait of a thinking man.

"Our relationship is the most important thing in the world to me," he finally said, struggling visibly to find the right words, "…but it's not the only important thing in my life. I have so many responsibilities now, to you, to my work, to our families and future children, to our cats, to our mortgage company, and to others. Where does it all end? Life used to be so much simpler, and in some ways, better. I do miss my carefree lifestyle a bit, so a part of me envies David. He doesn't have much tying him down."

"Well, thanks, I think," mumbled David, though he was getting tired of hearing what a "nobody" he was.

Defeat was rare for his sister, but the fight had left her eyes. A wave of sympathy washed over David, dragging him out to the sea in the undertow. He felt compelled to make her a peace offering, and he knew what it should be, but he just couldn't work up the courage to say the words.

After his flippant dismissal of Cassie's intrusion into his personal life, how could he tell her about the other reason he had pushed Stacy Weaver away? He couldn't even admit it to himself yet. Was he really infatuated with another woman?

If he said anything about this to Cassie, he would also be forced to reveal this other woman was out of his league and barely even knew he existed. She was even out of reach physically. Anyone could see their relationship was doomed from the start.

Cassie would jump all over him. She would claim this other woman was a fantasy, enabling his avoidance of relationships. Or she would crow that this proved his need for companionship. An even bigger argument would follow, one that would frustrate them both and wouldn't solve anything.

He opted for the cowardly way out, an innocent sounding half-truth. He said when his job with the Mars mission was over, he would try to settle down, marry a woman he loved and respected, buy a little house, fill it with 2.2 kids, find a long-term job, shop for stuff, sip coffee at Starbucks, and live the rest of his life in western capitalist bliss.

His empty promise seemed to satisfy her, at least for now. With a mischievous smile and wink, she pointed out that one of her new friends in California might be a good match for him. Then she tugged on his arm, leading him into a gentle hug across the table. They took their seats again and endured an embarrassed silence.

Finally, David's curiosity got the best of him. "So, what *did* you guys think about the party last night?"

CHAPTER 3
PRESSURE

MarsDay 1, 5:00 a.m.
(November 21, 1:28 p.m.)

As in her earlier dream, Anna floated before abruptly crashing to the Earth. A dull pain between her ears helped to clear away the mental cobwebs shrouding her senses.

Opening her eyes cautiously, she found herself on the floor of the EVA room, with her back against the exterior wall. Ollie was sitting next to her. He was wearing a counter-pressure suit, with the bubble helmet removed. She remembered helping him into his suit, but things were fuzzy after that.

She was surprised to find Commander Day towering over her.

"Sleeping on the job?" Evelyn's voice was strangely muted.

Anna swallowed, and her ears popped. Her hearing improved immediately, and her headache faded as well. The air pressure in the *Perseus* had obviously increased.

"Commander! I'm glad to see you're OK! Were you able to patch the leak?"

Rather than responding, Evelyn started to pace the EVA room.

Ollie answered her question, without enthusiasm. "There was no air leak." She strained to hear him add, "She faked the whole bloody thing."

"What?" She carefully rolled her head sideways to look at Ollie. His bubble helmet was resting on the floor nearby. He looked like he was a hundred years old.

"There was no bloody air leak."

Evelyn Day was not a large woman, but even during normal times, she projected a powerful presence. From Anna's vantage point near the floor, the commander appeared to be ten feet tall. Her pale face and nearly bald head made her look even more imposing. She was dressed in her standard attire, shorts and a loose fitting shirt. A logo on her shirt proudly proclaimed, "My best friends are Poly, Ethyl, and Ene," an advertisement for the chemical in the outer hull that reduced their exposure to cosmic radiation. Her left hand grasped a silver chain tightly, dangling a familiar pocket watch.

"No leak, this time," Evelyn admitted. "You were never in any real danger during this drill. But if the air leak had been real, you and I would be dead now, and Ollie would have a lonely voyage ahead. Needless to say, I'm very disappointed."

Anna searched for a good response, but couldn't think of one. Ollie also remained silent.

When asked if she felt well enough to hear a brief lecture on crew safety, Anna hesitated, and then nodded. She felt fine now, and she had learned a lot from Evelyn's frequent lectures in the past. The commander was usually a fountain of knowledge, an expert problem solver who could find a creative solution to almost any puzzle. She also oozed relevant experience, having served for five years as chief engineer aboard a U.S. Navy nuclear submarine and five more years as a civilian research base commander in Antarctica.

Evelyn cleared her throat. "I would like to see the surface of Mars before I die. To do that, I'll need your help. We must all be alert for the earliest signs of danger, no matter how small and insignificant they might appear to be. Mission Support will soon be too far away to make any difference during a real crisis. This little drill might not have been the best way to get your attention, but we have a boring, six-month journey ahead of us, and boredom breeds carelessness. Just because we made it through all the simulations and training back on Earth doesn't mean we can relax and let our guard down. Once a crisis is upon us, we need to react to it, quickly, intelligently, and efficiently. For example, the minimum recorded time for donning a pressure suit is just under a minute. Your time was over four minutes."

Her last statements were so unfair that Anna found the courage to interrupt. "The oxygen levels had dropped, and we couldn't concentrate. How could we have done any better in that situation?"

"A good diagnosis, and a fair question. How, indeed?" She studied her silver pocket watch intently, as if it was part of the problem or held the answer. "First, you were sealed in a room full of oxygen tanks. By opening the output valve on any of them, you could have increased the oxygen level in the EVA room."

Anna couldn't believe she had overlooked that solution. It was so simple, so obvious, and it had never even occurred to her.

"Second, as I watched you on the video surveillance camera from my quarters, I noticed that you started a debate in the middle of the crisis. Even worse, Anna, you almost opened the EVA room door! I appreciate your concern for my safety, but I would ask that next time, don't kill yourself in a foolish attempt to save me. In such a crisis, trust that I'm off doing my job, and be sure you do yours."

Anna resisted the urge to ask questions. Better to be quiet and get her verbal lashing over with.

"Third, in their internal design notes, the pressure suit architects express a belief that the human body can survive exposure to vacuum for several minutes if the flow of oxygen and pressure to the head is unimpaired. For obvious reasons, this has never been verified. I suggest at some point during your studies over the next few months, you should brush up on space suit science. Don't just read the advertised literature—read everything else you can find, too. We have an extensive library. Use it. Once we reach Mars and begin to explore the surface, our space suits are our lives. In an emergency where every second is critical, you might consider donning only the neck dam, bubble helmet, and respirator. This is not a safe procedure, and if anyone back on Earth asks, I did *not* recommend it. But it could cut your reaction time in half, or more."

Her pacing brought her near the EVA room door, where she paused. "I'll leave you now to store the suit components and go about your day. Oliver, get some sleep. You need it."

Evelyn pivoted crisply on her left heel, in military style, and marched out the doorway. A moment later, they heard her cabin door click shut.

"Thanks for your concern," Ollie called after her.

Not trusting her legs yet, Anna crawled over to Ollie and rolled onto her back, using his lower leg for a pillow. The two of them rested like that for a minute, gathering their strength.

Since Anna was still fully clothed, Ollie hadn't gotten very far in his attempt to dress her in a pressure suit. When she asked him about that, he explained, "No time. When you started acting all weird, Evelyn burst into the room, clucking like a mother hen. What a loon."

"Me, or her?"

"Her, of course."

"But she's right about putting the suits on," said Anna, feeling a need to defend the commander. "We didn't do very well, or rather, I didn't do very well. If the leak had been real, I would have been a goner."

"Yes...well, she's still a loon."

Anna smiled at him. "You know, lots of people back on Earth think all three of us are loony. I have to go on television soon and persuade them that we aren't. If they could see us now, they would be convinced it's true. Here we are, Doctor Oliver Sainsbury and Doctor Anna Schweitzer, two-thirds of the brave, highly-skilled Mars exploration crew, pinned to the floor by a simple emergency drill. Are we complete losers, or what?"

They shared some much-needed laughter while helping each other to their feet. After carefully removing and storing his space suit, Ollie retreated to his cabin for some well-earned sleep.

Then she was all alone. For the first time of many, Anna had the entire ship to herself. As she fully realized that she would soon be the only conscious person within more than 300,000 kilometers, disturbing images flashed back from her dream and the alert. She shivered and tried to dismiss them, but they wouldn't go away.

The EVA room had enough open floor space to attempt some simple stretching exercises. After a short, light workout, she assumed a lotus position and tried to meditate for a few minutes. Exercise and meditation usually chased her demons away, but they were more resilient this time. Eventually, she was able to enter a shallow state of relaxation where the dark creatures, though unconquered, were banished to peripheral shadows. She cherished the few moments of peace because they would probably be her last all day.

MarsDay 1, 6:29 a.m.
(November 21, 3:00 p.m.)

Like a heat-seeking missile, David rocketed into his apartment with Cassie right on his heels. He blew warm breaths onto his frozen fingers, but it didn't help much. The six-block walk from the café, with a stiff headwind the whole way, had felt like a 60 mile death march.

Cassie bee-lined straight to the thermostat and turned the heat up, while David started a pot of coffee brewing in his small kitchen. Their warm drinks at the café were a distant memory.

As David surveyed the contents of his apartment, he noted with satisfaction that everything was in its usual state of spartan disarray. He had never been very good at collecting material possessions, and he didn't entertain guests very often. The small studio adequately met his needs.

His basic requirements were a modest kitchen with a small table, a television set, and a couch that pulled out into a sofa bed. The 36-inch television set was an ancient, bulky monstrosity that must have weighed nearly 20 pounds. A bay window facing south gave the living room plenty of natural sunlight. Lighter computer equipment on a wobbly table occupied the rest of the meager space. The beige walls were drab and unadorned.

Considering the minimal furnishings, he almost laughed aloud at the irony of his present situation. For the next two years, with this room as a base of operations, he would be performing one of the most critical tasks of the Mars mission. A NASA analogue to his Mission Support headquarters would have been a large control room in Houston filled with banks of expensive equipment and dozens of scurrying people. Using only a high-speed Internet connection and some customized software on a mini-notebook computer, he could direct his support team from almost anywhere, even this apartment.

David's support team was fairly small, but very experienced. After supporting simulated missions for many years, the non-profit Mars Society organization had built up a core team, along with a much larger army of on-call academic and engineering experts. Years ago, the SEA had been formed in a merger of the Mars Society, the National Space Society, the Planetary Society, Red Colony, and other non-profit organizations with compatible goals. The merger had greatly increased the financial health and talent base of the resulting organization.

Though relatively small in numbers, David doubted whether his support team would fit into a larger NASA control room. However, they had infinite space for interaction in a maze of virtual rooms on a network of secure servers somewhere in cyberspace. With only basic Internet access, each worker could support the mission from anywhere in the world, just like David.

Leaving her coat on, Cassie plopped onto the couch and fiddled with the unfamiliar remote control for his satellite television system. They were alone, for now. Ben planned to rejoin them after taking an insulin injection back at his hotel room.

"Did you buy Ben's excuse?" asked David.

Cassie laughed. "Sometimes he can be hard to live with, but inside, my husband is a prince with a heart of gold. He knows we have a lot of catching up to do."

David was grateful because he wanted to ask Cassie some questions that might have been embarrassing in front of her husband. Now was a perfect opportunity.

"So Cassie, how are you and Ben doing after your first year of marriage?"

"Just fine."

Uh-oh. That was an automatic response, devoid of feeling, far too easy.

David felt like the psychologist now. "Any good arguments lately?"

"We do have a few minor differences of opinion, now and then. Ben doesn't ever argue with me. But sometimes we disagree on things."

"Such as?"

"Such as where we want to live and how we want to plan for children someday." She sighed, and drooped her head. "Little things like that."

"Where do you want to live?"

"Longer term, we both want to live in the mountains near Pasadena. It's beautiful there, and it reminds me of happy times here in Boulder. But houses cost so much there! We can't afford to spend a million dollars on a one-bedroom cabin with a quarter acre of land. I think we should stay in our small condo or rent an apartment, while we save our money. "

David resisted the urge to comment about some people with student loans who had been trapped in low paying contract positions, namely himself, and couldn't even save any money while renting an apartment. Instead, he asked, "And what does Ben think?"

"He wants to buy a house right now, even if it pushes us way over our heads into debt. I just don't understand it. He's usually the one with all the financial smarts. I know we both have good jobs, but what happens when we have children? I'll want to cut back on my work hours, so I can stay home with the kids. Ben just seems to shrug that off. He says the future will take care of itself. Then he acts like he did at the café this afternoon, saying how concerned and committed he is. It's like he's another person sometimes, and it drives me crazy."

"Maybe he's planning on getting a promotion at work?"

"Not likely. He could have been promoted three years ago, after his previous manager died in a car accident. Unfortunately, he doesn't wear the 'management material' label. He's too good a technician. Since the aerospace field is hot now, he could probably get a better paying job somewhere else, like here in Boulder. If we bought a house, we might end up selling it in a few years, anyway."

David agreed that sometimes Ben's quirks and inconsistencies could be frustrating. He wished he could give his sister some good advice, but she and Ben earned more money each year than he had earned in his last five years. He had never even seen the inside of a million dollar house.

When the new pot of coffee was ready, he contributed to her thought processes and emotional stability by bringing two steaming mugs over to the couch. They both took a few cautious sips, and it was just how he liked it, strong and black. Cassie appeared to have some trouble with the taste, but she didn't complain.

"Eureka," said Cassie, as she finally located the USNN channel on the television. USNN, a popular news network, was scheduled to air a special program about the Mars mission soon. Cassie and David were both looking forward to watching it, and Ben had mentioned it earlier, too.

On the current show, a Catholic priest, Jewish rabbi, and Muslim cleric were debating the role of space exploration in God's plan. Surprisingly, these men of faith seemed to agree on many things. The discussion was relaxed and interesting, rather than fiery and divisive, as he would have expected.

During a commercial break, Cassie switched the channel over to CUSA, and then quickly to Lynx and a few other news stations. Since Mars was the topic of the day on every news channel, David didn't care which one they watched. She finally changed the channel back to the religious discussion on USNN and turned the volume lower so they could continue their conversation.

David glanced at his watch and brought his coffee over to his rickety table. Still listening to the extended version of Cassie's tale of woe, but with one eye on the television and the other on his 50-inch, wrap-around organic display, he entered the virtual Mission Support center by running a client program on his computer.

As he roamed through the rooms of the support center, he quickly gathered status information from various repositories. Fortunately, Cassie muted the television and asked what was going on with the mission. Her question allowed him to devote his attention to one activity, rather than three.

"There's not much happening right now. Commander Day staged a surprise drill, and she's not very happy with the results. I wouldn't want to be anywhere near her for the next few days."

"Yes, you would, and you know it," said Cassie. "You would give your left arm to be on that ship right now."

David sighed, and looked up at the ceiling, which was the only decorated surface in his apartment. He had taped several rolls of Christmas wrapping paper to a section of the ceiling, black paper with tiny dots of random color and location. The effect was similar to looking up at a clear, dark sky full of stars.

"OK, you caught me. I would give almost anything to be out there," he said.

"It should be a boring journey, though."

"Maybe, maybe not."

"Let's hope it is!" said Cassie. As he turned to look at her over his shoulder, she added, "On the psych team, one of our goals is to alleviate the crew's boredom. I'm looking forward to the challenge."

David said, "Officially, remote teaching, media sessions, training, and exercise will take much of the crew's time. Anna will also be running some biology and medical experiments. But yes, the psych team's job is critical, at least on the outward journey. Once they reach Mars, there should be plenty of excitement."

"And what will you be doing?"

"While my support team monitors the habitat equipment, looking for early signs of trouble, I'll be monitoring the support team. I'll also watch the crew, the media, the general public, and anyone else that becomes involved."

"Speaking of the media, the crew interview on USNN should be starting soon. That tardy husband of mine has been looking forward to it all day. I wonder why he's not back yet."

David glanced at his watch again. "He's still got plenty of time. I'm sure he'll stagger in, about two minutes before show time." He winked at her, and they shared a laugh at Ben's expense.

CHAPTER 4
PERCEPTION

MarsDay 1, 6:59 a.m.
(November 21, 3:30 p.m.)

    David's virtual persona, "Shepherd", strolled into the Communications Shack at Mission Support, where he eavesdropped on the chatter of the technicians controlling the live, two-way video feed from the spacecraft. Each technician's virtual persona, or avatar, was seated at a control console. Two large video screens occupied the entire wall in front of them. The screen on the left displayed the current video uplink to the spacecraft. The one on the right displayed the video downlink in the other direction.
    Both screens were currently idle, but David expected to see some activity soon. While the media sessions were in progress, anyone in this room could watch the transmissions directly from the hub of the high bandwidth communications pipelines. He decided to hang around, but he wasn't the only one with this idea. The room was crowded with other observers. A status display on the side wall indicated 187 avatars were present. David was actually surprised his team had that many members. Most of the off-duty workers were probably here, too.
    Each 3-D avatar, represented by a 2-D perspective projection, was a loose visual approximation of a real life support team member. Some were familiar to him, but most weren't. Many wore creative costumes and probably benefitted from slight exaggerations of various bodily proportions.
    Somewhere in realspace, software on a server had sensed the large number of avatars in the room and had automatically stretched the wall

dimensions to accommodate them. All four walls remained their usual peach color, and the physical layout had not changed, but internal floor space had been increased at least ten-fold over the room's normal size.

The avatars milled about, whispering among themselves, sometimes getting in the way of each other. He could hear the dull murmuring of their conversations on his speakers, occasionally interrupted by the clearer, louder voices of the comm techs. Only select personnel were authorized to speak aloud in this room, and David was one of them, but he didn't have anything to say yet.

Over the murmurings, a crisp feminine voice announced, "Attention everyone! Room layout change in ten seconds…nine…eight…"

Room layout changes were rare. David held his breath, awaiting the magic that the virtual world maintenance team was about to perform.

As the countdown ended, the walls of the Communications Shack shimmered, and the room returned to its smaller, original size. Most of the previous occupants were gone. Only the four comm technicians remained, plus one other avatar, probably the maintenance tech who had changed the room layout.

The others were now visible in a new room, a steeply sloped auditorium sequestered by a transparent divider. An overhead sign labeled the other room "Observation Gallery." As indicated by a wall icon, sound from the Communications Shack would be transmitted into the gallery, one way only.

Watching the computer display over David's shoulder, Cassie asked him about his own persona. This was her first visit to the cyberspace support center, so she had no idea what his avatar looked like.

Shepherd found a mirror along one of the side walls and inspected his reflection. He was a shepherd, with a staff in one arm, wearing a corded kaffiyeh on his head. A plain white robe flowed over his shoulders and down his torso. The face was his own, but it was hidden beneath a dark beard and scraggly hair, far from his usual, clean-cut appearance. Reflective sunglasses completed the disguise, while adding a touch of flair.

Cassie complimented him on his creativity. Their own mother wouldn't recognize him. Then she asked him for a quick tour of the facilities.

David, or rather Shepherd, left the room by sidestepping through a sliding door into a long hallway. His first stop was the nearby "Psych Ward," which Cassie would soon help to staff. The door was open.

As he entered the Psych Ward, he asked Cassie if she had decided on a name for her own avatar.

"Kahuna," she replied. "Since I'll be Anna's personal psychologist, I let her choose the name for me. It seems appropriate, since astronauts always perceive psychologists as witch doctors."

"What will your avatar look like?"

"I haven't decided yet. I'll do that when I get back home tomorrow."

He entered the waiting room of the Psych ward. It looked like a typical reception area at a doctor's office, with chairs, magazine racks, an unoccupied desk, and even a water cooler. A closed doorway was labeled "Offices." Shepherd tried pushing against that door, but it was locked.

"Too bad," said Cassie. "I was hoping to see my new office!"

"Ask, and you shall receive." David typed some words on his keyboard, and the door opened, revealing another hallway beyond. Shepherd possessed a skeleton key to any door in the complex. Being the boss had some advantages.

The door to Cassie's new office was already labeled "Kahuna." Inside, the room was spacious, but empty. She would need to choose some decorations and furniture, so he told her how to contact a technician who could help her get started.

They continued their tour, visiting the Hospital, the Security Center in a central atrium, and an administrative wing. Then he entered the Main Support Room, the heart of the complex. This room looked like the Communications Shack, but on a grander scale. Four rows of consoles sloped downward toward the front wall, which contained nearly a dozen display screens. Avatars staffed some console positions. Soft, terse voices buzzed throughout the room.

He showed Cassie his own position, a raised chair of plush velvet in an open area near the back wall. The touch of Victorian decadence looked out of place within the otherwise utilitarian, high tech room. His seat's appearance was a subtle reminder to his colleagues that he wasn't a technical expert. He was a bureaucrat, a functional exception.

Bypassing his seat, he moved toward a metallic rectangle along the back wall, the door to his office. David used his key and typed an archaic password. The door yielded to him.

His office was small and unremarkable. He felt at home there. In fact, he had designed the decor to match the layout of his apartment closely, right down to a starry section of ceiling.

Shepherd walked over to a computer console, in the same location as David's computer in his apartment. He touched a large, virtual button on its keyboard labeled "e-mail." Instantly, part of David's office view was replaced by a familiar e-mail client application.

"Just going to check my messages while I'm here," he explained to Cassie, who politely diverted her attention back to the television set.

David had a dozen messages. None were marked high priority, so they could wait. He did open two of them, however, when he noticed who had sent them.

One message was from <alice>, which was Commander Day's account name on the internal support network. By default, internal messages were private, completely separated from all the prying eyes and hackers on the external Internet. Commander Day had also sent this particular message to the steering committee members and the psych team, two aliases that expanded to many internal addresses.

To: <committed_ones>, <shepherd>, <psychotic_ones>
From: <alice>
Subject: Drill results
Priority: Medium

Well, that drill was pretty disappointing. I doubt it could have been much worse. I've posted details to the general bulletin board, with video and commentary to the psych and ops teams.

I'll schedule another surprise soon. Hopefully my timing will be better. I really should have let Ollie get some sleep first. He's probably not very happy with me at the moment. It will be enlightening to see how he responds.

Question to the psych team: Are you sure that unannounced drills are such a good idea????

Evelyn

The commander's brief message didn't contain any new information. He had already seen her note on the general status board, which any support team member could browse. Perhaps later, he would watch the video she referred to, just to satisfy his own curiosity.

The other message was from <microbrain>, which was Anna's account name. As he opened her message, a warm tingle raced from his toes up through his chest and back down to his fingers at the keyboard.

To: <shepherd>
From: <microbrain>
Subject: Personal Message
Priority: Low

Hi Shep,

Today will be a big day—many dragons to slay. Wish me luck against the Hydra!
 I'll try to visit the Comm Shack before show time. Hope to see you there.

Anna

David terminated his e-mail client and warped Shepherd directly back to the Communications Shack. As the background image of the room faded and came back into focus, his computer made a "whoosh" noise, recapturing Cassie's attention. He told her about warps, which allowed an avatar to move instantly from room to room, as long as the receiving room wasn't locked. Warping was usually considered a bit rude, but it could be useful when someone was in a big hurry.

Anna wasn't in the Comm Shack. Compared to his last visit, the amount of chatter between technicians had increased. The communications team had been preparing to work with the news media for months. All their hard work would now be put to the test.

Back in the real world, David commented to Cassie about the large amount of money riding on the upcoming media session with USNN, $25 million, to be exact. Throughout the mission, lucrative commercial contracts would provide the SEA with a steady stream of income. They needed the next few hours to be smooth ones.

Cassie remarked that the network was probably more worried about it than he was. "With the way USNN has been hyping up this program, you would think it's the Superbowl. I'll bet they intend to make a hefty advertising profit."

"Yeah, but I've been sensing some weird vibes from them lately." He considered saying more, but he didn't want to bad-mouth a sponsor based solely on his negative opinion of some programs he had watched on that network recently.

Instead, he returned his gaze to the starry ceiling of his apartment. Eventually, he remarked, "You know, Anna's media appearances might be my own best contribution to the mission, so far."

"How so?"

David addressed a particular pseudo-star, a bright red one that looked like Mars as seen from his bay window at midnight. "Several months ago, I asked the SEA steering committee to make her the primary media contact among the crew. Fortunately, they agreed, and so did she."

"Why was it so important to have Anna as the main media contact?"

"I just liked the thought of having a single contact. We always want to present the media with a consistent story."

"No. I meant, why Anna?"

"After I watched some tapes of the crew during their training, she was an easy choice. Compared to the others, she has a much better screen presence. She also has a knack for explaining complicated concepts in simple terms. She taped a program for third graders on astrobiology that totally blew me away."

"So her hot looks had nothing to do with it?"

Surprised, he looked at Cassie, and she grinned back at him. She still knew him well.

"Well, maybe just a little," he admitted. "OK, more than a little. Her physical beauty is no secret, and she radiates confidence and warmth out of every pore. Why shouldn't we take advantage of that? She also projects fragile human weakness. I like that combination, and I think the viewers will, too."

Cassie prodded, "You mean you chose her because she's a stereotype of a weak female who needs help and protection?"

"She's tough as nails, and anyone who knows her realizes it's a stupid perception. But the opinion of the masses is more important. Stereotypes can be powerful tools. If some of the men in the viewing audience become more interested in the mission out of a misguided sense of machismo, that's just fine by me. If some of the women see her professionalism and look to her as a strong role model, that's even better."

Cassie seemed upset, but David knew she was pretending. As an expert in human psychology, she knew the rules of the male psyche far better than he did.

She pouted, "Well, at least you aren't making it a total soap opera. There won't be any romance or childbirth on the mission."

"Right-o. The mission planners, though bold, obviously didn't want to tackle those issues right away. Who knows how reduced gravity and increased radiation exposure affects childbearing? It's too bad Anna's medical history prevents her from having children, but going to Mars is a wonderful consolation prize!"

David returned his attention to Shepherd in the communications shack. The screens at the front of the room were no longer empty. Anna's image was on the screen to the right, and the USNN program host was on the left. They were talking to each other, experimenting with the unavoidable two-second time delay of communications. Their initial attempts at dialogue were not very smooth, but they were learning quickly. David would have laughed at the awkward exchange had he not recognized the host of the program.

"Great. Just great. Skye Fontaine. The queen of weird vibes." He tried to keep the bitterness out of his voice.

"What's wrong with her? I've seen her shows before. She seems like a pretty good science reporter."

David turned down the volume on his speakers. "She's been a real, uh, thorn in our side." He toned down his real opinion, not wanting to curse in front of his little sister. "Fontaine has a lot of charisma, and she can talk a good talk. People believe her, even when she's wrong. Lately, she's been wrong a lot."

"In your description, you forgot to mention her long eyelashes, beautiful smile, dark French-Canadian features, and big boobs. Did I leave anything out?"

"Not above the waist," he confessed.

Cassie laughed at his embarrassment. "If you're trying to woo male viewers, Anna's got some tough competition."

"No way," David stated emphatically. "Honest flesh tops silicone any day. Besides, you overlooked Fontaine's poisonous fangs and hateful message. She's been obsessed with revealing the identity of our mission sponsors and uncovering their sinister hidden motives. I don't know where she formed that opinion, but now it drives everything she does and says. A good reporter looks for the truth, without letting her own personal opinions get in the way."

Cassie had always enjoyed debating with him, and she wasn't about to back off now. "Sounds like she's just being a good *investigative* reporter. I think the mission sponsors are making a big mistake by remaining anonymous. They're practically inviting her, along with everyone else, to question their identity and motives. Unless they really do have something sinister to hide, why don't they bring their plans out into the open?"

"Who knows? But do the words 'innocent until proven guilty' have meaning anymore?"

Cassie replied, "Don't say it to me. Prove it to the public! You said their opinion is more important, and they can be a pretty tough jury."

"Come on, Cassie! Give the mission sponsors a break. Think of the historical context of what they're trying to do!"

"The public doesn't care about historical context," she stated firmly. "Most people are too wrapped up in their own worldly concerns."

"Leave history to the historians?" Unfortunately, he agreed with her. To most people, history was as irrelevant as the future. The here-and-now was all that mattered.

Having scored a point, Cassie smiled at him with a mischievous gleam in her eye. "Speaking of history, you know who's really going to hate this mission the most? Future sixth graders. Their history textbooks will contain a whole chapter about the current Mars mission, just after the chapters on the voyages of Columbus and Magellan."

Having studied history for so many years, David knew exactly what she was talking about. "No, college undergrads will despise us even more. They'll have to suffer through an entire semester on the subject."

"I wonder what they'll say about the mission. And about its context, the world we live in. They'll have the benefit of hindsight. They'll know who created the mission, and why."

"Are we back to speculating about the motives of our sponsors?" asked David.

"I guess so."

"You know, even if our sponsors have greedy motives, those future sixth graders aren't going to care. Our major concerns and worldly events will seem trivial to them. Lines in a textbook. More figures and facts to memorize before the next test."

"Humph," responded Cassie.

David looked at her in surprise. "You don't sound convinced. OK, tell me, what were the personal motives of the Wright brothers at Kitty Hawk? Who were their financial sponsors, or their technical colleagues? Can you name the U.S. president at that time, or any member of Congress? What major wars were going on? What were the most pressing social issues of the time?"

Cassie frowned, and grudgingly admitted, "I can't. And it's true; I don't care about any of that. All I know is that I'm flying home tomorrow on an airplane."

"My point, exactly. With the benefit of hindsight, we see the first flight of the Wright brothers helping to shape the history of the twentieth century. But what were *their* motives at the time? Maybe they just wanted to impress some chicks on the beach. Or maybe they were part of an elaborate government conspiracy. Who cares? It's the results that matter. History books are filled with examples of profound actions taken for obscure reasons rendered meaningless by the inexorable march of time."

"Are you claiming the end justifies the means?" The frown on Cassie's face deepened. "That's a difficult position to support, brother. I can think of many counter-examples. Some are downright nasty. Napoleon? Nazi Germany? Bin Laden?"

David had seen this comparison coming, and winced. When history and philosophy collided, justifying an extreme viewpoint with examples of past tyranny was quite common. It was the "evil mankind" thesis, where all people and actions could be perverted. Most of the time, truth lurked in the middle, where the abstract concepts of good and evil were balanced. If the motivation for the Mars mission came from this wide swath of middle ground, Cassie's comparison was invalid and her fears unfounded. Unfortunately, without knowing more about the mission planners and their agenda, nothing could be ruled out. That bothered him.

Their budding debate was interrupted by a tone from his computer. David was being summoned.

Shepherd was still in the Communications Shack with the technicians, but a new figure had entered the room and was trying to speak to him. This avatar had flowing blonde hair and a feminine figure, tastefully softened around the edges. He had no doubts about her identity.

Anna's avatar was a wispy ghost. Her transparency was the server's way of indicating she wasn't present in real-time. Her movements would be clumsy, hampered by the time delay of communications. Anyone who came across a ghostly avatar would give it a wide berth, unless they wanted to be rude.

While he had attended meetings with Anna at the virtual support center several times, he had only met her in person once, at the crew's going-away party last month. Living up to his high expectations was nearly impossible, yet she had made such an impression on him that he remembered every moment, every comment, every laugh and smile. He often replayed the scene in his mind, trying to keep the feelings fresh and alive. She had touched something in him that had not been touched in a long, long time.

Seeing Anna in the virtual world just didn't have the same impact, but it was better than nothing.

Oddly enough, he was seeing her twice. Behind her avatar was her realspace image on one of the wall displays, more detailed and stunning, but frozen in time by her ship's computer while she interacted in the virtual world.

Shepherd constructed a "cone of silence" link around himself and her avatar so they could talk privately. He didn't want anyone in the room or the observation gallery to overhear their conversation. Two symbolic, transparent cones dropped from the ceiling until one enveloped each avatar down to its shoulders. A shimmering tube connected the cones; more symbolism indicating the audio connection was private and two-way.

After turning up the volume on his speakers and activating his microphone, he greeted her warmly. Then he apologized for his previous out-of-avatar experience, explaining he was having a philosophical conversation with Kahuna in realspace.

"Now why am I not surprised about that," Anna laughed. "You could talk philosophy with a brick wall. By the way, did you get my message? It's been a rough morning so far, and now I need to battle the Hydra armed only with Ginkgo tea."

Her reference to the Hydra was an inside joke, one that reminded them to respect the awesome power of the media. Months ago, during a break in one of their lengthy virtual meetings, he had learned about their shared interest in classic Greek and Roman mythology.

Hydra was a creature of legend, a vicious monster with many snake-like heads. If a Hydra lost a head in battle, two more would grow back. They likened media reporters to the Hydra because both were deadly, and a mere mortal just couldn't fight them. For each visible reporter, two more were lurking in the shadows, eager to ruin your day.

He advised her to be careful. "This particular Hydra is a nasty one, with the blood of many mortals dripping from her fangs. Inspect your armor carefully."

While elaborating on his concerns about Fontaine's reporting bias, one of the comm technicians approached them and tapped on Anna's cone. The live video transmission was scheduled to start in one minute.

Anna bid David a hasty farewell. She waved to the crowd in the observation gallery as her ghostly avatar faded away completely. The connected cones disappeared as well. After a few moments of transition, her realspace image on the downlink wall display became animated once again.

In realspace, a loud knock on David's apartment door caused him to jump. There was Ben, right on time!

Cassie rushed to the door and let her husband in. She parked him on the couch and placed a hot cup of coffee into his shivering hands.

Through chattering teeth, Ben apologized for being gone so long. He had wandered around the streets, trying to find the right apartment building. Cassie didn't respond verbally, but she rolled her eyes in a way that all but stated, "Yeah, that's my husband. A lousy liar, thank goodness."

Ben glanced at the television and expressed relief at not missing the start of the live broadcast with the Mars crew. A news show was airing on USNN.

"That's odd," said David. "The program should have started by now."

He checked the live feed in the Communications Shack. The session had indeed started already. On the television, the news program continued, and the anchor commented about a last minute programming change. The live session with the Mars crew would take place at 9:00 p.m. Eastern time, three hours from now.

"Have they lost their mind?" wondered David aloud.

The network had been building up the hype around this program all week. Apparently, at the last moment, they had decided to tape delay the broadcast. The USNN program wouldn't be live, and it wouldn't even be the first aired. A competing network had scheduled another live session for just over an hour from now.

At least the three of them could still watch the USNN program live, through Shepherd's eyes at Mission Support. David bumped up the sound volume on his computer and situated the flexible display where they could all see it. Cassie muted the television.

Fontaine: ...particularly, many of the experts at NASA claim your mission is one failure away from disaster. Their strongest warnings are about power production. They believe a small nuclear power plant is essential for living on Mars, and your decision to produce electricity using solar power was extremely ill advised. They also fault the choice of a dusty, windy landing site with uneven terrain, making your odds of landing safely near the Earth Return Vehicle slim. How would you respond to those expert critics?

<time delay>
Schweitzer: Pessimists will always tell you why something can't be done. They should get out of the way of the people who are doing it. Indeed, traveling to Mars is dangerous, and our mission might fail for a hundred different reasons. Power production is one of our biggest concerns. In fact, it's the main reason we're landing near the Martian equator—to maximize the efficiency of our solar panels. If we encounter unexpected issues, we hope to find ways of adapting. Fallback options are already built into our plans at each step, and every critical mission component is redundant. For example, if we land too far away from our Earth Return Vehicle, or ERV, we can eventually return home on a backup ERV, which will reach Mars several months after we arrive.

The discussion about fallback options triggered a pang of worry within David. While Anna's statement was true for the mission hardware in space, he wasn't completely convinced the same was true for his own Mission Support organization.

Organizationally, his team was very flexible and quite able to adapt to ordinary events like personal vacations and illnesses. Yet they depended heavily upon the Internet, which was prone to occasional disruptions from viruses. Their links to outside organizations and experts weren't guaranteed.

Fontaine: And if that second return vehicle crashes or lands too far away?
<time delay>
Schweitzer: Then we are the unluckiest people in the solar system. But we should still be OK. We would have to wait on Mars two years longer than we had planned, tightly rationing our food and water supplies. Eventually, more ERVs, habitats, and supplies can be launched from Earth.

For the next half-hour, Fontaine continued to steer the conversation toward topics related to mission risks. She speculated about equipment failures, radiation, unknowns with growing crops and maintaining a biosphere, psychological issues, dust storms, and back contamination. She often returned to a central mantra: "Why would anyone travel to Mars now, when waiting a few years would make the mission cheaper and safer?"

Anna acknowledged many of the risks, but she forcefully advanced her opinion: procrastination was a foolish, cowardly exploration policy.

Watching the dialogue, David could tell that she was starting to lose her patience. Outwardly, she continued to answer the reporter's questions politely, however.

Schweitzer: Safety is a function of simplicity. By waiting longer, the mission isn't going to be much safer, and it probably won't be cheaper either. More surface simulations would be useful, but the Mars Society and the Space Exploration Alliance, SEA, have been testing equipment in simulations on Earth for years. At what point do you decide to get off your butt and do the real thing? We've waited 40 years already. Should we wait another 40? Or would you prefer 400? What about 4,000? Traveling to Mars will always be dangerous. Accept it.

Fontaine: You said the mission wouldn't be "much" safer. So by pushing you into taking this journey now, rather than waiting another ten years, say, you do acknowledge that your mission planners value other things above safety?

<time delay>

Schweitzer: Their values are their own business, so you'll have to ask them that question. All I can say is that sometimes a risk is worth taking. Even if the planners value other things, too, I do know safety is extremely important to them. They made that fact perfectly clear two years ago. They launched a fully redundant habitat containing backup supplies and living space, in case our current habitat fails. If they didn't value our safety, they could have skipped that launch, sending only an ERV and cargo ship on ahead of us.

Fontaine: But what are their priorities? What are the goals of your mission?

<time delay>

Schweitzer: Our four objectives are very simple. Number one is to stay alive. Second is to search for life, past or present. Our third priority is to characterize local Martian geology, locating useful resources or areas for future missions to explore. And the fourth priority is to verify the operational capabilities of the field equipment and procedures.

Fontaine: Those are straightforward goals, but I have difficulty believing them to be true or complete. How do you explain the total secrecy surrounding the planners of this mission? If their objectives were really that simple and honest, why are they hiding? What are they afraid of?

<time delay>

Schweitzer: Again, you'll have to ask them. I can't imagine why anyone would want to avoid talking to you.

Fontaine: What they've done is downright impossible. Despite legions of investigators seeking to uncover information, no one has figured out who organized the mission, their real goals, or even how much the mission actually costs. We have ballpark facts and figures. A paper trail of money reveals a billion dollars of funding to the SEA over the past three years. One of the contractors spent at least three billion dollars on hardware and launches. Those figures are a drop in the bucket, to be sure. Where's the rest of the money? Who are the people behind the money? What are their real goals? Who provides technical support?

During the time delay before Anna's response, Ben slapped his shoulder. "You're in luck, David. Looks like Fontaine wants a date with you. The tech support guy."

"Over my dead body," growled David.

Schweitzer: I'm as much in the dark about most of it as you are. As you already know, the SEA coordinates the mission. They arranged to build the equipment, launch the rockets, and support the mission. Perhaps the support team knows more of the details. I don't, and I don't particularly care to.

Fontaine: You mean to say you let someone launch you into space in a tin can and you don't care who they are and why they did it? That sounds incredibly naïve to me, and I'm sure most of our viewers would agree.

<time delay>

Schweitzer: I don't think it's naïve at all. The objectives are as I just stated. The SEA provides our support. As for who organized the mission, if they don't want to take credit right away, that's up to them. Even if they had some horrendous ulterior motive, as you seem to imply, how would they carry it out? We'll be the ones on Mars. They won't have any direct control over us. The crew will carry out the objectives I stated. No one can force us to do otherwise.

Fontaine: You sound certain of that. Yet the mission planners obviously belong to a wealthy and powerful organization. Who knows their capabilities? They might threaten to cut off your support if you don't cooperate. What about that possibility?

<time delay>

Schweitzer: It would be an empty threat. As I stated earlier, our mission was designed to be as self-sufficient as possible. What could they do? A lack of support from Earth would be a major inconvenience, but our ride home is already waiting for us on Mars. Besides, any type of death threat would be almost meaningless. Despite anything they might threaten to do, it is far more likely our mission will fail for unexpected reasons, and some or all of us will die anyway. Once you've accepted the possibility of your own death, threats lose much of their power over you.

Fontaine: They could threaten your families here on Earth. Many types of indirect pressure are possible.

<time delay>

Schweitzer: None of our crew has any immediate family. Look, I can't follow your reasoning at all. What would they have us do? Discover extraterrestrial life, and then declare war on it? It's crazy talk.

Fontaine: Further speculation on this program won't get us anywhere. If your support team has the answers, how do we contact them?

"There you go again, David," laughed Ben again. "She's really burning to meet you!"

"Yes, it appears that way," David replied, somberly. "And that might be a problem."

CHAPTER 5
WAVE

MarsDay 1, 8:30 a.m.
(November 21, 5:04 p.m.)

    The inflatable couch was cool to her touch, but Anna's excess body heat quickly warmed it up. She rested her head and shoulders on an air pillow at one end, while putting her feet up high on the other, determined to enjoy a few moments of leisure time between her media sessions. Sassy music by Annie Lennox was barely audible in the background.
    Placing her feet up on the couch didn't come naturally to her, but at present, it just felt like the right thing to do. From her early childhood, she recalled her German father scolding her severely on a train in Berlin after she had put her feet on a seat cushion. She had only been copying the relaxed posture of her mother, an American, but that excuse had only made the punishment worse.
    A four-inch gap separated the top of the couch from the bottom of the organic computer display above it. Her fingers danced lightly along this section of the outer hull. She visualized her hand passing outward six inches, through the wall. The icy cold of Old Man Void was that close. Her only protection was a thin shell of insulation and reinforced polyethylene plastic.
    The USNN media session, just completed, had temporarily changed her perspective. The immense gulf separating the *Perseus* and the Earth now felt more like a calming buffer, a sea of protection. Every passing second was welcome because it took her farther away from the insanity of life on Earth.

Some of the USNN reporter's questions had thoroughly tested her patience, but her tolerance seemed higher than usual, out here in her fragile refuge with its thin walls. Hatred and suspicion might dominate everyday life back on the Earth, but she refused to let them affect her in space.

I walk along the city streets, so dark with rage and fear...
And I—I wish that I could be that bird and fly away from here...

As a child, Anna had always envied the ability of Annie's "Little Bird" to take flight away from the troubles of the world. Hatred and suspicion were old childhood acquaintances. She knew them well. Closing her eyes, she thought about how her relationship with these old adversaries had evolved over the years. They had defined who she was and where she was going.

Around the time when she was 13 years old, her parents and older sisters were killed in an Autobahn accident. Whenever she recalled that time in her life, as she did now, what depressed her most was remembering so little from before the accident and so much from after it.

Her next ten years had been a whirlwind of distant relatives and an endless succession of schools. She remembered them all. Though the people in each place were different, her situation was always the same. The new kid was always greeted with hatred and suspicion. The streets of her youth had been dark places.

She had learned to make friends fast and lose them even faster. Each time she moved on, her friends were replaced by a new location and another dose of hatred and suspicion. The cycle repeated so many times.

Eventually, she accepted her situation and stopped seeking new friendships. She built a strong shell to protect herself from the world. The outer illusion of a cheerful, blossoming young woman remained empty inside.

Relationships were transient. She must never again let anyone come close enough to hurt her. That lesson was still an important one. Perhaps this was why her thoughts were dwelling on the past at a point in time when her future lay before her so clearly.

In her teen years, her happiest memories involved gymnastics or academics. Gymnastics, enhanced by martial arts and meditation, became her way of coping with her own humanity. Education was a quest for understanding and meaning in her greater universe of chaos. Both were solitary pursuits, safe from outside pressures. She could carry them with her on her present journey.

Later, she matured enough to break with the patterns of the past. Since she had learned many American customs and mannerisms from her mother during her early, impressionable years, a part of herself was strongly drawn toward America. She applied for a scholarship at the University of Michigan, and much to her surprise, the application was accepted. Looking back, that was a real turning point in her young life. In her first year as an undergraduate, she became hooked on microbiology.

The connection had seemed so clear at the time, as it still did today. The study of simple, honest forms of life resonated well with her inner pursuits. By understanding how biology worked, she hoped to better understand her own humanity and find her special calling within the unfriendly universe. As she studied and learned more, she encountered a new state of being: satisfaction.

And here I am. Guess what, Annie? This Little Bird has flown far, far away.

Caressing the fragile shell of the *Perseus* again, she imagined that she was touching her own internal, protective shell. Given enough time and distance from Earth, those two shells could easily begin to merge together, becoming one.

I must not let that happen. There are the others to consider.

The physical shell of the *Perseus* contained two other people. She did care about them, probably more than she had cared about anyone in a long time. She could cooperate with them and work with them, at least superficially. She even *needed* them, on many levels. But she would never let them close enough to harm her.

Completing the survey of her emotions, she found one other person she really cared about, too, back on Earth. She hardly knew him, but he seemed honest and kind, perhaps even a kindred spirit in some ways. Over the past few weeks, she had found herself thinking about him often. And she didn't even know his real name.

MarsDay 1, 8:41 a.m.
(November 21, 5:15 p.m.)

After listening to the USNN session, David fought a powerful urge to beat his head against his living room wall. In fact, his temples were throbbing as if he had already done just that. More likely, his headache was caused by too much caffeine, stress, and Fontaine-induced pessimism.

He no longer cared whether the USNN session was tape delayed or not. Now he wished it wouldn't air at all. If there was any cosmic justice, perhaps the network would lose the recording or someone would edit out the worst parts. The former was unlikely, and the latter was impossible because nothing would remain.

Practically every question asked by the host was openly biased, cynical, or downright rude. She had ridiculed nearly every aspect of the mission, exaggerating risks, while downplaying the benefits. Most of all, she had attacked the motivations of the mission relentlessly. Appealing to childish fears in her audience, she had even referred to the mission planners as the "Mars Bogeymen."

In hindsight, David regretted the time and effort his support team had invested in the session. Was the public relations damage worth the $25 million the network had paid the SEA? He doubted it.

The others were equally upset. Cassie, with a thoroughly disgusted sigh, returned the television to the Lynx News Network. Another interactive session with Anna was scheduled on that station in about 20 minutes. After the previous program, David's hopes for the next one were more subdued.

While they waited, they watched the tail end of a feeder news segment about initial reactions to the Mars mission from around the world. Thus far, the opinion of the American public seemed to be overwhelmingly positive and optimistic. That sentiment was shared in many other nations, a welcome exception to years of escalating anti-Americanism. For a brief period of time, the world celebrated as one.

Serious troubles still remained, however. Some were even exasperated by the Mars mission. The next news story showed legions of Middle Eastern university students taking to the streets with signs proclaiming "Science—Yes! Repression—No!" Military troops and tanks confronted some of the protesters, and the results were painful to watch. Yet somehow, the media was right there capturing it all, in full sound and color.

At the appointed time, the Lynx news program transitioned into a live feed from the *Perseus*. The host of the session was an older man with gray hair and a tiny, pointed goatee. Immaculately dressed and very professional looking, he might have just stepped off the set of Masterpiece Theatre. A caption identified him as Stewart Aarons. David had never seen him before, nor had the others.

As the program began, David peeked at the front wall of the Communications Shack through Shepherd's eyes. This time, Shepherd's view matched the image on the television seen by the rest of the world.

Despite her earlier problems with the USNN host, Anna appeared quite relaxed. David was captivated by her presence all over again. Her aura of confidence was overpowering, while her angelic smile, with its suggestion of hidden depth, melted his heart.

Aarons: Doctor Schweitzer, welcome to the program. It's an honor to speak with you on this historic day.
<time delay>
Schweitzer: I'm very pleased to be here.
Aarons: Could you tell our viewers how far your spacecraft has traveled?
<time delay>
Schweitzer: We will soon be 400,000 kilometers away from the Earth, which is about the distance from the Earth to the Moon. Every second, we are traveling another five kilometers farther away.

Anna's image on the television was briefly replaced by a spectacular view of the Earth with the Moon in the background. The view was centered on a point just off the southern coast of India. The day-night terminator shrouded the Middle East in darkness, while China and most of Australia were illuminated brightly. A similar terminator divided the moon, as well.

David marveled at the crispness of detail in the still image. A full motion video, if taken from the whirling *Perseus*, would have captured a blurry Earth and Moon in its view for only a few seconds at a time.

Aarons: Some of our viewers might be wondering how you can be that far away, after traveling for only one day. The Apollo astronauts took three days to reach the Moon. Were you launched on a more powerful rocket?
<time delay>
Schweitzer: Actually, our rocket was less powerful than the Saturn V rockets of the Apollo program. Since the 1970s, the thrust of launch technology, no pun intended, has been toward smaller, cheaper rockets.
Aarons: Then how could you be so far away, so quickly?
<time delay>
Schweitzer: The Apollo astronauts could have traveled this fast, but the Moon has little gravity and no atmosphere, so they would have been unable

to stop! To reach the Moon, one travels slowly and brings plenty of extra rocket fuel for braking. When we reach Mars, its stronger gravity will capture us, and its atmosphere will slow us down like a nice, fluffy airbag. Our fuel tanks are almost empty now, so our ship is coasting light and fast.

Aarons: Assuming all goes well, where will you land on Mars?

<time delay>

Schweitzer: 181 Earth days from now, on May 20th of next year, we will land in the "Medusae Fossae" region of Mars. The Medusae Fossae formation spans over 1,000 kilometers along the Martian equator. Our landing coordinates should be near 3 degrees north latitude, 168 degrees west longitude.

Aarons: The Medusa region? Now I understand why your ship is named the Perseus.

<time delay>

Schweitzer: Yes. In Greek mythology, Perseus was the slayer of Medusa, the evil Gorgon. All who looked upon Medusa were turned to stone.

Aarons: Why was that landing site chosen?

<time delay>

Schweitzer: Since the Medusae Fossae region is close to the equator, the day/night cycles will be fairly even throughout each season. The steady supply of sunlight and warm temperatures should make crop growth and solar power generation feasible. The landing site is low in altitude, so the atmosphere will be dense enough to protect us from much of the radiation hitting Mars. The Medusae Fossae region is located along a natural boundary line between the low northern plains and the southern highlands. We believe the soil in this region contains adequate ground ice to meet our water supply needs.

Aarons: Your expertise is microbiology. Professionally, are you happy with this site?

<time delay>

Schweitzer: Not completely. Any living microbes will most likely be found in underground aquifers. Near the equator, those aquifers will be at least a kilometer deep, far out of our reach. However, I might detect signs of ancient or dormant life in the ground ice layers above the aquifers.

Aarons: What about geology?

<time delay>

Schweitzer: Geology is a different story, much to the delight of my crew mate, Doctor Sainsbury. Southeast of the landing site, a network of dry lake *beds and outflow channels originate from a huge impact crater named Nicholson Crater. We assume glaciers or liquid water carved the channels. Since the channel floors are craterless, they were formed recently, in geologic terms. We're also curious about the "yardangs," deep grooves in the surface most likely caused by wind erosion. And finally, far to the northeast is the mighty Olympus Mons volcano, the highest mountain in the solar system!*

As Anna described the geology of the Medusae Fossae region, David rummaged through some papers on his desk and dug out a photograph mosaic of the area near the landing site. The image was old, dating back to the *Mars Global Surveyor* orbiter in the late 1990s.

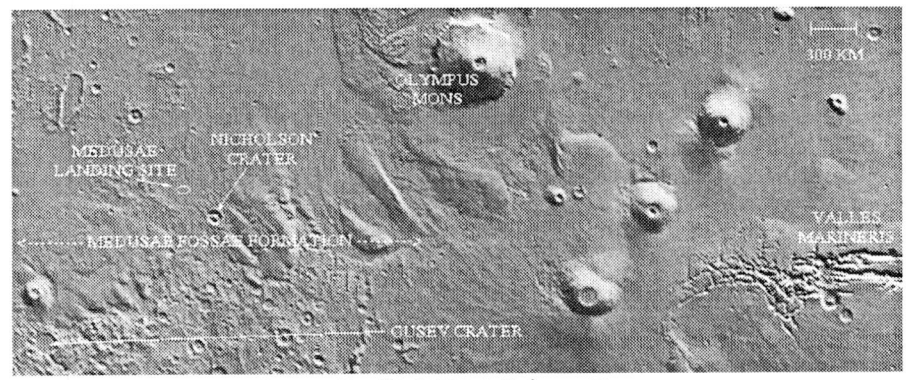

Image Credit: MOLA Science Team

Aarons: Some scientists favor exploring Mars using only robotic probes, as we have for the last 40 years. Why do we need people there?
<time delay>
Schweitzer: Robotic probes can't answer the really interesting questions. They can only scratch at the surface. Humans are far more capable, at a reasonable risk and cost. Of all the planets and moons in the solar system, Mars is by far the most Earth-like. It is a treasure chest, waiting to be opened. Who knows what we'll find there?
Aarons: How long has your mission been in the planning stages?
<time delay>
Schweitzer: I don't know when the plans for the mission were developed. It could have been five years ago, or fifty. The clock has been moving very

slowly since the end of the Apollo era. We could have sent people to Mars in 1975. In some ways, our mission would have been easier back then.

Aarons: I'm not sure I understood your last statement, Doctor Schweitzer. Exploring the moon was a great challenge in the early seventies. Surely, reaching another planet must be orders-of-magnitude more difficult. How could it have been possible in 1975? And if it was, why didn't it happen?

<time delay>

Schweitzer: The missing ingredient was a good plan. Rockets were more powerful back then, as I already explained. We could have sent more explorers, equipment, and consumables to Mars than our current mission is bringing. The space agencies around the world had more political and public support, financing, technical experience, momentum, and confidence. In fact, one could argue that our current mission has only three advantages over a hypothetical 1975 mission. Thanks to planetary scientists and robotic probes, we know more about the surface of Mars. Some of our internal systems, like computers and life support, are more advanced and perhaps more reliable. Our biggest advantage is having a better strategy.

Aarons: Could you tell us more about that strategy, Doctor Schweitzer?

<time delay>

Schweitzer: Our mission is based upon an older blueprint called "Mars Direct." We had to make some changes to streamline it for a three-person crew.

Aarons: I'm somewhat familiar with the background literature about Mars Direct and several NASA plans derived from it. Correct me if I'm wrong, but the NASA plans require a crew of six explorers. A crew of three seems less than optimal.

<time delay>

Schweitzer: It is, indeed. We downsized, while NASA upsized. It's true that six Mars explorers would accomplish more than three. However, a larger crew would require a bigger habitat, more food, more equipment, and more rocket fuel to return home. Mission costs and complexity would skyrocket, literally.

Aarons: Interesting. Tell us more about your plan for reaching Mars.

<time delay>

Anna's half of the screen split, with her image sliding to the top right corner above an animated graphic of the Mars Direct plan. David knew the technicians in the Communications Shack had inserted the animation, but he was surprised at how seamlessly it was integrated into the program.

Schweitzer: Although we just launched from Earth yesterday, the mission started two years ago. An Earth Return Vehicle, or ERV for short, was launched from Earth to Mars, along with a supply vehicle and backup habitat. After landing in the Medusae Fossae region, an automated process began to manufacture the rocket fuel for our return trip home.

Aarons: How was this fuel manufactured?

<time delay>

Schweitzer: The ERV brought several tons of hydrogen from Earth. Three solar powered Sabatier reactors combined the hydrogen with carbon dioxide from the Martian atmosphere, creating a huge amount of methane, water, and oxygen. Further processing converted the methane into benzene fuel, which is safer to store. As for the byproducts, the oxygen and water will replenish our supplies after we arrive. Everything is stored in tanks near the ERV, and these supplies are sitting on Mars, waiting for us to arrive.

Aarons: So that brings us to the current situation. The ERV is waiting on Mars, and you are on your way there. Can you show us what the landing site looks like?

<time delay>

Schweitzer: Unfortunately, we only have satellite images. Extreme temperatures and airflow during the landing damaged the external cameras on all three vehicles at the Medusae site. It was a minor design flaw, but a huge disappointment because we're eager to see our new home. The cameras would also have revealed vital information about the local terrain and dust levels.

Aarons: How long will you explore Mars?

<time delay>

Schweitzer: We'll explore for 18 months before returning to Earth in the ERV.

Aarons: Despite an extra cargo launch and a smaller crew, it sounds like you are essentially following the Mars Direct plan. Are there any other differences?

<time delay>

Schweitzer: The weaker launch vehicle required several more changes to the plan.

Aarons: Could you have built or found a more powerful rocket somewhere?

<time delay>

Schweitzer: We used the most powerful rocket existing today. Four years ago, the Raytronics Corporation partnered with SpaceX, an innovative startup aerospace company, to develop a powerful new rocket aimed at the large military satellite market. With the financial backing of Raytronics, SpaceX created an "ultra-heavy" version of their successful Falcon rocket. We happily used this RSX-1 rocket for our Mars launches, but it can only lift 100 metric tonnes into low-Earth orbit. The older Saturn V could lift 140 metric tonnes.

Aarons: What about on-orbit assembly?

<time delay>

Schweitzer: For a private mission like ours, on-orbit assembly is impractical. It would have added considerable cost, complexity, and risk.

Aarons: The difference between 100 metric tonnes and 140 doesn't seem like much.

<time delay>

Schweitzer: It's huge. To make up the difference, we shrank the size and mass of our crew, habitats, and ERVs. We also added two additional launches for cargo—like more solar panels for power generation.

Aarons: Wouldn't a portable nuclear reactor have saved a lot of mass?

<time delay>

Schweitzer: It certainly would have. Our mission is energy-poor, compared to Mars Direct. That's possibly our greatest concern. Mars Direct was originally intended to be a NASA project, with strong governmental support at every step of the way. Since the United States government isn't running our mission, a nuclear power source was completely out of the question. With the threat of terrorism and dirty bombs so great, Uncle Sam won't allow any private group or individual to become a nuclear entity. This required some creative changes to the plan...

As the session wound its way toward completion, the host asked for more details about their plans to find water and grow food on the surface of Mars. The tone of the conversation remained pleasant and amicable, a far cry from the previous USNN session.

David looked over at Cassie and found her staring at the fake stars on the ceiling. She seemed distant and distracted, as if she was pondering the meaning of life or some other deep cosmic mystery. When David offered her a penny for her thoughts, she mumbled something about trying to make sense of the optimism in this program, given the pessimism of the earlier program.

David admitted his own confusion. Seeing the programs back-to-back emphasized some glaring differences in the style of each network. He vastly preferred the Lynx network's operational, how-to approach to journalism over USNN's how-to-fail dramatization.

When the Mars mission succeeded, USNN's ratings would crash and burn. David wouldn't shed any tears if Fontaine's reporting career met with the same fate.

CHAPTER 6
THUNDER

MarsDay 1, 9:25 a.m.
(November 21, 7:00 p.m.)

"Are you sure you wouldn't like to go out to eat tonight?" asked David.

"Sit back and relax, Mars man," said Cassie. "It's probably been months since you've had a home cooked meal. Tonight you're eating Lasagna Bolognese, just like Mama used to make!" She and Ben had invaded his kitchen, searching for more raw materials to accessorize the groceries they had purchased earlier.

"I cook for myself all the time," David countered.

Cassie sniffed. "What? Frozen pizzas? TV dinners? Soup cubes?"

"You probably have work to do, too," added Ben, shooing him out of the kitchen. "So go do it."

David raised his hands in resignation. Retreating to his computer, he started a new virtual support session.

His guests cooked and chatted. Occasionally, Cassie interrupted him with a "Where do I find..." question. David's frequent answer was, "I don't have any of that."

Meanwhile, he rechecked his work messages more thoroughly. In particular, he was puzzled by one he had just noticed, though its timestamp revealed it had been sent a few hours ago.

To: <shepherd>
From: <chicken_little>
Subject: Advice
Priority: High

Shepherd -
The sky is falling.

This message surprised him so much that he muttered, "What the...?" a bit louder than he had intended, drawing the interest of the others. He showed them the message, and they shared his bewilderment.

Though the message looked like a harmless joke, David didn't find it very funny. He sent a terse response back to "Chicken Little" asking for his identity and an explanation. He also forwarded the message to the support team's internal security department, requesting they determine the identity of the sender and take appropriate action.

Then he returned to the task at hand, reading more messages. Most were status updates from the workers who monitored the various systems of the *Perseus*, looking for trends in the telemetry that could indicate future trouble. He had already read those messages earlier. Since all was well, he just filed them away. Other messages were related to the commander's surprise drill, notes from the psych team, or memos about upcoming media events. None required any personal action on his part.

Just as he had finished reading the last message, another arrived. Happily, it was from Anna.

To: <shepherd>
From: <microbrain>
Subject: Personal Message
Priority: Medium

Hi Shep!
My armor is dented, but holding. Hydra has been appeased. I think the Lynx show went well, at least. Thanks for the warning about Fontaine. You were right about her, and next time I'll be better prepared to respond to all her gloom and doom scenarios.

Other demons have given me a lot of trouble today. I might need a long talk with Kahuna. Unfortunately, I'm tied up with media

events most of today, and Ollie will be sleeping in, so I can't use my cabin to talk to her. If she's still there, please ask her if she's available tomorrow morning at 4:30 a.m. [1:37 p.m. MST].
Anna

He relayed the latter part of Anna's message to Cassie verbally. She reminded him of her travel schedule for tomorrow and suggested a different meeting time, which David then forwarded to Anna. He added some words of praise about how well she handled both media sessions.

The aroma of the lasagna simmering in the oven was mouth-watering. With Cassie checking its progress and tossing a green salad, Ben had taken a short break from the kitchen. He watched David send the message and asked about the curious references to Mars time.

David explained that an intelligent filter translated all time references into local time, Universal Metric Time (UMT), or Greenwich Mean Time (GMT), based on user preferences. The filter easily allowed his support team members around the world to synchronize their local schedules to Mars time.

Ben agreed the system might be convenient for the crew once they reached Mars. However, he also thought it would be tedious for the controllers back on Earth, whose daily schedule would shift by over 30 minutes every day. Ben's team at NASA normally worked standard shifts and used UMT to synchronize their far-flung probes.

Compared to a human crew, David pointed out, NASA probes usually had plenty of idle cycle time while doing their preprogrammed tasks. The Mars crew would be extremely busy once they reached the surface of Mars. One of the primary goals of Mission Support was to offload mundane work from the crew in the field, leaving them more time to concentrate on important matters.

Cassie, slicing mushrooms in the kitchen, paused long enough to inject a psychology remark into their discussion. "To alleviate symptoms of isolation, we want the crew to feel like they're at the center of the Universe. Making time relative to their own frame of reference is a simple trick that can help."

Reminded by Ben's reference to his team at NASA, David asked about the current situation there. "I've heard some rumors describing management's reaction to the mission as, uh, rather poor."

Ben said, "I think they're just embarrassed. They'll get over it."

"They deserve some embarrassment. They've been promoting the Moon over Mars for years because Mars is 'too hard.' Now someone comes along, out of the blue, and attempts a Mars mission. It can't help NASA's ego or credibility."

With his antagonistic remark, he sought to repay Ben for the earlier feistiness at the café. Being called a "faceless nobody" still turned his ears a bit red. A little harmless teasing might even the score.

Ben didn't take the bait. He had returned to his normal behavior, calm and insightful. "At least we still have a chance at the Moon," he said. "And we keep sending better, more capable robotic probes and landers to Mars."

"You mean more expensive, less reliable, and less predictable. Or should I say, more human," chided David, immediately regretting the unfair swipe. The NASA robotics teams had developed some amazing vehicles. It wasn't their fault that these marvels of technology were still inadequate for the job of exploration when compared to a human body, with its long history of successful exploration. Automatons had existed for only a few decades and had a lot of catching up to do.

Perhaps in another hundred years, humans might become more like machines and machines more like humans. If the two species met in the middle, would the resulting biomechanical mush amplify their strengths or their weaknesses? Time would tell, but David wasn't very confident. The current trend was alarming. In situations calling for a symbiotic relationship, unfettered competition could be dangerous and messy.

Ben yanked David out of his philosophical detour. "I do hear a lot of grumbling in the hallways, now more than ever. At least the people on my telemetry team are happy. We're involved in both types of programs, human and robotic."

"So overall, morale is pretty low?"

"I'd say it's holding steady," said Ben. "NASA's a pretty good place to work. The future is still bright, if we can just move past the recent accidents in the lunar program."

"At least no one's been killed," said David, trying to atone for his earlier remarks. "Things could have been worse."

Ben agreed, adding that his colleagues didn't mind if the lunar program paused for awhile to determine exactly what caused the Aitken Basin lander to explode as it was descending toward the Lunar South Pole. A year of delay was too long, however. When a major research program started and stopped so many times, morale suffered. As critical engineers lost hope and left, quality and efficiency would suffer, too. Unless they got back up on the horse soon, a sharper downward spiral was inevitable.

Sympathizing, David expressed hope that the Mars mission would be a positive influence. "At least some NASA engineers can take consolation in knowing their expertise and experience have really helped us. We couldn't have gotten this far without their support, even though much of that support was done under the table."

David finished reading his messages. A few minutes later, they sat down to a delicious meal of Lasagna Bolognese, green salad, and toasted garlic bread. Thoughts of Mars were delegated to the background.

Time flew. Before he realized it, Ben and Cassie were putting on their coats and heading back to their hotel room. David wasn't sure when he would see them again. Their farewells were lengthy, as was inevitable, given the majority of native Minnesotans involved.

MarsDay 1, 11:41 a.m.
(November 21, 8:20 p.m.)

After surviving three lengthy media sessions and recording two short educational clips about space science, Anna was looking forward to her next break. Only half a day had passed, yet it felt like a whole month since she had been "killed" in the commander's drill.

First, she had to finish another important duty, checking the status of the microbes in their *Living Machine* biofiltration system. However, that task would only take a few minutes once she retrieved her portable test kit.

The *Living Machine* allowed them to recycle over 80 percent of their water. They used the recycled gray-water to wash dishes, take Navy showers, and flush toilets. Once they arrived on Mars, gray-water would be used for growing plants in the greenhouse. Without the *Living Machine*, they would run out of drinking water only a year into their mission.

Though she would probably grow tired of checking the system's health twice a day for the next two and a half years, Anna found herself looking forward to the task today. It was the first useful job for which she was uniquely qualified and trained.

Afterward, she went upstairs and checked her messages in the *Perseus*-local version of the Mission Support virtual world. Several dozen congratulatory messages from various heads of state or other prominent people had survived the support team's filters, but she put them aside for now. The reply from Shepherd was more interesting. She glanced through it and sent him another note.

To: <shepherd>
From: <microbrain>
Subject: Personal Message
Priority: Low

Hi Shep!
Just wanted to say, thanks for being there! I really appreciate it.
Please send my thanks to Kahuna, too. I'll meet her at 1:00 p.m. tomorrow in the Psych Ward. I can already tell that being so isolated for the next 30 months is going to be real tough, though it will have its advantages, too. I hope you will hold my e-hand occasionally and keep lifting me up when I'm drooping.
By the way, I'm not sure if I ever told you how much I enjoyed our dance at the going-away party. Patsy Cline moves me. Even though I've never been a very social person, I do wish we could have spent more time together. The way things worked out is probably for the best, though. Maybe it will make the mission go by a little faster if you promise me another dance when I return.

Anna

After sending the message, she instantly regretted adding the last paragraph. She really didn't know why Shepherd fascinated her so much, yet for some reason, she kept thinking about him. Sure, he was very handsome, but more comely men had repulsed her before. Perhaps it was something subtle in his character. She just seemed to trust him, and that trust somehow allowed him to invade her outer defenses.

A few minutes later, Evelyn trudged up the ladder and entered the kitchen to fix herself a late breakfast. Anna logged off the computer and stretched onto the couch again. She kicked up her feet, and observed her fellow traveler's movements.

If she used her imagination, she could almost believe she was watching a female version of Ollie. Both were 5' 6" in height, with athletic bodies, buzz cut hair, and similar angular facial features. Their ages were similar, too.

Several photos of Evelyn in her youth had revealed an attractive woman with curly, dark hair, a charming smile, and a rich copper tan. Her predominantly Scandinavian features were accented by subtle traces of African and American-Indian influence.

Years later, Evelyn had kept the tan, but her hair had grayed and her smile was rare. Her face was a bit weathered and wrinkled, but the rest of her body had aged well. She was strong and fit. Like Ollie, she floated about the kitchen, wasting no energy. The reduced gravity environment added to the illusion.

Anna knew she should take advantage of her upcoming time alone with the commander to reconnect with her. Over the final few weeks of hectic preparations for departure, they had drifted apart a bit.

Unfortunately, the previous hours of media sessions had sucked away most of Anna's interpersonal skills. She just wasn't feeling very social. Her embarrassing performance during the depressurization drill decreased her willingness to speak to Evelyn, too.

Softly humming a tune as she went about her food preparation activities, Evelyn seemed unburdened by the events of the past. She asked Anna how her day was going.

With a sigh, Anna decided she might still have one more conversation left within her. She told the commander about the USNN and Lynx sessions, as well as another one with Amazon Sat in Brazil. Two out of three had gone very well.

Evelyn cheerfully thanked her for running the media sessions. It was an important responsibility, and one the commander was reluctant to do herself because "it just wouldn't work out very well."

Nearly 20 more live appearances were scheduled for this first week. Anna looked forward to later weeks, when the time delay of communications would become lengthier. Media sessions would turn into a series of pre-recorded questions and answers. Hopefully those sessions would be less formal and would leave her more time to recover. She had been warned by the support team to expect the opposite, however.

Anna worried about her workload. Keeping up with her media appearances, as well as her physical exercise, biological training activities, *Living Machine* maintenance, and medical responsibilities would be a real challenge. She voiced these concerns to the commander.

"I know you will do the best you can, and that's all I can ask," said Evelyn. After a moment, she added, "I know you did your best during my little drill a few hours ago, too. I'm sorry if I was abrupt with you. As you know, my job will require pushing you and Oliver very hard, sometimes. It's necessary, but I won't like it, and I'm sure you won't either."

Anna closed her eyes and considered her next words carefully. "I'll try to do better next time, but I have a request. Actually, I have two requests."

She heard a familiar whoosh as Evelyn sat down across from her. The inflatable couch adjusted its form to accommodate her weight. Anna peeked at her through nearly closed eyelids. Evelyn had brought a cup of juice and a warm bagel with her from the kitchen. A raised eyebrow on her face implied, "Go ahead."

"First, please try to work future drills around my media appearances. It would look bad if we have an emergency while I'm talking live with a hundred million viewers. Second, would you consider apologizing to Ollie, too, when he wakes up? He had a long day yesterday, and toward the end, he was really struggling. I've never seen him that low before."

Evelyn pulled out her pocket watch and examined it carefully, frowning, as if she was sitting by the railway platform trying to determine why her train was late. When she finally responded, her voice lacked much compassion.

"I can't make any promises about the timing of our drills, but I'll keep your request in mind. If I get the impression you aren't being attentive or careful, even during your media sessions, I might have to send you another reminder."

"Fair enough. And Ollie?"

"I probably do owe him an apology, but he won't get one. You shouldn't have gotten one just now, either. Anna, we aren't girl scouts on a camping trip. This is the longest journey in the history of mankind, and we are several crew members short of a full deck. Our nearest help is a half million kilometers away. If something goes wrong, there's not much anyone back on Earth could do about it anyway. We'll need to deal with it ourselves, fast! I'll push us all to the edge and beyond, if that's what it takes to prepare us for what's ahead."

Anna reminded her that they were all under a lot of personal stress. Psych issues were just as important as those in the physical world. They needed to take care of themselves before they could take care of the mission and each other. As the ship's physician, she could potentially override the commander's orders whenever the health of the crew was at risk.

Evelyn frowned again, but said nothing. This was a touchy subject. The commander actually had no direct power to force the others to do anything they didn't want to do. They needed to cooperate in order to survive, and a command hierarchy with a firm leader issuing orders was often far more efficient than alternative democracy or anarchy based leadership models. Yet if the crew rebelled, the commander could do nothing to prevent it. Evelyn would somehow have to issue her heavy orders with a light hand.

With the conversation veering into uncomfortable topics, they mutually agreed to change the subject. For the next ten minutes, they exchanged some inconsequential small talk. The ship traveled onward another 20,000 kilometers.

MarsDay 4, 7:44 a.m.
(November 24, 6:15 p.m.)

As Shepherd attended the SEA steering committee meeting in the virtual conference room, David was glad his avatar wouldn't show any signs of his own fatigue. Two nights of restless sleep were starting to take their toll on him. Something had been bothering him, upsetting his sleep patterns, and he didn't know exactly what it was.

Could it be the weird message from <chicken_little>? Or perhaps he had been infected by the negativity in several USNN news programs covering the Mars mission? Maybe the source of his unease was something unrelated to the mission, like the stormy discussion with his sister about relationships?

Regarding USNN, he lay awake at night wondering why that one network was so openly hostile in its mission coverage while the other networks took a more balanced, wait-and-see approach. Was something weird going on behind the scenes at USNN? Or did fault lie within all the other networks?

This issue seemed minor, compared to his other concerns. Yet part of his subconscious mind remained fixated upon it. He liked his world to be tidy. When he came upon a glaring discrepancy like this one, he couldn't leave it alone. He acknowledged this character trait, or perhaps flaw, as the driving force behind his insatiable urge to study philosophy.

The message from <chicken_little> was just as cryptic. His security department had been unable to trace the source of the crank email message from three days ago. According to their records, the <chicken_little> account didn't exist. Furthermore, they couldn't find any record on the support servers of the message ever being sent to him. They concluded that David was playing an elaborate joke on them, testing their abilities for some purpose of his own.

The sky is falling.

What did the message mean? Was it just a harmless joke? Since David had genuinely received it, something odd was going on within Mission Support. Their servers were supposed to be secure, but could a hacker gain access? Could he trust everyone he worked with? He was becoming obsessed with deciphering the meaning of the message, but such a short message could mean almost anything.

The most obvious connection was to Fontaine, with "sky" referring to her first name, "Skye." His shallow dreams had been disturbed by images of the reporter smirking, piercing him with daggers or tormenting him in more provocative ways.

He forced his wandering attention back to the meeting. Other avatars were seated in plushly upholstered chairs around a long mahogany table or along the two side walls. All 20 committee advisers appeared to be present today. The nine voting members on the board of directors were at their usual table positions, near the front of the room.

Including himself, these were the 30 people who were opening a new world for human exploration. He banished his nervousness, thankful to be seeing these distinguished celebrities in cyberspace. Interacting with these people in reality would have been far more intimidating. Many had impressive lifetime achievements within the space science community, politics, the environmental movement, or the entertainment industry. Here, they were all two-dimensional avatars, and one avatar was pretty much like another.

When it was his turn in the spotlight, he linked his local computer to the front wall projector, displaying his OpenOffice-7 presentation where the others could see it. He gave his five-minute status report, finishing early. Since his support team was running smoothly, he had little to say. He chose not to mention the message from <chicken_little> until he knew whether it was a harmless prank or a real problem.

With time left over, David talked about some future issues. Everyone was already aware of his biggest concern, that communications and interaction with the crew would become ever more difficult due to the increasing time delay. He also stated his concern about their relationship with the media.

A committee member seconded his latter concern, mentioning USNN by name. She called their attention to a USNN program scheduled to air a half-hour from now. The program was advertised as an impartial panel discussion about the Mars mission, but the three invited "experts" were all people who had been openly critical of the mission in the past. She predicted another public relations bloodbath.

David hadn't been aware of this program. He inquired about the identity of the guest experts.

"Tyler, Greene, and Rodriguez."

Several members of the audience groaned aloud, sharing David's dismay. The network couldn't have picked three worse people. All had been extremely critical of the Mars mission.

More discussion followed, but didn't lead anywhere. Shepherd gave up the platform to the next speaker, and David lost interest in the rest of the meeting.

Tyler, Greene, and Rodriguez.

Each of them was quite vocal and visible lately. Tyler, a United States senator, had opposed funding for every scrap of NASA research related to human spaceflight over the last four years. Greene, a prominent environmentalist, CEO, and political wanna-be, often griped about how space exploration distracted attention away from problems here on Earth. Both were five-star idiots, in David's estimation. Slightly better was Rodriguez, the director of NASA's Office of Exploration Systems, a strong advocate of human space exploration, but only if nuclear-powered rockets were developed and used.

Eventually, David left his computer, turned on his television, and heated up two leftover slices of sausage and mushroom pizza. By the time he returned, the steering committee meeting was over.

With pizza in hand, he plopped down on the couch to await the start of the USNN program in ten minutes. The couch was comfortable, and his eyelids grew heavy.

He imagined himself addressing the next steering committee meeting. As he tried to convince them of how dangerous Fontaine's propaganda could be, his speech was eloquent and his arguments powerful. Yet one of the committee members, a shapely female avatar dressed in a skimpy white outfit, questioned each fact that he presented, mocking him thoroughly in the process. He recognized her voice. As he studied her image more closely, he concluded that she had to be Fontaine.

"How did you get into this meeting?" he asked.

She responded with cruel laughter.

Awaking from his brief daydream with a shudder, he shuddered a second time when he noticed Fontaine's image staring at him from the television a few feet away. He glanced at his watch and realized he had missed the first 20 minutes of the panel discussion. His pizza plate was on the floor, and its contents were cold.

One of the other guests spoke. The camera angle focused on the new speaker, Jillian Greene, a petite, stylishly dressed woman with closely cropped blond hair and a permanent scowl tattooed on her face. He recognized Senator Tyler and Director Rodriguez to Greene's left. Both were older, graying men wearing business suits and intense expressions. Fontaine hosted the program, seated apart from the others on the right. David snapped awake and alert.

Greene: ...a trillion dollars is a lot of money. By comparison, a thousand dollars each year would support a family in a developing country. A trillion dollars could support a billion families!

Tyler: That's an excellent point, and one that is often overlooked when glory-seeking scientists demand money from the government. Every wasted American taxpayer dollar is food taken out of a starving child's mouth.

Rodriguez: I'm not even going to try counting how many numerical errors she just made. Let's avoid ridiculous exaggerations, please. This current mission didn't cost a trillion dollars. In fact, it didn't cost the American taxpayers a single penny. As far as NASA is concerned, it's a revenue-generating venture.

Tyler: That figures. Leave it to NASA to try to justify massive cost overruns. Your accounting stinks, always has, always will.

Rodriguez: It's true that NASA ran $30 million over budget in its contract to build some of the hardware for this mission, but let's put that amount into perspective. Technology kickbacks from the Mars mission have already saved ten times as much from our lunar program's R&D budget. All these figures, including the entire NASA budget, are petty cash to our government, as you both well know. NASA's total allocation in the US budget is less than half of one percent. That's what the American taxpayer should care about.

Greene: But it's still a waste of money, any way you slice it.

Fontaine: If space research is frivolous, how should this country spend its research dollars? Ms. Greene?

Greene: Environmental research is far more important, in my opinion. My corporation is constantly looking for ways to repair fragile ecosystems damaged by unethical scientists in renegade corporations. But we can never get enough funding for our programs because of all the money NASA wastes. I say that instead of exploring dead planets, we should maintain our living one!

Rodriguez: Without NASA's satellites and probes to provide data, environmental scientists would be back in the Stone Age. We're all on the same team. Comparative planetology has already led to great breakthroughs in our understanding of ozone layer depletion, global warming...

Tyler: But most of that so-called science is done with robotic probes and telescopes. Why should we waste money sending humans to do a machine's work? That's what I can't understand. As long as I'm an elected senator of this great nation, I pledge to stop the bleeding of taxpayer dollars. What has human spaceflight ever done to justify its cost?

Rodriguez: Give me one good human on the Moon or Mars over a hundred of the most intelligent robotic probes that we could ever...

Greene: What about one dead human? How many people would you kill on your little joyrides in space?

Fontaine: A good question, but the answer will need to wait until after a station break. When we return, I'll ask our guests about the morality of manned spaceflight.

As David reheated his pizza in the microwave again, his thoughts were a bit muddled. Greene, Tyler, and Fontaine were living up to his expectations. But what about Rodriguez? He had often been very critical of the Mars mission. Tonight, he sounded almost like one of its most fervent supporters.

Perhaps he had missed something important during the first part of the program? Later, he would play back the entire program from the archives in Mission Support. His team was recording the mission coverage from most of the popular media outlets "for the sake of posterity." A hundred years from now, school children might study the recordings in their history class. He could use the information a lot sooner.

He was also forced to acknowledge another possibility. Perhaps he had greatly misinterpreted Rodriguez's position. The man could be a very useful ally.

The commercial break ended. David poured himself a cup of coffee to go with his pizza. Then he returned his full attention to the program.

Fontaine: Ms. Greene brought up a good point before the break. My next topic for our guests to debate is the morality of human spaceflight. The current Vegas odds of any Mars crew member returning safely to Earth are no better than 50-50. Many experts believe the odds should be much worse. I'll ask each of you, do you view this mission to Mars as a suicide mission? And if so, is it justified? Senator Tyler?

"Uh oh," said David to himself. "She comes out of the commercial break with a vengeance."

Tyler: Yes, it's a suicide mission, absolutely, and it is totally unjustified. It is an abomination.
Greene: I agree. Whoever is behind this mission should be held in utter contempt. They are murdering three people while promoting the waste of trillions of dollars, money that could feed billions of people. Until our problems here on Earth are solved, spending money in space is recklessly wasteful.
Fontaine: Doctor Rodriguez?
Rodriguez: When exactly will we solve all our problems here on Earth? No, I wouldn't call it a suicide mission. But I wouldn't want to be on it, myself. Our best engineers and risk management analysts just can't make the numbers add up. In the past, I've warned about the risks. NASA would never run a mission like this. We give the crew a 20 percent chance of returning safely to Earth, but only a five percent chance if they actually land on Mars. These people have courage, for sure, but they just don't have the right equipment to do a safe, professional job. I wish they had waited a few more years, until nuclear propulsion was fully developed and tested.
Greene: They are fools, doing a fool's errand. Evil people have taken advantage of them, using their childish dreams to lure them into danger.
Rodriguez: Melodramatic statements can't...
Greene: You know the least ethical thing about sending humans into space? The ones giving the orders and reaping the benefits aren't the ones who lose their lives. I would like to think our modern society is more enlightened than that and will not accept it. When this crew dies horribly, we must find their killers here on Earth and bring them to justice. We must prosecute them to the full extent of the law.
Tyler: Well said.
Rodriguez: Now, wait a...

Tyler: In fact, we should begin a criminal investigation right now. Why wait? Those people in space are already as good as dead. Waiting will just give the guilty parties more time to cover their tracks.

Agitated, David got up and began to pace the room. He felt another cup of coffee calling. As usual, he heeded the call.

A little voice of intuition inside his head was screaming at him. As a highly-creative person, David would often seek out this inspirational voice, listen to it, and learn. It sometimes led him astray, but not very often.

Could Greene and Tyler actually be right? What if the mission planners know there is little chance of the crew surviving the mission? Is this why they remain concealed? If the mission fails, could I be prosecuted as an accessory to murder?

His rational, unemotional, calculating side scoffed at his willingness to listen to his intuition. Sometimes, the two voices waged open conflict within him, trying to pull him in one direction or the other. Now was one of those times. His rational side called this theory pure baloney.

Politicians like Tyler are all bluster. Even if the crew dies and the mission planners are labeled as murderers, along with my support team, the charges would never stick. If anything, remaining concealed would cast an unnecessary shadow of guilt upon the planners and my support team.

Still, he couldn't retract his intuitive thoughts. The nature of intuition was persistence.

Fontaine: ...of the mission planners. Who's giving the orders? Any suspects you would care to mention, Senator Tyler?

Tyler: That is indeed the real question, isn't it? They might be working for a foreign government. Possibly an unfriendly one.

Greene: Concealing themselves as well as they have is no small task. It implies considerable resources and a strong, secure base to operate from. A governmental base.

Tyler: Many terrorist groups would love to get their hands on advanced rocket technology, as well as chemical and biological research results to help them develop weapons of mass destruction. This mission represents an extremely dangerous transfer of technology and information. In the future, such transfers must be tightly controlled. Locating the mission sponsors and thwarting their plans is a national security imperative!

David groaned in dismay. Now Tyler was calling him a terrorist, too. The accusation was amusing when it came from his brother-in-law, but quite chilling when promoted by a U.S. senator.

Despite the fact that Tyler's argument was absurdly simplistic, some of the program's viewers might actually believe it. Often in the past, the U.S. government had taken great pains to limit technology transfers to potentially hostile countries like China, even when the transfers had little military value. Such blanket policies had already caused the demise of several promising start-up aerospace companies that couldn't afford to hire legions of attorneys to comply with every regulation.

But then again, what if Tyler was right?

Greene: I firmly agree! I believe our government needs to do a much better job of protecting the American public from the consequences of such dangerous scientific research. As you know, I've announced my candidacy for the Senate in my home state of California. If elected, I vow to work with Senator Tyler to make this matter a much higher national priority.

Rodriguez: But what if the crew survives and returns home safely? What if the planners are honest philanthropists? Aren't you jumping...

Tyler: We must slow down and control the pace of technological advancement! For example, look at all the problems the Internet has created. People have no privacy anymore, identity theft is rampant, online morality is impossible to enforce, hackers can attack businesses and good citizens at will. We need to tighten our controls on improper Internet usage, and...

Rodriguez: What does that have to do with...

Greene: We need to focus our efforts on restoring our planet's ecosystem, while helping third world nations develop their economies in a sustainable, environmentally friendly manner. Global stability is under attack by new terrorist threats every day, and our supplies of energy are endangered. Meanwhile, NASA is wasting money in space...

David started to lose interest in the rest of the program, since the participants repeated the same opinions over and over. Even though this wasn't an election year, the two political aspirants seemed to be campaigning.

Interestingly enough, he agreed with some of the statements all three guests had made. However, the best lies are often hidden within half-truths. Wasting taxpayer dollars was something to be avoided, and sustainable, environmentally responsible development in third world nations was an important goal. Politicians and environmentalists had been talking about these issues for decades without coming up with any new solutions, or even many original ideas. Perhaps a radical new approach was needed, a forward looking, optimistic approach, rather than one based upon the usual doctrine of guilt, hostility, despair, and managed deprivation?

As the program finally ended, David resolved himself to another night of restlessness. The caffeine from his coffee wouldn't help him to sleep, either. He made a mental note to switch to decaffeinated coffee tomorrow. Then he tucked that note away with all his previous, identical ones.

He reclined on the couch and covered himself with his favorite blanket, a worn, plaid eyesore made of a thick wool-cotton blend. During his years as a starving student, he had bought the blanket from the surplus Army-Navy store on Pearl Street. His head rested against an equally worn polyester fiber pillow at one end of the couch.

Once comfortable, his inner voices began to battle each other again. It started with a relentless whimper.

The Mars mission must not fail.

A worst-case scenario was if the Mars mission failed due to something he could have prevented. He would have to live the rest of his life with a heavy burden of guilt. How could he ever accept the loss of Anna and the others?

Why is USNN always so pessimistic?

Who is <chicken_little>? What is he or she up to?

How can I protect the crew from all this earthly crap?

Sleep came eventually, but the questions didn't leave. They mingled in his dreams, interwoven by a dark haired, impossibly beautiful seamstress. The woman watched his struggles, and laughed.

CHAPTER 7
DIRECTION

MarsDay 5, 5:33 p.m.
(November 26, 5:00 a.m.)

    The bandwidth on the communications link to Earth continued to drop.
    By now, Anna was totally perplexed. While talking to Russian, Egyptian, and European Union media correspondents for the past two hours, her technical difficulties had steadily grown worse. She instructed the ship's computer to make the necessary adjustments, dropping the bit rate again.
    Similar problems had been expected later, as the *Perseus* traveled farther away from the Earth. With constant power, the bandwidth of their omnidirectional transmitter and receiver dropped with the square of the distance. Her communications bandwidth should have been adequate for several weeks.
    She apologized once more to the program's host for the poor picture quality. Concurrently, she instructed the computer to page Commander Day. Both her crew mates were scheduled for study periods.
    Before the bandwidth problems, the first part of her media session had gone very well. Anna had thoroughly enjoyed talking to Der Spiegel in her native German language, despite several Euro-centric questions. Relations between Europe and the United States had been quite "competitive" lately. The reporter sought to emphasize that two of the three crew members were European.
    More like one-and-a-half Europeans are aboard. I'm such a mutt.

The next question was about their intended landing site. Anna had fielded this one many times before. She answered it by triggering a pre-packaged movie, a 3-D flyby of the Medusae Fossae region on Mars based on their best satellite imagery. The movie would last for three minutes, giving her time to concentrate on the communications problem. Even better, the movie was transmitted directly by Mission Support on Earth. The graphics would be crisp and sharp.

As Evelyn responded over the ship's intercom system, Anna silently rejoiced at her lucky timing. Her audience on Earth wouldn't hear their conversation.

Anna told the commander about the drop in transmission power. Since the computer couldn't find a power drain in any of the subsystems, she was at a loss to explain the situation.

Listening in on their conversation, Ollie offered to come up and take a look right away. True to his word, he appeared on the ladder within a few seconds, setting a new speed record for repairmen making house calls.

"Have you contacted Mission Support?" he asked immediately.

"I did that immediately when I noticed the problem. They're running some system diagnostics, both here and on their end."

"Let's take a closer look at the power usage levels."

With Ollie watching, Anna's fingers danced over her keyboard. The computer obediently followed her commands. She displayed a status page showing the power used by the major subsystems. All levels were still within normal bounds, although the cooling system gauge was inching up from green status toward yellow.

"I just don't understand it," she said. "Assuming the problem isn't with the receivers on Earth, or our transmitter, or our power usage, what else is left?"

"Aliens jamming our signal?" Ollie suggested, with a wink.

She appreciated his attempt to calm her nerves and rewarded him with a sideways smirk. "Then they aren't doing a very good job of it." Getting back to business, she asked, "What if we aren't generating enough power?"

"Then the batteries would kick in and a dozen alarms would sound, both here and at Mission Support...but it wouldn't hurt to check."

She accessed a new control page to check the status of the power generation and distribution systems. Ollie's grip on her shoulder tightened.

"Bollocks! Our power generation is down to 60 percent of normal. The problem must be at the source, our solar cells!"

Anna looked back at him. "How can that be? Unless…have we drifted out of alignment with the sun?"

"That, or some kind of physical problem with the cells themselves, which would be a real bugger to find and fix. We'd have to send one of our robots outside. An alignment problem would explain why the cooling system is running hot. Check the orientation of our spin axis."

She visualized their tiny habitat, spinning through space on its lonely journey, with one side always facing the Sun and Earth. Photovoltaic solar panels on that side of the *Perseus* were their primary source of power. If the angle of their spinning changed, the cross section of solar cells catching sunlight would be reduced. Power levels would drop, and intense sunlight would start to warm newly exposed parts of the *Perseus* exterior.

Anna accessed yet another control page, and the problem was immediately obvious. Their spin axis was off by 20 degrees.

"A steady lateral thrust is required to change the spin axis," stated Ollie. His voice contained the detached coolness of an engineer analyzing a serious problem. "If we're lucky, a maneuvering thruster is leaking propellant."

"And if we're unlucky?"

"The *Perseus* is leaking air."

She flashed back to the terrors of the air loss drill. This time, however, no alerts or inflating balloons were in evidence. Holding her breath, she checked the current air pressure and found it to be normal.

"Assuming we're lucky and it's a thruster problem, can you correct our alignment?"

"Sure. That's the easy part. The real problem will be to seal off the propellant from the bad thruster and replace it. Since we only have one spare unit, repairing the fault is critical. Also, we might have lost a lot of thruster propellant."

The lucky alternative didn't sound very good after all. "Can we afford a shortage of thruster propellant after only five days of flight?"

Ollie gravely shook his head. "I'll inform the Commander. Then I'll realign the *Perseus* from the console in my cabin."

He darted over to the ladder. Then he turned back to her, scratching at the stubble atop his head. "You know, for this to happen would require independent failures of our batteries, alarms, and maneuvering thrusters. Mission Support should have noticed a dozen serious alerts in their telemetry right away. Figuring this out is going to take some time and hard work." He disappeared down the ladder.

His parting words had sent a shiver racing down Anna's spine. Her shell of isolation was feeling extremely fragile at the moment. She forced her attention back to the media session.

The flyby movie, or at least her local version of it, was just ending. Her playback was apparently in perfect sync with the version shown on Earth, as it should be, for the host immediately commented on the exciting graphics and asked her a follow-up question about the landing site. Putting her best smile on, Anna responded casually, as if nothing had happened.

Ollie soon worked his magic, and her bandwidth increased. She didn't even feel or hear the gentle firing of the thrusters. Life in the *Perseus* was good, once again, at least for now.

MarsDay 9, 6:52 p.m.
(November 30, 9:00 a.m.)

Rubbing his eyes, David got up from the couch and wandered aimlessly about his apartment. He had intended to wake up two hours ago, but last night had been his first solid night of sleep in over a week. Fortunately, one of the best privileges of being the director was flexibility. As long as his pager behaved, he could sleep an extra hour or two without feeling too guilty.

Before going to sleep, he had visited with Anna in his office at Mission Support. She delivered a brief status update. Then the two of them talked about other things. Time had flown by quickly.

Normally, David had difficulty socializing with women as attractive as Anna. He never seemed to know what to say or do, and he would always, always end up making a complete fool of himself.

But not with Anna. Her gentle nature put him completely at ease. He was discovering they could talk, laugh, or cry about a wide range of topics. Perhaps the extra safety, due to their physical distance, made all the difference? Yet she had the same effect on him, or rather almost a lack of effect, the one time they had met in the real world.

Since today was Monday, his favorite day of the week, he planned to work a half-day and devote the afternoon to strenuous outdoor exercise. A group of former college friends played Capture the Flag every Monday afternoon in the foothills west of Boulder.

Cassie had always considered the game extremely childish. A bunch of grown men and women shouldn't be running around the mountains wearing Army fatigues and brandishing fake weapons, she would say.

Long ago, his sister had factored his love of adventure gaming prominently into his psychological assessment. She always sought the underlying motivations. What she didn't seem to appreciate was how much he looked forward to the exercise and the fresh air. David loved the mountains. Many people living near Boulder hiked the scenic mountain trails for their outdoor exercise. David hiked, too, but he also ran, crept, ducked, hid, and sometimes slithered.

As he started to plan his work schedule this morning, his mood soured. Over the past few days, progress on his top "to do" items had been elusive.

His most troublesome concern continued to be the mysterious <chicken_little> crackpot, who was still at large. Repeated inquiries to the security department over the past week had come up empty. He hated to believe he couldn't trust the people within his own organization, yet that was his leading conclusion. Either the security department was compromised, or someone on his team had helped a hacker bypass the elaborate security protocols. Either prospect was alarming.

In close second place was the biased mission coverage on USNN. The quality of their coverage had recently plunged to new depths. David checked the program listings often, and several suspicious documentaries or investigative reports had come to his attention.

One USNN program quoted "evidence" that major outbreaks of disease were caused by alien microbes raining down into the Earth's atmosphere from outer space. Another recounted the making of Capricorn One, an old movie about a fake mission to Mars. Other programs covered the various aspects of engineering needed to construct a spacecraft, with special emphasis on how easily people could die out in space.

Each program, by itself, was fairly harmless. Put them all together, add frequent references to the current Mars mission, stir, knead, and bake, and the final recipe further aroused David's suspicions.

At least the negative programming hadn't spread to other networks. Not yet.

Before he could do anything about either of his top concerns, he had to deal with breakfast. His normal morning meal of cold cereal wouldn't work because he had run out of milk.

What else do people eat for breakfast?

Whatever it was, he was pretty sure he didn't have any. Since he hadn't left his apartment in three days, his fridge and cabinets were more barren than usual. He was also down to his last can of Folgers Premium coffee, and his leftover pizza supply was depleted. With a hunger pang and a sigh of futility, he resolved to skip breakfast and get straight to work. Later, he could replenish his food supplies at the grocery store.

On his computer, he entered the virtual support center. After getting an update on the mission status from Major Tom, who was the senior duty officer in the main support room and his most reliable backup, he checked his messages in his office. Luck was with him today, and his message queue was nearly empty. Some of the headlines in the daily news dump to the crew looked interesting, so he took a few minutes to read the text version of the articles:

- "Mars Mission Sponsors Still Elusive" (usnn.com)
- "Looming Energy Shortage or Surplus on Mars?" (cnn.com)
- "Vegas Odds for Mars Mission Rising" (Reuters)
- "Heepah/Davis Divorce Shocks Hollywood" (e.com)
- "Medusae Landforms Confound Experts" (space.com)

After reading his messages and the news articles, he decided he had enough time for a quick run to the grocery store.

Leaving his apartment, he felt a cold fall breeze knifing through his Minnesota Vikings jacket. The morning air was crisp and deeply refreshing. Gray storm clouds hovered over the mountains to the west. Snow was on the way, just in time for his afternoon adventures. In anticipation, he whistled a happy tune as he jogged to the newly expanded Lolita's Market, three blocks from his apartment.

The store wasn't very crowded today. Only one checkout clerk worked the front registers.

Shopping was high on the list of activities David hated the most. His goal was to get in and out of the store as quickly as possible. He grabbed two cans of coffee, a gallon of milk, and six frozen pizzas. Next to the coffee, he noticed a wide assortment of Pop-Tarts. Thinking they might go well with his coffee, he added a few boxes to his cart. He also snared several other food items that might taste good with spaghetti sauce on them.

A short wait at the checkout counter allowed him to browse the tabloids on a newsstand. He usually enjoyed laughing at the covers, and today was no exception. He took special interest in the bold headline of the World Weekly Express: *Mars Mission Doomed!!!*

Gee, that's nice to know. I wonder what their renowned experts say? Can't be any more twisted than USNN's coverage.

He grabbed the tabloid and thumbed through it. On page 14, he found a full-page spread:

UN SHOWDOWN OVER MARS MISSION !!!
(Martians Vow Retaliation)

A furious Martian ambassador stormed out of a closed-door United Nations session last week after learning three human astronauts were recently launched towards Mars. Later, with the help of a translating device, Ambassador Gleekup-Chuk granted an exclusive interview to the Express.

Express: Ambassador, thank you for talking with us. Tell us your reaction to the news of three human astronauts heading to Mars?

Gleekup-Chuk: We will not tolerate trespassers. These Earthlings were not invited, and they are not welcome. If they attempt to land, we will shoot them out of our Beautiful Red Sky.

Express: How did the governments of the Earth respond to...

Reaching the front of the checkout line, David met the checkout clerk's amused gaze, grinned, and placed the tabloid back on the news rack. The young clerk had a shiny eyebrow ring, long rainbow-colored hair, and a fondness for giving advice about tabloids. In a loud voice, she announced, "Good move. They got the Mars story all wrong."

"How so?"

"Everyone knows there isn't any Mars mission!" she stated confidently. "It's all fake, a big Hollywood production."

David was tempted to respond rudely, but he stopped himself in time. Feeding the fire might be more fun. He asked her innocently, "Why would they do that?"

The look on her face turned more serious, almost conspiratorial. "I'm guessing they're promoting a new movie. Those rich Hollywood people are always doing wild stunts to sucker more people into buying tickets."

Still playing along, he muttered, "Greedy scum, all of them. But what tipped you off?"

"Easy. I watched this big show last week on USNN where they talked to one of the crew, a blonde chick. What a bimbo. Like, totally an actress, fake boobs and all. And like, there weren't any beeps, or static, or anything spacey about the show. They probably filmed her from the next room down the hall. Hello, they must think we're really stupid."

David was surprised to feel a strong surge of anger. People were entitled to their own opinion, as ridiculous as it might be, but the clerk's description of Anna had crossed the line. How could anyone in their right mind perceive Anna as fake?

Once again, he barely smothered a blistering comeback. Instead, he replied softly, "Yeah, one of us is really stupid."

Nothing would change the woman's opinion. This was Boulder. Once such a weird idea entered circulation, it would spread like wildfire.

"Aw, it's OK, mister. Don't take it so hard. They've got a lot of people fooled."

The clerk rang up his purchases, and David hurriedly signed the credit card receipt. He left the store quickly. Given more time, the clerk might try to convince him that all Republicans were spawned by the Devil, another popular misbelief in Boulder.

He didn't remember much of the cold walk home. His carefree attitude had evaporated. The morning sky now seemed gloomy and oppressive.

Back at his apartment, with a few minutes to spare before his appointment, he brewed a pot of coffee and put his groceries away. Then he sat down to a rushed breakfast. Once it had brewed, the coffee perked up his spirits a bit. He tried dunking a cherry flavored Pop-Tart into the coffee, but discovered the Pop-Tart got too soggy and oozed into his coffee cup, leaving an unappetizing film of sugar and what appeared to be deadly toxic chemicals floating on the surface.

Slouching in a folding chair by his computer, with a fresh cup of coffee in hand, he used the Mission Support software to place an untraceable phone call to Patricia Collins. Patricia was a volunteer who had assisted him with various projects in the past. She answered on the first ring, and they exchanged friendly greetings.

Like many of the outside experts assisting Mission Support, Patricia was always looking for more ways to help. In her day job, she was an account executive for a high-profile advertising agency in Manhattan. David had asked her for this appointment because he wanted to tap into her vast experience working with the media. Perhaps she could shed some light on USNN's biased programming.

Patricia got right down to business. "The media is fickle. One day they're your friends. The next, they're your worst nightmare. That's just the way they operate. It's also why my most successful advertising campaigns bombard television viewers with commercials."

"I'm not sure I see the connection," said David.

"We schedule runs of commercials to last anywhere from six weeks to six months. By doing so, repeatedly, for different products, my firm establishes a longer-term financial relationship with the network. An understanding is reached. We pay them to advertise, and they don't slam our products."

"Sounds a bit deceptive."

"It's the way the industry works. It's all very predictable and capitalistic."

David considered the meaning behind her words. "Are you implying we would get more favorable news coverage if we paid the network?"

Patricia laughed, and advised him that an outright "bribe" would most likely backfire. "Most media companies actually believe their ethical standards are high. They strive for journalistic integrity, at least until it clashes with their bottom line. You have to manipulate them gently to establish a better relationship with them. Seek a commitment where both sides benefit. When the financial risks are high or their reputation is at stake, the commitment needs to be a long-term one."

"Other than cold cash or guaranteed mission coverage over the next two years, what other long-term benefit or commitment could we provide to USNN?" asked David.

Patricia hesitated before replying, and when she spoke, she seemed to grasp for the right words. "I don't know. Your commitment to allow mission coverage for two years ought to be adequate. It is for the other networks. Prime mission coverage increases viewer levels. Over time, the network charges advertisers like me more money. You're already paying them, indirectly."

"So the other networks give our mission positive coverage because we pay them for it?"

"You could look at it that way," she replied.

"Then what's different about USNN?"

They both lapsed into silence. Thus far, the discussion wasn't very surprising. David had always assumed the media worked in this manner, but it helped to hear the whole cycle outlined so clearly. It was merely a series of assumptions leading to a conclusion. If one observed a different conclusion, obviously one or more of the assumptions were faulty or incomplete. But which one?

He outlined the basic assumptions again, for Patricia to confirm. A long-term commitment on both sides was required. Program content interested the viewers and increased ratings. Advertisers paid the network, which profited handsomely. The cycle seemed solid.

Based on her agency's latest data, Patricia was able to confirm that viewers were interested in the Mars mission coverage—in a big way. "The ratings numbers have skyrocketed. My agency has already paid huge advertising fees to various networks, including USNN."

"How much money are we talking about?" asked David.

"All together, around $100 million, in the past month alone."

"From just one advertising agency."

"Yes."

"That blows my next theory out of the water," said David, disappointed.

Reading his mind, Patricia said, "If you're wondering whether someone is paying the network to provide negatively charged coverage, it's unlikely, but it's happened before. I wouldn't rule it out completely. With negative coverage, the network still receives advertising revenue. One wouldn't have to add much to tip the financial scales. But there are two huge problems with that line of thinking."

"You said before, a bribe would be frowned upon."

"Right, usually," she said. "That's the first problem. But there's an even bigger problem. The network's advertising revenue would drop off over time. Negativity only works for a short period of time before the viewers revolt. As the mission continues, USNN will lose advertising revenue."

"So if the viewers are interested and the advertisers are paying top dollar, what's left? The long-term commitment?"

Patricia pointed out that if an accident scuttled the mission or viewers grew apathetic over time, the long-term commitment might be the part that was lacking. However, each media network shared the same risks. She doubted whether USNN would view the long-term situation much differently than their competitors.

David tried to think of other alternatives. If deliberate bias on the part of the USNN network was unlikely, what about a single, rogue reporter? He suggested the possibility that Fontaine was going off on her own, trashing the mission for some personal reason.

Patricia thought this was even more unlikely. "A big network like USNN keeps most of its reporters on a tight leash. If they start to violate the orders from above, jeopardizing lucrative advertising contracts, they're slapped back into line quickly. If they don't conform, they get fired. That's part of what I meant earlier with my comment about journalistic integrity."

"Does a reporter get fired like that very often?" asked David.

"Oh, yeah. You just don't hear about it."

David took a deep pull from his coffee, making a loud slurping noise as he did so. He was starting to get a glimmer of an idea.

He asked, "Rather than bribing an entire network, perhaps someone bribed a reporter? The reporter might risk being fired if the bribe was large enough."

"Possible," Patricia conceded, "but how would you ever prove something like that? You're talking about Fontaine, right? Hasn't she been trashing the mission for months? If she was going against the wishes of the network, bribed or not, surely she would be searching for a new job by now."

"Yes, which brings us right back where we started," said David. "She must have the support of her management at the network."

They talked longer without coming up with any new ideas. David thanked Patricia and ended the phone call. Then he looked back through his notes.

Any bias on the part of USNN must come from high levels within the network. But why?

Long-term commitment, viewer interest, or advertising revenue. Which of these three assumptions is wrong, uniquely for USNN? Does any of this really matter? Why do I care what they think and say?

This last bit of speculation prodded a flash of intuition.

It does matter. It's important for some reason. I just don't know why yet.

MarsDay 9, 10:00 p.m.
(November 30, 12:13 p.m.)

Once again, bees pounded on the door, the walls, and the ceiling. Anna had suffered through the same dream almost every night, but this time it was a little different. The bees were smarter and quicker. Their droning had more meaning. In fact, yes, it was true, they were actually communicating! They were talking to each other, conspiring about how to reach her.

Have you looked for cracks around the door? Can you fit through an air vent?

She was more terrified than ever. Hearing the cold voice in the dark was almost a relief because on some inner level, she knew that she would wake up soon afterward. She had to wake up! She had to...

...wake up! With a strangled gasp, Anna flew out of bed and huddled in the corner of her tiny cabin. She reached back and grabbed the thin blanket off the bed, wrapping it around herself tightly. She remained that way, trembling, for several minutes. The demons of her unconscious mind eventually retreated, but conscious echoes replaced them.

Something is wrong!

She leaped back into bed and pulled down the thin computer display and keyboard so she could communicate with the ship's computer. Her fingers flew over the keys as she checked the current status of the key systems in the *Perseus*. Life support was OK. Power supply and consumption was within the normal range. Computers, communications, crew location, and activity logs...all were fine.

The temperature was a few degrees low in her cabin, so she bumped the electronic thermostat up a bit. Other than that, everything was normal. She pushed the display and keyboard away, roughly.

Why do I feel this way?

She had a long time to think about it. Her sleep, so rudely interrupted, failed to return quickly.

CHAPTER 8
STABILITY

MarsDay 10, 3:55 p.m.
(December 1, 6:37 a.m.)

Host: Cynthia?
Cynthia: Thank you. Doctor Schweitzer, I've heard speculation that your medical supplies will deteriorate after a few months in space. Is this true?
Schweitzer: We don't know for sure. The rumors you heard are based upon some research conducted on the International Space Station. However, no one knows if radiation was the main culprit. The medicines might have deteriorated due to zero gravity or some combination of environmental factors. I'm keeping my medical supplies well shielded, just to be safe.
<time delay>
Host: We have time for one more question from the lounge. Doris?
Doris: Over all the other people who wanted to go to Mars, why were you chosen?
Schweitzer: For the biologist position, my recent Ph.D. in Microbiology just got me into the running. Athletic skills, EMT training, and field medical experience didn't hurt my chances. But hundreds of people were still in line in front of me. I may have been chosen because many of the others were actually too qualified. Practically every top biologist in the world wanted this assignment. Many had theories to prove and worldly responsibilities to uphold. But consider what our conditions will be like on Mars. We expect the scientific community back on Earth to bombard us with requests for

information, field samples, and targeted research. I believe the mission planners wanted a generalist, someone with no prior theories to prove, someone who is impartial and willing to collaborate with any scientist on almost any topic.

<time delay>

Host: Doctor Schweitzer, thank you for being our guest today. We wish you and your companions a safe journey. Until you return to Earth, our hopes and prayers are with you. That concludes today's Afternoon Tea. Tune in tomorrow when Ian Holst will join us, in person. Ian, as we all know, is the captain of our semi-finalist World Cup soccer team. BBC news is next.

Anna killed the connection and glanced at the commander. Evelyn had been relaxing at the table, barely out of camera range, since their earlier, private session with the Queen of England. Talking to the BBC was nice, but a rare audience with the Queen was a high honor.

"Well? Do you feel any different, now that you've received an Order of the British Empire award?" Anna asked.

Anna redirected her gaze toward the curvature of the wall beside the computer display. She lost herself in sky-blue, the color of the day. By choosing such a tranquil shade for the walls, the psychologists at Mission Support were probably trying to calm the crew. They had even added some fluffy clouds higher up. She could almost imagine a warm breeze blowing through her hair.

"I feel alive," Evelyn said. She put her cup of tea aside and studied the elaborate engraving on her pocket watch. Then she commented, "You have an amazing talent with words, my dear. A real gift."

"The Queen asked some good questions."

Evelyn laughed. "Her no-good science advisor was probably lurking nearby. Still, it seems like she's following the mission with great interest." Her fingers lightly explored the circumference of her watch.

"And great concern," added Anna. With a shallow smile, she added, "During most of my outreach activities, like the one with the BBC, I'm just floored at how eager everyone is to talk with us. I guess that's what it's like to be a celebrity."

Evelyn looked up from her watch sharply, a curious expression on her face, something close to a scowl but not quite. "Celebrities sometimes end up living lonely lives. All that publicity often comes at an expensive price, and exposure can be negative, just as easily as it can be positive."

"Of course. I'll try to keep that in mind. Shepherd said we haven't been smeared too badly in the tabloids yet, but he thinks it's just a matter of time."

"Let's hope we stay on their good side," said Evelyn, with a bemused shake of her head. "Public opinion needs to remain positive. The tabloids usually pick on celebrities who have fallen out of favor." She hesitated before adding, "I wonder what the tabloids will say about our audience with the Queen?"

Anna laughed. "I got a kick out of watching 'Doctor Oliver Sainsbury, O.B.E.' when he was up here earlier. When he addressed the Queen, you would think he had been introduced to God!" Ollie's nearly bald head had beamed like a beacon from his divine encounter.

They lost themselves in the memory. Eventually, Evelyn said, "I wish Morgan had been here to see it. He would have been just as deeply touched. He was a Brit, too, or rather, a Scot."

Her gaze was focused upon some distant place for a few moments. Anna fought the urge to follow her stare. Instead, she looked at the pocket watch. Evelyn held it gently, as one would hold a newborn baby.

Anna knew that Morgan Day, the commander's husband, had died a few years ago in some kind of accident. She had danced around the topic several times, but Evelyn was never willing to talk about it, and Anna had always respected her friend's privacy. However, with Earth behind them and Mars ahead of them, perhaps Evelyn would now be more willing to discuss the past.

"Tell me more about Morgan. What was he like?"

Evelyn's lower lip quivered a bit. "He was the most courageous, honest man I've ever known. And the most compassionate. I try to draw strength from his memory whenever I can."

"Through the watch?" Anna asked. She had always known the silver pocket watch held deep meaning for Evelyn. Perhaps there was a connection.

"He gave me this watch for my birthday, four years ago. He said as long as I had it, he would be with me." Barely audible, she added, "That was just before he went away."

Though Anna felt guilty, by now her curiosity was thoroughly aroused. She heard herself asking, "How did it happen?"

Silence, and then a hesitant answer.

"We were stationed together at McMurdo Base in Antarctica. Morgan led a team of engineers who were expanding the facilities. As the base commander, working for Raytronics Polar Services, I was actually his superior officer."

Another pause, as if she had trouble recalling. More likely, she didn't want to remember.

"Two of his engineers, a married couple, had been working on some faulty sensors at a remote weather station twenty miles to the south. They contacted us by radio when they couldn't get their trawler started. I could hear the panic in their voices. They knew a storm was approaching because winds were picking up and the temperature was dropping fast."

After a sip of tea, she continued. "Morgan begged me to let him rescue his people. At first, I wouldn't let him, but he was very persuasive. Finally, I agreed. That was the last time I saw him."

Anna waited for more, but the commander remained silent. Finally, Anna worked up the courage to ask, "No one made it back?"

Evelyn shook her head. "Antarctica can be a very unforgiving place. We think he reached the weather station because we didn't find the bodies of the others, either. Our best guess is that on the way back, he was blinded by the storm and drove off a cliff. His tracks were buried, and we never found his trawler."

She clutched the pocket watch tightly before placing it into her hip pocket. The silver chain dangled from her belt, a symbolic reminder that some links can never be broken.

Anna shared the commander's pain. She knew what it was like to care deeply about someone, only to have that person cruelly ripped away. Years after the car accident claimed the lives of her family, she had longed for their return with every fiber of her soul. She had dreamed about them almost every night for years, convincing herself at times that they still walked beside her.

She also regretted pressing the commander for information and reopening her old wounds. "I'm so sorry," she mumbled, trying to inject some of the compassion into her voice that she felt inside. "I, I just don't know what else to say…"

"No words are necessary, my dear. Time heals most wounds, or at least allows us to manage." She stared into Anna's eyes. "I hope you never find out what it's like to order someone off to their death. That decision has haunted me. I lost my life that day, too. But I gained experience. Just remember that, when I ride you so hard you hate my guts. Now you might have a better idea of why I'm doing it."

Anna considered those last words carefully because they could be interpreted several ways.

Does she want to protect us? Or is she trying to distance herself from us, as I'm so good at doing myself, thereby lessening her pain if we don't survive this mission?

Evelyn rose and placed her empty teacup in the kitchen sink. "If you need me, I'll be in my quarters. Let's take a rain check on our game of three-handed pinochle tonight. I need some time to be alone."

"Of course."

Evelyn moved over to the ladder, just as Ollie was climbing up to join them. "Just a minute, commander," he said, brusquely. Jumping off the ladder, he grabbed her right arm, attempting to pull her back into the room. "I would like a word with you both." His earlier reverence was gone.

"Can't it wait?" Anna interceded. "This isn't a very good time right now."

"It has already waited long enough. Four days, in fact," he replied. "I just figured out our solar alignment problem. As you know, I've been retracing the events and talking to some colleagues at Mission Support."

The commander lashed out at Ollie's wrist with her left hand, hitting a pressure point. Ollie immediately lost his grip on her other arm and grimaced in pain.

"Later!" the commander growled. She descended the ladder, leaving behind an angry crew mate holding his wrist.

"Why that, that..." Ollie spluttered, before reining in his anger. He turned toward Anna. "Well, would you like to hear what I found?"

"Sure. Pull up a chair and tell me all about it. And by the way, Ollie, your timing really stinks."

Her comment gave him pause, but he would not be deterred for long. He flopped into the inflatable chair across from Anna's couch and glared over his left shoulder at the empty ladder.

"It was all another one of her stupid drills." The scowl on his face surprised Anna in its intensity. "The *Perseus* was never out of alignment. We were locked into a simulation. She disabled alarms, rerouted the battery power, and thrusted the ship out of alignment. But it was all simulated within the main computer. She even simulated my sealing off the propellant to the bad thruster unit. Bloody Mission Support had to be in on it, too. They probably sat back and had a good laugh about it afterward, at our expense."

Anna smiled thinly at him, wondering how best to respond. "That's not too surprising," she said, finally.

Failure to provoke an angry response seemed to rile Ollie even more. "Well, what are we going to do? Her drills are going to drive us insane!"

Anna sighed, and leaned back, scratching at the itchy stubble atop her head. She had never liked the Sinead O'Connor look. At the moment, she didn't care about such trivial matters. She didn't care about much at all. Her emotional roller coaster had parked itself at the terminal.

"I take back what I just said, Ollie. You have very good timing. Let me tell you a little story I just heard, not five minutes ago..."

MarsDay 11, 8:11 p.m.
(December 2, 11:40 a.m.)

"The world runs on patterns. A broken pattern is a clear warning sign."

The biting words of Doctor Snodgrass, his "Theory of Everything - 501" professor and mentor from years ago, echoed in David's mind as he surveyed the usual lunchtime crowd at Old Chicago, his favorite restaurant in Boulder. He came here every Wednesday afternoon, his one day of the week to splurge by eating out.

A warm breeze graced the day, a far cry from the howling winds he had encountered up in the mountains two days ago. The unseasonable temperature had to be approaching 70 degrees Fahrenheit. Festive aromas of popcorn and hot dogs wafted from a portable fast food cart in the middle of the mall.

He sat at his favorite table outside the restaurant, dressed in a short-sleeved t-shirt and ragged, knee length cutoffs. He preferred this table because it was a good place to watch people at the busy, T-shaped intersection of Pearl and 11th.

The streets were crowded. A young mother scooted her two children along to wherever they were going. A flock of street musicians, beggars, and peddlers competed for attention. Some local students idled the afternoon away on a park bench, oblivious to their surroundings. Tempers flared, and pleasantries were exchanged. Mostly, shoppers passed by with bags bulging from their purchases.

The waitress approached with his lunch. From his frequent visits to the restaurant, he knew her on a first name basis. She remembered him, too, well enough to know he had not ordered his usual meal.

"Yeah, Donna, I know," he responded to her inquiry. "I'm taking a break from pizza today. I have to eat something healthy, occasionally."

Donna was his favorite waitress. Compared to the other wait staff at this restaurant, she was older and far more outgoing. She was also a bit overweight, in a delightful, motherly way. David loved hearing Donna's throaty laugh.

He heard it now. "David, you're a strange bird if you think a calzone is healthy!" She returned inside, still laughing, no doubt ready to share this little story with her co-workers.

He tasted the calzone, sipped his merlot, and let his thoughts wander on the afternoon breeze. What was Cassie doing now? She was probably helping one of her needy clients. Ben would probably be at work, about to take a lunch break. Anna would soon be sleeping. He wouldn't trade places with any of them, though he would gladly trade places with Ollie or Evelyn.

Thinking about Anna anchored his thoughts to the current status of the Mars mission. Since he hadn't heard from the mysterious <chicken_little> again, he had almost convinced himself the earlier message was a harmless practical joke. He still didn't find it very funny, though.

Of greater concern, Anna's most recent "Health and Safety" report had contained some red flags about crew interactions, particularly between the commander and Ollie.

Let the psych team handle that. Worry only about the things you can control.

Doctor Snodgrass often repeated this advice to students who were in danger of "worldly washout," as he called it. Many philosophy students were overwhelmed by the magnitude of the issues they pondered, as they applied their lessons to the real world around them.

His old mentor's advice was actually, "Worry only about the important things you can control." Snodgrass believed half of a person's worries were about trivial matters. Of the remainder, half were about things they had no control over. Therefore, the list of important worries a person could control was only 25 percent of the total set of possible worries. A wise student cast off the rest, freeing his mind and soul for better things.

Though the psych team should handle crew interaction problems, David was still the Mission Support Director. Encouragement and empowerment were well within his job description. He resolved to send the psych team a happy memo stressing the importance of crew psychology to the success of the mission. The psych team would promptly ignore the memo because they already knew their own supreme importance, but that was fine. It was how the management game was played, sometimes.

After removing psych issues, the USNN mission coverage had regained the top spot on his Worry List. Once again, he recalled his mentor's advice about patterns. In the general pattern of positive media coverage, USNN was still a lone anomaly. This was a clear warning sign...of what? And what was the real question, anyway?

As he watched the shopper migration and listened to chirping birds that should have migrated south long ago, he let his mind drift back to a USNN program from the night before. Fontaine had hosted this program, too. She seemed to be everywhere lately, attacking and posing biased questions to skeptics in the engineering and scientific communities, the political ranks, and the general public. If any wolves were out there circling the pasture, she was certainly the pack leader.

Why is she so fixated on her bogeyman theory and upon potential mission failures?

As Fontaine questioned various self-proclaimed experts and analysts on her programs, each stated their own opinion about why the mission was likely to end in disaster or why it was such a bad idea in the first place.

The guests on the program last night were worse than usual. One was a "quality" expert who estimated the odds of each unmanned vehicle landing safely on Mars at no more than 50-50, making the odds of six safe landings less than two percent. No mention was made of the three unmanned vehicles landing safely at the Medusae site two years ago. Besides, humans could guide the next three landings.

The other program guest was an aerospace engineer who claimed to have thoroughly analyzed the schematics and capacities of the fuel generation system within the ERV on Mars. In his opinion, the available solar cells and batteries were incapable, by at least a factor of two, of creating and storing enough electricity for the fuel generation system to run at full capacity. This engineer conveniently bypassed the fact that a fully fueled ERV was already sitting on the surface of Mars, awaiting the arrival of the crew.

Scientists and engineers are usually far more cautious. Doesn't Fontaine realize that if the mission goes according to plan, she and her "experts" will end up looking like idiots?

Given the risk, why would her "experts" encourage her insane agenda?

Perhaps she's putting words in their mouths by asking biased questions and editing the answers? Or she's choosing dubious, hostile speakers in the first place? Or she's paying them off? Or she's leading them with pessimistic data? Or...who knows?

But why?

Because...it's safe for her to do so. Somehow, she's totally convinced the mission will not go according to plan. It's doomed to catastrophic failure.

But that's insane! USNN would need to know more about the mission than the other networks, or even myself. I'm probably better aware of the internal operations and status of the Mars mission than anyone else in the world. How could a two-bit reporter possibly know more about the mission than I do?

Yet if...

What if Fontaine's network has a unique, closely guarded source of inside information—someone with the ability to guarantee the mission will end in failure? Would this explain USNN's negatively biased media coverage?

It just might!

If the network firmly believes their source, they might be willing to align themselves with the failure-mongers, risking a potential public backlash. When the mission fails, USNN will be light-years ahead of the competition. Their ratings will soar, and Fontaine will be famous.

And three people will die in space. Including Anna.

Startled by this horrible conclusion, he shot upright in his seat, bumping his glass of merlot and sending it to shatter on the brick pavement beneath his table. The spilt wine was the color of blood.

Donna was at his side immediately. "David, what happened? You look like you've seen a ghost!"

"Maybe I have," he mumbled. "Maybe I have."

Then he snapped back into the present, apologized, and offered to pay for the broken glass.

"Don't be silly, dear," replied Donna. "Accidents happen, even to very healthy people like you." She reached down to pick up the largest pieces of glass before retreating back inside.

Accidents happen...

Don't be silly, dear. How could USNN possibly know an accident will scuttle the mission? Their analysts and reporters are idiots, and at the moment, you're being a bigger idiot than they are.

But what if they're right? Even idiots are right, sometimes.

Lost in thought, David barely noticed when a busboy cleaned up the mess and Donna brought him a new glass of merlot. He eventually finished his meal, paid the bill, and left an extra five dollars for Donna in his tip. As usual, he wrote her a little note on the back of the bill: "But the calzone contained veggies, and veggies are healthy!"

He started back to his apartment, taking the long way, enjoying the beautiful winter day and watching the world go by. He needed time to think.

After taking a few steps along the pedestrian mall and brushing off a peddler selling watches, he glanced across the street at the BookEnd Café. Business was heavy there, as usual, and many patrons were sitting outside. He thought of Cassie.

Perhaps I should call her when I get back. She might spot something I'm missing, or confirm I'm totally crazy.

He took a few more steps down the mall. Hapa, the Japanese restaurant adjoining the BookEnd, was almost deserted. Almost...he froze in his tracks.

You're losing it, David. You're obsessed...with Fontaine. You're even starting to see her outside your nightmares now, in the real world.

After blinking a few times and moving closer, he studied the woman sitting outside Hapa. It was her! Either that, or Fontaine had a twin sister. She was less than 20 feet away, seated next to the thin railing separating the tables from the foot traffic on the mall. Her short red dress sparkled in the sunlight.

Sitting across from her was a middle-aged man in a polo shirt and gray slacks. The tall, slightly-balding man was quite handsome, in a rugged sort of way. His chiseled face was striking, and his frame was muscular. Both diners were eating sushi with chopsticks.

David shook his head, trying to clear his thoughts. Could this really be the woman who had plagued the Mars mission with her pessimism? The woman who had turned his dreams into nightmares? Why was she eating lunch in Boulder, of all places? He had to find out.

David approached the restaurant, intending to claim a seat outside and listen to Fontaine's conversation. A pang of ethical guilt threatened to halt his forward progress, but his curiosity brushed it aside, firmly.

Where guilt failed, rationality succeeded. He halted.

No, this won't work. She'll see another customer nearby, and they'll talk too softly for me to hear. Or they'll just leave. For this to work, I would have to be invisible.

Invisible. Hmm.

Back on the south side of the street, David spied an older man sitting with his back to a music store window. The man's ruffled clothing, gray hair, and a long, unkempt beard gave David an idea. As he approached, the strong smell of body odor on the pleasant afternoon breeze was almost overpowering. With a shaky hand, the man held out a shiny metal cup to him and asked, "Friend, could you spare a few dollars? I haven't had a decent meal in awhile."

Before this stranger could launch into his life story, David replied, "Sir, could I rent your cup for a few minutes?" He removed a crisp, new $20 bill from his wallet. The man looked startled, as if seeing David for the first time, but he quickly slid some coins into a pocket in his tattered jeans and handed the empty cup to David. Having "rented" the cup, David hastily retreated.

He ran a hand through his hair, tousling it a bit, and wiped some dirt from a nearby flowerbed onto his forehead and shirt. Fortunately, he had worn some older clothes today. Inspecting his makeshift disguise in a mirror would have added to his confidence, but he settled for using a shop window.

Walking slowly westward along the far side of the street, he worked his way back toward Hapa, trying to blend in with the background stream of humanity. When he drew near Fontaine, he sat down on the ground against the thin railing, his back to her table. An icy shudder coursed through his veins as he considered her proximity and recalled his earlier nightmares.

With his cup raised to all passers-by, David perked his ears and tried to listen to her conversation. This turned out to be more difficult than he had expected because she was already talking to her companion very softly. Still, there was no mistaking that voice. She was indeed Skye Fontaine, his ethereal antagonist.

"I've paid you a lot of money," she said. "How do I know the disk is genuine?"

"You'll just have to trust my sources," her companion responded, a bit louder and easier to understand. He sounded annoyed.

Her voice dropped even lower, barely above a whisper, and he could only hear bits and pieces of her reply. "But I don't even know who those sources...can trust me to...anything...Mars mission... very unusual."

"You don't need to know any more," the man replied. "You probably know too much already. If you stick your lovely neck out any further, it might just get chopped off."

With those last words, the man slapped his hand on their table, a bit too close to David's ear. David tried not to jump, but the hand holding his shiny cup might have wavered slightly.

Apparently, the two diners hadn't noticed. After a short pause, their conversation continued.

"I don't take kindly to threats." Fontaine's voice was colder now, and louder.

"Then call it advice. Don't forget who owns you. Do your job and don't ask any questions."

"But asking questions is my job."

"Asking the right questions is your job," the man replied.

Her dining companion pushed his chair back, grating the legs harshly against the concrete. The piercing metallic shriek sounded like fingernails on a chalkboard, and David flinched again. Retreating footsteps were followed by silence.

He was about to glance over his shoulder to see if Fontaine had left, too, but he heard her mutter softly, "Looks like I picked the wrong day to quit sniffing glue."

Her reference to a line from one of his favorite comedy movies surprised David almost as much as the earlier conversation had. He laughed under his breath, while waving to a lady who had just placed a dollar in his cup.

Sniff all the glue you want, sister. Maybe it will straighten you out.

After another short period of silence he heard her say, "Cheapskate didn't even leave a tip." As she picked up her purse, David peeked under his left armpit and tried desperately not to stare at her oh-so-long-and-shapely legs.

Then, in a louder voice, she said, "Aw, heck, you need this more than they do." The smell of Chanel No. 5 perfume suddenly overpowered him as she leaned over the railing and placed a green bill into his cup. "Don't spend it on booze, OK?" she added.

The number ten was visible above the brim of his cup. "Thank you, ma'am," he stammered, not wanting to turn around, afraid that he would fall under her devastating spell if he met her eyes. For some reason, he felt compelled to add, "I don't drink." Then he winced inwardly, realizing how pathetic his lie had sounded, even without the musky smell of wine on his breath.

"Yeah," she said, "and the Pope ain't Catholic, either." Then she left. He studied her closely as she walked away from the café, heading east. Gliding over the street's uneven bricks, her high heels never faltered. Her tight red skirt swished sensually with every step.

Behold, the great seductress. She must be Satan, herself.

David needed a moment to regain his shattered composure. Eventually, he removed Fontaine's $10 bill from the cup and slipped it into his pocket. That money was his, payment for a tiny piece of his immortal soul. He didn't touch the other coins and bills except to estimate their value at over $5. Not bad, for ten minutes of work. Perhaps he had been foolish to go to school all those years.

He rose to his feet, crossed the street, and returned the cup to its previous owner. Then he walked home via his alternate route, slowly, deep in thought.

Though he hadn't heard all her words, Fontaine had clearly referred to the Mars mission. The rest of the conversation had made no sense at all.

The only thing he knew for certain was his Worry List had grown.

CHAPTER 9
REFLECTION

MarsDay 14, 1:00 a.m.
(December 4, 5:56 p.m.)

    The dream was the same again. Bees...then a shiny trailer and a sinister voice.
    Anna was well into her scheduled sleep interval, but she wasn't the least bit drowsy. Instead, she was terrified, as she always was after awakening from The Dream.
    Despite two sessions with Kahuna in the Psych Ward, she had endured the same nightmare four times during the last two weeks. Kahuna, only mildly concerned, had suggested some reading material related to Nightmare Disorders in the online version of DSM-VII, version 7 of the Diagnostic and Statistical Manual for Mental Disorders.
    In Kahuna's opinion, which matched the DSM literature, the recurring dream wouldn't lead to any "social or occupational impairment" unless it caused her to lose sleep.
    Anna needed more. She needed explanations, answers! There had to be a reason she kept having the same dream over and over.
    Kahuna always seemed to answer her by asking other questions like "What do you think about that?" and "Why do you feel that way?" Such typical psychobabble might be useful at times for other people, but Anna didn't feel it was helping her any.
    She was growing more convinced this dream was different, somehow. It felt almost external, like she was receiving a real message from someone or

something unknown. The frequency and intensity of the message gave it a sense of urgency. After the first time, she always awoke rapidly, fully alert, fearful, and anxious.

Pulling her computer's flexible pedestal down to her bedside, she logged on the support team's virtual world. Since she was in her quarters in reality, the computer dropped her online avatar into a representation of her crew quarters.

She immediately composed a message to Kahuna outlining her latest frustrations. When she couldn't think of anything else to add, she sent the message and went to get a soothing cup of instant valerian tea from the kitchen.

Her avatar would remain patiently in its virtual quarters. However, she knew her real-world location marker would now be moving out the door, up the ladder, and into the kitchen area. Markers were used to constantly update the crew's real position and activities at all times. The psych teams back on Earth used the markers to study the interaction between habitat design and crew dynamics.

She glanced down at the thin bracelet on her left wrist, the one containing a location marker microchip and transmitter. She usually ignored the left bracelet, at least when conducting daily physical exams on herself and the others. A matching bracelet on her right wrist monitored her bodily vital signs at all times.

Ten minutes later, she returned to her cabin, tea in hand. Her avatar checked for new messages but didn't find any. Kahuna probably hadn't even seen her message yet. Summoning her reserves of patience, Anna fought the urge to page Kahuna.

Perhaps she should read a book while she waited, something fun and light. The ship's computer had access to a digital library containing thousands of short stories and novels. She stepped through the "A" section of the lengthy index, spotting Alice in Wonderland immediately. As a child, this had been one of her favorite books. Evelyn also quoted little passages from it quite often.

She read a few chapters and felt a bit more relaxed, though sleep still eluded her. Then she reached the part where Alice was trying to find a way to enter the beautiful garden, a part she didn't recall, for some reason. While pondering how she could have forgotten this key part to the story, she rechecked her messages and found three new ones. The first was from Kahuna, who offered to meet Anna in her Psych Ward office immediately.

Anna warped her online avatar into Kahuna's private office, a large, airy room with white pine paneling and plush furniture. Mona Lisa contently stared down from a corner, one of many classic art masterpieces beautifying the walls. Sculptures like Winged Glory competed for floor space with an army of potted ferns, some reaching upward to the artificial skylight above.

Whenever she visited this room, Anna wanted to explore the decor for a few minutes. But that wasn't why she was here. After greeting Kahuna, she plopped her avatar down onto a familiar old Victorian couch.

Kahuna locked the office and pressed a nearby button marked "Privacy." Then she sat in a chair near Anna's couch. Hampered by the time delay, they traded small talk before easing into a more serious discussion.

Kahuna was very interested in Anna's growing perception of her dream being a real message of some kind, and moreover, an urgent one. "What elements of the dream make it feel that way to you?"

"I'm not sure. It's not really a specific element, or even an emotion. I think it's simply because I've had the same dream over and over again. I feel like I'm back in my freshman biology class, where the professor spent a whole month going over the same chapter in the textbook until the daily quiz scores improved. I remember his explanation: 'Until you understand this material, you aren't ready to go on to anything more advanced.' This dream feels the same way, like there's more I need to know, but I'm not ready for the advanced stuff yet."

She twiddled her thumbs, waiting for Cassie's next question to arrive.

"How do you see yourself in the dream, in relation to the events happening around you?"

That was an easy question. "Small, insignificant, a toy for others to attack and abuse."

"Do you control the environment in any way?"

"I have no control over anything. I feel like I have no way to affect the outcome or shape the events. All I can do is react. I run, I hide, and I feel pain and terror. And frustration."

"How do you regard the passage of time, in the dream?"

Anna stopped to think, hoping Kahuna wouldn't notice her hesitation. The time delay of communications probably made all of her responses seem overly thoughtful or contrived anyway, but that was unavoidable.

"I suppose I don't feel the passage of time at all. Each part of the dream is separate and seems endless. The only thing holding it all together is the terror I feel. It washes over me in powerful waves."

Kahuna said, "Dreams come from the subconscious mind, which is extremely observant, but often very cryptic. Sometimes, the subconscious does have a message to tell us or teach us. One bit of advice is to be open to learning, just as you were open to learning in your freshman biology class. As the dream happens, try to ask each element or character, 'What are you trying to teach me?'"

Anna cleared her throat to comment, but Cassie continued. "The subconscious mind is also timeless and has a strange notion of past, present, or future. Messages from it usually feel like either a flashback or a premonition. Which does your dream feel like?

This was another easy question, and her response leapt forcefully from her throat. "The dream definitely feels like a premonition. A dark, sinister one. Something is wrong. No, everything is wrong. In the dream, everything is wrong!"

Anna's agitation was growing again, but she forced herself to keep her voice down, barely above a whisper. Evelyn would be trying to sleep in her cabin directly below. She took a few deep breaths, calming herself a bit.

"Ahh, now we're getting somewhere," Kahuna replied quickly, or as quickly as the speed of light allowed. "Everything is wrong, yet you have no control, no ability to affect change. A 'lack of control' dream is understakable for someone in your current situation. Let's talk about this lack of control. When you were a child, tell me about the first time you can remember feeling totally helpless?"

Anna sighed and answered the question, describing once again her deep feelings of anger and frustration when her parents and siblings died. Then she answered several more questions that followed. She knew the psych team had heard all this before, a dozen times, during the crew selection process. All the while, she felt close to realizing something profound, but it continued to elude her.

Kahuna's last bit of advice was, "Try to get some sleep! These recurring dreams are only harmful in their ability to interrupt your sleep patterns. I can't prescribe medication, but if you aren't able to sleep on your own, I could ask our team's psychiatrist to do so."

Prescribing medication was another difficult ethical dilemma on the mission, another gorilla in the room, because Anna was not a real doctor or pharmacist. Though she had completed several condensed courses in each discipline, a full EMT program, and over three years of part-time field medical work as a volunteer with the International Red Cross, she would rely upon earthly experts for most medical advice, including prescriptions.

In reality, however, the crew was several million kilometers away from Earth, far outside all bounds of jurisdiction. The law of the frontier was the only law that mattered. A lack of formal credentials wouldn't stop her from dealing with any emergencies that arose.

Fortunately, Anna wouldn't need any medication to help her sleep, at least not tonight. The last part of her discussion with Kahuna had been boring. She dozed off into a deep slumber. In her book, Alice had not yet reached the beautiful garden. This time, in her dream world, Anna did.

MarsDay 14, 2:31 a.m.
(December 4, 7:30 p.m.)

Shepherd waited patiently, admiring the artwork on the cream colored walls of the Psych Ward's waiting room. David wasn't an art scholar, but he did recognize some of these classical pieces from his studies of medieval history. In fact, he recalled writing a lengthy essay about how religious art had played a fundamental role in lifting mankind out of the dark ages into a more enlightened renaissance of scientific advancement.

While he waited for Cassie to appear, he decided to reread his old history essay, refreshing his memory on the topic. Finding the paper should have been easy because his school projects were saved on his computer. However, he couldn't find the assignment he was looking for.

Splitting his display in half, he skimmed through a different paper he had written for the same course. The medieval history course had been one of his earlier undergraduate classes, and many of his arguments and examples now seemed simplistic. Had he been grading the paper himself, today, he would be quite critical of several points.

Despite its shaky foundation, the paper had reached a proper conclusion. A prevailing misconception in modern times was that religion fundamentally opposed science. The seeds of this ironic belief could be traced to the trial of the great astronomer Galileo, who had been convicted and sentenced to house arrest by the religious powers of his time.

In his paper, David had researched clergy motivations having little to do with religion. The astronomer had been caught in a political and economic power struggle between the Vatican and some Italian city-states. In fact, Galileo remained a devout Catholic to the very end, as were many scientists who built upon his work with funding from Papal grants.

As he finished reading the paper, Cassie's avatar finally approached him in the waiting room. "Hi Kahuna!" he said, cheerfully. "You're running late! I was on your schedule at 7:00."

"I'm sorry, Da...er...Shepherd. I had an appointment that ran over. It was urgent and unavoidable. But I can stay as long as you need me to."

Kahuna led the way into her office and pressed her "Privacy" button again. The button was a symbolic trigger guaranteeing their communications would take place on an encrypted channel. Since psychology interactions were often intimate and personal, great care was taken to ensure privacy.

After catching up on the latest family news, David told Cassie about his lunchtime encounter with Fontaine in great detail. He wanted to get her opinion about what he had witnessed, but it had taken him two days to work up the courage to ask her.

Fortunately, upon returning home that afternoon, David had drafted some notes about what had happened and what each person had said. His transcript of the dialogue might not be word for word, but it should be close enough.

"Wow, David, I can see why you wanted to talk about this. But I'm curious...did you want to talk to your loving and supportive sister? Or to Kahuna, the dispassionate psychologist?"

"Maybe both, since they are conveniently the same person," he said, after giving it some thought. "I keep going through the dialogue in my mind, and I just can't make any sense out of it."

"We could walk through it again, together, but I doubt if it would help you much. I'm hearing your confusion, and it's probably coming more from actions than words."

"I'm not sure I follow you," said David.

"She surprised you with an act of kindness, even though your preconceived notions about her are hostile. In fact, you were the one who was being deceitful, violating your own rigid code of ethics at the time you overheard her conversation. How does that make you feel?"

"I see it's going to be Kahuna, then. Would you like my avatar to move over to the couch?"

"If it opens you up, you can have your avatar grow, shrink, stand on one leg, or sit wherever it wants to. Let's try to keep reality and fantasy separated here, OK? You have this picture of Fontaine in your mind, based upon her media image, and it seems to be clashing with what you've observed in reality. Does it surprise you that a television celebrity might be a real person too? With real hopes, fears, and some occasional, compassionate feelings?"

David thought about how he viewed Fontaine and how quick he was to judge her. "Maybe it does surprise me. When I see her on the television, I usually loathe her message. When I see her in my dreams, I despise her actions. As much as I try, how can I hate her as a person when I don't even know her? Others might shape her media image. I'm still finding that part of me really does want to hate her, personally. Perhaps that's what bothers me the most. I hate hating people. It's not my way."

Cassie barely let him finish before she pounced. "Dreams? What dreams?"

After a mild, inward curse or two, he told her about some of his dreams. He hadn't intended to, but it was unavoidable. Cassie the freight train would be appeased by nothing less.

They ended up talking for over two hours. While he didn't have any miraculous revelations, he eventually left her office feeling less agitated.

MarsDay 14, 6:30 p.m.
(December 5, 11:55 a.m.)

"It's frustrating, but not as bad as the time delay of direct communications has become. I tape each response, and invariably a few moments after sending it, I'll come up with a better way to say it."

Anna meticulously cleaned the dishes from their evening meal with a sonic scrubber, a tiny amount of water, and lots of elbow grease. Then she placed them into a sterilization chamber. All the while, she tried to fill the silence in the *Perseus* with idle chatter.

When the items in the daily news dispatch from Earth failed to trigger any serious discussion, she moved on to other topics. Now she was telling Evelyn and Ollie about her recent media sessions. Her audience didn't seem to be paying attention.

The spinning habitat, now far away from Earth, had increasingly become an isolated oasis. For people with patience, some interaction with Earth was still possible. Indeed, Anna could still enter the virtual Mission Support world and interact almost as well as before, assisted by sophisticated software algorithms that constantly synchronized certain events and predicted others.

Communicating with the media was a different matter, however. For the media, time was money, and 20 seconds of dead air time was an abomination.

Anna was tired of all the dead air time within the *Perseus*. She had held several normal conversations with Evelyn and Ollie, but not with the two of them together. As far as she could tell, they hadn't spoken to each other in several days.

Dinner tonight had been especially difficult, but she had tried her best. This rift needed to be repaired before it impacted the mission in some tangible way.

"On the bright side," she prattled, "I've discovered it's possible to hold conversations with more than one party on Earth at the same time. One of my talks today ran long, and I was able to overlap it with the next one. I figure tomorrow, I'll try for ten at a time, maybe more. That's if I'm still alive, of course. I've already contaminated our water supplies, and I figured that after breakfast tomorrow, I would de-spin the *Perseus*, shut down the main computer, and go outside to do some serious stargazing."

"I wouldn't advise that," Evelyn replied, softly.

"She speaks! I thought you two had fallen asleep over there. Or perhaps you've simply fallen into apathy? That's a common ailment, affecting most of the human race these days. What do you think about that, Ollie?"

Ollie slumped further, his head sagging over the back of his chair to the point where he could see her, upside-down. "I agree. I think you should shut down the main computer. Save our commander the trouble of doing it herself, as part of her next bloody simulation."

At least she had them talking now. The door had opened, just a crack, and she wasn't about to let it close again.

"So what do you say to that, Evelyn? I've already told Ollie most of what you said a few days ago, about the motivation for your drills."

Evelyn slammed her fist on the table and turned toward Anna, with sudden fire in her eyes. "When I tell you something personal, I don't expect you to broadcast it to the whole world. I thought you had more sense than that."

Anna returned the commander's glare with as much open defiance as she could muster. She was fed up, and she let her frustration show.

"Take a good look around you! Our whole world consists of three people. One, two, three." Anna pointed as she counted. "You stated yourself that we're several crew members short of a full deck. We don't have the luxury of keeping any secrets from each other. If we start holding things back, we're all going to die out here!"

She gave them a few moments to reply, but they remained silent. Evelyn looked especially thoughtful.

"Well?" Anna finally prompted. "Are we all going to grow up and talk about this like adults? Or should I mention this insane, suicidally stupid behavior in my next Health and Safety report?"

Evelyn pushed back her chair and started to pace the room, as she always did when she was about to deliver a lecture. This time, Anna resolved to control her level of intimidation. She was not going to back down.

"OK, I agree, this has gone on long enough." The tone of Evelyn's voice was casual, almost airy. "I probably should have sat down with Ollie earlier and told him what I was doing, but I didn't. The psych team thought it would be therapeutic for him to have a directed challenge. But I can't hide behind them. Perhaps I let my own feelings get in the way. Or maybe I was waiting for him to make the first move. Regardless, it's time to clear the air and move on."

"Why?" asked Ollie. He cleared his throat. "I mean, why do you or the psych team want us to think we're in danger during your wonky drills? And what if a real emergency had happened at the same time? Would you have known the difference? There are other ways to challenge us…better ways."

"More simulations? Training? Reading books?" asked Evelyn, dismissing these things with a wave of her hand. "Those are all fine and safe, but you greatly exaggerate the risk of my unannounced simulations. None of those alternatives tell me how the two of you are going to react in a real crisis. They don't tell me how you'll react afterward, either."

Anna raised an eyebrow, and Ollie threw her a glance indicating he was just as surprised. "Afterward?" he asked.

"Yes, afterward." Evelyn continued her pacing. "I've learned a lot about both of you, over the past few days, things I suspected from our training back on Earth. Much of it pleases me. Anna focuses on human aspects and psychological healing, as she should, being our doctor. Ollie checks the nuts and bolts, finding the root cause of the technical problems, as he should, being an engineer. You've both done your jobs well." She smiled at them.

Anna felt her cheeks warming a bit. She refused to be placated so easily. Of course they had done their jobs. What else could they do?

Evelyn leaned over the back of her empty chair. "Ollie, it took you several days to figure out my last simulation. What else did you learn during that time?"

He hesitated. "Well, I guess I learned more about the computer systems. I also got to know some of the people at Mission Support better. Is that what you meant?"

"That's exactly what I meant." Evelyn resumed her pacing. "If you learned even one thing that might avoid a problem later, or you made one new working relationship that will help you to become more efficient, then it was all worth it. And don't forget I'm testing Mission Support just as much as I'm testing you. They have similar issues, on their end."

"But at what price?" Anna heard herself ask. Some of her anger and defiance had faded away, but she wasn't quite ready to accept the commander's words at face value, either.

"Are you asking whether saving our lives is worth a few days of silence?"

"I'm saying, if a real emergency had happened during the last few days, we wouldn't have been mentally prepared to deal with it because you two were off in your corners pouting. I'm also asking whether you've given any consideration to our absent crew members?"

In answer to Evelyn's questioning stare, Anna continued. "I was wrong earlier when I said our world consisted of three people. It also contains the hundreds at Mission Support and the millions of others on the Earth who have placed their hopes, dreams, and possibly their futures upon our shoulders. That's a heavy burden for us to carry."

"I know all about carrying heavy burdens," Evelyn said, softly.

"Do you? You don't interact with the public every day, like I do. You don't see the looks of eager anticipation battling their fear of the unknown and their unwillingness to change. I record at least two educational sessions every day. The children of the world look up to us. They're all here with us, too, to some extent. What would be the effect on them if they knew of our petty, unprofessional squabbles?"

Evelyn countered, "What would be the effect on them if we all died, due to something we could have easily prevented?"

"In that case, they might regroup and try another space mission in a few years. I've been preaching to them that our mission could fail for a hundred different reasons, but the attempt mattered most. They might accept our deaths much sooner than they would accept our unwillingness to cooperate, to work together as a team, to represent the best of humanity."

"Cripes, you sound more idealistic than Irena," Evelyn responded eventually. "Still, I'm starting to see your point. There are some intangibles pertinent to our current situation. I'll give this some thought. But only if you don't shut down the main computer tomorrow."

They shared a nervous laugh. Anna had gained a bargaining chip. "That depends," she said, with a fiendish giggle. "While you two have been pouting, I've been doing the dishes every night, all week. Perhaps I really am insane. It's time we went back to playing cards, with the loser doing that task the next day. Anyone up for a quick game of pinochle?"

They all agreed. Now that they were talking to each other again, the evening was a bit more pleasant. Anna lost the game again, much to the delight of her companions. The dishes would await her attention again, tomorrow night.

If the others suspected she had lost on purpose, they would never be able to prove it. And she would never tell them.

CHAPTER 10
FREE FALL

MarsDay 16, 11:08 p.m.
(December 7, 6:00 p.m.)

To celebrate their highly-improbable upset victory during the afternoon session of Capture the Flag, David's friends on the Green Team had chosen to eat at Old Chicago. David wouldn't be ordering a calzone tonight. The champions would dine on deep-dish pan pizza, loaded with grease and artery clogging toppings.

Thoughts of work were far from his mind as he stopped back at his apartment to check the status of Mission Support before meeting his friends.

Upon reading his messages, he found a very encouraging response from Manny Rodriguez, NASA's Exploration Systems Director. In the message, Director Rodriguez clarified his attitude about the Mars mission. Before launch, he had bitterly opposed the mission because he had believed it to be unsafe. Since the mission was now en-route, Rodriguez promised to lend his support. His office at NASA would assist the mission and help the explorers return to Earth safely.

David was only mildly surprised at Rodriguez's response, given his statements during the USNN panel discussion. He was most happy to accept the director's assistance, subject to approval and terms negotiation by the SEA steering committee.

Ever since Anna's first media session with Fontaine, where she commented about every aspect of the mission having a good fallback plan,

David had been concerned that Mission Support didn't. If someone like Fontaine or <chicken_little> completely disrupted their systems, the mission might be jeopardized. In hindsight, he was actually quite surprised the mission planners hadn't taken more steps to minimize this weakness.

With the help of Rodriguez, he hoped to set up a backup support center at NASA. If an online catastrophe happened, Rodriguez's computer networks and experienced support teams in Houston might save the day.

Secure in the knowledge that he was making progress toward completion of his goals, David felt free to celebrate with his friends. He put his coat back on and walked to the restaurant.

The gathering was held in a back room. Paraphernalia from Chicago sports teams littered the busy walls. Each square-foot was covered by some little touristy knickknack or photograph. Michael Jordan was still worshipped here, despite his frequent retirements from the NBA so many years ago. The overall effect was gaudy, but no one seemed to mind. Gaudiness was almost expected in a place like this.

Reggie Kingston sat on his left. Reggie was a head shorter than David, 50 pounds lighter, and far more agile on the playing field. He and Reggie had been good friends through much of grad school, though outwardly, their personalities were quite different. Reggie, with his boisterous sense of humor and confident swagger, had partied his way through grad school. Afterwards, they had gone in their separate directions, so tonight was a good opportunity to reconnect.

To David's right sat Jennifer and Bill Smith. David pretended not to notice the newlyweds holding hands under the table. The happy couple lived 20 miles west, near the serene little mountain village of Nederland. Long ago, he had harbored a serious schoolboy crush on Jennifer. Now they were merely good friends.

As the leader of his squad, Jennifer looked out of place in her street clothes. Her dirty blonde hair was still pulled back into a tight, military style braid. Without her green fatigues projecting a rugged image, one might almost believe she worked as an engineer at one of the many aerospace companies near Boulder, which in fact she did.

Bill's husky frame seemed much more natural in fatigues than blue jeans, however. He was an outdoorsman and another long-time friend, despite his preoccupation with sports and his notoriously short temper. David had never actually seen Bill resort to physical violence. While his size and strength was impressive, he had always been a talker, not a fighter.

Three opposing "Generals" sat across the table, enlisted men who led the Army, Navy, and Marine reserve squads. They would be buying the pizza this evening. The "real" warriors usually didn't socialize with David's civilian squad. In fact, the only reason for including the Green Team in the military maneuvers was to add a dose of real world randomness to the outcome.

The Green Team wasn't expected to compete well, and they certainly weren't expected to win. However, tonight was the final week of the fall season, and a brilliant string of tactical decisions by Jennifer had propelled the Green Team into first place. Their victory pizza was well deserved. Each member of the squad had burned a lot of calories today.

As the three opposing leaders discussed tactics with Jennifer, the rest of the 12-member team conversed along the narrow table. Most were reliving the afternoon's adventures with a high degree of animation.

An approaching waitress carried their first pizza. She placed it in front of David. Leaning over his shoulder, she whispered into his ear, "A healthy guy like you shouldn't be eating this stuff."

David groaned. He now had a new reputation among the wait staff here.

He served slices of pizza to his friends before digging into his own. As everyone started to eat, much of the table talk became muffled, though no less animated. These friends had no qualms about talking with their mouths full.

Soon, Reggie got to his feet, holding his mug of Coors Lite high. He proposed a toast to Jennifer. "I'm glad she's still alive," he said. "After our flag was taken today, I thought she was going to fall back from our superior offensive position to recover it, and then I would have killed her!"

His toast was greeted with laughter and more toasts. David was the target of several accolades, too. His desperate dash back to their home base carrying all four flags was lionized. Jennifer roasted him about letting the rest of his team get shot while he grabbed all the glory.

When the proceedings were at their rowdiest point, their waitress reappeared and gave David a big bear hug from behind. "Hey everyone," she announced, "we have a celebrity in our midst, and he's all mine!" Not having the faintest idea of what she was talking about, David turned and gave her a questioning look. "You're on TV!" she explained. "And on USNN, no less!"

"What?" He shot to his feet, giving the woman his full attention. "Please show me, now!"

She went over to an old, flat screen television hanging on the side wall unused. Earlier, she had turned it off so it wouldn't be a distraction to the party. Now she clicked it back on, and there was David's face on the screen, along with the images of two other people he vaguely recognized. The sound volume was high, and they listened to the announcer for a few moments.

Again, if anyone knows the identity of these people, please contact our network immediately at the phone number or e-mail address on the bottom of the screen. A $5,000 reward will be offered to anyone who provides information helping us locate these people. Your name will be kept in the strictest confidence.

Some short video clips appeared on the screen—a young woman in a blue party dress applying lipstick in a mirror—a bearded man self-consciously adjusting his tie and tacky sport coat—David dancing with Anna.

"Oh my God." His legs gave out beneath him, and he fell back into his seat as if he suddenly weighed 500 pounds. His chest was heavy, and he couldn't breathe.

"That's David, all right, looking sharp!" Reggie announced, pounding him on the back. "Way ta go, friend! You made the evening news!"

"Yee-hah!" That would be George, a native Texan, at least in his own mind. "Who's that cute little filly with you, boy? She's a knockout!" His words prompted several hoots and whistles from around the table.

"Hey, that's the space lady! That Mars astronaut, Doctor Whats-her-name!"

David had no idea who said this because his face was buried firmly in his hands. He wanted the sudden, intense nightmare to end, but it wouldn't. He endured more hoots and wolf whistles.

Peeking through his fingers, he noticed that Jennifer and Bill weren't joining in with the others. Jennifer put her arm around him and whispered in his ear, "This is a bad thing, isn't it?"

He could barely speak, so he nodded and whispered back, "Very bad."

His shock gave way to action, and he suddenly knew what he had to do. He reached over to his left and gave Reggie a friendly clap on his shoulder. "Gotta go, friend. Glad we could catch up on things."

Then he turned to Jennifer and Bill. "I need to speak with you both. Outside. Right now." He waved to the others as the three of them grabbed their coats and moved quickly towards the exit.

Mars Day 17, 4:44 a.m.
(December 7, 11:45 p.m.)

Anna was surprised when Ollie trudged up the ladder. His sleep period had begun less than an hour ago.

"Early bird gets the worm, eh?"

He didn't respond to her teasing. After rummaging around in the kitchen for a few minutes, he plopped down on the inflatable couch with a cup of tea in his hand. His eyes were half closed.

Anna continued to study the schematics of their *Living Machine* biofiltration and water purification system on the computer display above him. Her next media session was scheduled for two hours from now, so she was taking this time to do some homework. The *Living Machine* was simple in principle but complex in detail. An intimate knowledge of its inner workings was critical to their survival.

Ollie had continued to struggle, even after they cleared the air with the commander a few days ago. Occasionally, he lapsed into somber moods, quite unlike the man she had come to know during the last six months of training. She hoped it was just a phase he was going through, one that would pass quickly. She put her keyboard aside and studied him more closely.

Ollie squirmed on the couch, well aware that he was the object of her scrutiny. He grumpily asked her to redirect her attention back to the computer.

"No can do, my friend," she replied. "You're talking to Doctor Schweitzer, now, and the doctor has noticed you haven't been eating or sleeping well. It's time we had a little talk."

Ollie reclined and rolled over, blocking her stare firmly with his shoulder blades. Eventually, he rolled over again, faced her, and acknowledged he was having some troubles. He couldn't sleep because his cabin was too stuffy and the mattress was uncomfortable. The bland meals were grating on his nerves, too.

Anna noted his shallow complaints, but believed his moodiness must have deeper causes. He acted like he was slipping into a mild state of depression. She tolerated the same mild discomforts every day without nearly this much effect. Besides, she knew that Ollie had lived in far worse conditions before. She asked what else was bothering him, hoping for some clues to the real issues.

"I've been feeling on edge for days," he soon responded, "and I don't know exactly why. Maybe I'm just uneasy being stuck out here, so far from Earth, with no real work to do! I'm a geologist, a rock hound, a person of the soil. My whole life, I've been deeply connected with the Earth." He looked around. "At the moment, there isn't a rock within millions of kilometers!"

Anna could sympathize because she shared these feelings, to some extent. She longed for some real biology work to do. Sure, she had the usual reports to fill out, medical procedures to run, and experimental cell lines to culture for later use in determining how organic material adapted to Martian surface radiation, pressure, and atmosphere. But the real interesting work wouldn't begin until they reached the surface of Mars. They would have to endure 23 more weeks of isolation before they reached their geological and biological paradise. In the meantime, they would have to cope with the current situation.

While she couldn't do anything about the underlying isolation, perhaps she could alleviate Ollie's symptoms. She returned her attention to the computer. On the chance his sleep cycle had not yet adjusted to the longer Martian days, she made a note in her medical log to reinstate his daily dose of melatonin supplement for two more weeks. She also canceled his wake-up call for tomorrow morning, modifying his schedule so he could sleep an extra two hours and take a medical exam an hour after waking.

His tea contained caffeine, so she took it away and brewed a fresh cup of soothing chamomile tea. Then she sent him off to bed, handing the covered cup down the ladder after he had descended to the level below.

Having dealt with her first little medical crisis, she smugly settled back into her chair and gazed at the wide computer display in front of her. Studying ship schematics was a poor way to counteract her own growing feelings of boredom, so she started up a game of Save the Microbes, a fun microbiology simulation programmed by someone at Mission Support.

She played well this time, better than usual. Her simulated habitat life support system kept two people alive throughout the six-month journey back to Earth.

MarsDay 17, 5:03 a.m.
(December 8, 12:05 a.m.)

    David probably wouldn't be returning to Boulder anytime soon. Fortunately, Bill and Jennifer had driven their Chevy Tahoe hybrid to the celebration. The cavernous cargo area now held a small mountain of equipment, clothing, kitchenware and other personal possessions from David's apartment. His friends offered to let him stay at their home in the mountains until he figured out what he was going to do.

    USNN would quickly track down his name and address. After the way they had covered the Mars mission thus far, he doubted they would be very courteous once they found him. They had already attacked every visible target they could find. Now they obviously intended to dig into his support organization.

    He wondered about the other two unlucky people on the broadcast who were about to be thrust into the media spotlight along with him. Who were they? He vaguely recalled seeing them at the going-away party for the Mars explorers, but he knew nothing else about them, not even their names. Could they be members of his support team?

    That party had been an awkward, formal affair. David arrived late, remained hidden in a corner for most of the evening, and left early. Most of the other guests were members of the SEA, or so he speculated. He hadn't socialized much, fearing people would ask about his own involvement with the mission. The highlight of the evening was meeting the three members of the Mars crew, and of course, dancing with Anna.

    Bill and Jennifer were both space exploration enthusiasts who had attended several Mars Society and SEA conventions over the years. He asked them about the other two people on the broadcast, and they were able to supply some names and background information.

    Kristin Colcheck was a greenhouse technology expert at Purdue University. Ahmed Tarraz was an aerospace engineer who worked at Pioneer Astronautics in Lakewood, a few miles to the south. They were two of the people who had worked with the SEA to develop hardware or procedures for the mission. Both would be easy for USNN to find, check out, and dismiss.

    Then there was David, a man with two PhDs, no known job, and a solitary lifestyle. Due to the incriminating video, his lack of obvious connections to the SEA or the mission would look very suspicious.

He could have stayed behind in his apartment and feigned ignorance. Sure, it was some other guy in the photograph. The investigative reporters would see through that lie in about two seconds. Public records would incriminate him. How could a guy with no known job and few assets afford an apartment in downtown Boulder, credit cards, and a high-speed Internet connection?

No, he was wrong. It wouldn't take them even two seconds to figure out he was the person they were looking for. Then they would turn his life into a living hell. He would be spied upon and preyed upon. His every move would be analyzed and fed to the public in whatever manner the media desired.

Due to the termination clause in his contract, he would certainly lose his job. The wolves wouldn't care. They would continue to dig into every last detail of his life, talking to people who knew him, searching for connections. To them, he would be their best link to the mysterious Mars bogeymen. They would yank him in any direction they desired, until they moved on to juicier prey.

He hated to think about what would happen to the mission after that, or to himself.

They couldn't stalk him if they couldn't find him. By going into hiding, he might still keep his job, too. It was the only reasonable option. He could run Mission Support from almost anywhere, so he had many potential hiding places.

"You're very quiet tonight," observed Bill, while keeping his eyes focused on the twisting mountain road. Boulder Canyon was difficult to drive at night.

David apologized again for ruining their evening. He glanced at Jennifer, resting in the back seat with her eyes closed. The moonlight danced through her now unbraided, shoulder length hair, and he thought about…Anna. He felt her heart beating in the distance. She was so alone, but trying to be so brave. They had visited several times in his virtual office over the last two weeks, and under her tough exterior, he could readily sense how scared she really was. He wanted to reach out to her, comfort her…

Angrily, he squelched his distracted thoughts. He had other friends to be concerned about, too, including the two who had gone out of their way to help him tonight.

"Are you sure it's OK if I stay with you for a few days?" he asked. "I know you newlyweds probably want your privacy, and I don't want to intrude…"

"Don't be silly," Jennifer scolded him. Apparently she had not been asleep after all. "You know we would give you the shirts off our backs if you needed them. But I'm not sure why."

"Why we would help him?" asked Bill, surprised.

"No, dweeb, I'm not sure why he needs our help tonight, and why he was on TV earlier. What have you gotten yourself into, David? And how could you possibly know Doctor Schweitzer?"

He pondered how to answer her question before cautiously replying, "I wish I could tell you everything about it, but I can't. However, I think it's safe to assume that a lot of people will be looking for me soon. It's important they don't find me."

"And this is somehow related to the Mars mission," she stated, more than asked.

David couldn't lie to his good friends, and he didn't see any easy way to avoid the directness of her question. "Yes, it is. But please don't ask me any more about it. At least, not yet. I need time to think, first."

That seemed to satisfy them for the moment, and they promised to help however they could. Through his job at the forest service, Bill knew of some remote cabins, good places to really get away from it all. Unfortunately, David would still need access to a high-speed Internet connection.

Jennifer said, "Then it's settled. You'll have to stay with us until you can find a place to rent in town or elsewhere. High-speed access is sparse out here in the boonies. Fortunately, we live on a ridge overlooking Nederland, so we get our high-speed access from a wireless Internet company. It's a private system, maintained locally, but I get better bandwidth from home than I do at work in Boulder!"

"Sounds perfect. I really owe you guys, big time."

Jennifer brushed off his words. "David, with this Mars mission going on, you probably don't realize what it's like around the hallways at Ball Aerospace. Everyone at work has been on Cloud Nine! We're so pathetic that we digest and trade every little scrap of information about the mission we can find on the Internet. Mars mission trivia has become a new form of water cooler currency. We just can't believe that after so many years of talk, someone is really doing it! We're finally going to Mars!"

Bill winked at him. "I happen to think they're all pretty selfish. They see the new golden era opening up, and with their cushy aerospace jobs, they'll be right in the middle of it."

Jennifer whacked him lightly on top of his head.

"Ouch! OK, seriously, the guys at the forest service are probably just as excited about it as the people she works with."

Their light banter continued until the vehicle entered a dark driveway in a secluded, heavily wooded area. Reflecting off a lake, the lights of a small mountain town gleamed in the peaceful valley below. As they got out of the car, David gave an appreciative whistle.

Bill said, "Wait until you see it in the daytime. The view takes your breath away, every time."

They started to unload his gear, and he realized Bill had been speaking literally. The thin mountain air made him stop to catch his breath more than once. Nederland's altitude was almost 3,000 feet higher than Boulder, and they were probably another 500 feet above the town.

He paused to look upward, and his reward was a stunning view of a million stars, as can only be seen in a dark sky on a clear winter evening. Among the twinkling stars, in the constellation of Leo, a steady crimson beacon had been gaining in brightness every evening. He felt the intense, primal chill in his bones that ancient natives must have sensed when gazing at the wondrous heavens. The spectacular pinpoints of light seemed so close he could almost reach out and touch them. Anna and her fellow travelers were out there somewhere in all that vastness, their only shelter a tiny, fragile shell of plastic. He shuddered in awe and wonder.

MarsDay 17, 12:46 p.m.
(December 8, 8:00 a.m.)

Despite the dry chill in the basement guest room, David slept well his first night as a fugitive. The bed was comfortable and the sheets were clean and warm. Compared to his apartment, he felt like he was staying in a posh hotel.

The smell of pancakes and maple syrup helped him to wake up. He ate a hearty breakfast with Bill and Jennifer, waited until they left for work, and set up his equipment in the basement. He was able to connect his computer to the local network with minimal effort. Upon reaching his office at Mission Support, he checked his messages. All was quiet, at least in cyberspace.

Before reading logbook entries and clearing out the usual busy-work that often claimed several hours each morning, he sent messages to inform his four senior duty officers of his current situation. One of the senior team members was working at all times, whether David was present or not, so they needed to be aware of any information critical to the mission.

Without going into any details, he mentioned that he would be hiding out until things cooled off. He also advised them to be extra cautious in their personal dealings and not call any undo attention upon themselves. His warning was probably unnecessary since this was their modus operandi anyway, but still he felt better having issued it. Each of his closest colleagues was a potential media target, too.

He also asked the security department to locate Kristin Colcheck and Ahmed Tarraz. They deserved to be warned before the media descended upon them.

Thoughts of the media prompted him to check the daily news dump to the crew.

- "Reward Offered for Mars Sponsor Information" (usnn.com)
- "Tensions Flare as New Gaza Fighting Erupts" (cnn.com)
- "Global Warming Fears Spur Liverpool Riots" (cnn.com)
- "Terror Summit Draws Record Attendance" (Reuters)
- "Wrigley Field Demolition Cures Cubs Curse?" (Reuters)
- "Latest QUAKE Blockbuster Shocks, Entertains" (e.com)
- "Lunar Accident Investigation Board Enters 10th Month of Deliberations" (space.com)

The first headline caught his eye, and he quickly browsed the article. Negativity seemed to be the media theme of the day, so David didn't bother to read the others. He understood the need to keep the crew informed about current events transpiring back on Earth, but he wished his team could find happier subject matters to choose from. If he was out in space and bombarded with these negative stories, he wondered if he would want to return to Earth.

Reading the first article made him realize his family might be concerned about him. He thought about calling his parents, but decided against it. With so much uncertainty in his current situation, they were the last people he wanted to deal with. Since Cassie already knew about his involvement in the Mars mission, he sent her a message containing the details about his getaway and comfortable hideout. She knew Bill and Jennifer better than he did, so she would be relieved that he was in good company. He also asked her to let their parents and siblings know he would be out of reach until further notice.

The rest of the morning was devoted to catching up on logbook information. The logs were usually dry reading, but by browsing them, he always gained valuable insights into the status and concerns of the crew.

Thoughts of crew status reminded him to inform them of USNN's latest actions, too. While he didn't want to worry them, they needed to be told about anything degrading the effectiveness of Mission Support. With his camera set for audio-only, he recorded a cautious verbal message.

CHAPTER 11
PROXIMITY

MarsDay 17, 5:30 p.m.
(December 8, 12:52 p.m.)

The previous evening, Anna had lost at cards again. She hadn't even tried to lose this time. The others were much better pinochle players. She needed to find a new game or resign herself to losing often.

The penalty routine was one she knew well. Clear the table, sonic scrubber, a bit of water, then the sterilization chamber.

As she cleaned, the others chatted in the lounge area. Anna was still concerned about Ollie's health, even though his longer sleep period this morning seemed to have helped. Some of his usual cheerfulness had returned. His medical exam hadn't revealed any obvious physical problems, even after the biometric data was relayed to experts back on Earth.

He did admit forgetting to take his vitamin and mineral supplements several times. She scolded him about his carelessness. Those supplements were vital to maintaining his health. Without them, drinking pure water regularly would suck the minerals right out of his body, leading to any number of serious medical and psychological conditions. He promised to be more careful in the future, and she made a bold entry in his weekly medical schedule to verify he was taking his supplements.

She tuned out most of the conversation in the lounge because Ollie appeared to be preaching on his favorite topic: environmental science. He could talk for hours about how technology, economics, politics, and environmentalism needed better integration within modern society. To him, "responsible development" was the answer to every problem the world faced.

Anna had been his solitary congregation several times already, and she didn't care to attend his sermon tonight. However, she did take note when Ollie stopped talking in mid-sentence. When he commented "That's odd," he gained her full attention.

"Odd, indeed," said Evelyn. "We seem to be getting an audio transmission from Mission Support, but we don't have any events scheduled for this evening. Maybe something unexpected has happened back home."

Anna put the remaining dish aside and joined them in the lounge. Audio messages uploaded quickly, so the full message had already arrived. As Ollie played the message, she immediately recognized Shepherd's deep, husky timbre, a voice she had come to know and trust so well over the past few weeks. Her heart skipped a beat.

Greetings, dear friends, from Mission Support! This is Shepherd. Sorry for the unexpected message. I'll try to keep it brief so you can get on with your evening plans. A situation has arisen that might not affect you directly, but I felt you should be aware of it.

The issue is related to network media coverage of our mission. USNN is still doing everything it can to stir up trouble and controversy. Keep this in mind, Anna, the next time you talk to them.

Now they have taken things to a new level. They are about to learn my personal identity. Needless to say, if the identity and effectiveness of the support director is compromised, it will have repercussions for the whole support team.

I've already taken some temporary steps to conceal my location. Mission Support will continue to operate normally until further notice.

We still don't know what motivates USNN to behave as they do. Their end goal might be merely to gather information. As reporters, that's their job, after all. However, I'm starting to become suspicious. They might have other designs. Their latest actions certainly fuel my speculation.

I'm working on a new fallback option to handle the worst-case scenario, if the entire support organization is compromised, hacked, or smothered. More on that will follow, after I flesh out the details.

That's all for now. Sorry to hit you with this news, but please try not to be too concerned about it yet. Our team here is resourceful and determined, and

we will deal with whatever transpires. *You can't affect what's happening here any more than we can affect what happens on Mars.*
Best wishes...Shepherd, out.

The three of them stared at each other until Evelyn broke the silence. "He's right—we can't affect what's happening at Mission Support. So who wants to deal the cards first?"

MarsDay 17, 6:36 p.m.
(December 8, 2:00 p.m.)

After a late lunch, David rechecked his messages at Mission Support. Several had accumulated, but the priority of each was marked "low." As he scanned the list, a new "Emergency" priority message arrived. The sender and subject line information caught his eye, and he immediately read the message.

> To: <shepherd>
> From: <chicken_little>
> Subject: Current affairs
> Priority: Emergency
>
> David -
> The sky is still falling.
> You have a secret. TELL NO ONE.

So, Mister Chicken was still out there, after all. Now they were even on a first name basis. This time, however, David was ready.
I've got you now, fowl. Let's find out who you really are.
One of the experts on his security team had created a command for him to run, in the event that <chicken_little> showed up again. The command retrieved and stored the contents of a restricted raw data file. Viewing the contents of this file would tell him who was in the virtual world and where they were. His security team guaranteed that in order for a user to perform any

function within the system, that user must have a valid account name and location entry in this file.

As he opened the file, his triumph turned quickly into dismay. Only 15 account names were listed, including his own, but <chicken_little> was not one of them.

Blast it all! You aren't getting away from me so easily this time.

He studied the contents of the file more closely, checking off valid accounts he recognized. Five were very familiar, belonging to people who often worked in the main control room and were currently on duty. Commander Day, Anna, and Cassie were also present. Of the remaining six accounts, one was a generic security login and the other five were system maintenance daemons.

OK, locations, locations, where are these people?

The five control room avatars were all at their stations in the main control room, as he had expected. Commander Day was in Conference Room 4. Anna and Cassie were both in the Psych Ward, in Cassie's office. The security avatar was at his normal post, the security desk in the central atrium. The five system accounts had a location marker of <mission_support>, which wasn't surprising, since they probably required access to the entire system.

David sat back to think. Had <chicken_little> left the complex immediately after sending the message? Everyone was where he would have expected them to be, all except...

What was Commander Day doing in Conference Room 4, all by herself?

The simplest way to find out would be to ask her, so he typed a command to jump his avatar into Conference Room 4. The server responded with an error message: *Conference Room 4: Cannot enter: Size capacity exceeded.* Puzzled, he tried using his universal key, the one granting access to any room in the facility. The result was the same error message.

He tried jumping to her location in a different way, using a macro. Once again, the system responded with a similar error message: *<location <alice>>: Conference Room 4: Cannot enter: Size capacity exceeded.*

The error message seemed to indicate the room was full of avatars, yet he knew the commander was alone. In frustration, he warped into Conference Room 1, a very familiar place to him. This was the largest conference room, the site of the SEA steering committee meetings.

Moving out the door and down the hallway, he encountered a set of blue doors, one to either side, their color a stark contrast from the beige walls. He fingered the door to the left, and it identified itself as the door to Conference Room 3. Likewise, to the right was the door to Conference Room 2.

Proceeding farther down the hallway, he found himself entering the central atrium where the four wings of the support complex met. He turned around and retraced his steps but couldn't find any other doors or rooms. Conference Room 4 didn't exist!

At about this time, he expected to see an avatar of Rod Serling slink around the corner from the Twilight Zone, accompanied by eerie music. Whatever was going on was well beyond his limited technical abilities, so Shepherd walked over to the security desk and talked to the guard on duty. It was time to get some expert assistance.

The guard's avatar looked like Arnold Schwarzenegger, which was quite appropriate. In terms of system capabilities, each member of the security team was a machine-gun-toting muscleman. David hoped to put those muscles and weapons to good use.

Based on David's error message, Arnold confirmed the room must be full of other avatars or it was too small to hold more than one avatar in the first place. He asked Shepherd to wait while he did some more checking.

David patiently browsed the atrium, appreciating its appearance. Someone had gone to great lengths to make the cavernous expanse resemble a space museum. The ceiling was a high dome, black as night, spangled with thousands of twinkling, starlike pinpoints of light. It was like his old apartment ceiling, only magnified in brilliance a thousand times over.

Hovering above the guard's desk was a towering replica of the telescope Lowell had used to view his infamous canals on Mars. An Apollo lunar lander graced the empty wall space between two of the hallways leading to various rooms in the support complex. The other three open wall sections were dedicated to Mars probes: the 1976 *Viking* landers, the 2001 *Mars Odyssey* orbiter, and the *Perseus*. Going clockwise, the pseudo exhibits thoughtfully progressed through 40 years of space frontier exploration, in chronological order.

"Aha, I've got something," the guard replied finally, ripping David's attention away from the *Viking* display. His voice was squeaky, nothing at all like his avatar's appearance would suggest. "Your Conference Room 4 is one of the buffers between the other rooms. These buffers are a special class of room, derived by the security team to isolate each base room object from certain types of hacker attacks. Conference Room 4 is located between Conference Rooms 1 and 2."

"So how do I enter that room?"

"You can't. Nobody can—that's the whole point. None of the real rooms adjoin each other contiguously within virtual-space. Except for the generic hallway, of course, which has other safeguards built into it. The width of each buffer room is hard-coded to a really small value, a floating-point number between zero and one, actually. Since base object dimensions are always positive integers, it's impossible for any base object, like an avatar, to fit inside. Therefore, a hacker attack using spatial utilities can't propagate directly from room to room."

"So how did Commander Day get in there?"

"She can't be in there. Like I said, it's impossible for anyone to enter that room, or any of the other buffers like it. I'll query her real location."

Though David's patience was slipping, he calmly gave Arnold his restricted data file and explained how he had tracked Commander Day's location. Then he went back to browsing the museum exhibits.

After several minutes of working in silence, Arnold shared his results. He had verified that Commander Day was still present somewhere within the system. Digging deeper, he had also proven her avatar was a proper ghost receiving its input from an active data connection with the *Perseus*. However, he couldn't pinpoint her location. Since he still claimed no one could enter a buffer room, Arnold was convinced some kind of programming bug must be hiding her true location. He promised to open a software trouble ticket right away.

Then David told the guard about the messages from <chicken_little>. Arnold did some more checking, but he failed to find any trace of that account or even the incoming message.

Having lost some confidence in his security team, David thanked the guard for his efforts and returned Shepherd to his office.

He decided to test the theory that one couldn't shrink themselves to a height, width, or depth between 0 and 1. Sure enough, passing non-integer dimension values like 0.5 into the standard "resize" command always led to an error message: *Resize Error: Unit dimensions must be positive integers.* He browsed the system manuals, looking for other ways to change the dimensions of an object. All related tools seemed to call the resize primitive, and were therefore subject to the same limitations. Arnold's advice was holding up. Access to the buffer rooms appeared to be impossible.

The impossible was becoming fairly routine today. Could Commander Day and his <chicken_little> adversary be one and the same? The connection between the two was extremely fragile, probably mere coincidence. He needed more to go on. Much more.

OK, <chicken_little>, you got me again. But this isn't over yet. I'll figure you out, and then, you're mine.

Perhaps the message content contained a clue. He looked back through the message and tried to fathom its meaning.

"You have a secret. TELL NO ONE."

David had many secrets, so those words could mean just about anything. Since the subject line was "Current affairs," perhaps the message referred to his attempt to hide from the media?

He had told several people about his current situation already, but only Cassie knew the details, as far as he was aware. Might the message be warning him not to tell anyone else?

If the message was meant to be a helpful warning, it should have been something like "Go, Run, Hide!" Could the sender know he was already going, running, and hiding? That line of reasoning seemed weak, too, but it would certainly cut down his list of suspects. He made a mental note that Commander Day would still be on this shorter list.

But why would anyone send a message warning him to keep his location a secret? He wasn't planning to tell anyone else where he was staying.

Wait, I also asked Cassie to inform our family that I was OK.

That information was a link in a different chain, one that didn't lead back to him directly, but would certainly lead back to Cassie. When the media figured out his identity, it wouldn't take them long to question his family. His parents and siblings didn't know where he was, but they might suspect Cassie did.

Stupid—that message to Cassie was stupid! If I'm going to play this little spy game, I'm going to have to do much better than that.

He quickly sent Cassie another message asking her to ignore his previous message. She should tell the rest of their family nothing. He explained his reasoning and invited her comments.

Then he leaned back in his chair and stretched his arms and legs. He needed more time to think and plan, yet he also needed a break from the virtual world to clear his mind.

Since Bill and Jennifer were still at work, the main level of the house was deserted. Much to his delight, a partial pot of coffee remained from this morning's breakfast. He poured himself a cup, heated it in the microwave, and breathed the heady aroma that had rejuvenated him so many times in the past.

While he awaited the return of his friends, he absorbed the sights and sounds of his surroundings. The middle level of the house was a single, spacious room with an open floor plan. This one room had to be over a thousand square feet in size. Plush furniture subdivided the area into a kitchen, dining area, and large living room.

Triple-paned windows facing south, east, and west allowed plenty of illuminating sunlight to enter. Jennifer obviously had a fondness for living greenery. Each window was surrounded by a plethora of potted ferns and indoor dwarf trees. The musky smell of the foliage was subtle, but it completed the illusion of a luxurious rain forest. The only thing missing was a flock of macaws.

And the views—oh, what views! Bill had been too modest. Each window opened onto endless stands of Ponderosa pine trees. A gentle afternoon breeze made the crowns tremble ever so slightly. Distant patches of white marked the shoreline of a frozen reservoir below. To the west, the waning afternoon sunlight silhouetted the cozy town of Nederland, nestled inside a long, narrow valley. Farther up the valley, the backbone peaks of the Rockies towered in the distance. David's keen eyesight detected wispy strands of smoke curling lazily from numerous fireplaces, piercing the alpenglow. Even indoors, he could smell the pine fragrance.

North was the only direction that was disappointing. The direct view of the reservoir below should also have been spectacular, but the windows on the north side of the house were too small. Whoever built the house had obviously been a firm believer in passive solar heating. Larger windows to the north would have sacrificed too much thermal energy to the frigid winter winds.

He sat on the couch, sipping his coffee and absorbing the transient splendors of the setting sun. Crimson streamers accentuated a thin layer of clouds in the distance, clouds promising to bestow a fresh blanket of champagne powder later in the evening.

In the midst of all this serenity, his thoughts wandered back to the events of the previous evening. He calmly speculated about how his current fugitive status had come about.

The short video clips airing on the network must have been taken at the crew's going-away party two months ago, just prior to the start of their quarantine period. That party was supposed to have been a private affair, but one of the guests or wait staff had probably concealed a button camera.

Button cameras, sometimes called "cameras on a chip," were simply computer microchips that accepted direct optical input. These cheap devices could be almost microscopic in size. Power requirements were minimal. David owned one himself, and he was quite familiar with its operation and capabilities because he often used it to record his video messages.

The proliferation of these units was becoming a major cause for concern within the general public. Spies and voyeurs could easily tune the camera input to enhance certain frequencies of the spectrum or filter out others, allowing the operator to see through air, thin walls, and clothing with ease. Some button cameras, like David's, even came equipped with sensitive microphones to capture audio input as well. Personal privacy had been under vicious attack for years, and no one was safe, as David had just discovered firsthand.

His team must have several spies within their midst. While <chicken_little> had invaded the support system computers, Button Man had attacked him personally and emotionally. These immediate threats worried him, but he didn't know if they were any more dangerous than the distant ones. After all, Fontaine continued to cause trouble, too, and other, worse threats might be lurking in the shadows. His list of concerns continued to grow longer.

Since the SEA was an open organization, anyone could join and participate. Most of the members had good intentions, but others with less noble designs were still capable of becoming members as well.

His support team was quite different, however. The steering committee had constructed his team carefully, and he trusted its members until proven otherwise. In his opinion, this made <chicken_little> the more dangerous of the two internal threats. Any bad sheep on his inner support team could endanger the mission.

The systems aboard the *Perseus* had been designed to allow the people in the field to override any remote orders from Earth. However, he couldn't rule out the possibility of gaps in the software being exploited and used against the crew. Ample evidence had proven the system programmers were capable engineers. Still, everyone made mistakes. As he pursued this line of thought to its natural conclusion, he recalled his last remark to the field team.

You can't affect what's happening here any more than we can affect what happens on Mars.

With this feeble addendum, he had hoped to raise the morale of the Mars crew a notch or two. However, it certainly didn't put his own mind at ease. At the time he said the words, he had assumed the statement was obvious and true. But was it? And if not, which part was false?

By the time the front door opened and Jennifer stepped through, the ruddy glow of the evening sun had faded to a faint flicker above the western horizon. In the entryway, she shook hardened clumps of snow from her hiking boots. David jumped off the couch and helped her with a bag of groceries.

While she removed her boots and purple parka, David placed a kettle of water on the stove and lit the burner underneath. Jennifer was a tea drinker in urgent need of a hot drink. Her walk from the bus stop was at least two miles in length. Judging from the blast of cold air entering the house with her, the temperature outside had plummeted with the evening sun.

Putting the groceries away, Jennifer bombarded him with questions about his day. Unfortunately, he couldn't tell her very much. He mentioned setting up his computer equipment in his basement bedroom and enjoying the views outside. Then he changed the subject. The transition was abrupt, but he had a few questions he needed to ask her, too.

"Jennifer, I've been trying to figure out what I'm going to do for spending money. I'm not sure how long I'll need to stay here, and I'll gladly pay you for rent and expenses. But at this moment, I have two dollars in cash."

"Let's figure that out later, when Bill is here," she suggested. "I doubt whether we'll charge you for rent. But you eat like a horse, and it would be nice if you could help with the grocery bills while you're here. You still have access to your bank account, don't you?"

"Sure, for now. But each withdrawal might create a trail that the media can follow back to me. If I withdraw money here in town, people will know I'm staying around here. If I do it in Boulder, Denver, or anywhere else, I have to get there first. With bad luck, someone might spot me. Same problem with credit cards."

"You'll figure something out."

When the kettle on the stove screamed its readiness, Jennifer steeped a cup of oolong tea and brought it over to the couch in the living room. David followed, and parked in a leather reclining chair to her right. She turned on the television, intending to watch a national evening news program, but finding the end of a reality game show instead. After muting the volume, she sipped her tea in silence. Together, they watched the last golden threads of sunset cross the western sky.

A few minutes later, Bill staggered through the front door. David was happy to see him carrying a cardboard box of well-known dimensions.

"I thought you might like some Neo's pizza as a welcome to the neighborhood, David. Unless you had your fill last night. Our 'za up here is better than any of the crap in Boulder."

"You're a sight for sore eyes, my good friend," said David, eyeing the box. He added, with a wink, "It's great to see you, too, Bill."

While Jennifer parceled out the thin-style sausage pizza, Bill went upstairs to change his clothes. His coveralls were grungy from a long day of outdoor forestry work. After he rejoined them, they settled down to eat dinner and watch the evening news.

The Mars mission was no longer the lead news story, but David had been expecting that. At this point in the mission, their ratings had started to decline. Hopefully, public interest would revive as the crew neared Mars.

The choice of a replacement lead story was a graphic description of some serial murders at three colleges in Indiana. Each of the eight victims had been a female student, strangled near her place of residence. Nothing seemed to connect the victims except their method of death.

News stories like this had always annoyed David to no end, and he was more upset than usual tonight. To have the Mars mission coverage replaced by a story like this was almost a direct slap in the face. He couldn't think of a topic more diametrically opposed to everything Mars exploration stood for. He visualized the tiny flames of hope, faith in humanity, and compassion for the sanctity of life dimming within millions of viewers. No wonder so many people lived their lives in the past. The future was dark.

When the Mars mission was finally mentioned, a brief video clip showed Anna taking some radiation measurements and drawing a blood sample from Ollie. Another clip showed Commander Day exercising with some makeshift barbells that looked far too heavy for such a tiny woman to be lifting.

Then a short segment aired about the search for three potential members of the shadow organization sponsoring the mission. The searchers had already determined the identity of all three of the leading suspects. Names, photographs, and some brief bio statistics were flashed on the screen. David was forced to give the investigative reporters credit for moving quickly and accurately. All three people had been identified correctly.

The airing of this news segment led to a new barrage of questions from Bill and Jennifer. At least David could clear up one misunderstanding right away. He assured his friends he didn't belong to the organization that planned or financed the mission. He didn't know the sponsors' identity, either.

They found his denials hard to believe, due to all the recent media attention. He tried to explain once more that he was involved with the mission, but in a minor capacity. His words rang hollow, even in his own ears, especially since he couldn't reveal what that "minor capacity" was.

Downplaying his role in the mission was close to lying, but he could weakly justify it by invoking relativity. Compared to the crew members out in space, all Earthly participants were involved in a minor capacity.

An inner voice urged caution, however. *David, this is your ethics speaking. Don't stray any farther. Lies are like slices of pizza. Many small ones add up. And once you start eating, it's hard to stop.*

CHAPTER 12
RESPONSE

MarsDay 19, 4:10 a.m.
(December 10, 12:29 a.m.)

Anna climbed the ladder to the upper deck and was immediately taken aback by a foul odor. "Ugh! Something smells like rotten eggs!"

Ollie was in his usual morning position, typing on the keyboard in front of the large computer display screen.

"And good morning to you, too!" he announced cheerfully. "Do I need another Navy shower?" He grinned, and then added more seriously, "I don't smell anything, love, but I've been up here for hours. If there's some delightful new fragrance in the air, I probably wouldn't notice it. My sniffer has always been poor, anyway."

Anna was astounded. "Geez, Ollie, you can't have a nose at all! I'll bet we have a ruptured food package, and it's probably some sort of dairy product. Nothing else would smell that bad so quickly."

She pulled up one of the floor tiles near the kitchen sink. Underneath was the primary storage area for most of the vacuum packed, dehydrated dairy supplies. Other small dairy caches were concealed all over the ship, in case some accident happened to their primary supply.

After removing the floor tile, the odor became stronger. She was probably close to the source.

In the back of her mind, she eagerly planned what to do after finding the spoiled food. A subsequent examination would be necessary, and it would also relieve some of her increasing feelings of boredom.

Carefully removing each plastic package from the food cache, one by one, she found the bad container near the bottom. As suspected, a pouch of concentrated milk had not been sealed properly. After being exposed to air and humidity for almost three weeks, a moldy fungus had begun to grow throughout. Fortunately, none of the surrounding packages appeared to be affected. Holding her breath against the pungent smell, she carefully removed the container and sealed it properly.

By her reckoning, the moldy container had several immediate implications. Obviously, the crew had lost some vital food supplies. They also had definitive proof of spores still sharing the *Perseus* with them, despite the best efforts of the pre-launch sterilization team. Forward contamination, the act of bringing some earthly organism with them and allowing it to proliferate on the hostile Martian surface, had always been a serious concern. Once they reached the surface of Mars, they already planned to use procedures designed to prevent the spread of Earthly microbes into the native environment.

Of greater concern, mold spores could potentially find shelter and grow in less accessible areas near the ship's internal plumbing and wiring. This could lead to health problems and equipment failures further down the road.

Still, Anna smiled. She had some real work to do. In her possession was a sample of living microorganisms requiring isolation, study, and ultimately sterilization.

Due to weight and storage volume limitations, her science equipment was inadequate for a thorough study. She did possess a microscope, and she could temporarily clear other supplies out of a sample box to hold her mold spores in quarantine. Her small "sickbay" area at the bottom of the ladder on the lowest level of the *Perseus* was too cramped, so she could use the fold-down emergency medical table in the EVA room as a temporary workbench, minus the thin mattress.

Her newly formulated plan had other benefits, like testing their procedures for sterilizing the contents of the sample box. Sterilization would be a critical, frequent procedure once they arrived on Mars and started to perform science EVAs on the Martian surface.

After cleaning the surrounding food packages and spraying them with a mild antifungal disinfectant, she repacked the supplies and replaced the floor tile. Then she grabbed a nutrition bar for breakfast and carried her prized mold culture down the ladder toward the sample boxes in the EVA room. For the first time in two weeks, she felt truly content.

MarsDay 19, 10:11 p.m.
(December 10, 7:00 p.m.)

Checking his messages after dinner, David was cautiously happy to find a message from a technician on his communications team. Another of his side projects was bearing fruit, though it was one of several that his inner voice of ethics had recently protested.

Following David's carefully considered "suggestion," the comm techie had contacted an engineer in the company that outsourced Information Technology support to USNN. The outsource engineer "accidentally" left a data file sitting unprotected on USNN's internet site, a data file containing a list of dates, addresses, and subject lines for every e-mail sent or received by Skye Fontaine over the past six months.

The comm techs had originally come up with this idea, suggesting it to David as little more than a prank, a way to "get back at Fontaine" for her biased news coverage. Many of the communications team members at Mission Support were extremely upset over USNN's perversion of their own time and efforts.

At first, David had vetoed the action on ethical grounds. He didn't want any trace of impropriety to smear the support team.

However, the comm techs soon convinced him to take a chance. Part of the outsourcer's job was to police the usage of USNN's equipment. If someone happened to be careless about where certain data files were left, that was their own impropriety, not David's. The information he would read was openly available to the public.

The ethical foundation for their actions still seemed weak, but in the end, his curiosity wouldn't let him pass up an opportunity to gather some inside information about Fontaine. He had originally hoped to find some clues about the identity of her lunchtime guest at Hapa, or even some traces of bribery or other skullduggery at the network. Now that USNN had made him a personal target, his motivation was stronger. Perhaps he would find a link to some member of the SEA who had ratted him out to the media.

Though he was eager to begin this latest task immediately, the list was so lengthy that it would probably take him several days to scan it. After looking for obvious connections to Mission Support or the SEA and not finding any, he forced himself to put the list aside. This huge task could wait until tomorrow.

First, he had another list to browse. If he was lucky, this other list might lead back to the identity of <chicken_little>. His security team had provided him with a list of dates and times that Commander Day's <alice> avatar had visited the Mission Support complex, as well as the rooms she had visited and the commands she had executed.

Spying on the commander's whereabouts also felt slightly unethical. However, each user of the virtual world was fully aware the security team could monitor their locations and actions, with approval from the support director.

The first day of the mission was of special interest because that's when he had received the first message from <chicken_little>. He discovered that Commander Day had spent a few minutes in Conference Room 4 again but had run no commands. Then she had warped into the main control room and remained there for over an hour, probably implementing the air leak simulation.

"Hey, workaholic!" Bill shouted down the stairs. "It's nine o'clock, time for the news!"

"Already? I'll be up in a minute!" Watching the late edition of the USNN evening news had become a nightly ritual.

Before signing off his account, he took one last look at Commander Day's activity list. She had visited Conference Room 4 frequently. In fact, she had been there almost every evening, at approximately the same time. While there, she never ran any commands, and she always warped directly from the central atrium. He could find no evidence of her ever running a "resize" command before entering the room.

As he bounded up the stairs, Bill and Jennifer greeted him without their usual enthusiasm. They sat quietly on the couch, staring at the television set, though a commercial was playing.

"What did I miss," he asked.

"Oh, nothing much," said Bill, finally looking up at him. "The League of Shiite Martyrs just nuked Jerusalem again, a few hours ago."

David collapsed heavily into the leather rocking chair, his usual spot for watching the news. The realworld disaster forced his virtual world headaches back into their proper perspective.

"How did it happen?" he finally managed to ask.

"They smuggled another dirty-bomb into the city on foot. It spread around enough radioactive dust to lethally contaminate ten square blocks."

"How many dead?"

"Only the terrorist. But soon, thousands of innocent civilians, tourists, and pilgrims will wish they were dead."

"Crap." It was the only appropriate thing he could say.

"Yeah, big time crap," Jennifer agreed. "So why do you think they call themselves Shiite Martyrs when their only goal is to make martyrs of everyone else?"

"Who knows," grumbled Bill. "Nothing makes any sense in that part of the world. Since the third Gulf War and the Great Rebellion, I've given up trying to fathom Middle Eastern politics. They play by their own rules, and everyone becomes a victim."

David asked, "What's the President going to do? Or the U.N.?"

"Probably more talk," answered Bill, without trying to hide his disgust. "That's what they're best at."

For the next half-hour, they watched the scenes of suffering in silence. Towards the end of the program, the news didn't get much better. The stock market had plummeted on the news from the Middle East, and the Indiana Strangler had claimed a tenth victim. Jillian Greene declared victory in her fight to persuade Congress to outlaw a chemical used in the production of cheap, translucent plastics. After the new legislation was signed into law, a major cellular phone manufacturer and three promising solar energy companies immediately declared bankruptcy.

The only mention of the Mars mission, other than a passing reference to "dangerous technology" in a boisterous speech by Greene, was a brief note that all three mission sponsorship suspects could not be located. So now David was a suspect. Since he was past the point of caring about it, he just noted this skillful use of language without comment. Hopefully the other suspects had found as nice a place to wait out the storm.

After the news program ended, he bid his hosts a good evening and retired to his basement hideaway. Tomorrow would be a long day. He couldn't do anything about the insanity in the rest of the world, but with the information he had just received from the USNN mole, perhaps he could find some answers closer to home.

MarsDay 20, 1:45 p.m.
(December 11, 11:00 a.m.)

After several frustrating hours of poring through Fontaine's e-mail correspondence list, David's eyelids were getting heavy. Morning sunlight poured through the window of his basement office, dulling his senses.

How could one person communicate with so many others, while also running interviews, traveling to Boulder, and hosting news programs? It seemed humanly impossible, yet the proof was right before his weary eyes.

Could Fontaine have three clones? More likely, she had a busy secretary who handled her e-mail and managed her obligations.

The correspondence list undoubtedly contained valuable patterns and clues, but he hadn't detected any yet. His most obvious tactic had been to search for e-mail origins or destinations on his support team's servers. However, if she was talking to people inside his organization, like <chicken_little>, her contacts had covered their tracks well.

His empty coffee cup sat beside the cold, untouched remnants of breakfast. Leftover sausage pizza topped with Rice Chex was usually his favorite way to start the day. Offering an extra energy boost, the distant call of caffeine enticed him to take a short break. He pushed his work aside and climbed the stairs, two at a time. A nearly full urn of liquid energy awaited him in the kitchen.

After filling his cup and turning to head back downstairs, he heard the heavy thuds of footsteps on the front deck. Then the doorbell rang. As befit his fugitive status, he immediately ducked behind the island of cabinets separating the kitchen from the rest of the open living area. Peeking out from his low vantage point, he could see a sliver of cloudy daylight through the thin windowpanes to either side of the front door. He also glimpsed a van in the driveway and a bearded man in a bright blue uniform at the door.

He decided to wait. After a few seconds, the man bent down near the door, got back up again, retreated to his van, and drove away. At least two more minutes passed before David worked up the courage to open the front door. He grabbed an envelope sitting outside and slammed the door shut again.

The brown, letter sized delivery envelope was addressed to Bill and Jennifer, without a return address. It looked harmless enough, though its midsection bulged outward. In the movies, bombs always ticked, so he placed the package to his ear. It was soundless and inert. With a shrug, he placed it on the kitchen table where his friends would be sure to see it when they got home.

Opting for a quick lunch, he grabbed a frozen pizza from the freezer, threw it into the cold oven, and set the temperature to 420 degrees. The pizza box was made of a material that disintegrated in the growing heat of the oven, adding a subtle hint of extra flavor to the food inside.

As he grabbed his cup of coffee and retreated to the basement, the pager in his watch began to vibrate. The unexpected sensation was so surprising that he almost spilled his drink on the off-white carpeted stairway.

His high-tech watch, with passive pager and cell phone functions, had been a perk of the job. He had worn it religiously since starting his assignment over six months ago. The pager had been activated only once before, after a rock-climbing accident had taken the life of one of the crew members in training. His thoughts instantly jumped to the current mission status.

Has something gone wrong in the Perseus?

He reached his computer. Shepherd was still in his virtual office, so he opened the door to the main support room, immediately bumping into another avatar. A runner had been waiting outside the door.

The runner said, "Sorry to page you, but there's a problem with the mission. We've lost contact with the Earth Return Vehicle on Mars."

Though David was dismayed, he also felt some relief. This news sounded serious, but he had been prepared for much worse. The crew was still safe— Anna was still safe.

He took a deep breath, forcing himself to remain calm. If there was a problem with the mission, it wouldn't be solved by panic or by jumping to wrong conclusions. His team might have lost contact with the ERV for any number of reasons. Some might be trivial and easily corrected.

Shepherd followed his colleague into the main support room and took his usual position in the velvet chair along the rear wall. Status information bombarded him from various displays scattered about the walls of the room. What the displays didn't tell him, he could learn by asking the technicians.

Several of the avatars in the support room milled about a console labeled ERV, conversing with the harried operator for that station. David resisted the urge to join the crowd. Instead, he pressed a button on the side of his virtual chair. His own personal bank of computer displays slid upward from the floor, partially enveloping his avatar. Now Shepherd could see and hear more from his own support position than he could from anywhere else.

Accessing the ERV console logs from the last hour, he could see that all had been normal until about five minutes ago, when NASA's Deep Space Network of ground-stations lost the telemetry connection. Sinbad, the avatar at the ERV station, had already made some useful annotations to help him decipher the cryptic information in the logs. The signal loss had been sudden and complete. The weather station feed, fuel status telemetry, and navigational beacon were all gone.

He turned up the volume on his speakers and listened to the discussion around the ERV station before interrupting. "Sinbad, Shepherd here. Do you see anything in the previous telemetry indicating the cause of the problem?"

"No, nothing," Sinbad replied. "It's mid-day at the Medusae site on Mars, sunny, with the usual light breeze out of the northwest. Everything was looking fine. I've already double-checked all the sensor readings in the logs. Power levels were nominal, fuel tank pressures were nominal…then, wham! We lost everything. It's like someone turned off a light switch."

"You've verified all our connections here, I presume?"

"Affirmative. The final checks are completing now, but everything looks normal."

David asked, "Could the problem be with the NASA ground-stations?"

A different tech chimed in, "JPL reports everything looks good on their end. They have a clear line-of-sight window with the Medusae Fossae region, and they still have contact with all their other Mars probes, as well as the backup habitat on Mars. Our own link with JPL looks fine, too."

Sinbad added, "I suggest we switch the ERV to a backup transmitter."

"Do it," said David, knowing they would have to wait 15 minutes until they knew if the switchover was successful. Mars was approaching its point of closest proximity, with Earth struggling to overtake its sister world in their respective orbits, but the two planets were still separated by almost 90 million kilometers of void. Even at their nearest, a round trip signal would take ten minutes.

"OK. So we wait, unless anyone has any other suggestions. In the meantime, I need everyone to save their logs and recheck them…all of them, even the ones having nothing to do with the ERV. Look for anything unusual, no matter how insignificant."

Could the problem have been caused by something or someone here on Earth? David examined his duty roster and paged both on-call software engineers. He left them a brief message requesting they recheck the control software thoroughly for bugs. Though he didn't mention <chicken_little>, he asked them pay special attention to entry points where hackers could get into the control systems. He also told them to treat this matter with the highest possible priority and urgency, pulling in whoever was needed to help.

Stupid, stupid, stupid. I should have asked them to do this before. If they find an open back door, I'll have no one to blame but myself.

Despite the chill in the basement, he wiped a bead of sweat from his brow. He accessed an overview document describing the major ERV systems at a high level. Embedded within the document was a section titled Communications Contingency Plans. The section was lengthy, but he read it quickly, using speed-reading techniques mastered long ago in grad school.

According to the documentation, if the integrated primary transmitter and receiver unit on the ERV was totally shot, a secondary unit should automatically activate itself 24 Mars hours after last contact with Earth. That would happen around 11:55 a.m. tomorrow, Earth time.

Although the ERV transmitter and receiver were integrated, a problem might affect only the transmitter portion of the system. In that case, a secondary unit should kick in immediately after receiving the switchover command.

As for other possibilities, he scanned a checklist inconveniently located on the final page of the section. An internal problem with the main ERV computer or the power system could lead to a sudden signal loss, as could some more catastrophic events, like an explosion of the fuel tanks. However, a sudden, total power loss was very unlikely due to the redundant design of the power generation systems and batteries. A computer system failure should trigger a cascade of reboots and self-diagnostics during the next three days, a scenario that was still possible. A benzene fuel storage tank explosion was unlikely, but couldn't be ruled out completely.

The communication signals might also be lost during transit. Excessive solar radiation and terrain features were among the most likely causes, though both had been ruled out.

Other, more radical causes of signal interference were possible. Several scenarios in the overall mission plan dealt with various aspects of encountering LGM, a widely used acronym for Little Green Men. The crew and support team was even encouraged to take those scenarios seriously.

Until Mars was thoroughly explored, the LGM potential had to be considered.

Also within the realm of radical causes, he recalled hearing a lecture by a prominent geophysicist about a region on Mars called "Stealth." During the mid-nineties, an extensive radar survey of the Martian surface had detected a mysterious anomaly. A large region west of the Tharsis bulge showed unusually low radar reflectivity. The ground material in this region, whatever it was, behaved similar to the way a military stealth aircraft absorbs radar signals, hence the nickname "Stealth" had been applied to that region. The most popular theory to explain this region required the presence of large quantities of radar-absorbing, pyroclastic ash left over from the eruption of the huge Tharsis volcanoes.

The nearest boundary of Stealth was well over a hundred kilometers east of the ERV landing site, yet its relative closeness had greatly concerned some of the researchers in the geophysics community. The ash, magnetically supercharged "Foo-Foo" dust, or whatever else dominated that region might have other mysterious properties and cause unforeseen problems during the mission. Perhaps a storm of Foo-Foo dust had somehow damaged the ERV or temporarily interfered with its transmissions?

Fifteen minutes passed, and the ERV remained silent. His team waited several more minutes, each more tense than the preceding ones.

The runner had been busy. By now, the main support room was fully staffed. Several more avatars lurked around the periphery of the room, silent but watchful. *Bad news travels fast,* David surmised. He considered calling security and asking them to clear the room of nonessential personnel, but since everyone already seemed to know what was going on, he might as well allow them to stay.

The outside world was another matter. Later, if his team wasn't able to reestablish contact with the ERV, the SEA would need to issue a press release to inform the public of the current situation. Though that action could wait until after they had exhausted all remaining possibilities, he did ask the runner to contact the steering committee members.

Over the next three hours, he set up individual cone-of-silence sessions with some of the support technicians to solicit their opinions. Later, he met with them as a group in one of the conference rooms. The general consensus was to wait until the 24-hour timer had expired, hoping the ERV would switch over to its backup systems and reestablish contact on its own. If that didn't happen, they could begin monitoring backup frequencies, along with some other drastic measures.

The only useful short-term suggestion came from Sinbad. NASA might be able to boost the strength of their transmission signal and the sensitivity of their ground-station receivers. He explained that if they needed the ERV to adjust its transmission frequencies, they wanted to be sure it could receive their instructions clearly. This might avoid a classic "Byzantine General" problem, a computer science dilemma when two groups are trying to coordinate plans with each other but some of their messages are lost or corrupted.

He wasn't about to second-guess the engineers who knew the most about such matters, so he authorized Sinbad to make the necessary requests of NASA-JPL. He also jotted down a reminder to send a message to his brother-in-law, Ben. Having a close ally within the JPL telemetry team was a potential advantage in a situation like this, one he was prepared to use.

Ben had once mentioned some technical tricks allowing his team to keep NASA's ground-stations in partial contact with the two distant Voyager spacecraft out on the fringes of truly interstellar space. Perhaps a similar technique might be useful to allay Sinbad's fears about signal strength.

After the meeting with the technicians ended, he and Sinbad met briefly with the steering committee. The committee members decided to issue a prompt, but terse, press release describing the current situation and outlining some of the plans to regain contact over the next few days.

Throughout the meeting, he couldn't shake a feeling of uneasiness. He had forgotten something. He tried to focus his thoughts upon the discussion, but the feeling persisted.

Immediately following the steering committee meeting, David sent a message to the crew in the *Perseus*. He told them as many details as possible and assured them his team was giving the matter their highest priority. He carefully avoided speculating about any consequences to the mission. It was too early for that, and besides, the crew would already know the potential impact of the ERV signal loss better than anyone else.

After sending the message to the crew, David leaned back in his chair and put his feet up on the sturdy desk serving as his base of operations. The bland ceiling of the basement office was a stark contrast to his apartment's starry sky, which had often helped him to relax and concentrate in the past.

A few minutes later, he heard the front door open, followed by a loud screech. "David! Did we forget to mention, no campfires allowed in the house?"

David raced upstairs to find Jennifer bracing open the front door. Throughout the main level of the house, a light haze hovered near the ceiling. The sharp odor of smoke was unmistakable.

"What the...oh, cripes—my pizza!"

He dashed into the kitchen and grabbed two potholders. As he opened the oven door, thicker plumes of dark smoke billowed into the room, setting off a smoke alarm nearby. The remnants of his pizza were charred beyond recognition. Coughing, he removed the oven's center rack and carried it outside, where he flung the burnt mess into the nearest snowbank.

Jennifer went upstairs to open some windows, while David slid open some windows on the main level. By the time she rejoined him near the dining room table, the smoke was beginning to clear, assisted by a frigid breeze blowing throughout the house. He could tell she was upset, but trying to hide it.

"Good thing we don't have any close neighbors," she said. "They would probably call the fire department."

"I'm glad you came home early," said David.

"I was worried about the weather."

David looked out the living room window and saw the reason for her concern. A cloud bank had completely obscured their view of the town. The entire range of mountains to the west was shrouded in a heavy mist. Light snowflakes were floating sideways, their dance frequently interrupted by powerful wind gusts.

He apologized profusely. "I totally forgot about the pizza. It's been a very bad day, all the way around. Is there anything else I can do to help clean up?"

He expected a response of, "You've helped enough." Instead, she replied more politely, "We'll just have to let the smoke clear. Not much else we can do. I hope it's better by the time Bill gets home."

As she glanced around the room, she saw the envelope on the dining room table. "What's this?"

"Oh, that's for you. It was delivered a few hours ago, by some guy in a van."

Jennifer opened the envelope and pulled out two thick, white envelopes from inside. One was addressed BILL AND JENNIFER. She tore it open, and her eyes grew wide.

"Zowie! Look at all the money!" she cried. Her hands were filled with $50 bills, a lot of them.

David had never seen so much cash in one place before. He joked about her having a secret admirer.

"Someone must like you even more," she replied.

The other envelope was thicker, and it was addressed DAVID. He opened it and found another stack of $50 bills. While this was certainly a pleasant surprise, he was tired of surprises.

Who knows I'm here? Other than Cassie, only Bill and Jennifer. Did one of them mention something to a co-worker?

Ridiculous. Neither have the kind of co-workers who could quickly part with several thousand dollars in cold cash, even if they had a reason to do it.

Jennifer blasted him with another look of disapproval. "OK, David, I think it's about time you told us what's going on. You said you aren't doing anything illegal…so how do you explain this?" She waved the stack of money at him.

With the sharp tone of her voice, she sounded a lot like Cassie the Freight Train. His sister had used that tone on him often, melting away all possible resistance. Cassie and Jennifer had shared an apartment for three years, during their graduate studies. During that time, Jennifer must have adopted some of Cassie's mannerisms.

David pulled a chair out from the table to rest upon while he deliberated. Jennifer followed suit, waiting patiently, her eyes never leaving his. Her fingers played with the braid in her hair, another Cassie-ism.

Eventually, he replied, "OK. I'll tell you what's going on. Now that someone else obviously knows I'm staying here, I can't keep you in the dark any longer. And if you decide you don't like the situation, I'll pack up my stuff and hide out elsewhere. But let's wait until Bill gets home, OK? He should hear this, too."

"Fine." A look of concern remained on her face, partially masking the blank, patient stare he knew so well. He had seen that trance-like expression often when they were playing Capture the Flag, lurking in the wilderness together, waiting for the right moment to pounce upon the enemy flag. Jennifer was an expert at waiting.

"In the meantime, I do need to get some more work done this evening, so I might not come upstairs for awhile. Other than the delivery, today really has been a bad day, and I'm scrambling to pick up all the pieces."

He rose from the table and headed for the basement stairs with his enigmatic envelope of money in hand. Identifying his mysterious benefactor could wait until later. At least his financial liquidity worries had been solved.

Jennifer called after him, "Poor boy. I'll fix you some healthier food. No more pizza for you today."

CHAPTER 13
ENTROPY

MarsDay 20, 5:39 p.m.
(December 11, 3:00 p.m.)

As Anna listened to the end of the taped message describing the ERV signal loss, the rounded walls of the *Perseus* closed in on her, just a bit. The tranquil wall color, sky-blue again, didn't seem to help. She decided that she might just hate that color. The psychologists overused it every time they thought the crew needed pacification.

She studied the faces of her companions, trying to assess their reactions, looking to them for an injection of vital confidence.

Written upon the commander's expression was indifference, perhaps even apathy. Evelyn looked like she had just received another piece of fan mail, like the hundreds of electronic postcards each of them skimmed through every day. If she was concerned about the loss of the ERV telemetry, she sure didn't show it.

Ollie was much harder to read. Like Evelyn, he also didn't reveal any of the surprise or concern she would have expected, or that she herself felt. His eyes were cold and distant, while the quivering corner of his mouth hinted at something else. What it was, she couldn't venture to guess.

The message had arrived just as Ollie was serving the evening meal. At least hearing Shepherd's voice again had been reassuring.

No, the message was from David, not Shepherd. David. It's good to know his real name now, even if everyone else does, too.

Anna was always a bit moody on an empty stomach. Now, her appetite had disappeared. Bite by bite, she forced herself to eat the reconstituted meatloaf and vegetables on her plate.

As the ship's doctor, she was closely monitoring everyone's daily intake of calories. Her own count had been a bit low each day over the past three weeks, partly by design. Until the crew was fully committed to landing on Mars, past the point when they could return to Earth using a "free return trajectory," they needed to conserve their food and water supplies. After all, they might encounter more spoiled food packages when they dug deeper into their supply caches.

Working up some courage, she asked Evelyn for her opinion of the current situation. The commander didn't respond right away. Instead, she pushed her food around her plate, arranging her peas in perfectly separated rows. When she finally spoke, her voice was calm and confident.

"Convincing the media that this is no big deal might be a tough challenge for you, but I have confidence in your abilities. For Ollie and me, this turn of events changes nothing."

Ollie dropped his fork. Unguarded irritation had replaced his neutral gaze. "What do you mean, it changes nothing? If there's a serious problem with the ERV on Mars, we have no guaranteed trip back home. I'd call that a bloody big change. Shouldn't we at least consider our options?"

"Not yet," said Evelyn. "It's too soon for that. I'm not going to worry much about a faulty ERV transmitter. Worst case, we can replace it once we land."

"I can think of several cases a lot worse than that," said Anna. She had crashed headlong into worst-case scenarios many times in her young life, enough to make her extremely cautious about tempting fate. No matter how bad a situation was, it could always get worse. "What if the ERV isn't there anymore?"

"And just where would it go?" asked Evelyn, amused. "It's a pretty big piece of hardware. I doubt it could float away on a gentle afternoon breeze."

Anna persisted. "And if the fuel tanks exploded? What then?"

"Due to the safe design of the ERV, that stretches the imagination. And let's not forget about the second ERV following us to Mars. Even if the first ERV was turned to stone by the mythical Gorgon herself, she can't touch our second ERV."

"And if the Gorgon remains?" asked Anna. "What if Medusa messes with our second ERV, too?"

Evelyn snorted, loudly. "Once we land, I'll slay the ugly bitch."

Ollie started to reply, then apparently changed his mind. He pushed his half eaten meal away and leaned back in silence, with his arms folded solidly across his chest.

Anna found her own spirits rising, along with her appetite. The commander was right. Anna had been preaching to the world for three weeks about all their wonderful contingency plans. Did she not believe her own words?

Besides, their final contingency plan would handle any unforeseen combination of events. She was under no illusions. She knew the commander possessed a securely sealed bottle containing a dozen small red pills. If Mars thwarted all their efforts, and death was their only recourse, she would sleep soundly thereafter. Her dreams would be free of bees forever.

MarsDay 21, 12:57 a.m.
(December 11, 10:30 p.m.)

The evening news program had been kind to their mission. Most of the media attention was still focused on the unrest in the Middle East. Even with the blizzard outside degrading the reception on their satellite television system, the violent images still came through loud and clear.

Several hours ago, the SEA steering committee had issued a short press release about a "temporary" loss of signal from the ERV on Mars. The newscast only contained the briefest mention of it. When given a choice between a news story about Mars and one filled with scenes of death and destruction on Earth, death and destruction was an easy winner.

The crew appeared to be taking the latest setback well. In her response to his message, Evelyn pointed out that if the ERV remained silent, Anna could promise the media a full investigation after they had landed. A human crew was uniquely qualified to land on Mars, examine the ERV, and repair whatever part was defective. Such tasks were well beyond the ability of robotic rovers or orbiting satellites.

If advertised properly, the loss of the ERV signal could almost become a publicity-generating event, she had reasoned. What better way to show the world the power of human ingenuity, and how that ingenuity would soon spread across the face of a new world?

The news program credits rolled onto the screen, and David leaned back in the brown leather recliner, fighting to stay awake. It had been a long day, and he was utterly exhausted.

While Bill turned off the television, Jennifer cleared her throat to speak. David already knew what she would say. It was time for him to confess.

So be it. As a strong gust of wind shook the house, David began his tale by telling his friends about a conversation with his brother-in-law almost a year ago. Ben had heard about openings for the SEA Mission Support team through some colleagues at NASA. Many of Ben's friends were seeking part-time technical positions, although details of the positions were ambiguous. A shroud of secrecy had already surrounded the support organization, and reliable information was hard to find.

Ben did some research. He learned the position of Director was still open. He also heard that "outsiders" were strongly encouraged to apply for the position, following the example set by corporate America in hiring external CEOs who could enter a company with an unbiased perspective. Ben had immediately thought of David for the Director's position and suggested he apply. David's diverse background and exceptional critical thinking skills might appeal to the SEA hiring board.

Though Ben had been confident, David had assumed that applicants with some sort of relevant technical experience would be preferred. The interviews were rigorous. He thought he had made a good impression on the panel, but even so, he was completely surprised to hear he had landed the position. His long shot paid off handsomely.

Turbulence from the storm outside rattled the windowpanes, but David's captive audience didn't seem to notice. They frequently interrupted with questions. He reminisced about months of intense training, working with the other paid and unpaid volunteers on the support team. Eventually he met the Mars crew in person at their going-away party. As he reached the present, the others remained silent, reassessing their long-time friend within a new perspective.

Bill eventually broke the silence. "One thing I don't understand is why your support team needs to be so secretive. Why not come out into the open and make your activities known? An army of people would help you."

David considered how to answer the question that had cost him so much lost sleep. "I know of several reasons, but none carry much conviction.

Perhaps it's best to turn the question around and ask, why would the support team ever want to work within the public spotlight? We already have an army of people who help us, and we can call upon practically any expert in any field, as needed. It's doubtful we would gain much by going public. Also, my team can make decisions and take actions without the media scrutinizing every move. I'll bet that's a luxury NASA really envies."

Jennifer frowned. "You're talking about the failed Aitken Basin lunar lander, right? What a witch hunt. Even though that probe was unmanned, the media circus has been almost as bad as the Columbia space shuttle aftermath."

David nodded his agreement. "NASA managers have been bogged down for months answering inane media questions and sitting in on endless presidential review boards. It must be impossible for them to get any real work done. Not that there's much for them to do, with the robotic Moon and Mars programs temporarily halted."

"Of course, the final result will be some plausible theory about why the lander exploded, plus a hundred other, potential concerns requiring a complete redesign of the whole robotic exploration program and several years of delay." Jennifer's frown deepened, and her voice grew bitter. "Meanwhile, President Fletcher has already threatened to cancel the entire space program, and the Chinese will soon be thumbing their noses at us from the south pole of the Moon."

Bill cleared his throat. "Jennifer and I should discuss what you've told us, and what it means. Speaking for myself, I don't have any problem with your staying here for as long as you want to."

"Sounds fine to me, too." Jennifer flashed David a mischievous smile. "But I must insist on two conditions. First, I don't want to come home to any more burnt pizzas in the oven." Then her smile widened, becoming feral. "Second, you can't keep us in the dark. I want to know everything that's going on with the mission, before my zealous colleagues around the water cooler hear about it."

David had no problem with this arrangement, as long as his friends didn't spread any inside information. He also stated a concern about the money on the dining room table.

"Those envelopes didn't appear out of thin air. Someone knows I'm here, and I have no idea who it is or what their intentions are. They probably mean us no harm, and we can take their gift at face value. But after all that's happened in the past few days, well, I just don't know anymore. I'm glimpsing movement in the shadows, and it troubles me."

MarsDay 29, 6:30 a.m.
(December 20, 10:30 a.m.)

With Christmas approaching, most of Anna's public outreach activities adopted a holiday theme. After recording short segments for at least a dozen different programs, she was tired of hearing the phrase, "Peace on Earth and Mars."

Some of the programs were more enjoyable than others. Her favorite was a holiday skit for the Saturday Night Live comedy show where she pretended the *Perseus* was already on Mars and some unexpected visitors were knocking on the airlock door. The final product was titled "Coneheads Bearing Gifts."

After extensive Earth-side editing, her acting debut had turned out quite well. Hopefully the more astute viewers would forgive their taking some liberties with reality. The *Perseus* had several "suitports" and two side panels that opened, but no traditional airlock.

Other programs were not nearly as pleasant, like the one currently locking her firmly within its grasp. Eight days had passed since the last signals were received from the ERV on Mars. With NASA releasing new orbital images of the Mars landing site the day before, the topic was now timely once again, and USNN had purchased more media time to discuss it with the crew. Fontaine was on the prowl.

Fontaine often smirked by lifting one corner of her mouth ever so slightly, a facial twitch that annoyed Anna to no end. As usual, the reporter was dressed immaculately. Her bright red outfit would probably have cost Anna a whole month's salary back when she was bussing tables at a trendy Ann Arbor restaurant to earn spending money during grad school. The reporter's flashy clothing seemed intentionally designed to overwhelm Anna's simple maroon coverall, the one she usually wore when appearing before the media.

At yesterday's NASA press conference, Anna had no problem finding Fontaine in the front row. The reporter had enjoyed the spotlight, asking several difficult questions of the NASA imaging team.

Even the highest resolution NASA orbiter images were still too coarse to detect any clear signs of the ERV. The terrain appeared normal and untouched, as if the craft had never landed. An orbiting neutron spectrometer instrument had also failed to detect any sign of the hydrogen in the fuel tanks, but that wasn't surprising. Detecting the ERV's fuel signature from orbit was improbable, due to the modestly high background readings of hydrogen in the soil of the Medusae Fossae region.

The NASA images of the Medusae Fossae region came from the *Mars Odyssey* orbiter, with its camera resolution of ten meters per pixel. They were fortunate that this aged spacecraft was still alive. Its supply of fuel was critically low.

Three other probes were still in orbit about Mars, but all were crippled by a lack of fuel. The resolution on the *Mars Reconnaissance Orbiter* camera was a hundred times better than the *Mars Odyssey* cameras, but without fuel for realigning the spacecraft, the camera was useless. Likewise, the high-resolution cameras on NASA's *Mars Global Surveyor* orbiter and the European Space Agency's *Mars Express* orbiter were retired long ago. The current Mars mission had caught the planners at NASA and ESA by surprise, right in the middle of a funding gap for Mars orbiters.

Fontaine's initial questions to Anna this afternoon made it clear that yesterday's press conference was not over yet. The topic of this session would be all things related to Earth Return Vehicles.

Anna emphasized the mission would continue with their plans mostly unchanged. Unless contact with the ERV was restored later, they would rely upon the backup habitat's navigation beacon to guide their precision landing. Then they would scoot over and repair the ERV.

Anna was surprised at the depths of Ollie's unhappiness with this plan. He almost seemed ready to throw in the towel, privately pointing out several times that they could still use their free return trajectory back to Earth. This argument probably didn't earn him any points with Evelyn, and Anna was disappointed in him as well.

The computer uploaded the next message from Fontaine.

Fontaine: Has your support team determined what caused the ERV to explode?

Anna saw right through this loaded question immediately. Fontaine often interjected her own opinion into her questions as if it was a given fact.

Obviously, the reporter had jumped to the conclusion that an explosion destroyed the ERV. Answering her question without addressing the unlikely explosion theory would seem evasive.

Nevertheless, Anna wasn't going to let herself be led around by the nose, not this time. She would stick to her script. She adjusted her button camera and began to record.

Schweitzer: We still don't know why the ERV is silent. Mars Odyssey detected neither debris nor any chemical residues. An explosion remains unlikely. Unless the ERV resumes transmitting, we probably won't know the cause of the communications interruption until we land on the surface and investigate in person.*

She reconsidered her answer and glanced over to Commander Day for a second opinion. Evelyn gave a slight nod, so Anna sent the reply back to Earth. The time delay of communications would give her a few moments to relax before she received the next question.

Evelyn and Ollie had been lurking around this morning, just outside the range of the camera. Neither was very talkative, but she was glad they were there. If she had trouble with a question, they might be able to help. Also, with them in attendance, she felt more like she was responding for the whole team.

The computer chimed the receipt of a new message from Earth. She held her breath.

Fontaine: Why don't you accept the possibility that an explosion destroyed the ERV? Several NASA experts have pointed right away to an explosion as the most likely cause of the ERV's disappearance. With almost 80 metric tons of rocket fuel detonating, very little of the vehicle would survive intact.

Ollie leaned over and asked, "Same answer again?"

Anna agreed, sighing loudly. "Same answer, but phrased differently. You know, after doing a lot of these media presentations, I've started to appreciate the skill it takes to become a successful politician. There's a real talent to saying as little as possible in so many different ways, slipping your evasive answers past the public without them noticing."

After taking a moment to compose herself, she activated the camera.

Schweitzer: We do accept the possibility that an explosion might have destroyed the ERV, just as we accept many other unlikely explanations. Very little has been ruled out. Until we have more information, your NASA experts are just guessing.

Ollie scowled at the commander and asked, "I know we've been discussing this for two days now, but are you sure this is the right approach? The *Mars Odyssey* image resolution is borderline, but it should have detected the reflection of sunlight from the ERV's solar panels. Based on those images, there's hardly any chance the ERV pods are intact. We should acknowledge at least that much."

Evelyn replied sharply, "You're talking about a single pixel going undetected within a huge regional image. We don't know what happened. Until we do, we have an obligation to investigate, using any means at our disposal." She paused for dramatic effect before adding, "That includes landing and checking things out, in person."

Ollie frowned, and was about to reply when the message icon on the computer flashed again.

Fontaine: Let me phrase my question differently. If...if, an explosion destroyed the ERV, what could have caused it? And what traces would remain?

"Persistent, isn't she?" said Evelyn.

Anna looked to the others for some help because this question encroached on a topic they wanted to avoid. "Should I tell her why an explosion is unlikely? Or perhaps I should just answer the last part by saying we would expect to see widely scattered fragments with a large, central component intact?"

"Either way, you're in hot water with her next question," warned Ollie. "I'm guessing she already knows about our radical ERV design, and she's just playing games with you."

Evelyn got up from the table slowly and entered the kitchen. She poured more hot water into her teacup. Only when she had retaken her place at the table did she respond. "It does sound like this reporter might know more about the ERV design than she's letting on. Someone Earth-side might have slipped her some information, but we won't know for sure unless we play along. Let's let her lead us where she wants to go."

"Dangerous, dangerous," moaned Ollie.

Once more, Anna asked how she should respond to the question.

Evelyn advised, "Tell her that the engine nozzle substructure should survive any explosion intact, and it might be large enough to be seen in the photos from the orbiter. That much is at least remotely possible, and it dodges the real issue."

"And the first part of her question?" asked Anna.

"Just ignore it. Let's see how she reacts."

Anna did as Evelyn instructed, and the three of them awaited the reporter's response. Anna got up to refill her teacup, too. She lingered in the kitchen for a minute, trying to refocus her thoughts upon their original script.

In her mind, she recited the three "money phrases" they had all agreed upon. These short phrases would make ideal newspaper and television quotes. Because Fontaine had focused all her questions on the explosion theory, Anna had only been able to use one of her money phrases and had not repeated it yet.

Eventually, Fontaine responded. Anna reclaimed her seat in front of the computer display and camera.

Fontaine: What about the crew cabin? It should be much easier to see in the images than the engine nozzles.

Cursing, Evelyn smacked her palm loudly on the tabletop, causing the others to jump. "There we have it. She's either the world's best psychic, or someone slipped her the design of our ERV."

Anna didn't see any way to answer the reporter's question honestly, not without diving headfirst into delicate issues. They had wanted to avoid the topic of ERV design until much later in the mission.

Judging by her directed questions, Fontaine probably knew already that the ERV wasn't really a "vehicle" at all. Instead, the volume that would have been taken up by a crew compartment was a carefully planned, modular jumble of engine nozzles, fuel generation equipment, fuel tanks, and solar cells. The crew would assemble the ERV once they arrived on the surface, bringing with them the most critical component of all, their own life support habitat.

Anna desperately longed to be relaxing on a beach in some remote place like Key West where the world couldn't intrude upon her peace of mind.

Though the *Perseus* was far more remote than the most isolated tropical island, it sure didn't feel that way right now.

In contrast to Anna's dismay, Ollie almost seemed happy. A thin smile lit his face as he arched his back and stretched his arms. He probably felt vindicated. His position all along had been one of complete disclosure. He had frequently tried to convince Evelyn about the need to reveal all aspects of the mission to the public.

Ollie liked to speculate about the mission sponsors remaining hidden because they wanted to avoid public scrutiny when the truly risky nature of the Mars mission was finally revealed. Anna strongly doubted his theory. It seemed too simplistic. It didn't explain why the sponsors hadn't disclosed all the mission details up front, waited for any public uproar to die down, and then revealed their identity.

Unless that's what is happening now. Perhaps the mission sponsors tipped off Fontaine, intentionally?

"Now what do we do, oh brilliant public relations guru?" Ollie asked the commander. "You've successfully painted Anna into a corner."

"And what would you suggest, Ollie?" asked Evelyn, softly. "I'm open to your ideas, as always."

He shook his head. "We need to reveal the full story, including an accurate description of our plan to assemble the ERV on the surface of Mars, the reasons why we're doing the mission this way, and the secondary consequences to the overall mission plan and objectives. What's so bad about telling people we won't have a full year-and-a-half to explore the surface? Isn't a year enough time for us to look around?"

"You're overlooking the real problem again," Evelyn replied. "It's not the time it takes to assemble the ERV. It's the risk. It's never been done before…and that equates to 'it can't be done' in many people's minds. This reporter has already been attacking us based upon the risky nature of the mission. If we give in, we lend credibility to the rest of her pathetic drivel."

"Swaying Fontaine does seem unlikely," Ollie agreed. "But what about the public? If we emphasize the innovative nature of the ERV design, people might believe the mission planners are hiding because they want to protect their bag of technological tricks. This happens in the private sector all the time."

"Now who's being deceptive?" Evelyn snapped. "You don't know the motivations of our sponsors. Perhaps they could care less about protecting their intellectual secrets. Also, we've convinced 90 percent of the media and the public that we're following the Mars Direct mission plan, plus a few minor enhancements. The cornerstone of Mars Direct is the premise that the ERV is awaiting our arrival on Mars, fully fueled and ready to fly. Now you want to tell everyone, 'So sorry, we forgot to mention, some minor assembly is required.'"

Ollie's words had swayed Anna's opinion, to a certain extent. She couldn't see any other way out of her corner, and she dreaded the thought of lying to the media deliberately.

Besides, what was the big deal about shipping some of the ERV components to Mars separately? The public had already witnessed the construction of the International Space Station in low-Earth orbit, a job orders-of-magnitude more complex than the ERV assembly task awaiting the crew. They could probably grasp the thought of an assembly job on Mars.

The biggest difference was the presence of gravity. For moving the ERV components around, all the crew needed was a set of low tech, inflatable tires. Their pressurized rover would pull the modular engines and fuel tanks over to the *Perseus* easily enough, even if bumpy terrain was in the way. Overall, the weak gravity of Mars would greatly assist their construction efforts.

They wouldn't even have to go outside during most of the construction interval. Tele-operated robots would do much of the work.

Anna meekly offered her opinion. "I think Ollie's right. We need to be honest. I don't see any other options. We have this reporter right where she wants us," she punned.

Evelyn didn't reply immediately. She swished the tea in her cup, studying it intently. After taking a cautious sip, she put the cup down and reached for her familiar pocket watch.

"OK, we'll try it your way," Evelyn finally conceded. "I don't see any other options either. Nevertheless, I fear we're making a big mistake, one that might cost us later."

Anna smiled and relaxed. The rest of the media session was still painful, but she felt much better about it. The prospect of misleading her public had been weighing on her conscience. If the mission sponsors had wanted someone to lie for them, they should have hired a different spokesperson.

CHAPTER 14
CHARGE

MarsDay 33, 12:13 p.m.
(December 24, 6:00 p.m.)

David sat in his newly favorite chair, a recliner facing the window with the western view. Outside, glistening snowflakes pierced the last rays of the fading sunlight.

The weather forecasters were correct, a rare event in the mountains. A winter storm blew in from the Pacific Northwest two days ago and stalled over Colorado, just as predicted. Winds were calm, and the snowfall had been light and steady ever since. Mother Nature worked gently, but persistently. Four feet of fresh champagne powder blanketed the slopes of the mountain valley.

According to Bill, the latest weather forecast called for at least two more feet of snow over the next 48 hours. This storm promised to dump the biggest snowfall on the mountains west of Boulder in over 25 years. The town of Nederland was completely isolated, awaiting the return of clear skies and the commencement of the digging out process.

All was white and surreal. The only noise outside was an occasional crackling when a pine branch collapsed under the weight of its pristine cloak.

Bill and Jennifer welcomed the rare moisture, even though it forced them to cancel their Christmas holiday plans. They had intended to visit Jennifer's parents in Castle Rock, just south of Denver.

Any travel tonight was clearly impossible. Even if work crews cleared all the snow from the winding canyon road to Boulder, the risk of avalanche would keep the road closed for days. The north and south routes out of town would only take a hearty traveler to places even more isolated than Nederland's valley. To the west, the road passed the Eldora Ski Resort on its steep climb to the continental divide. An outlet in that direction was unthinkable. Even the ski resort was probably inaccessible for the duration of the storm.

The soft hum from a 15-kilowatt Generac in the garage, barely audible over the crackling of the fire in the wood stove, lulled David's senses, making his eyes heavy. Electrical service had gone out two days ago, and the solar cells on the roof were useless when covered up by this much snow. However, the generator could easily handle all their power needs until its supply of LP gas ran out. Bill thought they would have heat and power for several days. After that, at least they would still be warm. His ample firewood supply should last all winter.

David's friends used their forced isolation to put the finishing touches on some last minute Christmas presents. He watched Jennifer knit the final rows on a wildly colored afghan destined for her parents. Bill crocheted a pair of wool slippers for his sister. This "domestic" vision of his friends contrasted with David's vivid memories of frantic dashes and other escapades during their Capture the Flag outings. He never would have believed Bill's strong, stubby fingers could be so dexterous.

Exhausted by another long day at Mission Support, David fought to stay awake by chatting with his friends. He shared his amazement that the wireless Internet connection, his lifeline to the world, was unaffected by the severe weather outside. He had even completed the last of his own Christmas shopping earlier in the day, online, using his still functional credit card for payment.

As was so often the case over the past few days, their conversation drifted toward the Mars mission. Bill commented on the latest news, the continued lack of signals from the ERV on Mars, which had been reported very briefly on a program earlier in the day. While the location and progress of Santa Claus was plotted in three dimensions down to within an inch of accuracy, references to the Mars mission were obscure.

Bill concluded that the loss of signal from the ERV was a non-event for most of the media. With holiday distractions in the way, the Mars mission wasn't likely to get much air time. Only a few vocal voices of dissent were heard, from predictable sources.

This state of affairs suited David just fine. Press coverage was good, but only when things were running smoothly.

When Jennifer asked about the view from the inside, David acknowledged that the trend of signal losses was alarming. Of the three initial navigation beacons at the landing site on Mars, only the beacon on the backup habitat was still transmitting. The cargo vessel beacon had gone silent soon after the vehicle landed two years ago.

The crew's morale was suffering, too. Anna had ventured forth some private concerns about her two colleagues. Both were acting oddly, and on opposite ends of the spectrum.

Olie continued to have trouble sleeping and was sometimes moody and irritable. Evelyn was calm, cheerful to the point of excess, and seemingly in denial that the mission had some serious problems to be addressed. Evelyn's carefree attitude wasn't consistent with her previous paranoia over uncovering potential mission problems.

The overall assessment from his psych team was that the crew didn't seem to be bonding very well. They believed the main culprit was stress, exacerbated by hard feelings left over from the commander's unannounced drills. David wryly commented that the drills had been mostly their idea in the first place.

Still, the psych team remained confident. Things could have been a lot worse, and the upcoming weeks would undoubtedly provide plenty of opportunities for teamwork to gel.

David lapsed into silence, thinking about Anna and worrying about her state of mind. During their ever more frequent conversations in his virtual office, Anna wouldn't tell him much about her own feelings. However, her voice trembled often, and her easy confidence seemed more fragile than usual. She avoided talking about the mission or her two companions unless he asked her pointed questions. They conversed readily on almost any other subject, however.

When it came to personal relationships, David had always felt woefully inexperienced. He suspected if Anna were here with him on terra firma, he would be head over heels in love with her. She infatuated him in ways he never thought possible. As he discovered each new facet of her personality, he was increasingly delighted. Her endearing quirks, hopes, dreams, and desires blended so well into a symphony of deep rapport. They seemed able to talk for hours about anything, or about nothing.

What cosmic cruelty had placed the woman of his dreams on a journey to Mars? Had he done something to upset the divine powers that be? Was his sentence of separation proper punishment for a serious infraction of some kind?

Even worse was the uncertainty. Did she share his feelings? He thought she might, but he couldn't just come out and ask her. She was under enough stress already. If he was wrong, it could damage their relationship and add one more burden on her shoulders. The uncertainty was tearing him up. He had almost considered asking Cassie for advice, truly a last resort.

Respecting David's somber mood, Bill and Jennifer had returned their full attention to their projects. The only sounds in the room were the crackling of the fire, the hum of the generator, the ticking of the grandfather clock in the corner, and the soft squeak of David's recliner chair as he rocked gently.

He might have nodded off for a few minutes before his serenity was interrupted by the sound of a motor outside. The sharp staccato whine increased in volume until it sounded like the source was right outside the front porch.

"A snowmobile?" asked Bill, incredulously. "What idiot would be driving around on an evening like this?"

"Time for me to disappear into the basement," said David, rubbing the weariness from his eyes.

He jumped to his feet and rushed over to the basement steps, keeping low to the ground until he was far enough down the stairwell to straighten up and descend the rest of the way with more dignity.

The basement office was just as he had left it, a bit cluttered after many days of work. Disjointed notes on small white slips of paper had proliferated to cover every flat surface within reach of the desk in the corner.

Since he had some time to kill, he set about straightening up the room a bit. He had never been a very tidy worker, though he knew exactly where everything was. While he cleaned, he left the door open so he could hear what was happening on the level above.

The front door opened, and Bill talked to someone on the porch. Their conversation was too muffled to understand. Then footsteps sounded on the floor above, and two people entered the house, probably Bill and their mysterious visitor.

A sharp feminine voice declared, "Oh, he's going to want to see me."

"I'm telling you, there's no one else here but my wife." Bill's voice was raised an octave above its natural depth.

The visitor was apparently not deterred. "Would I have come all the way from Boulder on a freezing snowmobile if I didn't know he was here? He's been your house guest for the past two weeks."

Now the conversation had David's full attention. He couldn't make out Bill's reply or the next few bits of conversation until the stranger stated loudly, "I'm not leaving until I talk to him. I can wait a long time. It's a lot warmer in here than out there in the storm."

After a few more seconds, he heard some soft footsteps on the basement stairs. Then Jennifer peeked her head around the frame of the open doorway.

"David, it looks like you have a caller who isn't going to take 'no' for an answer."

"Who is it?" he asked, matching her low whisper.

"Beats me. She just calls herself a colleague of yours."

Someone from his support team, perhaps? But they didn't know where he was. Another thought occurred to him. Could this be one of his mysterious benefactors?

Either way, he had better hear what the caller had to say. He trudged up the steps behind Jennifer, hoping for the best, while fearing that no good could come from the unexpected visit.

Rounding the corner of the stairwell, he caught his first glimpse of the stranger in the foyer. She wore a black, one-piece snowsuit, shapeless, but fairly slender. The narrow visor on her helmet was open. Thick, black ski gloves rested on the floor nearby. She had just taken off her heavy boots, also black. Apparently, she intended to stay.

As David drew closer, she removed her dark helmet completely. A cascade of brown hair flowed over her shoulders, and her whole face lit up when she saw him. It was a face he recognized immediately. His jaw dropped, and the bottom fell out of his stomach. There was no mistaking the identity of this visitor.

Skye Fontaine.

His friends obviously recognized the reporter as well, and were equally speechless. David blinked, hoping the image in front of him was an illusion that would disappear. She remained.

Fontaine's nostrils flared. Her dispassionate stare pierced him, delving deeply into his skull and revealing all his inner thoughts for her to analyze. This woman seemed able to outmaneuver him at will. He felt naked and inadequate before her, yet her presence also mesmerized him even more than the last time he had seen her in person.

The reporter finally broke the awkward silence. "You, Doctor Debacco, have caused me a lot of trouble." She said his name as if it left an unpleasant taste in her mouth.

David found his voice. "The feeling is mutual, I assure you."

Bill moved forward, his back tense and his face beet red. "I don't care what it's like outside. You're leaving, now. Resist, and I'll kick your butt so far that you won't have to drive back to Boulder." His lumberjack muscles rippled under his thin shirt in anticipation of carrying out his threat.

David grabbed Bill's arm in a weak grip that could easily have been broken. "The damage is done." David measured each word calmly and deliberately. "Throwing her out isn't going to help. She's gone through some trouble to get here. Let's hear what she has to say."

David studied Fontaine more closely. Contrary to his initial impression, she didn't seem very daunting or arrogant at the moment. Perhaps Bill's words had shaken her a bit. She fiddled self-consciously with a gadget on the belt of her suit. Reflected light from the fire in the wood stove danced in her defiant eyes, but her lower lip trembled.

"Perhaps we should all be more comfortable?" she suggested, while gesturing toward the living room.

As she stepped in that direction, Bill moved to block her. Fontaine glanced at Jennifer, clearly appealing to a higher authority. She found little support, however.

"Look, I'm not going away. While we talk, we can be comfortable, or not. It's up to you."

After a brief but intense non-verbal exchange between Bill and Jennifer, Bill slowly backed away. His face remained hardened, and he flexed his muscles again, this time in helpless impotence.

"Fine, but when you're done, you're gone," he said.

Fontaine seated herself in the rocking recliner chair, David's favorite. With an arm around his waist, Jennifer led Bill over to the couch. David remained on his feet, pacing in front of the hot wood stove.

Fontaine unzipped the top section of her coverall and slid it off her shoulders and arms, revealing a thick, red turtleneck sweater underneath. Even disheveled by the ravages of the storm outside, her beauty was still devastating.

"You picked a nice hideout."

David closed his eyes and tried to concentrate. All around him was blackness and despair. With his hideout no longer secure, only two options were left: disappear again, or give up his job and become a media target. Either way, the future looked bleak.

"How did you find me?" he asked.

She laughed, with musical timbres in her voice, an impish chuckle that might have been quite pleasant under different circumstances. Her outburst certainly seemed out of place, given the macabre atmosphere in the room.

"Is that a question I hear?" she asked. "How convenient, because I have some questions for you too. Shall we play a little game? I'll answer a question of yours, if you'll answer one of mine."

David reckoned that if he was forced to move on to a different hiding place, he needed to know the answer to his question. Otherwise, Fontaine would probably find him again.

Besides, what could he tell her that she didn't already know? He had seen her interview with the crew, a few days earlier. She seemed to know as much about the Mars mission as he did, possibly more. She was infernally omniscient, or more likely, she had excellent sources of information that somehow rivaled his own. He would give anything to learn what those sources were. A cold rage built up slowly within, clearing away his mental fog, as he rebelled against Fontaine's seemingly effortless manipulations.

"Fine," he barked. "So answer the question. How did you find me?"

"You have lots of friends." Fontaine glanced briefly toward Bill and Jennifer, who were glowering on the couch, watching the reporter closely. "One of them has loose lips and a looser libido."

At first, David didn't understand. Then it was all so obvious.

"Reggie!"

"Yes, your friend Reggie thinks the world of you, but he'll do anything to score. He'll tell a woman anything she wants to hear. One of my more attractive associates paid him a visit. Once his lips started flapping, she couldn't shut him up."

"I'll kill the little shithead," threatened Bill, under his breath, but loud enough to be heard clearly.

David stopped his pacing and collapsed heavily in a loveseat next to the wood stove. Fontaine's answer was actually good news. It proved the reporter wasn't omniscient. The option of finding a new hideout and disappearing successfully was still open to him, if he severed all ties to his friends and family. He couldn't leave the slightest clue behind.

"My turn," said Fontaine. She leaned forward in her chair, her eyes gleaming with an intensity that he recalled seeing often in her reporting sessions on the television. "Tell me, who is sponsoring the Mars mission?"

Now it was David's turn to laugh, and he did so deeply and at length. A great weight had suddenly been lifted from his shoulders.

The issue of motivations haunted him since the day his wine glass shattered on the red brick pavement of Pearl Street. The alarming possibility that the network knew the mission would fail had since been eclipsed by a prospect even worse. What if Fontaine already knew the planners' agenda? If the sponsors really were "Mars bogeymen" with sinister motives, the network coverage might simply reflect what inside sources were telling them.

This theory seemed weak from the start, and it appeared even less likely now. Fontaine wouldn't have asked her question if she already knew the answer. Since she didn't know the identity of the mission sponsors, she probably didn't know their motivations either.

David carefully considered the best way to answer. He looked at the reporter and sensed the impatience written all over her features. Most likely, she had been waiting to learn the answer to this question far longer than he had.

Should he string her along, protracting her torment while he had the opportunity? Part of him liked the thought of that, but he still had some other questions he wanted to ask the reporter, so he opted for the most honest and direct answer he could think of. He did wait a few more moments before speaking, however, savoring Fontaine's discomfort.

"I don't know."

"You don't know?" she said, without bothering to hide her irritation. "What do you mean, you don't know? How can you work for someone without knowing who they are?"

"That sounds like a different question or three." David smiled. He was starting to enjoy the mental fencing, slipping into his comfortable, philosophical debate mode. The tables had turned. Now he felt like the hunter, and she the prey. "I'll answer them later, if you want...but it's my turn to ask you another question."

"But you didn't answer my first question! 'I don't know' isn't an answer! It doesn't tell me anything!'"

"Sure it is, and it does," he replied smugly. "Sometimes, those three simple words are the most profound answer possible. Ask any scientist or philosopher."

Fontaine didn't wear her frustration very well. She sputtered and fumed, but finally conceded the point. "My next question won't be so closed-ended. Given your background, I had assumed I would need to keep you tightly focused so you don't go rambling on about meaningless philosophical rubbish."

Jennifer said, "Don't assume too much about David. He'll surprise you every time." Visibly relaxing a bit, she picked up her afghan and began to knit, keeping one eye on her project and the other on Fontaine.

David said, "Let's see, where were we. Oh yes, it's my turn to ask a question." He paused, trying not to appear overly eager. He wasn't about to hand control of the situation back to Fontaine. "Your strong opposition to the Mars mission is no secret. If you don't even know who planned the mission, why are you so opposed to it?"

She frowned. "I don't oppose the mission. Opposition implies a biased viewpoint, a mistake that a rookie reporter would make. I do admit that personally, I'm very skeptical of the means and motives of whoever planned this Mars mission. Also, I still don't understand the justification for sending anyone to Mars in the first place. As an investigative reporter, it's my job to understand. I need to ask tough questions when things don't add up. With this Mars mission, nothing adds up."

"Untrue, but honest sounding," said David, judging her response. It wasn't the answer he was hoping for, but it was probably all he could expect.

Fontaine's cheeks flushed. "Whatever. Doctor, tell me, what is your function on the mission. In detail, please. I'm not going to settle for any three word answers this time."

Ouch. He had known this question was coming, and had dreaded it. Now that he glimpsed the limits of Fontaine's knowledge, he regretted his willingness to play this verbal game with her. It looked like he knew a lot more about the mission than she did, after all. That meant he had more to lose.

Still, he had more questions, ones that she might be very reluctant to answer. He had spent several weeks chasing shadows, and now that Fontaine was solidly in front of him, he wasn't ready to let her get away yet.

He sighed. "I'll answer that, but a truthful response is almost paradoxical. My employment is subject to strict non-disclosure terms. If the media discovers my involvement, my job will be terminated, rendering my answer false."

Fontaine's jaw twitched, but she remained silent, waiting for him to continue.

"I'm the Director of Mission Support."

"Hot diggity!" Fontaine jumped almost to her feet, so visible was her surprise and delight. "I figured someone like you would be on the periphery, perhaps doing something related to the mission justifications, goals, or propaganda. This is so much better! But you aren't an engineer or even a trained manager, are you? How in the world did you ever end up running Mission Support?"

"That's a long story, and two more questions."

Fontaine closed her eyes for a moment before refocusing her attention on him. Perhaps he imagined that her stare was a bit more respectful, but he read something else in her expression and body language, too. A touch of hesitancy? Or perhaps even fear? Barring Bill's earlier threats, why would she suddenly be afraid of him?

She said, "Look, why don't we scrap this silly game. Now that I know more about your val...er, position, I have ten times as many questions as before. Let's cut a new deal."

"What do you have in mind?"

"If you need to keep your job a secret, that's just fine by me! Why should I give my competitors equal access to you? If you agree to answer my questions, all of them, to the best of your ability, you'll remain a confidential source."

David considered her tempting offer carefully. Perhaps it was a way out of his quandary, a way for him to remain involved in the mission while avoiding the disruption of a regime change. But what strings would be attached? Though he didn't see how, could she harm the mission with her subsequent questions?

"I see a few problems with your suggestion," he said, neutrally.

"Such as?"

"You didn't seem to have much trouble finding me, so other reporters won't, either. And once they locate me, they would gain access to the same information you have. You'll lose your incentive to keep your part of the bargain."

"True...so we're both motivated to make sure that doesn't happen, aren't we? I think you should have a talk with your friend, Reggie. There might be other subtle clues leading to you, but he's like a large billboard advertisement."

"Leave the little weasel to me," growled Bill. "How many pieces would you like him ripped into, David?"

David pretended to actually consider Bill's offer, before responding, "Just one piece is fine. If you want to have a little friendly chat with him, that would be very helpful. Thank you."

"Consider it done," Bill said.

Fontaine added, "Keep in mind, I'm a bit more persistent than some of the lackeys out there. Regarding this Mars mission, most of my fellow reporters seem to be groveling at your feet, terrified about doing anything to upset the public or the crew. They're the real weasels. Some might still be capable of independent thought, but I'll bet that most of them won't go too far out of their way, searching for the bigger story."

David still wasn't convinced. "OK, that all sounds reasonable, but would your higher-ups go along with all this?"

"Leave that to me. They've always given me a lot of wiggle room in the past."

"What about the Mars mission planners? They're still out there somewhere, and they tracked me down a lot faster than you did. If they find out I'm talking to you, I'm still toast."

"Yes, about that..." A deep frown creased her brow, as her mood darkened perceptibly. She started to speak, stopped, and restarted. "I think before we finalize our little arrangement, I should tell you the real reason I came all this way out here tonight in the middle of a blizzard, and on Christmas Eve, no less."

"Go on."

"I, I took a big chance, but I had to. I didn't want to lose you, too."

David couldn't make any sense out of her statement. How could she lose him? Before she had appeared from the depths of the blizzard, proving the insecurity of his hiding place, he wouldn't have considered leaving. This woman was full of surprises and contradictions.

She explained, "When I sought your other colleagues, I wasn't fast enough. They had already disappeared. Now they are permanently out of reach, of course."

"What other colleagues?" asked David, totally lost. Surely, she was speaking some other language.

"Tarraz and Colcheck, of course."

"Who?" he asked.

"Ahmed Tarraz and Kristin Colcheck. What were their roles on the mission?"

His puzzlement remained, until he recalled that these were the other two people fingered by the USNN program. "Oh, them! Their involvement is over, as far as I'm aware."

Fontaine coughed, and he waited for her to recover. Her hand reached for the gadget on her belt again, as if making sure it was there. The gadget was a small, black box with two glassy protrusions. It looked like some sort of solid-state, data storage device. She was probably recording every word he said.

Unfazed, David shrugged and added, "From what I've pieced together, Colcheck and Tarraz helped design some of the equipment and procedures. But that was years ago. They might be hanging around to provide some support, and I probably met them briefly at the going-away party for the crew, though I don't remember either of them. Why do you ask? And what do you mean when you say they are permanently out of reach?"

"You really don't know?" She studied his face intently. As she did so, the creases on her forehead deepened, but her hands relaxed. "I'm sorry to bring you bad news, but they're both dead."

David and his friends cried out in unison, "What?"

"Their bodies were found yesterday. It was all over the local news this morning, though neither death has been connected to the Mars mission yet. Ms. Colcheck's death is being linked to the Indiana Strangler murder spree because she attended Purdue University in West Lafayette, Indiana."

"But you don't buy that?" asked David.

"No. The chances of her being a random murder statistic are slim to none. Someone didn't want either of them talking."

"My God!" David sagged in his chair. The earlier weight on his shoulders was back, crushing him as never before. With help from Bill and Jennifer, he bombarded Fontaine with more questions.

Tarraz's case was believed to be a suicide—he hanged himself in his downtown Denver apartment. The police weren't releasing many details until his family could be contacted.

On the surface, Colcheck's death did resemble the other Strangler murders, though some of the finer details didn't match the previous killings. For instance, she had been abducted from her apartment, rather than a remote back street.

Fontaine concluded by stating, "Doctor Debacco, I'm actually glad to see how surprised and shocked you are. When you revealed you're the Director of Mission Support, I thought you might have ordered their deaths. And when

I came here tonight, thinking you might be one of the mission planners, my concerns were even deeper."

"Call me David. I hate being called 'doctor'—it sounds so stuffy. And I don't have the faintest idea why anyone would want to kill either of those people."

"You don't strike me as being a very good actor, so I happen to believe you. Besides, I already know the reason they were murdered. It's obvious. They knew specific details about the mission, details that could somehow disrupt the plans of the mission sponsors if revealed too soon. When they became liabilities, your employers terminated their contract, just as you claimed they would do to you."

"If that's true, then why am I still alive?"

"Maybe you aren't as big a threat to them, for some reason. They might believe you don't know anything useful."

David was tempted to make a snide remark, but it wasn't the proper time or place. Instead, he asked, "If I don't know anything useful, then why are you so interested in me?"

"On a story this big, I can't overlook any obvious leads. Someone in your position, with your unusual background, might know more about the mission than the planners suspect. You've probably seen or heard things that might be helpful. Perhaps casual remarks in passing, stray rumors…anything."

David placed his hands over his face, trying to block the outside world from intruding. He couldn't believe some of the things he had just heard. Could the reporter be lying? Not likely. Her claims about the deaths of Colcheck and Tarraz could be verified too easily.

Fontaine yawned, and glanced at her watch. "It's getting late. Perhaps you should consider my collaboration proposition and let me know your answer in the morning."

"Fine. How can I reach you?"

She laughed. "Oh, I brought an overnight bag. I'll sleep in one of your extra rooms tonight. I don't make a habit of allowing my leads to get away. Until you make your decision, the two of us are joined at the hip."

Bill erupted from the couch. "No. Not a chance. You'll get right back on your snowmobile and rent a hotel room in town."

Half-heartedly, Jennifer pointed out that whenever a really big snowstorm hit the valley, the hotels in town were filled with stranded skiers. Driving 20 miles to Boulder in the dark would be too dangerous. They couldn't throw someone out into the storm, not even Fontaine.

Bill would not be swayed. He stormed to the front door and held it open, defiantly glaring outside to make his point clear. Unfortunately, his timing was poor. A strong gust of wind whipped him squarely in the face and blew a cloud of snow crystals into the foyer. He braced himself and slowly closed the door.

"I guess we don't have much choice," he said, softly. His powerful hands squeezed the doorknob, as if trying to strangle it.

David walked over and placed an understanding hand on Bill's shoulder. "Letting her stay is the right thing to do," he said, with a confidence he didn't feel inside. Moving closer, he whispered in Bill's ear, "…but I'm barricading my bedroom door tonight."

CHAPTER 15
PERIGEE

MarsDay 33, 6:03 p.m.
(December 25, 12:00 a.m.)

David replayed the events of the last few days, searching for an escape from his current predicament. He longed to run off to a place where no one would find him, yet something was holding him back.

Perhaps he was tired of being in the dark. He wanted some answers.

Part of the problem was Fontaine's persistence. She had surprised him repeatedly with her sleuthing abilities. He wouldn't underestimate her again. If he was to disappear again, his new hiding place had to be well considered in advance.

I should have figured out a good backup plan already. Another mistake.

Dread permeated his soul as he thought about the deaths of Kristin Colcheck and Ahmed Tarraz. He found himself agreeing with Fontaine's conclusion, at least partially. The odds of their deaths being two random, unconnected events were astronomical. He would sooner believe that Fontaine had killed them herself.

What about that possibility? Could Fontaine have found them and killed them when they couldn't tell her anything useful? Or after they had told her all she wanted to hear?

He didn't know how far she would go to get her Big Story. That thought kept him awake for at least another hour, before he finally convinced himself that she was an unlikely killer. Hating her words on television was a far stretch from believing her to be capable of murder.

He rolled over and looked at the clock on the night stand. The time was 1:30 a.m. Sleep continued to be elusive, as new thoughts kept rolling in.

Why were Colcheck and Tarraz murdered? They weren't important to the mission. Their deaths make no sense.

Fontaine's belief that the mission planners killed them was based on the assumption that they knew critical secrets about the mission, secrets that might be revealed to the press. A flimsy assumption...but one that would be difficult to disprove.

OK, assuming her assumption is bunk, who would benefit from their deaths?

To answer that question, he needed to know more about them and about their past involvement with the mission. He had some homework to do.

Which of my own assumptions are bunk? Could the mission planners really be capable of murder? To what lengths would they go to protect the mission? Why can't I characterize this philosophical landscape? I've faced tougher logic problems, way back in Philosophy 101. Are my own assumptions about the importance of Mars exploration making me too subjective to see the facts clearly?

At some point during the next few hours, as he considered his own belief system more objectively, he reached a conclusion regarding Fontaine's proposal. With an almost audible click, his mind slipped onto a new track, and his immediate course was determined.

With this change came some relief. He found an uneasy slumber.

The alarm clock punctured his dreams abruptly. Rolling over, he slapped the snooze button a bit harder than usual.

It can't be 7:30 in the morning already!

But it was. He sat up in the bed and wiped the sleep from his eyes. Casting the covers aside took longer, but eventually he was on his feet and somewhat functional.

Taking care of his usual morning business, he verified the status of the mission and read a few messages. Then he checked the morning news headlines. He had avoided the online media lately, though the media obviously hadn't been avoiding him.

- "Reward Increased for Mars Sponsor Information" (usnn.com)
- "Truce in West Bank, but Tensions Still High" (cnn.com)
- "Global Warming Riots Organized, Effective" (cnn.com)
- "Terrorist Summit Releases Radiological How-To Papers" (Reuters)

- "Vegas Odds for Mars Mission Plummet" (Reuters)
- "Which Movie Stars Have Police Records?" (e.com)
- "Lunar Accident Investigators Expand Scope of Inquiry" (space.com)

David didn't bother to read any of the stories. They all seemed the same as the last time he had checked the news dump, two weeks ago. Instead, he shook his head and trudged his sluggish mind and body upstairs to see if anyone else was awake yet. His aching shoulders, arms, and legs conspired to make him feel much older than his 32 years of age. The next few hours might be rough ones, and he wasn't looking forward to them. However, if things went well, he might finally get some answers to his most troubling questions.

Perhaps I fear what those answers might be.

He found Bill cooking omelets on the kitchen stove, one of his favorite hobbies. Bill's helper, wearing a "Love the Chef" apron, was...Fontaine. So she was still here. It wasn't all just a bad dream.

Fontaine chopped onions on a cutting board, with tears rolling freely down her cheeks. The aroma of scrambled eggs and pork sausage helped to clear David's head a bit, along with...ah, coffee.

"Good Morning! Need coffee. Am dying for coffee. Must have coffee now."

Bill greeted him and wished him a Merry Christmas. David was taken aback for a moment. Somehow, while wrapped up in his own worries, he had forgotten what day it was.

While bantering with Bill, he assisted the breakfast preparations by setting plates and silverware on the dining room table. Fontaine finished her prep chef assignment and said, "David, it looks like you didn't sleep well last night. Was it something I said?" Her smile seemed friendly enough, but beneath it, she probably savored his weariness.

"Yeah, it was everything you said, and much more." He sat down at the table. "I have some thoughts I want to run by you, as well as an answer to your proposal. But let's have breakfast first."

He looked out the window. The snowstorm continued, as strong as ever. Skies were overcast, and now the snow level covered the lower foot of the windows on the southern side of the house. Dull reflections gave the scenery a surreal appearance.

As the omelets neared completion, Jennifer wandered into the room from upstairs. The ears on her pink bunny slippers flopped with every step she took, as did the rest of her. After the usual Christmas greetings were exchanged, she sat beside David in silence. Her eyes drooped, and her attention seemed fixated upon his coffee cup.

As they ate breakfast, their conversation was awkward until Bill and Fontaine discovered a mutual interest in sports. Bill, a big Colorado Rockies baseball fan, taunted Fontaine with a prediction that her Atlanta Braves would finish their division in last place again.

The others joined in the conversation. Somewhere along the way, they started to call Fontaine by her first name, Skye. David held out the longest because calling her "Fontaine" reinforced his belief that he was talking to a wily reporter rather than a gorgeous, young woman. Eventually, his casual nature betrayed him, and he joined the others.

Skye's praise for the Braves turned into general condemnation for the city of Atlanta. With over 25 million people living in the greater metropolitan area, Atlanta was bursting at the seams. Too many people, too few services, and too much crime had led her to move to southern Tennessee. She commuted to Atlanta on the days when she had to go into the office. Fortunately for her, she only needed to make the trip once a week. The rest of the time, she was traveling on assignments or reporting from a local affiliate studio near Chattanooga.

David commented that "Hot-lanta" didn't seem to be much different than many other American cities. Vast swathes of the country were bursting at the seams. Almost 400 million Americans lived mostly on the east coast, west coast, and southern sunshine belt. Too many of them were unemployed and happily living on an ever rising welfare stipend.

Skye didn't see the overcrowding problem in quite the same way, however. She took a tourist's view of the situation, focusing on the short-term opportunities for entertainment and culture in many cities, but leaving the long-term outlook to future generations. The megalopolis concept was fine with her, as long as she wasn't forced to live there.

After everyone had finished eating breakfast, David refocused his thoughts on more immediate concerns.

"Skye, it's time for us to discuss the Mars mission. Let's find a place to talk, in private."

With the four of them confined indoors, the 3,000-square-foot house almost felt crowded. The basement was off limits to prying eyes. Fontaine might absorb some of the information on his scattered notepads, although he wrote most of his personal memos in Latin, a little game he liked to play to keep his language skills up to date. Assuming she wasn't able to read Latin, she could probably still decipher some content from all the modern terms and technical acronyms without a Latin equivalent.

He suggested they put on some heavy clothing and take a walk outside, wearing Bill and Jennifer's snowshoes. This seemed agreeable to everyone, especially Bill, who asked them to trample some paths to the woodpile, the roadway, and the external doors.

While Skye went upstairs to change her clothing, David donned his warmest winter coat and insulated hiking boots. His aging, slightly tattered lime green parka, with its double layer of insulation, wouldn't win any fashion shows, but it would keep him warm.

The break allowed him to gather his thoughts. It also gave him an opportunity, possibly his last, to change his mind about the upcoming decision that would affect his future so greatly.

His internal struggle was brief, but vicious. He desperately sought a new direction, something he hadn't considered yet. By the time Skye joined him again, wearing her one-piece coverall, his decision remained unchanged.

They went into the garage and put on their borrowed snowshoes, carefully adjusting the straps. Skye had obviously done this before. Her blunt response to his questioning stare was, "We get snow in Tennessee, too."

When they were ready to go outside, they opened the garage door and scrambled their way to the top of the six-foot blanket of powder. Falling snowflakes immediately coated David's hat, turning it from blue to white.

Skye's earmuffs exposed her long hair to the elements, but she didn't seem to mind. The temperature was bearable, with no wind.

David set course immediately for the woodpile, about 30 feet away, on the left edge of the driveway. The snowmobile, buried under at least a foot of new snow, earned a wide berth. Forward progress was difficult. Even wearing snowshoes, he slipped into the snowpack about two feet deep with each step and had to pull his feet above the top of the snowpack for the next step. He felt like he was trudging up a long, very steep flight of stairs.

Following behind, Skye's traverse was easier. She stayed in his tracks, compressing the snow further and widening the path a bit.

They were alone. The towering forest was silent and peaceful, except for the crunch of snowshoes and the sounds of labored breathing. David was humbled by the cold, wondrous serenity and remorseful about disturbing the absolutely perfect blanket of whiteness. They had entered nature's cathedral, and he desired to show the utmost respect.

He couldn't tell whether Skye felt anything similar, but he doubted it. After they had covered no more than ten feet of distance, her sharp voice shattered his illusion. She was ready to get down to business.

"So what's it going to be? Will you collaborate with me and answer my questions? Or shall we do things the hard way?"

"And what exactly is the hard way?" he asked. "Remember, if you reveal my location to the media, I'll lose my value to you."

"The hard way is when I start to bug you, literally. My people are good at retrieving information from unwilling parties. Eventually, I'll learn everything I want to know," she said, smugly.

"And if I find somewhere else to hide?"

"I'll just locate you again. While you still have your job, I'll be near you, whether you like it or not." Almost as an afterthought, she added, "Oh, and don't forget your friends, family, and second grade school teachers. They're all fair game, too. We'll make you a star—a real celebrity villain."

"You would throw me to the wolves, even after what happened to Colcheck and Tarraz?"

"It wouldn't be my first choice, nor my happiest," she replied, puffing from exertion. "I would have to give it some careful thought, since I don't want you to be harmed. But if other tactics aren't working, I would consider it."

David didn't try to hide his disgust. "You sell your principles easily, it seems. That makes my decision much more difficult." He paused a moment to catch his breath. "You know, Skye, until a few days ago, I was convinced you were the Devil incarnate. I'm not as sure about that now, but it's still a possibility. And that's a real problem because my decision must be based partly upon trust. Right now, I don't trust you very much."

"Trust is earned," she said, candidly. "Since we've just met, it would be stupid for you to trust me. However, you can certainly trust me to make your life miserable if you don't cooperate. So what's it going to be?" she pressed. "Will we be collaborators? Or will I be your worst nightmare?"

"You're already my worst nightmare, and you have been for weeks." He renewed his course toward the woodpile. Realizing his previous statement wasn't true, he corrected himself. "No, you've been my second worse nightmare."

He turned to look Fontaine squarely in the eyes. He could feel her claws gripping him by the neck, squeezing his last options away.

"Will I sell my soul to the Devil?" he asked. "Yes. But..." he added hastily, "under three conditions."

She laughed. "You aren't in a very good position to impose any conditions."

"I'll impose them anyway. Here's the deal—take it or leave it." David tried to sound forceful, but she probably wasn't fooled for an instant. "First, you won't reveal my location or job function to anyone, especially not to the people you work with. You'll have to figure out something to tell them. Be creative. The fewer people who know of our arrangement, the better. I'll explain why that's so important in a minute."

"OK, that's difficult, but possible," she said. "There's only one other person who knows where you are, and she worships the ground I walk on. If I told her you had moved to Tahiti to start a new life selling cheap trinkets to the tourists, she would probably believe it."

"Good." He turned back toward the woodpile. "Second, you need to answer my questions, too—accurately and completely. This can't be a one way street."

She grabbed the back of his coat, stopping him. He turned to her again.

"Why?" she asked. "I thought you used up your questions last night. What else could you possibly be wanting to know from me?"

"I'll get to that in a minute, too."

She shook her head, but agreed. Then she added a condition. "I have non-disclosure agreements with some of my other information sources. I won't do or say anything to violate those other agreements."

Unfortunately, that type of information was part of what David wanted to learn more about. While he had hoped for more flexibility, her reluctance to reveal her sources might also indicate that she would keep her word with him. Ultimately, that might prove to be far more important. It would be foolish for him to enter into an agreement with someone who would betray his confidence at her first opportunity.

Even if she wouldn't reveal the identity of her sources, knowing a source existed, within a given framework, might tell him a lot. It all depended on the questions he asked. While "I don't know" was often a powerful answer, "I can't answer that" could potentially be just as useful.

He nodded his agreement, before revealing his final condition. "We need to find a place to sit down, so I can share my thoughts about the deaths of Colcheck and Tarraz. I want you to listen, and consider what I have to say with an open mind."

They reached the woodpile and trampled snow in front of it, firming a larger area. She finally stopped and turned to him.

"Fine. I'll give you a chance to defend your beloved mission planners. You can tell me how noble they are, and how they would never, ever stoop to murder to protect their little secrets. I'll try to keep an open mind, but forgive me if I'm a tough audience. The evidence points squarely at them. Unless you have some new, convincing angle or facts, I doubt whether you can change my opinion."

She offered her hand. Before he could change his mind, he grasped it, shaking it firmly. She matched his strong grip, symbolically sealing his fate. A few days ago, he had cursed the ground that Fontaine walked on. Now he would be forced to trust her.

Their hands remained in contact a moment too long, and David backed away. Despite the cold, his cheeks felt flushed.

She knows how to manipulate people in so many ways. Never forget that. She does it so effortlessly that it's easy to overlook.

She looked at him and smiled, innocently. "OK, so let's hear what you have to say about Colcheck and Tarraz."

They cleared the snow from a small area atop the woodpile, and she sat down gingerly on a flat log. The wood held her weight, making a good seat.

He turned away and studied the trees, the clouds, and the falling snowflakes. The meditative quality of the scene gave him strength and helped to clear his thoughts. When he turned back to her, he knew exactly how he wanted to proceed, though a lot would depend upon his second condition being met—and upon some assumptions about her character.

"Before we talk about Colcheck and Tarraz, I need to ask you some questions. Please consider them carefully and answer as honestly and completely as you can."

"Again, as long as they don't violate my other agreements," she said.

David trampled some more snow. Then he took a deep breath. "Let's go slowly, starting with chapter one. Tell me, how did your crusade against the Mars mission begin?"

Her nose crinkled, and she said, "I'm not sure I understand. You want to know when I started conducting interviews and doing news reports about the mission? That was years ago!"

"No, I want to know *why* you got involved. Who gave you your first assignment, and what did they ask you to do? What were your thoughts going into it? And what were *their* ideas."

She didn't answer right away. He hoped that she was trying to recall the past, rather than inventing a convenient answer.

"Two years ago, my 'Science and Technology Road Show' was dying," she said, in a low, melancholy voice. "Perhaps you recall that weekly, half-hour show, where I interviewed some of the top scientists within various fields?"

"Sorry, I don't remember it."

"I'm not surprised. Nobody else does either. It was buried in the listings at a pathetic time slot, and the network wouldn't spend any internal money to advertise it. My ratings were poor and not likely to improve. I was stuck in a vicious loop. Without better ratings, I couldn't request the large chunks of time from leading researchers that I needed in order to make the content a lot better. The result was a hacked-together, shallow, forgettable experience for the viewer, which killed my ratings even more."

"Sorry to hear that," David responded, with genuine sympathy. "It sounds like the premise of the program was a good one. It could have worked."

"I firmly believed it, too, at the time. But this was three years ago. I was so naïve regarding how one makes a splash in my field. Good reporting skills, ideas, and drive are only a beginning. More important is having a strong technical production team behind you. And most important of all, you need the support of management. The higher-ups must be willing to invest mountains of cash into your program, and along with it, your personal image."

She paused again, longer this time. David gave her plenty of time. He wasn't in any hurry.

"My 'big break' came after the program was canceled, two years ago. The network retained me as a field reporter, on a per-assignment basis. I got a new production team, one that had done some very good work in the past. My new producer had closer ties to upper management, so he was more willing to take some chances. He encouraged me to seek out controversial topics."

"Such as missions to Mars?"

"Such as missions to Mars. Right away, my producer pushed me on the Mars bandwagon. The first three equipment launches were coming up, and nobody else in the media seemed to be paying much attention. The SEA had a reputation of being long on words and ideas, but perpetually short on funding. No one really took them seriously until the three launched vehicles were successfully heading toward Mars. Then they announced a manned mission would commence two years later. That got everyone's attention, and it's been a media circus ever since. But I was there first."

By now, David's pacing had compressed a 50-square-foot area of real estate in front of the woodpile, plenty of room for Bill to access the firewood supply. He continued to pace, however.

"So your new producer pushed you on the Mars bandwagon. How exactly did he do that? What did he say?"

"As I recall, he basically told me to go out and stir up trouble. Look for stories behind the story. Ask a lot of questions. And above all, play up the mystery aspect, the fact that no one knew who had provided the funding for the SEA to construct and support the Mars launches."

"And that's what you did."

"That's what I did. It was hard at first, because this wasn't my usual reporting style. Later, it became much easier. I've always loved a good mystery. When I started to dig deep, I discovered that a lot of details about this mission just weren't adding up."

"So you dug even deeper. And your producer supported your efforts."

"Yes, and yes, completely. The initial ratings from my stories were excellent. Management was involved right from the start, and we had an unlimited supply of funds to do our early work. I did other stories, too, but I always came back to the Mars mission."

David paused his pacing for a moment, reviewing her responses. He was quite shocked at how close his earlier speculation had mirrored reality. But there was still a missing piece, a very important one.

He said, "You've gotten a lot of mileage out of the mystery aspect. But what about your focus on mission risks?"

"I wish I could take the credit for that, but I can't. That was actually my producer's idea, too. Early on, he suggested emphasizing the mission risks in my reporting. He said it would grab and hold the attention of the younger generations of viewers. And it has."

"Indeed, it has," said David. "And you've confirmed my suspicions. Regarding the deaths of Colcheck and Tarraz, I have a new theory to propose."

"This I've got to hear," Skye mocked. "How is anything I just said related to two people being murdered?" She scooped a snowball and threw it at David. The champagne powder didn't pack well, so her missile fell apart well short of its target.

David was not as happy. Since that day on Pearl Street, he had been trying to convince himself that his wild thoughts were nothing more than crazy speculation. Yet the pieces of the puzzle continued to fall into place. A grim picture was emerging, possibly not the only picture, or even the right one. But it was one he could not afford to ignore.

He started to walk away from the woodpile toward the street, which was also buried under six feet of powder. He motioned for her to follow, and she did. Having reached this point, David knew exactly what he needed to say.

"Philosophers like to speculate about fundamental truths," he said. "We've done this for as long as the human race has existed."

"Yes, you weirdos have confused and confounded the masses for a long time," Skye agreed.

"Consider balance, as an abstract concept. Our universe has very few hard and fast laws, but in many philosophical systems, balance is a fundamental assumption. Good and evil, right and wrong, yin and yang. Two sides to every coin. To a physicist, every action has an equal, opposite reaction."

Skye frowned. "Of course. But I don't see the relevance."

"You believe a powerful, hidden organization exists, one that has constructed the Mars mission for undisclosed reasons. Evidence suggests you're correct. The mission didn't just spring into existence overnight, and its secrets aren't maintained by accident. Years of planning, major resources, and persistent motivation were required. Each implies the presence of a powerful organization, probably a whole underground movement."

"Of course. And your point is?"

"To maintain the balance, counterforces must exist."

"Counterforces? What do you mean?" He heard her stumble behind him.

David smiled as he explained his theory. "Forces in fundamental opposition to the principles, motivations, goals, and desires of the Mars mission planners *must* exist. These forces might merely be aspects of society, like fear, apathy, greed, and paranoia. Lord knows there's enough of those things to go around, these days. Or...they might be physical entities."

"Physical entities?"

"Yes, one or more groups that oppose the first one directly. After all, if one hidden organization exists, why can't a second one exist as well?"

"A second hidden organization." Though she sounded interested, Skye's voice contained deep overtones of skepticism.

The roadway was about 50 feet beyond the woodpile, so the traverse took much longer than their initial segment. David was getting tired, too. Breathing heavily, he continued his lecture.

"Let's assume a physical counterforce exists. We need to give both entities a name. The one favoring and sponsoring the Mars mission is Alpha, while the opposition is Beta."

"Why don't we call them Alpha and Figment?" she asked, scoffing at him openly.

David winced. "Ha, funny. I admit most of it is speculation, but I've been seeing movement in the shadows for some time now. Each new fact coming along seems to be consistent with the theory, including what you just told me."

"Now you lost me again. I never said anything about a Beta group."

David paused to switch mental gears. "Let's talk about your network, and its coverage of the Mars mission. Other networks have presented a fairly balanced picture of the mission, weighing the opportunity and challenge against the physical obstacles. USNN is different. Your coverage is one-sided, and I don't mean just your own reporting. Other shows on your network are just as bad."

"I would prefer to think my coverage is realistic. It's the mission that's flawed, risky, and suspicious."

"Fine, call it what you want. The relevant fact is that your coverage differs from that of the other networks. Why?"

Skye stared at him, defiantly. "We're way ahead of the others. I told you last night, I'm more persistent than the lackeys out there. I've been asking better questions and doing better field work."

"I'm sorry, but this obviously has very little to do with you. Again, other programs on your network are the same way. Your management set your direction, through your program producers. You're merely a tool carrying out their wishes. Were this not true, you would be out on the street looking for a new job."

"Now wait a minute! Management supports me because my ratings have been good!"

"Then why haven't other networks followed? You just told me that stirring up controversy was initially your producer's idea, and your new producer has close ties to management. He also 'suggested' you emphasize the risks of the mission. Your management has given you funding and latitude. They cranked you up, pointed you in the right direction, and sent you out to do their bidding."

Skye grabbed his arm and twisted him around to face her. She took a step back. Her face was a most unattractive shade of crimson.

"OK, smart guy. If you have this all figured out, why don't you answer your own question. I've been quite successful in my reporting. Why haven't the other networks followed?"

"I was getting to that. It's the most speculative part, and also the most disturbing."

David looked down at his feet, pausing to catch his breath. He had a sudden twinge of doubt. If there was a flaw in his reasoning, now was his last chance to back away.

He could see no flaw, however. His reasoning was solid. It was based upon assumptions that couldn't be proven yet, so there was no guarantee it led to a true conclusion, but the process was sound.

He proposed to Skye that the actions of USNN's upper management were consistent and predictable if they had inside information guaranteeing the Mars mission would fail. This private knowledge gave them the confidence to chart their own course, risking public ridicule and future ratings decay. The other networks couldn't follow, because they didn't know the final outcome with as much certainty.

Skye was silent for several minutes, frozen in place. This gave David time to finish treading his path to the roadway. When he returned, she still hadn't moved or spoken.

As he compressed a bypass around her, she finally hissed, "This is all guesswork. It's groundless. Why should I believe it?"

"I'm not asking you to believe it," David replied over his shoulder, as she followed him back to the woodpile. He rested on the log Skye had cleared earlier, and looked down at the powdery snow. He said, "I agreed to your collaboration because I need your help in order to prove the underlying assumptions. Do you know if any part of my theory is true? Or false?"

Her only answer was a blank, frigid stare.

Interpreting her lack of response as a negative, he continued his probing. "You work at the network. You know the producers and others who might be involved. If you really wanted to, you could find out if it's true, or whether I'm blowing smoke rings."

"Why should I help you prove or disprove your lunatic theories?"

David looked up at her sharply, curbing a spike of anger. "Because the fate of the Mars mission might depend upon it, of course. If my theory is true, those three people out in space might die because of something we could prevent."

Skye stomped around in front of the woodpile. She fumed and huffed. Finally, she agreed to ask her producer some guarded questions.

"But don't try to lay any guilt trip on me," she stated, firmly. "Those three people out in space are already dead. This Mars mission is far too risky, whether your suspicions are true or not."

David confirmed the mission was obviously risky, but added, "If someone at your network has inside information that the mission will fail, it practically proves the Beta organization really exists, as a physical entity."

"And why should I care about your Beta organization?" she snipped.

"Because after two years of searching, you still haven't found Alpha. There's probably not much I can tell you about them, either. However, finding Beta might be much easier for you. Wouldn't a better approach be to use the identity of Beta to deduce Alpha?"

Skye said, "Now that's an interesting thought. Still, what if Beta doesn't exist? It would all be a big waste of time."

David stood, and trudged a few feet away, turning his back to the reporter. He debated whether to share a different theory with her, one that was even more speculative than the last. He decided against it, but he would throw her a bone.

"In that case," he said, turning back to her, "your theory about an Alpha organization with a diabolical hidden agenda gains some credibility. I might also be more motivated to help you dig up information about Alpha's intentions. After all, there's no guarantee Alpha and Beta aren't the same organization. It might all be simply a matter of perspective."

He noticed the surprise in her expression again. Waving for her to follow, he trudged a new path through the snow around the side of the house. This course was more treacherous because the overhang of the garage roof had blocked some of the snow from reaching the ground below. A steep, snowy crevice, three feet deep, bordered the side of the garage.

He paused again to rest, looking back at Skye, a few steps away. The signs of her earlier anger had vanished, but she still seemed quite disturbed.

She stated, "You do realize I have a conflict of interest here." Then she elaborated that her own credibility as a reporter was firmly tied to the failure of the Mars mission.

David didn't have a good response. She was right. If she helped him to uncover the existence of Beta, and he used her assistance to aid the mission, she might be dooming her own career. This was an aspect of the situation he had overlooked. He had been too focused on the bigger issues and what the reporter knew about them, or could find out about them. He hadn't given her personal motivations enough thought.

Had he made a serious mistake? He could only appeal to her character, hoping her ethics weren't as warped as he had once believed.

"I guess you have a difficult decision to make," he said, cautiously. "You can do what is right, or you can do what sucks up to your management. When you decide, remember those people out in space. Also, if you're as good a reporter as you seem to think you are, you'll have other opportunities."

"I guess my reputation would recover, eventually," she said.

His confidence returned as he realized that he had successfully snared her. Her vanity and arrogance would prevent her from backing away. He egged further, "You might even come out of this as a hero, with your Big Story."

The trees on this side of the house seemed to be listening intently to their conversation. Their thick trunks had taken on a shadowed, gloomy appearance. He wondered if they approved of his clumsy attempts to manipulate the reporter.

Charting a new course, he trudged around the side of the deck and down the hillside, to the clear patio beneath the deck. A doorway led from the basement to the patio. He might need this path as an escape route soon, if Fontaine changed her mind and decided her career was more important than her ethics.

Skye laughed, recovering more of her normal, brash irreverence. "You're right. If your wild accusations are true, it might lead to one heck of a story. How can I resist? I told you earlier, I love a good mystery. It won't hurt for me to ask some questions."

"Good," David sighed, deeply relieved for the moment.

"But I still don't understand what any of this has to do with Colcheck and Tarraz."

David turned back to his task, slowly working his way down a steeper stretch of the hillside. He pounded the snow into a series of wide steps. Meanwhile, he continued to voice his speculations.

"You believe Alpha killed them to keep them quiet. But what about Beta? Might they make good suspects, too?"

"Why?" asked Skye, immediately. "If they already know the mission is going to fail, why would they care?"

"That's a tough question to answer without knowing more about Beta, their plans, and their true motivations."

As David reached the clear area under the deck, he turned back to look at Skye on the hillside above. She was frowning.

"I still don't believe any of this. But just in case you're right, if I'm going to ask some questions of my colleagues and sources, I'll need to be real careful."

David agreed that extreme caution would be warranted. Then he asked, "By the way, regarding your sources, do you know anyone who goes by the alias <chicken_little>?" He held his breath, awaiting her answer.

"I can't talk about my other sources. But, Chicken Little? Why do you ask?"

"Never mind."

The tone of her voice implied she didn't know his feathered adversary. He carefully stepped back up the hill. The makeshift stairway held his weight.

"How about the guy at Hapa in Boulder a few weeks ago? Did your producers put you in touch with him?"

"How did you know about that?" She jerked her head up so quickly that she lost her balance and nearly flopped over into a deep snowdrift.

"Oh, I have my ways of gathering information, too," he said. "It's amazing how invisible a street person can be. You might consider using that tactic sometime. I'll give you back your ten bucks, if you want it."

She swatted some snow in his direction and spat, "Keep it."

"Why so upset?" he asked, laughing softly. "You said your people were good at retrieving information from unwilling parties. Now you know how it feels to be on the receiving end."

"I've never sunk that low before."

"Sure you have. You just let others do your dirtiest work for you. Like your friend who seduced Reggie so you could learn where I was staying. Did you script her lines?"

Her eyes darted around, as if afraid the trees might overhear and start to spread rumors about her. "My aide's actions were completely up to her. I gave her an assignment. I didn't tell her how to carry it out."

"Just like your producers gave you an assignment to carry out."

She hesitated. "Well, yes. I suppose so." Haphazardly, she brushed snow away from one of the steps leading up to the deck, clearing a small area to sit down. Then she parked herself, pouting. Her eyes were like laser beams, almost melting the snowpack in front of her with their blazing intensity.

David apologized for hurting her feelings, but he wanted her to realize just how easily her producers might have used her talents to further their own schemes. He knew he was pushing her, perhaps a bit too hard, given that they were now co-collaborators.

She reached for David's hand and pulled him down to sit beside her on the step. "Let's not argue. We have other things to talk about." She kept her hold on his hand and slid a little closer.

Watch it, boy. More manipulations. Now she's going to be all peaches and cream...but remember who she is and what she's after. The snake always coils before it strikes.

He said, "You probably have some questions for me, but first, I really need to know more about that guy at Hapa. You don't have to tell me who he is. I would like to know what he gave you, though. What was on the disk?"

She looked at him, frowning. "OK. If we're still on that topic, fine. For the low, low price of $10,000, he gave me a videodisk of the entire party with the Mars astronauts. Later, my staff matched faces to known names and occupations, except for you and the other two mystery people. I used his disk to find you, and I would do it again. Satisfied?"

"Not quite. The guy seemed awfully arrogant. Do all your paid weasels and back stabbers behave that way?"

"No, they don't. The whole thing smelled fishy, but I let it slide. The disk contained everything he said it would."

"Did he mention where he got it? Or who ran the camera?"

"No."

"And his threats?" he asked.

"Macho arrogance, probably. But now it's my turn. Here's what I want from you. Complete access to your system manuals, design specification documents, engineering notes, and internal communications between mission support members and the astronauts. I want to know everything about the mission that you know. And I want everything you learn in the future, too."

David leaned back, with a smile on his face. His head and shoulders imprinted the snow on the steps above. "Is that all?" he asked, half seriously. "I agreed to answer your questions. I never promised to give you all of Mission Support's proprietary manuals."

"You agreed to collaborate. That means we share information, in any form. If you don't like those terms, you're free to start running, anytime."

David's smile grew wider. "Let me rephrase my remark. I have no problem with sharing some of that information with you. But I never promised to 'give' you anything. You see, most of the information you requested really *is* proprietary. All seven levels of commercial copyright safeguards protect it. The documents can only be read on my computer, or those of my colleagues. They can't be transmitted or copied to other media. Heck, I can't even give you my computer! To operate the machine, you need a constant retinal scan!"

Skye leapt to her feet and turned to face him. Her face was flushed again. "You can't be serious! What kind of paranoid lunatics would set up safeguards like that?"

"As far as I'm aware, only terrorists, Mars mission planners, and your wealthy colleagues in the music and electronic publishing industries," he answered, winking. If his grin was any wider, it would probably have wrapped itself around his face.

Skye stared at him angrily, but gradually seemed to calm down a bit. She soon remarked, "Maybe I don't need to see this information. You can just tell me what I want to know."

"Better be specific," David advised. "Our support procedures manual has ten volumes, each with over 2,000 indexed pages."

"I don't care about that sort of information. Not directly, at least. I just want to know about general capabilities. Like, what equipment did the crew bring with them? In fact, what I really want to know is, how much did it cost the mission sponsors to create the Mars mission, launch it, and support it?"

David's grin finally broke into a hearty chuckle. He got to his feet, and motioned for her to follow. "I can tell you what I've heard. But why do you care?" He plodded around the front of the house, back to the woodpile, where he grabbed a few pieces of firewood and carried them into the garage. All the while, he listened to Skye's response, as she followed closely behind.

"Because I want to pinpoint the financial resources of Alpha, the organization pulling this all together. Over a dozen private individuals, groups, or governments have the ability to organize a $30 billion mission while maintaining some level of secrecy. My team has put together detailed profiles on all of them. But how many could manage a $100 billion mission? I can count them on one hand."

David laughed again, as he dumped his armful of wood in an unused corner of the garage and went back to the woodpile for another load. Skye sat atop her flat log once more, watching him closely.

"And how many could manage a $1 billion mission?" he asked.

Skye frowned. "What do you mean?"

"If you want to narrow your list of suspects based on financial capability, I'm afraid I have some bad news. It costs petty cash to support the mission because we rely so heavily upon volunteers. We use off-the-shelf equipment, too, wherever possible. Other costs, like launch costs, are closely guarded secrets."

"And those other costs must be significant. The R&D alone had to cost tens of billions of dollars."

"Good heavens, why? You're assuming a lot of new technology was needed. It wasn't. We had most of what we needed back in 1969, when the Apollo astronauts landed on the moon."

"That's not what my sources at NASA tell me."

"NASA engineers have a reputation for modesty and caution, especially when they seek research funding. For some of the old-timers, I'll bet it's real painful to recount the good ol' days of the Apollo program. But I'm just a starving historian and philosopher. I shouldn't contradict what your experts tell you. All I know is what I've overheard."

"And what's that?"

"I've heard SEA steering committee members state a firm dollar amount twice: $1 billion."

"But that's insane! Completely impossible! We've spent a lot of time and effort following the paper trail of money flowing around, in and out of the SEA, over the past few years. We've been able to track about $3 billion worth of transactions, over the past three years, but there has to be more. Much more. NASA spent more to develop their Crew Exploration Vehicle."

"That's money spent by NASA. Not the mission planners."

"What about rocket development? Rovers? Space suits? Greenhouses? Training facilities? Supplies? This is a complex mission. For a completely redundant, automated control system, the computer work alone should run in the billions."

"All private, I'm told. And cheap. I see signs of this in my day-to-day job. Sometimes, our equipment and procedures aren't quite synchronized to the nth degree, or situations could have been planned better ahead of time. The glue holding it all together is people-power, at Mission Support and inside the

Perseus. Humans tend to be far more flexible than the most sophisticated multi-billion dollar..."

The pager in David's watch started to vibrate wildly, a technological intrusion that broke his train of thought. "Pardon me, let's continue our talk later. I'm being paged, and duty calls." He dumped his armful of wood and took off his snowshoes in the garage.

Before retreating inside the house, he glanced back. Skye remained where he had left her, seated on the woodpile, probably pondering the sorry state of her investigation. If a dozen potential mission sponsors could afford to run a $30 billion mission, hundreds, or perhaps thousands, could organize a one billion dollar mission. She was faced with a difficult task. Momentarily, David's grin returned, wider than ever.

His happiness lasted until he reached his computer and activated Shepherd. Another runner awaited him, with news that the transmitter on the backup habitat had failed.

CHAPTER 16
INERTIA

MarsDay 34, 3:45 p.m.
(December 25, 10:18 p.m.)

Anna glanced up at the digital clock display, on the wall of the EVA room. *Three forty-five. Where's Ollie? He's never this late for our exercise sessions.*

The EVA room was the only open area in the *Perseus* large enough for calisthenics. Although it was a tight squeeze when two people used it at the same time, she still enjoyed exercising with Ollie. Three to four o'clock in the afternoon had been their usual "date" time.

Part of her job as the Health and Safety officer was to ensure that each crew member spent a minimum of one hour each day doing cardiovascular fitness exercises. She hated being so inflexible, however. They all knew the one-hour requirement was based on a NASA study in a weightless environment on the International Space Station. No one had ever experienced Mars gravity for extended periods of time before, but partial gravity was obviously much better for the body than no gravity.

Still, they needed a guideline to follow, something to add structure into their daily schedule without being too excessive. An hour seemed reasonable. To Anna, her exercise period was more than just a time for physical activity. It helped to cleanse her mind, provided a readily achievable goal, and gave her some much-needed stress release.

Exercise caused some problems, too. She hated taking frequent Navy showers, almost as much as she hated hand-washing her sweaty clothing. Those time and water consuming tasks made her feel guilty, so she usually lowered the thermostat in the EVA room to 45 degrees Fahrenheit during her exercise periods, hoping to minimize her sweating. She wore only what was functional, a sports bra to keep her bosom from bouncing about, and some thin shorts to cover the other parts of her body that she didn't have the nerve to display in front of Ollie.

The others probably didn't care what she wore when she exercised, especially when she was alone, as she was now. But she was never truly alone, anywhere in the *Perseus*. Button cameras were everywhere, relentlessly feeding their input into millions of terabytes of cheap crystalline storage located deep in the innards of the protected computer core. Far less than one percent of these images would ever be transmitted back to Earth, due to bandwidth restrictions. Upon their return, however, the entire quantity of data would be available to armies of psychologists, and possibly others.

Despite the chill in the room, she sweated profusely. Her workout had reached a new peak, and her heart rate was ten beats per minute higher than her target rate. Her immediate goal was to dissipate some of her frustrations through furious activity. So far, it seemed to be working. She was starting to feel better.

A few minutes later, Ollie trotted in. Apologizing for being late, he disrobed down to a pair of Spandex shorts and jumped into the other exercise harness beside Anna. He set the controls for "uphill, vigorous" and began to climb, fighting the resistance of the elastic bands holding him firmly in place.

"Hey, Bruce Jenner, slow it down!" Anna advised. He should be starting out slowly until his body was ready for more activity.

Ollie dropped his pace to a more reasonable warm-up setting. He confessed that he had some frustrations to work out, too. He had just come from the lounge, where he had been discussing the latest mission developments with Evelyn. Summarizing their conversation, his conclusion was, "She's still unreasonable. She won't even consider the option of using our free return trajectory back to Earth."

"Why should we?" Anna asked innocently. Perhaps it would help if she goaded some of Ollie's anger out into the open, where they could deal with it.

"Look, the ERV on Mars is still not responding. For all we know, it's gone, along with the fuel and the power generation supplies we need so urgently once we land. Now the signal from the backup habitat is gone, too."

Anna upped the intensity notch on her harness yet one more level. Ollie was voicing her own doubts. Her fears had been plaguing her all day, since hearing David's message about the signal loss from the backup habitat. That news had not been a very welcome Christmas gift.

She continued to advocate the commander's position. Perhaps if she did it well enough, she might convince herself it was the best course of action.

"Yes, we already knew the ERV wasn't communicating. Now the backup habitat is silent, too. So what? The *Perseus* is working just fine. It's doubtful whether we can salvage anything from the biosystem in the backup habitat, anyway, except perhaps the food and water supply. The only other things we might need are its batteries, solar panels, and extra living space. We can conserve our power and water for the first two months until the next ERV lands. And our cozy living quarters aren't that bad."

He reminded her, a bit condescendingly, that she wasn't an engineer. "Despite the simple design of most of our systems, it requires almost constant effort from Evelyn and me to keep them running smoothly."

Anna puffed, "Is that what Evelyn meant, way back on our first day in space, when she claimed that something could go wrong anytime and we have to be prepared?"

Ollie glanced at her and nodded. "Though I deplore the way she over-stressed it with her pathetic, inane drills, I happen to agree with her on that point. We need the backup habitat! Otherwise, when we get to Mars, any serious problem with the *Perseus* is likely to kill us."

Anna's fear abatement plan was failing miserably. She had known the *Perseus* was fragile, but she had been thinking of the danger mostly in terms of its fragile biological ecosystem. The wider range of engineering problems held less worry for her, since that was the domain of her two colleagues. Hearing Ollie voice his concerns so bluntly was unnerving.

He continued, "On the other hand, if we use our free return trajectory to return to Earth, it will cut almost a year from our total mission time. That's one less year the *Perseus* needs to function."

"Return home with our tails between our legs? After two years in space, without even seeing the surface of Mars?" She puffed again from overexertion, and she lowered her workout intensity dial a few notches. "I don't know if I could live with that. I think I would rather die on Mars."

"Would you?" he asked. She noticed him staring at her, and he had a strange expression on his face. With one raised eyebrow, he resembled a character from an old sci-fi TV show. Doctor Speck? Spook? She couldn't remember. Growing up, she had never watched much television.

They exercised in silence for a few minutes. Then Anna took a brief rest break. She jumped down from her harness and did some gentle stretching exercises on a floor mat, leading into more strenuous positions.

As she was in the midst of a handstand, Ollie commented, "You know, there's a much bigger concern, too. A more immediate one."

She really didn't want to hear any more concerns. She wanted to concentrate on her handstand. Slowly, she removed her right hand from the mat and supported all of her body weight with the left. Thanks to the lighter gravity, her arm strength was more than adequate for doing a one armed handstand, something she could never do back on Earth.

In the spinning habitat, Anna's balance was more of a concern than her strength. Living in simulated Mars gravity, the occupants of the *Perseus* endured minor Coriolis forces. Normally, these effects were slightly disorienting, but negligible. They became quite noticeable when she was trying to balance on one hand, however.

Ollie seemed oblivious to her current difficulties. He continued his gloomy dialogue. "Without communications from the landing site, our triple-redundant navigation beacons can't guide us to a safe landing. That's a scenario the mission planners couldn't possibly have expected. We need the homing signal and weather information from at least one of those beacons. Otherwise, we'll be landing blindly. Even if each vehicle is fine, just sitting there on Mars waiting for us, we could easily land hundreds of kilometers away."

Anna grunted, lost her balance, and fell to the mat, rolling gracefully into a sitting position, facing Ollie. "Yeah, I know. But we shouldn't write off the backup habitat yet. Mission Support hasn't given up hope. And even if they can't figure out what's wrong, aren't we back at the same worst-case scenario? It would be like the backup habitat was gone. One of Evelyn's golden rules of Mars states, 'What we can't reach doesn't exist.' Assuming we land safely, we would need to live on our own resources for two months until the next ERV and cargo vehicle land nearby."

Ollie responded, but she barely heard him. She resumed her handstand and removed her left hand from the mat this time, balancing on her right arm for 30 seconds. For added flair, she did a few scissor kicks in the air. Then she regained her upright footing via a cartwheel and a tight back flip. Back flips were almost too easy in the lighter gravity, though the trick, as always, was to miss the side wall and land on her feet, not her head. She longed for more floor and ceiling space. Then she could really show Ollie some moves.

She jumped back into her exercise harness and resumed a lighter level of activity. She was ready to cool down her session. Much of her energy was gone, sapped either by the strenuous workout or the disturbing conversation. Talking to Ollie wasn't going to make her feel any better. Perhaps she would have better luck with the commander.

MarsDay 35, 1:26 a.m.
(December 26, 8:15 a.m.)

Skye's rented snowmobile, now clear of snow, was resting under a protective roof overhang near the open garage door on the north side of the house. As she hopped on, David actually heard himself asking if she could stay any longer. Travel down to the flatlands was dangerous until the main highway was opened. That might take days, given the risk of avalanches in Boulder Canyon.

She was in a hurry to get back to work, and her vehicle was a new model that was probably equipped with all the latest safety features. The float-drive should keep her moving high and steady above any amount of powder. Also, an eco-switch could toggle the engine into a dual hybrid mode that emitted less pollution and ran much quieter, thereby minimizing the avalanche danger.

Skye assured him that in case something happened to her, his location would remain a secret for awhile. She had taken some steps to hide her tracks, and her ICID files no longer contained the relevant information either.

When he asked what ICID was, she explained that most field investigators kept electronic "In Case I Disappear" files in a remote, secure location. Her ICID files always contained information about where she was and when she should be returning. She could update the files by telephone from anywhere in the world, as she had done the night before. If she didn't return and cancel a timer within two days, the contents of her ICID files would be sent to three trusted colleagues. That would still happen, if she met with a fatal accident in the canyon, but David's exact physical location was no longer included.

To reach town, she would need to negotiate a series of confusing turnoffs along the forested access roads. However, the road signs were all buried under at least two feet of snow. When he asked how she would navigate, she just laughed and said, "You'll see."

Though she had already bombarded David with questions about his support organization the night before, Skye vowed to return in a week or two. No doubt, she would have more questions. She took lots of notes during her guided tour of Mission Support, but David suspected very little of this material would ever see the light of day. Mission Support was not a very "sexy" topic to her. Skye remained focused upon determining the identity of the Alpha mission planners. She seemed to consider the daily running of Mission Support as a mildly interesting distraction, little more than the topic of a future documentary. David wasn't about to try to change her opinion. It might buy him some freedom.

Of greater interest to Skye was their discussion following the loss of communications with the backup habitat on Mars. His team had invoked the same procedures that had failed to restore contact with the ERV. After several déjà vu filled hours, David resigned himself to the likelihood that all three of the surface vehicles on Mars would remain silent for the duration of the crew's outward voyage.

Skye considered the loss of communications a prime example of the shoddy, penny-pinching attitude prevalent within the Alpha organization. She had even formulated a new theory that Alpha remained in hiding because they didn't want to face lawsuits and criminal prosecution over their risky plans and decisions.

Given his prior beliefs about the low cost of the mission, David found some of her arguments persuasive. He completely believed her basic premise. Any organization willing to undertake a daunting project like a Mars mission would be the brunt of numerous frivolous lawsuits. Whether their plans and equipment were faulty or not was irrelevant.

The breakdown of the American legal system had reached epic proportions. Courtrooms were quagmires. Corporations and prominent individuals lived in fear. Dishonest, greedy opportunism was seen by many as the quickest and easiest way to obtain personal wealth. Harmful side affects permeated throughout the economy and society.

However, he advised Skye to avoid jumping to conclusions. While her new theory made sense, it might be a mere coincidence, rather than a primary motivation. Anything she stated on the air would be idle conjecture. Given her past track record, he doubted she could keep her opinions to herself for very long, though.

Before Skye started up the snowmobile engine, he repeated his advice.

"Yes, I know, I heard you last night," she yelled, as she revved the motor. Then she put her helmet on, gunned the motor again, and raced off.

Earlier in the morning, Bill had trampled a new track down the driveway allowing the vehicle to gradually rise above the top of the snow pack. As she accelerated down the narrow slot, her front skid dug into the wall of snow on the right. The snowmobile careened sideways, coming to an immediate halt. Skye arced high over the handlebars and disappeared from his view.

The snow in the driveway was at least ten feet deep, and David couldn't see up to the level where she had landed. He ran along the track toward the sideways snowmobile, but after taking a few steps, his legs sunk deeply into the snow pack. Bill had compressed the snow in the track so it would support a person wearing snowshoes, or a snowmobile, but not a person in regular hiking boots.

Floundering in the snow, he worked his way back into the garage and grabbed Bill's snowshoes. Then he trudged back to the scene of the accident.

With his head above the level of the snow, he could better assess the situation. Skye's boots were visible a few feet beyond the snowmobile, just to the right of the track. They protruded from the snow at a steep angle. He noted with dismay that she must have landed headfirst.

The capsized vehicle blocked his progress. Stepping over it, in snowshoes, turned out to be a difficult maneuver, but he soon accomplished it and moved onward.

At this point in the track, the height of the snow was only three feet above shoe-level. He kicked into the snowbank and dug his way toward Skye's boots. Grabbing them, he pulled with all his strength, lifting her out of the snow as directly as possible. His snowshoes sunk a few more inches, but held.

Soon, he had extracted her. He gently placed her limp body upon the firmer track of snow, crouched, and cautiously removed her helmet. As her long strands of dark hair cascaded atop the white blanket of snow, she opened her eyes and grabbed his arm.

"Why David," she cooed softly, "I didn't know you cared!"

He brushed aside her sarcasm. "Don't try to move yet. Can you feel this?" he asked, as he squeezed her left thigh firmly, as far down her leg as he could reach.

Skye's right foot lanced out, striking him in his hindquarters, sending him sprawling forward into the snow beside her.

"Can you feel that?" she laughed. Then she sat up and rolled over on top of him, pinning him down. "I'm fine, my dashing hero," she said. "Just a bit embarrassed."

Obviously her reflexes were OK. When he asked where she had learned to kick like that, she said a girl living on her own had to learn a few tricks in order to survive, especially in her profession.

Still laughing, she rolled off him and tried to rise to her feet. She immediately discovered what David had learned previously—her legs sank deeply into the snow, and she couldn't move.

He watched her struggle, and commented, "The big city girl seems to be in a situation that's a bit tougher than she is. Should I leave you there until the spring thaw? Or would you like a little more help from the person you just kicked in the hiney?"

"Help, please."

He slowly got to his feet, and pulled Skye up by her arms, draping her over his right shoulder in a fireman's grip. His snowshoes sank deeper into the snow again, but with some effort, he was able to carry her over to the snowmobile and set her down safely on the seat.

After resting for a few minutes, Skye claimed that she was ready to resume her journey. David tried once more to convince her to stay longer, but without success. They eventually freed her snowmobile, and she was on her way, with a promise to be more careful.

Skye waved goodbye over her shoulder and proceeded up the chute, slower than before. As she reached the level, untouched expanse of whiteness beyond, he breathed a sigh of relief. His sigh quickly turned into a groan of disbelief as Skye gunned the engine, spun the machine in a tight half circle, and rocketed back toward the garage. She whizzed past, 20 feet to his right, charting a new course through the pine forest while dodging branches laden with snow.

After losing sight of her around the corner of the garage, he returned inside the house and kicked off his snowshoes. Then he rushed to a window facing north, overlooking the lake.

Far below, her vehicle emerged from the forest and zipped straight across the snow-covered reservoir. She was probably traveling at least 60 mph. The highway to Boulder, her obvious target, ran along the far, north shore. Her only deviation was a single tight donut turn in the middle of the lake. Snow flew in all directions.

Reaching the other side in less than a minute, she climbed the steep bank and continued onward, down past the dam on the uncleared highway.

David sat down in the nearest chair. He was physically, mentally, and emotionally exhausted.

Why did I want her to stay longer?

MarsDay 41, 7:00 a.m.
(January 1, 5:55 p.m.)

"Your avatar is looking more transparent than usual, today," Shepherd stated bluntly.

Anna had already come to the same conclusion about David's avatar. Over the weeks that she had been meeting Shepherd in his virtual office, she had noticed subtle changes. Some of the differences were physical, caused by the increase in the time delay of communications as the *Perseus* traveled farther from the Earth. Interactions were becoming more difficult. As a reminder of the physical constraints, the computer made the avatars appear more transparent.

Yet, she suspected the real differences were psychological ones. As her remoteness increased, the other avatars just felt farther away. In fact, Anna perceived the entire Earth being just as transparent as Shepherd's avatar. Her whole universe was two other people, both asleep at the moment, and a thousand square feet of real estate.

"So I'm doing my best to mediate, but the gulf between Evelyn and Ollie just seems to get wider and wider," she complained. "And as I try to bring them together, I become the bad guy. Whenever I mention Ollie's views or opinions to the commander, we get into a big argument. It's the same with Ollie, though not quite as bad."

She waited for him to respond, knowing she could just go on talking if she wanted to. They were getting pretty good at this technique, though it took lots of practice, and occasionally one of them would say something that seemed wildly out of context. However, a short break felt more appropriate. She needed some time to think.

Oddly enough, she found herself craving a yo-yo. She hadn't touched one since she was a child, yet she yearned for a mindless task to occupy her hands and release her nervous energy. Since the nearest yo-yo was millions of kilometers away, the next best thing was a deck of cards. She grabbed one from the drawer under the kitchen table and started to play a game of solitaire.

Eventually, his response caught up to her. He asked if she had told the psychologists about these problems. Kahuna knew all about them, she responded.

They interwove snatches of conversation for another half-hour before the computer reminded her of a media event scheduled in ten minutes. She bid Shepherd a reluctant farewell.

Yes, Shepherd had seemed a bit more distant and quieter than usual today. This was probably another psychological red herring. Given her own problems, she needed him to be closer. Best of all would be if he was right here in the *Perseus*, with her.

The rest of the day seemed to pass by in a blur. That night, she slept restlessly. Her dreams were filled with bees.

CHAPTER 17
APPEARANCE

MarsDay 82, 1:53 p.m.
(February 13, 4:03 a.m.)

    Anna's cabin felt extra small and dull today. As her eyes glazed over, she yearned for a distraction, anything to take her away from her studies. Her search through gigabytes of images and data covering every facet of hydroponics in excruciating detail was important, but it was also extremely boring.
    Once they reached Mars, any crop growth oversight on her part could prove fatal to them all. They wouldn't have enough pre-packaged food to survive if they couldn't reach the supplies in any of the backup vehicles. Even if they were able to reach those other shipments, they only wanted to consume the supplies within as a last resort. Some future Mars explorers might need that food more than they did.
    While she knew the importance of her studies, she also had confidence in her knowledge of the greenhouse materials and usage plan. She had been studying crop growth issues for years back at the University of Michigan and was well versed in the latest NASA and SEA techniques.
    With her attention wandering, she pondered the past three months of their journey, dreaded the next three months, and cherished warm thoughts of Earth and Mars. Planets were definitely one of the Creator's best ideas. They sure beat living in a tin can.

Her memories of the last six weeks were particularly painful. Boredom had descended upon the crew like a dark shroud, straining their relations even more than before. Frequent, heated confrontations with both Evelyn and Ollie had failed to get the two of them back on better terms. In public, they were civil to each other. Privately, Ollie continued to lambaste the commander and her decisions.

Anna's welcome distraction came in the form of a chime from the computer. An intercom message was pending. She snapped back into the present and read another paragraph of material while she waited for the message.

"Anna, Ollie, we were expecting a CME alert from Mission Support, and it just arrived." Evelyn's voice on the intercom sounded as emotionless as ever.

Two days ago, the boredom of their voyage was briefly interrupted when Mission Support warned that a solar flare was highly probable. Sure enough, sunward sensors in the outer hull soon detected a sharp increase in high-energy radiation, indicating the eruption of a solar flare. After stowing items that were sensitive to radiation exposure, the crew took shelter in the most protected part of the *Perseus*, their sleeping quarters. For a few hours, they had a common, outside threat to worry about. They were able to put their disagreements aside.

The effects were temporary, however. Yesterday, Ollie was as cynical about their mission's outlook as ever.

She had been expecting Evelyn's announcement for the past two days. Coronal Mass Ejections, or CMEs, often accompanied solar flares. In a typical CME, the Sun might hurl billions of metric tonnes of solar material outward into the solar system. The most dangerous material would be in the form of charged protons, which moved more slowly than the initial burst of radiation. The crew would have several days of notice, plenty of time to prepare.

Evelyn forwarded the details of the CME alert, briefly and concisely. The message from Mission Support was mostly good news. The CME was a small one, and only the fringes would hit the *Perseus*.

Instruments aboard NASA's SOHO-2 sun-monitoring spacecraft had detected the CME several hours ago, and the first wave of charged particles wouldn't reach the *Perseus* until over a day from now. The initial flare had been a major X-class event, but large flares didn't always produce large CMEs. Powerful solar flares, though uncommon, were expected with increased frequency as the "solar max" part of the sun's eleven year activity cycle approached.

Having run frequent drills, Anna was well prepared. When the CME reached them, she would ride out the storm in her sleeping quarters again. This time, she might remain sheltered for days, if necessary.

Her only immediate responsibility was to take an inventory of the redundant caches of microbes and seeds stored within their storm shelter. If a massive CME sterilized the *Living Machine* wastewater recycling system, she could use these microbe samples to repair and restart the biosystem once the storm had passed.

In all reality, however, the backup microbe samples would be nearly useless in recovering from a massive CME. The main wastewater tanks formed part of the protective buffer surrounding the crew quarters. A CME powerful enough to completely sterilize the wastewater tanks would almost certainly kill her and her companions, too. Fortunately, a CME that powerful had never been detected before.

Anna started her verification task by releasing the velcro that held the seed and microbe containers firmly in place above her bunk. Each small, flat container was present and undamaged, as expected.

Then she left her quarters and performed the same check in the cabin on the level below. The backup sample containers, stored under Evelyn's mattress, were harder to reach. They were also in perfect condition.

Anna yawned. *Now we wait. Again.*

The next few hours would probably be filled with numerous media appearances. She would reassure the world, over and over, that the threat from this particular CME was minimal.

She briefly consulted some crib notes in the computer related to solar flares and CMEs, preparing for questions from scientifically savvy reporters. For example, they might ask her to explain why an increase in solar flare activity usually meant a decrease in overall radiation exposure.

"Flares and CMEs aren't the Sun's only emissions," she practiced. "The Sun produces a solar wind that partially shields the inner solar system from a steady bombardment of interstellar cosmic rays. Cosmic rays, entering our solar system from all directions, are so energetic that many pass right through our ship's hull. Fortunately, during periods of high flare and CME activity, a stronger solar wind should protect us from the most of the harmful cosmic rays. Because the solar wind just traces out magnetic field lines coming from the Sun, it can act sort of like a magnetic buffer."

Too much technical jargon in the answer. Make it simple, Anna, or you'll lose your audience.

Given a choice between flares and USNN, Anna would rather put up with a few minor flares. Despite its temper tantrums, the Sun remained her friend, the nurturing and protective guardian of the solar system.

MarsDay 88, 11:36 p.m.
(February 19, 6:00 p.m.)

Something strange was going on. Once again, David was in the dark. This time, however, the source of his suspicion was readily apparent. Jennifer and Bill had been acting oddly ever since they got home from work.

Perhaps they were simply looking forward to the weekend. If so, he could attribute their inquiries about his health, workload, and state of mind to the Friday evening euphoria shared by the vast majority of the American workforce. But what about Jennifer's immediate beeline to the kitchen? Or her announcement that the prime rib on their dinner menu this evening was non-negotiable?

Then there was Exhibit A, the beast itself. Jennifer had removed a huge, undoubtedly expensive slab of beef from a Whole Foods wrapper. It was big enough to feed half the neighborhood. When he asked why she had bought such a large portion, she explained it was "on sale." Once the beast was in the oven, she prepared enough Stovetop Stuffing and mixed vegetables to feed the other half of the neighborhood.

Bill just laughed and commented about having savory leftovers for lunch next week. But his actions were just as suspect. He went outside to refill the woodbox and sweep away an inch of blown snow on the front porch. Then he came back inside and started a roaring blaze in the fireplace.

Later, their signals became more obvious. Bill turned on the outside porch lights, and put five plates on the table.

Aha. They're having company for dinner.

David asked, "Who are your two guests? And when should I expect them, so I know when to hide out downstairs?" They just snickered, and winked at each other.

Soon afterward, bright auto headlights bathed the driveway and front windows. "Right on time," said Bill.

As David moved toward the basement steps, Bill grabbed his arm. "Why don't you answer the door this time, David?"

By now, he was thoroughly confused. Their guests must already know he was staying here. But who could they be?

Fontaine? No way. They would never roll out the red carpet for her.

Reggie? Or...could it possibly be, Cassie?

He rushed to the door and opened it. Ben and Cassie were just stepping onto the front porch, and David gave his youngest sister a warm, smothering hug. Then he lifted her feet and spun her around, for good measure. While she was recovering, he gave Ben a similar welcome, without the spin.

They came inside and greeted Jennifer and Bill. Then Cassie asked, "Did we surprise you, David?"

"Totally," he admitted. "What in the blazes are you two doing here?"

Ben smiled. "Cassie says her big brother has been working too hard. We decided to make a quick weekend visit so we could correct that deplorable situation."

David agreed that he could probably use a day off tomorrow, his first real break in over three months. The crew's journey to Mars had just passed the halfway point, and the mission would be in another period of low activity for the next several weeks. His deputies could easily handle the workload. No one would miss him for a day or two.

His other peripheral investigations were stagnant as well. Rodriguez at NASA was balking on details. Fontaine hadn't found any incriminating evidence at USNN. He was no closer to finding <chicken_little>, nor Conference Room 4. The three transmitters and navigation beacons on Mars remained silent.

Perhaps he did need some time off to recharge his batteries and figure out a new angle from which to attack his problems. Ben and Cassie might even have some ideas for him, though he resolved not to tell them about his deal with Fontaine. Hopefully, Bill and Jennifer would keep silent about that, too.

The evening was pleasant and relaxing. Thoughts of work were distant, and the prime rib was perfectly prepared. The five of them barely consumed half the food.

After eating, they relaxed and visited. David got caught up on everything happening in his family. Ben described their latest house searching efforts, and Cassie complained about high mortgage interest rates, which were well over 12 percent now.

Later, David watched the two couples battle each other in a game of Trivial Pursuit. They tried to get him to play, too, but he knew his limits. Except for the history category, his trivia knowledge was woefully inadequate. The game, and a rematch ordered by the losing team of Ben and Cassie, lasted well in to the early hours of the morning.

The next morning, David slept until eight o'clock. After visiting Mission Support briefly to make sure his substitute had everything under control, he went upstairs to check on the others. Nobody had risen yet.

He decided to take a walk outside. Most of the snow from the large storms earlier in the winter had melted away, though two-foot drifts still remained in shaded places. According to Bill, the south shore of the reservoir would hold traces of its snowpack well into June or July. The bright morning sun had already melted a light dusting of new snow from the previous evening.

David set a fast pace, staying on the cleared dirt roads. He followed a steeply climbing path toward the top of the mountainside. Soon, he was puffing from exertion.

To remain in hiding, David had retired from his Capture the Flag team. With his lack of exercise for the past few weeks, he had already lost some of his conditioning. Dismayed at how quickly this had happened, he resolved on the spot to wake up earlier and take a short jog every morning, as he had done back in his early college days.

Getting out more often and inhaling the thin mountain air ought to do wonders for his mental health and clarity, as well. Problems had a way of evaporating at high altitude. Creative solutions sprang from the forest, the streams, and the wispy clouds above.

He returned to the house an hour later, feeling completely exhausted, yet totally refreshed. The others were now awake. Bill and Ben were cooking up a breakfast of waffles, eggs, and hashed brown potatoes.

As he sagged into a chair at the dining room table, Jennifer noted his weariness and commented, "I hope you saved some energy. After breakfast, we were planning to hike one of the trails along the foothills overlooking Boulder."

"Great! Let's do it!" He had never been very good at pacing himself when it came to physical activity. If one hike was beneficial and fun, two hikes were even better. Besides, the altitude near Boulder was lower, and the air thicker, so he might have more energy there.

That evening, as he reclined in his favorite chair and chatted with Ben, his body was in open rebellion. His feet were sore, his legs ached, and his lower back muscles were a tight ball of agony.

Ben looked like he was feeling even worse. "It's the altitude," he explained. "How do you people breathe up here in the mountains?" He popped another Diaspan tablet to help relieve his symptoms of altitude sickness. He had been swallowing pills all afternoon.

Their conversation eventually returned to the Mars mission, and Ben recounted some of the activities going on at JPL. His communications team had tried many times to reestablish contact with the ERV and backup habitat on the surface of Mars, but to no avail.

David reciprocated, telling Ben how little progress he had made in resolving his various problems and concerns. At least things were going reasonably well within the *Perseus*, and that's what mattered most.

Cassie joined them in the living room. She overheard David's last comments and disagreed with him. She had a completely different opinion of the situation in the *Perseus*, and hers was much more pessimistic. The Mars crew didn't seem to be bonding yet. The psych team had been busily dealing with each new factor that arose.

The most serious problems had started back when the ERV signal was lost. What could have been an opportunity for the crew to come together under adversity had turned into a polarizing event. Regardless of the merit in the commander's decision to press on with the mission, she had pushed aside the concerns of her crew too brusquely. As a result, Anna and Ollie felt powerless and alienated. Their frustrations were readily apparent during their regular sessions with the psychologists.

Cassie's prognosis was not good. Unless the situation changed for the better, the conflict and bitterness would continue to escalate. The end results were unpredictable.

As Anna's personal psychologist, Cassie was most concerned about Anna's mental health. She had pieced together enough information from the other crew members, through their psychologists, to formulate a clearer picture of Anna's personal issues. Cassie couldn't reveal many details without violating patient confidentiality, but she could summarize the conclusions of the psych team.

Over the past month, Anna had shown increasing symptoms of Separation Anxiety Disorder. A mild case of this ailment was to be expected, and was probably unavoidable, given the crew's forced separation from everything familiar to them. However, each crew member had been chosen with this concern in mind. Great care had been taken not to select anyone with significant attachments to people or places on Earth.

So Cassie was quite puzzled. Why was her patient having these symptoms after only three months in space? She had some suspicions, based upon clues she had gathered. Her sleuthing job was made more difficult by her inability to just come right out and ask Anna certain questions. Open tactics would have put her patient on the defensive and jeopardized the free flow of information.

Cassie suspected that Anna was having a long-distance relationship with someone back on Earth. The relationship was probably very important to her, and very real, within her active fantasy world. Anna was desperately holding on to that person as a lifeline, an "attachment figure," despite the utter irrationality of doing so within her current situation.

As David listened to his sister, a new feeling of dread descended upon him. Had she ripped his heart out of his chest and stepped on it, she probably wouldn't have caused him any more pain.

Am I responsible for this? And why didn't I notice it before? Am I clinging to Anna as much as she is clinging to me? And what about the mission? Am I endangering it?

Since Cassie knew that David had some interactions with Anna in the past, she asked if he had any idea who her attachment figure might be. It would probably be someone at Mission Support, she speculated. David feigned ignorance, while feeling her questioning eyes boring holes into his skull.

Does she suspect anything? Probably. It's hard to tell, and even harder to fool her. She sees everything.

Fearing the answer, he cautiously asked about Anna's symptoms. He framed his question in the dispassionate context of guarding against future problems on the mission. His real interest was far more personal, of course.

Cassie hesitated. She didn't want to discuss the specifics of the case, but she could describe the clinical disorder using generalities.

"Any crew member with a serious case of Separation Anxiety Disorder might have difficulty bonding with the rest of the crew. The individual might show a powerful yearning to return home, eventually resulting in subconscious, compulsive activities that maintain a closer connection with the attachment figure. On Earth, a classic symptom in adults would be frequent phone calls home, or in a child, the desire to sleep next to the parents at night. This disorder is usually a childhood ailment, but adults can be afflicted too. The individual is often preoccupied with fears that injuries or illnesses will befall the major attachment figure, or themselves. If the individual perceives someone else coming between them and the attachment figure, they can show anger and frustration. In the most extreme cases, they can even lash out violently."

"Not a pretty picture. So what do we do about it?"

Cassie advised letting her psych team handle the situation. "However, given the remote potential for violence, I do strongly suggest you should warn the commander. She should watch Anna closely for symptoms. Her psychologist can tell her what to look for. There's also a more important reason to warn her, too. Any future violence might be directed against the commander, if she is perceived as the person who is coming between the patient and the attachment figure."

David was doubtful. He couldn't believe Anna to be capable of violence. Overall, her work record and attitude had been excellent. The only problems she ever mentioned in her reports were some recurring nightmares and occasionally getting caught in the middle of disagreements between Evelyn and Ollie.

According to Cassie, outward appearances and perceptions could be extremely deceiving, especially given the psychological unknowns assailing the Mars crew every day. This was a unique situation, without prior precedent. "We can't make many assumptions about how Anna might react. Her work might be flawless while the problem lingers, slowly reaching the boiling point."

David shook his head. He didn't want to talk to the commander or anyone else about this problem. Yet he could see no way out. He fidgeted in his seat, weighing his options.

"OK, I'll bring this up with the commander," he finally conceded. "But I need to hear more of the details first. I don't care about patient confidentiality. This issue could wreck the whole mission. What good is confidentiality if the patient is dead?"

Cassie was silent, obviously waging her own internal battle. When it came to professional ethics, she was just as idealistic as he was. David wondered if she could step over the line, in this case, as he had already done.

"OK, fine." Unhappiness was written all over her face. "But we have to talk in private. I don't want anyone else hearing the details. Also, you have to promise not to tell anyone what I reveal to you, especially the commander.

We can tell her what symptoms to watch for, but we can't have her invading Anna's privacy to the point where Anna becomes suspicious and shuts herself off from her support base. This is a very delicate situation, and it needs to be handled tactfully."

"I won't tell anyone," he vowed, knowing this was one promise that should be easy to keep. "And when it comes to the commander, I'll let you do most of the talking. This is your area of expertise, certainly not mine."

He got up from his seat and waved her to follow him. They could talk privately in his room downstairs.

Reaching his desk, he logged on his computer and immediately set up a half-hour appointment with the commander in the morning. Their timing was poor because Evelyn's sleep period had just begun. Had they been two hours earlier, they would have hit the four-hour block of time when Anna was asleep and Evelyn was awake.

David turned to his sister. She had been sitting on the edge of the bed, waiting patiently for him to finish. "OK, Cassie, spill the beans. What are you seeing that alarms you so much?" He edged his chair closer.

"Like I said before, I've been piecing the story together with the help of the other psychologists. Actually, we talk amongst ourselves quite a bit, though we're always mindful of the same confidentiality issues. It's so hard to get accurate information from the *Perseus*! I would give a month's pay to have Anna on the couch in my office, for just an hour."

"So this is all based on second-hand or third-hand gossip?" David barked, immediately wishing he used a softer tone of voice. He needed to maintain his air of impartiality.

Besides, Cassie wouldn't have brought this matter to his attention if she wasn't as certain of her facts as she could be. Her annoyed expression verified that conclusion, and David hastily apologized.

She quickly regained her focus. "You've apparently read Anna's reports, where she mentioned her recurring dreams. I'm not sure how much she included, but I find the dreams to be quite interesting. Detailed dream analysis is tricky stuff, but general patterns are often obvious, especially in recurring dreams. Some of the patterns in Anna's dreams are feelings of helplessness, apathy, pain, and personal danger. She dwells on the statement, 'You should not be here.' This indicates a strong attachment to some other place, time, or person."

"That sounds reasonable for someone in her situation," David said.

"Agreed. That was what I thought at first, too. Then the ERV signal loss happened. It's hard to interpret all the conversations and interactions that followed, but the psychologists have done the best they can. A shift in crew dynamics seems to have occurred almost two months ago, around Day 34. According to Evelyn, prior to that time, Ollie had been lobbying to abort the mission and return to Earth. Since then, he has accepted the decision to proceed. However, he also seems to have planted the seed of that thought in Anna's mind, and now she has adopted the same argument. She even claims to be representing Ollie's position and voicing his concerns. When Evelyn talks to Ollie directly, she gets a different story."

"Sounds like an inconsistency between Anna and Ollie. Could it be Ollie who's in denial? Or could he be lying, outright?"

"Why would he lie about it?" Cassie asked. "It's possible, but unlikely. He hasn't exhibited any behaviors his psychologist considers unusual, other than some occasional sleeping problems. As for being in denial, it goes against his character. He is quite forcefully blunt about such things. No, it's far more likely that Anna is deluding herself, conveniently projecting her own feelings and ideas onto someone else."

David still wasn't convinced, and he voiced his skepticism, more cautiously this time.

"There are other indicators, as well," said Cassie. "My psych team gets regular reports on how the crew is spending their time and how well they are keeping up with their activity schedule. The reports are very high level, but there's enough detail for us to determine that Anna has been logging more hours on the computer than she should be. That's a clear sign she's drawing inward, away from the others. Her computer time includes frequent avatar sessions at Mission Support. Some of those sessions have been with me, but not all of them. If you wanted to help, you could try to get me some details on those sessions. I need to know where she goes and who she is with."

"I'll see what I can do," responded David. He hoped he had managed to keep a straight face.

Yeah, fat chance, sis. I might ask security to send me a report, but unless it contains some surprises, that's one report you will never see…

David could literally feel his blood pressure rising. His ethical nature, which he cherished so deeply, found his recent actions deplorable. He had neglected to tell his sister about his interactions with Fontaine, but that was only a minor lie of omission. Then he had lied similarly about his involvement with Anna. Now he was lying more boldly to her face, and at a time when she was trying to be honest with him.

My God, I hate myself today. What am I becoming? Some day, Cassie, when you find out what I've done, I hope you can find it in your heart to forgive me.

Cassie continued on and on, revealing other subtle things that she and others had noticed, but David didn't want to hear any more. He had reached the point of saturation, and he couldn't absorb any more of her discomforting words. He floated through the rest of the evening on autopilot, feeling hollow inside.

CHAPTER 18
SHIFT

MarsDay 92, 6:30 p.m.
(February 23, 3:24 p.m.)

Ollie softly hummed a tune as he dealt the cards. His swift hand movements were synchronized with the airy melody. When Evelyn asked about the name of the song, he replied, "Oh, it's just something I made up."

Anna had noticed a major improvement in Ollie's attitude since their two days of hiding in the storm shelter. Even a subsequent, more potent solar flare yesterday hadn't bothered him. In fact, he almost seemed delighted that the sun had entered a new pattern of furious sunspot activity. If they received another CME alert from Mission Support, which they were expecting at any time, she wondered if he would jump for joy.

Perhaps he just liked playing cards, reading, and studying. If they were forced to hide in their storm shelter again, there would be little else for them to do.

Anna thought she knew the real reason for Ollie's improvement. When she asked about his recent prescription of sleeping pills, he remarked, "They've made a world of difference. This past week, I've been sleeping like a log!"

While they played the first three hands, Evelyn updated them on today's news from Earth. The latest test firing of the RSX-2 rocket, a more powerful successor to the rocket that had lifted them into space three months ago, had created a spectacular fireball in the Texas desert. Violence in the Middle East and Southeast Asia dominated the headlines, as it always seemed to. A new strain of SARS had appeared in China, after many years of dormancy. Corporate scandals, government scandals, environmental scandals…the list of bad news seemed endless.

Evelyn remarked that she was so glad to be out here in space, away from all the madness on Earth. Something in the tone of her voice sounded peculiar. Anna glanced up from her cards to find the commander staring at her.

She felt compelled to reply, "Well, there have always been problems on Earth and always will be. Let's try not to overlook all the good things there, too."

"Of course."

The rest of the hand was played in silence. As he was dealing the fourth and final hand, Ollie asked about the cause of the RSX-2 test failure. According to Evelyn, the Raytronics Corporation had not yet determined what went wrong. Her disappointment was obvious, as was the reason for it. The future of human space exploration was probably riding with the RSX-2.

If it ever got off the ground in one piece, the RSX-2 would be capable of flinging 170 metric tonnes of mass into low-Earth orbit, dwarfing the 100 tonne limit of the RSX-1. It would even surpass the 140 tonne capacity of the Saturn V rockets back in the Apollo era.

The RSX-2 would be the only rocket powerful enough to boost an intact nuclear-powered spacecraft into orbit. Nuclear engines were quite massive, due to the additional radiation shielding a crew would require. Without the RSX-2, assembly of a nuclear spacecraft in low-Earth orbit would still be possible, but at far greater cost, complexity, and risk.

Even after hearing the terrible news, Ollie seemed happier than ever. He said, "If all else fails, we can keep doing Mars missions with the RSX-1, despite what some people might think." He glanced at Anna and smiled.

Anna was shocked to hear him say this. Lately, after the setbacks with the ERV and backup habitat on Mars, his complaints about the limitations of their low-budget, low-capacity mission had often marred their exercise sessions. Along with his improving attitude, might his confidence in the mission finally be returning? She fervently hoped so.

Something didn't feel quite right, however. She had a disturbing flashback to the third grade, when she grappled endlessly with her mathematics assignments, despite her best efforts. In the classroom, her friends seemed to do the equations far more easily and quickly than she could.

They knew things she didn't know. She felt slow and dim-witted. It had taken her years to "catch up," and even longer to shake her feelings of inadequacy.

When they finished the last hand of their card game, Ollie had the fewest total points. Unless they were hiding in the storm shelter the following evening, he would be tasked with cleaning the dinner dishes.

Anna's feelings of unease wouldn't go away, and she found herself needing some time to think. Claiming to be tired, which she was, she bid the others a good evening and retreated to her quarters.

After using the restroom, she peeled off her clothing and snuggled under the warm Demron blanket on her mattress near the floor. Using the computer display overhead, she retrieved her personal medical logbook and started to review her notes on Ollie's physical condition. Before she got very far, a soft knock on the cabin door broke her concentration.

"It's open," she said.

The door slid aside. Ollie entered, carrying a steaming beverage in a cup. Anna rolled over and sat up to greet him, holding the blanket tightly against her chest.

"I thought you might like a spot of valerian tea." He offered the cup to her.

She gratefully accepted, taking the drink in one hand while keeping a firm grip on the blanket with the other. She took a cautious sip. The tea was hot, but not scalding. It did taste a bit strange, but everything else had seemed a bit strange this evening, too.

Ollie must have noticed the puzzled look on her face. "I added a dash of stevia. It's an unusual mixture, but I find it helps to improve the flavor of the valerian blend. It also hides the bitter taste of all the NASA cancer-fighting chemicals, too."

She took another sip and agreed the mixture was effective, though it would take some getting used to. Then she asked, "Ollie, earlier, what did you mean with your remark about the RSX-2? All along, you've been wishing the *Perseus* was twice as large and carried twice the supplies and people. You should be the RSX-2's biggest supporter."

"We don't have an RSX-2," he replied. "We have what we have. So we do what we have to do."

That's a reasonable response. Why am I still so uneasy about his sudden transformation? It's exactly what I wanted!

Between sips of tea, she asked him a few more questions, trying to better assess his health and general state of mind. His answers didn't reveal much.

The valerian root extract worked its soothing effects, and she nodded off to sleep, almost in mid-sentence. Just before succumbing to her weariness, she dimly perceived Ollie crossing over to her bedside and removing the empty cup from her limp fingers. "Uncle Ollie" looked down at her with an intensely thoughtful expression on his face. Then he straightened the sheet over her relaxed body, turned out the light, and left the room.

Anna's sleep was deep and restful until her dreams turned once more into nightmares filled with bees, trailers, and darkness. This time, she had no trailer to hide in, and she couldn't wake up.

MarsDay 93, 11:38 a.m.
(February 24, 9:00 a.m.)

Eighty-six messages had accumulated overnight. David only had an hour to read them before leaving, if he was to meet Skye at their scheduled time. He needed more time to mentally prepare for the encounter, but at least the long walk to town might allow him to gather his thoughts.

Today was supposed to be another day off from work, his second this week. Skye had suggested they go snowshoeing, most likely a shallow pretext for getting him into a private location where she could pummel him with more questions.

Both of their previous meetings had been in a public location, where he could easily curtail the conversation if it veered into uncomfortable topics. Those sessions had gone well, and the reporter had behaved herself, so David was willing to try something different.

To save time, he decided to read only emergency or high priority messages. This cut his list down to only five. But first, he read his customary "Good Morning" message from Anna.

> To: <shepherd>
> From: <microbrain>
> Subject: Good Morning
> Priority: Low
>
> Good Morning, Shep!

My wheels are rusty this morning. Ollie let me oversleep—he's been such a dear fellow the past few days. He even brought me a cup of tea in bed last night. Perhaps I'll ask him to read me a bedtime story tonight.

Crew relations seem to be improving. Last night was almost pleasant. Most of this is due to Ollie's transformation. I can't believe how he's turned his attitude around 180 degrees. It's actually a bit creepy, to tell you the truth. I'm waiting for him to unzip his face and turn into an ugly monster, like the zipperheads in that old sci-fi movie we like to joke about.

So all is well here, for now. I am missing you almost as much as I miss an ice cream sundae, or anything else with tons of processed sugar in it. Do you think our sponsors planned ahead and included a gallon of vanilla ice cream in our supply stash on Mars? After all, keeping it frozen wouldn't be much of a problem. And the SEA must have tons of ice cream sitting around after their big media campaign asking people to donate one out of every hundred ice cream cones to fund the Mars mission. It's so hard to imagine Americans and Europeans consuming $50 billion worth of ice cream every year, but I checked the data in the ship's library, and it's true.

Don't answer the question about the ice cream in our supplies—I want to keep the hope alive. It gives me yet one more thing to look forward to, after our arrival. I can't wait to get some solid ground beneath me again.

If Ollie really is a zipperhead, he might have some magic trick that can cut our remaining travel time. I'll ask him about that, but only after he reveals himself. Ha Ha.

That's all for now. Keep smiling, and have a great day. We will be doing our usual routine here, but we will also be watching for the next CME alert. I hope the sun gets over its bellyache soon.

Anna

He reread the message, looking for any obvious signs of Cassie's psychological concerns. Most of her words seemed to support the opposite viewpoint, that Anna couldn't wait to reach Mars. The only phrase giving him a momentary pause was "I am missing you." Normally, that would have been a harmless little nicety, especially within the context of her joke about the ice cream sundae. But now he wasn't sure. Anna was always making these little jokes, and he adored that aspect of her personality.

How can I appreciate her quirkiness if I'm constantly on the alert for signs of mental illness?

More messages waited. He looked at the sender fields and realized one was from <chicken_little>. The fowl could wait. Instead, he opened two messages from Commander Day, addressed to both him and Cassie.

The commander had been observing Anna more closely and had noticed some subtle comments or behaviors that she certainly wouldn't include in her "official" crew reports. Her second message, sent just a few minutes ago, mentioned that Anna had overslept by several hours this morning. This was one of the specific warning signs Cassie had alerted the commander to watch for, one that David believed to be a bit extreme.

Oversleep for a few hours and all of a sudden you're labeled an axe murderer. Poor Anna. I would never want to live my life under a microscope, like she is. Might Cassie be overreacting just a wee bit?

The third message, from the coordinator of volunteers on the telemedicine team, further increased David's level of unease. Having talked with the psych team, the medical coordinator was deeply concerned about the level of stress within the *Perseus*. He emphasized that reducing crew tensions needed to be a high priority.

Over the past five years, great advances had been made in better understanding the role of neural feedback in triggering the onslaught of latent diseases. Unless tensions were reduced, the medical team believed the crew risked serious health issues.

David sent back a brief request for more details, including statistical probabilities. He questioned how often similar health issues had occurred among small groups of isolated people in high stress situations, like on US Navy nuclear submarines.

The next message was from the science team. For a change, it contained some welcome news. During the overnight shift, the solar science community had forwarded a weather forecast. The latest solar flare had not yet produced a CME. The sun was still in a period of heightened activity, but for now, danger to the crew was minimal.

Finally, a good break. We've been overdue for one.

With slightly renewed optimism, he opened the final high priority message, the one from <chicken_little>.

To: <shepherd>
From: <chicken_little>
Subject: The latest...
Priority: High

David -

The sky is still falling.
Know who you trust, and trust who you know.

Another cryptic piece of pseudo-advice from <chicken_little> was just what he didn't need right now. David's temples started to hurt. The dull throbbing would probably lead into a stronger headache if he thought about this message too much. Yet he couldn't help himself. He enjoyed challenging mind games, and he desperately wanted to decipher the enigma of <chicken_little>.

Know who you trust? Trust who you know? But I no longer know who I can trust.

He composed a short list of the people closest to him, people he knew well: Cassie, Ben, Bill, and Jennifer. He could trust them.

What about Anna? I thought I trusted her, but how well do I really know her? Isn't that the big question here?

And why are Anna and Cassie on a collision course? Is it my fault for not being more honest with Cassie? Probably, but surely, that can't be the only reason.

Of the three people in space, he knew Anna far better than the others. Since reliable information from the *Perseus* was so difficult to obtain, he tended to trust Anna's words and opinions over that of her companions.

Might someone else in the Perseus *be deliberately misleading Cassie, too? Evelyn? Or Ollie? Or both?*

Both had ample opportunity, but neither had a good motive. He thought back to Cassie's previous disclosures. Some of her information had come from Ollie and his psychologist, while other bits were straight from Evelyn.

What else do I know about either of them? What other actions might throw suspicion upon one or the other?

Ah, yes, Evelyn's fondness for frequenting tiny buffer rooms at Mission Support. Highly suspicious.

This memory released a whole flood of related thoughts, including the ironic realization that an earlier message from <chicken_little> had led to his discovery of Evelyn's impossible location within Mission Support. Was this merely a coincidence? He still couldn't explain the mystery of Conference Room 4. Perhaps it was time to revisit that problem. But first, what could possibly be the motive of <chicken_little>?

Theorem: <chicken_little> is throwing suspicion on the commander, trying to drive a wedge between the Mars crew and Mission Support.

Supporting Postulates: <chicken_little> wants the mission to fail. He somehow knew I couldn't trace Commander Day's real location when he sent his "tell no one" message. He also knew I would read his message soon enough to spot her strange location. Furthermore, for his latest message to implicate the commander instead of Anna, he knows about my relationship with Anna.

Conclusion: Of these postulates, only the first is likely to be true. The motives, identity, and message of <chicken_little> remain unknown.

He quickly reasoned through several similar theories. None matched the known facts any better.

Frustrated, he put the problem aside and vowed to return to it later. His meeting with Skye was in less than 30 minutes. It was time to deal with other problems.

After packing some sandwiches and putting on his hiking boots, he enjoyed the usual walk to town. Skye was already waiting for him in the small parking lot tucked behind the Once Again Books new-and-used bookshop. She was driving a blue Saturn Vue hybrid with Utah license plates. The windows and sunroof were open. As he approached, the sweet sound of Rebecca Folsom music drifted over to him on the warm mid-day breeze.

Upon seeing him, Skye removed her bare feet from the dashboard and called out, "You're five minutes late. Throw your stuff in the back."

David shook his head, still unable to make sense of this woman who could be completely relaxed and friendly one minute, then impatient and demanding the next minute.

He had gotten to know her better during the past few weeks, and she no longer seemed so demonic, though he did wonder if she might have a split personality. She was constantly oscillating between her personal and professional personas. Sometimes the transitions were abrupt.

Skye had decided on their snowshoeing destination without telling him. He surveyed the dirt parking lot, noticing the meager remnants of snow in the shadows trying to hide from the harsh rays of the mid-day sun. Other than a light dusting once or twice, they hadn't received any new snow since the mammoth dump at Christmas. She must be intending to travel to a higher altitude.

Today's warm, windless conditions might make a long hike very pleasant. Fortunately, he had remembered to pack sunscreen. Despite his naturally olive complexion, a gift from his Italian genes, his skin still burnt easily.

He carefully placed his borrowed snowshoes, ski poles, and backpack into the SUV and closed the hatchback. Then he climbed into the passenger seat and greeted Skye with a lukewarm, "Good morning." His purple and gold Minnesota Vikings coat and blue jeans starkly contrasted with Skye's stylish coverall.

She didn't waste any time leaving. The SUV stirred up clouds of billowing dust as it careened out of the parking lot. Spinning her tires on the gravel, she pulled onto the main highway through the sleepy mountain town and immediately squealed to a stop at a crosswalk. Three monks in brown habits slowly crossed the road in front of them. "Gotta keep the Lord on our side," she quipped.

Heading east through the downtown area, she greatly exceeded the posted 25 mph speed limit, barely slowing down for a roundabout. Apparently, she had been in town long enough to notice that the speed limit wasn't enforced.

The highway curved northward. David held tightly on to the door handle as Skye took a hairpin turn at 60 miles-per-hour. Closing his eyes, he tried to avoid thinking about the 1,000-foot-deep chasm to the right.

"Where did you learn to drive? Italy?" he asked.

Her reply was, "There are times to slow down and times to speed up." Hitting a short straightaway, she pushed the gas pedal to the floor. "No one's going to be following us. I didn't like the looks of some of the people hanging around town."

"I thought I was the paranoid one."

Skye confided that she was a bit disturbed by some recent happenings at work. In her daily reporting, she had backed off her openly critical coverage of the Mars mission a bit, per their plan to determine the response of the network. That response had been swift and clear. Her producers had immediately pressured her into restoring her rhetoric to its previous levels.

Then she had made a mistake, a rare slip of the tongue. In a conversation with a colleague, she had casually referenced the Director of Mission Support. This news quickly reached her producers, and their response was even swifter and clearer. She was ordered to reveal everything she knew about David. She was also instructed to arrange a formal interview with him in their studios.

Holding his breath, he asked, "So what did you tell them?"

And by the way, where are you taking me? Somewhere you chose, or your producers?

"I told them about our agreement, of course. Not all the details, but enough to make it clear that I could not do what they wanted."

"I'll bet they didn't like that," he said, somewhat relieved.

"No, they didn't. Not at all."

They lapsed into silence. Ten minutes later, she pulled into a parking lot near the Brainard Lake Recreation Area. David opened his eyes, jumped out of the vehicle, and kissed the ground. When Skye commented that she had saved them at least five minutes by driving so fast, he replied that it would take him at least five minutes to recover from her driving.

He took in the familiar surroundings. The parking lot held only half its usual legion of cars. He had come to the Brainard Lake area often with his college friends. This area, with its sprawling network of trails around numerous small, scenic lakes, was a local favorite for hiking in the summer and snowshoeing or skiing in the winter. During his early college years, when he had jogged for exercise, his toughest challenge had been the strenuous dash from the 10,000-foot high base area to the towering peak of Mount Audubon, 3,000 feet above.

They put on their gear and set out upon the roadway. A low barricade blocked the highway leading to the lakes and campground above, as was normal during the winter months.

Skye stepped around the barricade, but David called her back. "I have a better idea," he said, pointing toward a sign 50 feet to the left marking the trailhead to Left Hand Reservoir.

During the winter months, reaching the best trailheads around the base area required a three-mile trek down snow-packed roadways. David remembered the trail on the left was a mile shorter, narrower, and more heavily wooded. Left Hand Reservoir was several hundred feet higher than the base area, so the hike would be more strenuous, but a better view would await them.

They proceeded along the alternate trail, mindful of the tall pines gracing both sides and the occasional larger rock protruding from the packed snow. With the forest peacefully still, David listened to the crunching of their snowshoes, the swishing of the liquid in Skye's oversized canteen, and the gasping of their lungs as they hungered for oxygen.

Breathing the thin, chilled air was obviously difficult for Skye, as it was for most flatlanders when they hiked at the higher elevations. Though she didn't complain, he stopped several times so she could rest.

During their first stop, David asked if she had made any progress tracking down the Beta organization. She hadn't learned much, other than the extreme reaction of her producers, which didn't prove the existence of Beta nor their involvement with it.

Their conversation continued until they approached the reservoir. The trail widened, and the proud pines on either side gave way to scraggly, twisted shrubs. Shorter remnants of trees were wind-blasted to such an extent that branches and pine needles grew only on the leeward side of the tortured trunks.

Snow and ice covered the reservoir. The area was just as David recalled—a desolate, snow covered wonderland, ringed by a distant swath of lush pine trees reaching upward half way toward the peaks of the surrounding mountaintops. Jeweled sunlight glistened, reflected by the snow atop the summits.

Several new, sturdy picnic tables lined the eastern side of the lake, the side with the best mountain view. They claimed the nearest table and took off their gear. David unpacked the food in his backpack, minding the occasional wind gusts that threatened to blow away their plates and napkins.

Not another soul was in sight. Despite the picnic tables and the remnants of tracks in the snow around the lake, he could easily imagine they were the only people ever to have discovered this beautiful place.

While they ate their chicken salad sandwiches, they talked about the Mars mission. Eventually, David brought up the topic of <chicken_little>. He hadn't intended to reveal any details about his feathered antagonist, but the message from this morning still weighed heavily on his thoughts.

Skye appeared to be quite intrigued. "People can use various tricks to achieve anonymity within online communities," she offered, "but they always leave footprints. Trust me. I've had a lot of experience with this."

When he asked how she was so familiar with the workings of virtual worlds, she shyly admitted, "How else can a celebrity like me find a date with someone who's not a groupie? I'm usually the one trying to be anonymous."

"You hang out in online dating clubs?" He doubled over in laughter. Though Internet dating was more popular than ever, the thought of Skye

Fontaine skulking around in a virtual world, seeking companionship, seemed totally ridiculous. This flashy, cosmopolitan woman undoubtedly kept a long list of male suitors at her instant beck and call. With her carefree, on-the-edge lifestyle, she was a walking advertisement for the allure of short-term relationships.

Skye blushed and turned away. The sincerity in her reaction was plain to see, and David's conscience got the better of him. He ended up apologizing to her, at length. His assumptions about her personal life were nothing more than shallow, vicious stereotypes.

He found himself wondering if Skye might be <chicken_little>. If she was so good at remaining anonymous within virtual worlds, perhaps she had found a way to infiltrate the Mission Support center. This scenario didn't fit the known facts very well. Nevertheless, he filed it in his mental folder, the one overflowing with other unlikely speculations.

David lost himself in the icy tranquility of the surroundings. A small Clark's Nutcracker flew past and landed on the table next to their food. He tossed a morsel of bread to the dainty, gray plumed bird, which immediately grabbed his gift in its long, pointed beak. His new friend flashed its black and white tail feathers as it flew back across the lake.

Skye soon turned back to the table and resumed nibbling at her sandwich. Between bites, she mumbled, "The people who maintain your world must have a way of tracking down your Chicken Little character."

"Why?" asked David.

"The days of the anonymous superhacker are over. Nowadays, people always hack from the inside. He must be someone on your team. Most likely, he's one of the people who created the virtual world in the first place."

Early in his investigations, David had considered <chicken_little> might be someone on his security team with the ability to cover his tracks well. However, he had not yet considered the possibility that his adversary might be one of the people who had created the virtual world in the first place.

At first glance, this seemed to make some sense. Though he was no software expert, it seemed reasonable that a founding programmer might have installed a hidden account. Such a person could also possess other unknown but powerful abilities. In fact, the whole scenario reminded him of the plot of an old movie, in which a nuclear war almost started when a teenager hacked into a military computer using an account concealed by the original programmer.

The mysterious Conference Room 4 anomaly might be explained if <chicken_little> could assume Commander Day's identity and resize rooms at will. Most likely, someone with insider powers would be in the employ of the Alpha organization. It was a real stretch, but this meant <chicken_little> was trying to pass David useful information. Yet if that was true, why were the messages always so cryptic?

Skye must have interpreted his silence as a sign of disinterest because she changed the subject. Her new topic was one they had discussed several times before, one that bothered the reporter to no end.

"My team has crunched the numbers and done more digging," she said. "To make a long story short, there is no possible way this Mars mission could cost only $1 billion."

"Why don't you make a long story long, and prove to me why it can't?" asked David.

Skye inundated him with her latest facts and figures. The company making the rockets charged the U.S. military a half billion dollars per launch, so right up front, the cost of the six Mars launches would approach $3 billion. Even with the radical design of the Earth Return Vehicle, which Skye knew all about, her team estimated the cost of the ERV design, component manufacturing, integration testing, and training to be at least five billion dollars. Each habitat would be pretty cheap, probably only $1 billion, all-inclusive. The other field equipment would probably be even cheaper, but there was a lot of it, and it all needed to work under harsh conditions. She guessed another $2 billion there.

Skye's speculation turned to software, mission integration, crew training, and other major overhead costs that were unavoidable on a project of this magnitude. She would probably have kept spouting figures for ten minutes, but David had heard enough.

"I don't feel like doing any math today. What's your latest, bargain basement estimate?" he asked.

"At least $20 billion. We're guessing it was spread out over five years, so that's $4 billion a year."

David laughed again, and this time, his conscience approved. "Do you realize that even if your estimates are correct, $4 billion dollars is petty cash? Our country's Gross Domestic Product last year was over $20 trillion!"

"I know," she sighed. "When it comes right down to it, despite all the propaganda to the contrary, exploring Mars is cheap. At least 20 organizations could easily afford it, and that's being extremely conservative.

Some corporations, like General Motors or Walmart, make that much money in sales every day. Dozens of investment firms and insurance companies have a hundred times as much cash sitting around."

"What if you only include groups with a special interest in space exploration, as well as the means to keep the mission concealed from the public?"

"We already have. For each entity in our list, we threw out ten others that didn't meet those conditions, and a few others."

Curious, David asked who was on her latest list.

"Four aerospace companies, two government agencies, five wealthy non-profit foundations, one religious order, and at least ten private individuals." She buried her face in her hands and pleaded, "Can you tell me anything else that might help us to narrow our search? Anything at all?"

"Can't think of a thing," he replied, honestly.

And if I could, I probably wouldn't tell you, anyway. Watching you struggle with it is far too much fun.

Self-pity didn't seem like Skye's style. She rebounded quickly, stating with confidence, "We'll find them. It's just a matter of time." Then she frowned again. "I have another question. Allow me to be blunt."

"By all means," said David, wondering when she had ever not been blunt.

"Since there's no way the Mars mission could have cost $1 billion, someone on your precious steering committee is feeding you bad information. Who would do that? And why?"

He thought for a moment. "Since I don't have any reason to know how much things cost, they could tell me anything they want to...or they could tell me nothing. I still believe the slip-ups were accidental."

"What if your steering committee is being lied to? The people you overheard might actually believe what they were saying."

David said, "Now that's really odd."

"What's odd about that?" asked Skye, throwing her arms into the air for added emphasis. "Everyone else is being lied to. Why not them?"

"No, I was referring to our friends over there." David tilted his head, gesturing to the right.

Farther along the lakeshore, two men wearing brown monastery habits were sitting at another picnic table, well out of hearing range. Two sets of cross-country skis were on the ground nearby. The men gazed at the lake, apparently meditating with the help of music from a portable holocrystal player on the table in front of them. Their hoods were down, and David's sharp eyes could barely discern a receiving device over the ear of the nearest man. Wireless audio receivers were a normal accessory for such rugged, solid-state music players.

He wasn't sure how long the men had been sitting there before he had noticed them, but they could have been there forever. They seemed a natural part of the environment, like the water, bushes, snow, and rocks around them.

Skye glanced at the monks and immediately drew in her breath, partially stifling a gasp. She leaned over the table to David and silently mouthed, "Let's go." Then she placed a finger over David's mouth and gestured to the trail back to the parking lot. Her meaning was clear. She thought they were being spied upon.

They crammed the remnants of their lunch into the backpack, none too gently. Putting on his snowshoes, David was all thumbs. He finally managed, and they started back the way they had come. He tried to walk normally, but hastily at the same time.

He sneaked a peek over his shoulder. The two monks had not moved an inch.

Once they had put some distance between themselves and the monks, David asked Skye what was going on. In a low voice, she referred to the device on the monks' table. "That's a directional microphone. A top of the line Lucy model, in fact. We call them TM-87's. I've used them often."

"Then we're in trouble. And there were three monks back in town, right? If Moe and Larry are back there by the lake, where's Curly?"

They both agreed they didn't want to find out, so they quickened their steps down the path toward the parking lot. Running in snowshoes proved to be impossible. Their jerky gait burned up their energy but didn't add very much speed.

Panting, David glanced back over his shoulder again. Two brown figures leisurely kept pace with them in the distance.

CHAPTER 19
ELEVATION

MarsDay 93, 4:01 p.m.
(February 24, 1:30 p.m.)

    Sunshine had given way to dark storm clouds. A few snowflakes began to fall, buffeted by light gusts of wind. The forest branches came alive, ceasing to be objects of beauty, reaching out toward the hikers maliciously. The wooded ridge had become a dreary, foreboding place.
    David's lungs burned from exertion, but his legs still felt strong. He had stuck to his plan, jogging for an hour each morning for the past five days, and the results were already beginning to show. While he still struggled to take in enough oxygen, the rest of his body seemed willing to work on what was available.
    Unfortunately, Skye was unable to keep up with his pace. She fell a few steps behind, gasped for air, and finally begged him to stop. "I just can't breathe," she moaned. Her chest heaved, as she dropped to her knees in the packed snow of the narrow roadway.
    Their two pursuers stopped as well, a few hundred feet farther up the path. They seemed to be talking to each other. One was drinking from a plastic bottle. They gazed all about, while avoiding eye contact with David.
    Were these the men that killed Colcheck and Tarraz? He looked around for anything that might improve their situation.
    Fifty feet downhill, a colorful sign advertised a fork in the trail. Their trail bent to the left, and the Little Raven Ski Trail worked its way through the trees off to the right.

As if reading his mind, Skye asked, "Perhaps we should take the other trail? We could lose them in the trees."

David studied his map of the Indian Peaks Wilderness Area, pondering the question carefully. Toward the left, they would reach meager traces of civilization and safety only a mile ahead. To the right was a hundred thousand acres of rugged wilderness, though the Little Raven would soon cross the Sourdough Trail, which could also take them back to the parking lot. Even if they shook their pursuers somehow, they could easily become lost in the process and freeze to death at night, especially if the looming storm worsened.

He voiced his concerns and concluded, "They're too close behind for us to shake them very easily. Let's keep going toward the parking lot."

"I don't feel in any shape to scramble off the main trail, anyway," Skye agreed. "I just want to get back to the truck."

"Still, they can run circles around us while we're on the main path." David glared back at the monks. "I don't like this one bit. It smells like a setup, a trap."

"Is that your wargames experience talking?" she asked.

"Oh, you know about that, huh?"

"I probably know more about you than you know yourself. I've done my homework, Mister Almost-Had-To-Repeat-Fifth-Grade."

Suppressing a blush, David studied their immediate surroundings again. He noticed plenty of large boulders and new pine tree growth along both sides of the trail. The terrain might provide adequate cover for eluding their pursuers, but if they left the trail, the thick foliage would also hinder their progress.

He wished Jennifer was here. With her tactical prowess, she would find a way out of the predicament.

He looked down. Rocks could be a useful weapon, if one was desperate enough. He uncovered a few small stones and stuffed them into his coat pockets.

"Good idea," said Skye. "I also know you used to pitch on your high school baseball team."

David grimaced at the painful memory. "Then you must also know I set a school record for the highest walks-per-game ratio. I could never find the plate. 'Wild Dog Debacco' was my nickname."

Her breathing had nearly returned to normal. Reaching for his closest arm, she whispered, "David, I don't like this setup. But what can we do?"

She actually looked scared, but a brief flash of annoyance jolted him as he considered a new possibility. What if the monks were Skye's colleagues? Could she be using them as a false source of danger, trying to get closer to him, beating down his defenses so she could pry more information from him later?

As he helped her to her feet, he looked deeply into her eyes, where he saw genuine, unmistakable fear. His doubts melted away. He held her a little closer and a few moments longer than he should have.

"I didn't think anything could scare you. After all, you're a tough city girl. You've probably been in worse situations."

Skye shook her head. "This city girl is better at acting tough than being tough. And we aren't in a city. I'm totally lost here."

Fueled by her closeness, a warm, hormonal rush penetrated his chest deeply. He fought the unwanted feelings, while picking up his ski poles and looking down the path toward their destination.

"Let's get moving," he said. "Slower, this time. We might need our strength when we reach the end of the line."

Skye clung to him tightly, then eased away and took a few steps down the trail. David soon caught up to her. They took the wider roadway to the left, continuing their trek side by side at a slower, more sustainable pace.

Light snow continued to fall, blanketing the older, dirtier crust beneath. The woodland scenery continued its devious contradiction, sublimely beautiful, yet ominously silent. David would have welcomed sleigh bells and a multitude of happy, frolicking people, but the path remained deserted.

The trail flattened and widened a bit. Eventually, rounding a bend, he spied the parking lot only a short distance away. "At last," he sighed, while glancing back over his shoulder. Their pursuers had closed the gap and were less than a hundred feet behind.

"Get ready to jump into the truck, fast," he advised. "We might have the element of surprise briefly, if Curly thinks we took the other road up to the Brainard Lake base area."

"His buddies probably let him know exactly where we are."

David frowned. "Yeah. If they did, then they hold all the cards. We'll just have to see what game they're playing." He felt the reassuring weight of the rocks in his pocket.

As they reached the snow packed pavement, they hurriedly kicked off their snowshoes. Their equipment would only get in the way, from this point on. David concealed the shoes and poles behind a bush along the side of the road.

He hesitated, then took off his Vikings coat and added it to the pile. He hated to leave his arsenal of rocks behind, but the bright purple coat would be far too visible during the next few minutes. In their quest to reach their vehicle, stealth and quickness would be their best allies. His white t-shirt would blend with the color of the snow much better. Skye's black snowsuit stood out a bit, but that couldn't be helped.

He glanced back down the trail they had just left. The monks were nowhere in sight.

With Skye following closely behind, he carefully traversed several crusty snow banks along the near side of the roadway. To reduce their exposure, David didn't want to cross the road to the parking area on the other side until they were opposite their vehicle. The road curved gently to the left, so if Curly was lurking near the main barricade farther ahead, he might not see them until they were nearly home free.

Drawing opposite their vehicle, David drew up short, in dismay. Both rear tires of the vehicle were flat, and it appeared the front ones had been sabotaged as well. They had been completely outmaneuvered.

He pulled Skye closer to the trees along the side of the road. One look at her pale face told him that she had reached the same conclusion. They weren't going anywhere.

"What now?" she asked.

"There are other cars here. Maybe someone will come along soon, and we can hitch a ride."

"Or I could hotwire one."

David looked at her, surprised. "You know how to do that?"

"No," she sighed. "But I've seen it done. Once. And I've never been as motivated to try as I am right now."

Snowflakes accumulated on David's shoulders, dampening his light t-shirt and causing him to shiver. He needed to find shelter soon.

He studied the scene again, looking for anything that might be useful. He paid special attention to a blue, full-sized van parked next to their vehicle. Perhaps the rear or side door had been left unlocked.

Skye clutched his arm and gestured to the left. Two figures approached from the barricade area, one much taller than the other. Perhaps the couple was a man with his son.

"Here's our ride!" she said. "And right on time."

David fought an urge to step onto the roadway and race toward the newcomers. He held Skye back, as well. Their minimal concealment on the edge of the trees was still their best ally. The monks could be anywhere.

As the strangers drew near, David realized the "son" was actually a young man, probably in his early twenties. A wide grin and short, dark hair accentuated the exotic Asian lines carving his face. The taller "father" appeared to be a few years older. He possessed similar features, though his head was bald and he was much broader about the shoulders and waist. His face held a stern expression, adding to the father-son illusion. Both men wore faded parkas and thick boots.

When the men were a few feet away, David took a step toward them. This time, Skye pulled him back.

"They were at the rental car company when I rented the Vue," she hissed in his ear. "Coincidence?"

Her question was answered immediately, but not by David. The shorter man approached them and said, "Please to be coming with us."

"That was too easy," whispered David. Louder, he replied, "I don't think so. We'll catch the next taxi, thanks."

"Is so. You come with us," the shorter man stated confidently. The grin on his face was wider than ever. He tapped his parka pocket, which bulged outward slightly from a solid object inside. His massive friend circled and edged closer as well, cutting off their retreat.

A Subaru wagon pulled up beside the men, driven by another man with Asian features. The happy-faced man opened the rear door and gestured for them to enter. "We talk in car. Then you go."

"Then you go," his big friend repeated, with a hint of a smile cracking his face too, for the first time. Friendliness was obviously not the larger man's strong point. His expression looked strained and artificial.

The situation seemed hopeless to David. The others had superior numbers, weaponry, and tactics, even though their monk colleagues had vanished, if in fact they were colleagues. He and Skye had, well, nothing. David wasn't even wearing a coat.

"I guess we go," he said blandly, glancing at Skye in case she had better guidance to offer. Her blank stare and viselike grip on his upper arm confirmed that she didn't.

As they took a step toward the Subaru wagon, the back doors of the blue van across the roadway burst open. Three new figures in dark blue windbreaker jackets leapt to the pavement and moved to quickly surround their potential abductors. The new arrivals carried lethal looking, semi-automatic weapons.

"FBI! Nobody move!" barked one of the newcomers, an older man with a healthy crop of white hair and a no nonsense attitude of authority about him. He circled the Subaru and approached their group cautiously, with his weapon raised. A short blonde woman dashed around the front of the car. Her weapon was pointed at them as well. The third agent covered the driver of the car.

Caught completely off guard, their abductors had no choice but to raise their hands, very slowly.

Stunned silence led to awkwardness. David wasn't sure if he should raise his hands, too. He remained motionless, as did Skye, who still held his arm tightly. The Feds didn't seem to notice. They had eyes only for their abductors.

When he had recovered his voice, David commented wryly, "This parking lot is getting awfully crowded."

"Good timing," added Skye. "And you are..."

"FBI Special Agent Grissom," the white haired agent replied. "This is my partner, Dell." He gestured toward the woman who was instructing their abductors to place their hands on the hood of the Subaru. "The others are, uh, Mays and Thomas, I believe." He nodded toward the third agent, who was herding the driver of the car to join the others, and a fourth agent, whose side profile was dimly visible in the back of the van. The third agent took up a watchful station behind Dell.

"I doubt your timely appearance was accidental," said David. "So who are these other guys? And what about the monks?"

"Monks? I don't know anything about monks. These guys, I know only too well." He swatted the shorter abductor lightly on the ear. "Isn't that right, Trinh, my good friend. We've been watching you for weeks. I almost broke down and bought you some English language lessons."

The man responded, "You not hold us long. Diplomatic immunity."

"Yeah, they sure do look like diplomats, don't they, Dell?" The two closest agents shared a cynical laugh.

"We do nothing. Just go for walk." Trinh's glare pierced the agent.

"The last time I checked, carrying a concealed weapon without a license was against the laws of this great nation. And I know you don't have a license, my friend. Also, if Miss Fontaine and her friend are willing to testify, we can hold you on attempted kidnapping, too. That should be enough until we can dig up the evidence to charge you with murder. After we dangle that gem in front of your boss, he'll leave you sitting high and dry."

Trinh spat at the agent's foot. "You crazy! Mad! We not killers. We civilized police."

Grissom scoffed, "How many Falun Gong practitioners have you tortured and murdered lately? Oh, that's right. You and your 'civilized' thugs wiped out most of that peaceful movement years ago."

As he listened to the exchange, a hundred questions flooded David's mind. All he could put into words was, "Did they kill Tarraz and Colcheck?"

"That's what we figure," replied Grissom. "Am I to assume you're the third guy they were looking for, uh, Debacco?"

"Yes. David."

The agent nodded. "They would probably have killed you, too, if you had gone with them."

"Why?" asked David. "Who are they? And what do they want?"

Before replying, Grissom glanced at the other agents. "They work for the Chinese Ministry of Defense. We don't know exactly what they're up to, but we assume their objective is to interfere with the Mars mission in some way. Though it's been a real challenge, the FBI and CIA have pieced together some inside information about your Mars mission. So have others, like our civilized friends here. Perhaps you can help us fill in more of the missing pieces."

Skye still held David's arm tightly. With her other hand, she was fiddling with a button on a front pocket of her snowsuit, a button that looked a bit too large and opaque. He predicted that she was about to launch herself into investigative reporter mode. As a source of information, Agent Grissom was too good to pass up.

By this time, a thick layer of newly fallen snow covered Skye's hair and shoulders. David shivered, recalling his own coatless condition. Larger snowflakes fell more rapidly now, and the wind had died down.

He answered the agent, "I'll consider helping you. But first, I need to retrieve my coat. If you don't mind."

"Of course. But don't wander off too far."

He walked along the roadway toward the place where he had stashed his coat and their other equipment. Skye asked Grissom another question. The man responded at length, but David's attention had moved on to other matters. He was peering into the forest.

Through the snow and the trees, he barely discerned a man in a brown habit peering over the top of a large boulder. The monk watched the commotion on the roadway intently, while holding a small device near his mouth.

David reversed his direction and returned to the group. The fourth FBI agent had left the van to join the others, too. This new agent, armed and clothed like the others, looked very familiar. Apparently, Skye thought so, too. Upon noticing him, her voice stumbled and halted in mid-question.

Seeing their surprised expressions, Agent Grissom started to turn towards the fourth agent, but not quickly enough. The man raised the butt of his weapon and smashed it against the back of Grissom's skull. The impact made a dull, sickening noise. At the same time, the third agent, Mays, raised his weapon and shot Dell three times in the back. Gunfire echoes reverberated from the nearby mountain peaks as both agents dropped to the ground.

David had watched many soldiers "die" during his wargames. They always rose back upon their feet and slunk off the battlefield. Dell and Grissom didn't rise. His jaw dropped, and he knew he must have a stupid look on his face, but he didn't care. Two people had just been killed in front of him, for real, and he hadn't raised a finger to help them.

He tensed up his muscles, ready to leap at the nearest agent, the familiar-looking one. The man must have guessed his intentions because he stepped back and warned David not to do anything stupid. A semi-automatic rifle was leveled squarely at David's chest. The other agent continued to cover Trinh and his friends, who appeared to be just as surprised at the sudden turn of events as David was.

Skye found her voice first. "You do get around a lot. I didn't know you were an FBI agent." Her hands crept toward the ever-present gadget on her belt.

"Shut up!" the man barked, in a deep, husky voice, before redirecting his wrath toward the other agent.

"Moron! You were supposed to hit Dell from behind or shoot her in the chest. How are you going to explain an agent being shot in the back with another agent's weapon?"

Mays came to attention and saluted, while keeping his weapon leveled. "Major, Sir! Dell struggled with a chink, after Trinh surprised Grissom and took his weapon away. Then he shot her in the back. Sir!"

"Lose the salute, Mays. I'm not in the Army anymore." The man stepped toward Skye and ripped the box from her belt. "You won't be needing your stun gun."

David looked at Skye in surprise. So she hadn't been quite so helpless after all. Not today, on the occasion when they first met, or anytime between.

With her weapon removed, he didn't see any point in asking her about it. Instead, he refocused his attention upon Thomas, the Army Guy. As he did so, he suddenly remembered where he had seen the man before.

"I know you," he muttered to Thomas.

His short statement had an unintended effect. Army Guy leapt toward David and snaked out his leg. Before he knew it, David was lying flat on his back in the roadway, with an assault weapon pointed at his chest.

"How do you know me?" the man snarled.

David was too stunned to answer right away. Fortunately, Skye spoke for him. "He saw us together in Boulder, when I met you at Hapa a few months ago. Back when your name was Timmons, instead of Thomas."

"Oh." As unexpected as the man's initial overreaction had been, his immediate placation by Skye's words was even more dramatic. He backed away, looking clearly relieved about something.

Skye helped David back to his feet. He rubbed his knee where he had been struck, and cautiously put his weight upon it. His whole leg throbbed in pain but seemed pretty solid.

"So why did you kill them?" Skye asked, gesturing to the two FBI agents on the ground.

"They were in the wrong place at the wrong time. Too bad."

"And what are you going to do with us?" she asked.

"I don't have any orders concerning you, and your talents might still be useful. Maybe you'll get a second chance, if you're lucky. I warned you about sticking your neck out."

"What about David?"

Army Guy snorted. "He won't be a problem for much longer. But look at the bright side. When he's out of the way, I'll be up for a big promotion. Just in time, too."

"And what about these other guys?" Skye asked, gesturing to the three foreigners with their hands still on the hood of the Subaru.

"They'll be free to go, but they won't get very far. The FBI protects its own. After all, they did murder two agents and a civilian in cold blood."

Assuming he was the "civilian" who "won't be a problem for much longer," David's personal prospects were looking totally bleak. His only hope was to keep the man talking until he could find a means of escape. It was a desperately thin thread, but he clung to it, since it was all he could do.

"Didn't they kill Colcheck and Tarraz, too?" he asked.

Both men shared another good laugh. Army Guy finally said, "Sure, why not. But that was actually the beautiful work of my friend Mays, here. Ol' Grissom was wrong about a lot of things."

Mays added, "Suicides are easy. Colcheck was an extra challenge. I wanted to make it look like she was a real victim of the Indiana Strangler." The man's wide grin revealed that he enjoyed his work far too much.

Army Guy checked his watch and stated, "We've wasted enough time." He pointed at David. "Mays, after you kill him, leave the weapon for our fall guys without the ammo clip. Leave Dell's weapon without the clip, too."

Skye embraced David tightly around the waist and cried, "Wait! If you kill him, you won't find out who's running the Mars mission. You need him alive!"

Army Guy grabbed Skye by the wrist and ripped her away from David roughly, leading her toward the van. She struggled against him, but to no avail. He must have been stronger than he looked. Over his shoulder, he taunted, "Shepherd, the Mars mission, and its planners will soon be irrelevant. Kill him."

David frantically looked around for some miracle that might save him. Once again, the situation appeared hopeless. Mays was several feet away, out of his reach. The three Chinese men were closer, but they would be of no help. Judging from their earlier conduct, they would probably be delighted to help Mays pull the trigger.

Seeming nonchalant about the whole situation, Mays said, "Don't worry. I'll make it quick and painless."

As he started to raise his weapon, his eyes glazed over. Then he dropped to his knees and fell to the roadway, head first.

David couldn't believe what had just happened, but it didn't shock him quite as much as it should have. The day had already been filled with surprises. Somehow, he had a new lease on life, but he needed to act quickly to extend that lease.

With a snarl, he launched himself toward the Army Guy. Oblivious to what had happened, Skye continued to struggle, and the two had only covered half the distance to the van. David tackled the man from behind with the force of all his weight. They fell to the ground in a tangled heap. The semi-automatic weapon slid away, coming to rest near the back left tire of the FBI van.

David found himself atop the heap. Pressing his advantage, he pummeled Army Guy with several punches to the face, connecting twice. Then his opponent shifted his weight, raised his foot to David's stomach, and kicked him away. David lost his grip and crashed against the side of the Subaru. He managed to stay on his feet.

Skye was crouched beside the van. Looking over his shoulder, she yelled, "David, run!"

He didn't pause to turn around. Instead, he bolted forward, following Skye as she dashed between the van and their useless Saturn Vue. They both kept their heads low to the ground. Skye plunged into the forest on the other side of the vehicles, with David right on her heels.

They continued running for a few yards before David took the lead and veered to the right, following a narrow gully. Keeping his head down, he scrambled forward, his movement hampered by knee-deep snow drifts. A hail of bullets impacted some of the tree trunks and boulders nearby. He pushed Skye to the ground and covered her with his body.

A strange "twang" sound from ahead was followed by more bullets from behind. Then a loud explosion shook the ground. Back at the parking lot, chaos was breaking loose.

Not waiting around to watch the fireworks, he pulled Skye forward through the snow, keeping low. They continued along the gully, deeper into the forest.

Blood rushed furiously through his veins, bringing an almost euphoric sensation. He was alive and in his element, a situation where his wargames experience was useful. David was the runner on his Capture the Flag team, the person whose job was to quickly return a captured flag back to the home base while avoiding enemy ambushes along the way.

Though the current situation felt similar, the weapons were real. Also, he didn't have a home base awaiting him. In fact, he had no idea where he was going.

A small rock outcrop offered a good hiding place while Skye caught her breath and he considered their situation. They couldn't go back to the parking lot, and the roadway would be too dangerous as well. To make matters worse, David had started to shiver uncontrollably. He still had no coat to wear.

Though his blue jeans repelled most moisture, his legs and t-shirt were still sopping wet from melted snow, chilling him to the bone.

Could they find a backwoods cabin for shelter before he froze to death? Skye's warm snowsuit should protect her longer, but they would both perish if exposed to frigid, sub-zero temperatures overnight. With the coming of the snowstorm, the temperature had already plummeted within the past hour.

He recalled that the area northeast of Brainard Lake was almost as undeveloped as the wilderness to the south. Their chances of finding shelter in that direction would be poor. Even if they did find an isolated cabin, an overzealous landowner might shoot them for trespassing before they could explain the reason for their intrusion. People around these parts liked their privacy.

To the east, the small town of Ward offered their best prospects for reaching civilization. The town was five miles away, however, and he didn't know if he could walk that far before succumbing to the elements. Unless they followed the roadway, they would have to traverse rugged terrain.

Another explosion shook the earth, and an automobile hubcap whizzed past their rock outcrop. Surprised, David peeked over the top. The parking lot was still visible, only a hundred feet through the trees.

Skye climbed the rock and crouched close beside him. "We're right back where we started," she observed. "Only now you don't have a coat, and neither of us has snowshoes."

David spotted a brown and red patch on the forest floor only a few feet away. "Looks like one of the monks didn't make it." The man lay on his back, motionless. His brown habit was soaked in blood from a chest wound. "Perhaps he was carrying something useful. I'll bet he won't mind if I borrow his cloak, too."

"Be careful," Skye advised needlessly, as he slithered through the snow toward the fallen monk. David already intended to be careful, at least as careful as one could be while doing something so foolish.

Back at the parking lot, more shots were fired. He ducked, unable to tell where the bullets were aimed. All he knew was that none had hit him.

Reaching his target, he crouched and studied the dead man, noting his white hair and full beard. The man looked much older than David had expected. The brown, blood-soaked habit, slightly tattered around the edges, appeared authentic. A white shield logo, with two crossing keys, embellished the right shoulder.

As he gripped the garment, intending to slide the body back toward Skye behind the rock outcrop, one of the monk's hands locked onto his wrist. David's heart skipped a beat in surprise. The man was still alive. His heart skipped another beat when he saw the monk's free hand digging in an inside pocket. David jumped backward, easily freeing himself from the injured man's weak grip.

"Wait!" gasped the man, raising his head slightly and removing an object from his pocket. It wasn't a weapon, as David had feared. In fact, it was clearly a set of car keys.

"Take," the man said, flipping the keys feebly toward David. His head sank back to the ground. "Down the road, yellow van." Every word from the wounded man was clearly an effort. "Go with haste, brother."

David clutched the car keys and scrambled back to the outcrop. Along the way, he picked up the monk's weapon. The miniature crossbow-like device was half buried in the snow. Giving the keys and weapon to Skye, he left the safety of the rock again, crawling back towards the monk.

"What are you doing?" asked Skye.

"I'm taking him with us. We can't just leave him to die."

"Are you crazy? Let's get out of here!"

Following his instincts, David ignored her advice. When he reached the monk a second time, the man appeared to be unconscious, but breathing shallowly. David carefully lifted him onto his shoulder and limped back towards Skye.

The man wasn't very heavy, but the added weight made each step treacherous. David's injured leg screamed at him in pain from what he hoped was a deep bruise rather than something far more serious.

Through the dense underbrush and deep snow drifts, Skye forged a trail parallel to the road. David followed as quickly as he could. By now, the main parking area was quiet.

Keeping the roadway in sight, they dashed eastward. Another parking lot loomed ahead through the trees, slightly off the main pavement. Two identical yellow vans were parked side by side. The rest of the lot was deserted.

Skye pressed a button on the monk's key chain, and they heard a very welcome "click" from the farthest van as its doors unlocked. She dashed to the vehicle and slid open the side door. Then she jumped into the driver's seat and started the engine.

David followed, moving as fast as he could on his injured leg. He carried his burden to the open side door. With Skye reaching back to help, they gently laid the monk on the middle row of seats. Then David dove inside and slammed the side door shut.

Skye jammed the manual gearshift into drive and gunned the engine. As she turned on the main roadway, the van hit a patch of ice and skidded sideways, careening toward a shallow ditch. Fortunately, she regained control quickly and continued more cautiously, respecting the road's icy surface.

Kneeling beside the injured monk, David found a lever that reclined the middle seat to create a flat, bed-like surface. He carefully repositioned the monk and checked his injuries more closely. The man remained unconscious, and the only wound David could find was a bullet hole in his chest near his left shoulder. Judging from the rate of bleeding, the bullet had probably severed an artery.

David wasn't sure what he could do to help, but he took a chance that pressure on the wound might help to stop the bleeding. He ripped a strip of cloth from the bottom of the monk's habit, wadded it up, and held it against the wound. The man groaned loudly, but was otherwise unresponsive.

The next few minutes seemed like hours as David repeatedly glanced through the back window of the van, expecting to see a pursuit from behind. However, the roadway remained deserted. He relaxed a bit when they reached the Peak-to-Peak highway and Skye turned south towards Nederland. Conditions on the main road were better, and her speed increased.

"What are we going to do when we reach town?" asked Skye, breaking the tense silence.

They finally decided to go directly to the local medical center. Skye would seek help for the injured man. Remaining as inconspicuous as possible, David would walk back to his hideout. After Skye stashed the van, she would follow him.

The only problem with this plan was his lack of a coat. He wasn't about to walk around town in a blood-soaked t-shirt or brown habit, either. Fortunately, Skye found a thin wool coat liner on the floor of the front seat. It matched the one that the monk wore under his habit, right down to the strange monogram near the right shoulder. Removing his wet shirt, he put on the wool liner. It was scratchy, but warm.

With their plans made, David relaxed a bit and watched the majestic mountain scenery go by. Neither of them said much, as they internally processed the events of the past few hours.

David's leg still throbbed. He wasn't looking forward to the two-mile hike awaiting him after they reached town. Still, the walk would give him plenty of time to think, and possibly even some much-needed time to forget.

CHAPTER 20
REFLECTION

MarsDay 94, 1:55 a.m.
(February 24, 11:41 p.m.)

    Unable to sleep, Anna climbed the ladder to the lounge where Ollie was working on the main computer. She wore her usual staple, a maroon jumpsuit. Had she still possessed her long, blond hair, it would have been bedraggled this morning. Still half asleep, she had bypassed most of her morning wake up routine.
    Ollie commented on her early rising. She told him about her usual nightmare, but once again left out the part his voice had played. He was sympathetic, as always.
    While she moved slowly in the kitchen, fixing herself a cup of green antioxidant tea, Ollie invited her to watch the daily news dump with him. Prying her eyes open required a physical effort. She squinted at the wall display. A special "news upload" icon flashed in the lower right corner, indicating the computer was still receiving the regularly scheduled transmission from Earth. After the upload was complete, she settled down to watch the program next to Ollie on the couch, her tea in hand.
    The daily news program was always entertaining. Mission Support took great care and pride in seamlessly merging segments from television programs around the world. She usually enjoyed the special annotations, which added an appropriate touch of humor to even the most serious of events. Anna suspected the commentator was probably a secret member of the psych team.

The topic of the first news clip was usually relevant to the Mars mission, and today was no exception. The lead-in to the first clip was a short cartoon with an animated Queen of Hearts caricature screaming "Off with her head!" Fontaine's face was morphed with the image of the queen, to hilarious effect. Anna braced herself for another anti-mission diatribe.

Fontaine had chosen a dark setting for her report today. By the looks of it, she was in a parking lot. Anna could barely discern some pine trees in the distance. Fluffy snowflakes gently fell to rest upon her shoulders, glistening in the reflected light from the camera crew spotlights.

The parking lot resembled a war zone. Firefighters carefully doused the area around at least two smoldering vehicles, mindful of yellow police-tape streamers roping off the area. Sirens wailed in the distance.

Fontaine wove a fanciful story about FBI agents and Chinese spies. Her report also contained jerky footage from a button camera. The footage clips implied that several brutal murders had occurred, and the reporter made a vague reference to sabotage of the Mars mission.

Anna found the news segment interesting, but also confusing and largely irrelevant. Scenes of violence from Earth usually triggered her mental "off" switch.

One of the figures in the video clip caught her attention. It looked like David!

Another man confessed to two more murders. Then he received terse orders: "Mays, kill him." It wasn't clear who "him" was, but by now, her attention was riveted.

Some desperate pleas and a tantalizing reference to "Shepherd" confirmed Anna's growing fears. She watched a brief struggle, and the person wearing the camera ran into the woods. Then Fontaine's smirking face was back on the screen again, telling the world that one of the alleged Mars mission planners had just been murdered.

The circular walls of the *Perseus* closed in upon her, crushing her with relentless pressure. She felt helpless, isolated. If David was in trouble, or had been in trouble, what could she do about it? Absolutely nothing.

Ollie didn't calm her fears. "Looks like we might need a new Shepherd," he stated, bluntly.

Anna stared at him, horrified. Her whole world was turned upside down. She lurched to her feet and staggered over to the ladder, trying to reach the safety of her quarters where she could replay the news clip again.

David can't be dead. He can't be.

I'm the one taking all the chances. I'm the one out in space on the "dangerous" mission.

But people die every day back on Earth, too.

As she reached the safety of her cabin, her grief burst to the surface as wracking sobs. She buried her head in her pillow for a few minutes, until she regained some control and could think more clearly.

She didn't know for sure that David was dead. After replaying the news clip on her computer several times, studying the frames carefully, a glimmer of hope remained. It looked like he might have escaped his attackers. Was he killed later?

She had to find out, right now. Connecting her computer to the Mission Support virtual world, she queried Shepherd's location, but learned he wasn't online. Then she paged him and waited outside his office door in the main control room.

With each passing moment beyond the mandatory twelve-minute time delay of communications, her glimmer of hope faded. Soft Chopin music from the ship's library failed to soothe her fraying nerves.

Finally, mercifully, the ghostly image of David's avatar appeared before her. After watching Fontaine's report, Shepherd's transparency startled her, and she had to remind herself that his wispiness was only a computer artifact.

Shepherd invited her into his office, where they could talk in private. "David, is it really you?" she asked. Her trembling voice was barely above a whisper. At this point, she wasn't sure of anything. She counted off each second until he could reply, knowing she should have sent a longer message, but not trusting herself to say anything else yet.

"Of course it's me," he finally responded. "Aren't you supposed to be sleeping now?" David sounded the same as always, but a stifled yawn hinted that he had been sleeping.

She took a deep breath, willing her tense muscles to relax. After apologizing for waking him, she recounted the contents of the news dump.

Wait, wait, wait. This time, his response was even slower. He must have needed extra time to reflect upon her tale of woe.

"Good Lord, what can she possibly be up to, now?" he eventually said. Then he retold the earlier events, at length. He ended by stating that Skye was supposed to follow him back to his hiding place. She never showed up, and he had fallen asleep on the couch while waiting for her.

"That witch," hissed Anna, as her anger resurged. Fontaine's false claim was infuriating, but David's casual use of the reporter's first name caused her almost as much distress.

David continued, stating he had not seen Fontaine's report yet, so he would play back the news dump to the crew while he waited for her response.

She overlapped the end of his message with a few simple statements about how happy and relieved she was to find him still alive. Their communications medium, worse than a telephone connection, seemed grossly inadequate for projecting her true feelings. Besides, Anna had always been very uncomfortable with intimate phone conversations. While she had dated several men infrequently over the years, she had never found anyone she could bare her soul to, over the telephone, or any other way.

While waiting for David's next reply, she considered going back upstairs and telling Ollie the good news about Shepherd still being alive. But then David was back, talking in her earplug, assuring her all would be fine.

"As for Skye's schemes," he said, "if she wants the world to think I'm dead…fine. Who knows what her real intentions are, but her misdirection might buy me some breathing room."

"Playing dead is a pretty drastic step, don't you think?" she inserted.

His voice continued, "Things are getting out of hand back here on Earth." His voice was riddled with frustration. "It was bad enough when I was chasing shadows, like tiny little conference rooms, hackers offering cryptic advice, and reporters with hidden agendas. Now, I've got real Chinese agents, Army majors, dead G-men, and bleeding monks with spy toys all running amok."

"Army majors?" asked Anna. David hadn't mentioned anything about the military being involved.

Wait, wait. "Yes, I know playing dead is a drastic step…but it sure beats being dead." After a few more moments, he responded to her second question. "Thomas apparently used to be a major in the U.S. Army."

"And who was this Major Thomas? One of the FBI agents?" David had woven so many new characters into his story that Anna couldn't remember all of their names. While waiting for his reply, she replayed his earlier narration. Yes, Thomas was indeed one of the FBI agents.

"Yeah, he was one of the Feds, the fake one. Major Thomas was the guy who gave Skye the disk leading her to…wait a minute!"

Anna longed to know what David was thinking. Her own mind remained a confused jumble of murkiness, as she waited for him to continue.

Finally, he said, "Anna, I need you to do something for me. Promise me you won't tell anyone I'm still alive." His voice was soft, but filled with urgency.

"You mean, Ollie and Evelyn? Or the media?"

He continued, obliviously. "I don't want anyone to know, except Skye and the people I'm staying with. I suppose I'll have to tell Cass—er, Kahuna, too. Otherwise, she'll be out here on the next airplane, causing a huge ruckus."

"But your job?" she asked. "How will you run Mission Support if people think you're dead? What will you tell your support team?"

Her questions caught up to him. "Yes, exactly, don't tell Ollie or the commander. They don't need to know." A pause, then "I don't know what I'll tell my team. I'll think of something. Maybe I can reincarnate myself as a new avatar. That might work, if my security team goes along with it. I might be forced to tell them my plans, too."

"You don't trust your own security team?"

Anticipating her question, David revealed his earlier fears. Members of his support team might have been compromised, including security. He wasn't convinced his security team had done all they could to track down the details of Commander Day's incursion into Conference Room 4.

"And now we have another amazing coincidence," he continued, with grim overtones accentuating a hesitant voice. "My most reliable backup director goes by the alias, Major Tom. Could his real-world identity be Major Thomas, former Army guy, fake Fed, and murderous thug?"

Anna was speechless. The resemblance in names was uncanny. If his suspicion was true, David's paranoia was fully justified. Who could they trust, if his own backup director was trying to kill him?

She felt the *Perseus* shrinking again, but this time it was much different. The outer layer of the polyethylene shell was a security blanket, protecting her by wrapping itself around her. The immensity of the void beyond insulated her from the madness taking place back on Earth. Conspiring with David in hushed tones as she was, it felt natural to wrap her shell around him, too.

In the midst of her spiraling journey inward, a tiny voice of reason yanked her back to the present. "I don't buy it, David. It's too much of a coincidence. If Major Tom was really plotting against you, would he have chosen such an obvious alias? Given the popularity of the David Bowie song, surely anyone on the support team could have grabbed that name!"

Wait, wait, wait. "There was nothing obvious about it. I didn't learn about his background until I already had one foot in the grave. Dead men tell no tales."

"And loose lips sink ships," Anna responded, her way of admitting his speculation sounded reasonable. The consequences were alarming, though. If members of the support team were conspiring to carry out some agenda at odds with the mission plan, what could it be?

She asked if Thomas said anything else linking him to the Mission Support team, but her words overlapped his next statement. David planned to ask Skye for the raw footage from her button camera. The whole encounter with Major Thomas had happened so fast. He might have missed other vital clues.

Anna fumed again at the mention of Fontaine's name. Though she recognized her irrational, petty jealousy for what it was, her suspicions had also been aroused.

Just how close are David and the reporter?

Is this how she learned some of her inside information about the mission dangers and the ERV design?

Do I really know David well enough to trust him? What if Fontaine seduced him, physically?

What can I possibly do from afar to prevent her from sinking her hooks deeper into him?

Silence stretched for an eternity, while she considered their situation carefully, in light of David's previous remarks. Realizing he hadn't answered a very important question yet, she asked him why he didn't trust Evelyn and Ollie.

Wait, wait, wait. When he replied, he stumbled over his words in a most uncharacteristic fashion, as if ripping each syllable from his throat required a conscious effort.

"There are some other things going on—some contradictions. I don't know what to believe anymore. It's all so confusing. I wish I could share the details with you, but I can't. Please believe me—I want to—I want to share everything with you."

She had never heard him sound this way before. Perhaps his near-death experience had shaken him more deeply than she had realized. His contagious confidence seemed to have vanished. She wanted to hold him in her arms, comfort him, and tell him everything would be OK. But holding him was impossible, and she was certainly in no position to predict the future.

At least she could still comfort him. Uttering some soothing platitudes, she suggested perhaps he should talk to someone on the psych team.

Wait, wait, wait. "No! They're the ones who...well, I guess I don't trust them, either." David's reply had started boldly, and ended in a whimper.

"Geez, David, is there anyone left that you do trust?"

She cursed the delay of communications. How was anyone supposed to hold a conversation when you had to wait so long for each reply?

To fill the gap of silence, she started to say she trusted Evelyn and Ollie completely, despite some of the interpersonal problems they had run into. However, David was speaking again, too, so she paused in mid-sentence to listen.

"Regarding your shipmates, I have few hard facts, but there is one matter I can safely mention." He went on to describe the message from <chicken_little> leading him to discover the commander's location within an impenetrable room at Mission Support.

Intrigued, Anna immediately proposed a possible explanation. She had noticed that previous room layout changes didn't propagate back to the *Perseus* very well.

Suppose a support technician grew Conference Room 4, via a layout change. Then later, the technician shrank the room back to its original size. Due to the painful time delay of communications, the shrinkage wouldn't propagate to the *Perseus* instantly. The larger conference room would still exist locally within the *Perseus*, and Evelyn could enter it or remain inside. To David on Earth, it might appear she was located in a too-small room. Once the software update reached the *Perseus*, her avatar might even become trapped within the room.

After another time delay, David speculated about other permutations. Perhaps the room would continue to retain its larger size locally until the commander left it, or the software update might immediately warp her avatar into a "safe" room.

However, when the commander took her foray into the twilight zone, the round trip time delay was less than a minute. Anna's scenario was unlikely.

Despite this flaw, David's responses were much more enthusiastic than before. Though his avatar didn't reveal his emotions, Anna knew her theory had excited the man behind the mask. They traded more speculation along these lines for several message iterations.

What seemed to thrill him most was that her theory could be verified. All they had to do was set up an exact time to run a test. David would ask a support technician to create a new room for their exclusive use. Anna's avatar could enter the room, and a few seconds later, the technician could shrink the room down to less than one unit of size in each dimension. Then they could see what happened to her avatar in the virtual world on Earth, and also within the *Perseus*.

He did note at least two serious problems with their test plan, however. Buffer rooms might behave differently than regular rooms. Worse, the plan depended upon David successfully "reincarnating" his avatar first. While he was presumed dead, he couldn't ask the technicians at Mission Support to assist with any special projects.

They ended their conversation by trading some cautiously optimistic remarks. All would be well, with all mysteries ultimately revealed. She knew he was just trying to cheer her up, but she went along, willingly.

Sleep called to Anna. Her eyelids drooped as she checked the local time in the corner of her computer display. It was a few minutes before 4:00 a.m.; almost time to relinquish her quarters to Ollie.

She groaned in dismay. Sleep was out of the question until four hours from now, when Evelyn could take over the important duty of monitoring the ship's functions locally. Perhaps later, Anna could take a long nap on the couch in the lounge upstairs. Evelyn probably wouldn't mind.

CHAPTER 21
MASS

MarsDay 100, 4:00 p.m.
(March 3, 5:05 p.m.)

Wait, wait, wait. Within her media sessions and her conversations with David, it was what Anna did best these days.

Any second now...

Whoosh!

The background of the room containing her avatar faded, and a new room appeared. She was in the entryway to the central atrium at Mission Support, staring at the security guard and Lowell's telescope replica. Again.

She sighed. This was going nowhere. She and David had tried three different scenarios attempting to explain how Commander Day's avatar had gotten into a room too small to hold it. All had failed.

A soft tap on the door of her quarters broke her concentration. Ollie's voice said, "Workout time. Are you coming?"

"Be there in a minute."

Due to a mid-course trajectory adjustment earlier in the day, they had decided to shift their regular 3:00 p.m. workout back an hour. She finished a message to Shepherd, adding a description of the test failure to the end. Then she logged off and followed Ollie down to the EVA room. Her stress level had been high today, and she looked forward to a strenuous workout to burn off her nervous energy.

MarsDay 100, 4:54 p.m.
(March 3, 6:00 p.m.)

As he read about Anna's eventful day, David's thoughts crept back to his own busy schedule. Since his "death" a week ago, he had gone to great lengths to convince his support team colleagues the Shepherd avatar was now guided by a different real-world human controller than before. He had kept his old account because creating a new one would have required mapping all of his access codes. That would have been difficult without assistance. The act of creating a new account would have left footprints and unanswerable questions, too.

His first task had been to answer Cassie's fretful messages. She had heard the news about his death but had not believed the messenger. That hadn't stopped her from sending five messages, over the course of several hours. Each was more desperate than the previous one.

After Cassie was placated, she had helped him to word an emergency memo to all support personnel describing Shepherd's demise, in vague terms. David explained that the Shepherd account was a "group" account, so a new Shepherd had taken over the helm, one of several people with access.

Next, he set up a series of individual meetings with key staff members to "educate the new Shepherd" about the current status of the mission. He claimed that he was already somewhat familiar with the mission status, having worked closely with the previous Shepherd in the background as a contingency plan. David even used an audio algorithm on his computer that deepened his voice until it bore little resemblance to his own.

These meetings were mostly a waste of time, but he wanted to maintain the illusion of transition. Because of his new suspicions, he also wanted to review his staff, searching for other wolves in the pasture.

Most of the staff went along with the new arrangements without raising many questions. He had expected the security team to closely question the transfer of authority, but other than a brief interruption of his login abilities, security also seemed willing to accept their new leader. The only real difficulties came from the SEA steering committee, which didn't like being kept in the dark about contingency plans, and Major Tom, who had assumed he would be next in line to assume the directorship.

David had deliberated, at length, what to do about Major Tom. His first instinct had been to pull the plug on Tom's account immediately. However, he couldn't prove his able assistant was really former Army Major Thomas, nor could he readily see any way he could ever prove it unless Tom slipped up. Therefore, he decided to keep Major Tom within the fold and watch him closely for signs of disloyalty.

Retaining Major Tom was also motivated by practical considerations. If he was a bad apple, he wasn't the only one in the barrel. Tom could continue accessing the support team's virtual world through an accomplice. Removing his account would only warn him that his cover had been exposed. It would also clearly indicate that David was still alive, since only he and Skye could possibly know Tom's real-world identity, and Skye had no collateral with the rest of the support team.

No, it was much better to let his unknown opposition believe they had scored a victory. Besides, if Tom was innocent, David would still need his help running Mission Support.

David heard voices upstairs. Bill and Jennifer were probably home from work. A few minutes later, Jennifer poked her head through the doorway and asked what he would like for dinner.

"Something easy, that I can eat down here, please," he said. "I'll be busy for awhile."

She retreated, and David refocused his thoughts on the latest message from Anna.

> To: <shepherd>
> From: <microbrain>
> Subject: Test results
> Priority: High
>
> Hi Shep!
>
> What a day.
> Of course, you know our mid-course trajectory change maneuver was successful. I can't tell you how nervous I was about that. I'm not an engineer, and the very idea that one can modify the course of a spinning, tethered spacecraft goes against all intuition. Evelyn has explained the physics to me three times now, but still, I doubt and worry.
>
> The maneuvers just felt, well, wrong. Each time a thruster fired, it was like rising in an elevator shaft. There were a few gentle sideways bumps, as well. It actually felt a lot like the Space

Mountain ride at Disney World—a roller coaster in the dark, with hidden bends and rises. Scary. I'm glad we stowed away all loose items beforehand. Otherwise, we would have had quite a mess to clean up.

Evelyn and Ollie sure didn't do much to put me at ease. Talk about nerves—both were literally climbing the walls before and during the thruster firings. Ollie and I are about to do a late workout session. Maybe it will help him to relax. And me, too.

Our latest room resize test was a failure again, I'm afraid, at least from this end. It was just like the first two tries. I steered my avatar into the Daycare Center at the appointed time. A few minutes later, the ship's computer warped me from that room to the entryway in the central atrium. I tried to re-enter the Daycare Center, but it was too small.

It sure seems like the software synchronized the room shrinkage pretty well, without any bugs. If this is how the Conference Room 4 thing happened, the software must have been fixed over the past few weeks. Or Evelyn hit some scenario we haven't considered yet, like resizing the room so it would hold her, but no one else.

By the way, whose idea was it to name our test room the Daycare Center? Very funny. Talk about a useless room, within a virtual world...

Gotta run. Hugs...

Anna

So, Conference Room 4 remained a mystery. Perhaps he should just come right out and ask the commander what had happened. The direct approach still seemed like a mistake, though. If <chicken_little> and the commander were somehow connected, the wisest course was to tread carefully until he had fathomed their intentions.

Anna's description of the trajectory change maneuver interested him more than the results of the failed tests. David had probably been more worried about this event than the commander and Ollie put together. His team had worked around the clock, verifying the *Perseus* star tracker was constantly locked on to at least five guide stars. During his private meetings with the software technicians, he had asked each of them to check their systems again, looking for signs of infiltration or sabotage. They probably hated the new Shepherd by now, but the trajectory change was too good of an opportunity for potential saboteurs like <chicken_little> or Major Tom to pass up.

Stepping back, he forced himself to reconsider the facts. The thruster burn worked, so his fears had been unjustified. He had no proof that any saboteurs existed. The *Perseus* was now on a tighter trajectory toward Mars, though a free return to Earth would still be possible until a few days before arrival, when another minor course change would target the spacecraft for a precise aerocapture.

While the techies hadn't found any problems with the thruster timing software, they did uncover some minor, unrelated issues. Biometric and crew location data from the *Perseus*, for the evening of Mars Day 92, were found to be corrupt. The source versions of the data files, on the main computer in the *Perseus*, were also corrupt. Recent software changes had disabled the radiation sensor alarms in Commander Day's sleeping quarters, too. They attributed this problem to a simple coding error, but after the code was fixed, several sensors returned marginal readings and needed to be recalibrated.

Facts relating to Skye's report of his "death" warranted greater examination, too. He hadn't seen the reporter during the past week, and her media coverage of the Mars mission had been sparse.

Through Bill, he had received a short, snail-mail letter from Skye a few days ago. The note had helped to explain the reporter's actions on that eventful night seemingly so long ago. Elegantly handwritten sheets grabbed his attention from a corner of his desk. He picked up the letter and read it again, for perhaps the tenth time.

Bill,
    Please forward this letter to David. Contacting him this way seems safest at the moment. A paper letter can't be traced very easily.
    Thank you,
    - SF

David,
    I'm sorry if I worried you the other night. Rather than stashing the van and walking back to the house, I drove down to Boulder and

picked up a film crew from a local affiliate station. What excuse can I offer? I'm a reporter after all, and a story was beckoning.

I got back late and checked into a hotel in Boulder. Returning to Nederland might have seemed suspicious, if anyone was watching me. With you dead, I don't have any reason to be there. I hope you understand. It's time for me to be a good girl. Until we know how all those people found us at Brainard Lake, we should set up any future meetings very carefully.

You are probably wondering why I worded my news report the way I did. To avoid violating my journalistic integrity,...

David always laughed aloud when he read this part. He still couldn't reconcile the word "integrity" with some of Skye's past actions.

...I was intentionally vague. If people misinterpret my words and believe you are dead, perhaps it will steer unwanted attention away from you. Officially, I was referring to the monk guy that you tried to save. I'm sorry, but he died from his injuries, not five minutes after we arrived at the medical center.

Was he in league with Alpha or Beta? Who knows? But it's possible, and I'm leaning toward Alpha, so I labeled him an "alleged Mars mission planner." I've tried tracing his identity, without any luck. He carried no I.D., and his fingerprints didn't match any known felons. The van was reported stolen from an observatory parking lot in Tucson, Arizona, of all places. No leads there, either.

I'm mentioning these details in case they trigger some connections in your own mind. Perhaps you can spot something I'm overlooking.

Regarding Thomas and Mays, if they are still alive, I'm betting they will report back to their superiors that you were killed in the shootout. Watch the enclosed microdisk of our encounter with them, and note that Thomas referred to getting a "big promotion" after your death. That man seems like such an egotistical bastard that he might truly believe he killed you. Of course, if he checks the dead body at the morgue, he would immediately know otherwise.

Even if they remain suspicious, any lingering doubts might be enough to delay future violence. We should both be much safer until they can prove you're still alive.

I hope you caught my lead and figured out something to tell the people you work with. Sorry if this causes you any problems with the support team.

I'll contact you soon to arrange another meeting. We have a lot to talk about. I just got a new, scorching hot tip to follow up on. If it checks out, your Alpha friends have been very naughty.

- SF

The enclosed microdisk contained footage from her button camera, with the audio and video enhanced in some places. If he had read her letter ten times, he had probably replayed the footage 20 times. He felt that if he replayed it yet once more, he would gain some new insight.

He resisted the urge to play the recording again, referring to his notes instead. Mays identified Thomas, and they argued. David said, "I know you," prompting Mays to attack him.

David interpreted the unexpected response as another indication Thomas was Major Tom. Perhaps Major Tom had been worried that others on the support team already knew his real world appearance or identity?

Next, Skye referred to Thomas as Timmons. Either name by itself was meaningless to David.

Then Thomas mentioned the big promotion awaiting him after David was out of the way. David's interpretation of this remark differed from Skye's. He thought the choice of words made more sense if Thomas was Major Tom and was referring to his virtual workplace. Once Shepherd was out of the way, Major Tom expected a promotion. He would become the new Director of Mission Support.

Yet, why was that so important to him? Would sabotaging the Mars mission be easier for him if he was the director? If so, then how? David couldn't think of any way the director could uniquely and decisively sabotage the mission. His job reflected the efforts of the technicians who really ran the show, accomplishing the directives of the steering committee. By implementing those directives poorly, a bad director could gum up the works…but the crew in the *Perseus* would hardly be inconvenienced. The mission would continue.

The flip side of the coin still made more sense to David. A director could influence the mission more by the things he "didn't" do. If others had already found a way to sabotage the mission, all Director Tom had to do was sit back and let it happen. This line of reasoning strongly implied an active director like David had the ability to piece together subtle clues and figure out what was going on.

Back in David's notes, Mays confessed to murdering Colcheck and Tarraz. Then Mays was ordered to kill David. Thomas said some tantalizing words about the mission and its planners soon being irrelevant. More than anything else, this statement had fueled David's paranoia about sabotage during the mid-course trajectory change maneuver.

But it wasn't. What could Thomas have meant? Was something else plotted? Something unrelated to the mid-course change?

If so, it would probably happen very soon. But what could it be?

Another solar flare? While more flares were likely, they couldn't be predicted in advance, and the crew had already survived one.

Unless...

What if the software error disabling the radiation sensors was deliberate?

Who cares? The radiation sensors are simple warning devices. The shielding around Commander Day's sleeping quarters is still intact.

Or is it?

The technicians had recalibrated several sensors because their radiation counts were skewed toward the high end of the normal range. If the sensors had been correct, the real problem could be a lack of radiation shielding around Commander Day's quarters.

He quickly fired off a message to the technicians who had worked on the problem, asking if this scenario was possible. Immediately, he regretted sending the message. Surely the technicians had already considered this possibility and discarded it. He was slipping into micro-management, a style he had tried desperately to avoid.

Jennifer brought him a heaping plate of beef stroganoff. He had barely started eating when the reply came.

His scenario was impossible. Nine water tanks provided most of the radiation protection around the sleeping quarters. Draining any of these tanks would require a crew member to manually close a valve in a hard-to-reach corner of the EVA room. Excess water would also be detected in the main holding tanks. The crew activity logs indicated the last person to go near the valves was Ollie, on Mars Day 78, during a monthly maintenance check. The solar flare and CME occurred later, and the commander was still alive. Therefore, the valves must still be closed.

Ah, but some of your crew data was corrupt for the evening of Mars Day 92. Therefore it's NOT impossible. Only extremely unlikely.

Unfortunately, the crew data from Day 92 couldn't be restored. His line of speculation seemed to have reached a dead end.

Feeling another headache coming on, he decided to take a break and finish his dinner upstairs. He sat down at the table with Bill and Jennifer, eating in silence until Jennifer asked how his day went. Once he told her about the trajectory change maneuver, everything after that spilled out as well. When he got to the part about his dead end with the radiation shielding issue, Jennifer sat back and laughed.

"What's so funny?" he asked harshly, more than a bit irritated by the whole matter.

"You are. You can't see the forest because all the trees are in the way, David." His stare became more questioning, and he invited her to continue.

"Two things," she said. "First, Cassie told me her psych team gets all the crew location marker information, too. They probably have a good copy from MarsDay 92."

He had completely forgotten about the psych team. They were always watching the crew's movements closely, running the raw data through their sophisticated, black-magic behavioral models. He promised to send Cassie a message, immediately.

"And the second thing?" he asked, hoping it wasn't as glaring an oversight as the first had been.

"If you want to find out whether those water valves in the *Perseus* are closed, just ask Commander Day to check them."

As another oversight, this was far worse. David symbolically beat his forehead on the kitchen table. "I can't believe I could have overlooked that," he groaned. "I guess I'm too wrapped up in all the internal Mission Support, virtual world stuff that's going on."

He thanked Jennifer and excused himself from the table. "I have some messages to send," he called over his shoulder as he headed downstairs, two steps at a time.

That night, David didn't sleep well. Drifting in and out of a light, restless slumber, he speculated about the responses to his inquiries from Commander Day and Cassie. Would either of them find anything? Or was he on another wild goose chase? The urge to get up and check his messages almost overpowered him several times.

Could the commander have planted these vague clues as another phony drill? Perhaps she was testing Mission Support's problem solving capabilities? She or Ollie had run several drills, though after the first week of the mission, each simulation had always been announced in advance.

When morning arrived, his feelings of unease persisted. A strong cup of coffee perked him up, masking some of the weariness in his body, but doing little to calm his nerves.

Back in his office, he circled around his computer display, sizing it up, as if it would bite him if he got too close. That display might soon tell him the answers to the disturbing questions causing him to lose sleep. If he was piecing the right clues together this time, the ramifications for the Mars mission would be devastating.

He connected to Mission Support and found his incoming queue contained 35 messages. One from Cassie had an "emergency" priority label, as did another from the commander. His uneasiness deepened.

Anna's regular wake-up message would have to wait. He opened the emergency message from the commander first.

To: <shepherd>
From: <alice>
Subject: Valve status
Priority: Emergency

Shepherd -

I checked the cutoff valves in the wall between the EVA room and my sleeping quarters. You were right. One of them was closed, and the corresponding water tanks were dry.

Obviously, we have a serious problem. There's no way anyone back on Earth could have done this. Either Ollie or Anna must have closed the valve by hand, intentionally. Or both of them.

There's no mistaking their intent, either. Whoever did this wants the next solar flare to kill me.

Yet, they also messed around with the sensor software. Ollie could probably have done that himself. Anna would have needed an accomplice back on Earth, perhaps the person she has been spending a lot of time with at Mission Support? The previous Shepherd was investigating that connection. Kahuna can provide details, if you haven't been informed about that issue yet.

My gut instinct leans toward Anna being the guilty party. Her attempt to kill me would fit the pattern the psych team warned me about. Also, she is intimately familiar with the freshwater tanks and the wastewater recycling system.

What do we do next? Unless we want to scrub the mission right now, which I'm NOT prepared to do, I suggest we keep Anna and Ollie in the dark. Rather than having an immediate confrontation, let's wait and see what happens. The guilty person might slip, and we might find a way to salvage the mission. Or...motivations may change, after we pass the point of no free return.

I'm tempted to open the valve and restore the shielding to my quarters. Taking an extra dose of solar radiation for the rest of our voyage doesn't sound too appealing. However, the dose should be harmless, well within safe limits, until radiation from the next flare or CME hits. Therefore, I suggest keeping the valve closed, and the status quo preserved. Again, let's just wait and see what happens. If we do encounter radiation from another flare, I can open the valve quickly and flood the water tanks.

Perhaps I'll schedule another unplanned drill soon: a flare alert. Whoever did this, let's feed them some rope and let them hang themselves.

By the way, I've verified the excess freshwater is indeed stored in the overflow tanks in the dome above the lounge. Those tanks are supposed to remain empty until we reach Mars and fill them with melted ground ice. Anna should notice this eventually, during her biosystem verification task, if she's careful enough. Ollie should also notice the closed valve in his next maintenance check. It will be interesting to see if one of them alerts me to the problem.

These next three months will be long ones, assuming Anna's psych issues are what's behind all this. If Ollie is guilty, well, this might be a short trip. With his engineering skills, he could do almost anything. Maybe he won't, if he thinks I'm living on borrowed time.

- Commander Day

With his worst fears confirmed, David sat back to ponder the situation. His first reaction was a sense of amazement at the commander wanting to continue the mission, sharing her tiny habitat with a potential murderer. On the other hand, what choice did she have? Even if they used their free return trajectory, their slingshot around the Sun and voyage back to Earth would last more than 20 months.

He could readily understand why the immediate suspicion fell upon Anna, given the beliefs of the psych team. However, David was reasonably certain Anna didn't have an "accomplice back on Earth" amongst the support team. He had checked the logs. Most of her virtual world connection time had been spent with himself or Cassie.

Besides, closing the water valve and recalibrating sensors were deliberate, premeditated acts. Mentally disturbed or not, could Anna have been so coldly calculating?

He recalled the second emergency message, the one from Cassie. Perhaps it would help him to prove Anna's innocence. Hoping for the best, but fearing the worst, he opened the message.

To: <shepherd>
From: <kahuna>
Subject: Crew activity logs
Priority: Emergency

Shepherd -

The psych team copy of the crew location logs for MarsDay 92 is intact. I'm attaching the annotated summary. The logs speak for themselves.

Let me know what you want to do. Sounds like you are going to need some serious advice, if Commander Day confirms your suspicions of sabotage.

- Kahuna

The attached logs revealed the crew shared the lounge and kitchen area for two hours, on the evening of Mars Day 92. At 7:30 p.m., Anna retired to her quarters. The commander worked on the computer in the lounge, and Ollie was in the kitchen. A few minutes later, Ollie visited Anna in her quarters, stayed briefly, and returned to the kitchen and lounge area.

At 10:00 p.m., the commander relocated to the EVA room, where she exercised for an hour. She spent the rest of the evening in her quarters. Ollie remained in the lounge until 5:00 a.m. the next morning, an hour after his shift was supposed to end.

Meanwhile, just before midnight, Anna left her quarters. For two minutes, her location bracelet placed her in the EVA room near the section of the inner wall containing the water valves. Then she returned to her cabin, staying there until 5:00 a.m. the next morning. After 2:00 a.m., the contents of the crew activity log matched the version at Mission Support exactly. Internal checksums were consistent throughout.

David reviewed the activity log several times, looking for some hidden ambiguity to cast doubt upon its stark, incriminating evidence. He willed the text to be different, but the words remained, and the conclusion was clear. Anna was the only person who could have sabotaged the radiation shielding around the commander's quarters.

Yet, this scenario didn't make sense. Or at best, it was incomplete. Anna didn't possess the technical skills to reprogram various sensor systems. She would have needed help from someone at Mission Support. Her accomplice couldn't be Cassie, for the same reason—his sister didn't possess the right skills, either. Who else had Anna spent a lot of time with?

He looked through the support team logs, noting Major Tom was on duty the night of Mars Day 92. No big surprise there, though any connection between Anna and Major Tom led immediately to alarming implications. He sent the security team a note, asking them to look for potential linkages between the two accounts. Proving Anna couldn't have reprogrammed the sensors would be difficult, but it was currently her only defense, and he vowed to leave no stone unturned in pursuing it to its conclusion.

Having several pieces of hard evidence staring him in the face had proven to be even more frustrating than sifting through the murky innuendo of the past. The facts seemed to fit together in obvious ways, but were they the only ways? With his philosophical training, he was all too aware that reality was often a fleeting illusion, a specter given substance by personal preconceptions.

Examining his biases coldly and rationally, he came to a swift conclusion. *I'm in love with Anna. Head over heels.*

He wasn't sure exactly when their online relationship stopped being a harmless activity, a mild breaking of the crew fraternization rules, and became so much more meaningful to him. Yet it had. And now, he needed to face the consequences.

A second fact was just as obvious.

I've been lying to the commander and Cassie about the relationship. My tiny little fib has been growing, and the lying must stop. Now.

He sent Commander Day a response to her previous message, supporting her decisions and her intended future actions. He also attached the incriminating crew activity log, but he urged her to keep an open mind about Anna's involvement. Anna's only "accomplices" at Mission Support, people she spent a lot of time with, were Cassie and the previous Shepherd.

His conscience forced him to continue typing a painful death march of one word at a time. He explained the previous Shepherd's online relationship with Anna, leaving nothing out, at least from a pseudo-second-hand point-of-view. Before he could change his mind, he included Cassie on the message and sent it.

The deed was irreversible, and his conscience applauded, yet the rest of him felt like the worst scoundrel in the universe. His relationship with Anna was a private matter, and therefore, he felt he had betrayed the woman he loved. When she found out, she would probably be hurt and offended.

Or worse. David realized he had just made a mistake. His confession was a subtle trap. If Anna learned about it, she would wonder why the "new" Shepherd felt the need to tell everyone about the "old" Shepherd's relationship. Assuming she would ever talk to him again, how could he justify the urgency? Would he be forced to explain, "Oh, sorry, honey. I did it to give you a flimsy alibi, because someone is trying to murder the commander, and you're the prime suspect. I hope you understand." Or would he be forced to lie directly to Anna, too?

Tell a lie, confess, tell more lies, and confess. Oh, what a tangled web we weave...

He sent another message to Cassie and the commander, imploring them to keep the contents of his previous message in the strictest confidence. He included his "don't let Anna know we suspect her" excuse to explain his request.

In for a penny, in for a pound...

What other tired clichés could he apply? What other dirty laundry should he air? After more deliberations, he composed a third message to Cassie and the commander, revealing the relevant details of the previous Shepherd's interactions with Skye. He also asked the commander about her incursion into Conference Room 4.

As his hand hovered over the key to send the message, he hesitated. The employment clause in his contract was still a sword of Damocles, hanging over his head. Besides, the commander still courted her own mysteries that he didn't understand completely. He deleted the message without sending it.

Mental exhaustion forced him to take a break. He wandered upstairs to the kitchen and solemnly pulled three Fat Tire beers from the refrigerator. One was for Anna, one was for Cassie, and one was for the commander, the three people he had wronged the most.

He put on his coat and stepped onto the large wraparound deck on the west side of the house. The deck provided a comfortable place to sit and enjoy the sunny winter afternoon. A chilled breeze wafted through the pines. He imagined himself carried away to happier destinations.

After arranging his three beers in a straight row, he twisted the top off the nearest one, the one for Anna, and took a cautious sip. When it came to alcohol consumption, David knew he was a total lightweight. At this high altitude, one beer counted as two. Later in the day, when Cassie raked him over the coals, he planned to be quite drunk.

CHAPTER 22
SIZE

MarsDay 141, 4:11 a.m.
(April 14, 9:00 a.m.)

On mornings when David was having trouble concentrating on the latest mission status reports, he almost regretted how "efficient" his schedule had become. Over the past six weeks, he had read reports every morning. At 11:00, he went jogging. After he returned, he ate a light lunch. The afternoons were always filled with meetings, planning, and whatever other work was necessary. Every evening, if he had time, he visited with Bill and Jennifer and watched the news.

His jogs took him through some remote, heavily forested terrain to the south of Nederland. He liked late-morning because he wouldn't meet many people on the trails. His schedule also provided him with a solid deadline to finish reading the morning status reports.

Today, however, the plan was breaking down. Though he had two hours left, his present state of distracted apathy almost guaranteed he wouldn't finish the reports on time.

He missed his freedom. He also missed the innocence in his relationship with Anna. Following Cassie's advice, he had tried to distance himself from Anna emotionally. Lately, he even found himself daydreaming about Skye more often than Anna.

His relationship with Skye remained strictly professional, but he had glimpsed brief moments of sensitivity behind her brusque, annoying facade, enough to make him long to know her better. Objectively, his feelings for her oscillated wildly between contempt and adoration. He recognized the signs. Such abrupt swings could only mean he was slipping, falling under her spell, becoming her pawn or worse. He was starting to make up excuses for her past actions, or even agree with them in some cases.

Grunting with open distaste, he sat up in his chair and swivelled over to his computer. It was time to enlist the assistance of the Love Doctor. He checked Cassie's public schedule and made an appointment to talk with her later in the day.

With a few more keystrokes and pointer movements, he browsed Fontaine's web site, looking unsuccessfully for any new messages. Since Skye believed some of her network colleagues were watching her moves closely, they had worked out a discrete communications protocol where she would leave subtle pointers to encrypted messages on her USNN web site. He would respond by meeting her in a singles room on the Internet at a time of her choosing, where their verbal chatting would be difficult to trace.

Most of their recent message exchanges had been about cargo manifests, a safe but extremely unromantic topic. Due to a tip she received a month ago, Skye was investigating whether some of the engine nozzles and science equipment in the initial cargo shipments to Mars had been left behind on Earth. Even after visiting a dusty warehouse near Colorado Springs and failing to find the equipment, Skye pursued this new angle vigorously, embarking upon an effort to track the flow of all mission supplies through the SEA. She hoped to learn more about the goals of the Mars mission planners based on what equipment had been sent to Mars.

For probably the tenth time, David reconsidered his decision to provide her with all his relevant cargo and supplies information. Was he simply honoring their agreement? Or was some part of his decision based upon a weird, psychological need to be of value to her?

No, he hadn't sunk that far yet, though it might be just be a matter of time. More than anything else, Skye's latest investigation seemed like a harmless distraction. It would keep her busy asking questions that led nowhere.

The cargo wasn't in the warehouse because it was on Mars. He had talked to a half-dozen SEA inspectors who had signed various manifests prior to the cargo vehicle, ERV, and backup habitat launches two years ago. All vital equipment had been present and accounted for. Also, his orbital mechanics team boasted that the flight trajectory of each vehicle was nearly perfect, a feat only possible if the mass of each vehicle was exactly what it was supposed to be. The laws of physics guaranteed that no mass was left behind on Earth.

Seeking a distraction from his muddled thoughts, he turned online, to the daily news dump.

- "Senator Tyler (R – Co) Believes Firm Terrorist-Mars-China Link" (usnn.com)
- "DoE Abandons Wave Power Generation Plan Over Endangered Turtles" (cnn.com)
- "NASA Management Protests Budget Cuts" (cnn.com)
- "Greene, Eco-Activists Praise DoE's Turtle-Friendly Decision" (Reuters)
- "Latest Reality Show Sizzles: 'Green Mile'" (e.com)
- "Lunar Accident Investigation Board Targets NASA Culture" (space.com)

Reading the USNN article, his thoughts slipped back to Skye. He wondered what she was doing at this moment. Probably, she was hard at work, badgering some unsuspecting scientist or putting words into the mouth of a little old lady in Boca about the evils of spending public tax dollars to fund NASA's second attempt at lunar exploration.

Or maybe she was doing something really useful, like following up on her previous leads about the three Chinese "policemen." He recalled being quite impressed that her media connections had tracked the men down so quickly. Within a few days of their encounter, she had learned the men worked for a branch of the Xinhua News Agency, a legitimate organization and the propaganda arm for China's ambitious manned space program. They quickly dropped out of sight, however, and Skye's sources had been unable to find them. Either their employers had arranged for them to disappear back into the teeming throngs of one billion countrymen, or the FBI had found them first, as Army Guy had predicted. Either way, David didn't expect to see them again.

Their motives were of far greater interest. Why would they try to abduct him? What could they hope to gain? If it involved the Chinese space program, why did they care about the Mars mission at all? China would soon have its own planet, or rather, a small moon. Within four years, the Chinese were expected to establish a permanent research outpost near the south pole of the Moon, annexing the entire polar region.

NASA had restarted its own lunar efforts too late and lost too much of their aging workforce from the Apollo era. Barring any unforeseen catastrophes within the Chinese program, NASA would never catch up. Once China claimed the only piece of prime lunar real estate, the game was over...on that world, at least.

For the near future, Mars would be a different story. With a surface area equal to the Earth, a 24-hour day/night cycle, a thin atmosphere, and abundant water supplies, no nation could blockade another by occupying all the prime development sites. If one knew where to find and utilize them, energy and resources would be freely available over most of the planet. Knowledge, technology, and "strategies for living" would become valued treasures on Mars, as well as the most lucrative product exports.

If the Chinese hoped to stifle this juggernaut by interfering somehow in the initial exploration mission, they were due for disappointment. They might as well try to stop the flow of the mighty Yangtze River with a cork.

Oops—bad analogy, David—they completely dammed that river years ago.

Shaking his head again, he returned to the mission logs and high-level summaries. As usual, he searched for patterns, and for connections between what might seem to be unrelated events. This was how he had found the problem with the radiation shielding around the commander's quarters, and he was convinced it was how he would find the next problem as well.

Fortunately, that next problem had not yet materialized. The Mars mission logistics proceeded according to plan. Several minor equipment failures had been encountered, but these were quickly diagnosed by the support team and fixed by the crew. The hardware issues seemed to be caused by normal wear and tear, and were well within the realm of statistical probability.

Mother Nature had also cooperated. The space weather forecasters had observed two large CMEs last month, but both had been directed away from Earth, Mars, and the tiny speck of plastic and humanity coasting between. The impact on the crew had been minimal.

Today, the crew continued their regimen of planning, study, exercise, and communications with Earth. Their interpersonal relationships had been more relaxed lately. If David hadn't known about the underlying psychological issues or the incident of attempted sabotage, he would have believed the crew was coming together as a functional team.

He searched the daily logs for new clues about the relationship between Anna and Ollie, but didn't find anything useful. The psychologists at Mission Support were deeply concerned that they were forming a close alliance against the commander, whose aloofness didn't help in breaking down barriers. David longed to talk with Anna about it, but Cassie had insisted he let the psych team handle the matter.

Besides, the time delay of communications made two-way, real-time conversations far too frustrating. He and Anna still traded recordings or text messages, but these exchanges did little to further their relationship and bring them any closer. If anything, the one-way messages starkly emphasized the growing physical distance between them.

The font on his computer display started to drift in front of his eyes again. Some of the words and ideas in the logs partially registered within his consciousness. Much was lost. Out of necessity, he found himself reading the noteworthy passages several times. Frustrated by his lack of focus, he decided to take a break.

Shepherd left his office and plopped down into the velvet director's chair near the back wall of the main support room. He watched the bland interactions of the support technicians for a few minutes. The staffing level was lighter than usual.

Will history remember these good people, and their dedicated efforts? Will the entire mission be marked as a turning point for humanity? Or will we become a footnote within the history texts, grouped with other failed exploration attempts?

After brooding on these questions, an urge to change his real-world scenery overpowered him. His jogging time wasn't until another hour. Having nothing better to do, he went upstairs and refilled his coffee cup. Then he returned to his desk, only slightly refreshed, but ready to get back to work.

As he directed his avatar to rise and pivot toward his office, David sensed a shimmering in the corner of his field of view. The disturbance was near the open doorway between the support center and the hallway outside. By the time he turned his avatar back toward the doorway, however, the door had closed and the ghost was gone.

That looked like a transparent avatar. One of the crew members?

He queried the location of Commander Day. Not only was she online, but to his dismay, her avatar was located in Conference Room 4. Out of habit, he tried warping into that room and failed again. He shrank his avatar as far as possible, and the warp action still produced the same, familiar error message.

If Commander Day was in limbo within Conference Room 4, who was in the hallway outside the main support room? Ollie's sleep period had just begun, and he wasn't online. Anna was, however, and her avatar was located in an adjacent hallway.

So I saw Anna. Her daily duty shift has just started. I wonder why she's roaming the halls? And why didn't she stop and visit?

Could she be spying on me?

He decided to do a little spying of his own, by warping his avatar directly into the hallway where Anna was last detected. A moment after he warped, he almost fell out of his chair in surprise. Anna's avatar was right in front of him, nose to nose. Then she was gone, vanished. David looked around and spotted a rapidly retreating figure farther down the hallway. She had passed right through him, rudely, without even pausing.

Of course, stupid—she didn't see me. In her local, Perseus *copy of the virtual world, I won't be in this hallway until the one-way time delay has passed, over nine minutes from now.*

Perhaps she hadn't seen him in the main support room earlier, either. But she should have, since he hadn't moved for some time.

Using the time delay to his advantage, he followed her and watched her movements, hoping she wouldn't remain in one place for a long time. Her avatar halted and opened a door farther along the hallway. Then she turned, rounded a bend, and raced down another hallway. Shepherd was right on her heels.

This pattern repeated for several minutes, until she had paused in front of almost every accessible doorway in the support center. Anna was obviously searching for something or someone.

Her travels eventually brought her into the atrium at the center of the complex, where she paused in front of the security desk. Then she abruptly disappeared. David queried, and found she had warped to the lounge within the virtual *Perseus*. In fact, her physical reality location now matched her virtual location.

The virtual *Perseus* was usually off limits to casual Earthly avatar visits. Since David didn't have any official reason to be there, he warped back into his office, where he monitored the location of Anna and the commander for several minutes. Neither moved, and he soon gave up the diversion.

While reading his messages, he was surprised to receive a new one from Anna.

To: <shepherd>
From: <microbrain>
Subject: It's happened again...
Priority: Medium

Hi Shep!

Soon after starting my solo shift, I logged on the support computer to check the status log. But first, on a whim, I queried Evelyn's location. Even though it's the middle of her sleep period, she's online too, in Conference Room 4 again. Since that's impossible, she must be somewhere else, so I looked around the complex for her. I don't have access to every room, but I checked wherever I could. I couldn't find her anywhere. And no, I couldn't enter Conference Room 4, either.

I'm really tempted to page her or go downstairs and knock on her door, but what if the support system is screwy and she's not online? She's probably sound asleep, and I shouldn't wake her unless it's an emergency. So here I sit, feeling silly, wondering what I should do.

What do you think—should I disturb her? Or...since you have permission to access more rooms at the support center, could you look for her?

This is just like something crazy out of Alice in Wonderland. If that conference room had been labeled a "Garden" instead, I would soon expect to see the Queen of Hearts running around the hallways of Mission Support. And I don't mean Fontaine.

Time for me to check my little microbe friends and see how they are feeling today. Probably the same as yesterday, I hope.

Hugs...

Anna

Anna's message solved one mystery, but added another footnote to the buffer room saga. David checked the commander's location again and was partially relieved to find she was no longer online.

He responded to Anna's questions, suggesting they drop the issue for now and focus on today's tasks. He also included some fluffy, Cassie-induced wordage meant to refocus Anna's attention upon the mission.

Now that Cassie was finally speaking to him again, she had agreed the online relationship between David and Anna must continue. Obviously, Anna strongly needed companionship. Cutting off their relationship abruptly might trigger a severely negative reaction. Instead, his sister had advised him to gradually wean Anna's attentions away from the relationship by refocusing her excitement upon Mars, emphasizing the anticipation of their arrival and the thrill of what they might find during their future explorations.

For at least the fourth time, David tried to concentrate on clearing his backlog of messages. This time, however, his tingling intuition was getting in the way. He couldn't shake a feeling he was overlooking some tiny detail related to Anna's pursuit of the commander. The whole episode seemed strange and surreal.

He eventually reread her message. Then he leaned back in his chair, closed his eyes, and lapsed into thought. Soon, he realized what had been bothering him. It was the reference to Alice in Wonderland.

He hadn't read that story since he was a child. Obviously, the commander was fond of it, since she had named her avatar <alice> and made occasional references to the storyline or some of the colorful characters.

Sifting through his childhood memories, he recalled Alice had wanted to reach a beautiful garden but was too big to fit through the doorway. The similarity to his current situation was uncanny. Was the commander playing a game with the support team? If so, the book might contain some clues. He couldn't remember how Alice had reached the garden, but it had something to do with shrinking and growing.

He found a copy of Alice in Wonderland on the Internet. Then he sat back to read.

MarsDay 172, 7:00 a.m.
(May 16, 8:21 a.m.)

After sending her last media transmission for the morning, Anna looked around the empty lounge area. Something seemed out of place, but her casual inspection came up empty. An icy shiver raced down her spine. The *Perseus* seemed colder than usual this morning, but she checked the computer and found the temperature was a normal, balmy 72 degrees.

The most likely cause of her unease was the upcoming *Perseus* course correction, but some of her dread might also have been an artifact of restless sleep the night before. The bee dream had returned, after a two-month reprieve. Tension knotted her neck and shoulder muscles, remnants of her desperate flight and struggle.

She glanced at the time. Only one hour to go until the final trajectory change maneuver. The next hour would see the *Perseus* placed on a final approach trajectory to Mars. Five days from now, that course would lead to either a safe landing in the Medusae Fossae region or a spectacular crash. Either way, they would be making history, and the media back on Earth would be deliriously happy.

Anna began to pace the circumference of the lounge and kitchen, looking for loose items not stowed properly, while rubbing and stretching her neck, back, and leg muscles. She longed to work out the kinks with a vigorous exercise session, but there would be plenty of time for that later.

"Computer, audio play Holst, The Planets. Selection: Mars, The Bringer of War. Volume: 75."

She chose the Holst selection because it matched her mood. As the music began to play, Anna looked forward to the inevitable buildup, the powerful transformation from a somber dirge into a sweeping crescendo of untapped energy and potential. The music evoked an ominously powerful image of Mars the harsh warrior. Between the notes, she heard the planet calling to her, saying, "I'm close to you, and I'm reaching out to capture you."

Unable to resist the call of the planet, Anna unsealed one of the insulated porthole covers and peeked outside, into the depths of space. She hadn't done this very often during the voyage. When viewing the silent, spectacular, and immovable background of stars, the spinning motion of the *Perseus* still made her nauseated after a while. She waited.

Have I missed it, this time around? No, there it is!

A brilliant, apricot-colored half-sphere came into view. Mars appeared the relative size of a half Moon back on Earth. It glowed like red embers of a dying fire, waiting to be rekindled. Though it appeared motionless, her new home sped through the night at an incredible rate. Attempting to catch her, it drew three kilometers closer with each passing second. The planet was eager to greet its first tenants.

Atmospheric distortion blurred many of the surface features, but some landmarks were still unmistakable. The arm-like western end of Valles Marineris, the deepest valley in the solar system, stretched from around the sunward side of the planet. Its open and craggy fingers, Noctis Labyrinthus, groped westward toward three stunning volcanoes rising far above the fractured highlands of the Tharsis region. From this distance, Anna couldn't perceive height directly, but their summits were dark rings of detail extending far above the hazy mist of the dust-laden atmosphere.

A bit farther to the west, a fourth volcano, Olympus Mons seized her attention. Aptly named after the home of the Greek gods, Mount Olympus, this granddaddy of all volcanoes was truly the divine ruler of the Martian surface. It had all the impressive attributes of the other volcanoes, plus a white beard of wispy clouds adorning its lower slopes, an unusual event in the Martian mornings.

Yes, oh bearded one. You're the crusty old man of Mars, and you always will be. I hope you don't mind if we pitch our tent on your doorstep. We promise to be good campers. We won't pollute or destroy. We just want to share.

The spin of the *Perseus* pushed the planet out of view. Holding her breath, she eagerly awaited its return. In space, certain events were guaranteed. A body in motion stayed in motion.

Soon, the planet swung back into view. This time, Anna searched for different landmarks. She looked past the glittering jewelry of this exceedingly beautiful planet, focusing her attention on a bland area near the day-night terminator, to the southwest of Old Man Olympus.

Medusae Fossae. Our new home.

The only surface features visible in the Medusae Fossae region were some random dark and light splotches. Early astronomers had placed great significance upon patterns of light and dark on the Martian surface, interpreting them to be changes in vegetation or other ground cover. Sensitive orbiter cameras had eventually revealed the truth. Most of the splotches were simply patterns of dust.

Anna strained her eyes, looking for Nicholson Crater, one of the largest fixed landmarks in the Medusae Fossae region. It marked the invisible line of the equator. However, Nicholson itself was still invisible from this distance.

The planet swung out of view again. Anna turned and slumped to her knees, slowly dragging her head and shoulders down the outer bulkhead. For several minutes, shudders wracked her body, and she was otherwise unable to move. Her tears flowed freely, as if in synch with the passionate Holst music in the background.

The brilliant beauty of Mars was a cold spear, piercing her heart. Her remoteness and insignificance had never been more obvious. She and her crewmates, the only humans within a hundred million kilometers, would be the first people to ever view its virgin vistas with their naked eyes. Yet, compared to this proud planet, with its 4.5 billion-year history, they counted as less than nothing. They were ignorant savages, dancing around a campfire.

Dear Lord, is mankind ready for this knowledge? This true awareness of context and meaning? Yet, if we aren't, we never will be. Soon, our ignorance will kill us, or our indifference will smother us.

We need you, Old Man Olympus, as much as you need us.

Eventually, her legs found their strength anew. Brushing aside the dampness on her cheeks, she resealed the porthole cover and returned to the main computer. Viewing Mars from space was a profound, life-altering experience, but if she was ever going to reach its surface in one piece, she and her companions had a lot of work to do.

She took a long sip of tea, while checking the schedule of control triggers within the main computer. The result would be the same as the last four times she had checked, but she needed to reassure herself the trajectory change maneuver would occur on schedule.

What the…

Her tea took a wrong turn, and she coughed, trying to clear her windpipe. The orbital insertion maneuver had been removed from the schedule. She checked the trigger list again, and then a third time. Clearly, the schedule had been changed.

"Evelyn, please respond." She spoke tersely into the microphone on her wireless headpiece, while trying to keep her voice sounding smooth and calm. Then she realized she had pulled a classic Star Trek blunder by speaking before she had opened a connection to Evelyn's audio pager. After correcting her oversight, she repeated her request, and the commander responded immediately.

"Sorry to wake you, but it's an emergency. I've just noticed the trigger for the orbital insertion maneuver has disappeared from the schedule!"

"I changed the schedule," Evelyn replied. Her voice was crisp, alert, and calm. "I've been talking to Mission Support for the past hour. They're concerned about a suspicious change to the TV table last night. No software updates were scheduled."

"TV table?" asked Anna, wondering what televisions or furniture had to do with software or orbital maneuvers.

"The TV, uh, transfer-vector table is a simple list of 64-bit pointers to software functions. Whenever a function is called within our control software, a transfer vector redirects the function call to the appropriate segment of code. However, the techies back on Earth believe one of our transfer vectors is screwed up."

"But how could that happen?" Anna asked. "And what does it mean—in English?"

"Unknown...and it means I'll trigger the trajectory maneuver manually. We won't be able to rely upon the scheduler. I'm already warming up the thrusters, and our star tracker has been stable for days."

"But isn't the timing of the thruster firings too precise for a human to control?"

"The low level software seems to be OK, but there's no way to call the correct entry function, except manually, through a direct pointer reference. Once I do that, the computer should do the rest for us."

Evelyn ended the conversation rather brusquely, assuring Anna she would handle everything from the computer console in her quarters. Anna was told to sit back and enjoy the ride.

The commander's words didn't ease Anna's fears. Given David's deep concerns about sabotage from within the Mission Support team, Major Tom, or some co-conspirator, could have corrupted their software in a hundred different ways.

From Evelyn's description, the software change sounded subtle. Perhaps the saboteur still strived for secrecy, which limited the actions he could take. David's misdirections and increased vigilance might be paying off.

After checking the status of the *Perseus* systems, she set an alarm to sound just prior to the originally scheduled time for the trajectory change maneuver. In case Evelyn fell asleep, as unlikely as that was, the alarm would tell Anna when to alert her. Anna wasn't about to let some silly oversight prevent their course correction. The choice between staying in space for four more days or 18 more months was obvious and overpowering.

She stretched her taut muscles again, seeking elusive relaxation. The computer was playing other Holst music tracks, since she hadn't provided any instructions to the contrary. The current selection sounded soft and fragile, which again matched her mood, so she left it harmonizing in the background.

With her short-term obligations completed, Anna had some time for other activities. But what? Her edgy nerves wouldn't allow her to concentrate on technical studies. She had already checked the status of the biosystem earlier. Playing another round of her frustrating biosystem computer game didn't appeal to her at the moment.

Perhaps some light reading would help her to relax. Looking for a fun distraction within the lengthy list of novels in the ship's computer, the Alice in Wonderland title caught her attention again. She had started reading this book months ago, but other matters came up and the story had been put aside until now.

She started reading where she had left off, in the section where Alice was trying to reach the beautiful garden. This was the scene Anna had mentioned in a message to David, at least a month ago. Since then, they had traded several messages speculating about the coincidence of <alice>, i.e. Evelyn, fitting into a room too small for her to enter. David had even scoured every room at Mission Support, looking for bottles one could drink from, or signs labeled DRINK ME. His search was unsuccessful, and they had given up the silly game.

As Anna read the passages related to the garden dilemma, she couldn't help looking for additional clues. Perhaps David had overlooked something.

Could it have something to do with poison? Alice drank from the bottle because it wasn't labeled as poison. Stupid little girl.

She read the section again, from the start of the chapter. Alice had unwisely tipped the bottle because she wanted to "shut up like a telescope." The interesting choice of words created a hilarious visual image in Anna's mind.

Wait...Like a telescope...No, it can't be that simple!

Armed with insight, Anna minimized the book and initialized a new virtual world connection. She immediately warped her avatar into the central atrium of the support complex. The massive replica of Lowell's telescope hovered above the security desk, defying gravity. She had seen this telescope probably a hundred times before, and had never considered its unusual prominence within the room. The other museum exhibits were spacecraft, probes that had been to other worlds. Yet Lowell's telescope, slowly turning, was the room's centerpiece.

OK, Alice, just how does one shut herself up, like a telescope, in a virtual world?

Searching for the right syntax, she issued several versions of commands like "shut <microbrain>" or "shut up <microbrain> like a telescope." Each time, the language parser returned a syntax error. Just as she was about to give up, she found a simpler command, shut telescope, which passed the parser. Her view of the atrium changed, dramatically. The telescope towered over her, along with the guard's desk. Her avatar's perspective had clearly changed.

Yet, she hadn't moved at all. The room had grown, or rather, her avatar had shrunk. According to her personal statistics, her size was still 1620 units tall. One virtual unit normally corresponded to a real-world millimeter, but Anna strongly suspected the telescope command had shifted her spatial context to some other measurement scale, possibly microns or nanometers.

With the thrill of success racing through her veins, she queried Evelyn's location. The commander was in the main support room, probably collaborating with Shepherd and the technicians. Anna might never find a better opportunity to investigate Conference Room 4. While Evelyn was distracted, Anna could warp herself into the room, take a quick look around, and leave undetected. Without stopping to second-guess herself, she issued the warp command.

Conference Room 4: Cannot enter: This room is locked, and you do not possess a key.

"No!" she cried aloud. The error message struck her almost like a physical blow. Had she figured out Evelyn's secret, only to be thwarted by a simple, locked door? If a key was needed, she might never gain admittance. <alice> was probably the only avatar with the correct key.

In the children's book, she recalled Alice encountering the same problem. She had shrunk herself to a height where she could enter the garden but had forgotten to bring the door key with her. Unfortunately, in the virtual support center, the security team issued all keys. How could she ask them for a key to unlock a room no one should be able to enter in the first place?

While she pondered her next move, her timer alarm went off, and she immediately paged Evelyn to remind her about the course change. Evelyn was already in the process of triggering the maneuver. She sounded quite surprised Anna had sent her a reminder.

"Just trying to be helpful," said Anna, a bit puzzled that she even needed to offer an explanation. Of course she would remind Evelyn about the maneuver. It was her job to think of such things, especially while she was the only crew member officially on duty.

A minute later, her body felt a gentle upward nudge. The sensation felt familiar, from the last time the *Perseus* thrusters had fired. Anna killed her connection to the virtual world and returned her attention to the control software on the ship's main computer. She watched their trajectory change, ever so slowly, until it perfectly matched the desired course projection.

All systems still appeared to be functioning normally, and soon her thoughts returned to the locked room quandary. How could she enter that room? She couldn't—it was that simple. But what about <shepherd>? David had once commented that his avatar possessed a universal key able to open any room in the support complex.

With renewed optimism, she sent David a message containing the good news about the successful telescope command. Hopefully, he could figure out the rest of the puzzle on his own. Though Anna longed to see the inside of Conference Room 4 herself, this had been David's mystery, right from the start. It seemed appropriate that he should be the one to enter the garden.

MarsDay 172, 5:36 p.m.
(May 16, 7:15 p.m.)

"Listen to your heart, as well as your instincts, David," advised Cassie, through her Kahuna avatar. "If your instincts tell you to pursue this other woman, and she's interested in you, too, then go for it. Your isolation and your need for job secrecy are temporary conditions. Don't let them ruin your chance for a good, lasting relationship."

"But what about Anna? I still love her!"

"You can't possibly be truly in love with her. You've only met her once."

"There's no such thing as love at first sight?" asked David.

"I've never seen it," said Cassie. "Your relationship with Anna is unrealistic and unhealthy for both of you. You won't see each other again for at least two more years. That's a long time to wait, David."

"So you don't believe in long-distance relationships either, Sis?" he responded, sarcastically. "When you and Ben were dating, you had a thousand miles of separation. You were lucky if you saw each other twice in the same month."

Cassie paused for a moment, and he could tell he had finally scored a point, albeit a weak one. So far, the discussion had gone just about how he had expected. Cassie remained firmly opposed to his relationship with Anna, and she had plenty of good reasons to support her opinion.

Of course, Cassie might be singing a different tune if she knew the identity of this other woman. David wasn't prepared to reveal his feelings for Skye, however. He fully admitted hiding his relationship with Anna had been a big mistake, since Cassie was Anna's personal psychologist and urgently needed to be aware of such details. The situation with Skye was different. There was no link between Skye and Cassie, and he preferred to keep it that way.

Cassie eventually replied, a bit defensively, "When Ben and I were dating, we could talk on the phone anytime. Despite the distance, we could still visit anytime we wanted. Since Anna is completely out of reach, she's little more than an excuse for you to avoid relationships with other people. I wish you could see that as clearly as I do, David."

"So even though my new friend lives over a thousand miles away, and I've only seen her on a few hastily arranged occasions, you're OK with that?"

"Absolutely," said Cassie. "So tell me more about her! Is she someone you work with at Mission Support?"

"You might say that."

"What's she like?"

David searched for a truthful response that wouldn't give much away. "To be honest, when I work with her professionally, she can be quite rude at times. She's also focused, aggressive, impatient, and sometimes manipulative. Yet privately, I believe she's very different."

"It's astute of you to recognize the difference between public and private facades. The pressures of the working world can often create illusions, for better or worse. If you get along well enough privately, her work demeanor is probably nothing to worry about."

They talked longer, with David deftly dodging Cassie's attempts to pry more information out of him. She warned him about the dangers of getting involved with someone he worked with, especially if one of them was in a position of authority over the other. Since this didn't fit the current situation, David only pretended to show interest.

Eventually, their conversation moved on to other topics. By the time they said their farewells, two hours had passed. In hindsight, he didn't mind the long conversation because they had so much to catch up on. However, he also had other things to do this evening.

In particular, David longed to see the inside of Conference Room 4, and he knew he wouldn't get any sleep tonight until he had tried Anna's "telescope" command. Checking the time, he decided he could still make a quick attempt before watching the evening news with Bill and Jennifer. But first, he checked his messages and found one from his old adversary.

To: <shepherd>
From: <chicken_little>
Subject: Weighty matters
Priority: Emergency

David -

Riddle: When the sky falls, where does it land?
Answer: Does it matter?

After talking to Cassie for so long, David wasn't in the mood for more mental games. He filed the message away and vowed to come back to it later. The commander had also sent him a message, and judging from the subject line, it promised to be an interesting one:

To: <shepherd>, <psychotic_ones>
From: <alice>
Subject: Crew interactions
Priority: High

I wanted to inform you of two crew interactions I won't be mentioning in my official daily reports. As with all other psych matters, please hold it in strictest confidence.
Ollie came to me earlier today, and he was quite upset. During his pre-landing maintenance check, he noticed the problem with the radiation shielding around my quarters. He seemed genuinely distraught, and he swore he had not closed the water valves. I urged him not to confront Anna about this, but it's possible he will anyway. If he didn't do it, then he must suspect she did.
At least the timing of his discovery is fortunate, since the successful trajectory change maneuver has now made our aerocapture at Mars inevitable. If Anna closed the valves as part of an irrational attempt to return to Earth, she no longer has the return option available to her.

> The other interaction was with Anna, during the trajectory change maneuver. She actually reminded me to initiate the maneuver manually. If our theory about her wanting to return to Earth is correct, then I'm at a loss to explain her attention to detail. I feared she would try to interfere somehow, but she didn't.
>
> I'll look forward to any recommendations from the psych team on how to proceed from here. I must admit I'm quite confused. Might the valve closure have been unintentional? Perhaps we are imagining problems that don't really exist?
>
> - Commander Day

He fervently hoped the commander was right. If the whole issue with the closed valve had been a false alarm, he could give some of his paranoia a rest, along with his guilty conscience over not revealing his relationship with Anna earlier. Unfortunately, this solution seemed far too convenient. It didn't explain the recalibration of the radiation sensors in the commander's quarters, the corruption of the crew activity logs, the transfer vector changes, or Major Tom's fateful words.

Whether the closure of the valve was intentional or not, David needed to assume the worst and plan accordingly. Or did he? The only hard evidence, from the crew activity logs, still implicated Anna. Perhaps now was a good time to confront her about what she had done on Day 92? He mulled over the current situation for some time before sending a message to Cassie and Commander Day to propose that course of action.

Earlier, Cassie had told him to trust his instincts. Those instincts were telling him the situation was still dangerous, and they needed more information. The best source of information was Anna. He couldn't believe she would intentionally harm anyone, especially the commander, whom she revered so much.

And what about the commander, and the games she was playing? It was time for him to see what she was hiding in Conference Room 4.

He consulted the crew activity log and found the commander was currently in the lounge with Anna and Ollie. In a few minutes, Anna's shift would end, and their evening gathering would probably break up. Commander Day would probably log onto her computer account shortly thereafter, so David needed to hurry, while she was preoccupied.

After warping his avatar into the central atrium, he ran Anna's shut telescope command and observed the same effect she had described in her message. The telescope seemed to tower over him. He paused briefly to admire the scenery from his new perspective, before attempting to warp into Conference Room 4.

His view changed again. He was now inside a normal conference room, complete with a short oak table and six plush chairs. The brightly colored walls were decorated with space related artwork. A potted fern in the corner added a touch of earthiness. At the front of the room was an audio/visual hookup wall for viewing presentations. The lighting level was normal, as well. Had he not known differently, he would have thought this was Conference Room 2 or 3, the small meeting rooms his team used occasionally.

He glanced quickly in all directions, to verify he was alone. Then he walked around the room, looking for anything unusual. Other than the lack of a door, the room still seemed normal. He could detect no hints of past room usage, which was to be expected. Unlike real rooms, virtual rooms didn't show wear and tear, and people rarely left items sitting around.

Since he had accomplished his goal of entering the room and having a quick look around, he killed his computer connection and reflected on what he had discovered. At first, it didn't seem like much. His entry into the buffer room hadn't revealed any huge secrets, like the identity of <chicken_little> or clues about the motives of Beta or the mission planners. Yet, the room's contents being so unremarkable spoke volumes.

Virtual rooms within the support center were created and furnished according to need. Why would anyone create an ordinary conference room, unless they intended to use it for a conference?

To hold a conference, several avatars were needed. David wondered who might attend such a clandestine meeting. The commander was almost certainly involved, and possibly his feathered adversary. Who else? Major Tom and other Beta conspirators? Perhaps members of the steering committee? What about the mission planners, themselves?

If the planners used the room, they could undoubtedly access other areas of mission support, too. They might be walking past him in the hallways every day, without his even being aware of their presence. The thought of that made David shudder.

CHAPTER 23
LOCATION

MarsDay 176, 7:00 a.m.
(May 20, 11:00 a.m.)

"I thought I would find you there," Evelyn's voice announced, from behind. Anna glanced over her shoulder as the commander stepped off the ladder into the lounge area, but she immediately returned her gaze to the view outside the porthole.

"Isn't it just the most beautiful sight you've ever seen?" Anna's eyes felt moist. "This is my last chance to see Mars from space until our journey back to Earth, so I'm trying to make the most of it."

"And what is Mars telling you?" asked Evelyn.

Anna was surprised at the commander's insight. Mars was indeed speaking to her, welcoming her and warning her at the same time. She confessed her regular rapport with Old Man Olympus. The mountain had told her to watch her step. Mars was an unforgiving place.

"Yes it is," Evelyn whispered, as she moved closer and watched the spinning planet with Anna. Neither spoke for a few moments.

Eventually, Evelyn asked, "Loose items?"

"All stowed," answered Anna. "The *Perseus* is ready for both zero-G and high-G."

"It's a good day to die."

"Native American philosophy? Dakota?" She recalled the commander's ancestral roots.

Anna glanced back at Evelyn again and was surprised to find herself the object of the commander's scrutiny, instead of Mars. At first, she didn't know how to respond. Then she returned her gaze to the window and mused, "We're all going to die, someday. If today is my last, then at least I've lived long enough to see this glorious sight. No one can take that away from me. Not even Old Man Olympus."

As she moved over to the kitchen area, Evelyn hissed, "You might be surprised at what Old Man Olympus can take away from you."

Anna turned again. Without explaining her comment further, Evelyn grabbed a nutritional bar for breakfast and rummaged through the cabinets. She obviously intended to double-check the kitchen articles had been properly secured.

Anna fought against a flash of irritation. Evelyn was only doing her job, only being cautious. She wouldn't find anything out of place. Anna had already checked each room in the *Perseus* twice except the commander's quarters.

Evelyn soon finished her inspection of the kitchen and descended the ladder to the lower levels. Anna turned back to the view of Mars, just as the planet was swinging around again.

Minutes later, Anna heard a terse announcement over her ear-receiver: "Brace yourself for zero-G." From the computer control console in her quarters, Evelyn was about to explode the bolts securing the rotational tether to the dome of the *Perseus*. Afterwards, the *Perseus* would be without gravity until it hit the atmosphere of Mars.

Saying one last, hasty goodbye to the view of the planet from space, Anna closed the porthole cover and moved to a nearby section of nearly empty wall space. She crouched, wrapped a thin zero-G net around herself, and clipped several fasteners to the wall and floor. Her Anna-sized cocoon would keep her safe if the *Perseus* tumbled after the upcoming tether separation.

She informed Evelyn that she was ready, while wishing she had checked on Ollie one more time. The last time she had looked in on him, he was soundly asleep in his bunk, under a similarly netted cocoon. Unless he unfastened the clips manually, he would be safe, too.

She felt, more than heard, a dull thud coming from above her head. Immediately, her stomach lurched, and she was falling, falling, falling. As she fought to regain control of her rebellious senses, her feet left the floor and her nose brushed up against the top of the safety net. She was completely weightless.

"Status," barked Evelyn in her ear.

"All OK, up here," she answered. "Glad I ate a light breakfast this morning."

"I'll do the next procedures from down here, with confirmation from Mission Support. Get ready to awaken Ollie if I run into any problems and need his help."

Anna floated over to the area in front of the computer and hooked the display into slave mode so she could follow the commander's actions. The lights dimmed as Evelyn switched their power supply over to batteries, isolating the solar panel circuitry. Then she began the slow, methodical process of retracting the solar arrays and heat radiators on the outside of the *Perseus*. Each bank of four solar panels folded like an accordion along grooves in the exterior hull, before locking into a flattened, shielded reentry position. All except one.

"Anna, I can't seem to get bank seven to retract completely," said Evelyn over the ear-com. "I'll need your help."

"I'm on it. Should I wake Ollie?"

"Not yet."

Anna kicked off from the table toward the outer hull, landing clumsily beside the netted shelves where the computer equipment was stored. She grabbed one of the tele-robotic operator helmets and slipped it over her head. Using the helmet as a data interface, she seized control of a spiderbot in the external robot storage area.

Each six-armed spiderbot was only about four inches in length. The arms could be customized for specific tasks. Anna chose a spiderbot previously equipped with tiny "hands" able to navigate around the exterior hull by grasping regularly spaced protrusions.

To control the spiderbot appendages, she placed thin gloves on her own hands. Sensors embedded within the gloves would allow her to move the bot almost like it was an extension of her own limbs. A high definition wireless video feed between her helmet and the bot's two external button cameras would allow stereoscopic visual feedback during each movement.

Software completed the connection. She ran a quick diagnostic on the algorithms in the spiderbot's memory. The bot reported full health and control.

Then she opened the robot bay doors and steered her bot along the underside of the hull, moving cautiously at first, since she wasn't too familiar with maneuvering in zero-G. Back on Earth, she had often practiced using the bots for biology research. Moving dirt around with a "scoop" attachment was easy, with the assistance of gravity. Fortunately, with help from the ship's computer, the zero-G movements were equally as intuitive. By the time her bot reached the non-retracting section of solar panels on the side of the hull, her confidence in her abilities had increased.

She reported, "I'm in position. Looking around."

"Move over, nine o'clock, about one meter. Pan the image slowly. We have lots of time. Let's not overlook anything." Obviously, the commander had tied into her video signal and intended to help search for the problem.

Anna maneuvered the bot around the panel, slowly, focusing the camera on the grooves near the solar panel. The most likely cause of the retraction failure was some form of debris clogging a groove, but she was unable to find anything.

They switched to a new plan, with Anna moving the bot back to a safe distance and switching to a wider-angle view while Evelyn tried to retract the panel again. Evelyn commented, "If this doesn't work, I'll have to get Ollie's opinion. We might need a second spiderbot out there, too."

The panel slid along properly until it reached a certain point in the folding process where one of the corners slid upward, out of the grooved slot. "Looks like one of the sliders is damaged," commented Anna calmly, as she telescoped the bot's vision to study the corner of the panel outside the groove.

Evelyn laughed, and Anna felt her own tension released. "We're in luck," Evelyn said. "Those sliders are simple, ten-cent hooks, and we have dozens of spares. Take the old one off. I'll put a new one in the top sample box."

Anna moved her bot forward until she could grasp the hook, which had clearly snapped in half. With coaching from Evelyn, she removed the old hook, retrieved the new one, and replaced it. Then she moved her bot back to a safe distance again, while the commander tried retracting the solar panels again. This time, the retraction worked.

"Nicely done, Anna," Evelyn said, warmly. The words brought a satisfied flush to Anna's cheeks, which were already puffed because her heart no longer fought against gravity to pump blood into her head.

Evelyn added, "We're a half-hour behind schedule, but that means we still have almost two hours of contingency time. Let's let Ollie sleep another half-hour. I want him to be alert when we start our plunge."

Anna stored the spiderbot back inside the robot bay. Then she returned the gloves and helmet to their storage shelf and watched on the computer display as Evelyn completed the next tasks on the checklist.

By the time she woke Ollie, Evelyn had already started her final external inspection. All antennas had been retracted, except for a tertiary, expendable transmitter that would squirt a series of telemetry blips to the *Mars Odyssey* orbiter during their plunge. If something went wrong during their descent, the technicians back on Earth should still collect plenty of data, along with some dazzling photos of their fiery demise.

Ollie moved a second spiderbot onto the hull to assist the commander with her inspection. Anna followed along visually, using the computer display in the lounge. With both engineers working, the inspection was soon completed successfully.

"Let's send the bots back to the barn," said Evelyn, her voice purring with optimism. "We've got another hour to kill before we hit the atmosphere. I want to triple-check all our systems. After we start the plunge, we won't have time to react if something goes wrong. We can't take anything for granted."

The next hour passed quickly. Ten minutes before their anticipated intersection with the thin Martian atmosphere, Anna strapped herself to the floor in the middle of the lounge. A foam mattress would distribute some of the high-G deceleration forces. Evelyn and Ollie were similarly protected in their quarters.

As she thought about what the next few minutes would bring, a cold knot worked its way into the pit of Anna's stomach. Her crewmates were undoubtedly engaged in similar self-reflection, since their intercom chatter had died off to nearly nothing. They awaited the first bump of atmosphere, the first tendril of greeting as Mars reached out to capture or destroy them.

The lounge was quiet, and the sky-blue walls felt closer than normal. Dimmed lighting gave Anna the unwelcome feeling of being trapped inside a mausoleum. She forced herself to take some deep breaths. Inhale, exhale, inhale. She focused on slowing her pulse rate through meditation. Slowly, her body responded.

Part of her problem was her lack of responsibilities during most of the landing sequence. The initial, ballistic phase of the descent was in the hands of the engineers, though they probably couldn't do much to affect the outcome, either. She could only watch the computer display from her position on the floor. Software plotted the actual and optimal trajectories, and Anna prayed the little green line would remain firmly locked onto the dashed, blue one.

A solid jolt slammed her body into the foam mattress before releasing her back into gentle weightlessness. "We have first contact with the atmosphere," commented Evelyn softly. "Hang on. This will be the bumpy part."

Several jolts later, Anna was ready to have solid ground under her feet. The turbulence quickly merged into a continuous, smothering pressure. Soon, that pressure would approach five gravities at its worst. Breathing became an ordeal. Not trusting the strength of her neck muscles, she kept her head focused straight ahead, while watching the computer display out of the corner of her eyes.

Was the green line diverging a bit? It was hard to tell.

Evelyn resumed a dry, methodic commentary, interspersed with terse notes from Ollie on the status of the systems in the *Perseus*. Ollie sounded a bit nervous, but Evelyn's voice was rock solid.

"Hypersonic chute is deployed. In case you hadn't noticed, we're slowing down."

"Exterior temperature beneath the heat shield is a bit high, but well within acceptable limits."

"As expected, E-M interference has blocked our signal from the *Mars Odyssey* orbiter. We're sending simple tones, but we'll be blind for awhile."

After what seemed like days, the deceleration pressures eased a bit. Evelyn flatly announced their speed was now subsonic. Another strong jolt shook the *Perseus* as the commander jettisoned the hypersonic parachute and opened a larger, subsonic chute. The G-forces increased again, almost reaching a so-familiar level of normal Mars gravity. The worst of the descent was over.

Anna unbuckled herself from her acceleration mattress and studied the computer display more closely. The green *Perseus* trajectory line had turned yellow. As the computer's image recognition algorithms more accurately updated their position, possibly assisted by telemetry from the *Mars Odyssey* orbiter, the line turned red.

Evelyn provided more commentary, this time with a touch of restrained emotion. "Our trajectory is taking us well outside our ten kilometer wide landing ellipse. We're about 80 kilometers too far south-southeast."

"How could that have happened?" Anna asked.

"Save the questions for later. Anna, find us a smooth landing spot."

Anna crawled over to the exterior hull and uncovered a porthole facing their direction of travel. Her first close-up view of Mars was surprisingly familiar. Far below, the ruddy landscape almost fooled her into thinking she was flying over Arizona in an airplane. The ground rose gradually to the right, making that direction undoubtedly south, and their trajectory mainly eastward. The southern plain, wide and smooth, was framed in the distance by a jagged row of mountains.

The terrain beneath the *Perseus* was chaotic, with numerous ridges, valleys and mesas. As Anna saw the walls of a deep canyon cutting across their direction of travel, she practically drooled. Multicolored layers were clearly visible, even from their current altitude. This beautiful canyon might become her biology playground for the next 18 months. Ollie would certainly be drawn to this place, as he sought to understand the complex geology of this region.

Thrusters slowed their descent, but the *Perseus* was still dropping fast. They would easily clear the walls of the upcoming valley. However, along their course farther ahead was a solitary, towering mountain. Anna alerted Evelyn that they wouldn't clear the top of the mountain. They would have to steer around it.

"Which direction?" asked Evelyn. With the heat shield gone, her radar view was focused downward, giving her a limited view of obstacles farther ahead.

"Right, er, south, and hurry." The wide, flat plains to the south would make an ideal landing area.

Anna watched closely as the mountain slid past. Surprisingly, they didn't come near it after all. She realized her depth perception was probably quite unreliable, even though she had done her eye-focusing exercises every day. Her eyes would need time to recover from six months of living in a tin can, where the farthest object was only several feet away.

As their altitude continued to drop, a strong breeze pushed them even farther to the south, toward the middle of the plain. She silently thanked Old Man Olympus for guiding their descent. The planet seemed to be apologizing for putting that mountain in their path.

The ground drew near, and Evelyn fired the thrusters of the *Perseus* to slow their vertical and horizontal velocity. Small boulders littered the plain beneath them, or rather, Anna hoped the boulders were small. Due to her earlier depth-perception problem, she no longer believed her visual judgement. Evelyn's radar and hazard avoidance software would be far more trustworthy. Anna continued to shout verbal directions over the roar of the thrusters, steering Evelyn toward what she believed to be the smoothest spot within her field of view.

The roar of the thrusters suddenly gave way to complete silence. Anna nearly panicked until she realized the *Perseus* was no longer dropping. They had already landed, so smoothly she hadn't even felt the initial contact. After a journey of several hundred million kilometers, the *Perseus* rested on the surface of Mars.

MarsDay 176, 12:51 p.m.
(May 20, 5:00 p.m.)

Tears of happiness streamed down Jennifer's cheeks as she handed David a slender flute of champagne. He had never seen her so emotionally overwhelmed before, and would not have believed it possible. Jennifer was usually as stoic as anyone he had ever met, a true disciple of Zeno, or perhaps simply a living stereotype of a logical engineer.

Bill, on the other hand, often wore his emotions on his shirt sleeves. Tonight, he and his wife were equally enthusiastic. Their nearest neighbors could probably hear their wild shouts of celebration, over a quarter of a mile away.

A brief toast by Bill turned into a lengthy affair, as each of them paid tribute to the Mars crew, the unknown mission planners, and the support team. David extended the accolades to include the current leadership at NASA, ESA, RSA, and the other great space agencies and aerospace companies of the world. These organizations had looked the other way while some of their best engineers and technicians had assisted his support team.

The top story on the early edition of the CBS evening news was the first-ever, almost-live report from Mars. David's media communications team had supplied the networks with footage of the fiery descent of the *Perseus*, captured clearly by the orbital camera on the *Mars Odyssey* probe. The footage included the first video message from Mars, transmitted by Anna over an hour ago. Her simple words were probably destined for immortality.

"*Mission Support, the* Perseus *has landed! Our arrival time was 10:08 p.m., UMT. That's 11:02 a.m., local time. Requesting orbiter confirmation of our location at 1.61 degrees north latitude, 167.42 degrees west longitude. We think we landed farther southeast than expected. Our atmospheric insertion point must have been a bit off. Also, winds blew us farther south, instead of north, as the* Mars Odyssey *telemetry had predicted. Wherever we are, the sun is shining high overhead, and the surface winds are calm. It's a beautiful day on Mars."*

Her message included images from the redesigned external cameras, which had obviously survived the stresses of the atmospheric entry this time. Panning clockwise around the landscape, Anna gave a brief description of the surroundings.

The *Perseus* had landed on a wide, flat plain. A light layer of dust or sand coated the ground. Due to a lack of landmarks, distances were hard to calculate, but the plain appeared to be devoid of any large rocks, crevices, or other distinguishing features for several kilometers in all directions. Smaller boulders were abundant, however.

To the south, a range of rugged mountains was clearly visible, far across the plain. A low ridge was implied, rather than clearly seen, to the west. Due north, a lone peak guarded the entrance to what Anna described as a deeply carved, layered canyon. Anna had already named the peak "Sentinel Mountain," and the canyon "Sentinel Canyon."

Though the crew had landed nearly a hundred kilometers off-course, they couldn't have picked a safer landing spot than the featureless plain. To some viewers back on Earth, however, the first glimpse of a human landing site on Mars would probably be disappointing. The scenery looked like the Pathfinder and MER-A landing sites, which had been thoroughly imaged long ago. Anna claimed to have captured some better footage during the landing sequence. Once their higher bandwidth relay through the *Mars Odyssey* orbiter was fully established, David looked forward to seeing the video of the landing.

The hum of the generator in the garage reminded David that his public relations team had other problems to deal with as well. Sadly, a large part of the country might not even have heard the news about the successful Mars landing yet. Electrical service in Nederland had been interrupted this morning, and had not yet been restored. The outage probably covered a wide region because some of the staff at Mission Support had suddenly dropped offline during the *Perseus* descent preparations. Most of his remaining workers claimed to be running on backup power supplies.

After less than five minutes of Mars coverage on the evening news program, another "top news story" confirmed his fears. Practically the entire North American and European continents were currently without electricity. An ultra-radical environmentalist group named Earth's Revenge had claimed responsibility for causing the outage by sabotaging several critical transformer and power relay stations. Oddly enough, the brunt of their attacks had targeted solar collection facilities and wind turbine farms. In their public statement, the group claimed the former were polluting the environment and masking the dangers of global warming, while the latter defiled the natural beauty of the Earth.

Despite the power outage, David's remaining staff had been adequate. He did wonder, however, whether a full support team might have caught the orbital insertion problem, allowing the crew to land closer to their target.

Back on the news program, the focus shifted to politics. Jillian Greene, the senatorial candidate and noted environmentalist, denounced the Earth's Revenge attacks almost as vehemently as she repeated her usual diatribe against the "distractions" of the Mars mission. Lately, Greene was quite visible on various television news programs. Her Senate campaign was in high gear, and many analysts already assumed her landslide victory almost six months before the election.

David had caught part of a rousing, surprising speech earlier in the week. Greene boldly advocated easing restrictions on coal mining, while severely curtailing fossil-fuel power plant emissions. The candidate claimed her plan would reduce energy prices while creating domestic jobs and protecting the environment, a win-win-win situation for the nation. David couldn't understand how her overproduction plan was sustainable, though he realized his view might be clouded by anger at Greene's opposition to the Mars mission. He had already made the mistake with Skye of confusing the message with the messenger. That was a mistake he didn't want to repeat.

Recollections of Greene's earlier debates prompted him to leave the room for a few minutes and place a phone call to one of her past sparring partners, Manny Rodriguez at NASA. He found the Director of Exploration Systems working late in his office at JSC, the Johnson Space Center, near Houston. Rodriguez had just come upstairs from a Mars party and was happy to receive David's call. He offered his congratulations on the success of the Mars landing.

Motivated by the power outages, David told the director about his current staffing problem at Mission Support. In the event the situation worsened, he asked whether a small JSC Mission Control team could provide backup support for the Mars mission.

Rodriguez had offered this option several months ago, and he repeated his offer now. The main JSC control room was currently controlling operations on the International Space Station, but the workload was light. The highly experienced JSC technicians would be more than willing to assist the Mars crew if any emergencies arose. Without detailed specifications for all of the equipment and protocols, however, Rodriguez warned their support would be minimal.

When the director asked about the crew objectives, David detected hesitation and unease in his voice. Rodriguez stated emphatically his controllers needed to know the overall mission plan in order to suggest judgement calls and priorities, should the need arise. David promised to forward whatever information he could, but he sensed the director's misgivings ran deeper.

"I suppose I do have some worries about it," Rodriguez said, in response to David's follow-up question. "I was initially opposed to the Mars mission, and am still highly doubtful. I've put a lot of effort into crafting a logical, progressive plan to move our public space program farther out into the solar system, starting with a return to the Moon. I don't want to see another repeat of the 'flag and footprints' Apollo missions, where the Nixon administration was able to turn its back on manned spaceflight because we didn't have an infrastructure in place."

"You're concerned that after the Mars crew returns, Congress will lose their interest in space again?" asked David.

"I suppose I am. I'm 65 years old. Like so many others, I witnessed the crushing disappointment of the Apollo program cancellation firsthand. This is my last chance. If our current lunar exploration program fails, I won't live to see another attempt, if there ever is one."

David appreciated the Director's openness and wished he had a way to assure the life-long space advocate his fears were unfounded. Unfortunately, he couldn't make any grand promises or predictions. All he could do was offer his own support.

"I completely agree. For what it's worth, I promise to do all I can to help keep the program alive."

"That's all any of us can do," Rodriguez replied softly. "That's why I'm helping you now. For this brief moment in history, the Mars mission occupies center stage. It must not fail! Afterwards, I'll just have to pray the future will take care of itself."

"It always does," said David. "Though sometimes not as we would like."

David ended the phone call, happy at achieving the promise of support he had been seeking, but also deeply disturbed at Rodriguez's pessimism about the future of the manned space program. Past history was already littered with major technological "breakthroughs" causing later grief and suffering. What would future history contain? Would his own efforts, and those of his team, be heralded as a major breakthrough in human development? Or something far more disturbing?

MarsDay 176, 1:00 p.m.
(May 20, 5:10 p.m.)

On the group comm channel, Anna asked, "Are we ever going to move on to the next task?" She couldn't wait to get her robotic hands and feet dirty.

As she flipped up the visor on her helmet and awaited a reply, her spiderbot switched itself into autonomous mode. Anna was using the telerobotics equipment in the lounge to control one spiderbot, while Ollie controlled another from their quarters on the deck below.

Together, they had carefully surveyed the exterior of the *Perseus*, looking for signs of damage. The *Perseus* appeared to be in perfect condition. They had also taken numerous photographs of the terrain to verify they were not in any immediate danger from their surroundings.

"Is Ollie back yet?" asked Evelyn.

After completing most of their external survey, Ollie had gone one step further. Outfitting one of the spiderbots with treads, he drove it onto the surface. His official reason was to study the dust fans around some of the larger rocks nearby, hoping to get a better idea of the strength and direction of the normal winds on this plain. Anna knew better, though. As a geologist, Ollie's urge to get his own robotic hands dirty undoubtedly surpassed her own, several times over.

Ollie said, "My spiderbot just returned. I had to move out far enough to get away from the dust disturbed by our landing thrusters."

"And the fans?" asked Anna.

"The dust fans spread out widely in both the upslope and downslope directions, with underlying trends to the east. That's exactly what I expected to find, based on the best atmospheric circulation models. Our winds should usually be light to moderate, flowing upslope in the mornings and downslope in the evenings."

"Just like the training camp near Colorado Springs," commented Evelyn, wryly. "But the scenery looks more like our camp in Utah."

Ollie added, "The underlying eastern trend indicates we'll have some pretty strong dust storms occasionally, though. They probably breach the valley of the larger outflow channel far to our southwest and gush across the plains, flowing eastward."

"Noted. We'll brace the *Perseus* with guy wires, after we weigh it down."

"The Robonauts are ready for action," urged Anna.

During Ollie's little robotic adventure, Anna had checked out the systems on the two larger "Robonauts" in the robot storage area. Back on Earth, operating the human-sized robots in their training sessions had almost been a mystical, out-of-body experience. Feedback crudely mimicked every sense except taste, and the overall experience was surprisingly similar to wearing a space suit. The robotic arms and legs even moved somewhat like her own, with Segway stabilizers keeping them from toppling over.

"Have you visually inspected Ollie's spiderbot?" If Evelyn was excited about being on Mars, her voice didn't show it. She was all business.

Sighing, Anna put her helmet back on and inspected Ollie's spiderbot. It appeared to be in perfect health, none the worse for its little traverse across the surface of Mars. The treads and moving joints were free of dust.

Finally, Evelyn gave the order to begin the next task, which was to manually adjust the hydraulics in the lander legs until the *Perseus* was level. Anna gave a small whoop of joy and raced down the ladder to the EVA room. She could have controlled a Robonaut from the lounge, but the machine's movements would feel much more natural if she was hooked into an exercise harness in the EVA room.

The original post-landing plan had called for a human excursion, the first-ever on another planet, immediately after the robotic EVA. At the last minute, Evelyn had canceled that part of the plan, however. She said they would have plenty of time to walk around later, after their most critical jobs were done.

Work before play, I suppose. I'll have to save my "One Small Step" speech for later. Besides, with the power outage back on Earth, no one would hear me anyway.

Ollie was already buckled into one of the harnesses. Anna quickly donned her bulky control gloves and slippers. These accessories would greatly enhance her sense of touch by providing reasonable feedback whenever her Robonaut used its hands or feet. Hindered by her new appendages, she lifted herself into the other exercise harness and clumsily adjusted the tension of the straps. Evelyn briefly entered the EVA room to help them make the final adjustments.

Anna reactivated her helmet and ran an initialization program. She became Robonaut One.

Her view was dark. Puzzled at first, she upped the brightness of her external "eye" cameras. Then she realized her Robonaut was still parked inside the unlit robot bay. Her practice sessions had always begun outside, during full daylight.

Slightly embarrassed, she returned the brightness level to normal. All signals and control commands from her Robonaut were automatically logged, so her mistake would probably be visible to others who replayed the logs and knew what to look for.

Though the official reason for keeping command and feedback logs was to assist with diagnostics and system upgrades, she strongly suspected the data would eventually be used by others back on Earth to recreate the experience of walking on Mars. The exercise harness and control equipment would soon be mass-produced for the consumer market. If they could be sold at a price comparable to other home exercise equipment, a new tele-robotics application would be born overnight. Strenuous hikes in some of the most scenic places on Earth or Mars could be sold to the masses on ordinary microdisks, crystal data storage, or even over the Internet.

If her suspicion was true, then every movement today might be replayed by billions of people, now and in the future. Her muscles tightened a bit, momentarily paralyzed by the implications, but she overcame her stage fright by concentrating on the simplicity of her immediate task. All she needed to do was step onto the surface without falling on her face.

Whether Ollie was having similar fears, she couldn't tell. After she signaled her readiness, he opened the bay doors for her, without comment. She slowly lowered herself onto the surface beneath the *Perseus*, sighing in relief as her feet touched the ground. Her descent had hardly been graceful, but at least it was successful.

Ducking her head, she stepped out from beneath the *Perseus*, allowing Ollie's bot to descend and stand beside her. They stood in silence for a moment, gazing at the side of the *Perseus*, the rocky plain, and the mountains beyond. It was a magical moment, one she hoped to remember for the rest of her life. For the first time, she was seeing the surface of Mars from an external, almost "human" point-of-view.

Though she couldn't feel hot or cold temperatures directly, she fought the urge to shiver. Sensors indicated the external temperature around her robotic feet was a balmy 50 degrees Fahrenheit, but the temperature around Robonaut's head was well below zero degrees. Such a disparity was to be expected, due to the extremely thin Martian atmosphere.

"Looks like we're in luck," she commented, smiling. "We got the best parking spot!"

"Early bird gets the worm, eh?" asked Evelyn over the comm channel, chuckling softly. She was probably back in her quarters, where she could monitor their telemetry on her computer.

"Do you have the car keys?" asked Ollie.

"I thought you did!" They shared a laugh over the old inside joke. Years ago, a contest had identified the most useless item to bring to Mars. "Car keys" was the winning entry.

Anna approached the nearest landing leg, gaining confidence in her walking abilities with each step. With guidance from Evelyn, the hydraulics on each of the six legs was adjusted until the *Perseus* was perfectly level. Only minor changes were needed, since the landing site was flat to begin with.

Then they began a more difficult task, lowering the solar cell arrays to the ground and angling them to catch the maximum amount of sunlight. Each section was able to tilt sideways, tracking the sun as it traced a path across the sky from east to west. The arrays had been designed with flexibility in mind, and the reduced gravity of Mars made the sections easy to handle.

As they made progress, the *Perseus* began to resemble the round center of a huge sunflower. Petals stretched outward in each direction except due east and due west, areas in shadow for nearly half of each day. The two gaps would also allow access to the robot bay, and later, to the suitports, when human-powered surface exploration started.

Within 20 minutes, this task was also complete. Anna moved her Robonaut back a few steps and studied the layout. All appeared to be well, and Evelyn reported the *Perseus* was receiving a strong, steady supply of power. However, Anna didn't relax until Ollie gave his approval, trusting his more experienced eyes to spot any potential issues she had overlooked. Power would be their greatest concern, until they gained the option of using excess fuel from the ERV to run a backup generator during times when extra power or battery life was needed. They couldn't afford to take any chances. Without a functional solar grid, they were as good as dead.

Now came the part of the post-landing procedures Anna had been dreading. During the next four hours, the two Robonaut workers would start the process of filling 1,200 plastic bags with nearly a hundred cubic meters of dust and sand. The "sandbags" would be placed on the roof and draped around the sides of the *Perseus*, weighing it down and shielding it from the radiation penetrating the thin atmosphere of the planet. They expected radiation levels to stay well within safe guidelines, most of the time, but extra protection would provide a better margin of safety.

Roaming farther away from the *Perseus*, Anna searched for deep drifts of the dust needed to fill their plastic sandbag shells. She found several places where dust and sand had formed shallow drifts near boulders or small gullies, but the quantity of loose material was lacking. Of all the problems she had expected to encounter on Mars, lack of dust and sand hadn't been one of them.

As she was nearing despair, Ollie gave a soft cry of "Eureka!" She trotted her Robonaut over to view his discovery.

A few hundred feet south of the *Perseus*, Ollie's robot studied a circular depression nearly ten meters in diameter. The dust in this area was rippled, and sizeable rocks were absent. Ollie's keen eye had recognized this area as the shallow indentation of an ancient crater. Most of the crater wall and sides had eroded away, leaving a dust-filled pit.

Congratulating themselves on their good fortune, they walked back to the *Perseus*. Ollie erected a light tripod designed to support a sandbag while it was being filled. Anna attached a roll of bags, which suspiciously resembled a double-layered, super-strength roll of Hefty garbage bags. She laughed at the thought of trash bags and duct tape probably being the two most useful supplies within their inventory. Both afforded maximum utility for a wide assortment of tasks, while minimizing mass and storage volume.

Unfortunately, their digging equipment was in the cargo vehicle, a hundred kilometers away at the primary Medusae landing site. They managed to rig two makeshift shovels and sleds from spare plastic sheets in the storage area. Ollie volunteered to take the first shift of digging. They established a system where Ollie's Robonaut would heap dust and sand from the shallow crater onto the sled, while Anna filled sandbags by the *Perseus*. When Ollie's load was full, he pulled the sled over to her position. Although the robots were designed to handle greater stresses, they moved slowly and carefully, like dancers in a bizarre, alien ballet.

Anna's mound of sandbags began to grow, but she didn't pile them around the *Perseus* yet. That was a task for another day. Instead, she arranged them in flat rows nearby, but well out of the way.

Soon, the Robonaut's intelligent learning algorithm signaled it was ready to perform the sandbag-filling task automatically. With a sigh of relief, Anna turned full control over to the machine and released the tension in her harness. The robot would repeat her previous actions until conditions changed or it was instructed to stop. Though the learning software had proven quite reliable during Earthly testing, Anna remained in her harness, ready to interrupt the robot's actions at a moment's notice.

She didn't need to. By the time the last rays of feeble sunlight retreated in the west and the temperature began to plummet, the robot had filled and stacked nearly a hundred sandbags.

"Time to head back to the barn, Ollie." She checked the power reserves on her Robonaut. "Good timing, too. My robot is running low on juice."

The rechargeable batteries on each Robonaut had enough capacity to last for several days under normal usage. However, today's exertions had been far from normal. Despite the lighter gravity, each sausage shaped sandbag still weighed 20 pounds. The manual movements required to carry and stack the bags had drained her robot's batteries at an alarming rate.

They returned their Robonauts to the thermally protected cocoons in the robot bay and set their batteries recharging. Then, finally, she extracted herself from the exercise harness. As Ollie did likewise, he complained his back was sore, probably from remaining in the harness for so long.

While Ollie retreated to his cabin, Anna joined Evelyn in the lounge. She paced the room, stretching and rubbing her tight arm muscles. Evelyn prepared two cups of green antioxidant tea.

"You two did good work out there today," said Evelyn. "But we have a lot more to do."

"I wish we had a third Robonaut to make it go faster," said Anna.

Evelyn agreed. "Or to use as a spare, in case one breaks down and we can't fix it."

They took their tea to the sitting area, where Anna reclined on the couch, leaving the chair for Evelyn. The wall color of the day was a surprisingly bold shade of crimson. Perhaps the psychologists were making a statement about the need to adapt to seeing various shades of red in her new Martian surroundings. She still enjoyed her game of outguessing the psych team.

"I'll take a shift tomorrow," said Evelyn. "We'll probably need only one person watching both robots."

"Mine filled nearly a hundred sandbags today. If you both take a two hour shift tomorrow, and I go for four hours, we can do at least twice as much."

The commander frowned. "We might need to work even longer hours. At this rate, the task will take almost a week. Until then, we're vulnerable to solar flare radiation at several sun angles throughout the day."

"This would be so much easier if we could use heavy construction equipment for the digging and hauling, as we had planned. Then both Robonauts could fill sandbags."

Evelyn silently stirred her tea with a spoon. Then she stopped and took a long sip. "We can't reach the cargo vehicle. It's too far away."

In her surprise, Anna nearly dropped her own cup of tea. "Why can't we tele-operate the pressurized rover and drive it back to the *Perseus*?"

The commander scowled, puckering her lips, as if her drink tasted bitter. "I haven't been able to establish contact with the rover yet, nor any of the three landers at the Medusae site. The signal interference must be a local problem, as well as a global one. If we could reach the rover or any of the other vehicles, we could probably fix whatever is wrong." She shook her head. "No, they're too far away. Recall my motto. What we can't reach doesn't exist."

Evelyn's cold conclusion left Anna more than a little chilled. She wasn't content to sit inside the *Perseus* and quote conservative mottos all day. Somewhere in their fallback options was a solution they hadn't considered yet, and she was going to find it.

"What about the ATV?" Their supplies contained a light All Terrain Vehicle, with enough fuel for a single, 100-kilometer trek, one way. It was sent to Mars along with the crew for exactly this reason, in case they landed so far away that they couldn't reach the other equipment on foot. "We could send a Robonaut driver to the Medusae site."

"The terrain is too chaotic. To keep in constant contact with the *Perseus*, the robot would have to drop data relays every few kilometers. We don't have enough relays for that. And what if there's a serious problem with the rover that we can't fix easily? We would lose the robot and the ATV. That's a desperate gamble, and a risk we can't afford. Remember, two months from now, we can direct our backup ERV and cargo vehicles to land near the *Perseus*. We might need the ATV to reach them, too. And we certainly can't afford to waste Robonauts if we're ever to construct the modules for the final ERV to take us back home to Earth.

Anna agreed these were all sound reasons not to send a robot, but then she suggested the next obvious variation, sending a human driver instead. Evelyn didn't take kindly to this idea at all. A human engineer could fix a wider range of rover problems, but the consequences of failure would be far greater. If sending a robot was too risky, sending a human engineer was out of the question.

Silence settled upon the room like a tangible cloud. Anna couldn't think of any other options, and the futility of their situation was frustrating.

"So we're just going to write off all that cargo and the pressurized rover?" Anna asked.

"Yes. For now."

"And what if the next cargo vehicle and ERV crash, or land even farther away?"

"If that happens, we'll reassess our situation." Evelyn placed her empty cup on the table behind her. Any wavering of her hand was imperceptible. "Then it might be time to take greater risks."

Anna lapsed back into silence. The only options she could envision were the ones she had already suggested. In fact, the situation was becoming quite clear. If the cargo vehicle and ERV failed to land nearby, one of the engineers would be forced to make a suicidal dash up to the primary Medusae landing site. Without retrieving the pressurized rover and plenty of fuel, the outlook for their long-term survival would be grim.

CHAPTER 24
ROTATION

MarsDay 219, 2:15 a.m.
(July 3, 10:30 a.m.)

"Beavis?"

"Yeah. You're right on time." David flipped up the tinted visor on his helmet so Skye could see it was really he. She had sounded quite worried on the chat line yesterday, and had insisted they avoid using real names when they met.

"Nice wheels!" said Skye, admiring the ATV on which David was sitting. Then she glanced back over her shoulder and moved closer to him, a bit too close.

"I figured it would get us out to the highway a lot faster. Butthead's waiting for us," he said, referring to Bill.

When Skye had suggested meeting David on one of the hiking trails behind the Gold Lake Resort, he had immediately asked Bill for advice. Gold Lake was a remote, private lake north of Nederland, and David had never been there before. However, Bill was quite familiar with the national forest lands on all sides of the resort. He suggested a good meeting spot, a tall outcrop of rock along one of the popular hiking trails.

"Do you have the goods?" she asked.

David handed her a bag of clothing strapped to the back of the ATV. "There's a small notch behind this outcrop, where you can have some privacy."

"Thanks. No peeking."

He had pieced together Skye's concern about having microphones or locational devices concealed in her clothing. This worry seemed a bit extreme to David, unless she was keeping some secrets from him. Much could have happened in the two weeks since their last rendezvous.

David flipped down his visor and prepared the ATV for departure. He had chosen this parking spot because it afforded a good view of the trail for several hundred feet in either direction. If a hiker happened along, he could give Skye plenty of warning. As bad luck would have it, he didn't have long to wait.

"Someone's coming," he hissed loudly, hoping Skye would hear.

The hiker was tall and bulky, but he jogged down the path with a catlike grace. His trendy jacket and jeans seemed too heavy for the warm spring day and too fashionable for the wooded surroundings. The only part of his ensemble really belonging on the remote trail was his well worn, military-style hiking boots.

As the man moved closer, a chill of recognition raced down David's spine. It was Major Thomas. Despite the change in outfit from FBI garb to street clothing, there was no mistaking his identity.

Thomas was quickly upon him, but he made no move to attack, nor any sign he recognized David. Instead, he asked curtly, "Did'ja see a woman come down this path? Long dark hair, jeans, and sweater?"

David almost removed his visor to reply, but caught himself in time. His tinted helmet provided him with anonymity. Instead of speaking, he gestured down the heavily wooded path in the direction the man was heading.

Thomas rushed on by and continued jogging down the trail. If anything, his pace was faster than before. He soon disappeared through the trees, farther down the rutted path.

David realized he had been holding his breath throughout the entire encounter. Exhaling forcefully, he hopped from the ATV and, on suddenly gelatinous legs, raced around the outcrop to where Skye was dressing. She was completely naked, with her back to him and one leg lifted. Her hands held a pair of jeans.

Normally, the sight of her long, tanned legs leading up to the rest of her sensuous body would have stopped him dead in his tracks. At the moment, however, he had other matters on his mind. Quickly averting his gaze, he whispered, "Hurry up! We have to leave. Now!"

With a few mild curses, she threw on the rest of her clothing. He soon heard a zipping of the leather jacket. "How do I look?" she asked.

He turned to inspect her new apparel, which had been loaned by Jennifer on short notice. "It'll do," he said. The jeans were obviously a few inches short and a bit loose in the midsection, but now was not the time for perfect fashion. "Let's get out of here."

Crouching, they silently crept around the outcrop, but Thomas was nowhere in sight. David shoved a spare helmet into Skye's receptive hands. Then he leaped onto the ATV and started the engine. She climbed up behind him on the snug two-person seat, clinging firmly to his waist with both arms. The motor revved, and tires spun in the loose dirt. David sent the vehicle careening down the narrow path in the direction Skye had initially come from, swiftly at first, and then a bit slower as they put more distance between themselves and the murderous thug behind them.

Soon, they emerged from the trees and neared the lake. The Gold Lake Resort was on the northern shore, a short distance to the right. With today being the Saturday in the middle of the long, Independence Day holiday weekend, the resort was quite busy. Several vacationers lounged around the lakeshore on reclining beach furniture, fished from a short dock, or moved between the main lodge and cabins. Children splashed noisily in the clear blue water, watched by a flotilla of ducks in the middle of the lake. The smell of popcorn wafted to them on the gentle afternoon breeze, over the fumes of their ATV.

David felt quite conspicuous, but he forced himself to relax. To the people at the resort, they were just another young couple escaping the teeming flatlands for a relaxed weekend in the mountains. ATVs were a common sight here, as were riders wearing helmets.

He drove around the lakeshore on a dirt path, slowly approaching the cabins. Skye punched his arm and told him to stop. He killed the engine, allowing her to explain in a lower voice, "I stayed in the third cabin last night. That woman sitting out in front is Greta Burgess, my producer's boss, and a first class creep. She's a big mucky-muck at the network, and she's keeping me on a short leash."

David studied the woman out of the corner of his eye, without showing any overt interest to draw return attention. If Skye hadn't informed him otherwise, he would have assumed Burgess was just another white-haired grandmother waiting for her grandkids to return from the beach or hiking trails.

Shuddering, he asked, "Do you need anything inside?"

"No—let's go. The sight of her makes my skin crawl. I put a chair under the handle of my bedroom door last night, and I was still up half the night worrying she would burst in and kill me. I could use some sleep."

"Time for that later," David said, as he tried to restart the engine. The motor hesitated, and then roared to life.

He drove farther down the path. Passing the third cabin, he continued to watch the network bigshot out of the corner of his helmet. Skye's disguise must have been pretty good, because the woman looked at them and glanced away without showing any interest.

The path turned into a rough dirt road, the only access road between the resort and civilization. David kept going, picking up speed as he left the buildings behind. Soon, they were moving along at a good clip, bouncing over potholes and ruts with gusto.

Skye asked him to stop again, so he pulled off the road into a dense grove of aspens. The smooth white bark and tiny green leaves of the aspen trees offered poor concealment, but travelers along this road were few, even during the busy holiday season.

"What now?" he asked, as Skye removed her helmet and helped him remove his, too. Answering his question, she gracefully swung around to straddle him on the cramped seat and locked his lips in a brief, tender kiss.

"Thank you for saving me from my captors, my knight in shining helmet."

David soon forgot the corniness of her remark as their lips met again and their embrace became more passionate. He found himself swept toward places he was reluctant to go, yet they were enticing nonetheless. Returning her affections cautiously, and then with hunger, his arms encircled her, even as she reached around to draw him downward. She leaned back on the handlebars—and her shoulder blade hit the horn button.

The piercing shriek of the horn brought David back to his senses abruptly, and he slid away, giving Skye room to upright herself on the seat. Laughing, she pursued, kissing his neck and holding him close, but the brief spell was broken. He tolerated her embrace, but went no farther.

They remained entwined in a warm hug for some time before Skye swung off the seat and hopped to the ground. She looked confused.

"I'm sorry if that was a bit sudden, David. I thought my feelings for you were pretty obvious, just as yours were for me."

"I'm not sure what I feel. I'm...very confused."

Averting her eyes, she asked, "Is there someone else? I just assumed there wasn't."

"No, well, no, not really," he stammered. Skye's beauty, intelligence, and passion were all he could possibly desire in a soul mate. There was no denying he was strongly attracted to her. Yet, something held him back.

"Is it my job?"

"Maybe. Or I might just need a little more time. I really don't know very much about you."

"What do you want to know? I was born in Montreal and lived for 18 years in Quebec. I'm 27 years old and speak three languages. I graduated from the Northwestern School of Journalism four years ago, at the top of my class. Sometimes, I'm confrontational, headstrong, and intimidating. Always, I'm an inquisitive pain in the ass. My career is on the fast track, or it was. And of all the men in the world, I can't stop thinking about a handsome, strong, and courageous idealist who works too hard and overanalyzes everything. Enough?"

David laughed. "That's plenty, for now. But a real relationship needs time. Let's take it slow. After we know each other better, maybe we won't feel the same way."

She raised the corners of her lips into a little smile, as she jumped on the back part of the ATV seat and wrapped her arms around him, more firmly than before. "By now, you should know I don't do anything slow," she said. "But I'll try."

On the drive back to Bill's parking spot, David took back roads to skirt around the town of Ward. He was starting to hate this little town. Every time he came near it, he ran into Major Thomas.

As they pulled beside Bill's truck, Bill jumped out and greeted them. "You're late!" he shouted, over the roar of the ATV engine.

The truck and trailer were still parked near the ditch of a narrow dirt road where David had left him two hours earlier. Since the trailer ramps were already extended, David swung the ATV around and drove straight onto the trailer without stopping. Three minutes later, they were riding back to Nederland.

Skye slouched in the back seat, using the rolled-up leather jacket as a pillow. Soon, the sounds of gentle, steady breathing indicated she was asleep. Noting she didn't snore, David notched a mark to the positive, and then immediately scolded himself for doing so.

He shook his head, unable to believe he was thinking this way about the antagonistic reporter. Certainly, the ruffled woman in the poor fitting clothes couldn't be the same slick villainess that had haunted his nightmares earlier in the mission. She seemed scared and defenseless. Even her sleep seemed troubled. Something had changed, and she was like a new person. Or was he the one who had changed?

"So what happened back there?" Bill asked, reining in David's dangerous thoughts.

He gave Bill the short version of the events at the resort, leaving out the romantic interlude, and concluding with, "If Major Thomas is back in the picture, things might get pretty dicey around here. I'm putting you and Jennifer in danger. It might be time for me to go somewhere else."

"You don't hear us complaining," said Bill. "You're still free to stay as long as you want."

"I really appreciate that, my friend. But I thought I might call Cassie and see if I could hang out with her and Ben."

As they rolled into the driveway, he gently nudged Skye awake. She shot upright, wild-eyed and disoriented. Upon seeing him and Bill, and then their peaceful surroundings, she calmed down as quickly as she had awakened.

"What time is it?" she asked.

"Noon." David was surprised. "Don't you have your watch?"

"I left it in the forest, back at the resort, along with everything else that might be bugged. I even left my stun gun, and that rarely leaves my side. The only things I took were my driver's license, credit cards, and this." She removed a thin leather pouch from her back pocket. From behind her driver's license, she pulled out a thick, featureless blue card. "I'll need your computer to play what's on this data storage card."

They entered the house, and Jennifer greeted them from the kitchen. She immediately noticed Skye's outfit. "Hey, hey! My sweater never looked better! But with my jeans riding so low on your hips, you look like you're into the latest weird children's fashions."

"I could use a belt," Skye agreed.

As Jennifer went upstairs to find a belt, David called to her, "We'll be downstairs in my room." He turned to Skye and added, "That didn't sound too good, did it? I'm going to ruin your reputation."

"I didn't think I had much of a reputation around here," Skye replied.

"It's pretty poor, but it's been improving steadily over the past few months. We've noticed you've really cut back on the viciousness of your Mars mission attacks."

She looked downward, as if studying an insect on David's shoes. "Yeah, you're not the only one who's noticed. That's part of why I'm here today. My producer is really ticked off, as is Burgess the creep, and probably others I don't even know about. Their pressure has been intense. And now they've gone around me...but I'll get to that later. First, the card."

They went downstairs, and David held the card near his computer. A popup application allowed him to download the contents of the card. It held several megabytes of audio files.

"I've indexed them by time and content," said Skye, watching over his shoulder. "Some of these are pretty good. Select that one." She pointed to one of the files.

David opened the audio file and turned up the volume on his machine's built-in speakers. A raspy voice almost made him jump. *"It's Sid. What's the latest?"*

"That's my producer's voice," explained Skye.

Surprised, David turned to look at her. "No. You didn't."

"Yes, I did," she said. "I bugged his office."

"Does he suspect anything?"

"Yeah, I think so. He might not be certain it was me, but he found the bug a few days ago, and he's not stupid. This is one of the last recordings, in fact. His suspicion might be part of the reason why Burgess forced her way onto my vacation weekend at Gold Lake. But there's more. Much more."

Her producer was obviously talking on the phone with someone, and they could only hear one side of the conversation. David had missed several sentences, so he returned to the start the file.

"It's Sid. What's the latest?"
"Yes, I know the content has been light lately. I'm taking care of it."
"Yes, I know."
"Yes, I know!"
"Well, you can tell her to kiss my... Never mind. She probably would. She kisses everyone else's."
"I said, I'll take care of it."
"How would she like it if we turned our attention on her? That might be worth a few ratings points."

"No, I'm not serious. I'm just a bit upset, that's all. She's promised us a lot, you know, and hasn't delivered much. I'm starting to take some heat."

"I understand. I'll take care of that, too."

With a loud click bordering a slam, the producer hung up the phone. He added "Bitch!" at the beginning of a longer string of expletives addressing Skye, the network, and the Mars mission.

"I assume the boss lady isn't very happy." That was a new voice, a woman, who sounded quite young.

"No, she's not. OK, kid, you're in. Fontaine's out. That's the edict from above."

A sigh, of contentment? "I won't let you down."

"See that you don't. And don't tell Fontaine, not yet. She can finish gathering the footage for this latest piece. We'll spin it, and you can host the show as your coming-out party."

"When's the target?"

"Next Friday, on the July 4th weekend. That'll give people something to stew about, as they roast their weenies around the backyard barbeque."

As the conversation ended, Skye suggested a different audio file. She pointed to a file recorded after her last trip to NASA-JPL, near the end of May, right after the Mars landing. Her producer was talking on the phone again. After some introductory remarks, he commented:

"I met her little weasel on the inside and hand delivered her bribe. Is she happier now?"

"Good. Try to keep her off my back, please. The Babylon show is coming along great. We'll air it next week."

The clip ended. Skye pointed to another file and explained that it was an earlier recording, one she had overlooked until a week ago, when she had reorganized the files. "Had I heard it earlier, I might have done some things differently," she said, wistfully.

This time, her producer was talking to another man in his office. Skye identified the second man as a secretary. The two were discussing travel plans for his trip with Skye to Pasadena for the Mars landing.

The conversation sounded quite normal to David, and he gave Skye a questioning glance. She told him to replay a short segment again.

"Should I try to book you on an earlier flight coming back? The 23rd is a Sunday, and I know you hate to travel on Sundays."

"No. I'd end up changing it anyway."

"Stop!" Skye stared at him intensely. "Well? What about that?"

"Sounds normal to me."

"Sid is not a patient man. Why wouldn't he want to return earlier? After the Mars landing, the party that night, and a scheduled press conference the following morning, we should have been out of there. We could have returned on May 21st, two days earlier."

David had a flash of insight. "You think he expected a serious problem with the Mars landing? One that might take several days to sort out?"

"No. But I suppose that's possible, too. Indeed, I did spend those extra days poking around JPL, digging into the reason the landing was off-course. By the way, their first guess was some bogus telemetry got uploaded. I'm sure you already know about that."

"Yes, that's still the best theory. Someone at JPL screwed up."

"Sid couldn't care less who screwed up, unless it made his Decadence in Babylon feature a bit juicier. You probably saw that show about the NASA celebration after the landing?"

"Nope. I was busy."

"Well, you didn't miss much. He pulled me away from my cargo investigation to have me do a stupid fluff story. Later, he cut my best interviews and background segments. The remnants made their modest celebration look like a big frat party on taxpayer dollars. But that's a different topic. Why else would Sid hang around for two more days?"

"In one of the phone calls, he mentioned delivering a bribe. Perhaps he needed some time for that?"

"I haven't figured out the bribe stuff yet. Come on! What else happened? Think big!" she added, impatiently.

David leaned back in his chair and thought for a moment. Then the bottom fell out of his stomach, and he swivelled around to face her. Skye sat on the edge of the bed. Her hands fretted nervously. One glance at her confirmed what she suspected. "The power outage?"

"The outage. Practically the whole country was in the dark for several days. Communications, food distribution, emergency services, and mass transit systems were all disrupted. Airline flights were grounded for nearly three days, until Saturday night. Things were a real mess, and we were stuck in California, in the middle of it all."

"But your producer couldn't have known about the outage before it happened. No one could have predicted it!"

She lay back on the bed and stared up at the ceiling. "Except the people who caused it."

"Except...well, yeah, I suppose. So you're implying a link between your network and the terrorists who caused the outage? Forgive me, but that's hard to believe."

Skye replied sadly, "It's no harder to believe than some of your own theories. You said no one could guarantee the failure of the Mars mission unless saboteurs were working to make it happen. I forget your exact words." She rolled onto her elbow and looked him in the eyes. "I didn't believe in your crazy conspiracies at the time. Now, I do."

"But Skye, if this is true...my God. What are we caught in the middle of?"

He leaned back, and the room spun around him. Actually, he was spinning in his chair. It was an old nervous habit.

"Whatever it is, we're in it deep, David. And now I've lost my own program, replaced by a piece of eye candy with no talent."

David moved over and sat beside her on the bed. She sniffled, and the tiniest glimmer of a tear traced its way down her cheek. Fiercely, she brushed it aside. He saw the old fire returning in her eyes.

"They won't get away with it," she said, sitting up. "I have not yet begun to fight. Who said that, oh great history expert?"

"John Paul Jones, in a Revolutionary War naval battle. He's dead now," David added, dejectedly. "He lost his ship, his flag, most of his crew, and almost the battle. Skye, we're way out of our league, here. We're just two people, with powerful enemies, and we still don't know who they are. What can we do?"

"I think we're sitting pretty good, as long as I have this little gem." She picked up the blue data storage card and held it lightly in her fingers. "Remember what I do for a living. Investigative reporters have brought down some powerful people before."

"Without a network, you aren't a reporter."

"I'll find another network and go back on the airwaves. And you already have a network. A strong, hidden one. Now that your people have landed on Mars, you have a whole planet to back you up, too."

David rolled his eyes toward the ceiling and shook his head. "At the present time, Mars and a dollar might buy you a short phone call." Still, Skye's optimism was contagious, and he felt his own confidence rising a few notches. "Perhaps you're right. The situation might not be hopeless after all. Almost hopeless, but not entirely."

"That's my David!" she said, clapping him on the arm, before embracing him much more tenderly. "And I remember another thing you said when we first met. You talked about balance. You said Alpha was a powerful organization with resources and motivation. Won't they help us?"

"We don't know who they are, either," David reminded her.

"Then we need to find them. Fast."

A flash of suspicion worked its way along David's synapses. Could everything Skye just told him, and everything they had recently experienced, be a great big lie? What if all this was merely the latest attempt by her network to learn the identity of Alpha? Might she be using him, contriving her affections, while pumping him for information?

Nonsense. I'm already helping her, and I've told her everything I know about Alpha.

Unless she doesn't believe that.

Fool! You could sit here and argue with yourself all night. Meanwhile, there's a beautiful woman in your arms. It's time for you to trust her.

He held her closer, and neither spoke for awhile.

Later, when they wandered back upstairs, they found a belt on the kitchen table. Jennifer and Bill were watching a sitcom on the television. Jennifer looked up and frowned. "You two must have had a lot to talk about! It's nearly four o'clock."

"Oh!" gasped Skye. "Then we missed it. The program that's being hosted by my replacement. It was supposed to be on at two."

"Replacement?" asked Bill.

David held up his hand to halt any further questions. "It's a long story."

He turned to Skye. "If you really want to watch the program, my support team records everything it can find that's of relevance to the Mars mission. I can play it back on my computer."

"Wonderful! I can't wait to see the little tart's debut. I hope she gets the hiccups or has a booger hanging out of her nose."

Laughing, David suggested, "We might pick up some more hints about what's been going on, too."

"I doubt it," said Skye. "They removed the meat and potatoes from that program, too. What's left probably isn't worth much."

Jennifer spoke up. "Mind if we watch? And by the way, since you skipped lunch, what would you like for dinner?"

"Lunch?" David suddenly realized he was famished. He hadn't eaten anything all day. He had also neglected to check his work messages since early that morning.

David excused himself, asking everyone to wait an hour before watching the USNN program on his computer. That would give him plenty of time to catch up on his work. Before heading downstairs, he grabbed a granola bar from the kitchen.

It turned out he needed every minute. Several minor work matters required his attention. He also sent a long message to Cassie asking if he could visit her in California for a week or two, until things settled down in Colorado.

Just as he had completed these tasks, the others filed into the room, ready to watch the USNN program. They brought a few slices of warmed pizza for David, along with several bottles of beer. He chose an Oasis Oatmeal Stout, a local brew he had always enjoyed. If the upcoming program was as bad as Skye claimed, he might need a few beers to calm himself.

He reentered the mission support center and soon found a pointer to the recorded program on the "Rank and File's Rank and Vile" list on the bulletin board in the central atrium. "Wasting Time and Money on Mars" had already been voted into the number two slot on the list, just below Skye's "Decadence in Babylon" program from several weeks ago.

After more support team members had time to vote, "Wasting Time and Money on Mars" would capture the top spot. Watching the first half of the program was enough to convince David of this. Skye's earlier description had been quite accurate.

Devoid of any real substance, the program was far more one-sided than any he had ever seen before on USNN. The whole premise of the program was to suggest the only accomplishments of the Mars crew, after several weeks on the surface, were making grandiose speeches, covering the *Perseus* with sandbags, and digging a hole.

In reality, despite the shortage of field equipment, the first few weeks of the mission were a resounding success. The crew had verified the usefulness of tele-robotics, explored the plains around the *Perseus*, deployed a simple ground penetrating radar to detect ample reservoirs of liquid water about a kilometer beneath the surface, collected samples of porous layers of rock, established their NASA-dictated "zones of minimal biological risk," ruled out the existence of deadly chemical, biological, and organic toxins in the dust and sand, verified the habitat's dust filtration system, baselined the radiation spectrum, and begun detailed studies of biology, geology, and atmospheric dynamics.

These tasks had been accomplished from the comfort of the *Perseus*. The crew had stepped foot on the surface in person only once, briefly, for PR purposes. Anna had delivered a beautiful speech about the "New World" being open for exploration and settlement. Billions of people around the Earth had celebrated, even as USNN did their best to ignore the monumental event.

Best of all, the crew is still alive.

In the science community, theories of planetary creation and evolution had already been reexamined vigorously, given the sudden abundance of in situ surface data from Mars. The queue of science requests had grown, and David's advisors in the Mission Support "science backroom" were forced to make some difficult priority calls.

Requests for data about solar radiation, atmospheric water vapor content, and greenhouse gas composition had been given the highest priority, since these areas of study had direct, immediate implications back on Earth for longstanding theories of weather prediction, ozone layer depletion, global warming, and SETI, the Search for Extra-Terrestrial Life.

The geology community clamored for more information about sediment layering. Much of this research needed to wait until the crew visited places like Sentinel Canyon. Until then, Ollie placated the earthly geologists by gathering some data from a rock outcrop inside the small impact crater just south of the *Perseus*.

The rock outcrop had provided some tantalizing clues in support of a "high obliquity" theory of Mars orbital mechanics. In the high obliquity model, every few million years, Mars wobbled enough to make the equator the coldest place on the planet. The model predicted that the regions to the west of the massive Tharsis volcanoes, where the crew had landed, should have seen frequent, glacier-dominated ice ages. If the theories were true, the crew was five million years too late to witness the last ice age, but the evidence of its passage would be preserved in the sediment layers.

The astrobiology community and SETI were captivated by Anna's measurements of methane in the atmosphere. In most of the models, naturally produced methane broke down much faster than it was created. The new methane readings seemed to verify less precise, remote measurements from years ago. Somewhere on the planet, perhaps in isolated underground niches, microbial life forms might be thriving. Finding these colonies of microbes would be a difficult quest, a holy grail for future generations of Mars explorers.

As Skye had warned, the USNN program mentioned none of this. Even her description of the replacement host, Maria Tavish, turned out to be correct. Tavish looked sleazier than the program content. She stumbled over her lines more than once, much to Skye's delight.

Some reused JPL party scenes were credited back to the "Decadence in Babylon" piece. A camera panned around a large, dimly lit ballroom. Well-dressed people lurked about the outer edges of a central dance floor. An impressive crystal chandelier dominated the high ceiling above. Beyond the dance floor, pockets of partygoers congregated at several tables or talked in smaller groups near the plushly ornate walls. Noise and energy levels were high, alcohol flowed freely, and some of the dancing was a bit rowdy.

Jennifer's sharp eyes detected a familiar face. "Hey, there's Ben! He's sitting at a table in the back." She pointed at a corner of the display.

David squinted his eyes. The man looked like Ben, but in the poor lighting, it was hard to tell. "I wonder if there's any way to enhance the contrast?"

"Here, let me try," said Jennifer. "I've done some video imaging work before."

Skye offered to help, too. Working around David, who remained in front of the machine to satisfy its security algorithms, they toggled some settings and backtracked through a shorter clip several times to view the results. Each time, the image became sharper and brighter.

Meanwhile, Skye asked, "Who's Ben?"

"He's my…friend." David was about to say "brother-in-law," but while he had accepted Skye as an accomplice and more, it was not yet time to introduce her to his family. "He works on an important telemetry team at JPL," he added.

Jennifer made another adjustment and played the clip again. Though the foreground lighting was saturated, the brightness of the background had improved dramatically. Ben's features were easily seen now. Someone had just departed from his table, leaving him alone with two drinks. Ben moved the far drink, grabbed the coaster or napkin beneath, and slipped it into an inner pocket of his sport coat.

"That's weird," said Bill. "I wonder why he took that napkin?"

"Maybe he's collecting souvenirs?" offered Jennifer.

Bill laughed. "We'll have to give him a hard time about that. Why don't you save that clip so we can send it to him?"

David ran a command to save the video output into a file. To be sure he got the right segment, he replayed the saved version, which began a bit earlier than the sequence they had just watched. This time, Ben's drinking companion showed up clearly.

Skye gasped, "That's Sid! My producer!"

The meaning of her words took some time to sink in. When they did, David felt sick to his stomach. "It can't be!" he said, feebly.

"Play it back again!" Skye ordered.

He slowed the playback to half speed and reran the clip. They watched as Ben's drinking companion removed an envelope from his pocket, folded it, and placed it on the table under his drink. Then he left, and the rest of the scene played out as before.

David froze the playback and stared at the static display. No one spoke for some time.

Eventually, Skye said, "I guess that explains one little mystery."

"No. I don't believe it," said David. "I can't believe it." He flashed back to some of his earlier conversations with Ben. They had discussed various aspects of the Mars mission in depth on several occasions. Always, always, they were in agreement on the most important points. Ben's fraternizing with the producer of a radical anti-Mars mission TV program was simply impossible. Yet he had just seen it with his own two eyes.

"Skye, could the video have been altered? Could Ben's likeness have been superimposed on top of someone else?"

"I suppose it's possible. But why?"

"To throw us on a wrong track. To make us suspect someone who's innocent."

Simultaneously, Bill and Jennifer asked, "Suspect?" Jennifer continued, "Did we miss something? All I saw was your producer leaving something, and Ben picking it up. Maybe Ben asked for a handkerchief. Perhaps they placed a bet on what dance couple would stay on the floor the longest. Who knows what really happened?"

A lengthy discussion followed, where Skye and David revealed the contents of the recordings on Skye's blue datacard. They even replayed some of those audio files, hoping to find a discrepancy and remove suspicion from their friend.

The clincher was when Skye revealed her datacard also contained gigabytes of raw video footage from various past programs. She explained her intention to create a video résumé from the footage, as part of her future job search process. Some of her original interviews and background shots from the "Wasting Time and Money on Mars" program were present, including the scene with Ben, which she claimed could not have been altered. Her producer's face also appeared during the setup of several scenes.

"But this just doesn't make any sense! Ben knows I'm still alive, he knows my job, and he knows where I'm hiding. If your producer is bribing him, why haven't any unexpected visitors shown up on the doorstep like you did last winter?"

"They still might, David," warned Skye, her eyes round and glassy. "We have to assume they know where you are. I don't know why they've waited, but you shouldn't stay here any longer. None of you should."

Calmly, Bill spoke up, in his deep, lumbering voice. "No. Your producer doesn't know anything about David because Ben wouldn't tell him. Ben hates USNN more than I do, and he's a lousy liar. If he's on their payroll, it's for some other reason."

Jennifer agreed. Unless Ben offered information about David freely, there was very little to connect the two of them. "Except Cassie, of course," she added.

"Cassie?" asked Skye.

David brushed off her question and continued along this new line of speculation. "So you're implying Ben is doing some other service for the network. If so, what could it be?"

"You said he's on a JPL telemetry team?" asked Skye. She called his attention to the likelihood that a telemetry error caused the *Perseus* to land 100 kilometers off-course. "Perhaps your friend caused the error? Or he helped to cover it up afterwards?"

"No way," Bill stated again. Ben would never help the network, and he would never sabotage the mission.

Skye forged on, as if oblivious to the consternation around her. "Think about it—it makes sense! Recall some of the earlier problems on the mission, like the explosion of the first ERV and the loss of telemetry from the other vehicles at the primary landing site. What if the JPL telemetry team was responsible for all of it, and they've covered their tracks so well that you haven't suspected them?"

"The ERV couldn't have exploded," said David calmly. "And my team would know if someone at JPL was messing around with the telemetry."

"Would they?" Skye had ramped up into high gear now. Openly agitated, she started to pace the room. "You once told me half your support team might work at NASA. Perhaps others used to work there and still have strong ties. If NASA is doing something behind your back, most of your support team might be involved!"

Jennifer frowned. "But why? Something that big would require an equally big motive. The NASA engineers I know, the people in the working ranks, tend to be idealists. Most would give anything for this mission to succeed."

"I can think of several reasons," said Skye, grimly. "The most obvious is jealousy. NASA isn't running the mission, and that really irritates some of the higher managers. They're very critical and suspicious, since they don't know the motives of the mission planners. Then there's the JPL-Ames-Houston triangle, too."

"Huh?" David had followed her reasoning, and could even concede that a few disgruntled NASA engineers might veer over to the dark side. But she lost him with her reference to a triangle.

Skye explained. "JPL, Ames, and Houston. It's no secret those three NASA centers often quarrel amongst themselves. Whenever I visit one of those places, I always have to remember where I am, so I can guard my tongue and say the right things or tweak people the right way. It all has to do with their philosophy of space exploration."

"Go on," spurred David. This was news to him, but he noted Jennifer nodding her head in agreement.

"Here's the triangle, in a nutshell." Skye continued to pace the room, lecturing to her class. "Houston is one extreme. They specialize in manned spaceflight. They use minimal robotics, only when required to support humans. Ames is in the middle. They sponsor cooperation between humans and machines, making both more efficient and effective. JPL is the other extreme, which believes humans are a liability in space, and should almost always be replaced by machines."

Jennifer now looked skeptical. "That's too simplistic. I know people at all three centers who aren't like that. However, now that I think about it, there's another triangle, too."

Jennifer became the teacher, as they asked her to elaborate. "Consider the scope of operations at each center. Houston is concerned mostly with low-Earth orbit and lunar exploration—things like the International Space Station, plans for lunar bases, medical studies, and so on. Ames focuses on astrobiology and planetary science. The whole solar system is their playground, but they like the inner planets best. JPL doesn't care about biology or medicine. They deal mainly with the outer solar system, the galaxy, and the universe at large. They come full circle, or full triangle, when you consider in-orbit telescopes requiring human service, or planned radio-telescope arrays on the far side of the moon."

"I'm...not sure I see the relevance," said David, feeling unusually dense.

"Simply put, Ames should solidly support the current Mars mission. Mars is an outer-inner planet with astrobiology potential. The mission is a showcase for human-machine interaction. It hits all their top priorities. However, at both JPL and Houston, you might find camps who strongly oppose the mission for wildly different reasons."

"I see," said David. He truly did understand a bit more clearly now, but he would also need some time to process these triangles and their implications. One conclusion seemed to jump right out. "So you agree with Skye. JPL might be working against us?"

Jennifer hesitated. "Overall, no, I would still be shocked if that were the case. Some of my closest colleagues work at JPL, and they're good people, every one of them. I trust them completely. But..." she paused again, and a decidedly unhappy cloud settled over her normally cheerful features. "...I do admit it's possible. Smaller groups of people at JPL or in Houston who feel their jobs are threatened in some way might refuse to help or even cause problems. But open sabotage? And Ben?" She shook her head, and stared at the floor.

David speculated about his next move. "Just before you came down here, I sent a message to Cassie asking if I could stay with her for a few weeks until things settled down in Colorado. It's been too long since I've seen her."

"Under the circumstances, that sounds like a real bad move," said Bill.

Skye questioned the connection between Cassie and Ben, so David revealed their two-year marriage. He described Cassie as a close confidante. A tiny, inner voice of caution tried to hold him back, but it failed, as he also explained Cassie was his sister.

A look of surprise crossed Skye's face, but David saw no open pleasure. If anything, she seemed sympathetic, as if finally realizing how deeply any deception by Ben would hurt David.

The discussion drifted into personal memories of Ben and Cassie together. Many of the joyful recollections were already tinged with doubtful sadness. If Ben was working against the mission in any way, relationships would be deeply affected.

Then Skye interrupted with a new thought. "Perhaps a trip to visit your sister wouldn't be a mistake after all. It would be dangerous, for sure, but it might also be a perfect opportunity to watch your brother-in-law and figure out if he's really involved!"

"He doesn't know we suspect him," said David, considering her idea carefully. The others expressed their doubts, but he thought Skye had raised a good point.

David was tired of hiding. If Ben was the next link in the chain toward identifying the Beta conspirators and thwarting their plans, perhaps it was time for him to adopt some tactics better suited to Skye's talents than his own. Probing Ben for information might turn out to be foolish or even dangerous, but it would certainly be a move the opposition wasn't expecting!

CHAPTER 25
MOVEMENT

MarsDay 219, 11:11 p.m.
(July 4, 8:00 a.m.)

By the time his alarm clock went off, David had already finished several hours of work. Sleep had been hard to come by. Eventually, he had given up, brewed a cup of coffee in the kitchen, and settled down in front of his computer.

Insomnia had its uses. Over the past several months, reports and data had flowed steadily into Mission Support from the Mars crew. Unless he constantly kept on top of the unread reports, they accumulated quickly. The effort required to process the backlog seemed to increase exponentially.

Throughout the mission, the crew submitted the same reports to Mission Support every day. A brief Commander's Check-in Report was always followed by a Commander's Log containing more detail about daily crew activities, mission status, and upcoming goals. Anna would send a Narrative Report suitable for release to the press after minor editing and formatting. An Engineering Report, Geology Science Report, Biology Science Report, Health and Safety Report, and indexed Multimedia Report would also be transmitted, though the contents of these reports varied according to need.

While sophisticated software helped the crew to generate the reports swiftly, the only help for David in reading them was his speed-reading skills. Sifting action items out of the volume of information sometimes took hours. He had long since given up on using software to create context links, though such aids would be useful later when the reports were distributed to the science community.

Fortunately, he could delegate most of the technical work to the technicians, while assigning various staff to follow up on the most important open issues. These management tasks also took additional time and effort, however. In fact, each solution tended to generate more reports from Earthly experts. The feedback loop could snowball if he allowed it get out of control.

With a satisfied grunt, he closed his last trouble ticket status report. Being caught up on his work was certainly a good way to start the day. If he was sleepy later, he could take a nap on the bus.

Last night, as the discussion with his friends continued, he had firmly decided to visit Ben and Cassie in Pasadena. His suitcase was already packed. Despite misgivings about this course of action, Bill offered to drive him to the bus station in Denver a few hours from now. David would catch a 1:00 p.m. bus to Los Angeles. They would drop off Skye along the way, so she could shop for clothing. Later, she would scout some of the downtown media branches and schedule interviews, even though she was more interested in the larger east coast media conglomerates.

For his plans to be complete, all David needed was for Cassie to confirm a visit was convenient. She usually checked her messages early in the morning, so he expected a response from her soon.

His nose told him to wait upstairs, where Bill and Jennifer were preparing a bountiful breakfast in the kitchen. The decadent aroma of scrambled eggs, bacon, and french toast wafted down the stairwell, luring him upwards. He almost bumped into Skye as she descended from the upper floor. She was still rubbing the sleep from her eyes.

A few minutes later, breakfast was served. Conversation around the table was sparse and contrived. After their lengthy discussions the night before, little remained to be said. Bill and Jennifer still considered David's plan to be too dangerous. They made a last ditch effort to talk him out of it, but their arguments failed to sway him. He was determined to get some answers out of Ben.

As Bill cleaned the dishes off the table, David excused himself to recheck his messages. Skye followed him downstairs. As he settled back in front of his computer, she sat beside him on the edge of the bed and lightly trailed her fingers over his arm in an openly flirtatious manner.

Slightly distracted, David guided his avatar into his virtual office, where he found two messages awaiting. One was a reply from Cassie. The sender of the other message, unfortunately, was <chicken_little>.

He winced and muttered, "Great. Just what I needed this morning. A dose of mental abuse, right when fortitude is needed." Choosing pain before pleasure, he opened the message.

To: <shepherd>
From: <chicken_little>
Subject: Weather report
Priority: Emergency

David -

The sky is still falling.
Winds are calm before a tornado strikes. A basement makes a good storm shelter.

As usual, David reread the short message several times. It seemed more ominous than most of the previous riddles.

Skye found the "basement" reference interesting. David's shelter was already a basement office in the mountains, probably the safest place in the world from any possible tornado threat. "But if that's what the riddle plays upon, then Chicken Little knows where you are."

David lifted his arms and spun around in his chair to face her. "Why not? Everyone else seems to know where I am." Skye's long, dark hair, swirling over her shoulders enticingly, threatened to become another distraction. However, his dismay easily overwhelmed his passion. He was forced to voice the inevitable conclusion. "It's time for me to move on."

"Yet..." Skye studied the brief message again. "If Chicken Little truly wants to help you, and the message is meant to be advice, then it's probably telling you to stay put."

"Don't run out into the storm?" The words dripped from his tongue like acid. "Any child would heed that advice. But how would he possibly know what I'm planning to do?"

"Perhaps he heard about our run-in with Major Thomas yesterday?"

"How?" David shook his head. His only certainty was <chicken_little> played mind games with him at a time when David needed to take decisive action. Angrily, he hit a key to display the next message, from Cassie.

To: <shepherd>
From: <kahuna>
Subject: Re: Personal Message
Priority: High

Hi David!

Sorry to disappoint you, but Ben just surprised me with a spontaneous get-away ski vacation to New Zealand! He knows I've always wanted to go there. The workload for the Mars mission is light, and I can shift my Earthly clients to another counselor while I'm gone.
We're looking forward to three weeks of fun in the snow, sightseeing, and no stress. Maybe we'll even do some family planning. *Wink wink.* We're leaving tomorrow morning, and we'll be gone for three weeks.
Our other big news is we just bought a beautiful wooded lot in the mountains near Lake Arrowhead. It's a pricey, newly developed area, but we're going to save some money by building only a small cabin. Then we'll add on later, when we can.
If not for worries about how we're ever going to pay for this trip, my world would be perfect right now. Perhaps you could come and visit when we return? Your work might be busier then, too, so I'll understand if you say you can't get away.
Love ya, bro...

Cassie

The impact of Cassie's message hit him hard. The room spun around him again, and this time, his chair was stationary. He fought his growing nausea at the prospect of his little sister cavorting for three weeks with, well...her husband. After all, they still had no real proof of Ben's involvement with the USNN network or the mission saboteurs. Today's strong suspicions might be sand castles, destined to be washed away by the next wave.

They discussed what to do, in light of this new twist of events. Skye's situation hadn't changed. She still planned an aggressive search for a reporting job at a different network. She had many contacts within her industry, and she planned to call in some markers.

David was in limbo, however. He still needed to leave, but he had nowhere to go. Yet, in reality, he could go anywhere. Any hotel with a high-speed Internet connection could serve as a temporary storm shelter. If he kept moving around, paying cash for his expenses, he might keep ahead of any pursuers for several weeks...until he made another mistake.

"With Ben vanishing for three weeks, do you really need to go anywhere?" asked Skye. "If he's already ratted you out, we wouldn't be sitting here right now, at least not alive. He probably won't be talking to anyone from a ski slope in New Zealand, either."

"Unless he wants to be far, far away when the dirty deed is done," said David, scowling. Yet he still couldn't grasp the prospect of Ben being so deeply involved in the Beta conspiracy as to throw David to the wolves. His only other incentives for leaving his comfortable nest were the close proximity of Major Thomas, the cryptic message of <chicken_little>, and his own growing need to take some sort of decisive action.

None of these reasons, by itself, was urgent enough to warrant a hasty decision. He decided to wait until Cassie and Ben returned. Then he would pay them a visit and do some investigating.

Unfortunately, the timing was less than ideal, due to the landing of the cargo vehicle and ERV during the first week of August. Beta probably intended to disrupt those landings, too, so David would need to assess Ben's involvement quickly.

MarsDay 245, 11:01 p.m.
(July 31, 1:00 a.m.)

Anna rolled over in her bed and checked the time. Three hours after retiring for the evening, her only sleep had come in short, troubled fits. At least the murmur of the wind had subsided, as well as the subtle trembling of the *Perseus* from sudden gusts. They had survived their first dust storm on Mars, though it was a mild one. Tomorrow, they would brush off the solar panels and assess any damage from the abrasive dust and sand. More severe storms would surely follow, so they needed to be prepared.

While the last remnants of the storm had lingered long enough to keep her awake, Anna was also distracted by the results of her latest water supply tests. After nine months of recycling their water, toxins and bacterial contamination were slowly accumulating. Meanwhile, helpful microbes had been dying at an unusually alarming rate. If the present trend continued, she could probably stretch their water supply to last another three months. They weren't in any immediate danger, but unless she figured out what was wrong, they would all be dead within six months.

Their plans had called for supplementing the drinking water with outside sources and processing their wastes more efficiently in a closed greenhouse system. Without one or both of these options, the quality of their water supply would continue to deteriorate.

Neither option was currently feasible. The greenhouse pods and heavy digging equipment were still out of reach, a hundred kilometers away. Her best option was simply to wait for seven more days. If all went well, their backup cargo vehicle and ERV would land safely, near the *Perseus*. Soon, she would have all the supplies she needed.

If both landings failed, her final option was to perform a miracle. Perhaps she could transmute rocks into water through sheer willpower. Miracles were hard to come by on Mars. Planning was usually more reliable. The commander would be expecting her to develop some solid backup plans.

They could manually dig a hole deep enough to reach the ice-rich layers of soil below, cover the hole with a plastic bubble, and bake the bubble with the sun's rays to promote evaporation and condensation. Technically, this plan should work. In the thin atmospheric pressure of Mars, water boiled almost immediately after it melted. A constant cycle of melting, boiling, condensing, freezing, melting, and collecting could be maintained indefinitely, with minimal equipment and only a modest input of solar energy.

Unfortunately, they had no real shovels, pick axes, or other equipment for digging. They also lacked an adequate plastic bubble, though they could probably improvise. Even with the proper equipment, the chore would be well beyond the abilities of Robonauts. The hardest work would require human labor, and the limited range of motion in their space suits would make the task daunting.

Worst of all, they had no way of telling how much water they could expect to mine with this technique. They might go through a lot of trouble, only to produce a few glassfuls of water.

Other than their water problems, the mission had gone as well as could be expected, given their lack of equipment. Upon reaching Mars, the crew had finally come together as a team. Verbal disputes were rare, so the psychologists seemed happy. Equipment failures had also been few. Apocalyptic predictions about dust contamination and radiation sickness had proven to be unfounded. A week ago, a radiation spike from a minor solar flare was hardly an inconvenience. The *Perseus* even felt larger, now that she slept in her own, private cabin. Had they landed at the primary Medusae site, all would be well on the new world.

If any miracle happened with the water recycling system, it would come from the environmental experts back on Earth. She still conversed frequently with Mission Support, borrowing strength and optimism from David when her own supply was running low. The finest researchers in all branches of environmental science assisted the support team. Each day, Anna spent several hours gathering, formatting, and transmitting new batches of data to satisfy various requests from Earth. The experts followed dreams of spin-off applications, research proposals, and new theories. Solutions were just a matter of time.

I'll be lying here awake all night, hoping others will solve my problems. I need to do something.

If her conundrums seemed impossible to solve, perhaps she should set her sights higher. She had learned a little trick during grad school, another good way to relax and adjust her focus. Throwing on a robe, she padded downstairs to an unobstructed window in the EVA room, where she gazed outside into the night sky.

At night, Mars truly became an alien world. A lack of reflected moonlight made viewing the landscape futile. Phobos and Deimos, the two moons of Mars, were just too small to be of much use.

Looking upwards, however, the dark sky glittered. A million multi-colored jewels blazed fiercely down through remnants of dust from the storm in the lower atmosphere. The same, familiar constellations greeted her as she would have seen on the Earth, but they were nearly drowned out by the brilliance of their neighboring stars and constellations.

The thin atmosphere of Mars had little turbulence, so the stars twinkled strangely. If she watched long enough, their movements would also seem odd. The stars here didn't spin around Polaris in the Little Dipper as they would if viewed from the northern hemisphere on Earth. The Martian axis of rotation was aligned toward a different point in the sky. North and south weren't the same absolute directions on Mars and Earth.

Somewhere out there in the alien sky was a solution to all of her problems. In fact, somewhere out there was a solution to everyone's problems. She had only to expand her mind and embrace the limitless possibilities. Some people called this "thinking outside the box," but Anna liked to call it "thinking inside infinity."

She remained at the window for ages, lost in the loveliness of the vast cosmos. When she finally tore herself away and returned to her cabin, sleep arrived soon after her head touched the pillow.

Though solutions to her problems remained elusive, responsibility now rested with the infinite intelligence of the universe. Pressure, fear, and stress had temporarily melted away. In her powerful new perspective, the universe was in harmony. All things were good. Events would transpire, and she would absorb whatever divine wisdom came her way.

MarsDay 247, 9:49 a.m.
(August 1, 12:45 p.m.)

From his vantage point in a corner of the spacious Union Station waiting room, David watched a clerk hand Bill a bus ticket through a thin slot at the bottom of a heavily fortified cashier window. Turning, Bill threaded his way back to him and Jennifer through long rows of wooden benches, dodging stacks of suitcases and sprawled, resting bodies. The station was surprisingly busy for a Sunday afternoon, as people came and went on busses or trains to destinations unknown.

Bill slipped the ticket casually into an outside pocket on David's light windbreaker jacket. "That should get you to Pasadena," he said, as they sank to a less conspicuous position, on the floor next to Jennifer. "Just remember to use my blurry park service badge, in case anyone asks for your photo ID."

"I hope the bus driver is far-sighted," joked Jennifer. "You two don't look anything alike."

"We'll see. It might be a short trip." David reached into his pocket. The texture of the paper ticket was reassuring.

Faking his identity was a violation of several recently enacted anti-terrorism laws designed to track the movement of suspects across state lines. Unfortunately, he had no choice. He needed to reach Pasadena without triggering any identification alerts to draw the attention of the FBI, Chinese spies, or the media. Traveling as Bill was the safest way to go.

"Your bus leaves in ten minutes through those doors," said Bill, pointing to a bank of glass doors on the other side of the waiting room.

"Last chance, David," said Jennifer. "Are you sure this is the right thing to do?"

"No, but I'm doing it anyway."

Wiping a moist tear from the corner of her eye, she said, "Give Cassie a hug from me, and call us when you're ready to come back." Then she gripped his forearms tightly. "And be careful. I have a horrible feeling about this."

David picked up his two light bags and walked casually across the crowded room. He turned once and smiled at his friends.

Once through the doors, a blast of hot air greeted him. The temperature in downtown Denver hovered near a hundred degrees, and the black asphalt of the street radiated heat in all directions. He removed his jacket and draped it over his arm. Then he sauntered down a sidewalk along the terminal until he came to a bus displaying "Los Angeles" in block letters on a side-mounted E-Ink billboard. A short line had already formed, so he took his place at the end and waited. Upon reaching the bus steps, a street-side conductor clipped his ticket without asking for a photo ID. David breathed a sigh of relief. He had passed another hurdle.

He took a seat near the back of the bus and waited for the other passengers to embark. He shared the back half of the bus with only three other people, until a tall man of wide girth lumbered down the aisle and sat across from David, one row behind.

The man's flowing brown robe immediately caught David's attention. He tried not to stare at a small insignia on the right shoulder. It was a white shield with two crossing keys. The monk in the woods near Brainard Lake had worn the same logo, so many months ago.

Despite the steady stream of cool air blowing from above, small beads of perspiration formed on his David's brow. The bus started its thousand-mile journey by lurching way from the curb. He snuck another glance back. The robe was definitely a monk's habit, and the man was watching David intensely. As their eyes met, the man smiled.

MarsDay 248, 12:45 a.m.
(August 2, 3:06 a.m.)

"Next stop, downtown Las Vegas, and the new Pair-O-Dice station!" the bus driver announced over the crackling intercom.

The message woke David abruptly from a shallow slumber. He had fought against sleep for hours, fearing he would wake up already dead. However, the long, dark ride through Utah had been too monotonous. The gentle swaying of the bus eventually lulled him to sleep.

He glanced over at the monk, whose eyes were closed and face expressionless. David wondered if the man was asleep or in a deep trance.

His question was answered when the monk spoke. "Is this your stop?"

David looked around, checking to make sure he was the one being addressed. The three other riders in the back of the bus had long since departed, way back in western Colorado. New passengers had embarked, but all were sitting at least five rows ahead of them. It was just he and the monk.

He was tempted to pretend he didn't hear the man's question, but he quickly changed his mind. Perhaps some conversation might be enlightening.

He replied, "No. You?"

The man laughed deeply and heartily, but his eyes remained closed. "Las Vegas would be an interesting place for a clergyman to call home. No, I'm going on to Pasadena."

David cursed inwardly. That meant he would share the bus with the monk for another 12 hours. Once more he was tempted to lapse into silence, but the man's words were an easy invitation to learn more about his background and intentions.

"You have family in Pasadena, then?" he asked.

"Sure do. Six brothers and three sisters." The man launched into a lengthy synopsis of his close relatives. By the time the bus left the Las Vegas station, on its way to a quick stop at the airport, David had learned the monk's name was Brother Matthew, he hadn't seen his family for over two years, and he enjoyed the dry climate of Arizona.

"Tucson is a long way from Denver," said David, fishing for information. He recalled the van driven by the other monk had been stolen in Tucson. "How did you end up there?"

"Well now. That's a long story."

A hint of a smile crossed the man's lips, and David waited for him to say more. Instead, frustratingly, he changed the subject. "Please pardon my intrusion. I noticed you seemed quite upset, earlier. You were also having trouble sleeping. Is there anything I can do to help?"

David searched Brother Matthew's face for any signs of malice, but he saw only genuine concern. The man had finally opened his eyes, tugging on his short, gray beard as he spoke. Wrinkles of concentration curled on his forehead.

He sure looks harmless enough. Put a red hat and suit on him, and he would make a great Santa.

Appearances can be deceiving, stupid.

Mister, you can help by telling me who you are, why you're here, and what you intend. But you won't do that, will you?

His inner dialogue might have continued for hours, but the man was waiting for a reply to his question. David guardedly responded, "Thanks, but I'm probably beyond your help. Unless you have a crystal ball under that habit."

The monk made a show of groping his pockets. "Nope, I don't seem to have one. However, help can come from many places, if one is receptive. I rely upon prayer when I'm in need. It's not as direct as a crystal ball, but it's much more reliable and satisfying."

David grunted, and politely nodded his head. He had been praying a lot lately, but answers had not been very forthcoming. He looked at Brother Matthew again, trying to see a representative, a pipeline to greater knowledge. Yet he saw only a potential imposter, a paid assassin who was toying with his prey before finishing his task. It was time to probe deeper.

"The emblem on your habit looks interesting. Tell me about it."

The monk smiled, and launched into another lengthy discussion about the history of the Vatican Observatory, of which he claimed to be affiliated. David interrupted frequently with questions, recalling his undergraduate studies of science and religion in the European medieval and renaissance periods. The man turned out to be quite a scholar on the subject, and their conversation became more relaxed and animated. David tried not to let his guard down, but he found himself warming to a kindred soul whose passion for knowledge appeared quite genuine.

The bus pulled into the Pasadena station at 11:00 a.m. local time. During the trip, David had learned more about the synthesis of science and religion than in all his undergraduate courses combined. The monk got up to leave, shaking David's hand as he passed by, and bestowing a blessing upon him and his endeavors.

With his head spinning from new ideas and connections, David reassessed the encounter. He was still alive, and the historian in him was deliriously happy. However, he had failed to gather much practical information about Brother Matthew, other than the interesting link to the Vatican Observatory.

Was that revered organization somehow connected to the Mars mission sponsors or the opposition? The proposition was reasonable because the Vatican did have a long history of providing skilled labor and financial support for the arts and sciences. He resolved to consider the matter further. Perhaps he would suggest the theory to Skye and see what a professional investigator could discover.

Looking out the tinted bus window, he was delighted to spot Cassie on the sidewalk outside. She appeared to be studying a schedule board. While David had been lost in thought, the other passengers had debussed. Cassie must be wondering if he was aboard, or whether his plans had changed. He lurched to his feet, grabbed his suitcase from an overhead compartment, and rushed to greet his sister.

CHAPTER 26
MOMENTUM

MarsDay 248, 11:30 a.m.
(August 2, 2:08 p.m.)

"How ya doing, Ollie?" asked Anna on the main comm channel, trying to keep her voice level.

By her calculations, she and Ollie were halfway up the smooth northern slope of Sentinel Mountain, the newly named, solitary peak standing guard over the deep valley north of the *Perseus*. This was their first extravehicular activity of any real distance and purpose.

The goal of the EVA was to deploy a communications relay atop Sentinel Mountain. A relay might help them to communicate with the vehicles at the Medusae landing site, much farther to the north. It would also provide useful wind and navigation data to help Evelyn land the cargo vehicle near the *Perseus*, two days from now.

Anna savored the vast open feel of the ruddy terrain to all sides. Had she not been constantly under surveillance by the cameras and sensors in her suit, she might have spun a few times and started to sing like Julie Andrews in an old movie filmed in the Austrian Alps.

The EVA had gone well, so far, except for Ollie's fatigue. Moving around in the suits was hard work, even in the lighter Mars gravity.

"You tell me how I'm doing," Ollie panted, in response to her question. "You're the one watching all the medical sensors."

On his back, Ollie carried a toolbox and two tanks of oxygen. The third member of their team, a Robonaut, was carrying the heaviest items. Operating in slave mode, the robot copied Anna's body movements precisely, stepping where she stepped until ordered to cease.

She checked her medical readout again, and it presented a grim picture of Ollie's condition. "Your pulse rate is elevated too high, and it only gets worse after that. Your faceplate is fogging up, too. Slow down your pace, OK?"

Evelyn broke into the conversation from her location back at the *Perseus*. She had been monitoring their progress closely by tying into their *Mobile Agents* data management and tracking system. Since the bulk of the mountain interfered with the transmission, her signal was almost swamped by static.

"Once you reach the summit, you'll...<static>... half-hour to set up the relay. Assuming a two hour descent and a three hour walk back to...<static>...leaves you an hour to reach the summit. Otherwise, you'll lose your daylight on the way back."

Anna struggled to control her temper. "I'm calling a medical override. Ollie won't reach the summit if he's dead. That's what he'll be in a few minutes, if we don't slow down."

"Confirmed, and logged." Even through the static, Evelyn's sigh of resignation was clearly audible. "Make the best progress you...<static>...cutting it close."

"Roger," Anna replied. Then she turned to Ollie. "Two minute break?"

Ollie found a smooth boulder to sit upon. Similar debris littered the slope, possible remnants of landslides from long ago. The smooth sheet of rock beneath their feet was somewhat slippery, due to a light coating of reddish dust.

"Smoke 'em if you got 'em," Ollie quipped feebly, much to Anna's surprise. He didn't use American slang very often.

Anna came around behind him, removed his toolbox, and clipped it to her own pack. She also replaced their empty oxygen tanks with full ones.

"Your pack should be lighter now, Ollie," she estimated.

"And what about you? How long can you carry the extra weight of my tools?"

She laughed. "All the way up, back down again, and around you in circles a few times, old man!" She playfully skittered further up the slope. "Catch me if you can!"

"Watch it, young whippersnapper. Respect your elders."

Anna laughed again and continued up the slope, glancing back to make sure Ollie was following at a reasonable pace. She slowed down and almost let him catch up.

Soon, she regretted her teasing. Ollie's toolbox was heavier than it looked, and it weighted down her every step. She started to sweat profusely. A small fan on the front of her suit began to whine, as it tried to remove her excess body heat and distribute her internal temperature evenly. The external temperature near ground level was approaching 60 degrees Fahrenheit, but her helmet was much colder, making her suit AI's temperature control task difficult.

She glanced at the vital signs monitor strapped over the right wrist of her suit, noting with surprise her own pulse rate was now elevated higher than Ollie's. However, youth had its advantages. Her tolerances were higher, so she wasn't in any immediate danger.

She paused to let Ollie catch up. Remembering their remote audience back on Earth, she panned her helmet camera around to capture a sweeping view of the lower ridges and the surrounding plains over a kilometer below. Ruggedly remote, the scenery was beyond spectacular, and she longed to share it with everyone back on Earth. Since the cheap stereoscopic cameras on her suit probably wouldn't do justice to the view, she narrated a brief description of what she saw.

"The valley to our west does appear to be deeply layered. Each layer is thick, but since it's a few kilometers away, I can't make out any compositional details."

"Looks like sediment to me," said Ollie, who now stood beside her, trying to catch his breath. "Layer upon layer of thick sediment. Gray, black, green, and white, but mostly red, possibly indicating a high iron content. If this whole area wasn't covered by an ancient ocean, I'll eat my helmet."

"Panning farther to the north, we can see several mesas off in the distance. They have smooth, sheer sides, with debris aprons suggesting recent erosion?" She ended her statement as a question and looked to Ollie for approval.

"Perhaps. Most likely, any recent erosion activity has been caused by the wind. It's really scoured the slope we're standing on."

Anna panned her cameras downward to film the smooth rocks and crevices around their feet. Then she twisted to the right. "More evidence of erosion to the east."

"Definitely fluvial scouring. And I can see Sainsbury Crater now! That's high on my list of places to visit, once we're more mobile. It's about three kilometers wide and only twenty kilometers away. Hard to tell from this distance, but it looks new. Probably only a few million years old."

"Sainsbury Crater?" asked Anna.

"You get to name the mountains. I'll name the craters. Deal?"

Evelyn broke in again. "Time to get moving. If...<static>...in 30 minutes, you'll skirt the east side of the slope and place the relay, once you have line of sight...<static>...Confirm, please."

"Confirmed." Anna looked ahead. "But we're in luck. I think we're near the top!"

The slope ahead converged upward toward an apex. Anna almost sprinted the final yards to the top. Then she halted in dismay. It was a false summit. Another ridge extended a hundred meters higher, along a saddle with steep sides, tapering to another apex. After all of her training in the Rocky Mountains, she should have been prepared for the cruel combination of geology and perspective.

She rechecked the health monitor. Her vital signs were elevated again, but not too badly. Ollie's were still high, too.

Anna made a decision. "Ollie, I'm going to dash up to the summit. It should take about ten minutes. If it's truly the top, I'll start laying out your equipment. You can catch up, as you're able, and just do the final connections. That should save us some time."

Evelyn barked, "Negative. Don't split up. First rule of hiking, even back on Earth."

That message came through loud and clear. Fuming inside, Anna sought a compromise. She hadn't come this far only to stop within sight of the summit. "I'll wait for Ollie to reach my position, and then I'll start my final ascent."

Evelyn agreed to this plan, and Anna waited. She walked around, studying the slope, while gradually working her way a few meters higher along the saddle. If Evelyn noticed, from the view through the helmet camera, she didn't say anything.

Finally, Ollie's head appeared over the ridge line. "Taxi!" he called.

"Take another break, Ollie. Then follow as you're able."

With the robot following, Anna climbed the remaining slope as fast as her weary legs would carry her. Now that she was so close to the goal, her pack actually seemed lighter. Ten minutes later, she had reached the top. This time, the summit was genuine. She halted, gasping for breath, and stunned by the beauty of the expanse below her.

In all directions, smooth plains trailed off toward the horizon. Occasional mesas and gullies textured the landscape. The sky was filled with emptiness, a paradox Anna didn't attempt to fathom or explain. The close horizon made distances tricky to calculate. On the wide plain to the south, far in the distance, a tiny sparkle of light reflected off some piece of machinery back at the *Perseus*, the only intrusion of civilization into this vast, untamed wilderness.

"Wow." She was unable to express her feelings any other way. "Hurry up, Ollie. You've got to see this view!"

The EVA had been a steady progression of ever more breathtaking views. It had started with the obligatory 15 minutes of pre-breathing back at the *Perseus*. While the helmet bubble of her outer space suit layer was locked into a habitat suitport mechanism, she had no view at all. Once her time in purgatory was over, she had stepped eagerly onto the surface and glimpsed the surrounding, rock-strewn plains. Upon leaving the shelter of the *Perseus*, she had seen the clear sky above and imagined the feeble sunlight attempting to warm her body through the layers of her space suit. Then came the long hike, with each step revealing new treasures. And finally, the even longer climb culminated in the spectacular view around her.

After another minute of sightseeing, she got back to business by checking Ollie's vital signs and progress. He was doing better, progressing along the saddle slowly and carefully. She removed her pack and started to deploy the equipment. The top of the mountain was a smooth, rectangular area about twenty by five meters across, offering plenty of room for their equipment.

She checked on Ollie's progress again, visually. He was hunched down on a steeper part of the slope, on his hands and knees, still far from the top. "Ollie!"

"I'm OK," he replied. "Just getting a closer look at a streak in the rock. I wish I had my geology equipment with me so I could get a sample."

"Your rock hammer is up here. Gather your souvenirs later, on the way back down. If we have time."

"Yes, Sir!" He mocked her drill sergeant attitude while issuing a subtle reminder. He was in charge of this engineering expedition.

Anna's words were effective, however. Ollie got to his feet and began the last part of his ascent.

While he climbed, she began constructing the frame to hold the communications relay in place. She assembled the telescoping poles for anchoring and stabilizing the equipment six feet above the ground. After choosing a flat site near the southern cliff face as a good location for the relay, she organized Ollie's tools nearby.

Ollie finally reached the top of the mountain a few minutes later. After catching his breath and admiring the view, he pointed to a different spot away from the edge. "Over here. It should catch a more accurate wind profile here."

Anna dutifully moved the equipment and tools away from the cliff face, starting with Ollie's drill, which easily weighed ten Mars pounds all by itself. He got right to work, drilling angled holes in the rock face and inserting the three structural rods. Where the rods met above his head, he clipped them together with a rigid plastic band. Then with more plastic bands, he rigged a small platform beneath.

As he was finishing this task, Evelyn interrupted on the comm channel. "Time's up." Without the mountain in the way, her voice was clearer.

"We need ten more minutes," replied Ollie.

"Make it five. Not a minute more."

"Five minutes, then." Through his faceplate, he flashed Anna a wink. She stifled a laugh.

Ollie hurried his pace. While Anna held the comm cube steady, he made the final structural connections. Then he opened a hinged door in the side of the cube, allowing him access to the interior. With a tool resembling a pair of tweezers, he poked around inside, grunted a few times, and cursed engineers back on Earth who had obviously never worn a space suit.

He backed away. "OK, it should be working now. Evelyn, how's our signal strength?"

"Much better! Now start back, pronto."

"It's Miller time," Ollie said, while sealing the door on the plastic cube with ultra-sticky adhesive tape.

Anna had already repacked the drill and the remaining tools, clipping them to the Robonaut this time. They carefully descended the slope, the way they had come. Any serious accident, so late in the day, would probably be fatal. Past field simulations indicated that 70 percent of Mars-fatal accidents would happen when an EVA team was on its way back to the safety of the habitat.

On the way down, they retested the communications link. Their connection to the *Perseus* was crystal clear. Unfortunately, Evelyn still couldn't contact the pressurized rover or any of the other vehicles at the primary Medusae landing site.

They soon reached the base of the mountain and began traversing the wide plain back to the *Perseus*. Daylight faded, and they used the last fleeting rays of twilight to cross the final kilometer. The temperature had already begun to fall, and Anna's suit now struggled to retain its internal heat. Her polypropylene liner had wicked most of the sweat away from her body, but the remaining dampness chilled her to the bone.

Upon reaching the *Perseus*, they scampered beneath and locked their helmets into the suitport clamps above. Then Evelyn released the airtight seals and helped them enter the EVA room, leaving the outer layer of their space suits below, ready for their next EVA.

Anna's first lengthy excursion onto the surface of Mars was complete. Her only plans for the evening were to relax and retire early. Tomorrow would be another long day.

Despite her weariness, she wouldn't trade the long hours for anything. A strange feeling of euphoria had been growing inside her slowly over the last two months. Today's EVA helped to bring it more fully into her conscious awareness. She was where she wanted to be, doing what she wanted to do.

MarsDay 248, 3:15 p.m.
(August 2, 6:00 p.m.)

A key turned in the lock, and Cassie's front door opened. The moment David had anticipated, yet dreaded, had finally arrived. He stood face to face with his brother-in-law. It was time to put up his deflector shields.

"Hello, David! It's good to see you!" Ben greeted him with a handshake and a half hug. David tried not to flinch. "I trust you had a good journey on the bus?"

"It was a long journey, but it went by just fine." He added another half lie, "It's good to see you, too, Ben."

It will be even better when you've answered all my questions.

Cassie got up from the couch long enough to give her husband a peck on the cheek. "David and I have been gossiping like two old mother hens. But he still won't tell me much about this new woman he's been seeing! I need your help, Ben."

"Smart man," Ben snickered.

Cassie slapped at his arm. "I'm glad you came home from work at a reasonable hour tonight."

"Things have been busy since we got back from our vacation," Ben agreed. "But today was better." He reached around the doorframe to pick up two brown bags on the porch outside. "I even had time to cook dinner. I know Chinese isn't your favorite cuisine, David, so I tried to stick with safe choices."

"I'll survive," said David. He gestured at the room. "I love the condo, Ben! Cassie gave me the ten cent tour."

The two bedroom, two-story condo was a detached unit, set well back from the busy street out front. Cassie had opened the ground floor windows to accept a cool summertime breeze from the west. Clean lines and plush carpeting gave the living room a modern, aesthetic look and feel. The walls were decorated with tapestries and one large painting, Cassie's favorite, a beautiful watercolor of a lakeshore scene. It had been David's wedding gift to her and Ben. David had practically stolen this Tamlyn Akins original for only $100 at a charity auction in Boulder two years ago, based upon advice from Reggie, who worked at an upscale art gallery. The modern masterpiece was easily worth a hundred times more than what David had paid for it, according to Cassie's later appraisal.

While Cassie and Ben cleared room on the kitchen table, David returned to the living room. He had been using a coffee table for a desk. Earlier, while visiting with Cassie, he had connected his computer to a local wireless network and started to catch up on his workload at Mission Support. He would need several more hours later in the evening to clear the backlog of messages. At least he had already processed the highest-priority items, like the daily crew logs.

He quickly rechecked the running transcript of dialogue between Anna and Ollie on their excursion to Sentinel Mountain. They had accomplished their objective and were on their way back to the *Perseus*. Commander Day believed they would return shortly before dusk.

The media had portrayed this EVA as a dangerous event. Truthfully, it was. As he forwarded the good news of the impending success to Cassie and Ben, he watched their reactions closely. Both seemed genuinely relieved, as he would have expected. If Ben was in league with USNN and the mission saboteurs, he didn't reveal any hints.

Before joining them at the table, David read a new message from Skye. She knew about his trip westward, and was checking to see if he had arrived safely. She also suggested he should watch a program later in the evening, her first special report on the Lynx network.

Skye had started working at the Lynx network two weeks ago, settling quickly into her old role as an investigative reporter. With their fear of eavesdropping by USNN or the Beta shadow group somewhat diminished, they had gone back to exchanging messages directly. However, they still used cryptic terminology and avoided direct references to places and times. In her latest message, Skye claimed to be baking a huge pizza with some unusual toppings, whatever that meant.

David shut down his computer and moved to the table. "A colleague just informed me of a Mars-related program on the Lynx network. She said we might find it interesting. Could we watch it at 7:00?"

"Sure!" said Ben, checking his watch, as David had already done. The program would start in less than 15 minutes. Ben went into the living room and turned on the television. He repositioned it so they could watch from the kitchen table. Then he returned to the table with the remote control in his hand.

David filled his plate with a generous portion of a mild beef-and-vegetable entree. As they ate, he asked about their vacation in New Zealand. Cassie's face glowed, and their discussion became more animated. She told him all about the great skiing, cold temperatures, and spectacular sightseeing. "The scenery was even more breathtaking than in the Lord of the Rings movies," she purred. "It was probably the best three weeks in my whole life."

Ben joined in, with similar comments and accolades. They promised to show him their digital photos later.

Time flew by, and the Lynx program began. Ben upped the volume on the television. They put their dinner conversation on-hold.

David recognized Stewart Aarons, the host of the Lynx program, from his frequent sessions with the Mars crew. The program began with a one-on-one conversation between Aarons and his guest, Skye Fontaine. As the identity of the guest was revealed, David again observed Ben's reactions closely. He appeared to be adequately dismayed. His ears even turned red.

"What's she doing on that network?" he asked, spitting out the word "she" like it was poison.

David remained silent. His connection with Skye was his trump card, and he intended to save it for a time when he could use it wisely.

Ben's question was answered during the first ten minutes of the program. A series of questions and answers between the two reporters outlined Skye's transition to her new network and her new responsibilities. She would be a field reporter with the freedom to investigate various science and technology events. The scope of her duties included filing reports about the Mars mission.

Based on past-shared experience, David knew several of Skye's responses were misleading or incomplete. Once more, he remained silent, even when Skye mentioned having a high level mole within the Mars Mission Support organization.

"I wonder who it could be?" asked Ben.

"It sure isn't me!" Cassie said. "I'd die before saying a single word to her."

David laughed, implying the same without actually saying it. Thus, he avoided another open lie, but continued his slide toward the dark side.

As the program continued, Skye got the viewers quickly up to speed by rehashing certain details and events related to the Mars mission. Though much of her recycled information was duly credited to previous USNN programs, her approach was far more balanced. She reported facts as facts, supposition as supposition, and personal opinions rarely.

She also speculated that someone might be trying to sabotage the mission. To the best of David's knowledge, his sabotage theory had never been mentioned in the public media before. Her background material about the loss of communications with the vehicles at the main Medusae landing site, as well as the telemetry problem causing the *Perseus* to land off-course, was skillfully crafted and cautiously ambiguous. Without going into any details, she left the viewer with a clear impression of more happening on the mission than the public was seeing.

Cassie fumed over the reporter's remarks about bad telemetry. "Does anyone still believe that crazy theory?" she asked.

"We've ruled it out," Ben confirmed. "There was no trace of any anomaly on our end."

David detected an opportunity. "Ben, if someone inside your team at JPL was trying to cover up the telemetry problems, how would they go about doing it?"

Ben looked surprised. He fumbled for an answer, in a most un-Ben-like manner. "Well, I suppose they could overwrite records of Mars-bound transmissions, play within the signal-to-noise ratios, or modify some bits in various files and change the checksums. There are several ways someone on my team could have done it, but they would leave footprints behind."

David was now in full pursuit mode. "Hypothetically, who would have the ability to try, with a reasonable chance of getting away with it?"

"Well, I suppose my team leader could do it, and maybe two others in my group."

"Could you have done it?" He hastily added, "Hypothetically again, of course."

"Well, I, I suppose I could…"

Having gotten the answer he was looking for, he decided to back off. "So the reporter's theory is still possible. Could it ever be proven?"

"All our transmissions and receptions are immediately duplicated on read-only media. I've personally checked, and everything is kosher. The only way around our record keeping would be to tamper with the direct feed to and from Mars, and that's hard to do. That's why so few people could do it. Once it's been done, though, any tampering would be almost untraceable."

"Almost untraceable?"

Ben looked up at the ceiling, apparently lost in thought. "NASA's not the only game in town. The Europeans have some sophisticated tracking stations, too, and they might have recorded some of the raw data from our Mars orbiters. But even if we compared their records and ours, proving anything would be hard. They would only have received signals sent from Mars, not transmissions to Mars."

"And bad telemetry from an orbiter could have caused the off-course landing."

"Yes, that was the original theory," Ben confirmed.

"It's still technically feasible?"

"Yes."

"Could the Europeans have caused the problem by sending bad instructions to the orbiters, or to the *Perseus*?"

"To the orbiters? No. We have algorithms to prevent unauthorized users from interfering with our transmissions. Our pipelines are secure."

"And what about the *Perseus*?"

Ben suddenly looked miserable. "I don't know. If the *Perseus* software engineers were lax, they might have left some loopholes. Any small flaw could be exploited."

David sat back and pondered Ben's answers. False instructions and orbiter telemetry could have been sent to the *Perseus*, especially if Ben and others on his own team were being paid to look the other way. It was the equivalent of the bank robbers paying off the local sheriff. If Ben was the local sheriff, David could ask questions all night and get nowhere. He needed undeniable proof of Ben's being bribed.

During their discussion, they had missed several minutes of the Lynx program. Skye's new topic included recordings of interviews with several surly cargo handlers. Without the ability to replay the program, he couldn't understand how these people were connected with the Mars mission. From later questions, the connection became obvious. Skye was continuing her investigation into the cargo manifests of the three vehicles now sitting at the Medusae landing site on Mars.

"Different network, same old crap," muttered Cassie. "Why does that reporter go to such great lengths to manufacture false news? Why does she hate us so much?"

The segment continued after a commercial break. Skye was back in the studio with the program host, showing some local animations of boxes shuffling around. She referred to engine nozzles, heat shields, hydrogen tanks, and other items of inventory.

Aarons: So, summarize all this for us. If this equipment hasn't been sent to Mars, where is it?

Fontaine: For almost two years, it was sitting in a warehouse near Colorado Springs. A year ago, it disappeared.

Aarons: What is the impact of this equipment being left behind?

Fontaine: With three metric tonnes of hydrogen missing, the crew on Mars can't generate enough fuel for their return trip home. Without the return vehicle's engine nozzles, heat shield, and tethers, there basically isn't any ERV to return in, anyway. The impact is clear. Those three people on Mars are stranded.

Aarons paused for a few moments, to let her words sink in. David was speechless with shock and disbelief, which was just as well, since it gave him another opportunity to judge the reactions of the others. Cassie whispered a few mild oaths under her breath. Ben didn't say anything, but his whole face was beet red, and his eyes were bulging practically out of their sockets.

Aarons: Have you determined what was sent to Mars in place of the missing equipment and supplies?

Fontaine: No. Cargo records were destroyed, so it's hard to even speculate. The memories of the cargo handlers are sketchy. The crew on Mars can't reach the Medusae landing site, conveniently, and the Mission Support team still can't contact any of the vehicles there. We might never know what's been sent to Mars in place of the critical equipment.

Aarons: But what about the second cargo vehicle that will land in two days? And the second ERV two days after that? Once the Perseus *crew can access those supplies, they could drive up to the Medusae landing site.*

Fontaine: I believe more accidents are about to happen. That's purely a guess, though, without any solid evidence to back it up. We'll know for sure in a few days.

Aarons: Is it possible the replacement cargo was some sort of weaponry or bomb? That might explain the loss of contact with all three Medusae vehicles.

Fontaine: More speculation, but it certainly fits the theory about someone trying to sabotage the mission. I'm still searching for similar cargo swaps on the other two Medusae vehicles, in addition to the ten metric tonnes of missing mass on the ERV. I've already found a half tonne missing on the Medusae backup habitat, and three tonnes missing on the Medusae cargo vehicle.

Aarons: Even if cargo was mishandled, your initial premise for sabotage seems quite speculative. Do you have any firm proof of a deliberate attempt to sabotage the Mars mission?

Fontaine: I do have some strong circumstantial evidence that a member of the JPL telemetry team sabotaged the landing of the Perseus. *That evidence is being kept in a very safe place, along with other evidence implicating executives at my former network. That's why I don't work there any longer.*

"My God." Cassie wore a different expression now, one that was harder to fathom. "Do you think there's any truth to what she's saying?"

David urgently needed more time to think, so he merely answered, "It's possible. Sabotage would certainly explain why we can't contact the equipment at the Medusae landing site. Even the amount of missing mass on each vehicle makes sense. Blowing an irreparable hole in the side of a habitat wouldn't take much explosive force. However, the ERV fuel production equipment is designed to spread out onto the surface of Mars. After landing, a huge explosion would be needed to destroy everything."

His thoughts turned to Anna. If Skye's suspicions turned out to be correct, the crew on Mars was in serious danger. Any failures during the next two landings might seal their fate.

"Huh?" Ben had asked him a question, but he had been too wrapped up in his thoughts to hear it.

"The reporter mentioned some circumstantial evidence about someone on my team." Ben's tone was sharp, almost accusative. "Any idea what she was implying? You brought this up before, too."

David lied again. "No idea. But it does fit our earlier discussion. Finding a saboteur on your team could explain a lot."

They watched the end of the Lynx program in silence, without hearing any more surprises. Then he traded more speculation with Cassie. Ben added a word or two, but was otherwise quite subdued.

Either he's guilty or he's pondering how to expose the saboteur. How do I bring his real thoughts out into the open?

He never got the chance. Ben announced he needed some fresh air. He grabbed his car keys and left the condo.

David stared at his little sister. He tried to wipe the concerned look off his face, but she would probably see right through him, as she usually did. He considered telling her about Skye's recording, the one implicating Ben, but he couldn't bring himself to do it. Without knowing what was in the envelope Ben had received, he couldn't risk damaging Cassie's marriage. If he was wrong about Ben's guilt, he would never forgive himself.

CHAPTER 27
MOTION

MarsDay 249, 4:53 a.m.
(August 3, 9:00 a.m.)

Cassie plodded into the kitchen, wearing a frumpy sweatsuit and rubbing the sleep from her eyes. David greeted her from the living room, once again the site of his work area. He made his "Good Morning" sound cheerful, but he didn't really feel that way inside. The guest bedroom was comfortable, but sleep had been elusive. Weighty matters were on his mind.

"How long have you been up?" asked Cassie.

"About four hours. I gained an hour because my body's still running on my Colorado schedule. Are you still taking the day off?"

"I sure am! How often is my big brother in town for a visit?"

As she poured herself a cup of coffee and refilled David's empty cup, she asked what time Ben had left for work.

"I thought he was still here," said David, voicing his puzzlement.

Cassie brought her coffee into the living room and sat beside him on the couch. Her sleepy squint was replaced by a look of concern. "He didn't sleep in our bedroom last night. I just assumed he got back late and slept on the couch, so he wouldn't wake me up. Did he come home at all last night?"

David rose and looked out the window. Ben's parking spot was empty; his little two-seat Chevy Centipede hybrid was nowhere to be seen. "Maybe not."

"I'll bet he went in to work last night. All that talk about saboteurs on his team really upset him."

369

"He's probably sifting through his data, trying to find evidence one way or the other," David speculated.

"I'd better call him." She pressed some buttons on her cell phone and waited for Ben to answer.

David went back to browsing a report from the commander about her plan to place a second navigation relay ten kilometers southwest of the *Perseus*. With the beacons and the *Perseus* carefully calibrated into a 3-point navigational grid, each with accurate, realtime weather sensors, the incoming cargo vehicle should be able to land with greater accuracy.

Two days ago, David had considered this deployment overly cautious. After hearing Skye's suspicions of NASA-JPL sabotage, the commander's plan now seemed quite prudent. Data returned from the weather and navigation relays could be fed straight to the landing craft, via the *Perseus*, without Earthly intervention. In fact, the commander already intended to monitor the descent of the cargo vehicle closely. She would be ready to seize control and tele-operate the vehicle toward a safe landing during the final minutes, if anything went wrong.

Cassie snapped her cell phone shut. "Ben's not answering," she said. "But I queried his phone's location, and it's somewhere near his office at work. Our car answered a locational query, too. It's in the JPL parking lot."

"OK, that's one mystery solved," said David.

But I wonder if he's searching for evidence of sabotage, or trying to bury that evidence.

David turned back to the commander's EVA plan and finished reading it. In an addendum, his EVA analysis group approved the plan. Subject to some guidelines, they also advised the plan was safe enough to be conducted as a solo human EVA, rather than a tele-operated Robonaut EVA. He forwarded this information to the commander.

He browsed the morning news headlines. Skye's program had become an overnight sensation.

- "Explosive New Theory About Mars ERV Silence" (lynx.com)
- "Inventory Control Problems on Mars?" (Associated Press)
- "Possible NASA Sabotage of Mars Mission" (Reuters)
- "No Return for the Mars Astronauts? Initial Viewer Ratings Skyrocket" (e.com)
- "Disgruntled Reporter Circulates False Rumor About Former Network" (usnn.com)

David laughed when he saw the final headline. After giving some thought to the reaction of the crew upon seeing these stories, however, his smile turned into a scowl. The damage was already done. He bitterly opposed censorship, and the news stories had already been transmitted. He would have to deal with the fallout proactively.

In an emergency message to the crew, including the entire support team and the SEA steering committee, he outlined Skye's suspicions while emphasizing they were highly speculative at this time. He urged each recipient to contact him if they had any information about the allegations or knew of any way to prove or disprove them. After appending some optimistic platitudes, he sent the message and also posted it on the support center's bulletin board. Then he prepared himself mentally for the swamping influx of replies sure to come. He had probably just tripled his workload for the next few days.

With a deep sigh, he leaned back on the couch and turned to Cassie. She was watching him.

"What?" he asked.

"Did you know you're an angry typist?"

"A what?"

"Some people scowl when they type, pounding the keys as if they want to break them. They get all stressed out, and it's not very healthy. Relax!"

David smiled, and told her about the message he had just sent. "I only pound my keyboard when I need some angry inspiration," he promised.

She started to reply, but was interrupted by the doorbell.

"Could that be Ben?" asked David.

"He would just come on in. I'm not expecting anyone, either." In a louder voice, she cried, "Who is it?"

"Newspaper delivery," said a muffled voice outside.

They stared at each other for a moment before Cassie approached the door and David slunk away to hide in a bathroom. From his observation post, with the bathroom door cracked open, he watched Cassie check the peephole before cautiously opening the front door. She talked to someone on the other side, and David strained to hear the conversation.

"Aren't you a little old to be delivering newspapers?"

A feminine voice with musical overtones replied, "News is my life. When I'm not making it, I'm delivering it."

"You look familiar, too. Do I know you?"

Another reply, "No, but I know your brother." In a louder voice, the visitor announced, "David, come on out! Call off your guard dog!"

He immediately thought of Skye. The voice sounded like her, and the visitor's brashness matched her modus operandi. Besides, few people knew he was here, or so he hoped.

Sure enough, he heard Cassie gasp, "Fontaine!"

He left his hiding place and approached the front door, not quite fast enough to prevent Cassie from slamming it shut. She slumped with her back against the door.

He motioned her away. "I almost expected Skye to show up. She's good at popping in uninvited."

He opened the door and greeted Skye. She was dressed in another stunning, shapely outfit, with a thousand-dollar purse dangling casually off her shoulder. Her dark hair was pulled back into a loose ponytail. Chanel No. 5 perfume assaulted him as she returned his greeting with a passionate kiss, making his whole body tingle. He felt his ears turning red.

"What are you doing here?" he stammered, once he had untangled himself.

"Just delivering the daily news." She held up a local Pasadena newspaper. The headline on the front page announced in bold letters:

New Mars Mission Sabotage Theory
Possible JPL Involvement

"So Skye, do you think your allegations could have made a bigger media explosion?"

"Only if I delivered them with a nuke. Did you enjoy my little coming-out party?" She winked. "I needed to burn my bridges so viewers will no longer associate me with that Other Network."

David chuckled, "I'd say you accomplished that rather well. But given our situation, do you think it was wise?"

"It was critical. I want USNN to think I've got a lot more leverage than I really do."

"But what if they come after you? After us again, I mean?"

"If anything happens to me, they risk my ICID files making an even bigger explosion. No, they'll hem and haw, and then they'll try to cut me a deal. When they do, I intend to make it very difficult for them. I'll insist on knowing everything."

"Remind me never to play poker with you," said David, in all seriousness.

"But that's not why I'm here. I thought I would share some other news with you, too. A surprising item you won't find in any newspaper. At least, not yet."

"Really? What might that be?"

"It concerns you both, and you'll want to be sitting down. May I come in?"

David looked back at Cassie, who had been watching their interaction in silent disapproval. She glared at Skye, but waved her inside.

"You have a lot of explaining to do, David," said Cassie. Her voice was ice.

David sighed. "Yes, I do." Skye sat near him on the couch while he recounted their past relationship and interactions at great length. He began with his eavesdropping outside the Boulder restaurant, which she already knew about, and continued through the encounters in Nederland, at Brainard Lakes, and finally at the Gold Lake resort. Throughout, Cassie remained standing, pacing the room and interrupting occasionally with knife-edged questions.

"So this is the new woman you've been seeing." She shook her head. "I can't believe you would have anything to do with a flashy tart like her."

David tensed up, and was about to fling a blistering reply when Skye's hand on his arm held him back. "It's OK," she said. "I get that a lot. It goes with the job. In my profession, one tries to be noticed."

"Cassie, don't make the same mistake I did," advised David. "There's a lot more to Skye than meets the eye."

"How poetic," said Cassie dryly. She crashed down into a sofa chair across the room. "When you told me about your new romance, I was all excited for you. And now I find you with…" She gestured at Skye, apparently unable to even voice her name. "David, how could you do this? She stands for everything you hate in the world. She's the ultimate user, with no vision, no long-term perspective. She'll use you, too, and then she'll throw you onto a slag heap."

David glanced at Skye. Inwardly, he had to admit Cassie was echoing his own, lingering concerns. Everything she had said was superficially or potentially true.

"Like I said, there's a lot more to her than meets the eye." He launched into another long explanation about the skullduggery at USNN and Skye's growing rebellion at being used to deliver anti-Mars propaganda for reasons unknown. He concluded with the program last night, though he didn't mention their suspicions about Ben.

When he had finished, he turned to Skye. "How certain are you about these inventory problems?"

"Enough to stake my reputation on it. I'd say, maybe 90 percent. Everything hangs together well enough, but it's still possible someone is intentionally leading me on. Even USNN's response fits, both then and now. You might recall I've been looking into these inventory problems for months. Whenever I started to get anywhere, my old program producer at USNN assigned me to work on fluff projects instead."

"I almost wish you had spent more time working on those fluff projects," said David, wistfully. "But that wouldn't change reality. If the three vehicles at the Medusae landing site have been destroyed by sabotage, or any other way, our friends on Mars are in deep trouble."

They lapsed into a moment of silence. Cassie got up to refill her cup of coffee without asking Skye if she wanted one. The snub was subtle, but visible.

Skye grabbed David's hand and gave it a gentle squeeze. "Speaking of fluff projects," she said, "I think it's time you told your sister about our video clip from the party at JPL. Actually, that's why I'm here."

David jumped in surprise, mixed with more than a little irritation. "I don't want to say anything about that until we have firm proof."

"Well, I've got proof. And it's solid enough for me."

"Proof of what?" asked Cassie, returning from the kitchen and reclaiming her sofa chair across the room.

Skye looked at David, waiting. She was obviously going to make him break the news to his sister, as was appropriate. Suddenly, he wished he was anywhere else in the whole world, even locked in a room with Major Tom. He took a deep breath and considered his next words carefully, words that might rip Cassie's life apart.

He reached for his computer and twisted the flexible display around to where she could see it. "Here's the video clip Skye mentioned." He explained about the "Decadence in Babylon" program, and Cassie angrily confirmed she had seen it. "Well, you probably didn't see this, in the background." He played the enhanced video, and once again, he endured the sight of a man clearly slipping an envelope to Ben. When he revealed the other man as Skye's old program producer at USNN, Cassie's face turned deathly pale.

"I don't believe it," she said. "It's a fake scene. You can do anything with video." She blasted Skye with a withering stare.

"It's real," said David. "I was right there when we found this, along with Jennifer and Bill. Skye didn't even know who Ben was, back then, and she also didn't know he was related to me."

Cassie harrumphed, still not convinced. "Even if it were true, it doesn't prove anything. We can't tell what really happened from a short video clip, without sound or context."

"That's why I didn't mention our suspicions until now." David turned and glared at Skye. "You'd better have some stronger evidence or Cassie won't have to throw you out of here. I'll do it myself."

Without saying a word, she removed some folded papers from her purse, handing them to David. He skimmed through them quickly, noting several dates and monetary amounts, along with handwritten notations along the margins. The last page was a real estate brochure for a modestly sized, ivy-covered house on a wooded lot.

"What am I looking at?" he asked.

"That's your sister's house."

"What?" Cassie yelped. "I don't own any house. We just bought some land a few weeks ago, but it's an empty lot." She crossed the room, and David handed her the brochure.

"Well, it's your husband's house, at least. The sale was recorded in his name only." She removed some more papers from her purse.

David didn't think Cassie's face could get any whiter, but it did. "I recognize this place. It's one of the houses we walked through, one I really liked, in the Lake Arrowhead area near the land we bought. But it was only a fantasy, way out of our price range. Way, way out."

"Apparently not." Skye pointed to the other papers David was holding. "Were you aware your husband also has a Swiss bank account?"

"Ben? Impossible!" Cassie plopped down on the floor near David's feet, still browsing the sale documents and the brochure for the ivy-covered house.

Skye said, "It took some doing, but I was able to view the records. I'd prefer if you kept that part a secret. The Swiss like to believe their records are secure from the media."

David scanned the typed bank records in his hands. Several major inflows of cash were listed over a span of three years, totaling almost $10 million. The last was dated a few months ago, two days after the off-course Mars landing. Some recent, large deductions made the current balance much lower.

He gave the pages to Cassie. As she studied them, tears traced down her cheeks. David crouched near her and gave her a firm hug. "We'll get to the bottom of this," he promised.

"Wait a minute," she sniffled, trying to regain her composure. "What real proof is there of Ben's buying the house? Records can be forged. His signature could be copied." She glared at Skye again.

"Call the real estate agent if you aren't convinced," Skye suggested.

"I think I'll do just that." She retreated upstairs, and they heard snatches of conversation for a few minutes. When she returned, her expression told David all he needed to know, but she elaborated anyway.

"I didn't tell the real estate agent who I was," she said, tonelessly. "Her phone number matched the one in my address book, and I recognized her voice. She described Ben perfectly but wouldn't give me his name. When I asked for a way to contact the new owner, she gave me Ben's work phone number. She even mentioned the house was supposed to be a surprise gift for the new owner's wife."

"Aren't you lucky," said David, half seriously. "You own a $6 million house."

Cassie grabbed the bank records from the floor and ripped them in half. "If this money came from USNN as bribes, I don't want it." She flung the papers to the floor and ground some of them into the carpet with the heel of her stocking-clad foot.

Skye said, "I've traced some of the transactions to one of USNN's offshore holding companies."

Cassie sat again, and buried her face in her hands. Her tears returned as a torrential downpour, and shudders wracked her body. David moved to her side and sought to comfort her, but he lacked the proper words. All he could do was hold her in a tight embrace.

An eternity passed within the span of a silent minute. Then Skye said softly, "If your husband is involved with the mission saboteurs and he learns we're on to him, you aren't safe here."

"She's right." David's brain started to work again, as he fought his way out of his own pit of despair. "You've got to disappear, Cassie."

"Where can I go?"

"Anywhere," said Skye. "I mean, we can reach anywhere, at least, without anyone knowing. I'm learning my new network can be quite extravagant. After I convinced my boss and the higher-ups that their new star reporter was tracking the story of the century, they loaned me the keys to the company jet.

That's how I got from New York to Pasadena this morning. Coast to coast is only a four-hour, ticketless flight."

"Sweet," said David. "How about Boulder?"

Boulder would obviously be the first place Ben would look for them. If they covered their tracks, they could buy a few days, perhaps enough time for them to figure out a better plan. Besides, Boulder was a place where Cassie would feel at home.

He voiced these thoughts and concluded, "After the cargo vehicle and ERV land on Mars, the situation will be different. Two successful landings would make the field team almost self-sufficient. That will tie Ben's hands, along with anyone back on Earth who wants to sabotage the mission." He didn't mention his lingering suspicion about one of the three crew members on Mars also sabotaging the mission. That potential weakness in his plan would have to be addressed later.

"Yes," said Cassie, almost dreamily. "I'd like to go back to Boulder. My friends are there."

Skye agreed too, adding, "Pack some bags, and take as much as you want. No luggage restrictions on the friendly Lynx airlines."

David put an arm around his sister and guided her up the stairs. While she packed some clothing into a single large suitcase and grabbed a smaller cosmetics case, he stowed her notebook computer and peripheral equipment into a padded satchel. Then he led her back downstairs, carrying her luggage and pretending it wasn't heavy.

He would need to keep a close eye on Cassie. Something in the tone of her voice worried him. A part of her was off on a distant plain, detached from reality. A casual friend might not have recognized it, but David was certain he saw the warning signs. One of the cars on her freight train had temporarily derailed.

He also worried about Ben's reaction. When Ben returned and found his wife gone, what would he think? What would he do? David whispered these concerns to Skye, and she agreed. They needed to invent a good cover story, one to buy them a few days, or longer.

"How about leaving him a note?" she asked. "You could say you and Cassie decided to drive back to Colorado."

David shook his head. The excuse was too lame. "Why would we do that? I only just arrived here yesterday."

Neither of them could think of a reason until David recalled Ben's heavy workload. "I could claim I don't want to be in his way."

Skye said, "That's weak, but it will have to do. We should remove any evidence to the contrary, of course." She picked up the torn remnants of paper from the living room floor and stuffed them inside her purse.

David packed his own suitcase and computer. Then he wrote a note for Ben and left it on the dining room table.

"Let's get out of here, before he comes back," said David. In the movies, the bad guy always appeared, just as the heroes were trying to escape.

They moved to the door and turned back one last time to study the apartment, making sure they didn't forget anything. Cassie's gaze fell upon her Akins painting on the living room wall.

She took a step toward it. "I have to take your painting, David. I can't bear to leave it."

"No," he said firmly, dropping her suitcase so he could hold her back. "Ben would notice it's gone right away. It would blow our cover story to smithereens. No one takes a painting with them on a long drive in a car."

They maneuvered Cassie outside and into Skye's rented Lexus. After David threw the luggage in the trunk and hopped into the passenger seat, Skye drove off, with a slight squeal of the tires. Her driving was more subdued than usual, and she obeyed most of the traffic laws.

An hour later, they were jetting through the air. David was heading back home again, yet he knew he hadn't escaped his problems.

The next 30 hours would be critical to the success or failure of the Mars mission. He had to assume Ben would attempt to sabotage the landing of the cargo vehicle. Perhaps he should have stayed behind and taken a more aggressive tactic, wringing the truth with his bare hands around Ben's scrawny neck.

It was too late for second guesses. Besides, he had his sister's welfare to consider. He had made a decision, and it was the right one. Upon his return to Boulder, he would find a way to deal with the consequences.

MarsDay 249, 9:00 a.m.
(August 3, 1:14 p.m.)

Anna's cocoon was dark and cold, but also snug and safe. As she sat on a retractable bench beneath the *Perseus*, with her feet dangling above the dusty surface and her outer space suit helmet locked into a suitport dock above, she watched the latest news clips from Earth on her Heads-Up Display. Evelyn interrupted occasionally, counting off the minutes until her pre-breathing activity was finished.

She could return to the EVA room anytime, simply by pressing two buttons on the hard torso of her suit. Bailing out would carry a stiff penalty, however. She would be forced to endure the entire pre-breathing interval again, prior to stepping onto the surface.

"Two more minutes."

As she watched the edited summary of a Lynx news program, Anna realized today's "simple" EVA might end up being quite difficult. She had offered to answer questions from reporters and schoolchildren during the long traverse to the site where she would place a second navigation, weather, and communications relay. Mission Support would paste her answers together with the initial questions into two seamless programs, one a press conference, and the other the latest in a long series of educational outreach programs that she had recorded from the *Perseus*.

Unfortunately, the allegations in the Lynx program would probably change the focus of the questions in the press conference. Even though she had no way to confirm or deny Fontaine's claims of potential lander sabotage, reporters would probably ask her for comments. She would have to redirect these difficult questions onto more constructive pathways, while remaining optimistic and enthusiastic for the children's program.

Despite the media distractions, her top priority would be to avoid tripping over rocks or slipping into pits of Mars dust. The latter was unlikely, but sometimes, buried craters were hard to spot, especially if one wasn't being careful enough. Mars undoubtedly retained many dangerous secrets.

"EVA One, you're free to descend," Evelyn finally announced, much to Anna's delight. "Remember, Anna, you're in command of this EVA. Keep Ollie's Robonaut from getting too distracted by all the geological wonders, OK?"

"Aye aye," she responded.

Anna climbed down from her perch and planted both feet on the cold ground, for the second time in two days. She felt good today, despite the strenuous workout the day before. Ollie had complained of numerous aches and pains, and she had strongly recommended he be allowed to take the day off. Unfortunately, Evelyn couldn't go on the EVA because she was practicing her remote piloting skills in preparation for the cargo vehicle landing tomorrow. That left the engineering tasks on the EVA to Ollie again, or to a tele-operated Robonaut, which might not have the necessary dexterity and situational awareness.

The only other choices were to postpone the EVA until early tomorrow morning, which Anna preferred, or to cancel it entirely, leaving only two surface points of reference when Evelyn piloted the lander tomorrow. According to Ollie, either was still a reasonable alternative. The beacon deployments had always been low on the priority list, which was why those tasks hadn't been done weeks ago. In hindsight, it seemed like a foolish scheduling decision, given the overall, critical importance of the upcoming landings.

Evelyn finally ordered a "mixed" EVA, with one human and one Robonaut. The machine would operate in slave mode again, following Anna until she reached the deployment area. Then Ollie would "enter" the Robonaut and direct her placement and activation of the equipment. The commander allocated plenty of time for the 30-kilometer round-trip excursion, in case Anna ran into trouble and needed a rescue.

She set out toward the southwest, with the Robonaut following her footsteps. As a navigational aid, Anna chose a tall peak in the distant mountain range across the plain and started walking toward it. The robot carried the beacon on its back, as it had the day before. This time, Anna took the tools from the outset, along with the telescoping frame and other necessary hardware. Her pack was heavy, but manageable.

She passed basaltic rocks, layered soil, and possible clumps of sediments during the first hour of the traverse. Had Ollie been along, he probably would have stopped several times for a closer look. Instead, Anna just kept walking, and the robot kept following. Low, smooth boulders punctured the firm soil at widely spaced intervals. Staying on course was easy and required little thought.

Her space suit's comm system downloaded the latest media questions over the wireless network from the hub in the *Perseus*. The first question was from a BBC reporter, who wondered if the 37 extra minutes in every MarsDay had caused any physical or psychological problems for the crew. Anna smiled and recorded a reply. This was an easy question, one she could confidently answer. Numerous physical and mental health studies over the past eight months had generated a wealth of data, most of which matched their benign expectations from simulations conducted back on Earth.

After several more questions she could also answer authoritatively, including three from a statewide competition for sixth grade biology students in Connecticut, she began to wonder whether someone at Mission Support had filtered out the harder, more stressful queries. In particular, she had expected some real zingers from Fontaine. She silently thanked whatever guardian angel was helping her behind the scenes.

During her first break, she pulled out a small plastic vial of gray-water and recorded a brief educational program. She discussed how water on Mars could exist in all three states, solid, liquid, and gas, all at the same time, due to the low air pressure. She also illustrated the difference between evaporation and sublimation by pouring the vial of water onto a shaded, flat rock. Some of the water boiled away immediately. A few beads remained liquid, and evaporated quickly. The rest froze, and would sublimate into the atmosphere over the next few hours or melt and evaporate as the sun angle changed.

After three hours of walking, she reached the general deployment area. Ollie entered the Robonaut and began to look around for a good, stable site for the beacon. He sought a place where the rocky layer under the thin dust coating was hard and durable, providing a firm anchor against strong winds. During their months on the surface, they hadn't encountered any windstorms yet, but scour marks on various rocks bore evidence of such storms.

Ollie directed Anna to pound at the ground with a rock hammer several times. Finally, after nearly half an hour, they found a site meeting his approval. Under his guidance, Anna repeated the assembly procedures from the previous day. Within another half-hour, the beacon was active.

"Evelyn, does the beacon telemetry check out?" called Anna. Initially, there was no response, but after several more tries, Evelyn finally replied.

"Evelyn here. Report, please."

"I was starting to worry. I'm all done, if the beacon checks out."

"Sorry about the delay. I was in the middle of a landing simulation. Mission Support threw me some nasty curves. I splashed the cargo vehicle, big time."

"I wish I hadn't heard that," said Anna. Earlier, Evelyn had expressed confidence. With a little more practice, she thought she could land the cargo vehicle on a dime in any situation.

Evelyn replied, "I don't think we'll encounter any 500 kilometer-per-hour dust storms in the middle of the landing sequence."

Anna noticed the Robonaut had strayed a few meters away. "Ollie's been dying to visit the rock escarpment a few kilometers from here. It's the one extending north, connecting with Sentinel Canyon. I can see it, but I still can't make out many details. It's probably at least another hour beyond our position. Do we have time to look?"

"Negative. You can explore your current position for 30 minutes, but then I want you to start back."

Anna walked eastward, joining Ollie's robot. She watched its camera lenses zoom and refocus, as he studied a series of parallel indentations in the soil. The disturbance was at least ten meters wide.

"What could have caused this?" asked Anna. "It looks like tracks from the biggest monster truck in the universe."

"It's a monster, all right," replied Ollie's voice. "I'm guessing the track was formed by a monster dust devil. I wish I was out there, so I could be more sure about it."

"I thought dust devils were supposed to be weak and harmless."

"That's what everyone else thought, too, but that's not what I'm seeing here. The top layer of soil is depressed in places and disturbed in others. What a mess. Given the low density of the air pressure, it's hard to imagine winds strong enough to do this. Hand the robot a trowel, please."

Anna complied, and Ollie started to excavate a narrow trench.

"What if one of these hit the *Perseus*?" she asked. Ollie didn't answer.

After the robot had dug several trenches, he said, "At least the disturbance in the soil isn't very deep. I'd still estimate wind speeds of well over a thousand kilometers-per-hour would be required, though. We weren't expecting to encounter anything over 300."

Evelyn interrupted, from the *Perseus*. "Anna? Please start back now. No delays."

"We could use some more time here," Ollie responded sharply.

"Negative. Mission Support doesn't like the latest forecast from the solar physicists. A new sigmoid region has just emerged on the limb of the Sun, and it looks like an active one. They think a solar flare is possible."

"Ouch," said Anna. "I'm starting back now."

"Can the robot stay longer?" asked Ollie.

"No," Evelyn replied firmly. "Our robots are almost as important as our humans, and they can't repair themselves if they're damaged by radiation."

Solar flares were nothing to mess with. Of all the dangers she could face while walking about the surface of Mars, X-rays from strong solar flares were the worst. They could strike without warning, building to a deadly intensity within ten minutes. Active sigmoid regions on the Sun were breeding grounds for flares. The crew would never consider going on a long, unshielded EVA if any sigmoids were present on the side of the Sun facing Mars.

"Sorry, Ollie," she said. "We'll come back later, once we have enough fuel to drive the ATV or the pressurized rover."

After some grumbling from its controller, Ollie's robot finally handed the trowel back to Anna. "Look at this!" he cried. The robot ran several meters farther south. "The monster even disturbed some small rocks!"

"Oh, for crying in the soup." Anna was starting to lose her patience. Ollie was securely within the *Perseus*, looking at rocks, while she was about to get blasted by a solar flare. She pressed a large button on her suit torso. The Robonaut instantly straightened and approached her. She started back toward the *Perseus*, muttering about crazy geologists, and the robot followed obediently.

Before leaving, Anna took a moment to survey the site for any litter containing unsterilized Earthly microbes. Forward contamination would ruin this site if she ever wanted to return here and conduct some biology studies. The only thing she wanted to leave behind was the relay, which had been thoroughly sterilized a few days ago.

Anna was probably almost as disappointed by the early departure as Ollie. She hadn't made a big fuss about it to her crewmates, but she had hoped to do some real science work on this EVA, too. Her chemical analysis kit was clipped to her suit. She had intended to measure the salinity of various types of dust, sand, soil, and rock.

Once the cargo vehicle landed, setting up experimental greenhouse pods would be one of her highest priorities. Eventually, she wanted to supplement their food supply with homegrown food, but her initial attempt to grow vegetables in one of the sample boxes had produced pathetic results.

She needed to find soils containing a better mix of nutrients. If she couldn't find better soils, then hydroponics—growing food without soil— was a possible backup option. She would try both approaches in her greenhouses.

As she drew near to home, Anna opted to remain outside and collect more samples. She wasn't very optimistic. Most of her new specimens would match her previous ones. To find soil samples with a different nutrient balance, she needed more mobility.

When evening approached, she went inside and tested her samples. As suspected, none looked very promising. She angrily emptied them into a box of earlier samples awaiting safe decontamination and burial outside. Once a sample was brought inside and exposed to the thriving airborne microbes in the *Perseus*, it was treated as an earthly material, subject to strict quarantine.

After pouting in her cabin, she ate a late dinner with Evelyn and Ollie in the lounge. Their tales of woe were just as bad, if not worse. Ollie fretted about monster dust devils, and Evelyn about the cargo vehicle landing. When Anna grew tired of the discussion, she retreated back to her cabin and wrote EVA, biology, and health reports.

She worked well into the evening, knowing she wouldn't get much sleep anyway. Except for the landing event, tomorrow was a routine habitat maintenance day. If the landing was successful, she could sleep afterwards.

And if the landing fails? Self, try not to think about that, if you want to get any sleep tonight.

CHAPTER 28
GRAVITY

MarsDay 250, 4:14 a.m.
(August 4, 9:00 a.m.)

"That should raise some eyebrows, brother!"

As Cassie commented on the message that David had just sent to the entire support team, he was happy to see some of the old fire back in her demeanor. She still had a long way to go, but the road to healing had begun the night before.

Leaving Skye at the Boulder airport, they took a shuttle to the bus station in downtown Boulder. Their intention was to catch a connecting bus to Nederland after verifying they could stay with Bill and Jennifer for the next few days. Upon leaving the shuttle, however, they immediately ran into Jennifer, who happened to be on her way home from work. The reunion between the two old college roommates had brought a brief smile to Cassie's face.

They had deferred Jennifer's questions until later, when they were sitting comfortably in her living room. After Bill joined them, the whole sordid story about Ben's secret spending spree was revealed. David had done most of the talking, while Cassie cried, Jennifer consoled, and Bill asked questions. Cassie's release of anguish seemed to have an immediate, visible benefit. By dismissing some of her inner pain, she had taken another step down the long road toward acceptance and recovery.

Upon hearing the confirmation of Ben's deeds, Bill offered his house as a place of refuge once more. David gratefully accepted, at least for now.

Cassie dragged David back into the present by adding to her remark, "And thank you for not revealing any names yet."

David's message to his support team lent his credibility to the rumors of JPL sabotage. He instructed his team to land the cargo vehicle without using any telemetry from the *Mars Odyssey* orbiter. He also highly recommended the commander control the final landing stages manually. After sending the message, he also posted it on the general bulletin board.

"Well, at least I've warned them. Hopefully it will do more good than harm. The *Mars Odyssey* orbiter telemetry could have pinpointed the moment to begin the entry, descent, and landing sequence better than we can back here on Earth."

Cassie completed his thought. "But it's smarter to use less accurate data than telemetry that's intentionally wrong."

David looked around the basement bedroom. Part of him was relieved to be back here, working, though he knew they couldn't stay very long. This place had come to feel like home.

He asked how the crew was coping with the stress of the landing.

"Reasonably well, so far. I checked Anna's report this morning. Ollie seems to be more worried about dust devils, though he might be redirecting his stress rather than relieving it. The commander has been practicing the landing sequence, giving her a constructive outlet."

"Actions speak louder than words?"

"In this case, exactly. Anna is probably more stressed out than anyone else. She's stuck using words to the media, in educational programs, and with Mission Support. She needs a better way to release her feelings."

"Exercise?" he asked.

"There is that, at least. The two recent EVAs have probably helped."

"And my message about sabotage probably hurt."

"Probably," she said.

"We'll just have to keep everyone busy for the next few days."

His last statement was directed more at Cassie and her own burden of stress. She didn't seem to notice. David was no expert in psychology, but if he had to guess, she was probably going through a stage of denial. She hadn't mentioned Ben's name all morning, and she seemed overly cheerful. He wondered if he should confront her with the painful issues right away, or wait until she was a bit stronger. Waiting seemed safer.

They went upstairs and found the rest of the house vacant. Bill and Jennifer had already left for work. David made a fresh pot of coffee in the kitchen, while Cassie climbed one more level to her guest bedroom. Her computer equipment was in her room, and she wanted to check for feedback on the crew's mental state from the rest of the psych team.

David was happy she had a useful task to distract her. Diving into her work was probably just another avoidance tactic, but it seemed quite healthy at the moment. On the practical side, he needed her skills. The task of closely monitoring the stress level of the crew was critically important.

He poured two cups of coffee, intending to bring one upstairs for Cassie. When he was halfway up the split stairwell, he heard a distressed cry from above. "No!"

Fear knifed through his chest. "Cassie? Are you OK?" he called, while hurrying his pace. She didn't answer.

He found her sitting at a small desk in the corner of her room, staring intently at her computer display. Her lips were moving silently, as if she was reading.

"What's wrong?" he asked, while placing the cup of coffee on the desk. He grasped her right arm and gave a gentle squeeze.

"Your message, David," she spluttered. He glanced at her computer screen. She had been reading the message he had sent to the entire support team earlier.

"What about it?"

"It's, it's...not yours!"

"What?" He took a closer look at the text on her screen.

> To: <mars_crew>, <support_team_all>, <committed_ones>
> From: <shepherd>
> Subject: JPL telemetry issue
> Priority: Emergency

> Many of you have heard persistent rumors that sabotage caused the off-course *Perseus* landing, and possibly the loss of the three vehicles at the Medusae landing site. In particular, the JPL telemetry team has been blamed for directing the *Perseus* to land a hundred kilometers off-course.

> These rumors are false. They are the fictitious work of a rogue television reporter whose hostility towards our mission has been

demonstrated countless times. We have full confidence in the quality of the telemetry from JPL, and in particular, from the *Mars Odyssey* orbiter.

The landing of the cargo vehicle will continue as planned, using all available telemetry. The final landing maneuvers may be overridden manually, at the discretion of Commander Day.

- Shepherd

David read the message three times before he believed his eyes. The first paragraph and last sentence were taken from his original message, word for word. The rest was almost completely different. His grip on Cassie's arm tightened, until she pried his fingers away.

"I was right there when you typed your message," said Cassie. "You didn't write this! How could it have changed?"

"I don't know. I wouldn't have believed a message could be altered once it's been sent. Obviously, it can."

Cassie crinkled her nose, a sign of concentration. "Could the security team have done it?"

"Perhaps. What about the bulletin board?"

Cassie warped her avatar into the central atrium, where she approached the bulletin board. The message from Shepherd had been changed there, too.

"What can we do, David? We've got to warn people about...about the saboteur!"

David noted she still hadn't referred to Ben by name. Perhaps she still held out hope of her husband's innocence, despite all the circumstantial evidence to the contrary.

"I don't know of any other way to broadcast a message," he replied. "But when my staff shows up in the main support room to monitor the landing in a few hours, I can talk to each of them directly."

"So you can warn them!"

"Yes, but it might not be that simple."

Sitting on the edge of the bed, he lapsed into thought. Since Ben was obviously working for the Beta organization, his friends who changed the wording of David's message must also work for Beta. These people, most likely members of the security team, had already demonstrated their power over events within the virtual world. What else could they do? Could they block his avatar from entering the support center? Since they could forge messages, they could easily appoint one of his backups, perhaps Major Tom, to direct the landing.

And the orders would all come from me, just like this last message. I've got to do something to stop them. But what?

First, he needed to make sure that his avatar was still alive. If security was involved, they could easily pull the plug on the Shepherd account or change his access passwords. If Shepherd was dead, his options were limited.

"Cassie, could you please query Shepherd's location?"

"Sure. But why?"

While she ran the query, he explained his concerns. Fortunately, Shepherd was in his office, still alive. He breathed a sigh of relief.

With Cassie following, he raced downstairs, back to his own computer in the basement. It was time for Shepherd to act, while he still could. He didn't know what he was going to do yet, but he might have only minutes until his access was blocked. He had to think of something, quickly.

Since his messages could be edited, he needed to talk to someone right away, someone with authority who could carry the torch for him if his account was terminated. He queried the list of avatars currently within the support center. As the names flashed by, he saw several familiar ones.

Arnold? No. He works in security. He might even be the guy who edited my message.

Major Tom? No way.

Sinbad? Possibly. He's not involved in the landing preparations, but at least he has access to the main support room.

Wait! Commander Day is online!

If there was ever anyone with a vested interest in the cargo vehicle landing safely, it was Commander Day. He could trust her in this matter, since her own life was at stake. When she talked, people listened. Even better, the security team would never even consider killing her account.

However, talking with the commander directly would be difficult. The time delay for communications to Mars was nearly 17 minutes, one-way. If she stayed in one place long enough, Shepherd could just stand in front of her and start talking. If she moved to a different room, she would never hear his message.

He had to try. First, he needed to find her, so he queried her location.

Conference Room 4.

Just when things couldn't get any worse, they did. His inward groan must have been audible because Cassie asked what was wrong. To her, a conference room seemed to be a perfect place to meet the commander.

He hastily explained his past experience with this conference room, and his theory about clandestine meetings being held there. Whoever used this room had gone to great lengths to conceal their activities, so they probably wouldn't appreciate his intrusion. Was he ready to confront them directly?

Cassie's excitement was tangible. "I think you should enter. You might actually meet the mission sponsors! They're the perfect people to receive our warning."

"But what if it's the saboteurs who meet there?" he thought aloud. "I might be confronting the very people I'm fighting against!"

"Then why would Commander Day be there?"

He conceded her point was a good one. Still, he hesitated. "Wait a minute. What about the earlier sabotage inside the *Perseus*?" Cassie already knew about the radiation shielding issue. "I never considered that Commander Day might have been responsible, since she was the obvious target. What if she was? What if she's been the source of all our problems on the mission?"

"You think she wants to die? There's nothing in her psych profile suggesting it."

"I recall reading in one of the psych team's reports about some unresolved issues with her husband's death. Might she be trying to join him?"

Cassie shook her head. "There are easier ways to kill yourself. You don't have to go to Mars to do it."

She had made another good point. He could dawdle all day in indecision, or he could act. Time was running out. He warped to the central atrium and ran the shut telescope command to shrink himself.

"Very cool," Cassie commented, as the visual perspective changed.

He typed the command to warp into Conference Room 4. Before he invoked it, he turned back to Cassie.

"One more thing," he said. "I don't know what I'm going to do or say once I'm in there, but it's important that you don't say anything."

"Why?" she asked defiantly. "I'm involved in this as much as you are!"

"Yes, but the people in that room don't know you're involved. They're going to see Shepherd warp in. Whether it's the sponsors or the saboteurs in there, I'm the one they'll retaliate against if things go south. If they kill my avatar, I'll need to borrow yours so I can still move around the support center."

"But even if I say something, they won't know who I am."

"That's probably true, but I don't want to take the chance someone will recognize your voice."

Cassie wavered, and finally agreed. She grabbed a pencil and a pad of paper from his desk, making it obvious she was still going to offer her input nonverbally.

Taking a deep breath, David ran the warp command.

Whoosh!

The background faded, and a new room came into view. It was the same conference room he had seen before, but this time, five of the six chairs were filled with colorful avatars. Several more loitered along the two side walls.

From the foot of the short oak table, David quickly scanned the bizarre collection of avatars. Many looked like characters from Alice in Wonderland. Commander Day's shimmering <alice> avatar was present near the head of the table, across the room from David. Standing near her was an outline of a human-sized, cat-shaped avatar, completely transparent, but with two solid, glowing eyes. Seated at the table were the King and Queen of Hearts, Tweedle Dee, Tweedle Dum, and the Mad Hatter.

"Weird," whispered Cassie.

The avatars along the walls showed more diversity. He recognized one, immediately: Arnold, the security guard.

With his true-surround speakers, he deduced the cat-shaped avatar, obviously a Cheshire Cat, had been speaking when he entered the room. "…while we're waiting for White Rabbit, we can discuss the land…Sweet Jesus!"

David almost laughed, as he imagined the effect of his robed avatar appearing in the midst of an unsuspecting roomful of people. He turned on his microphone and tried to inject confidence into his voice. "No, I'm a different Shepherd. The one whose job is to know what's happening in my support center. Someone threw a party and didn't invite me."

The Cheshire Cat spoke again. "Arnold, I thought you killed this avatar."

"I've been working on it, sir," replied Arnold's squeaky voice.

The Cat loped around the side of the table and approached Shepherd. "How did you get in here?" His voice was cold and brusque.

"The same way as the rest of you, probably."

"He has a universal key," Arnold explained, from the side wall.

"Kill his connection, now." This order came from the Cheshire Cat again. He was obviously a figure of authority within the group.

"Wait!" David had wasted enough time. "Look, I don't know who you people are, and why you're meeting in secret. But since Commander Day is here, I have to assume you want the Mars mission to succeed. If so, I have some urgent information for you."

The Cat figure muttered something about rabbits being late, and returned to his original position at the front of the room. "You've got two minutes," he said, louder.

Cassie had hurriedly scribbled, "Suck up to the cat, first!" on her notepad, and underlined it. He waved her off.

Before he changed his mind or they killed his avatar, David quickly revealed his evidence of JPL sabotage. He described the envelope transfer at the party, the purchases of real estate, and the highly incriminating bank statements. The saboteur had already boasted he had the ability to make the *Perseus* land off-course. David concluded the cargo landing needed to proceed without any direct involvement of the JPL telemetry team. Otherwise, the reporter was right. Another accident would happen.

"And why are you telling this to us?" asked one of the other avatars seated at the table. David couldn't tell which one spoke.

"I need to warn my support team. I already broadcast a message, but someone changed it." A low snicker from the side wall confirmed his suspicion. Arnold had changed his message. "I assumed that same someone would soon kill my avatar. If you do that, the cargo landing will be trashed, and the whole Mars mission might fail. Please, don't kill my avatar!"

A moment of silence followed his final outburst. Cheshire Cat broke the spell by asking, "Chicken, do our plans remain intact?"

A flat, toneless voice from the near wall curtly answered, "Yes."

David turned to face the latest speaker. He hadn't paid much attention to the three avatars standing along the nearest wall. One looked like a large, mangy, brown chicken, with a drooping beak and sad, dull eyes. Compared to the flashiness of the other avatars in the room, the chicken looked pathetic.

"<chicken_little>, I presume?" David asked.

The chicken remained silent.

"Kill Shepherd's account," the Cheshire Cat ordered. "Now."

"No!" David pleaded again. "Look, <chicken_little>, if your weird messages were intended to guide me, then help me once more. Don't let them kill…"

"...my account!" The tail end of his plea was directed toward a dark computer display. An unemotional text message on the screen announced, "Error: Remote connection lost. Attempting to reconnect..."

His computer repeatedly failed to restore a connection to the virtual support center. The error message mocked him, slowly scrolling off the bottom of the screen. Shepherd was dead.

David leaned back in stunned silence. His worst-case scenario had come true.

"That could have gone better," Cassie said. She took his hand in hers in a gesture of sympathy. It didn't make him feel any better.

For over a year, Shepherd had been a huge part of his life. He was an alter ego, a being of power and authority in the virtual world, sharply contrasting with David's own lack of status in the real world. Shepherd was his outlet for his dreams and aspirations. Now that Shepherd was gone, only small, insignificant David remained.

As if reading his thoughts, Cassie said, "Shepherd is still alive, you know." She tapped David's left temple. "He's safe in here."

"No, he's gone. I have nothing left."

Silently, Cassie knelt on the floor at his side. "You still have me," she finally said. Her voice was so low he could hardly hear her. With a pang of guilt, he recalled Cassie had recently endured a betrayal far worse than the death of Shepherd.

Her voice rapidly gained intensity. "The rest of your family and friends are still with you, too. You have your skills, your likes and dislikes, your knowledge, and your gentle nature. As much as I dislike her, you even still have Fontaine."

"Skye," he whispered, wondering if there was anything she could do to help. Probably not. She had already done her part, warning the media and public about the risk of JPL sabotage. She had no way to stop the landing or to block Ben from sabotaging it. He should at least send her a message to let her know what had happened. Perhaps he could use Cassie's account to contact Skye. Now that Shepherd was dead, David didn't even possess an active Internet account.

He fought a brief internal struggle against the shrouds of despair threatening to smother him, and won. He still needed to act. The lives of Anna and her crewmates still depended on him, now more than ever.

"Why wouldn't they listen?" he asked.

He was only thinking aloud, but Cassie answered anyway. "The group dynamics seemed straightforward. The big cat with the glowing eyes is in a position of autocratic authority."

"The Cheshire Cat," he corrected.

"Whatever. He's already made up his mind to trust NASA, for some reason. Perhaps he works there?" She shook her head. "It doesn't matter. Once he made his decision, nothing you could say would convince him otherwise. For some leaders, that's part of the psychology of holding absolute power over others."

"But why kill my avatar?"

"You challenged him. You called attention to his making some bad decisions. That's the worst way to approach an absolute dictator. I was trying to advise you to suck up to him, first. Changing his decision needed to seem like his own idea, not your demand."

"I really messed up, didn't I?" he asked, dejectedly.

"Well, no, it was all a long shot to begin with. Even with my training and experience in playing verbal games with patients, I probably wouldn't have done much better."

"So, what do we do now?" he asked, thinking aloud again. The blank ceiling stared back at him, answerless. He missed his stars.

"The encounter wasn't a complete waste of time. We did learn a few things."

"Yes, we did," he replied cynically. "We learned the cargo landing is doomed. Those idiots, living in their little Alice in Wonderland fantasy world, brought it on themselves."

"That's better. Let some of that anger out. It's good for you." Cassie's eyes flared as she spoke, perhaps an indication of an attempt to heed her own advice.

"Do you really think they were the mission sponsors?"

"Maybe," she said. "Don't forget Commander Day was there. Her having a direct link to the sponsors would make sense."

David shook his head. "I think I messed up right from the start. Those weren't the mission sponsors in that room. They were Beta, the saboteurs. That's why they wouldn't help me, and it's why they killed my login."

Cassie disagreed, due to the amount of work it would have taken to set up the hidden little corner of the support center where they could meet in privacy. Only the mission sponsors could have done that.

David responded that it wouldn't be very hard. He cursed his own inability to see the truth right in front of him the whole time. "I had already known that Major Tom was a bad apple." He noted Cassie's surprised expression. "And I had already suspected that others on the security and software engineering teams were involved too. The shut telescope command doesn't even leave an entry in the command history logs, so it must have been created by a combination of software and security experts. That should have been a big clue. Once they could shrink an avatar, Arnold could hand out room keys to anyone. That's all they needed. They met under my nose, plotting their evil little schemes throughout the whole mission."

"But what about Commander Day? She wouldn't sabotage the mission. It would be suicide!"

"That part doesn't make any sense," he agreed. "Could they be blackmailing her into cooperating? With your psych team connections, you know her past better than I do. Does she have any skeletons in her closet?"

Cassie thought for a moment, before cautiously nodding her head. "Her long military career was outstanding. But in her civilian career, some people died under her command in Antarctica, including her husband."

"Interesting. That could explain a lot, and I'm surprised the psych team didn't brief me. Haven't heard a word about it in the media, either."

"Fontaine missed that one," said Cassie.

David wiped his brow for effect. "I assume you have electronic access to the commander's psychological records. May I see them?"

Cassie stood, and started to pace the room. The small basement office had seen a lot of pacing lately.

"I can't do that, David. Patient files are confidential."

"But I'm trying to save the commander's life! What good is confidentiality if the patient is dead?"

"I remember you used that line on me once before, regarding Anna," said Cassie. "And I also remember you were lying to me at the time about your relationship with her." Cassie's nostrils flared, and she stopped her pacing long enough to stare at him, with her hands on her hips in open defiance.

"I'm not lying now. Don't forget, Anna will be just as dead as the commander if we allow Beta to wreck the cargo landing. Please, Cassie. Help me save her. If the commander is helping the saboteurs, something in those files might tell me why. I need to know, if I'm going to figure out a way to stop them."

She threw her hands up in the air. "Just fling all my ethics out the window? I can't do that, David."

"Difficult times sometimes require compromises." David stared at the floor. "I never understood that, before I took this job. I had an academic's view of the world, seeing only black or white. I didn't recognize all the shades of gray in between."

He could tell she was wavering, but not enough to change her decision. "No. I can't do it. You'll need to get your information elsewhere."

David glared at her and coaxed some more, but Cassie wouldn't budge. However, her remark, "get your information elsewhere," had ignited a new idea. Perhaps Skye, the information queen, could help after all. He could ask her to do some digging into the commander's background, including the death of her husband.

David quickly switched subjects, as he recalled another loose end. "Then there's <chicken_little>, if that's who was in the conference room. If he's involved with Beta, why would one of his earlier messages have thrown suspicion on the commander, his fellow saboteur?"

"You lost me there, big bro. I'll take your word for that. But what's this 'Beta' you keep talking about?"

"Sorry." He explained his shorthand notation for the hidden organization opposing the goals of the Mars mission sponsors.

They speculated about <chicken_little>'s involvement in Beta, but to no avail. The motives of his feathered antagonist remained as cryptic as ever.

"What about Anna?" asked Cassie.

"Anna? What do you mean?"

"Can't we send a warning to her?"

"And what could she possibly do about it?" he snapped. Anna was powerless to stop plots from brewing back on Earth. Confronting the commander about her involvement with the saboteurs would be equally futile, and possibly dangerous, too.

"I'm just trying to help! Don't get all huffy."

He apologized. After giving the matter some more thought, he even agreed with her.

"I guess we should warn Anna," he said. "But carefully. Who knows what the commander will do, once her involvement with Beta is revealed."

With several messages to send, they left the basement and climbed the two flights of steps back to the guest bedroom. Cassie sat before her computer display. Her Kahuna avatar was still waiting patiently in her Psych Ward office.

Cassie quickly typed an emergency-priority message to Anna. David dictated most of the text, which ended in a plea to be careful if she discussed this matter with the commander.

After sending the warning to Anna, Cassie checked her messages. Looking over her shoulder, David almost had a heart attack. A new message from Shepherd had just arrived.

"Open it!" he goaded, while fighting back an urge to grab the keyboard himself.

To: <mars_crew>, <support_team_all>, <committed_ones>
From: <shepherd>
Subject: Support for cargo landing
Priority: High

FYI, I'll be working on a special assignment, until further notice. While I'm gone, I've appointed Major Tom to direct Mission Support. He will oversee the landing of the cargo vehicle today, and possibly the ERV landing two days from now.

- Shepherd

David felt physically ill. Had he eaten any lunch, he probably would have lost the contents of his stomach immediately. Instead, he successfully fought off the wave of nausea and was able to put the message into a proper perspective. The contents made perfect sense. With Shepherd out of the way, Beta was pressing its advantage and taking no chances. They wanted their man in the driver's seat.

Cassie must have felt ill too because she hastily excused herself from the room. When she returned, her face was pale, and her legs seemed barely able to support her. She collapsed back into her chair by the computer, heavily.

"Are you OK, Cassie?" he asked, concerned.

"Fine. I've just been feeling queasy all morning. You wanted to ask Fontaine to check the commander's background."

David knew this approach was a long shot. Unfortunately, he lacked any better options. While he reflected back upon the disastrous meeting in Conference Room 4, searching for any strand of a new, helpful idea, Cassie began composing an external e-mail to Skye's new account at the Lynx network.

He interrupted, "Wait a minute. I'm overlooking something. Or rather, someone. Two someones, in fact."

Cassie paused her typing, allowing him time to get his muddled thoughts in order. Some pieces of the puzzle were still missing.

"In that meeting of Beta, where was Major Tom? Seems like he should have been there, since he's so involved in their plans. But even more importantly, where was Ben?"

"Ben?" Cassie held her stomach as if she was going to be ill again. David regretted his lack of tact at bringing up a painful subject, but it was necessary.

He said, "If Ben's carrying out Beta's sabotage, he should have been at the meeting, too."

"And since he wasn't?" As Cassie's question hung in the air, her eyes briefly lit up before glassing over again. "No, that doesn't mean anything, does it? He could have been off somewhere else, doing practically anything. Even if he was there, we wouldn't have recognized him."

"You're right. He could very well have been there. And if he was, or if the others tell him what happened..." David hated the conclusion he had blundered into, but the consequences of his previous actions were obvious.

Cassie finished his sentence. "...he'll assume I know all about it, too." She cringed. "And he can easily guess where we're staying."

"We have to leave," said David, getting to his feet. "The sooner, the better. But that's not the worst of it. He'll also know I still have access to Mission Support, through your account."

"Through my..." Cassie turned back to her computer. As if on cue, the display went dark, and a text message appeared. "Error: Remote connection lost. Attempting to reconnect..."

CHAPTER 29
VACUUM

MarsDay 250, 11:00 a.m.
(August 4, 3:57 p.m.)

The scraggly little bean sprout in Anna's hand seemed to look up at her and say, "I was doing the best I could. Why did you uproot me?" She wiped a tear from her cheek. Her plants had struggled valiantly to survive in the poor soil and lighting conditions of the sample box. This little bean sprout had fared better than its cousins. Her plants had all the nutrients and carbon dioxide they needed, but the high levels of salts and other toxins in the soil continued to stunt their growth.

After resealing the sample box and adjusting its atmospheric mix, she stepped down from the flexi-ladder and transferred the corpse of the bean sprout to her work area, a small nook in the EVA room. Along the way, she nearly bumped into Evelyn, who had been using the floor of the EVA room as a pacing platform.

"Are you OK, Evelyn?" Anna was starting to worry about the upcoming cargo landing. Evelyn rarely showed her emotions, but during the last few hours, she had been literally climbing the walls.

"Just nerves, my dear. In two hours, the cargo vehicle will either land, or it won't. We've done all we can."

Anna activated her microscope and placed a thinly sliced cross-section of bean sprout on a slide. She looked over her shoulder. Evelyn had resumed her pacing.

"It will land, and only ten feet away. We're due for a good break."

"I'll settle for ten kilometers away," said Evelyn. "In the meantime, I'm trying to prepare for our next activities." She waved a sheet of E-paper while she paced. "Mission Support sent a list of cargo and a longer list of recommendations."

"May I see?"

Evelyn handed her the paper. The cargo manifest section was just as Anna had expected. A pressurized rover, ten portable greenhouse pods, three larger inflatable greenhouses, nearly a metric tonne of medical and field equipment, and four tonnes of food and water were of primary interest. Christmas on Mars would be coming a few months early this year.

Farther down the E-page, she came to Mission Support's recommendations. The first few tasks involved verifying the integrity of the pressurized rover. A short geological excursion in the rover was listed as a later task, but she didn't find any mention of biology and soil gathering activities.

"What gives?" she asked Evelyn.

She had already explained her concerns about crop growth and her need for better soil several times. Mission Support was fully aware of the importance of her research, too.

Evelyn said, "I think they're worried about fuel consumption. We'll only have a 200-kilogram supply of benzene, initially. We can't take many trips until the fuel production plant is running. Our highest priority is to find accessible deposits of ground ice. Geology wins."

"That should make Ollie happy. But..."

But what? Evelyn's right. I'll just have to be patient. The pressurized rover is useless without fuel, and we might die if we don't find water.

She handed the E-page back to Evelyn and resumed studying her bean sprout under the microscope. While she worked, her mind was still on the conversation with Evelyn. Something was bothering her. After a few minutes, she finally realized what it was.

"Evelyn, all the fuel production equipment is on the ERV shipment, isn't it?"

"Yes."

"And if the ERV doesn't land safely...?"

Evelyn grabbed her pocket watch and checked the time. "We need both landings to be successful. Otherwise, we'll have food or fuel, but not both."

This was a surprise to Anna, a detail she had overlooked. "But once we have the pressurized rover, we can drive up to the Medusae landing site and grab more fuel, right?"

"Right. Assuming the fuel tanks there are still intact," Evelyn added.

"I guess we'll know soon enough."

Evelyn resumed her pacing, while Anna turned back to her microscope. Her courageous bean sprout revealed its secrets grudgingly. She saved some data and formulated some opinions, to be verified or debated by the experts back on Earth.

Back in her quarters, she transmitted her data and checked for incoming messages. Several media questions had arrived, and she recorded adequate responses. A message from Kahuna had also arrived, but it was just a courtesy message stating she was going to be out of contact for a few days.

She just got back from a long vacation, and now she's taking another? Must be nice. I wish I could be in her shoes.

No, I don't. I'm right where I want to be, in the middle of a three-year vacation.

MarsDay 250, 12:02 p.m.
(August 4, 5:00 p.m.)

David fiercely depressed the <hangup> button on Cassie's cell phone. Then he shook his head at the futility of his current situation. Events were unfolding, and he was powerless to affect the outcome.

"Well? What did she say?" asked Cassie, eagerly.

"Skye offered her condolences on the death of Shepherd. You heard me describe the meeting in Conference Room 4. Bottom line, she can't do anything to affect the cargo vehicle landing. As expected."

"Can't? Or won't?"

"What do you mean?" asked David, scowling sharply at his sister. He rose to his feet and walked over to the window. Their room at the St. Julien hotel was three floors above the bustling crowds on Walnut Street in downtown Boulder.

"She stated her belief, on national TV, that another landing accident would happen. Her reputation is riding on this."

"Oh. I thought you were implying something else."

He pivoted and faced Cassie who had been sitting beside him on the twin bed nearest the window. The light from the window revealed helplessness in her expression that matched his own. She laid her head back on the blanketed pillow and stared upward at the ceiling, the least interesting part of the ornately furnished room.

Their new hideout was comfortable, quiet, and luxurious. Slate tiles decorated the wall across from the twin beds, bestowing an earthy décor to the otherwise modern room. A small kitchen area offered utility, while the large, spotless bathroom contained a full tub, shower, and a jetted whirlpool. The whirlpool might be useful later, as a way of soothing his stress and frustration.

"She did offer to check Commander Day's background," he added, referring back to his conversation with Skye. "She also promised to contact us on your cell phone if her network's information hotline turns up any good leads."

"How likely is that?"

"Not very. They got a weird call this morning from a solar physicist at the Southwest Research Institute who read the transcript of yesterday's EVA. She was puzzled about why the EVA was cut short. With so many degrees of separation between Earth and Mars, the newly active sigmoid region on the Sun wasn't a solar flare threat for Mars until just a few hours ago."

"What do solar flares have to do with sabotage of the cargo landing?" asked Cassie.

"Absolutely nothing." David batted at the curtains beside the window. "But at least they're getting tips from reputable sources. Maybe someone else out there will report something that's more helpful."

"In the next 45 minutes? I don't think so."

David glowered at his watch. The landing would happen at exactly 6:00 p.m., but the media wouldn't confirm the disaster until a few minutes later. Bad news from Mars traveled just as slowly as good news.

Cassie asked, "Can we contact anyone else on your support team?"

He shook his head. "I don't know anyone's real identity or how to reach them. Our secret community was designed to prevent outsiders from knowing who was involved and what they were doing. Now that we're the ones on the outside, we're completely cut off."

"What about other outsiders? Like the FBI? Or those Chinese agents who tried to kidnap you?"

"No way." David would sooner shoot himself than go to either of those groups for help.

"How about other SEA members?"

"Perhaps, but it would take far too long to contact them." Local groups of SEA members around the country held frequent meetings, and three chapters in Colorado were among the most active. If he could attend a future meeting and alert them to Beta's hijacking of Mission Support, he might find allies who could help. Ideally, if he was incredibly lucky, he might even meet somebody who worked on the security team with the power to reinstate his login and kill Major Tom. This exceedingly remote possibility was still enough to sustain a tiny flame of hope.

Hanging on the slate covered wall, the muted wide-screen television began to display live footage from a control room at JPL. Cassie restored the volume so they could listen to the dialogue on the special Lynx news broadcast. Aarons, the reporter on the scene, claimed his network would cover the cargo vehicle landing sequence from the vantage point of the *Mars Odyssey* control room.

Behind Aarons, technicians staffed two short rows of computer displays. At the front of the room, part of a large display screen showed a live video feed from the *Perseus*. Commander Day was sitting by a control display of her own, typing, and occasionally speaking terse technical acronyms.

David sank down upon the other twin bed and resigned himself to watching the broadcast like any of the other billion ordinary viewers in the world. The program would be the ultimate reality TV show. The interplanetary disaster would be shown live, with full color and sound.

During a commercial break, Cassie rolled over and watched him. She asked, "What did you think I meant?"

"Pardon?"

She muted the television again. "Earlier, you got all upset when I asked if Fontaine couldn't help us, or wouldn't."

"Oh." David rubbed his eyes. Recalling that point in their conversation, he eventually answered, "I thought you were accusing her of getting rid of the competition."

"The competition?"

"Yes. Anna."

"I see." She added softly, "I thought you were past that."

David stifled a surge of anger. Lashing out at Cassie wouldn't do any good. Perhaps it was time for him to discuss the matter more openly. Doctor Contrato might be able to help.

"I still love her," he said, in a low voice.

"Anna? And what about Fontaine?"

"I think I love her, too. But differently."

She was watching his body language closely. "You mean, you love Anna, and you lust for Fontaine."

As she began the process of gently unwrapping the layers of David's troubled, conflicting emotions, Cassie still wouldn't address Skye by her first name. Fortunately for David, her psychological surgery was interrupted by a soft knock on the door.

Looking out the peephole, he spied Bill and Jennifer in the hallway outside and invited them in. Their timing was a perfect diversion from Cassie's necessary but uncomfortable probing into his screwy love life.

Jennifer's cheeks were flushed, and she was slightly out of breath. "Looks like we'll be neighbors tonight," she said. "We asked for the room next to yours."

David apologized for inconveniencing his friends. Before calling Skye, he had reached Jennifer at work and suggested that returning home might not be safe tonight. They probably still had some time, but if Ben's cronies came searching for him, the house in Nederland would be their starting point.

Cassie recapped the disturbing events of the day. They agreed that David and Cassie should leave town in the morning, without disclosing their plans. That way, if Ben showed up, Bill and Jennifer wouldn't have anything to tell him.

That part of the plan still sounded too dangerous. David thought his friends should stay at the hotel longer. Someone other than Ben might show up at their house. Someone like Major Tom.

Jennifer shrugged off his concerns. "Once you've left, we'll return home. They aren't going to scare us out of our own house."

"And there's the star of the show, now," said Bill. He had been watching the television screen, which still showed images from the control room at JPL. Over the shoulder of the reporter, they spotted Ben at one of the control consoles, typing on a keyboard.

"I wish we could see what he's doing," said Jennifer.

David already knew what Ben was doing. He longed to be in that control room himself, so he could strangle his brother-in-law or pound him into a bloody pulp, a pre-crash spectacle for the huge television audience.

Aarons wandered about the control room, followed by the camera. For the most part, he stayed out of the way of the technicians except to ask an occasional question. When Ben started to announce their reception of "tones" from the lander, Aarons asked for clarification.

During the main landing sequence, Ben explained to the reporter, signal interference from the superheated Mars atmosphere would prevent any real data transfer between the cargo vehicle and the orbiter. Dull tones could still be received, however, as a Morse-code-like substitute. According to Ben, the *Mars Odyssey* orbiter just received a series of tones indicating the landing craft was entering the upper atmosphere.

Ben looked haggard, and his explanation was choppy and disjointed. Bags under his eyes implied he hadn't slept much lately. The man was a mess, but David felt no sympathy. Compared to the pain Cassie had endured over the last two days, lack of sleep seemed a minor inconvenience.

Other technicians chimed in. Telemetry readouts from the orbiter indicated the cargo vehicle was on course. "All looks good so far," added Commander Day, her voice perfectly timed though it had left Mars minutes ago.

The next five minutes seemed like hours, as the drama built up to its horrifying climax. David didn't really want to watch, but he was drawn to the program and couldn't tear himself away.

Ben confirmed the release of the heat shield and the final parachute deployment. Two new views were added to the frontal screen beside Commander Day's image. One was from an external camera on the *Perseus* scanning the skies of Mars, searching for a trace of the incoming lander. The other was a live feed of the rapidly moving Martian surface, taken from the cargo vehicle itself.

On the audio channel from Mars, Ollie's voice began a running commentary. "Slowing with full thrusters. Craft is right on target. Speed is now 100 kilometers-per-hour." By now, Commander Day might be steering the lander through the final stages of descent. "Fifty. Twenty."

The view from the lander stopped moving and remained focused on a single boulder. Commander Day's voice trembled with emotion as she announced, "Mission Support, we have a successful landing! Our new neighbor is only one kilometer southwest of the *Perseus*. I'd call that a bulls-eye!"

Cheers erupted in the *Perseus*, the *Mars Odyssey* control room, and David's hotel room. David rose to his feet with the others and celebrated without restraint.

Out of the corner of his eye, he glimpsed a surprising scene on the television. In the *Mars Odyssey* control room, Ben was leaning back in his chair with his eyes closed and a huge, twisted grin on his face. He looked even more weary than before, but also victorious, as if he had won some major battle.

Cassie, Bill, and Jennifer didn't seem to notice Ben's expression. They were all chattering a mile a minute, even as David was shivering. He tried to pay attention to their conversation, but his mind was far away.

Was I completely wrong about Ben? Or have I underestimated just how devious he really is?

MarsDay 250, 4:00 p.m.
(August 4, 9:05 p.m.)

After the excitement of the cargo vehicle landing, the past three hours had been completely anticlimactic. Anna had helped the others inspect the cargo for any signs of damage, using internal and external button cameras. Then they thoroughly studied the area beneath the vehicle for ravines or boulders large enough to snag the pressurized rover as it was deployed.

Long past the point where Anna was convinced the cargo was undamaged and the undercarriage was clear, Evelyn continued to pore over the data from the remote sensors. She was leaving nothing to chance. Anna finally left in frustration and exercised for an hour.

At some time during that hour, Evelyn finally dropped the pressurized rover to the surface. The next part of the operation would be a tele-robotics task.

Anna was more than ready. In fact, since she was already in an exercise harness, it took her only a few seconds to reset the equipment for remote tele-operation duty. While triple-checking her connections, she couldn't get the tune "Jingle Bells" out of her head. Today still felt like Christmas. A 21-metric-tonne package had just been delivered on her front porch, and she was about to go out and retrieve it.

Poor analogy, Anna. This package is about to retrieve itself. Christmas presents usually don't do that.

Activating the tele-robotics link, Anna found herself seated at the controls of the rover. They now had a third Robonaut at their disposal, sent to Mars inside the pressurized rover. The robot was already powered and awaiting her instructions. She ran some internal diagnostics, which came back positive across the board.

Satisfied, she started the rover's engine. The tele-robotics gear wasn't sensitive enough for her to feel any vibrations, but she could hear the sound of the motor, and her control panel gauges indicated a successful startup.

"Take it slow and easy," advised Evelyn's voice from nearby.

"Party pooper," Anna replied.

While she longed to gun the pressurized rover's engine and race back to the *Perseus*, Evelyn's advice would be followed to the letter. The time for fun would come later, when she could physically drive the rover, and when it wasn't loaded down with five metric tonnes of additional supplies. Today, she would perform every operation in slow motion.

The one-kilometer drive back to the *Perseus* consumed almost an hour. Coupling the rover to the *Perseus* by backing up, adjusting hydraulics, releasing dust shutters, and connecting an inflatable "tunnel" took nearly another hour. Finally, Anna deactivated the rover engine and placed her Robonaut driver into standby mode. Her task was complete.

She handed her tele-robotics helmet to Evelyn and released herself from the harness, rubbing her tense back muscles. "Nicely done," Evelyn said. "You've just added a new room to our cottage. Shall we take a look at what's inside?"

"I'll join you later," was the answer she surprised herself with. "I need a shower first." She left the EVA room and headed toward her quarters, passing Ollie on the way out.

After her shower and a change of clothing, she tried recharging her mental batteries with a few minutes of meditation. Her shortage of sleep the night before, combined with renewed surges of excitement, made the attempt futile, however. A Christmas present awaited.

She joined Ollie and Evelyn in the EVA room. They were all smiles. "All of the supplies are here!" said Evelyn.

"Of course they are!" said Ollie. "Was there ever any doubt?"

Evelyn placed a box of food gently atop a stack of similar boxes in the corner. "Well, with everything that crazy reporter was claiming, I was starting to wonder…"

Anna joined in their laughter, despite only eight metric tonnes of the shipment being present and accounted for. The other 13 tonnes remained back in the cargo vehicle, including the greenhouse materials and heavy digging equipment.

All of that equipment would be there, too, of course. Tomorrow, she would retrieve some greenhouse pods and place them near the *Perseus*. Her crop growth experiments could begin in earnest...if she only had some decent soil.

MarsDay 251, 3:36 a.m.
(August 5, 9:00 a.m.)

On this Thursday morning, the light breakfast crowd at the St. Julien Restaurant consisted mostly of well-dressed people who looked like business travelers. Many had already eaten and were in the process of leaving. David and his friends had no trouble finding a quiet booth in a dimly lit corner of the spacious main room. He felt a bit conspicuous, dressed in sweat pants and an old t-shirt, but at least his casual apparel matched that of his friends.

Since they had celebrated the successful Mars landing in David's hotel room until well past midnight, Jennifer had suggested the convenience of eating downstairs at the hotel restaurant this morning. Everyone had readily agreed.

They ate in slow motion, with subdued conversation. David realized they might not be seeing each other again for some time. Everyone acted like they were trying to delay their inevitable separation.

As he and Bill split the tab, Cassie and Jennifer excused themselves from the booth, seeking a restroom. Upon their return, Jennifer seemed mildly amused or happy about something. Cassie had rarely smiled in the past two days, but her expression was at least guardedly positive.

"Telling secrets about us?" asked David.

"You'll never know," was Cassie's reply.

David had been watching Cassie closely, looking for signs of improvement. He was still worried about his little sister. Besides her recent depression, which had obvious causes, she also appeared to be battling a stomach flu virus. Overnight, his own sleep had been light, and she had woken him up several times with her frequent visits to the bathroom.

"Are you feeling any better?" he asked, as she slipped by him to reclaim her seat near the dark, oak-paneled wall.

"I'm fine."

She glanced at Jennifer across the table, who added, "You're being a good mother hen, David." She winked at Cassie.

Rather than joining the teasing, Bill scowled, and kicked him under the table. He was looking over David's shoulder, toward the entrance of the restaurant. David slowly craned his neck to follow his friend's gaze.

Six new patrons had entered the restaurant. Two had seated themselves at a table near the entrance. Two moved to a different corner of the main room. The remaining two stood near the buffet area with their backs turned. All were hooded and cloaked in brown habits.

Jennifer was in the middle of a sentence when she noticed the newcomers and halted abruptly. David had no idea what she was saying because he hadn't been listening. He turned back to the others. "Coincidence?" he asked. Last night, he had shared the stories of his previous encounters with monks in great detail.

One of the figures near the center of the room turned, and approached their booth. As he drew near, he removed his hood, revealing a weathered face with a short gray beard and a full head of silver, closely cut hair. The man looked vaguely familiar, and David searched his memory for a name to attach to the gravely serious monk. Then he recalled several hours of stimulating conversation on a dark bus.

"Brother Matthew!"

The man smiled, thinly. He said, "I'm most pleased to see you again, David. However, I hoped our next encounter would be under happier circumstances."

"Why are you here?" David asked curtly. Alarmed, he glanced around the restaurant.

Brother Matthew reached for a chair from a nearby table. "Might I join your group? We have important matters to discuss."

He seemed to interpret their shocked silence as an approval. Pulling the chair over, he sat near Bill, but with some separation from their booth.

"And just what are these important matters?" asked David.

"A deeply troubled soul is in need of peace. Some past mistakes require correcting."

The echo of his words hung in the air as David sought understanding. The man didn't sound very threatening, but was his intention revenge? He ventured, "Past mistakes, like the death of your friend near Brainard Lake?"

Brother Matthew shook his head. "That unfortunate event has already been reconciled. Yet others remain. First, I must ask you to choose your next actions wisely."

"My next actions?" The man spoke in riddles. David felt like he was talking to <chicken_little>.

"All of you," Brother Matthew said, without really clarifying anything. "Many paths diverge from this point." His gaze swept the group, starting with Bill. "Some pass through violent regions and ultimately go nowhere." His eyes paused, lingering on Cassie. "Others traverse rocky, barren soil to most unappealing destinations. I pray you will all have the wisdom to choose a better course."

"I don't understand," said David. He had only one path: futile resistance, as he sought a way to regain control of Mission Support and interfere with the plans of the Beta organization. Yet that battle was already decided, and he had lost. Only the barest glimmer of hope remained. Was Brother Matthew suggesting he walk away and accept defeat? Or was he talking about something else entirely?

"Brother, it is time for your penitence." Brother Matthew directed these words over his shoulder, toward the cloaked, hooded man who still lingered near the central buffet area, but had moved a bit closer to their booth. The monk leaned back and snared a new chair from another table, pulling it beside his own. His colleague joined them, sat, and slowly pulled back his hood to reveal his features.

"Ben!" Bill's voice was a snarl.

David was too surprised to speak, let alone to move. Beside him, Cassie's sharp fingernails dug into his arm as her weak grip tightened.

While David remained frozen in place, Bill rose threateningly to his feet. Brother Matthew held up his hand and gently implored, "Remember, choose the better direction. The one of peace."

"Peace, right," growled Bill. His face darkened further. "Cassie, how many pieces should I rip him into?"

David recalled a similar, threat-filled play on words many months ago, when he first met Skye in person. It took all his willpower to suppress his own sudden, overpowering urge to wring Ben's neck, as he had dreamt of doing so many times during the past two days.

As he wavered, Cassie's trembling voice froze him. "Please don't. He's still my husband." The rest of her words were whispered so low they were almost inaudible. She might have said, "And I still love him."

He turned back to Cassie. Her deathly paleness alarmed him, as did the feverish intensity of her stare.

Her plea had halted Bill too, though he warned, "You'd better tell us why you're here, Ben, and fast." He slowly settled back onto his seat but remained leaning over the table towards Ben, with one clenched fist planted squarely in his plate of unfinished pancakes. He didn't seem to notice the sticky mess he had created.

David glanced about the restaurant. The business travelers had all departed long ago. If they required assistance, the only other diners were a group of six elderly women and two families with young children. All were seated across the room. Even the wait staff, usually so attentive, had disappeared.

Ben closed his eyes, slouching a bit in his chair. He seemed even wearier than he had appeared on television the night before. Had a strong breeze blown through the restaurant, he would probably have been swept away.

Reopening his eyes, Ben centered his gaze upon Cassie. "I'm sorry I misled you, Cass. I, uh, I should have told you about buying the house. It was meant to be a surprise, a special gift." He spoke slowly, as if reciting lines he had memorized. "It was something too important to keep secret. Please forgive me."

Cassie eased her grip on David's arm slightly. Her response was low, yet it contained a fierce intensity. "I don't care about any stupid house. You've been lying to me about a lot more than that."

Ben seemed to shrink even further into his chair.

"I've never, ever lied to you," he said. "I did...hide a few things, though. And I'm deeply sorry about that, too. It was necessary."

Jennifer butted in, "Things like taking bribes from USNN? Sabotaging the Mars mission? Putting the lives of the Mars explorers at risk?"

Ben shook his head, showing some vigor for the first time. "That's not true! I haven't done any of those things." He turned to David, almost begging. "I would never do anything to jeopardize the Mars mission. You know me better than that. Tell them!"

David shook his head, too, but slowly, and with great sadness. "I thought I knew you well, Ben. But we have video evidence. You accepted an envelope from Skye Fontaine's program producer on the night of the post-landing party at JPL. We also have evidence of transactions in your Swiss bank account. Your balance jumped, soon afterwards."

"Fontaine's..." A twisted look crossed Ben's face, and he seemed newly awake and alert. He turned to Brother Matthew. "If true, this would be an important development."

"Clearly," the monk responded.

David fought back a new surge of anger. "What do you mean, if true?" he snapped. "We know it's true. We've all seen the recording, and a whole lot more."

He instantly regretted his outburst. The encounter seemed peaceful enough, for the moment. However, Ben and the monks obviously shared a special relationship. Though Brother Matthew had acted most friendly in the past, things could still take a left turn if he decided to erase all the evidence of Ben's transgressions permanently. David might have just killed himself and his three friends.

If trouble erupted, he and Bill would be difficult to subdue, but how long could they hold off six men? Jennifer might also be scrappy in a fight, but Cassie? She had never squashed an insect in her entire life. The best he could hope for was to buy some time for his sister to escape.

On the other hand, Ben seemed genuinely surprised. Might David's facts be in error? Could the recording have been forged? It did come from Skye, whom he still didn't trust completely.

Could she have played me for a total fool? She could have doctored some video footage and created phony bank statements. But Ben had already admitted to buying a multi-million dollar house. JPL must be paying him a lot more than their other engineers.

His questions were answered immediately, as Ben turned back to him and said, "I was at that party. And I did accept an envelope from a courier. But I had no idea the man worked for USNN. Can you really prove this?"

David was tempted to yell, "No! We made it all up! Let us go!" However, he and his friends were long past the point of escaping that easily. He answered truthfully. "His identity was confirmed in other recordings. He definitely works at USNN."

Ben still looked genuinely surprised. How could he not have known the identity of his Beta conspirator? Something didn't add up, and David was beginning to have more doubts.

"You have other recordings of this program producer, too?" asked Ben, so excited he was practically drooling. "What do those other recordings reveal?"

David had made another mistake. He never should have mentioned the other recordings. Some were far more incriminating for USNN than the one Ben had starred in. If Skye intended to use them against the network in a dangerous game of bribery, he might have just weakened her hand. Perhaps he could divert the subject before any more damage was done.

"What does it matter?" he asked. "You still took the money as payment for sabotaging the *Perseus* landing. Or are you going to claim your drinking friend paid you to kill his wife?" Then he winced at his own words again.

That was a really bad idea to plant in Ben's mind.

Ben lowered his gaze and said, "I told you, I didn't sabotage the *Perseus* landing."

Cassie joined the interrogation. "Look at us when you say that. I want you to look in my eyes and say you didn't cause the *Perseus* to land a hundred kilometers off-course."

Some new diners entered the restaurant, but they sat across the room, near the other patrons. David suspected that any newcomers would naturally shy away from their monk-infested corner. Outside assistance remained unlikely.

He returned his attention to Ben, who hadn't moved. "I can't do that," Ben said. David was confused for a moment, until he recalled Cassie's demand.

"Honesty, Brother Benjamin," said the monk seated beside him. "The door is open to truth and understanding. Don't allow it to close again."

Ben looked up. "You're right. They deserve to hear the whole truth."

David waited for Ben to add, "...before you die," like all the villains in the old James Bond movies, but he didn't. Instead, with eyes only for Cassie, he stated solemnly, "I did cause the *Perseus* to land where it did. And the man you claim works for USNN did pay me for doing it. Five million dollars, in fact."

"I knew it!" cried Bill, pounding the soggy remnants of his pancakes further into oblivion. "What else did they pay you for? Destroying the other ships?"

As he answered, Ben's voice didn't waver. "Yes. They paid me to hide signals in the telemetry to the other three vehicles, signals to trigger some hidden explosives. That was all arranged three years ago, back on Earth, before those rockets were ever launched."

"Skye was right," moaned David, softly. They had slowly pieced together Beta's actions, over the past few months, and Ben had just verified their worst suspicions.

"The reporter?" asked Ben. "She was remarkably accurate. She's a dangerous loose end." He glared at Brother Matthew.

David was chilled by the ominous comment. If Skye was a dangerous loose end, what were he and his companions?

"Why did your employers wait so long?" he asked. "They could have destroyed those vehicles anytime, even before they were launched."

"I'm not sure, exactly," replied Ben. "I haven't been involved in their planning. Our relationship is strictly one-way. My sources tell me what to do, and I do it. I don't even know who they are."

"They want those people to die," Cassie confided sadly to the empty plate on the table in front of her. She looked up at the others and calmly explained, "It's obvious. They waited until after the human crew was launched because they want them all to die on Mars. Our suicidal commander refused to use the free return trajectory. They landed off-course, and no one will ever know what really happened to the other vehicles. The crew will die, and that will be the end of it."

With equal somber, Jennifer added, "The end of the space program, you mean. After NASA's recent setbacks on the Moon, congressmen are looking for any excuse to save a few pennies in the budget by canceling the whole space program. Robots are easy to forget about, but the politicians can't kill the program while we still have people alive, out in deep space. Their constituents would crucify them."

Bill muttered, "And Ben's given them exactly what they wanted."

David saw the cold fury in Bill's eyes, a dangerous look he had never seen there before. His friend was notoriously long on words and short on actions, but he might have finally been pushed over the edge.

CHAPTER 30
APOGEE

MarsDay 251, 4:34 a.m.
(August 5, 10:00 a.m.)

If Bill acted on his fury, David's best move would be to restrain his friend, a difficult task for sure. Despite Ben's heinous admissions of guilt, David didn't want this encounter to deteriorate into violence.

Brother Matthew and his colleagues were firmly in control of the situation, given their superior numbers and unknown capabilities. A peaceful outcome was to be preferred, though David was starting to doubt whether that was possible. Ben had revealed far too many incriminating facts.

"Wait," Ben pleaded, with his hands held upward before him, as if trying to ward off any assault before it was launched. "I know how bad this all must sound. But there's more to the story. Much more." His voice was low, and filled with emotion.

"Indeed, there must be," replied David, in an attempt to buy some more time to defuse the situation. The others stared at him. "Ben hasn't told us anything new. But there's that missing crater on Mars. The one the cargo vehicle should have created last night, when it crashed." He turned back to Ben. "What happened? Did you get cold feet? Or did Skye's story scare your friends into changing their plans?"

Ben nodded. "I got an emergency message yesterday morning. It instructed me not to hinder the landing of the cargo vehicle. Again, I don't know why. Perhaps the reporter's story changed their plans, or perhaps not. All I know is it was one of the happiest messages I've ever received."

"Happiest?" Wiping away some tears, Cassie struggled to ask, "Why?"

"Because it would have been my first divergence, the first instructions from those hidden bastards I openly disobeyed. It would have put all of our lives at greater risk, too."

David would have been less surprised if Ben had removed a hand grenade from under his cloak and tossed it onto the table. All he could utter was, "Wha—What?"

Ben smile was weak and flitting. "Let me back up a bit. As I've told you several times, I haven't sabotaged the Mars mission. That's the truth. So far, each time I've carried out an order from the saboteurs, we've been able to synchronize those orders with our own needs."

"Our own needs?" asked David, struggling to keep up. "Whose?" He gestured toward Brother Matthew. "Theirs?"

Ben replied, "No. The mission planners, of course."

"What?" This time, they all cried out in unison, and quite loudly. Some wait staff that were clearing away the breakfast buffet glanced in their direction, but quickly turned back and went on with their business. Ben urged them to keep their voices down.

"Wait a minute," said David, still reeling in surprise. "Now you're claiming to know the identity of the mission planners?"

"That's correct."

"And you're helping them?"

"Yes."

"Hogwash." David pounded his fist on the table, barely missing his empty plate. "You already admitted you caused the *Perseus* to land a hundred kilometers off-course. If that isn't sabotage, what is it?"

"It's a successful landing, right on target," chuckled Ben. His shoulders relaxed, as if he had just released a heavy burden of tension. "The *Perseus* landed almost exactly where I intended. Where we intended," he corrected, quickly.

"Away from the Medusae landing site," David prodded. "Away from the evidence of your earlier sabotage. And what about that? You expect us to believe the mission planners sent 60 metric tonnes of critical equipment to Mars, and then willingly destroyed it all? That's crazy!"

Ben glanced at Brother Matthew, who nodded slightly. Then he leaned toward David and lowered his voice further. "Nothing has been destroyed."

He explained that the explosives were removed from all three vehicles prior to their launch from Earth. "When I told the mission planners someone had offered me a very generous bribe to sabotage the mission, they were shocked. They already operated in secret, back then, but for their own reasons. My revelation opened their eyes to greater concerns, and forced them even deeper into hiding."

"So you were working with the planners from the beginning?" asked David.

"From near the beginning."

"But what about the signal loss from the vehicles at the Medusae landing site?"

Ben snickered. "As I mentioned, I embedded instructions in the telemetry stream to 'explode' each vehicle. When the signal was received, each vehicle simply turned off its transmitters and receivers. Poof! They vanished. It was all a piece of cake. We've known about that part of the plot long ago, so we've had years to prepare. Even covering my tracks at JPL was absurdly easy."

"And the images from the orbiters?"

Ben admitted to subtle doctoring of some early images from the *Mars Reconnaissance Orbiter* by directly tampering with the input stream. Once he was able to misdirect the probe to use up the last of its fuel supply, that problem went away. *Mars Odyssey* was the only working orbiter now, as David well knew. Ben claimed the *Mars Odyssey* cameras just didn't have enough resolution to reveal any clues contradicting the illusion of the three destroyed landers at the Medusae site.

Something about Ben's explanation didn't quite add up, but David couldn't put his finger on what was bothering him. He decided to move on to a new topic by gesturing toward Brother Matthew. "What about your friends here? Are they mission planners, too?"

"Oh, heavens no," said the monk, with a deep, throaty laugh. "We simply assist, as we're needed. We support their goals. It's noble work, and it gets us out of the Vatican Observatory from time to time. We also offer moral guidance when ethical or scientific issues arise."

Ben added, "When you and Cassie turned against me, I went to Brother Matthew for advice. I didn't know how to approach you."

Brother Matthew placed an arm around Ben's shoulder. "Benjamin was quite upset, and he thought you wouldn't allow him time to explain. He even predicted his own physical danger." The monk apologized for alarming them, claiming it was his idea to approach them as they had.

"Ben *was* in danger," said Bill softly, as he wiped pancakes and syrup from his still-clenched fist with a napkin. "And he still is, if he's lying to us."

David agreed, though he still suspected Ben wasn't actually in any danger. He had no idea what the monks were capable of, and he didn't want to find out.

He should have been overjoyed to hear Ben's confession, especially the part about the vehicles at the Medusae landing site still being intact. He desperately wanted that part of the story to be true, since it would mean Anna was much safer on Mars than he had been led to believe. He should also have been giddy with relief that the monks didn't intend to harm his friends. However, Ben had made several claims without offering any proof. David still had more unanswered questions, too.

"How did you find us?" he asked.

"The pager in your watch, of course." Ben smiled. "We gave it to you, so we know its access codes. It's GPS-enabled, and it will transmit as well as receive. While you're wearing it, we can locate you anywhere on the Earth, within three feet."

David studied his watch, seeing it in a new light. He had wondered how the monks had found him so easily when he was hiking with Skye at Brainard Lakes. In hindsight, he should have realized that his watch was a glaring beacon others could use to find him. GPS-coupled microtransmitters were so pervasive in society that he had never even given it a second thought.

Tracking him through his watch also offered the first independent scrap of evidence to support Ben's story. The mission planners had given him the watch, along with his laptop computer and his other office equipment. If anyone could use his own equipment to track his location, it would probably be them.

Jennifer asked why the planners remained hidden. The smile left Ben's face, and he sighed, deeply. He looked up at the ceiling for a few moments.

"I think they're scared," he finally said, lowering his gaze. "They don't know who's trying to sabotage the mission, so they didn't want to reveal themselves and their real plans until after the crew landed safely. After all, if the landing had failed, there would be no mission. They would have to try again, two years from now, and at a severe disadvantage if the saboteurs knew their identity."

"You assume the saboteurs don't already know their identity," warned David.

Ben was still somewhat confident they didn't. In fact, he believed their attempted retaliation against David proved the point. "They were probably looking for an easy target. Perhaps they wanted to send us a message, too."

David made no effort to hide his anger at this revelation. "In other words, you hung me out to dry, without any knowledge or protection. I was your cannon fodder."

"More like a lightning rod," said Ben, countering David's charge. "Or our first line of defense. It's what you've always..." He halted, shifting uncomfortably in his seat. "Look, I'm sorry. I really am. We probably should have told you more about what was going on, but you've always been in a vulnerable position. We couldn't risk telling you things that might end up in the wrong hands. In fact, I shouldn't be telling you so much right now." He looked at Cassie, pleadingly. "I need you to understand why I've hidden all this from you, Cass. You've always been more important to me than anything else, even the mission. I really, truly mean that."

Tears began to stream down Cassie's cheeks again. She said softly, "But David could have been killed." She gripped his arm tightly again, this time without digging in with her fingernails. His skin still throbbed from the scratches she had inflicted earlier.

"I know." Ben apologized again, saying how horrible he felt about that. "We had no way of knowing they would come after you."

Brother Matthew added, "They did ask us to protect you. We've always been nearby. And Brother Thaddeus gave his life to save yours, though we still don't know exactly how that happened."

David grimaced at the memory. So the dead monk was Brother Thaddeus. He hadn't even known the name of the man who helped him escape from Major Tom's ambush. If everything he had just heard was the truth, he owed these people a great debt, despite their putting him in danger in the first place.

As he processed Ben's tale, he found it did answer many of his questions. He also discovered he didn't like some of those answers.

He switched topics again. In a previous discussion with Ben, not far from this very hotel, Ben had speculated on the reasons David was hired. "So, Mr. Mission Planner, why was I really hired? The truth, this time. Was it only because you needed someone stupid and expendable? A 'faceless nobody,' as I recall?"

"No," Ben snapped, but then added, "...not entirely. There were other reasons. One, in particular. I don't remember exactly what I told you before, but I'm sure I didn't tell you that one. It would have given too much away."

"Well?" David had waited a long time to hear why he had really been hired. He fought to curb a sudden surge of impatience.

Ben shifted in his chair again. "I had to campaign long and hard to get the other mission planners to hire you. The main reason I did it was because I trusted you."

"That's it? You trusted me?"

No doubt sensing David's disappointment, Ben asked him to put himself in the role of the mission planners, back a few years ago. They were trying to create a genuine Mars exploration mission, a challenge even NASA had been afraid to attempt. Money and lives were at risk, and a whole lot more. Then out of the blue, they learned that someone might try to blow up their rockets. Perhaps NASA's lunar probe was later sabotaged under similar circumstances.

"Is that possible?" interrupted Jennifer, with her eyes wide. "Were the lunar missions sabotaged, too?"

"Who knows what our opponents are capable of? We still don't even know who they are. They've covered their tracks better than we have."

Jennifer persisted. If the lunar missions were sabotaged without Ben's help, the Mars mission could have been, too.

"Lunar missions use a different telemetry team," replied Ben. He returned to his previous line of speculation. If someone was trying to sabotage the mission, what could the mission planners do?

"I give up," said David. "What could you do?"

"We could go deeper into hiding, as I said before. But that would be difficult because we needed to staff a large support team back here on Earth, one that was somewhat visible to the public and could therefore become compromised by our unknown adversaries. We knew we could never trust the entire support team. But I knew," Ben emphasized, "that we could trust the person running the team. That was important, David. It was extremely important then, and it's even more important now."

"But I'm not running the support team any longer." If he sounded bitter, it was probably because he was.

"Yes, well, when your messages to the support team jeopardized our plans, the other planners began to doubt your allegiance. And when you burst into our private conference, claiming other things they knew to be false, your credibility suffered further."

"Were you there?" asked Cassie. "We were wondering."

"At the meeting?" asked Ben. "Yes, I was there. I had a hard time keeping silent when you stated your claims. If I had said something, it would only have made matters worse. You seemed to have your mind made up about a lot of things, David."

"Yes, I did," he agreed. "And I'm still not completely convinced by what you're telling me now. If you're working for Alpha, could you please explain to me why your group is helping a known Beta agent?"

"What's Alpha and Beta?" asked Ben, looking confused.

David apologized. Of course Ben wouldn't know David's shorthand way of labeling the mission planners and those who opposed the mission. He explained his terminology to Ben.

"Then you actually know someone who's working for, well, for Beta?"

"Of course!" said David. Ben stared at him blankly, as did Brother Matthew. "You mean, you don't know?" And in fact, he wouldn't, since Anna and Skye were the only other people who knew about Major Tom, until he told Cassie recently. He hadn't even shared his ever-increasing suspicions with Bill or Jennifer. He could only draw two conclusions from Ben's lack of knowledge. Anna wasn't involved with the mission planners, and neither was Skye.

"Tell me, who is it?" asked Ben.

"It's..." David was about to describe his previous encounters with Major Tom, in the virtual and real worlds, but he stopped. A new plan was formulating in his mind. When he spoke, it was to offer Ben a deal. "It's...something I'll only reveal to the mission planners, directly, after my job and my account have been reinstated."

Ben's cheeks flushed. Now he was the one who seemed impatient. He said, "David, this is important. We need to know who we can trust at Mission Support, and who we can't. The ERV will land tomorrow, so we don't have time to play any little games."

"Then you'd better hurry," was David's only response. He was tired of being kept in the dark. He might still be destined to end up as cannon fodder, but from now on, he would only do so willingly and knowingly. Now that he had some leverage, a scrap of information the planners lacked and needed, he intended to use it to his advantage.

Besides, if everything Ben had said was true, he still had a job to do. The three people on Mars needed his support more than ever. He couldn't do anything to help them from a restaurant in downtown Boulder.

"I'll...see what I can do," Ben said. He rose partially from his chair, but then sat again. "Cassie?" he asked, softly, with the same pleading tone as before. "Will you come with me?"

"No." Her reply was immediate, and the firmness in her voice lacked the pained edge David had been growing accustomed to hearing. "Even if what you've said is true, you're still so far in the doghouse that you'll be sleeping on the couch for the next five years."

"Five years is a big improvement over never," Brother Matthew said, slapping Ben on the back for emphasis. The monk wore a smug expression, well deserved, since his intervention had been fairly successful.

Cassie nodded, and smiled. "If your friends restore my Mission Support account, too, I might knock a few years off that sentence. Until then, I'm going to hang around with David. I need some time."

Ben nodded, and agreed to plead her case to the planners as well.

Bill and Jennifer immediately invited David and Cassie to stay with them in Nederland again. If they were now trusting Ben once more, there was no longer any reason for them to leave. David gratefully accepted.

Ben started to rise again, but David asked him to remain for a few more minutes. "I still have some more questions," he said.

"Shoot. But quickly. I need to get back. There's much to do."

David briefly recounted the story about his receipt of the money envelope at Bill and Jennifer's house, along with two later, similar deliveries. He asked, "Were those deliveries the work of the mission planners? And if so, how did they know where I was?"

Ben stifled a laugh. He winked at Cassie, which evoked a response from her. "That was you, wasn't it, Ben? I told you where David was, and what had happened to him."

The mischievous look on Ben's face was enough of an answer for David, but his nod confirmed his guilt. "I didn't want you to starve, so I got on the blower to Western Union."

That explained another one of the little mysteries troubling David over the past few months. Cassie had always been his prime suspect, since practically no one else had known where he was. His theory had never made much sense because Cassie didn't have immediate access to large amounts of cash.

After thanking Ben for his generosity, David scaled the ladder from small headaches to larger ones. "Is <chicken_little> a friend of yours?"

Ben's mischievous look remained, growing more intense, if possible. He said it was safe to assume <chicken_little> worked for Alpha.

"Then you know the fowl's identity?" asked David. Thinking back to the numerous times riddles from <chicken_little> had kept him awake at night, caused him to notice certain events, channeled his suspicions, or led him to consider alternate actions, he craved a satisfying answer.

"Actually," said Ben, "you know him, too. Quite well, in fact."

Him? That leaves out Cassie, Anna, and the commander, three of my earlier suspects. Who else is left?

Ollie? No. And it's not Major Tom, of course.

I don't really "know" anyone else at Mission Support, personally, except...

Suddenly, the answer was obvious, but David would do almost anything not to hear it confirmed. All he could say was, "Oh, no."

"Oh yes," Ben nodded. "He be me, too."

David reeled in shock from this latest surprise. It couldn't be true. In fact, it really couldn't. He pointed out Ben's presence, back when he received the first message from <chicken_little>.

"I was there when you *received* the first message," Ben clarified, smugly. "I sent it from my hotel room."

Sure enough, as David recalled the sequence of events from that afternoon so long ago, he realized Ben had been gone for longer than expected. Later, they had watched several media broadcasts before David checked his messages.

For at least the third time in the past two hours, he fought a strong urge to wrap his arms around Ben's neck and squeeze. Rather than explode in rage, he just filed away his new knowledge of the identity of <chicken_little>. There would be plenty of time to strangle him later.

He did ask other questions, however, which Ben promptly answered. Yes, Ben was the pathetic-looking, chicken-like avatar David had addressed in Conference Room 4. Why were his messages so cryptic? Because e-mail was a permanent record, and messages could be intercepted or used as criminal evidence later.

David knew he should ponder that last statement a lot more carefully because it probably revealed quite a bit about the psyche of the Alpha organization. However, there would be time for that later, too. Ben's mention of the secrecy within Alpha led him to his final question, and it was a whopper compared to the minnows he had landed thus far.

Before he could change his mind or lose his nerve, he asked, "Ben, who are the mission planners?"

Ben's smile faded. He shifted in his seat and shook his head. When he spoke, his voice was low, but steady. "I can't answer that, David. Not yet. I hope I've regained some of your confidence, because you're just going to have to trust me on this."

David was about to protest, but Jennifer was faster. "But you said they were going to reveal themselves after the crew landed successfully on Mars! Why didn't they?"

Shrugging Ben looked at David. "You know why, don't you?" he asked.

David thought for a moment. Yes, he did know why. "Because there might still be a saboteur aboard the *Perseus*."

"Right," said Ben. "You should have been at the meeting when <alice>, er, Commander Day, revealed that one of her crewmates might be trying to kill her. It was chaos. Utter chaos. The planners saw all their dreams going up in smoke. They almost overreacted, but calmer heads prevailed, eventually."

"And do you know who the saboteur is?" David held his breath.

"No. Do you?" asked Ben.

"I'm afraid not." With a disappointed laugh, David added. "At least we only have three suspects."

"Two suspects," said Ben. "The commander is above suspicion."

"I'm not so sure of that."

Ben forcefully repeated, "The commander is above suspicion. As for the others, we're betting Anna is guilty, but its even money as to whether she's really working for, um, Beta. Her problems might be purely psychological, or that might be only a cover story." Ben glanced at Cassie, who nodded her acceptance of both possibilities.

David shook his head, just as vehemently. "I can't believe Anna would harm anyone. And she would have needed an accomplice on the support team. I searched for links and didn't find any."

"We intend to settle the issue. Soon, we'll know for sure." He reached over to grasp David's arm, just below the left shoulder. "And we have you to thank for warning us. I'll remind the planners of that when I ask them to reinstate your account."

Rising to his feet again, Ben bid them farewell. He promised to be in touch soon.

David was still grumbling at Ben's refusal to identify the mission planners. He hooked the sleeve of Ben's habit as he moved to leave.

"One more question. Will the ERV landing tomorrow be successful?"

Ben looked around the room, before sliding closer to David and whispering in his ear. "Tomorrow is going to be a bad day on Mars."

MarsDay 251, 11:00 a.m.
(August 5, 4:36 p.m.)

Through the large windshield in the pressurized rover, Anna watched the terrain slowly slide by. She occasionally glanced down at the speedometer. The ground between the *Perseus* and the cargo vehicle was smooth, but some large boulders were scattered about. Eventually, they would clear a wide path. Until then, ten kilometers-per-hour was as fast as she wanted to travel on this first excursion. She could have walked to the cargo vehicle at half that speed, but since it was so close, her trip would only take about six minutes.

Part of herself wanted the trip to last longer. She now had some time to relax and sift through her thoughts. Lately, some of her emotions had been quite contradictory.

With one successful landing down, and one more to go tomorrow, her team's prospects for survival were looking better. She still loved almost every minute of living on Mars, despite the hard work and lack of time to do all the things she needed to do. Now that the cargo vehicle had landed, her workload would increase even more, and she faced some difficult priority calls.

The best part of the rover trip was her temporary freedom. She was tired of Evelyn watching her every movement. Especially during the past few days, she had endured quick glances, frequent questions, and the painful loss of personal space accompanying an object under scrutiny.

Am I imagining all this? Perhaps becoming a bit paranoid?
No. She doesn't treat Ollie that way.
At least she's not critical or judgmental. She's just always nearby!

Of course, some of Evelyn's watchfulness was necessary. Since their landing, the two engineers had spent much of their free time doing habitat or robot maintenance. Anna had volunteered to perform some of the simpler maintenance tasks around the *Perseus*, like occasionally taking a robot outside to sweep dust off the solar panels and heat radiators. She was glad to help whenever her own workload was somewhat lighter. While doing these tasks, she welcomed Evelyn's advice and supervision.

No. I'm making excuses for her. There's something weird going on, something more than just my overactive imagination.

Lying awake last night, as she listened to the normal nighttime sounds in the *Perseus*, she overheard the commander talking to herself or someone else in her cabin on the level below. Evelyn seemed to speak in lengthy phrases, so she was probably holding a one-sided conversation with somebody at Mission Support. Anna could understand only occasional references to things and people. Her own name was mentioned several times, or so she thought.

The rover's steady approach to the cargo vehicle brought an end to her quiet interlude. She chose a flat parking area and sent a message to the *Perseus*. It was time to get back to work. She was eager to get her hands on the greenhouse supplies in the cargo, among other items. Her six-minute vacation was over, but she should have six more minutes to herself on the return trip, too.

Controlled by Ollie back at the *Perseus*, a Robonaut detached itself from the side of the rover and loped toward the cargo vehicle. The first task, removing rocks from beneath the vehicle, didn't take long to complete. Ollie backed the robot away from the cargo pod and turned to face the rover. Flashing her a "thumbs-up" signal, he stated over the comm system, "Ready to drop." His robot's mannerisms were so humanlike that Anna had difficulty remembering Ollie was still back inside the *Perseus*, rather than standing near the cargo vehicle, a few feet in front of her.

"Looks good from here, too," she confirmed. With her wider visual vantage point, she looked for anything that might interfere with their operation. The ground beneath and around the cargo vehicle was smooth and featureless.

Anna tied the rover's computer into the cargo vehicle control systems and transmitted a signal to begin the cargo deployment. She expected an iris in the floor of the pod to open, and the cargo modules, attached to a central support beam, to slowly descend. Gravity would do most of the work.

Nothing seemed to be happening. She squinted out the viewport, looking for physical obstructions that didn't exist. Then, glancing down at the video display on the dashboard before her, she noticed an error message: *Insufficient power for operation.*

"Uh, Ollie," she called. "I think you forgot to hook up the power cord."

"Duh! I'm stupider than this robot." Ollie pulled a retractable power cord from the side of the rover and climbed up one of the landing legs to plug it in. The cargo vehicle operated on a minimal battery and solar cell power supply during its flight to Mars. Their current operation required a significant amperage boost from the powerful engine of the rover.

Once Ollie's robot had returned to the ground and backed away, Anna ran the deployment command again. This time, it worked. The cargo contents slowly dropped until the lowermost items rested on the ground.

He retracted the power cord, freeing Anna to back her rover near the cargo. The first items to be moved were mostly mining equipment. After Ollie hitched a small backhoe behind the rover, she towed it toward a flat section of the wide plain chosen for a parking lot. Then she backed up the rover again and dragged a bulldozer blade until it rested beside the backhoe. After that, Ollie attached a second blade to the front of the rover, hitched a light cart to the back, and stood upon the cart to reach other items stored higher.

An hour later, the entire contents of the cargo vehicle were laid out upon the plain, where each item could be retrieved whenever it was needed. Everything in the inventory list was accounted for.

As Ollie attached his Robonaut back to the side of the rover, Anna glanced back at the cargo vehicle. Externally, it looked the same as it always had. Someday soon, they would attach inflatable tires to the landing legs and tow the empty shell back to the *Perseus*. Then they would tip it over, creating a large, pressurized workshop and garage. Many other tasks needed to be accomplished first, however. At the moment, they didn't even have enough spare oxygen to pressurize the volume.

Patience. Do everything in order. Step by step, we're settling a new world.

MarsDay 251, 12:21 p.m.
(August 5, 6:00 p.m.)

As David waited on the phone for Skye to answer, he pondered the fact that "on-hold" music hadn't changed for the last 20 years, and probably never would. Cassie's cell phone beeped its protest at him as well, indicating its battery charge was low.

Cassie, waiting beside him in the lobby of the St. Julien, quickly dug through her purse to find a power cord that would recharge the battery. They moved to a couch near an elaborate pillar concealing a power outlet. As he had frequently done this afternoon, David looked around to make sure no one was watching them. The rest of the hotel lobby was empty.

The lobby resembled a neo-Roman palace, with a mixture of marbles interrupted by garish streamers draped from the ceiling. David wouldn't have been surprised if gladiators with trumpets walked through the front door and provided a floorshow. Meanwhile, the emperor Davidicus waited on the phone to talk to a lowly reporter.

Hanging around the hotel with a cell phone appended to his ear was a disappointing finish to what was otherwise a wonderful afternoon. In contrast to Bill and Jennifer, who were both extremely late for work and had left hurriedly, he and Cassie had leisured away the afternoon. They window-shopped on Pearl Street, ate lunch at the BookEnd, and talked for hours.

They continued their conversation in hushed tones until Skye finally, curtly, answered the phone. "Sorry if you were waiting long, David," she said, "but I was just getting a good tongue-lashing by my boss. He's not very happy."

David checked his watch, noting that he had been on-hold for a half-hour. He asked what was happening at the network.

Judging by the tone of her voice, Skye was decidedly upset. "I went out on a limb by predicting the ERV and cargo vehicle landings were going to be sabotaged, and USNN was somehow involved."

"And it wasn't," he concluded for her. "At least, the cargo vehicle didn't crash."

"Right. But I'm about to. Crash, that is. If the ERV lands safely tomorrow, I'm toast. I can kiss my whole career goodbye."

David laughed softly, which triggered an angry response from Skye. She reminded him of his sharing the blame for the wrong prediction.

He agreed, but added, "Since then, I've been reeducated. And I have some good news for you."

After pausing solely for dramatic effect, he revealed the implications of Ben's parting comment. She immediately asked where he had gotten his information, but he carefully avoided telling her the source of the comment, or any other details of the encounter with Ben.

As she probed him for more information, he found his resistance wavering, but holding nonetheless. He still didn't trust Ben's story completely. If the ERV landing failed, like Ben had predicted, then he would put more faith in the other revelations. Until then, caution seemed appropriate. He would reveal little, despite Skye's hunger for more facts.

She promptly reminded him of their disclosure agreement. "Trust me," he responded, adding, "Soon, you might have all the information about the Mars mission you could ever want."

Skye jumped all over his ill-advised statement. "Have you been talking to the mission planners?"

She continued to hammer away at his resistance, until he finally admitted his information had come from someone who claimed to be working for the mission planners. His source might in fact be working for Beta, he cautioned. There was no way to know for sure.

"So what am I supposed to do?" she asked, crossly. "Make a bigger fool of myself on national TV by quoting questionable sources?"

"What do you have to lose?" he countered. If she upped the ante, and the ERV landed successfully, nothing would have changed. A failed landing, however, might completely restore her reputation.

As they discussed the options, Bill entered the hotel lobby. "Your chariot awaits," he said, eyeing the lobby décor as he bowed and gestured sweepingly toward the door. He had come to drive them back to the solace of their mountain hideaway.

David ended the phone call and retrieved his luggage from the concierge desk. As they left the hotel, the pager in his watch began to vibrate. He glanced down at the display and noted a text message:

9:00 p.m. - CR4

As he interpreted the message, his heart leaped with joy. His account must have been reinstated. Apparently, he now had a date with the mission planners.

CHAPTER 31
ALTITUDE

MarsDay 251, 2:47 p.m.
(August 5, 8:30 p.m.)

    With three people watching over his shoulder, David typed the password for his account at mission support. After a normal pause, his computer display revealed a view of Shepherd's office.
    His alter ego had been resurrected. Until he had lost Shepherd, he hadn't realized how much a part of his life this virtual persona had become. Now that he was whole again, the online world already felt different. Shepherd was no longer as real or permanent.
    His first instinct was to send a message to Anna, but he had other things to do first, like checking his messages and looking for anything to indicate Major Tom's plans. His meeting with the mission planners was only a half an hour from now, and he intended to be armed with as much information as possible.
    Satisfied, Bill and Jennifer went back upstairs. Cassie remained at his side, watching him intently. Perhaps she suspected what he was feeling? She was so perceptive, and her online persona had been ripped away, too.
    He queried to see whether Major Tom's avatar was currently active. He was, and his location was the main support room. David warped to the security desk in the central atrium and asked the on-duty worker to send him a detailed report of every command run by Major Tom over the past two days. Then he warped back to his office. It was time to have some fun.

He must have been wearing his inner smile outwardly, too, because Cassie asked him what he intended to do. "Oh, I'm going to drop in on an old friend," he said.

The Shepherd avatar left his office and entered the main support room. Major Tom was sitting in his chair, except it wasn't his chair. It was dull and metallic, matching the other furniture and decor.

"He didn't waste much time before making changes," David growled to Cassie.

A bubble around Major Tom's head was connected to bubbles around two other, unfamiliar avatars. David fingered them both and recorded their identities. He would investigate them later. Perhaps they were uninvolved in Tom's ulterior activities, or perhaps not.

He walked up to Major Tom and rapped on his bubble, the accepted way to break into a private conversation. The bubbles disappeared. "What do you want?" Major Tom asked. His oh-so-familiar snarl practically screamed a confirmation of his true identity.

David let silence linger for a few seconds, as he convinced himself he had truly recognized the voice ordering his death so many months ago. That voice was quite different than Major Tom's usual, softer tone. No doubt, Thomas enhanced his voice with an audio algorithm, just like David did.

When he was finally ready to speak, David calmly asked for an update on the mission status.

In his "enhanced" voice, Thomas hemmed and hawed about how he thought Shepherd would be gone longer. Then he delivered a more concise status report, claiming all was well. The crew on Mars was healthy, and the ERV systems were in perfect working order. Nothing should interfere with the scheduled landing tomorrow afternoon.

David thanked him and traded a few harmless words about personnel scheduling before going back into his office. He hated leaving Major Tom back in charge again for even a single moment, but keeping up appearances of trust was more important now than ever. If Shepherd took immediate action right after Thomas's little verbal slip, it would practically be a confession: David Debacco, fugitive from USNN, was still alive. The timing was rather unfortunate because even before the slip, David had already been convinced of Major Tom's guilt.

Games within games.

Well, soon, it will be the mission planners' decision what to do about him.

At least, I hope they're the real mission planners. I'll have to hope they are. No time for any more second-guessing.

Yes, but...

Out of the blue, he finally realized what had been nagging him, in the back of his mind, since the encounter with Ben. It was a simple question, actually, but one requiring an answer before he could firmly believe Ben was helping the mission planners.

Why did the mission planners recruit Ben?

Perhaps he still had time to ask that question of <chicken_little>, assuming Ben had told the truth about his online identity. Upon checking his messages, he conveniently found one that <chicken_little> had just sent to him.

To: <shepherd>
From: <chicken_little>
Subject: Resurrections
Priority: Emergency

Shepherd -

Just confirming, 9:00 - you know where.
I'll say a few words of introduction. Then, you're on. Be brief.
Reveal the Beta agent, and we'll handle the rest.

The message washed away David's last doubts about the identity of <chicken_little>. Only Ben would refer to a Beta agent, in conjunction with the purpose of the meeting.

But still, his other doubt lingered. Was the rest of Ben's story true? He decided to respond to the message.

To: <chicken_little>
From: <shepherd>
Subject: Re: Resurrections
Priority: Emergency

I'll be there. But first, I need to know...WHY DID THE PLANNERS RECRUIT YOU?

Leaving the wording simple and direct, he sent the message. Hopefully, Ben would receive it in time to respond.

Other messages awaited, including one from the security team. A log of Major Tom's activities over the past three days was attached, as he had requested. He warned Cassie his review of the log might take some time, but she offered to stay and help, in case she spotted something that slipped by him. More likely, she didn't want to miss Ben's response.

They heard some light footfalls on the basement stairwell. Then Jennifer poked her head around the corner of the open doorway. "You guys should come upstairs and watch the evening news," she said.

"No time," David responded. "But why? What's going on?"

Jennifer laughed. "Oh, just the next chapter in the escalating war between Fontaine and USNN. She did a live phone interview with a space law expert who claims any crimes committed on Mars would be outside the boundaries of all recognized legal jurisdiction. Obviously, she's implying that acts of sabotage by USNN or anyone else might go unpunished."

"She's laying it on thick, huh?" asked Cassie.

"Very." Jennifer added an appropriate bread-and-butter sweep of her arm. "No backing down from her—she's still predicting the ERV will land off-course, crash, or both."

"And how has USNN responded?" asked David.

"I'm not sure. We just switched over to their news broadcast. I'll bet they're really pissed."

Jennifer went back upstairs, and David continued to browse the activity log. Major Tom had been busy during the last three days, meeting with a lot of people and traveling to many rooms in the support center. Nothing in his pattern of activity looked very incriminating, however. Cassie couldn't spot anything, either, other than noting a meeting between Tom and the psych team. David had rarely done that during all of his time as director.

Checking his messages again, he found a response from Ben.

> To: <shepherd>
> From: <chicken_little>
> Subject: Re: Resurrections
> Priority: Emergency
>
> I can't answer that question. Besides, you shouldn't need me to.

"I shouldn't need him to? What the heck does that mean?" David asked.

Cassie shrugged, and reminded him, "It's almost nine o'clock. No time to worry about it now."

"I suppose not."

He pondered this matter of Ben's real function for a moment before pushing it aside. Yes, it was too late for second guesses. Ben was either telling the truth or he wasn't. It was time for him to take a chance.

David warped into the central atrium and thanked the avatar behind the security desk for her quick response in forwarding the information about Major Tom's activities. Then he asked her to also send him activity logs for the two avatars that had been talking to Major Tom in the support center a few minutes ago, as well as the members of the psych team Tom had recently visited. The security avatar got right to work.

David stared at the towering replica of Lowell's telescope above the security desk. In the real world, he glanced at Cassie and said, "I've got déjà vu. Let's hope this works out better than the last time."

She squeezed his arm to show her support. Then she smiled at him. "Last time, you asked me not to say anything during the meeting. What about this time?"

"I guess it doesn't matter. I assume they already know your involvement."

Two avatars entered the atrium from a hallway, only to disappear without the characteristic bright flash of a warp command. David surmised they shrank themselves first. Then Commander Day's <alice> avatar entered the atrium and vanished in the same manner.

"Let's join the party," said Cassie. "This time, we have an invitation."

David resized his avatar as before and warped into Conference Room 4. His sense of déjà vu increased. Just as before, several Alice in Wonderland avatars were seated at the main table. Fewer avatars stood along the side walls than before, but Arnold and the scraggly chicken avatar were both present. The Cheshire Cat and <alice> were once again at the front of the room.

Most of the avatars were engaged in local conversations. Silence cones abounded. Not sure of what to do, David walked over to Arnold and wrapped a cone around the two of them.

"I assume you were the one who restored my avatar?" he asked.

Arnold responded, in his usual squeak-speak. "Yes. Sorry about killing it earlier, but I was just following orders. I'm glad you're back."

"Me, too. But let's see for how long."

The sharp sound of a wooden gavel called the meeting to order. The bubbles around the room disappeared, and the Cheshire Cat's eyes glowed as he prepared to speak. A futuristic, ringed space station in a piece of artwork behind the Cat made it appear as if he had a halo.

"Thank you for attending, on short notice," said the Cat. "We're here to finalize our plans for the ERV landing tomorrow."

As the Cheshire Cat spoke, three more avatars warped into the back of the room. Virtual meetings were just as prone to latecomers as real world meetings.

By now, the room was even more crowded than during his last visit. In all, he counted about 20 avatars in attendance.

He turned his attention back to the Cheshire Cat, who continued, "The first part of our meeting will be for public consumption. We've reinstated Shepherd's account and invited him to attend. He claims to have some important information to share. Guard your lips, everyone."

Though David felt uncomfortable as the object of everyone's notice, he saw no outward signs of discourtesy from any of the other avatars. Their expressions were as blank as ever.

"Then, we'll ask Shepherd to leave, take a break, and receive verbal status reports from Mars. Note the time delay of communications is now nearly 34 minutes, round trip. Chicken?"

Right down to business, David noted. He agreed with Cassie's earlier assessment about the Cat's methodology. This group was certainly not a democracy.

The chicken avatar waddled up to the front of the room, while the Cheshire Cat claimed the only empty seat at the table. "Thank you." Ben's voice was skewed, but still somewhat recognizable.

"We've restored Shepherd's login partly because of his past service to our cause. More urgently, we need his continued service in the future. We all know why he and most other members of the support team have been kept in the dark about our plans. They're too exposed, and the fragile buffer between us is our best protection."

He paused, catching his breath, before continuing. "We're approaching a critical juncture, and we need Shepherd's help more than ever. As a down payment on his future services, he has offered to reveal the identity of certain people in our midst who are not working in the best interests of the mission.

"I don't need to remind you how important this knowledge might prove to be. I'll also add that I personally trust Shepherd's judgement in this matter. We should take his advice seriously. Shepherd?"

So far, the meeting had played out according to Ben's concise script. It was now David's turn to speak. As Ben's chicken avatar resumed his place along the far wall, David steered Shepherd toward the front of the room.

He took a deep breath to successfully dissolve a small knot of tension in his stomach. As he pushed the [speak] button on his microphone, he felt surprisingly calm and focused.

"Thank you. As the chicken stated," he avoided using Ben's name, "there's a lot going on that I still don't know about. But there are also some facts I do know about. Being cannon fodder on the front lines can be quite revealing." His last remark probably didn't earn any sympathy, but he wasn't beyond trying.

He started to tell them about the incident at Brainard Lakes, but the Cheshire Cat interrupted him. "Our people were there. We know most of what happened," he said, brusquely.

"Very well. But you probably aren't aware that Thomas, the false FBI agent, works on my Mission Support team. His avatar is Major Tom, my backup director. When you killed my login yesterday, you put him in charge of the support team."

A muted buzz of conversation around the room was stifled by the rapping noise again. The gavel made the room feel like a courtroom, with the weirdest jury David could ever have imagined. He heard Ben's voice loudly and clearly over the din of the others, pointing out that the opposition might have canceled Ben's orders to sabotage the cargo landing at the last minute due to Major Tom's promotion and subsequent ability to sabotage the landing himself. The planners had been very lucky this hadn't happened.

"How certain are you of Major Tom's guilt?" the Cat asked, when everyone had quieted down.

David brushed aside the impression that he was the one on trial. Instead, he chose to believe he was a star witness for the prosecution.

"I'm almost 100 percent sure. I have quite a bit of evidence, though some of it is circumstantial."

The Cheshire Cat's response was swift and decisive. "Arnold, kill Major Tom's account immediately."

"Wait!" cried David. "I've left his account active for months, so I could watch him and learn of others who might be involved."

"And have you?" asked the Cat.

"Partially. I have a few suspects, but at nowhere near the same level of certainty."

The Cat hissed, "Irrelevant. At this point, we don't need certainty. We need action. After the meeting, tell Arnold who you don't trust, and we'll kill their accounts, too." The Cat's words were clearly a non-negotiable order.

"But..." David was trying to think of a good counter argument. The courtroom atmosphere was more pronounced than ever, except now the trial was beginning to resemble a closed-door inquest.

He found the thought of terminating other avatars as repulsive as his own virtual death had been. He might be fingering innocent people who had put as much effort and passion into their work as David had. Could he hang them, based on flimsy suspicions?

Cassie jerked his hand away from the microphone, muting his connection. "Don't argue," she said. "You'll alienate them. Later, you can do what's right, outside of the meeting."

He nodded, and then verbally gave his agreement to the assembled group.

"What can you tell us about their plans?" asked the Queen of Hearts.

"Very little, unfortunately. Just before he ordered me killed, Thomas said he would earn a promotion. I believe his goal is to run the support team, but I don't know why. Perhaps knowing your own plans would help me to figure out their intentions?"

"No," said the Cat immediately, without offering any further explanation.

David hadn't expected that ploy to work. In the real world, he shrugged nonchalantly. "No harm in asking," he whispered to Cassie.

"You hope," she responded.

Aloud, he called their attention to the prior sabotage of the trajectory software and the radiation shield around the commander's cabin. "At the time, I thought Major Tom's goal might have been to cover up those issues. If so, I wonder why he took the risk. His efforts backfired badly. My suspicions of Major Tom actually led me to discover those bits of sabotage."

"But only because he failed to kill you," said Ben.

"True," admitted David, reluctantly. Could he have almost been killed solely to increase the odds, by a tiny fraction, of those acts of sabotage going undiscovered? That motive seemed little more than an afterthought. Such was the life of cannon fodder.

"You've given us more to consider," said the Cat. "What else can you tell us?"

As the Cheshire Cat spoke, his eyes flared again. David uncomfortably recalled a favorite sci-fi television show from years ago, Stargate SG-1, in which evil alien imposters sometimes gave themselves away when their eyes flared in a similar manner. The timing of this memory was quite inconvenient.

He swallowed, and cautiously said, "There's the issue of whether or not there's a saboteur on the crew."

Since his words didn't trigger another outburst in the room, as he had almost expected, most of his audience must already have known the details about the act of sabotage in the *Perseus*. In fact, Ben had already told him about news of the sabotage nearly throwing the mission planners into a panic.

"Do you know who it is?" the Cheshire Cat asked, forcefully. David didn't need to hear the urgency in his voice. This was obviously a question of great importance to the group.

"I have an opinion or two, and I'd be glad to share them with you. Until recently, Commander Day was my prime suspect, followed by Doctor Sainsbury."

Several people responded, almost at once. The Cat said, "Commander Day's loyalty is beyond question."

The King of Hearts said, "Our own list of suspects is the reverse of yours."

Ben said, "Until recently?"

He chose to address Ben's response, since it was the only question asked. "Yes, until recently, I didn't know who was meeting in this conference room. All I knew was that Commander Day spent a lot of time here. That made me highly suspicious. Assuming your group really did plan the mission, then I agree she's no longer a credible suspect."

The King of Hearts spoke again. "I've been delegated the task of finding the saboteur. Let's talk about this outside the meeting. I'll contact you."

David agreed. In fact, he would be most eager to continue the investigation. Despite the evidence pointing squarely at Anna, evidence that he had helped to gather, he still couldn't believe her guilt. He looked forward to proving otherwise.

The Queen of Hearts spoke next. "And the public and media? What's the view from the front lines on how our mission is being perceived?"

"The public view is mostly positive, but guarded, due to all the secrecy. People around the world are following the mission to a far greater extent than I would have expected. Recently, the open warfare between media networks has fueled a lot of interest, too."

"Yes, there's Fontaine to worry about," said the Queen again. "Who else in the media is actively helping the opposition?"

The dissolved knot in his stomach reformed itself inside his throat. "Actually, I believe Fontaine can be trusted," he croaked. His statement started an even louder buzz than before.

After the room settled down, he explained that Fontaine had provided him with some detailed, highly-incriminating evidence against her former superiors at USNN. The evidence ties them to several past acts of sabotage. "I can't reveal any more, however," he added.

When asked why not, David stated bluntly that he couldn't reveal the information to anyone, even the mission planners. His unvoiced concern was Beta's learning how weak Skye's information was. For her to operate with the widest possible latitude and personal safety, her bluff needed to be preserved.

As expected, his words weren't received very warmly, but he refused to back down. Ben interceded by revealing his own connection with Fontaine's program producer. David had intended to avoid saying even that much, but apparently the group already knew about Ben's receipt of bribe money to sabotage the *Perseus* landing. They just hadn't known the source of the funds.

"And by the way," David added, "Fontaine traced the funds to an offshore holding company that's owned by USNN." That admission seemed harmless enough.

"That figures," said Ben. "But earlier, you mentioned other recordings?"

"Yes," said David.

The Cat spoke again, firmly. "People, let's get back to the basics. The media is irrelevant. Our most important priority is to determine whether anyone on Mars is working against us. If Shepherd's other recordings reveal that linkage, it's absolutely critical for us to know about it, right now."

"They don't," said David.

"Then we have no choice but to continue with the second ERV landing tomorrow as originally planned. Killing the accounts of Major Tom and his accomplices should fit well into our time line. If we remove their options, we might force the opposition to react. We'll know the truth one way or the other, and at a time of our own choosing."

David remained silent, absorbing these new, tantalizing hints. Earlier, Ben said they were about to "settle the issue." Apparently, a failure in the ERV landing was crucial to their plans for revealing Beta.

With the latest revelations still hanging in the air, the Cheshire Cat abruptly declared the first part of the meeting over. Shepherd groaned, as he was asked to leave, but he immediately ended his connection.

"I'd give anything to stick around longer," muttered David, staring at the blank screen. "We were just getting to a juicy part."

"Somehow, I don't think they would have taken too kindly to that," said Cassie. "Better quit while you're ahead."

But was he really ahead? Major Tom's account would soon be terminated, which might put his own personal life at greater risk if Shepherd was deemed to be responsible. He resolved to wait a few days before sending a message asking his support team if anyone knew where Major Tom had gone. Perhaps feigning ignorance would keep the wolves at bay.

Then there was the landing tomorrow. He assumed the mission planners intended to redirect the second ERV to a different landing site. The Mars Direct plan suggested that strategy as the best way to open a wider area on Mars for human exploration. Or did they have something else in mind?

Anna was still a prime suspect for sabotage, and the identities of Alpha and Beta were still as unknown as ever. Skye was off stirring up trouble. And Ben refused to disclose his own involvement with the mission planners. For David, being "ahead" didn't seem much better than being behind.

MarsDay 252, 2:00 p.m.
(August 6, 8:21 p.m.)

After checking her notes, Anna re-examined the image of the sedimentary outcrop in the exhumed crater just south of the *Perseus*. Ollie's Robonaut had easily found the right place, but now she needed to tell him exactly where to dig. Her goggles allowed her to see the exact same image Ollie saw, but it looked different than the image stored in her notes from when she had explored the crater several weeks ago.

She asked Ollie to brush away a loose layer of reddish dust near the bottom of the outcrop. A thin coating had accumulated since she had been here last.

After the dust was removed, she interleaved her previous image of the outcrop with the current image. They matched much closer now, so she was confident they had found the right place.

The specific layer she sought was darker than the other layers, and about five centimeters thick. Of all the sediments she had found within walking distance of the *Perseus*, this one showed the most promise as future topsoil for growing plants, according to the experts back on Earth. The salt and sulfur content was lower than in the surrounding layers, but plenty of pre-processing would still be needed to add nutrients, organics, and hydration.

Digging turned out to be easy for Ollie because the layer was soft and crumbly. His Robonaut was well equipped for the task. Before long, he brought a container filled with soil back to the *Perseus*.

Anna took the soil inside, through the sample box slot. She carefully cleaned and disinfected the outside of the box before touching it with her ungloved hands. Though her toxicity tests of the dust and soil continued to read negative, she didn't want to risk a cancer-causing substance like hexavalent chromium escaping her detection.

By the time her soil was thoroughly prepared and placed inside one of her three remaining portable greenhouse pods, Ollie had filled the sample box with another load of dirt and was standing by with a third load. "Put it in a different sample box," Anna directed. They had three sample boxes at their disposal.

"No can do," answered Ollie. "We're only supposed to use one box for soil samples."

Chaffing at the unnecessary restriction, Anna curbed a harsh reply. Even though they needed to make allowances for aspects of Mars they didn't fully understand yet, she could see no reason for some of the crazy guidelines the commander had insisted upon.

Yet she also had to admit their first two months on Mars had been remarkably accident-free. Evelyn seemed to be applying her naval and corporate experience in extreme environments quite successfully thus far. Nearly all of her decisions had been right on the mark, even when she lacked data. As they learned more about living on Mars, Anna's appreciation of the commander's wisdom and foresight increased daily.

Ollie said, "I'm going to leave this box here and move away from the *Perseus* for a few minutes. I want to get a good view of the ERV landing."

"Is it that time already?" A quick glance at the nearest wall, with its embedded time display, confirmed the second ERV would indeed be landing within ten minutes. "I'd better get busy sterilizing the outside of this sample box."

"Don't be late," said Ollie. "This will be your last chance to see one." No more landings were scheduled during the next 15 months of their habitation on Mars.

She quickly finished her task and left the sample box on the floor of the EVA room. Bypassing Ollie's human body, which was bundled in the Robonaut control harness, she crossed over to the ladder and ascended to the crew lounge on the upper level.

As she had expected, Anna found the commander using the main computer to monitor the landing of the second ERV. The wall display revealed telemetry from the ERV, most of which was unfathomable. Anna was almost tempted to put her goggles back on and watch the landing from the external viewpoint of Ollie's Robonaut, but that was how she had watched the previous landing. For this one, she wanted a human touch. She had decided to watch this landing from Evelyn's viewpoint.

Her seat at the table was barely in range of the camera pointed at Evelyn. She suppressed an urge to scratch at her wig, which she had worn almost constantly over the past few months because she had been filming so many media events. For some reason, it always seemed to itch at the most inconvenient times.

If Evelyn noticed Anna sitting behind her, she didn't say anything. The commander's attention was focused on the computer display. Within a small status window, Anna noticed a tiny prompt repeating: *Attempting to acquire ERV signal...*

After several minutes, Anna's mild feeling of unease began to evolve into a more tangible dread. The time for the landing had almost arrived, and Evelyn's display hadn't changed.

"Something's wrong," Evelyn stated tersely, confirming Anna's worst fears. "I haven't acquired a signal from the ERV. I'm switching to a backup frequency." She was speaking for the benefit of the countless number of viewers back on Earth, since Anna could already see what she was doing.

After another long minute, Evelyn's narration continued. "Backup frequency is silent, too. Scanning other frequencies and querying the telemetry from *Mars Odyssey*. Also querying mission support and JPL."

Over the intercom, Ollie's voice added, "I don't see anything outside." Unlike Evelyn's crisp sentences, Ollie's voice contained far more emotion.

Anna watched a series of small images march across the commander's screen. Each image was labeled as a time lapsed frame from the thermal camera on the *Mars Odyssey* orbiter, as it swept the horizon of Mars in search of the heat from the ERV's atmospheric entry. Some of the images might have contained a bright pixel or two, but Anna couldn't discern any details.

"Entry and descent confirmed in the *Mars Odyssey* images," said Evelyn over the intercom again. "Early telemetry indicates the ERV may have landed off-course, to the south."

Hearing these words, Anna's hopes began to rise. She had been fearing a much worse outcome than simply an off-course landing. Unfortunately, her recovering optimism was soon dashed.

"Most of the southern terrain is several kilometers higher," said Evelyn, as dispassionately as ever. "The atmosphere is much thinner. The ERV's autopilot and other descent systems weren't designed to land at high altitudes. If the early *Mars Odyssey* data is confirmed, then our ERV just made a big hole in the ground."

CHAPTER 32
LIGHTNING

MarsDay 252, 5:00 p.m.
(August 6, 11:26 p.m.)

"Obviously, we have a serious situation to deal with."

Evelyn's words were an understatement, if ever Anna had heard one. She didn't even know if the commander was referring to the situation outside the *Perseus* or inside.

Preparations for dinner provided a temporary distraction. Anna placed three nutro-meal portions in the microwave and set the temperature and timer without bothering to consult the container labels. After fixing similar meals every third day for the past nine Earth months, she could recite the recipe, ingredients, and portion size recommendations word for word. Today's dinner would be beef stroganoff ala Anna. Though the texture of the rehydrated beef cubes and vegetable ingredients left a lot to be desired, the pasta base was fresh, and ample seasonings could improve the taste as desired.

Joining the others in the lounge, she sat beside Ollie on the couch and watched him out of the corner of her eye. He hadn't said much to either of them, since the failed landing of the ERV almost three hours ago. Anna could tell he was not a happy camper.

She asked, "How certain is Mission Support about where the ERV finally landed?"

Evelyn answered, "With help from JPL, they've narrowed down the crash site to an ellipse that's about 500 kilometers wide, far west of Nicholson Crater."

On the computer display above Anna's head, the commander displayed a topographical map of the Medusae Fossae region and outlined the suspected landing area with a dashed red line. Anna strained her neck to see the map over her shoulder. Most of the ellipse contained high, rugged terrain, with numerous, steep crater walls.

Evelyn added a marker for their current location, and some concentric circles indicating distance. The middle of the estimated landing ellipse was 300 kilometers to the southwest of their current position.

"Can we reach that far with the pressurized rover?" asked Anna.

Evelyn shook her head. "Only if the rover had a full tank of fuel. Even then, we would have to pick our route very carefully. Without knowing the exact location of the crash site, it would be pointless to try."

Ollie broke his silence by barking, "Stop saying 'crash site!' We don't know for sure the ERV crashed."

"Denials won't change reality," snapped the commander. She shook her head again and added more sympathetically, "There's no transponder signal. No telemetry at all. Given the remoteness of the crash site, my golden rule applies. What we can't reach doesn't exist."

Anna wanted to put her hand over Evelyn's mouth to stop her from saying anything else. Couldn't she see how distressed Ollie was? His marked improvement in confidence and attitude over the past few months seemed to have evaporated completely. He appeared closer than ever to his personal breaking point.

She didn't sense the same desperation in Evelyn's behavior. It was probably there, but hidden beneath years of Navy combat training. As for her own feelings, worrying about Ollie's state of mind gave her something better to focus on than ERV crashes.

The commander continued, "Let's take stock of the big picture." Her voice was level, as if she were reading an abstract in a technical journal. "We have one pressurized rover with enough fuel for a round trip journey to anywhere within 300 kilometers. The *Perseus* is in good condition, but our solar and battery power reserves are minimal. Greenhouse pods are plentiful, but useless without water and soil for growing crops. We have heavy digging equipment and some explosives, but no spare fuel for digging."

"Our highest priority should be water," reminded Anna, recalling her earlier conversation with Evelyn on this subject. "Without it, we're dead."

Evelyn nodded. "That means we need fuel for digging, fuel from an ERV. Our best option is for me to take the pressurized rover up to the main Medusae landing site and bring back some fuel."

"And if the ERV and fuel isn't there?" asked Ollie. "What if it's blown up, like that reporter claimed?"

Evelyn got up from her chair and started to pace in front of the couch. By now, Anna knew Evelyn's fondness for pacing as simply an outward expression of her mental pacing. She came up with her best ideas while on her feet.

"If it's not there, then I'll return here, and fall back upon Plan B."

"Plan B?" asked Anna.

"There's always a Plan B," said the commander, winking at her. "I just haven't figured out what it is yet."

Better, better...Ollie needs to hear more optimism like that.

Unfortunately, the frown on Ollie's face made it very clear he didn't think much of Evelyn's joke. He cleared his throat to speak, and Anna expected a sharp, biting response. Instead, Ollie seemed to let the moment pass by meekly saying, "Plan A could still use some work."

"How so?" asked Evelyn.

"While you're at the Medusae landing site, someone should drive the other pressurized rover back with a second load of fuel. That means you can't go alone. But we shouldn't leave the *Perseus* vacant, either."

At moments like this, Anna regretted having only two crewmates on Mars. Even more, she regretted being the only non-engineer. Since standard operating procedures would often require an engineer to remain at the *Perseus* and two crew members to be on each long sortie in the pressurized rover, Anna was guaranteed a rover ride almost every time.

She sighed, accepting the inevitable. "Fine. I'll go, with one of you. Ollie?"

"No," said Evelyn. "I'm definitely going."

Since Ollie didn't object, Anna said, "Then it's the two of us. A ladies' road trip. No men allowed."

Evelyn smiled. "We'll leave tomorrow morning at eight o'clock. If we average 20 kilometers-per-hour, we should have plenty of time to reach the Medusae landing site before dusk."

MarsDay 253, 4:16 a.m.
(August 7, 11:00 a.m.)

David's late-morning jog usually started out with a modest climb, which would help him to reach his target pulse rate quickly. Today was different, however. Cassie had joined him, and they planned to walk, rather than jog. Though she exercised regularly back home, she deeply respected that ever-present adversary, the Rocky Mountain altitude.

Besides, he had been watching her closely enough to notice she still wasn't feeling well, physically or mentally. With the shocks induced by her husband's secret activities, David could readily understand that she might need more time to sort out her feelings. For the first ten minutes of their walk, she was silent and moody, but he could tell she wanted to talk to him about something.

As their feet crunched along the dry gravel of the path, he glanced up at the sky through an opening between the tall trees. Puffy cumulous clouds were building to the west, along the continental divide. A big storm was brewing, as was typical for the afternoons around this time of the year, but it would probably hold off for a few hours.

He hoped his weather forecast was accurate because neither of them had brought any rain gear. Their jeans were semi-waterproof, as almost all jeans were these days, but Cassie's light cotton sweatjacket atop her even lighter summer blouse didn't look very water repellant. His own t-shirt certainly wasn't, either.

Both sides of the forest trail were carpeted by a thick layer of dry needles extending into the arid pines in every direction, as far as the eye could see. The early-August monsoon rains had been late this year, but change was in the wind. A week from now, the dry tinderbox would likely be transformed into a lush tropical rainforest. A few weeks after that, winter would arrive, and the dryness would return.

Cassie finally broke her silence. "Any news about the ERV?" The tone of her voice indicated she was just making small talk. Whatever was bothering her remained unspoken.

"Nope."

David's team had been trying to contact the ERV for the last 14 hours, but without any success. All communication channels were silent. If the mission planners were following the Mars Direct plan, his team should have been able to contact the ERV right away. He desperately wanted to know whether the possible crash, and the certain silence following, was what they had expected. However, his inquiries to Ben last night and this morning had produced cryptic, <chicken_little>-esque responses.

His gut instincts told him the landing had gone horribly wrong, and the ERV crash was real. As an undeniable fact, the automatic ERV entry, descent, and landing systems weren't able to land safely at higher Mars altitudes. According to Anna, the commander hadn't guided the craft manually, either. Based on these firm facts, a single conclusion was obvious.

At least Anna can still return home on the first ERV at the Medusae landing site. But what about the next Mars crew? Or will there even be another one?

His silent moodiness wasn't helping to draw out Cassie's thoughts, so he voiced his suspicions about the ERV crash. She had been wondering the same things, too, but had also considered a more radical possibility.

"Ben referred to 'settling the issue' of whether there's a saboteur on the Mars crew. Did they crash the ERV on purpose?"

David considered this highly unlikely. The mission planners wouldn't jeopardize the future of Mars exploration by destroying such a valuable piece of hardware. Cassie reminded him, however, they didn't know the planners' real goals or what collateral damage they were willing to accept in order to achieve those goals.

"Besides, what else could Ben have meant?" she asked.

David mentioned the commander's plan to visit the Medusae landing site in the pressurized rover, speculating, "What if that's what Ben was talking about?" His support team was currently poring over high-resolution orbiter images to determine the safest route.

"But that trip might have been unnecessary if the ERV had landed safely."

She had a good point. Even if the second ERV had landed several hundred kilometers away, as in the Mars Direct plan, the crew could have waited until plenty of benzene fuel had been produced. Then they could have sent the rover to retrieve the fuel with less risk to the crew.

Along the trail, they came upon a large, square-shaped rock outcrop David had dubbed "The Castle." While jogging back to the house, he had often scaled the rocks and eaten his lunch atop the wide, flat surface above. Cassie probably wasn't in the mood for any climbing today, and they hadn't brought a lunch with them, so he walked on by.

"Interesting dynamics are happening," said Cassie, softly.

Her comment lost him. "You mean, with the ERV?"

"No, with Evelyn's trip. If there's really a saboteur on Mars, it seems very dangerous. Either Anna or Ollie might try to sabotage the rover. Or both of them."

"We're watching for that, as is Evelyn," said David. "Besides, Anna is going on the trip, too."

"Really? Then the dynamics are even more interesting. And more dangerous."

"How so?" he asked.

"I don't think I'd like being cooped up in a small rover with a possible murderess. Evelyn is either very brave, or very foolish."

Cassie had a good point, though it was one the commander must be well aware of. Besides, he still didn't consider Anna a credible sabotage suspect. If anyone was going to attempt something, it would be Ollie.

"There's also the dynamics of where they're going," added Cassie. "Evelyn knows an ERV is still sitting at the Medusae landing site, all safe and intact, but the others don't know that. If Beta believes they've already destroyed the three Medusae landers, any Beta accomplices on Mars would believe the same thing."

"They'll think Evelyn will find only wrecked vehicles at the Medusae landing site. That *is* interesting."

Will a Beta saboteur even allow the commander to reach the Medusae landing site? Finding evidence of the explosions would lead to repercussions back on Earth, especially now that Fontaine has raised the specter of sabotage. USNN might come under serious suspicion. Beta's plans, whatever they are, might be disrupted.

As David and Cassie came to Route 119, the main "Peak to Peak" highway running north-south along the eastern side of the Continental Divide, he spotted the Sundance Café down the road a few hundred feet. This cozy restaurant was a favorite hangout for the mountain locals. She smiled for the first time all morning and offered to buy him lunch.

"I can't turn down an such an offer from my rich sister," said David. Cassie's smile faded. David instantly regretted the remark.

As they entered the restaurant, David was glad to be wearing his less conspicuous street clothes, rather than his jogging apparel. They had a choice of sitting inside or outside. "Inside," decided Cassie, firmly. "I love the view, but it's easier to talk in here."

Inside suited David just fine, too. Several patrons were eating on the sundeck, but the inside tables were empty. He felt less exposed with four walls around him, though two of the walls were mostly windows and an open doorway.

As they sat, David looked out the wide windows, absorbing the breathtaking mountain views the Sundance was famous for. He compared the various purple-pointed peaks in the distance to a faded mural painted between the ceiling and the top of the north-facing window.

Refocusing his attention on Cassie, he decided to ask, point blank, what was bothering her. However, a waitress picked that moment to intervene with menus and a description of the daily special. The young woman was quite abrupt, almost to the point of being rude. After the distraction, David lost his nerve to confront Cassie.

She seemed ready to talk, however. "David," she said softly, "what do you think about Ben's story. Do you believe he's telling us the truth now?"

He didn't know how to answer, so he dodged. "What do you think?"

She shook her head. "I can't think right now. Or rather, I don't trust myself to think straight. This past week, I've been sick to my stomach half the time, ravenously hungry the other half, my hormones and moods are all whacked out, and I'm, well, I'm also two weeks late."

"Late?" asked David. "Oh! You mean..."

"Yes. I think I'm pregnant."

"That's wonderful!" cried David, reaching across the table to give her a hug. She didn't return his embrace with much enthusiasm, however. A bit confused, he sat back down and stared into her somber eyes. "That's why you're asking about Ben. Does he know?"

"No. The only other person I've told is Jennifer."

They sat in silence for a few moments, until the dour waitress returned and they ordered their meal. In his distracted state, David hadn't even glanced at the menu, so he just ordered the daily special. Then he remembered it was salmon, which he despised.

Oh well. Some things are more important than food.

He reached across the table and clasped Cassie's hands in his own. "You asked me whether I believed Ben. So far, his story makes sense, except for the ERV. We've already talked about that. If it really crashed, it might have been a genuine accident. Landing on Mars is hard. However..."

His voice froze, as he caught the briefest glimmer of a thought too troubling to speak aloud, especially to Cassie in her current state. He would nurture that thought, holding it safely inside. Later, it might blossom into a disturbing new theory, one that might cast doubt on the benevolent motives of Ben and his Alpha colleagues.

As Cassie fought her own demons, she didn't seem to notice the sudden turmoil David was going through. A tear rolled down her cheek, soon followed by several more.

"But he lied to me, over and over, since before we were even married!" she sobbed. "How can I trust him again?"

"You have to try." David replied with far more certainty than he felt inside. "If not for yourself, then for your child."

"I know. I know." Her voice had faded until he could barely hear her words. "That's the hardest part. I'm so…confused."

David promised to be there for her, in any way he could. He also advised her to tell Ben about her pregnancy as soon as possible. It was his child, too, and the miracle of newborn life might help to bring them back together.

If Ben can be trusted, added the tiny voice of doubt in the back of his mind. *But he won't fool Cassie a second time. No way.*

As they made some plans for Cassie to talk to Ben, her attitude slowly recovered. By the time their food arrived, she was even close to laughing again. He wrinkled his nose when the sharp smell of the salmon assaulted him. Noticing his reaction, Cassie switched their plates, trading her pork chops for his fish.

The waitress didn't seem to notice. Her attitude had improved remarkably, as well. She explained, "Some guys on the deck just ran off, leaving a $100 bill on the table. I've never seen an $80 tip before!"

The waitress returned to the kitchen. Between gestures and stories, they enjoyed their meals, eating slowly. Afterwards, Cassie covered the check as promised, despite David's objections that he should be buying lunch for the mother of his future nephew or niece. She even bought two pieces of cheesecake for dessert.

Eventually, they got up to leave. According to David's watch, they had been in the restaurant for just over an hour. It felt much longer. He needed to get back to work so he could coordinate his mapping team's route suggestions with Evelyn. Skye had scheduled a 3:00 phone call, too, and he found himself almost looking forward to it.

The narrow steps leading down from the Sundance to the parking lot were old and creaky. Cassie almost tripped on the bottom step. As David grabbed her arm to stabilize her, he bumped into a man wearing sunglasses who was heading up the steps. David turned to apologize, and felt a cloth pressed against his nose and mouth. His legs collapsed, and the world went dark.

MarsDay 253, 7:00 a.m.
(August 7, 1:49 p.m.)

Anna worked her way through the rover's pre-departure checklist carefully, but quickly. She couldn't wait to be finished. Evelyn had been hovering around for the past hour, helping and directing, but also watching every move she made.

Anna expressed her annoyance passively, with silent concentration on each specific task. If Evelyn thought Anna incapable of following the simple instructions on the checklist, she would soon be proven wrong.

Finally, she reached the last item on the list: the food supply. Without saying a word, she retrieved a crate of food from a supply area in the *Perseus*. Her shadow followed and lifted a second crate.

On the way back to the rover, they bumped into Ollie in the EVA room. "Two crates of food?" he asked, with open disapproval. "Are you planning on staying out there for several weeks?"

Evelyn responded, "If the ERV is damaged, we can't be sure how long it will take to repair it. One of our food boxes might become damaged, too, or its contents spoiled."

"That's ridiculous!" scoffed Ollie. "How could that possibly happen?"

"You tell me," Evelyn said smugly, as she finished placing her heavy burden in the rover and returned to the EVA room. "Or rather, prove to me it can't happen."

"What about all the food at the Medusae landing site?" asked Anna, intentionally taking Ollie's side. In her state of irritation, she wouldn't mind seeing the commander's logic refuted.

Evelyn turned to her. "Prove it's still there," she demanded, sharply.

Anna shook her head, sorry she had stepped into the middle of the argument. However, Ollie came to her rescue right away.

"I came down here to tell you, Mission Support can't agree on the best route to the Medusae landing site. They've recorded some options for you to choose from," he said, gesturing toward the ladder.

Sighing, Evelyn turned to follow him upstairs. Then she stopped and stepped towards the rover instead. "I'll take their message in the rover."

Anna followed and sat in the passenger seat while the commander replayed the message. She had looked forward to seeing David's image, or at least hearing his voice, but then she remembered the original Shepherd was still "dead" to the world. He had probably asked one of his backups to handle the presentation.

Most of the message consisted of old, high-resolution images from orbit, annotated by a faceless speaker who outlined various routes and hazards. As Ollie had implied, each route contained risks. The more direct routes, like the one heading almost due north through Sentinel Canyon, appeared to be choked with large rocks at various points. Other routes were less cluttered, but much longer, requiring lengthy detours to the east or west before heading north.

Evelyn studied the maps and raw orbiter images for a long time, rechecking the support team's conclusions. Anna reminded her that if they wanted to reach the landing site by nightfall, they would need to leave soon. Her words were brushed aside. Evelyn seemed intent upon finding the shortest, perfectly safe route, even if it took forever to do so.

Anna's frustration level began to rise again. She needed to get away from Evelyn, so she left. At the moment, the thought of spending several days in the cramped rover with the commander was intolerable.

She found Ollie sitting on the couch in the lounge, and he appeared eager to talk, if not openly distraught. Joining him on the couch, she finally got him to confess his worries about the upcoming rover trip. It was their first lengthy EVA, and they didn't know how well the rover would handle the long journey. Anna sensed his reservations ran deeper, but she could coax no more from him.

Finally, around 9:00, Evelyn made an announcement on the intercom. She had decided upon the best route, though it was a lengthy one. It looped far to the west before turning north. If they left now and exceeded their 20-kph goal, they might still reach the landing site by nightfall.

"Gotta go," said Anna, rising, and giving Ollie a warm hug. He held the embrace longer than she had expected. "Don't worry. We'll be fine, and I'll see you in a few days."

"I'll miss you," he responded.

As she left, she glanced back. He was still sitting on the couch, and his gaze, lingering upon her, was filled with sadness. She wondered if he would be OK, alone in the *Perseus*.

Of course he will. He's a survivor. Five minutes after we're gone, he'll be back to normal and studying rocks or something.

So why do I feel like I'll never see him again?

She descended the ladder, shaking her head at her warped intuition. Upon reaching the rover, she closed both pressure seals and began the process of purging the nitrogen from their rover's air supply. Then she settled back into the passenger seat next to Evelyn.

"Where were you?" asked Evelyn.

"Just talking to Ollie. He's very concerned about our safety. I hope he'll be OK by himself."

"I'm sure he'll be just fine," Evelyn said.

Twenty minutes later, when the internal atmosphere of the rover was nearly pure oxygen, Evelyn retracted their inflatable tunnel connection from the *Perseus* and began the rover on its journey. The first segment of their trip was a 20-kilometer sprint to the southwest. They followed the same course Anna had taken on her pedestrian EVA, when she had deployed the second communications relay.

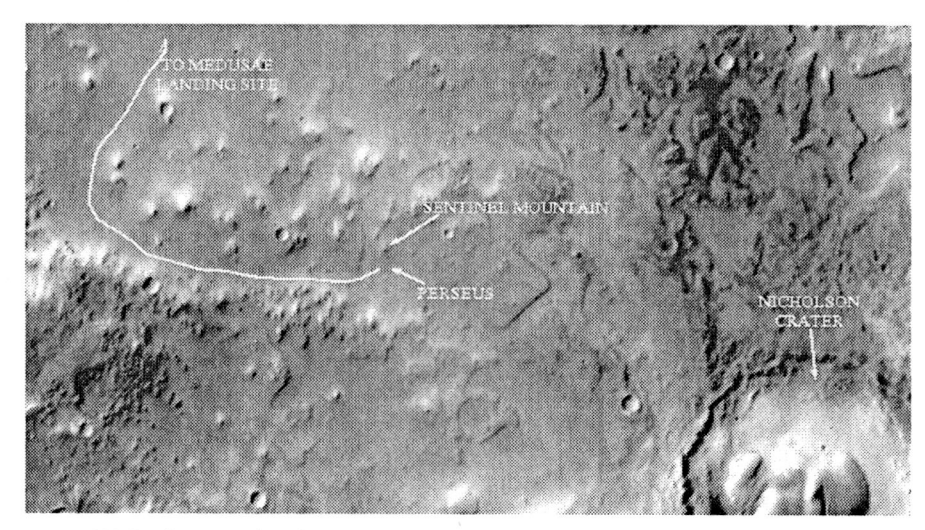

USGS image of region northwest of Nicholson Crater (public domain).

As they passed the relay, they also crossed the track of Ollie's monster dust devil. Anna knew that Ollie was dying to return here and study the trail.

Continuing onward, Evelyn increased the rover's speed to almost 30 kph. Such a speed was almost recklessly fast, given they were driving over unfamiliar terrain, but the area around them seemed smooth and unbroken. Soon, they approached the low escarpment extending northward and forming the western wall of Sentinel Canyon.

"I was afraid of this," remarked Evelyn, as she slowed the rover. "The images from orbit lacked the proper resolution and lighting angle to tell the height and steepness of this slope."

They were still over a kilometer away from the escarpment, and the adjacent terrain was littered with larger boulders. She reduced her speed farther, until they were crawling at only 5 kph.

"Can the rover climb that steep of a grade?" asked Anna, as she eyed the slope dubiously. It appeared to be at least 50 meters high, and some of the brightest crimson layers were eroded into near-vertical slices.

"Possibly," said Evelyn, "but we'd be foolish to try. The escarpment should taper off to the south. Let's look for an easier route."

She turned the rover to the left and cautiously threaded her way between the largest boulders, heading southeast. Ironically, their detour took them in the opposite direction than their true objective. Anna did some quick calculations. At this course and speed, they would reach the Medusae landing site six months from now, after circumnavigating the entire planet. Of course, their fuel and supplies would run out long before then.

Evelyn angled the rover farther to the east, toward smoother terrain. Gradually, the rover's speed increased until they were traveling parallel to the escarpment at almost 20 kph.

Anna studied the distant wall of rock for any sign of a safe route to the top. She also commented on the patterns she imagined in the beautiful rock layering. Her chatter was intended to help the time pass faster.

They proceeded in this manner for almost an hour, following the escarpment as it bent to the southwest and gradually dropped toward the plain. In reality, the plain was rising to cover the rock face, as layer upon disappearing layer indicated. The jagged peaks of the southern mountain range towered above them, though the summits now appeared to be lower in height than Anna had expected. Evelyn veered due west, slowed her speed, and easily climbed a modest slope to the flat plains beyond.

By the time they had completed their detour and reached a point about 20 kilometers west of the *Perseus*, it was almost noon, and Evelyn was ready to let Anna drive. Switching seats was unnecessary, since both positions had a full set of controls, but they did so anyway. American and German customs both placed the driver on the left.

Anna turned the rover westward along their originally planned route. She tried to drive as fast as possible, but 20 kph proved to be her upper limit.

Her co-pilot leaned back and dozed in the seat beside her, snoring loudly at times. Evelyn's sleep was sometimes interrupted when Anna hit larger bumps. After a short respite, the snoring would resume. Had Anna been trying to sleep, Evelyn's vigorous sawing of logs would have kept her awake. Since she was trying to stay awake and alert, the monotonous sounds sought to lull her into sleep. Her eyes became heavy, and her speed dropped further.

A loud beep from the rover's collision avoidance monitor jolted Anna into instant alertness. A large boulder had appeared in front of the rover, as if out of nowhere. She slammed on the brakes and veered to the right. Since her speed had dropped so much, she had no trouble missing the obstacle.

Glancing at the time, she was surprised to find it was almost 4:00. She couldn't remember the last hour.

Evelyn had also been awakened by the commotion. "Try to miss the mountains, please," she quipped.

"Sorry," said Anna. She felt herself blushing, which only added to her embarrassment. "I just can't seem to keep my eyes open."

Evelyn jumped up from her seat and moved to the back of the rover, where she checked the bank of equipment monitoring their internal environment. Meanwhile, Anna began to drive again. Fully awake now, she resumed her 20 kph westward pace.

"Everything looks OK," said Evelyn, as she rejoined Anna at the front of the rover. "Since I couldn't stay awake either, I was worried the carbon dioxide levels might be too high in here."

"Do you ever stop worrying?" asked Anna.

"Never," said Evelyn, laughing, but with an undertone of seriousness. "It keeps me alive. By the way, I turned down the heat a bit, to help us stay awake."

Anna nodded and continued driving, while Evelyn checked their current position by matching local terrain features to the rover's maps. They were about 80 kilometers west of the *Perseus*.

"At this rate," said Evelyn, "we won't make it to the Medusae landing site before dusk. In fact, we won't even get close."

"I know." Anna had been watching their progress closely, at least during those times when her eyes were open. She knew exactly where they were, and how far they needed to travel.

"We'll drive another hour," Evelyn ordered. "That should bring us to the point where we can loop up to the north. Then we'll camp out for the evening."

The next hour passed more quickly because Anna had someone to talk to. Rather than being upset at their poor progress, the commander seemed quite understanding and forgiving. They both agreed safety was more important than schedules.

When the sinking sun began to cast long shadows, making driving too hazardous, Anna had reached the bend in their route and started northward. Before halting for the evening, Evelyn reminded her to turn the rover so it faced west. Proper orientation was an important safety measure, in case a solar flare occurred overnight and lingered into the morning. They would soon be sleeping in two tiny bunk beds, with modest shielding from radiation. Realigning the rover would guarantee an angry morning sun, rising in the east, wouldn't catch them off guard.

With the rover's engine turned off, Mars became a very quiet, surreal place. Anna looked out the windshield at the Arizona-like desert. She could almost hear coyotes howling at the setting sun from the surrounding buttes. The scene would only become more serene after the sun set. She couldn't wait to do some serious stargazing.

First, she had other priorities. Her stomach had begun to growl, and she realized they had driven straight through lunch without eating anything all day. Doctor Schweitzer scolded herself for not monitoring their calorie and nutrient intake adequately. That task was still one of her most important responsibilities, whether she was inside the rover or back at the *Perseus*.

Evelyn must have been hungry, too, because she immediately volunteered to cook. Anna caught the commander's wink. Cooking would merely consist of heating two packets of field rations, so it was hardly a chore at all. Still, the ritual of dining together was what mattered most, as well as the fair sharing of duties, no matter how trivial.

While Evelyn "cooked," Anna contacted Ollie in the *Perseus*. Due to terrain and distance, the signal reception was poor. Ollie had been following their progress remotely for most of the day, and he seemed to be in better spirits than when she had left a few hours ago. They conversed until Evelyn announced dinner was ready. Then Anna said her farewells and promised to call back in the morning before they began their next day's journey.

After dinner, Evelyn asked for some help with astronomy. Gazing out the rover's main windshield, she was trying to identify various constellations but was overwhelmed by the sheer number of blazing stars. The sun had set a few minutes earlier, and the thin atmosphere was already pitch black. They turned out the interior rover lights and were treated to a spectacular display in the heavens.

Shining down upon Anna with brilliant intensity, the twinkling stars were almost forceful. They demanded respect. Their light had bathed the Martian landscape for billions of years, without any humans or other known life forms to appreciate it. The wonders in the vast heavens would remain, long after Anna and her companions were gone.

Several hours later, she retired to her cramped bunk bed along the north wall of the rover. Pessimistic engineers back on Earth had dubbed these beds "coffins." The rover's temperature had dropped, and she crawled under a warm blanket to ease her shivering. Since most of her chills were internal remnants of wonder left over from her stargazing, the blanket didn't help much.

Evelyn remained awake, working on the rover's computer. Eventually, the soft tapping of the keyboard dulled Anna's senses, and the warm fingers of welcome drowsiness embraced her. She became one with the silent stillness all about her. The cold, sterile plains outside were a comfort, buffering her from the rest of the universe. She was at peace.

Bump, bump.

Anna awoke with a start. She glanced at the time on a display above her: 3:00 a.m.

The noise had sounded like something softly bumping the hull of the rover. Had it been part of a dream? She didn't recall having any nightmares, or any other dreams at all.

The only sounds she could hear now were the commander's soft snores from across the cramped room. Obviously, Evelyn hadn't caused the noise.

She waited.

Gurgle, gurgle, gurgle.

This new, softer noise persisted. It was definitely real, and it sounded like it was coming from outside the rover.

But there are no other humans within millions of kilometers!

Except Ollie, and he's too far away. It's too cold for him to be outside at night.

Suddenly terrified to the core of her soul, Anna tried to get up too quickly and thumped her head on the low ceiling of her coffin bunk. She staggered to the front windshield and looked outside. The night was as dark as ever. By the starlight, she could see nothing unusual in front of the rover.

The noise outside became a scratching sound. Still soft, it was somewhat harsher and more grating, as if something metallic was scraping the rover's plastic hull.

Anna raced back to the rear of the rover and gazed out a small porthole in the closed doorway. Again, she could see nothing unusual outside. The gurgling and scraping noises were definitely louder at the rear of the rover, but as she listened, the gurgling died away. The scraping noise seemed to be coming from above her head now, on the roof.

She went to Evelyn's bunk and nudged her shoulder firmly. "Evelyn, wake up!" she whispered.

Evelyn's response was immediate and totally unexpected. Faster than Anna would have believed a person could move, the commander erupted out of her bed. Flowing like water, she pinned one of Anna's arms painfully behind her back. Evelyn's other arm was already locked around Anna's neck and squeezing tightly.

After an awkward moment of silence, Evelyn calmly stated, "It's dangerous to awaken a martial arts expert like that. I hope you had a good reason."

With her free arm, Anna weakly gestured upward. "Something's on the roof!" she croaked.

As if solely to confirm her story, the noise on the roof turned into a loud metallic shriek. This new sound was even more terrifying, since it led her to imagine something outside was trying to cut its way through the roof.

Another awkward moment passed. Then Evelyn moved just as quickly as before. This time, she released Anna and jumped away, toward the rear of the vehicle.

After collapsing to the floor in a surprised heap, Anna rubbed her shoulder and neck with her free arm. The pain in both places slowly subsided.

She remained on the floor. It seemed like the safest place, well removed from the whirling dervish she had unleashed inside the rover, as well as the threatening noises outside. The metallic shriek from above had been joined by some dull thumps.

"Get your suit on," ordered Evelyn.

By the time Anna's legs would move again, Evelyn had already donned most of her thin counter-pressure suit. Anna scrambled to catch up. Just as she sealed her neck dam and bubble helmet, the sounds on the rooftop stopped.

The silence was deafening, and she glanced upward to verify the ceiling was still there. It was, and Evelyn had just retracted a Robonaut control harness from it. Anna helped her leap into the harness. Then she reached for a control helmet before realizing it wasn't needed. Evelyn could already control the robot, using her suit.

"Stepping into the Robonaut now," Evelyn said, with her standard Navy terseness. "What the...it's outside already. In fact, the robot's on the roof."

Anna was almost swept away by waves of relief. The scraping, bumping, gurgling, and grinding noises must have been caused by their own Robonaut. She had been imagining something far worse, something totally alien.

But what was the robot doing out there?

Evelyn soon answered her question. "This looks bad. It's mangled our transmitter and receiver array into a slag heap. The damage is completely irreparable."

Some of Anna's relief evaporated. "But how?" she asked. "Its control signals are relayed through the rover. Once the array was damaged, its signals would cease."

"That's probably what happened. It must have finished its destruction autonomously."

Anna nodded. Robonauts did possess a limited ability to operate without any human controller. They didn't use that capability very often, and she had momentarily forgotten about it.

With a trembling voice, she said, "I wonder what else the robot did. Earlier, I heard some bumps and gurgles coming from the rear of the rover. That's what woke me up."

"Descending now," said Evelyn. Her arm and leg motions indicated she was guiding the Robonaut down the ladder to the ground. A few moments later, she added, "I don't see anything. No, wait! There's a patch of damp soil beneath the rover. That can only mean one thing."

At the end of her statement, Evelyn's military inflection cracked. For a brief moment, she stopped sounding like a robot herself and became a living, breathing human. For her, this brief slip was akin to a raging, emotional outburst. It washed away any remnants of Anna's relief.

"Our fuel?" asked Anna, fearing the answer.

Evelyn didn't respond. She crouched in her harness, as if she were peering intently underneath something. Anna imagined what the underside of the two fuel tanks must look like, to her robot's eyes. Whether empty or full, the tanks would look the same.

Kicking herself, Anna realized a simple way to resolve the matter. All she had to do was look at the fuel level indicators on the rover's dashboard. She did so, and it confirmed her worst fears. The gauge for each tank was pegged to the left: empty.

In a daze, she returned to the commander's side and reported her findings. Evelyn guided the Robonaut to its sheltered pod and stepped out of the harness. Then she removed her helmet bubble and neck dam, too, carefully storing everything away in a locker.

Anna removed and stored her suit as well. Under the watchful eye of the commander, she went forward and sank heavily into the driver's seat. She tried contacting the *Perseus*, without any reply. She also failed to receive a signal from any of the orbiting satellites. The rover was blind, deaf, and dumb.

She glanced back at Evelyn, who was inspecting the environmental controls intently. With a satisfied nod, the commander turned and climbed back into her coffin.

"What are you doing?" Anna asked, incredulously.

"Getting some more sleep," was Evelyn's calm reply. "With the comm array gone and the robot deactivated, no one's going to be disturbing us. It's 3:30 in the morning. Our environment is stable."

Anna couldn't believe what she had just heard. Sleep was the last thing in the world for them to be doing now. They needed to act. They had to find a way out of their dilemma.

Without fuel for the motor, the rover was crippled. Their secondary fuel cell system would keep them alive for only a few days, even if the power was devoted exclusively to life support. Without communications, they couldn't even contact Ollie for help.

Wait—there must be a replacement comm array in our spare parts inventory!

That's why Evelyn is so calm. She'll just replace the unit in the morning and contact Ollie. He'll drive out to meet us on the ATV, towing the rest of our benzene fuel supply.

It's a good thing we held some fuel in reserve, back at the Perseus. *Once again, Evelyn and her brilliant command decisions would save the day.*

Anna willed her body to relax by taking several deep breaths. She needed to remain calm. Sleeping would be difficult, but she would try. In the morning, if Evelyn needed her help to repair the damaged comm array, Anna would be ready.

CHAPTER 33
ALIGNMENT

MarsDay 254, 6:20 a.m.
(August 8, 1:47 p.m.)

Munching on a breakfast bar, Anna revealed her guesses about the commander's plan to return safely to the *Perseus*. She finished by asking, "Well? How close was I?" Then she leaned an elbow on the armrest of the rover's passenger seat and looked at Evelyn, waiting for a response.

To her surprise, Evelyn didn't answer. She returned Anna's stare with the sullen look of someone who had already admitted defeat. It was an expression Anna had never seen before on the commander's face.

Anna fought even harder to keep her own confidence from slipping away. If her plan wouldn't work for some reason, she would think of something else. Losing hope would be far too easy, and it would accomplish nothing.

"There are two problems with your plan," Evelyn finally said, holding up two fingers for illustration. "First, we don't have a backup communications array."

"Yes, we do!" Anna crowed, triumphantly. Since the comm system was so critical, and the transmitter/receiver array was exposed to the elements on the exterior of the rover, their inventory contained a full replacement array and a complete set of spare parts for any reasonable repair. Anna had just verified her facts by checking the inventory list in the computer only a few minutes ago.

"Try finding the parts," Evelyn suggested.

Anna consulted the computer again and retrieved a bin number. Then she went back to the supplies area and pulled the correct bin from the ceiling. It was empty.

"I don't understand," she mumbled, as she returned to the passenger seat.

"Empty, huh?" Evelyn asked.

"You mean, you hadn't looked?"

The commander shook her head. "No need to. Ollie wouldn't have bothered to sabotage the comm system if he knew we could repair it."

"What? Ollie didn't do this!" Anna couldn't believe Evelyn would even voice such an absurd accusation.

"Who else could have controlled the Robonaut? It wasn't you or me." Evelyn gestured toward the main windshield. The first rays of flat morning sunlight illuminated the desolate landscape beyond. "I don't see other suspects around."

"What about someone back on Earth?" Anna asked.

"Unlikely. Emptying the fuel tanks required both intelligence and dexterity. A human tele-operator on Earth would have been way too clumsy, and the robot can't bypass the safety mechanisms on its own."

Anna's mind raced, trying to think of some other possibility. Uncle Ollie couldn't have done this. He just wasn't capable of harming anyone.

But he was acting strange right before we left.

Anna banished this thought, shoving it right out her mental airlock. She asked, "What's the second problem with my plan?"

"Since Ollie obviously performed the sabotage, he won't come to our rescue, even if we were somehow able to repair the comm array."

"But maybe we could talk to him! Reason with him!" Anna realized she was speaking as if Ollie was indeed guilty. She slammed her palm into the chair's armrest in open frustration, at their situation, but also at her own disloyalty to her best friend.

Evelyn sat back in the driver's seat and closed her eyes. For well over a minute, she didn't move a single muscle. She might have remained that way indefinitely, but Anna couldn't stand the silence any longer.

"Well? Aren't we going to do something?" Anna asked.

"I am doing something," said Evelyn, still without moving. "I'm pondering our options. Would you like me to lay them out on the table?"

"Yes, please."

"We're too far away from the *Perseus* to return on foot. Since we don't have any fuel, the rover can't move. Without a Sabatier Reactor, we can't convert our small, on-board supply of hydrogen for the fuel cell into benzene for the motor. Nor do we have any other possible source of benzene, or any other chemical to run the motor."

"Could we construct a Sabatier Reactor from spare parts?"

"No." Evelyn explained that a dizzying array of pipes, fittings, pressure vessels, and catalysts would be needed, along with a way to construct the device. "Even if we could build the reactor, we would need energy to run it and time to produce enough fuel."

On the rover's computer, Anna called up some background information on the Sabatier reaction process. The vital chemical reaction to produce methane from hydrogen had been well known since the 19th century, but their 21st century rover completely lacked the materials to initiate and sustain the process. Even if they somehow managed to convert their hydrogen into methane, further processing would be needed to create benzene. She soon agreed with Evelyn. "Not even MacGyver could do it."

Evelyn cracked a thin smile, which vanished almost immediately. "If we could repair the comm system, we could contact Earth and tell them what happened. I'm sure they would send us a new habitat, if we wanted to wait around for two years."

The commander continued her blunt analysis. "There's the equipment at the Medusae landing site, including that nice, comfortable habitat and second pressurized rover. It's all just sitting there, waiting for us. However, I've checked our maps thoroughly. Reaching the area on foot within a single day would be almost impossible. Likewise for reaching the *Perseus*. We're stuck. And of course, anyone caught out on the surface overnight would freeze to death."

"Could we send the Robonaut?" Anna immediately realized the stupidity of her idea but recovered quickly, amending it before Evelyn could shoot it down. "Without the comm array, we can't control a robot that far away. But maybe I could go along and bring extra oxygen!"

"Possibly," said Evelyn, though she didn't show much enthusiasm for the idea.

Wrapping herself around this potential plan, Anna's mind began to churn through the details. Before long, her distracted gaze noticed a message logo in the corner of the console display in front of her. Sometime during the night, prior to the destruction of the comm array, she had received an incoming message. She pointed this out to Evelyn, who wryly commented, "Take a guess who it's from."

Anna played the message on her console, and Ollie's familiar face greeted her. He had made the recording in the lounge area of the *Perseus*. Enviously, she noticed a steaming cup of tea in his hand. The sky-blue wall color in the background mocked her.

Hello, Anna. I'm sorry to be greeting you in this manner, and I'm sad our relationship has to end this way. By now you've probably realized that you're out of options, and you have all the time in the world to listen to my message.

Any lingering doubts about Ollie's guilt were swept away. Once more, the commander was right. Anna curled her body into a tight ball on her seat, with her chin on her knees, and closed her eyes. She continued to listen, but she couldn't bear to look at Ollie's face.

In case you're tempted to try reaching the Medusae landing site on foot, don't bother. Even if you could somehow manage to walk a straight course without any navigational aids, you won't find anything there. That reporter was right. My colleagues destroyed all three vehicles.

Besides, I removed the oxygen flow regulators from both of your suits. I didn't want you trying to return to the Perseus. *Evelyn should have caught that. Sloppy to the last.*

You might be asking, "Why?" I suppose I owe you an explanation. That's the least I can do, given how things have turned out.

Very simply, we've always been concerned about the economic and political turmoil brought by robust space exploitation. Energy is power on Earth, but in space, nearly unlimited energy is freely present. Free energy, free power. Politically speaking, free, ubiquitous power is akin to anarchy. Solar physics makes this outcome inevitable.

Stability can only be maintained if access to space is firmly controlled. Would you like a glimpse of the future? In a few months, we'll force the Chinese government to cancel their lunar program. Little will happen in space for the next 30 years, until we begin to strip-mine the Moon ourselves, to serve the energy needs of a planet bursting at the seams. We'll also build massive solar, wave, and wind farms to supplement our declining supplies of fossil-fuels. These projects will be incredibly expensive, but money won't be an issue. Once we reach that point, the public will pay us any price to satisfy its thirst for energy. Energy credits will be the currency of the future.

Mocking the serious tone of Ollie's voice, Evelyn translated, "Those with all the power intend to dole it out to whomever pays the most."

Ollie's message continued in a similar tone as Evelyn's frequent lectures. She peeked at the screen to find Ollie's eyes staring at her, focused on the camera unmovingly. Anna hid from his penetrating stare again.

Mars will be bypassed. It's too dangerous. With a little help from some basic technology, people could live on Mars independently of Earth. If a self-sustaining settlement of humanity ever managed to plant a toehold on Mars, chaos would enter the system and anarchy would follow. The same could be said for settlements on near-Earth asteroids.

By contrast, a settlement on the Moon will always rely upon supplies of carbon and volatiles from Earth. We should be able to maintain complete control of it.

We were tempted to squash this Mars mission immediately, like we've killed other threatening projects at NASA and elsewhere over the past 40 years. Instead, we decided to use the mission as a way to end the Mars threat, once and for all. I infiltrated the crew by arranging a little "accident" for the previous geologist.

Again, I'm sorry it had to come to this. Anna, you should not be here. None of us ever should have landed on Mars.

Hearing these words, Anna curled up even tighter. Her struggling mind flashed back to recollections of her frequent nightmares. Ollie's words were uncomfortably familiar. In the background, she could almost hear the buzzing of bees, swarms of earthly woes trying to reach across the void, following her to Mars.

After losing contact with the equipment at the Medusae landing site, Evelyn should have used the free return trajectory back to Earth. The early abort would have provided us with ample grounds to discourage and ridicule any other fools who were tempted to try a similar stunt in the future. No one else would have been hurt.

Instead, the mission continued. Our commander's stubbornness boggles the mind. Even after we sabotaged software, sensors, and radiation shielding, she persisted. We expected a solar flare to remove her, but the Sun failed to deliver. She's the person responsible for your death, Anna, not me.

With you and Evelyn out of the way, I'll be free to reshape the public's perception of Mars. Our risk-averse society will digest my message without suspicion. By the time I'm through, everyone will be convinced that Mars is a hostile, toxic planet, totally devoid of life, past, present, and future. I'll eventually return to Earth a hero and continue my educational efforts there.

Thank you for failing so miserably at growing crops using Martian soil. If your experiments had shown any promise on their own, I would have needed to find a way of choking them off. Likewise, if you're wondering why you've been having so much trouble with the water recycling system, it's because I've been dumping anti-bacterial soap down the drain. I couldn't conceal much of it in my personal supplies, but a little bit has gone a long way. We can't have the environmental experts back on Earth thinking they can grow crops on Mars or sustain a closed ecosystem. It's too soon for that.

The water recycling system should begin to recover soon. I'll figure out some excuse to tell the experts. Maybe it just couldn't sustain three people. It only needs to keep me alive until more water and food supplies arrive from Earth, along with a new ERV, courtesy of our renegade mission sponsors.

About those sponsors, public pressure and outrage ought to crush them and their petty little ambitions, once their identity is revealed. We still don't know who they are, but we'll soon find out. I've just learned that my colleagues back on Earth have abducted Shepherd. This time, he'll tell us everything we ever wanted to know about the mission and its sponsors. He's been a real thorn in our side. Hopefully, the next Shepherd will be more cooperative.

The latest pain caused by Ollie's words was almost physical. If he was telling the truth, David was in trouble back on Earth, and she couldn't do anything about it.

I'll let you get along with your pre-death preparations. Don't worry about cleaning up after yourselves. No one will ever know what happened to you. I'll have plenty of time, fuel, and mining explosives to blow your rover to smithereens long after you're dead. Future robots might come poking around, wondering what happened to you. We don't leave loose ends.

Did I mention how sorry I am about all this? Anna, I really did enjoy your company. Evelyn can burn in hell for all I care, but at least you tried to be a friend, and I appreciate that.

By the way...

"Oh, shut up, already!" cried Anna, killing the message playback with a swat of her hand. She felt her inner walls rising to protect her. Of all the betrayals she had ever endured, Ollie's hurt the worst, by far.

Evelyn didn't seem to notice. She got up to check a spare parts bin in the back of the rover. Then she inspected the oxygen tanks on their space suits closely.

As Evelyn returned to the front and sagged into the left seat, her scowl revealed her findings. Anna pouted in silence for several minutes.

"I really messed up," confessed Evelyn.

"What?" Anna returned her attention to the commander.

"Ollie was right. I should have noticed the damage to our suits before we even left. I was too busy watching you and didn't pay enough attention to him. That was a mistake."

"Why were you watching me?" Anna felt her blood pressure rising even higher as she recalled how upset she was, prior to their leaving the *Perseus*.

"I knew there was a good chance that you or Ollie would try some sort of sabotage. You were my primary suspect, so I watched you the closest. I'm sorry."

Even after the magnitude of Ollie's betrayal, this lesser one still hurt, too. Evelyn spun a lengthy tale about open water valves, radiation sensor sabotage, Anna's emotional relationship with Shepherd, and psychological theories. It all made a convincing case that Anna was trying to kill the commander.

"And David knew about this?" Anna moaned.

"Yes. But you should know that he never doubted you. He defended you to the last. We just didn't listen because the psychologists' story was more believable and was backed up by the physical evidence in the crew logs."

Anna curled up into a tight ball again. Ollie and Evelyn had turned against her. Now, so had David. Evelyn's feeble defense of her long-distance companion and soul mate only made the hurt feel worse.

The droning of an angry swarm smothered her thoughts. Her walls rose higher than ever before, blocking the painful, cruel stings of the outside world. She never wanted to see any of these so-called friends again. Even death seemed a blessing, compared to the shocking blows life had just dealt her.

MarsDay 254, 7:31 a.m.
(August 8, 3:00 p.m.)

"It's time for you to wake up, Mars boy," a disembodied voice whispered from the darkness. The voice had been preceded by the foulest odor David had ever smelled.

"Wakes them up every time," a different voice said, louder and deeper.

David opened his eyes but was greeted by pitch-blackness. He felt something covering his eyes. As he reached to remove the obstruction, he found that his arms were firmly locked behind his back. Cold rings of steel bit into his wrists as he tried to free himself.

"Good luck trying to break those handcuffs," said Voice One. "I wouldn't even try, if I were you. You'll just start bleeding all over the place, and you might need all your blood later."

Voice Two added, "Your chair's sitting on a $10,000 rug, too. Be considerate to your host, will you? He might charge you for his cleaning bill." Both speakers seemed to find that last statement extremely funny, for some reason.

"Who are you?" David croaked. His throat felt like sandpaper. *And how long have I been unconscious? Minutes? Hours? Days?*

"We're nobody," the deeper Voice Two answered. "You'll meet the somebodies in a few minutes. But I wouldn't be in a hurry, if I were you."

"Need water," he rasped.

"I suppose we could do that for you, since you're going to entertain us this evening." said Voice Two again.

The room felt spacious, but slightly musty. Since he couldn't hear any external sounds, he guessed that he was in a large basement. Without his eyesight, there was no way to be sure. He could be anywhere, in any town, state, or even country.

After a few moments, he felt a glass pressed to his chapped lips. The water was refreshing, and he drank sloppily, spilling more than entered his mouth.

When he spoke again, his voice had recovered its usual smoothness. "I don't suppose you have a bathroom around here? Our host might be upset if I make a puddle on his carpet."

He felt a hood shoved none too gently over his head, and then his hands were released. When he lifted them to his face, he found he couldn't remove the hood.

"Let's just leave that alone," Voice One stated firmly, while grabbing his arm and leading him through the darkness.

The strong material of the hood allowed air to pass through freely. He took some cautious steps on shaky legs, supported by the body behind Voice One. He had obviously been unconscious for a long time.

Then he was locked into a small room. By touch, he found a sink and toilet. Once his most immediate concerns were taken care of, he washed his hands, rubbed his aching wrists, and stretched his legs. His only thoughts were of escape, which seemed unlikely unless he could remove the hood and see where he was going. That action proved to be quite impossible. The light fabric of the hood resisted all his attempts to tear it.

I guess I'm not going anywhere.

He found the doorknob and left the bathroom. Immediately, his arms were pinned behind his back and the handcuffs were reapplied. Then he was led back to his seat, and the hood was removed.

"Hello, David," a new voice snarled, from somewhere close in front of him. This voice was all too recognizable, especially since David had been expecting to hear it soon.

"Hello, Thomas. Murder anyone, lately?"

"Not today. At least not yet."

"I'd prefer to keep it that way," said David.

"That's the spirit!" He felt a light slap on right forearm. "You keep that attitude, and you will live longer. So will your little cupcake."

"Cassie?"

"That's right," Thomas said, casually.

"Where is she? What have you done to her?"

Thomas answered with a laugh that David had heard once before, and had hoped to never hear again. "She's fine, so far. How long she stays that way depends upon how well you answer my questions."

David found himself in a deep quandary. He had almost accepted his role as cannon fodder for the mission planners, and he would rather die than answer any questions from Thomas. But he couldn't let them harm Cassie!

His only option was to stall for time. Help had come from unexpected sources before. Brother Matthew claimed his monastery friends had always been nearby. They could find him again by tracing his watch…which was missing.

Those goons took my watch! Brother Matthew has no way to find me. He probably doesn't even know I'm in trouble.

With his brief surge of hope dashed, David felt more helpless than ever. If he and Cassie were going to get out of this predicament, they would have to do it themselves. The cavalry wasn't going to ride over the hill and save them. Not this time.

Yet, what could he do? His only hope remained in stalling. He doubted whether he could tell Major Tom anything that would be very damaging to the mission planners, anyway.

Except that secret about the vehicles at the Medusae landing site being intact. Oh, and that even bigger secret that I suspect is true, but I fervently hope it isn't.

"Here come the ladies now," Thomas said.

Some footsteps thudded slowly down a stairwell. Then some chairs were shuffled around.

"Cassie?" he asked, cautiously.

"David! Are you OK?" Cassie's voice was strong, and she didn't sound like she was in any immediate distress.

"Just fine," he responded. Then he addressed his captor. "Thomas, if you harm her, I won't tell you anything."

Thomas laughed again. "That's not the way the game is played, David. I'll harm her anytime I want to. If you want me to stop, you need to give me answers I'll believe."

"That won't be necessary," a new voice said. It was a woman's voice, and it sounded vaguely familiar, yet David couldn't remember where he had heard it before.

"Interrogations are my specialty," growled Thomas. "I'll decide what's necessary."

"No, you won't. Not yet, at least."

The woman spoke with authority. David waited for Thomas to issue another challenge, but he didn't, making it obvious who was in charge of the situation.

That's useful information. And very welcome, too. Unless they're simply playing "good cop, bad cop."

The newcomer went on to say, "David, I've learned a lot about you. I suspect you're a very intelligent and reasonable person. There are two ways you and your friend can leave this room. You'll either walk out of here on your own feet, blindfolded, exceedingly wealthy, and able to continue your work…or, we'll drag your dead bodies out and throw them in a dumpster somewhere. It makes very little difference to me, I assure you."

"How wealthy is exceedingly wealthy?" he asked, trying to buy some more time while sounding reasonable. Of the two options offered, one definitely sounded better than the other.

But at what cost?

"Wealthier than you ever thought you could be, even in your wildest dreams."

"I don't know," said David. "Some of my dreams are pretty wild."

"Good," the woman said. "I like a person with ambition. But big dreams require large sacrifices. I need two things from you." Her voice softened a bit and became more cajoling. "The first is merely honest information. You appreciate the value of honesty, don't you, David?"

"It's one of my highest values," David admitted. This person was quite skilled at the "good cop" routine. "What's the second thing you need?"

"I'll get to that," she said. "For now, simply concentrate on answering my questions honestly. I'll be verifying your answers later, after giving you a shot of TCS-44. A smart guy like you might have heard of the potency of that drug. You'll tell me everything I want to know."

"Why don't I just give him the drug now, and save some time?" Thomas whined. His ego still sounded damaged from the earlier exchange when he was forced to back down.

The woman responded, "Because honesty and trust are almost as important to me as information retrieval. There's been a disaster on Mars, and the sole remaining crew member needs our help to survive. He needs your help, David. Won't you help him?"

The soft voice pleaded with him, but he didn't believe a word she said. "What disaster?" he asked.

"Our worst fears have come true. Two of the crew members went exploring in their rover, and your team has lost all contact with them. They're presumed dead, killed by faulty equipment, murdered by the negligence of the criminals who sent them to Mars. I need your help too, David. Please help me find these monsters and bring them to justice!"

Ominous dread gripped him as he listened to the intensity in his interrogator's voice.

Anna and Evelyn, dead? I still don't believe her. But why is she lying?

"How can I help?" he asked, with hopefully an adequate amount of eagerness in his voice.

"I said I needed two things. One is information that will help us find and punish the people who are responsible for this recklessly wasteful mission.

The other is to save the last remaining crew member. We want him to return to Earth safely."

David was starting to understand the picture this woman was painting. It was a bold, troubling landscape where good was bad and right was wrong. She would have him believe she was acting in the best interests of the Mars crew, but he knew better.

Besides, the safety of the crew was only one of his concerns. Of even greater importance was the overall success of the effort to explore Mars and someday settle the planet. He doubted whether these people cared about the true portrait of human existence.

He asked, "If you value the crew's safety, why did you try to sabotage the *Perseus* and the three vehicles at the Medusae landing site?"

"We didn't want them to land on Mars. Mars is a dangerous, hostile place. The thought of sending people to die there was too horrible for us to imagine. We had to act. We hoped they would be forced to return to Earth if they encountered some serious setbacks."

That part sounds at least partially true. Mars is a dangerous place, and they probably did want the crew to return to Earth. The best lies are concealed in half-truths.

As David considered the line this woman was feeding him, he decided on a bold strategy. His plan relied upon telling some half-truths of his own, leading up to a theory his abductors might be willing to hear. He had started to formulate this theory back when he and Cassie speculated about the ERV crash, but it still contained some major gaps. Perhaps in their eagerness, this woman and her colleagues would overlook those gaps and jump to a faulty conclusion.

The woman began to ask him a series of questions. David answered honestly, while trying to steer the conversation away from dangerous topics.

When asked about Cassie's identity, he merely said, "She's my sister, and she's visiting me from California." They seemed to accept this answer at face value, probably because they could easily verify his claim later, under the truth drugs.

Much to his relief, they didn't ask about any potential involvement Cassie might have in the mission. This allowed him to bypass the subject of Ben's involvement, too, at least temporarily. Many of the subsequent questions focused on the identity of the mission planners, however, and David's knowledge of Ben's activities placed him on thin ice.

He maneuvered, dodged, and foiled, mostly by telling his captors everything he could recall about the planners and their methods. This was the topic they obviously wanted to follow, so he led them down that path willingly. He revealed that the mission sponsors met regularly in Conference Room 4. He disclosed how he had infiltrated their meeting, how the telescope command worked, and how one needed a key to enter the room. Then he described their Alice in Wonderland avatars in great detail, right down to the Cheshire Cat's glowing eyes. These disclosures were all fairly harmless, or so David hoped.

When asked about the planners' motivations and agenda, he claimed honestly to have formed some theories, but he couldn't prove them yet. Sensing his opportunity, he built a bridge to the next topic he wanted them to follow.

"They obviously know more about you than you know about them," he casually commented.

As expected, Thomas and his superior jumped all over that statement, demanding to know what the planners knew about them.

"They know your identities, or at least some of them. That's why they killed Major Tom's account. Apparently, they learned about your opposition to the mission when you tried to plant explosives on their rockets prior to launch. They removed the explosives, of course."

This revelation led to considerable consternation in the room, much to David's delight. He hoped they would focus on the physical act of detecting the explosives, rather than Ben's later involvement.

He revealed the planners' belief that all three vehicles at the Medusae landing site were still intact. "That means the Mars crew can return to Earth anytime," he concluded, leading them closer to the edge of the pit he had dug.

As his interrogator asked another question, he listened closely for any signs of her true intentions. Her voice seemed to emanate relief, however, which matched her earlier story. Perhaps they really did want to help Doctor Sainsbury return safely to Earth. With a full supply of fuel and ERV components sitting on Mars at the primary landing site, his return should be much easier.

By now, David's head was protesting in pain from prior abuse. He tried to remain focused on giving honest responses that wouldn't betray him later.

Finally, one of the woman's follow-up questions squarely hit the target David had been steering her toward. She asked why the mission planners had preserved the initial ERV, but had allowed the second ERV to crash. He answered at length, spewing his latest, gap-ridden theory about the planners' motives, while pushing his captors over the edge of the abyss.

"The crash of the second ERV was planned," he stated angrily. "The mission sponsors offered several hints about this in their meeting, but at the time, I was too blind to see their true motives. I now firmly believe that they intended a 'flag and footprints' mission right from the start. Call it a 'smash and grab' mission, if you want. They care nothing about long-term exploration or scientific research. They created the mission as cheaply as possible, they ran it as cheaply as possible, and now they intend to end it as cheaply as possible. The Mars crew will come home, and that will be the end of Mars exploration."

More excited questions followed, proving the allure of this theory to his captors. In particular, his interrogator wanted to know why the mission planners would go to so much trouble to organize a one-time-only Mars mission.

"Probably because they'll make an obscene amount of profit. They'll sell their soil samples and planetary science data to the highest bidders. That alone should earn them billions. For the science community, foreign governments, or anyone else who's interested, buying the data and samples at an outrageous price would still be cheaper than mounting a new Mars expedition."

David knew he was skirting the line between fact and fantasy. Mars is a big planet, and future scientists might be willing to mount new expeditions to acquire more data or samples. Since his captors obviously saw little value in exploring Mars, he hoped they would dismiss the possibility. If they had any business sense, they would focus on the true part of his statement. Buying data and samples would indeed be much cheaper than mounting a new Mars mission.

He continued to press his advantage. "The Cheshire Cat is a businessman, through and through. People like him only care about short-term profit, rather than long-term benefits to humanity. Other spin-offs, like tele-robotics advances, entertainment, and advertising, have probably netted him billions of dollars already. Some of these spin-offs are one-time events, too. The bastard will pocket his money, move on, and forget all about Mars."

As David wove his tale of woe, he found himself almost believing his own half-truths. Could this theory actually be true? The biggest hole was simply the fact that a "flag and footprints" mission wouldn't have required a second ERV at all.

But Skye's "experts" claimed the first ERV couldn't generate enough fuel for the return trip to Earth. What if they were right? What if a second one was needed to finish the job?

Telemetry from Mars revealed the first ERV's fuel tanks were full. Could the planners have faked the telemetry?

To do so, they would need someone on the inside at Mission Support, and probably at JPL, too.

Someone like Ben.

Oh, crap.

His interrogators asked a few more questions, but David answered on autopilot. Had he stumbled upon the true, ghastly secret the mission planners had tried so hard to conceal? Had all his hopes, dreams, and efforts gone to pad the wallet of some wealthy businessman who cared nothing about the long-term survival and prosperity of the human race?

The questions stopped, but again, he hardly noticed. He didn't even wince when a needle was stuck in his arm and the same questions began all over again. As his resistance to evasion melted away, his final, independent thought was one of irony. In attempting to lead his abductors toward a faulty conclusion, he might have inadvertently led them to the truth.

CHAPTER 34
CRITICAL MASS

MarsDay 254, 2:19 p.m.
(August 8, 10:00 p.m.)

Voices from the darkness assaulted him. He understood disjointed words, woven together by others that made no sense to the mush of gray matter between his ears. He couldn't remember who he was, where he was, or how he had gotten here. All he cared about was sleep.

Leave me alone!

Yet the background voices persisted softly. Some of the broken phrases began to meld into sentences. Greater structure and meaning could be attained if he wanted to concentrate, but he didn't.

"We can't trust him."

"Agreed. His goals differ from ours."

"And if other options were removed? After the true rollover?"

"Perhaps, but then the need will be gone."

"Yes. In the morning, take them out into the woods. Hurry back, and we'll leave for Houston."

"How much are you offering?"

"Ten. No more."

"Done."

Then the voices went away. Silence returned, and sleep followed shortly thereafter.

MarsDay 254, 4:00 p.m.
(August 8, 11:43 p.m.)

The rumbling of Anna's stomach soon drowned out any muted buzzing of bees infiltrating her thoughts. In the clash between inner reflections, dreamlike fantasies, and physical needs, her stomach and bladder won. She uncurled herself, got up, and moved to the back of the rover to prepare a field ration packet and take care of other necessary business.

"Would you like one, too, Evelyn?" she asked, as she warmed up her meal. "I'm having a beef and bean burrito."

"Sure, why not. Make it two. A burrito for my last meal."

As they began to eat, Evelyn commented, "You've been very quiet today."

"Yes. You've given me a lot to think about."

"Now you know how I feel."

Anna smiled, as she realized the truth in the commander's words. The 254 days since launch had been mostly happy ones, filled with challenging work and unsurpassed thrills. Occasional periods of boredom or frustration seemed petty in hindsight. Yet through it all, she never suspected Evelyn was carrying so much weight on her shoulders. "Perhaps ignorance is bliss," she whispered.

Evelyn disagreed. "Knowledge is usually better, even when that knowledge is so disturbing. Or just plain wrong."

"You mean the incident with the water-valve sabotage."

"Yes. How do you suppose Ollie managed to frame you for that?"

"I don't know." Anna thought back to that part of the voyage and couldn't recall many relevant details. An unusual act of kindness did stand out in her memory, however. "One night, he surprised me by bringing me some tea at bedtime."

"He drugged you, perhaps?" asked Evelyn.

Anna twisted in her seat. "I do remember oversleeping the next morning." She also recalled prescribing Ollie some sleeping pills. Did he use her own pills against her? "But why would he drug me?"

"So he could borrow your location tracking bracelet, do his sabotage, and make it look like you were the one skulking about in the middle of the night," Evelyn said. "It's all so obvious, in hindsight. The backdrop is harder to fathom, though."

"Backdrop?"

Evelyn didn't explain her remark right away, but she eventually alluded to Kahuna's theory about Anna's Separation Anxiety Disorder. She had mentioned this briefly before, but now she held Kahuna's diagnosis under a microscope. "Without the assumption of your mental illness, I might have realized Ollie's deception earlier. So the more interesting question," mused Evelyn, "is how Ollie was able to fool Kahuna so thoroughly."

Anna found that question too disturbing to be interesting. It was yet another betrayal, this time by her personal psychologist.

As she chewed her meal, savoring the warmth and stringy texture of the food, she reaffirmed her commitment to the difficult decision she had reached after hours of soul-searching. It still felt right, and it was still what she needed to do.

"Evelyn," she said, "I understand why you withheld so much from me, and I forgive you. I also forgive David and Kahuna. None of you had much choice, since you felt you couldn't trust me."

The commander nodded. "And what about Ollie?"

"That will be much harder," she sighed, "but I'll try to forgive him, too. I don't want to end my life holding grudges and carrying baggage to whatever lies beyond. That's not very, uh, tidy."

"No, it's not," Evelyn agreed.

"For what it's worth, I've always admired and trusted you, Evelyn. Even when you pushed me so hard, I always knew why you were doing it. Sometimes I was pretty angry with you, but I always respected you."

"Thank you. That means a lot to me." Evelyn took another bite of her burrito and chewed thoughtfully. Then she added, "As we sit here, about to die, I find myself filled with so many regrets—a whole lifetime's worth. Anna, I wish the two of us could wipe the slate clean and start over again. You've been a wonderful companion, and yes, a friend, despite all my groundless suspicions."

"You know I've always had trouble with friends," Anna sadly contemplated. "They never seem to be around for very long. Always leaving, or dying, or something. I had hoped it would be different with us."

"Who knows. Maybe it will be."

Anna looked up sharply, hoping that Evelyn had come up with a way to forego their fate. Her slumped, dejected posture hadn't improved, however. "Oh, yeah," Anna muttered, in understanding. "In the Great Beyond."

They finished their meals in silence. Then Evelyn got up to retrieve something from her personal belongings. When she returned to the front of the rover, Anna locked eyes with her and saw some of the old fire that had been missing all day.

"The mission," Evelyn said, "has progressed to the point where I can no longer give you any orders. I can only make a final request."

Evelyn opened a small container and removed two caplet-shaped pills. They were red and bore no markings, nor did they need to. She handed one to Anna and kept another for herself. Then she methodically placed the container on the dashboard and clenched her pill in her fist. Anna found herself doing the same.

"I don't intend to linger until our fuel cell dies and our air fouls," said Evelyn. "I've always been a person of action. That's how I've lived my life, and it's also how I'll end it. There's only one final action to take."

Anna opened her hand and studied the tiny pill. She took a deep breath. "You're the commander. You need to go down with the ship. That means I should go first."

"We're a team," Evelyn responded. "We go together."

Anna nodded. "As long as you don't leave me behind. I couldn't bear that. Not again."

"I won't leave you," Evelyn promised.

She won't leave me!

Due to the gravity of the situation, Anna had no right to feel the surge of relief that pulsed through her veins. She marveled at her almost-physical response, realizing that she was in the process of making a minor psychological breakthrough. Confronting her worst fear had never been so easy before, and she needed some time to reflect on what she had just learned. She wasn't quite ready to die yet.

"I need to see one last sunset," she said, making up an excuse that would buy her some time. "And I need to view the stars once more. Then, I'll be ready."

"I understand."

The sun slowly dipped toward the horizon, and the light outside the windshield faded. Boulders cast long shadows that cloaked some shallow, snake-like gullies a few dozen meters in front of the rover. As they watched, the veils of darkness deepened.

"If you had your choice between Earth or Mars, where would you live?" asked Evelyn.

Anna didn't even need to think before she responded, "Mars. It's less crowded, and almost every sunset is just as beautiful as this one."

"Life is much harder here, though."

"Not really. Life presents its challenges everywhere," Anna mused. "Here, the obstacles are mostly physical and intellectual ones. Back on Earth, it's too much comfort, fear, greed, mental and psychological stress, apathy, and endless self-destructive distractions. By comparison, Mars is a paradise. It's a place where a person can really live."

As the stars came out, Anna felt the sands of her life draining away. Her hourglass was nearly empty. She reflected on her past and found it filled with her own regrets. If only she had more time.

But most of my regrets are a whole world away. When I went to Mars, I left a lot behind.

Good riddance.

I do wish I could have helped David, though. If Ollie was right, David will soon be joining me. Though we couldn't be together in life, perhaps we can rest together in death.

Her only other deep, pressing regret at the moment was not seeing Venus, the Earth, or Jupiter in the evening sky. Her best celestial friends were all morning planets. Jupiter would rise just after midnight, followed by the Earth a few hours later.

Her consolation prize was Saturn. Moving to the back of the rover, she easily found the ringed world through the small porthole in the back door. It was high in the eastern sky, blazing fiercely upon her through the thin atmosphere above.

Eventually, she returned to the front of the rover and sat in the passenger seat. The red pill was still smothered within her fist.

"I'm ready." She looked at Evelyn and nodded slightly. They locked their hands firmly together, and Anna swallowed her pill. Evelyn did the same.

For a few moments, nothing seemed to happen. Then she felt herself slipping away. The slide was long and luxurious, and she enjoyed the journey.

MarsDay 255, 1:02 a.m.
(August 9, 9:00 a.m.)

The ride seemed to last forever, but David wasn't in any hurry for it to end. Cassie was seated beside him, and they exchanged cautious, whispered words. From the softened bumps and roomy interior, he guessed they were in the back seat of a sedan-sized car. Cuffed hands and blindfolded eyes thwarted any attempts to explore his surroundings, however.

His head still throbbed, but the pain was tolerable. He had felt worse before and hoped he would feel worse again, at some point in the future. Any outcome that didn't involve a bullet in the head was seeming quite attractive right now.

Thomas's voice occasionally broke the monotony of the trip, as he talked to someone in the front seat. His companion sounded like one of the men David had briefly encountered the day before, probably Voice One. Most of the discussion was about guns, rocket grenades, and creative ways of killing terrorists.

The car finally slowed to a bumpy stop. "End of the line, Mars boy," announced Voice One.

Doors opened. Then he felt some rough hands grabbing him and pulling him out of the car, none too gently. His blindfold was removed, and he blinked at the sudden infusion of bright sunlight.

He was on the side of a deserted dirt road, a few yards from a highway. A forest of tall pine trees rose on each side of the road. The ground was muddy, and low, green ferns glistened with moisture beneath the canopy of trees. This place looked familiar, somehow. All was serene, except for some bird whistles and the busy chattering of a squirrel.

"Move." He was shoved from behind toward a wide path through the forest. Glancing back, he saw Thomas's rugged face sneering at him. The point of a gun prodded him in the back. On the other side of the car, Cassie was receiving similar treatment from a man he had never seen before.

They climbed a low rise and he immediately recognized a large outcrop of rock. It was The Castle, his regular lunch spot on his jogging trail. He was back near Nederland, so close to safety, yet so far away.

His captors pushed him and Cassie off the trail, behind the rock outcrop. Jumbled slabs of granite cluttered the base. David had scaled these rocks many times.

Thomas led him to one of the granite slabs and told him to sit. Cassie was pushed down beside him. They faced Thomas, who selected a higher slab to sit upon. The other man moved away, around the outcrop, probably to stand guard in case any pedestrians wandered along the trail.

Holding his gun in his hand almost lovingly, Thomas pulled a silencer attachment out of his pocket. He glared at David and said, "You know, Mays was my friend. I'm really quite upset that you killed him."

Mays? Oh, the other FBI guy, on that day at the Brainard Lakes parking lot.

"I didn't know he was dead. And I've never killed anyone in my life."

"What about two of the three people you sent to Mars?" asked Thomas. "They're dead, and it's all your fault. If you had done your job, instead of constantly prying into my business, they might still be alive."

"Are you referring to your attempts to sabotage the Mars mission from within the support team, Major Tom?"

"Of course. If I'd had my way, those fools would still be in space right now, on a free return trajectory back to Earth where they belong. But no, you had to interfere."

"Prying into your business was part of my job. As director, I'm responsible for every aspect of the support team's actions."

Tom attached the silencer to the end of the gun. "I suppose so. But that's all water under the bridge now. We both know the current situation. Despite the shoddy negligence of the mission sponsors and planners, there's still one crew member alive on Mars. We need to get him home safely."

So you keep saying, but I don't believe you. Anna is still alive, too.

David looked at Cassie, and then back at the gun in Thomas's hands. "Hopefully the next Shepherd will do a better job than I have." Escape was clearly impossible. Without the use of his hands, he had no chance of overcoming two powerful, armed assassins.

"The next Shepherd was supposed to be me," Thomas growled. "That will never happen now, once again thanks to you."

"You're welcome," David sneered, defiantly.

Thomas gripped his gun tightly. "Do you have any idea how much I'm looking forward to pulling this trigger?" Then he sighed, deeply. "But my boss has other ideas. She wants to offer you one last chance."

Say, what?

"We have a tiny little problem," continued Thomas. "You said it yourself. The next Shepherd might do a better job than you have. Or perhaps the next Shepherd will be a fool. The position is too important to be left to chance. None of our remaining operatives on the support team are in the chain of command. My boss doesn't like being forced into a situation where she can't control the outcome. She wants to cut you a deal."

"I'm listening," said David, trying not to sound overly eager. He doubted whether Thomas would be fooled. The man was a professional, and he had gone far out of his way to show David his only two choices: living or dying.

"She wants to release you and your sister, so you can return to your job. You'll work with Doctor Sainsbury, forward his reports to the media, and return him safely back to Earth. As long as you do your job well, I'll leave you alone. If you don't..." He raised the gun and pointed it squarely at Cassie.

"I see," said David. A lot was happening behind the scenes. If he accepted the offer, he would become cannon fodder for two groups, instead of one.

David's intuition was actually screaming at him to refuse the offer. It sounded way too good to be true, and therefore, it probably was. However, his guaranteed alternative was a bullet between the eyes, and not just for himself. For Cassie, too.

"Oh, I almost forgot," Thomas drawled. "As another incentive, in case you needed one, we'll pay you a small fee for your services."

"How much?"

"Ten million dollars. Twenty percent now, and the rest when Doctor Sainsbury is safely back on the Earth. Take it or leave it."

David glanced at Cassie, but she was staring only at the gun. Surprisingly, she hadn't uttered a word throughout the whole encounter. He wondered what thoughts were going through her head, and what she made of this crazy offer.

"Ten million dollars is a lot of money," he said, cautiously. "Why do I get the impression that you require more of me than simply doing my job?"

Thomas laughed heartily, and lowered the gun. "To the people who fund our efforts, $10 million is almost an insult. It's less than nothing."

"So you think your boss is thumbing her nose at me?"

"That's right, shithead," said Thomas. "But what I think doesn't matter. What do you think? Shall I leave here with two fewer bullets in my gun?"

"No," he answered quickly. "I mean, yes, I accept her offer."

"That's too bad," sighed Thomas shaking his head. "Like I said, I was really looking forward to pulling the trigger." He placed two small keys on the granite slab beside him, before hopping off. "Keep your nose clean, kid. Remember that I'm out there just praying for an excuse."

Then he tucked the gun into a holster under his arm and casually walked away. A minute later, they heard two car doors slam, followed by a motor racing into the distance.

David leaped over to Thomas's granite slab and picked up one of the keys. Struggling to bend his wrists the right way, he forced the key into the lock on his handcuffs. They opened.

As soon as he had freed Cassie, she wrapped her arms around him and squeezed tightly. "My god, David, I've never been so scared in my whole life. Nor as hungry. I could eat a moose right now."

Laughing, David held his sister close. He said, "With all this talk about Anna and Evelyn being dead, I've got to get back to my support team right away."

"Do you believe it's true?"

"No way. But it's safe to assume that Ollie is the saboteur we've been looking for, and he might be about to take some action. I've got to stop him, if it's not already too late."

Cassie asked, "What about the guys who kidnapped us? They won't like it if you interfere."

"I told them I would do my job, and that's what I'm going to do. If they don't like it, they can launch their $10 million bribe into the Sun for all I care."

With David leading, they walked along the trail as rapidly as their unsteady legs would carry them. Reaching Bill and Jennifer's house, they found two strange cars parked in front.

"Looks like we have company," said David.

"I wonder if they're friend or foe."

"Or if we'll be able to tell the difference."

Something about the setting aroused David's suspicions. Perhaps the thought of their way-too-easy escape, coupled with the too-good-to-be-true offer, gave him a feeling that he was walking into an ambush.

But who's left? The FBI? The guys from China? Someone else?

"Stay here." He pulled Cassie down to the ground behind a grove of wet ferns. "I'll do some scouting around."

Keeping to the trees, he darted around the side of the house and peeked into a basement window. He couldn't detect any people or movement inside. Then he slithered onto the back deck and looked through several windows. The main level of the house appeared to be deserted.

A side door leading into the garage was unlocked, and he cautiously slipped inside. As his eyes adjusted to the dark, he noticed both of Bill and Jennifer's vehicles still inside their nest.

Very odd. Plenty of cars around, but where are all the people?

He grabbed an aluminum baseball bat from a pile of sporting goods equipment in a corner. The bat wouldn't make a very effective weapon, but he didn't want to enter the house totally unarmed.

The door from the garage to a utility room opened silently to his touch. He quickly scouted the main level of the house without finding anyone. Then he slunk upstairs and checked all the bedrooms, noting suitcases on the floor of Cassie's bedroom and another guest room. Intending to probe the contents later, he hastened downstairs and repeated his search pattern in the basement. His own computer equipment was still in the downstairs office, but some of his belongings had been shuffled around a bit.

Scratching his head, he went back up to the main level of the house, opened the front door, and beckoned to Cassie. She stumbled across the driveway. Once she was safely inside, he locked the door behind her.

"Nobody's home," he said.

David retrieved an assortment of nutritional bars from the pantry and brought them over to Cassie, who had already taken off her shoes and crashed on the couch. "I think I'm going to lie here for about a year." She stretched languorously. Seeing what he was holding, she added, "After I eat ten of those energy bars, that is."

He left some of the food with her and brought the rest downstairs. Logging on took as long as it always did, only a few seconds, but the delay this time seemed to last forever. Finally, he was back in control of Shepherd in his virtual office.

The bulletin board in the main atrium was his first stop. One of his backup support directors had posted several internal memos.

- Still no word from the rover...
- Doctor Sainsbury asks to conduct a rescue EVA.
- Shepherd, please phone home!
- Crisis team unable to determine status of rover.

David's heart nearly stopped beating as he read the linked reports. Apparently, his captors had been telling the truth. Anna and Evelyn had left the *Perseus* two days ago. Their last transmission had been a routine check-in with Ollie after stopping for the first night. All telemetry from the rover had ceased after 3:00 a.m. Orbital images, not surprisingly, had failed to reveal any clues about the rover's current whereabouts or status.

After making direct contact with his team again and inventing an excuse to explain his absence, David talked to his technicians for the next ten minutes. The last telemetry from the rover indicated a sudden drop in benzene fuel levels. They were unable to come up with any reasonable theory explaining both the fuel and signal losses. These systems were completely independent. An accident affecting both systems at the same time was extremely unlikely.

So...it probably wasn't an accident. No surprise, there.

While continuing to ponder the rover situation, David moved on to the problem of the missing ERV. Sinbad, his team's best ERV systems expert, informed him that the second ERV had maintained its silence. Nothing had changed in the two days since he and David had talked last.

His next target was the psych team. If Ollie had sabotaged the rover, then Anna was innocent and the psych team had led everyone astray again. David had tolerated many past mistakes from the psychologists, starting back on the very first day of the mission when they had recommended unannounced drills to help the crew come together as a team.

His patience was exhausted. He sent a message to Arnold asking the security team to "fire" everyone on the psych team except Kahuna. Once again, he despised killing the avatars of any innocent people, but the Cheshire Cat was right. It was time for action. His intuition told him the psych team was a nest of Beta vipers.

As he sent the message, David heard some thumping noises from upstairs, followed by shouts. He killed his connection, grabbed the baseball bat, and charged upstairs.

The living room was filled with people. Several wore monk habits. In the center of the group, Cassie and Ben were locked in a long, tender kiss. Ben looked even more haggard than the last time David had seen him. Tears of happiness rolled down his flushed cheeks.

"David!" A warm body nearly tackled him from the side. The body belonged to Skye. A steamy kiss from her made his knees weak and his head throb anew. She snuggled up against his shoulder, wiping away some tears of her own. "We've been so worried," she said.

Then Bill came over and hugged David. He was followed by Brother Matthew, whose greeting was more dignified.

"You've been gone for two days!" said Bill. "Ben arrived last night, assuming you had been kidnapped by Beta. Then Skye showed up because you missed an appointment with her. Where the heck have you been?"

"It's a long story," he answered, "but Ben was right. We had a run-in with Thomas and his thugs. I can't believe they let us go."

Skye immediately released him. Her eyes grew wide. "They might have bugged you. You've got to ditch your clothes right now! Cassie, too."

To make her point, she unbuckled David's belt and pulled it off. Then she carefully removed a tiny device embedded in a fold of the leather. A hairlike antenna was attached.

"This one's mine," she said, "but there are sure to be others. Some will track your location, while others record your conversations. Mine does both. It's been in your belt for several days."

"You bugged me?" David's face grew warm, and he clenched his fists reflexively.

"Of course!" answered Skye. "That's how we knew you had returned this morning and were somewhere within three miles of the house. But no more words now. Get moving. Bill, help him, and I'll help Cassie. Jennifer, start a fire in the wood stove. After they give us their clothing, we'll burn it all."

Skye was an effective drill sergeant. Several people moved at once to fulfill her orders. Shaking his head, David retreated to his bedroom in the basement, followed by Bill.

Wearing fresh jeans and a bold "Ski Copper Mountain" t-shirt, he returned upstairs to the main level of the house just in time to witness a heated confrontation between Ben and Skye.

"Open. Now!" shouted Ben. Two monks were holding Skye, one by each arm, and Ben was trying to pry her mouth open.

"I'll swallow it!" Skye mumbled, while shaking her head and keeping her jaw clenched.

"If you do, we'll lock you in a bathroom until it comes out the other end." David had rarely seen Ben as upset as he appeared to be now. "And that's a promise," he added, with his nose only an inch away from Skye's.

Bill and Jennifer were watching the exchange from the kitchen, where they had been boiling a large pot of pasta noodles. Both had amused expressions on their faces. David threw them a questioning look, and Bill motioned for David to join them.

"Looks like the tense, unholy alliance between Ben and Skye has imploded," Bill remarked, while casting him a wink.

Jennifer added, "Skye won't give them her bug. It probably has our discussion at the restaurant recorded on it, so Ben's never going to let her keep it."

David grinned, and clapped Bill on the shoulder. Then he crossed the open room and put an arm around Ben, gently pulling him back.

"Uh, Ben, it might interest you to know that when we were at the restaurant in Boulder, I wasn't wearing my belt."

Ben took a step backward on his own and looked up at David. "No kidding?"

"No kidding."

Ben glared at Skye again and asked, "Did you swallow the bug?"

She shook her head, keeping her jaw locked tightly.

"Now I wish you had," said Ben. "For all the harm you've done in the past, it would have been just what you deserved."

David did warn Ben that the bug might have recorded his meeting with the mission planners in Conference Room 4, as well as everything after Beta kidnapped him. The earlier meeting probably wouldn't reveal anything of consequence, however.

Ben agreed, and added, "I'll want to hear the rest of the recording, too. I'm sure we can work out a deal so we can both listen together. Right, Miss Fontaine?"

Skye glanced at the two burly monks on each side of her and slowly nodded her head. She obviously understood that she wouldn't be going anywhere until they had all heard the recording.

Ben made a gesture, and the monks released her. She immediately removed the bug from her mouth and attached it to her own belt. Then she sat in a chair by the fireplace, rubbing her arms and glaring at the monks, visibly pouting at her rough treatment.

Laughing, David returned to his office in the basement. His dour mood returned, however, as soon as he thought of Anna in trouble on Mars. He had to find a way to help her. There must be some option they hadn't considered yet.

The commander knows the vehicles at the Medusae landing site are still intact. If the rover suffered a mechanical malfunction, she and Anna might try to walk there.

Unless the problem happened suddenly, and they didn't have time to get into their space suits before losing cabin pressure.

Would they even be able to find the Medusae habitat on foot?

Wait a minute...

A simple idea occurred to him. If Anna was still alive, he *could* help her reach the backup habitat safely. But he needed Ben's assistance.

He ascended the stairwell three steps at a time and found Ben talking to Jennifer in the kitchen. David grabbed his brother-in-law from behind. "I need to talk to you alone," he explained.

Ben followed him downstairs immediately, but not before Skye noticed his abduction and followed them. David tried to shoo her away, but she wouldn't budge. Since he was loath to waste any time arguing, he gave in and allowed her to accompany them.

When Ben and Skye were seated on the edge of the bed in his downstairs workroom, he outlined the current situation with regard to the rover emergency. Ben already knew what had happened, but Skye appeared quite surprised. His support team hadn't released many details of the rover situation to the press yet. He could tell that she wanted to ask some questions, but she remained uncharacteristically silent.

David forged onward, almost forgetting she was there. He spoke only to Ben, pointing out that if Anna was still alive, she and the commander might attempt to reach the Medusae landing site on foot. By now, it was early morning at their location. If they hadn't left the rover on the previous morning, they might be leaving right now.

Skye said, "But nothing is intact at the Medusae landing site."

A loud peal of thunder accented her words, as did an instant downpour of raindrops drumming on the roof.

He shook off Skye's interruption. "Ben, I need you to send a transmission. You need to turn on…"

"Stop!" barked Ben. He glanced at Skye, who was still sitting beside him with eyes that were like digital recorders, hungrily absorbing and memorizing every word being said. She probably had an electronic recorder planted somewhere on her body, too.

"I know what you're going to ask," Ben said. "And the answer is a most emphatic no. I can't do anything to help them."

"Yes, you can!" shouted David, losing his patience. "You can send a signal to the Medusae habitat! If it's still intact," he predicated, in deference to Skye's presence, "you can give Anna a target so she's not wandering about, lost on the surface!"

"David, you don't know what you're asking." Ben buried his face in his hands for several seconds, and then trailed his hands upward through his wispy hair. His look of anguish was plain to see. "Evelyn and Anna have moved beyond our ability to help them. Their fate is out of our hands. This is the way it must be, and we have to accept it."

"But I can't accept that. We have to do something!"

"Trust me," uttered Ben softly, but forcefully. "David, let them go."

David's anger guided his words. "If you won't help, I'll turn to someone who might." He intentionally tilted his head toward Skye, making the meaning of his threat clear.

Ben buried his face in his palms again. Shaking his head, he moaned, "I never should have told you anything, David. I thought I could trust you, but I should have just walked away. Now my weakness could destroy everything. Did you tell Beta about anything I said?"

Cassie sauntered into the room and placed a heaping plate of spaghetti on David's desk. Then she sat on the edge of the bed beside Ben and wrapped her arm around him tightly. Her new outfit was similar to her old one, a light blouse with jeans. Since her favorite jacket was now ash in the fireplace, her shoulders were bare.

"I don't know what I told them," David said, answering Ben's question. "Most of the time, I was half conscious or drugged. I probably told them a lot, but I tried my best to redirect their attention away from certain things."

"You were amazing, David!" Cassie hadn't picked up on the somber mood in the room, so her joyful outburst seemed totally out of place. "You spun a story so believable that you almost fooled me! You played their own words and psychological games right back against them, better than even I could have. I think they bought your crazy story, hook, line, and sinker."

"Even while under the truth drug?" asked David.

"Yes, even while drugged. You gave the same story again, almost word for word." Cassie shivered. "The passion in your voice, and the conviction…I thought for sure that you would slip, and then they would kill us both. How did you manage to beat them, David?"

He shrugged. "Again, I don't know. I don't remember much, though I do recall actually starting to believe my own tale. Maybe that was enough to carry me through."

"Amazing," Ben said. "We have so much to discuss. But we need to resolve our current difficulty first." He glanced at Skye, directly implying that in his opinion, she was the difficulty.

David's anger resurged. "You still aren't going to help me, are you."

"I'll most certainly help you," said Ben, "by giving you advice. Or consider it orders from the mission planners, because this is also what they would tell you. Do your job. Run the support team efficiently. Forget about everything else I told you. That knowledge can only make the situation worse."

If one more person tells me to do my job, I'm going to explode.

"And what about Skye?" asked David. "I'm obligated to tell her everything I know about the mission planners, including some of what you told me."

Ben sighed. "I'll think of something. Perhaps we can cut her a deal to keep her quiet about certain things for just a little while longer."

"I'm always open to deals," Skye laughed, tossing her hair over her shoulder playfully. "But if you want my temporary silence, the price is high. I want to know everything about the mission planners and sponsors, from the inside, and from the beginning.

David felt some of his anger towards Ben melting away, though plenty remained. Ben was going to have his hands full, trying to negotiate with Skye. The two of them were perfect opposites, the ever-cryptic <chicken_little> and the insatiable information sponge. Each deserved the torments of the other.

How had Bill referred to them? A tense, unholy alliance? They were surely that, and then some.

CHAPTER 35
REALITY

MarsDay 255, 10:00 a.m.
(August 9, 6:13 p.m.)

    A warm breeze gently rocked Anna's hammock. She rested between the only two ash trees on her landlord's block, possibly all of southeastern Michigan, to survive the onslaught of the Emerald Ash Borer beetle.
    Her long hair dangled off to one side of her pillow. Songbirds serenaded her from the branches above. Fierce sunshine baked her pale arms, legs, and face relentlessly. SPF-10 sunblock protected her, as it usually did when she studied outside.
    Her open textbook rested heavily in her arms. The final exam in her last graduate class was tomorrow. Her college life was drawing to a close.
    With a happy sigh, she imagined what it would be like to hand in her completed test papers. Of course she would pass the course. The only question was whether she could maintain her straight-A average. This semester had been tough, but she was tougher.
    "Ow!"
    Anna's soft cry was one of surprise, rather than pain. Though the sudden impact of her head bumping a wall was enough to wake her, she had barely felt it.
    She longed to return to the pleasant safety of her dream, but her head bumped the wall again, pushing her closer to consciousness. Anna had never been able to wake up quickly. She needed more time.

What's a wall doing in my dream, anyway? Why am I even dreaming? I'm supposed to be dead.

She rolled over and cautiously opened her eyes. The interior of the rover was much brighter than usual, though the close ceiling of her coffin bed shaded her eyes from any direct glare of the overhead lights. Her bed rocked gently from side to side, which meant the rover was moving.

But that's impossible! We don't have any fuel!

Her thoughts were a murky fog. She felt drugged, like that morning after Ollie had served her tea in bed. A surreal incandescence seemed to emanate from the walls of the rover. She couldn't feel anything at all, not even warmth or coldness. Perhaps she was a disembodied spirit?

"You're awake!"

The voice was followed by footsteps. Then Evelyn's smiling face beamed down upon her from above.

"Evelyn, you're glowing!"

"Most likely an aftereffect of the drug," said Evelyn. "It's potent stuff. Two pills might have killed you. Three would take down an elephant."

Anna slowly digested Evelyn's words.

That must mean I'm still alive!

This knowledge should have made her profoundly happy, but in her groggy state of abstraction where she couldn't even feel the mattress beneath her, part of her still longed to return to her idyllic dream. That wish faded quickly, however. Being alive on Mars was far better than lounging on a hammock in Michigan.

"You didn't swallow your pill, did you, Evelyn."

"Nope."

"And why did you let me swallow mine?" Anna asked.

"Pick a reason. Consider it a final loyalty test, or rather a futility test. You might have hidden an oxygen flow regulator somewhere so you could walk back to the *Perseus*. Or perhaps, well…let's not go into the other reasons just yet. They'll be obvious soon enough."

"And our fuel?" asked Anna. "The gauges were wrong?"

With the materials available, Evelyn couldn't have created any fuel. Anna recalled that fact very clearly.

"The gauges were accurate," said Evelyn. "But I managed to find some fuel."

While Anna was pondering that remark, the rover tilted wildly. She was almost thrown from her bunk but managed to hang on by grasping a handle above.

"Sorry!"

The apology came from the front seating area. Anna had forgotten that the rover required a human driver.

Ollie? Ollie!

"You called Ollie!" Anna cried. "How did you convince him to help us?" She reached out an arm to hug the commander, but she backed away.

"No," Evelyn answered gently. Then she called to the front of the rover, "Mo, pull over, please. It's time for some introductions."

Anna reeled in confusion, even as the rover stopped swaying. She closed her eyes and listened as another set of footsteps approached. When she dared to look up, a strikingly handsome stranger was standing before her. He wore a faded, full-length maroon coverall that matched her own. His shining skin was darker than coal. Slightly taller than Evelyn, his wispy body and rugged features looked very familiar.

As Anna gaped, Evelyn wrapped her arm around the stranger's slender waist. Their pose mimicked a photograph taped to the wall of Evelyn's cabin. Realizing the man's identity, Anna was overwhelmed with dread.

Evelyn confirmed her fears. "I'd like you to meet Morgan Day," she said. "My husband."

Morgan gently shook Anna's limp hand. "Pleased to meet you," he said, in a deep voice containing warm, rich harmonics. "Call me Mo. Everyone does."

Anna moved her mouth, but no sounds would emerge. After several tries, she managed to whimper, "But you're dead!"

"That's right. I'm just as dead as you are."

"I was afraid of that," she moaned. She closed her eyes again, and laid her head back on her pillow.

Evelyn and her dead husband traded some whispered words. They assumed Anna needed more time to recover from the drug. Footsteps moved to the front of the rover, and the vehicle began to move again.

"Please pardon my husband's teasing," Evelyn's voice cooed. "Drink some water and get some rest. We'll talk later." Then she stepped away.

Anna didn't want to rest. She wanted answers. Her mind churned through several possibilities, each more bizarre than the last.

Perhaps heaven is a place where one's deepest wishes are granted. That must be what's happening!

Evelyn sought a reunion with her dead husband. She also wanted to explore Mars in a fully fueled rover. Both wishes have come true in her afterlife.

Testing my theory should be simple. All I have to do is wish for something that I desperately desire.

Anna concentrated on visualizing her mother's face. She would give anything to visit with her parents for a few minutes. She didn't know what she would say to them, but it really didn't matter. If her theory was true, she could talk to them anytime.

When she opened her eyes, the midsection of the rover was still deserted. She sighed with disappointment.

A water bottle was tucked under her arm. A few cautious sips helped to clear her thoughts. Gaining courage, she sat upright and downed the contents of the bottle in several large gulps. Her spinning head slowly stabilized. The objects around her lost their lustrous glow, but she still couldn't feel her own body. She tried to stand, but her legs were too weak, and she collapsed heavily to the floor.

With Evelyn's help, she staggered up front to the passenger seat. The resurrected Morgan Day was still driving the rover, cautiously navigating through a narrow valley fraught with large boulders and treacherous side-slopes. Ranges of tall mountains lined both sides of their route. The specter seemed to be following a set of parallel grooves, possibly the remnants of a large dust devil.

"You're still here," Anna acknowledged, more to herself than to the man who drove the rover. "I didn't imagine you."

"Still here, and still dead." He looked at her and winked. "At least as far as most people back on Earth are concerned. Welcome to the club."

Standing behind the passenger seat, Evelyn slapped at her husband's shoulder. "No more teasing, Mo." To Anna, she said, "You're alive. We all are."

Still alive, again!

Since the sun was high overhead and slightly in front of them, she surmised the time was just before noon, and they were traveling east. One glance at the clock on the dashboard confirmed part of her guess.

"Are we near the Medusae landing site?"

"We won't be going there," said Evelyn.

"Why not?"

Their driver took his eyes off his route for a moment to glance back at his wife. "We should start from the beginning," he said.

Anna released a lever on the side of her chair and spun it around backwards. Since the rover only had two seats, Evelyn retreated a few steps and sat on the edge of her coffin bunk. Though more relaxed, her posture hinted at inner turmoil. Such hesitation was rare for Evelyn. Lack of eye contact was the most obvious indicator, along with minor tugs and pulls on her jumpsuit.

Encouraging her to begin, Anna asked, "What really happened in Antarctica, four years ago?" This question seemed reasonable, given Morgan Day's surprising presence. If they were still alive, she hadn't heard the real story of what happened there.

Antarctica was a good place to start, Evelyn agreed. "Morgan's accident was a sham, the first of many. Our mission sponsors whisked him away, along with the two members of his engineering team, long before they were in any danger from the storm. They began their training in isolation, and now they're here on Mars."

Anna searched the commander's face for any signs of deception, but found none. Her story was simple, and it began to explain the presence of her husband in their rover. But it was also impossible.

She asked, "How did they get to Mars? By taxi?" Literally, people couldn't appear on Mars out of thin air.

"On our backup habitat, of course."

Whoa. Now her tale is losing all credibility. Or is it?

Three years ago, the launch, voyage, and landing of the backup habitat was intended to be a full dress rehearsal for their own mission. The only thing missing was a crew. Could three people have snuck aboard and survived the journey, without anyone knowing?

"So you're claiming that ours wasn't the first human expedition to reach Mars?" As Anna fought her disbelief, she also suppressed a slight pang of disappointment.

"Technically, that's not quite correct," said Evelyn. "Right from the start, our mission sponsors planned to send a six-person expedition to Mars. And that's exactly what they've done. They could have done it the NASA way, by waiting until they could send six people together in a huge, expensive, and fragile habitat. Instead, our sponsors simply split us into two groups and staggered our launch window by two years. We're all part of the same expedition."

"Our mission patches even match." Mo pointed to a patch on the sleeve of his jumpsuit. The simple design matched the patch on Anna's sleeve. He added, "From day one, we were deeply concerned about a perceived weakness in most of the earlier Mars exploration plans. Despite the redundancy built into various hardware and software systems, the most important component of the mission was also a single point of failure."

"The crew?"

"Right," said Evelyn. "Many of the more probable failure scenarios, like a serious design flaw in the habitat, could easily kill an entire crew. It wouldn't matter how many people were aboard. Once a whole crew died on Mars, the exploration program would be subject to the brutal slashing of vultures and naysayers back on Earth."

"We can't allow a single stupid mistake to kill the program," Mo said. "It's too important. People can die, but the program must go on."

He slowed the rover and stopped on a relatively flat area. Then he activated the comm system. "Wendy, ten minute break. Over."

"Roger. Ten minute break," came a woman's crisp reply over the speakers. Obviously, the communications array had been repaired while Anna was unconscious.

Mo turned his chair to face hers. "You see, Anna, I'm not going back to Earth."

"Never?"

"Never," he firmly repeated. "Why should I? Everything I ever wanted is right here. And everyone." He smiled at Evelyn, who nodded her approval.

Anna gawked in disbelief. How could he be so enamored by his surroundings to say he's never leaving? Yet, her own brief excursions onto the Martian surface had left her with similar feelings. This was a powerful, harsh place. She still longed to tame it.

"You speak with such certainty. What have you and your crew been doing on Mars for these past two years?"

Mo laughed, grimly. "Mostly making mistakes. And learning from them. Since we're all still alive, I'd say we've done rather well. That was our top goal, after all. Learning how to stay alive on Mars, so we could pass that information to your crew, and you could do better. All other concerns were secondary."

"I've been in constant contact with Mo," admitted Evelyn, "since before we even left the Earth. We've benefitted a lot from his experiences."

That explains her amazing ability to make good decisions despite a lack of data. She cheated!

If Mo and Evelyn had been sharing information for so long, he must have the ability to send messages to others on Earth, too. She desperately hoped so.

"Ollie mentioned David, er, Shepherd, in his gloating farewell message. He's in trouble, back on Earth! Is there anyone you can contact and ask to investigate?"

"Already done," said Evelyn. "It was one of Mo's first actions after hearing Ollie's message. Yes, he was listening to everything we said and heard, through my space suit comm unit. His rover was parked only a few hundred feet away, out of sight, the whole time. We were never alone."

Evelyn went on to explain their desperate gamble. By taking a long excursion in the rover, she had risked her life to prove the loyalty of her crewmates. She had also hoped to elicit information about the identity of the saboteurs. "Alas, Ollie only spoke in generalities. We'll forward his message to our sponsors, and we can use it to make some better assumptions, but he revealed less than I had desired."

"They must be a large energy cartel," speculated Mo, "since they have such a keen interest in preserving the status quo when it comes to long-term energy production and distribution. Since so many energy companies and cartels have merged lately, there aren't many suspects left."

Evelyn nodded her agreement, and she traded more guesses about the identity of the saboteurs with Mo. Anna was less interested in this topic. Now that she had a reasonable assurance someone back on Earth was trying to help David, her thoughts returned to Mo's earlier statement about his intention to remain on Mars for the rest of his life.

"Mo, you said you weren't going back to Earth. Did you mean you can't go back? Can I still return, if I want to?"

Frowning, Mo claimed that none of them could return, even if they wanted to. "Remember the SEA slogan, Anna. 'Going to Mars is easy, living on Mars is easy, but returning to Earth is really tough.' Our return systems require a lot of testing, including at least one full practice flight where we plan to send a massive quantity of geological samples back to Earth. Developing a reasonably safe return capability will take at least 10 years, and possibly a lot longer."

Anna was forced to agree with his conclusion. She had always dreaded the return part of the mission. Using any way of measuring risk, the return trip was the most complex and dangerous part of their mission plan, by far.

Why did I always assume I would be returning to Earth? Now that I'm here on Mars, why not stay for a while?

The urge to stay was powerful, but she had conflicting emotions too. Anger dominated the mix. She had been misled, yet again. In countless media appearances, she had told everyone listening on Earth about their plans to return. It was all another big lie.

Her anger continued to rise and finally boiled over. "You never asked me what I want! What if I don't want to stay?"

"You do want to stay," Evelyn calmly replied. "You said it yourself, last night. One reason you were chosen for the mission was because you didn't have any firm attachments back on Earth."

Yes...but, you still should have asked me! And what about David? Will I ever be with him?

Mo added, "Besides, dead people don't have many options."

"We can still send you back, eventually, if you really want to go," said Evelyn, "But even in the advertised mission plan, an ERV problem might have delayed your return to Earth. You've already accepted that risk, so nothing has changed."

She saw the truth of Evelyn's statement, but it didn't calm her much. What gave her greater pause was Mo's comment about dead people having few options. What did he mean by that?

Once I swallowed that red pill, I gave up any hope of returning to Earth. I really am dead. And yet, I also have a second chance. I can still make a difference here.

As she pushed her anger aside, Mo's choice of living on Mars suddenly seemed obvious. People chose to live in Colorado or Alaska or France all the time. Why not Mars?

Pondering the enormity of the challenges ahead, she found herself in awe of the man driving the rover. He had shown incredible courage. Before leaving the Earth, he knew he would die on Mars, even if he managed to reach the surface alive.

But why had he and his crew taken such risks? Prior to the first habitat landing, no one knew whether the landing systems would work properly. What was their hurry?

She voiced her thoughts. "Why didn't you wait until your landing systems had been fully tested and you had acquired more knowledge of the environment at the landing site?"

Mo winced and shook his head. He raised his hands to his temples, as if he was in great pain. "You said the four-letter word, Anna: wait. People have been saying that filthy word for 40 years. Wait for this. Wait for that. Wait until we know more—but there's always more to learn! Wait until the trip is safer—but it will never be safe enough! Wait until all our problems on the Earth are solved —but we'll always have problems on Earth! Wait until the triple-rotating blapschnick is cheaper, or we can use nuclear propulsion, or we've created a base on the Moon in order to learn how to live on Mars, or the electronics are more advanced, or whatever. We could delay and add complexity forever! Hey! Why not save everyone the trouble and confess right up front? We're never going to do anything!"

Evelyn reminded her, "You've said these same things yourself, Anna. To the media."

"I suppose I have. My own words have come back to bite me."

She had often preached about the need for society to get off its collective butt and do a real Mars mission. Their true enemy had always been complexity. In the face of technical uncertainties, governmental inertia, and public skepticism, mission complexity would continue to increase over time. A Mars mission involving human explorers would become ever more dangerous and therefore less likely to happen. A breakthrough event was urgently needed to change the paradigm.

Mo said, "Seriously, about running more tests, the Mars Society ran hundreds of simulated Mars missions years ago, complete with rovers, habitats, and surface EVAs. Almost anyone in the world could spend two weeks 'on Mars.' Later NASA lunar simulations even used a huge pressure chamber back on Earth. They couldn't simulate the lighter gravity, but everything else was very realistic. We've already learned a lot, without even going anywhere. At some point, you have to draw the line."

"But you could have tested the landing, at least. Right?"

"How? And why?" Mo erupted into a heaving belly-laugh.

Evelyn grinned as she explained, "Unless you send human pilots to Mars, how can you fully test a human-rated landing system? Automate everything and do a trial run? A fully automated habitat landing system is about as useless as a hole in a space suit. It's way too complex! And it will never be used again! It's a great way to waste time and throw money out the airlock."

As the last remnants of Mo's mirth subsided, he pointed out that airplane landings still weren't fully automated back on Earth, despite major economic reasons for doing so. "And that's a much easier task. Again, reduce the complexity. Send people, instead."

The counter side of the argument made even better sense to Anna. She had wondered often what would have happened if the first habitat landing on Mars had failed. It would have been a spectacular, expensive failure, and it might have led to delays, frustration, and pessimism in the space program. NASA was currently suffering this problem, due to their failed Aitken Basin probe on the Moon.

And what would the final lesson have been? Don't send machines to do a human's job?

Yet sending three test pilots to Mars carried even greater risks. NASA shuttle launches had been grounded for two years after the Columbia reentry accident. Had the first habitat crashed while landing on Mars, the public outcry would have been far worse if the media had known that human pilots were aboard.

Aha! I know the mission planners' little secret now. And it's totally brilliant!

The mission planners had bypassed the whole public relations dilemma by sending an already-dead crew to Mars. If they had crashed during landing or died while exploring the surface, no one back on Earth would ever have known.

Despite her renewed sense of wonder, Anna continued to play the devil's advocate because she loved a good argument. Stubbornness was a deep part of her German heritage. Her father had refined the ability to argue the paint off a house.

She coyly stated, "Even with humans guiding a landing, things can go wrong. We just saw an example of that a few days ago, when the second ERV crashed. A better, automated landing system might have made a difference."

Mo and Evelyn exchanged amused glances. Then Mo said, "Actually, that landing was completely successful."

She yelped in surprise. "But it was way off-course, to the southwest! There's nothing down there but steep crater walls and rugged highlands terrain!"

"And our new home," laughed Evelyn. "I guess I didn't mention that yet."

Now the picture was perfectly clear. Anna realized that Mo and his crew had been very busy. Over the past two years, they must have used their rover to move their habitat, cargo, and ERV equipment. Their new base could be anywhere within 500 kilometers of the original Medusae landing site.

Mobility had always been an important part of their published plans. The cargo manifest included several sets of inflatable tires. Officially, these were needed for towing the empty cargo vehicle near the *Perseus* so they could use it as a garage. Later, they had planned to transport the ERV fuel tanks and rocket engines near the *Perseus*, too, prior to constructing the final Earth Return Vehicle.

"Wait until you see the base!" cried Mo, with enthusiasm. He recounted how they had constructed the base underground, using mining equipment to expand a lava tube running deep into the side of a thousand-meter-high cliff. Explosives and tele-operated robots had done most of the work.

"Choosing the right location was the most important task, and the most difficult," he explained. "Among other criteria, we looked for layers of porous rock beneath layers with more density and strength. Finally, after months of searching, we found a spot that satisfied Zen. The lava tube was an unexpected bonus."

"Zen Honda is their geologist," Evelyn added. "His wife Wendy, a doctor, is the other crew member. Both are engineers and fellow Navy brats. I've known them a long time, and you'll get along great with them."

"Wendy is a real doctor?"

Evelyn nodded, adding, "She's primarily a field medic and combat surgeon."

"Thank you, God!" One of Anna's greatest fears had always been a crew member suffering a serious illness or injury. She had never performed a real surgery, and part of her doubted whether she could.

Anna closed her eyes and leaned back in her seat, tilting her head upward. Stretching her neck muscles in this manner helped to relieve some of the tension building in her shoulders. It also gave her a chance to think for a few moments, uninterrupted.

If everything she had just heard was true, and she had no reason to believe otherwise, some aspects of her own situation had clearly changed. She would soon be living in a different habitat. Rather than fitting into a three-person crew, she was now part of a six-person crew.

Well, a five-person crew, most likely.

She tallied the functions of each person on Mars. The others were all engineers, with dual experience in geology and medicine.

"Am I still the only microbiologist on the crew?" she asked.

"Yes," answered Mo. "We're very fortunate Doctor Sainsbury was the guilty party instead of you. His geology experience would have been useful to us, but not as critical as your microbiology and botanical skills. We desperately need your help to jumpstart our crop production."

A loud beep from the dashboard served as a reminder that the ten-minute break was over. Mo opened a comm channel again. "Wendy, time to wake up. I'll take point. Over."

"Roger, waiting for you to take point."

Morgan lurched the rover forward. This part of the valley was smoother and wider, and he was able to build up some speed. The only serious obstacles were some sand dunes, which proved easy to avoid.

They soon approached a stationary rover. As they passed, Anna caught a brief glimpse of the driver. Her new crewmate had pale skin and short, dark hair. She looked older than Anna, but perhaps a few years younger than Evelyn. Her friendly wave, which Anna returned, left a good first impression.

I never imagined meeting new people on Mars.

They ate lunch on the move. Soon, the valley narrowed until it tapered to a bottleneck less than a kilometer wide. Sheer cliffs towered on both sides of the rover. Mo reduced his speed to a crawl as they pierced the narrows. Then they were in the clear again. Wide plains awaited them, and Anna could see forever. The rover's speed increased as they paralleled the cliff face to the right about a kilometer away. Their direction of travel remained southeast.

Anna sat up in her seat and stretched. She noticed a tingling sensation in her arms and legs. The tranquilizing effects of Evelyn's drug were finally wearing off.

She had been lost in thought for the latter part of their journey. While assimilating all that she had just learned, her thoughts kept drifting back toward speculation about the mission planners.

I still didn't know who they are, or what their true intentions are.
Why don't I just ask? Perhaps Mo and Evelyn already know.

She cleared her throat. "Evelyn, who are the mission sponsors? And why did they send us to Mars?"

For a moment, Evelyn didn't answer. She had placed a crate of food on the floor behind Anna and was using it as a third seat. Anna swung her chair around to face her again.

"I'll call our main sponsor Cat," Evelyn finally said. "I don't know his real name. He seems to genuinely care about the future of humanity. Saving our environment and our species is important to him."

Mo agreed, adding that in his numerous private discussions with Cat, the topic of the future was always a central theme. "He's a visionary. When you talk to him, he stretches your mind, and you come away happy. He yearns for a future of unlimited potential where mankind unfurls its sails and takes flight throughout the solar system, tapping into the staggeringly abundant resources that surround us. Many of the unsolvable problems plaguing society, like terrorism, poverty, warfare, and environmental incompetence have no place in his future. They're swept away by a tidal wave of universal wealth, knowledge, and freedom."

"So in other words, he's a Trekkie?" Anna scoffed.

"You might say that," agreed Mo. "But Cat's also a firm realist. He accepts that society will probably fill the void by inventing new problems. Also, his roadmap won't be easy to accomplish. Quite the opposite. He sees all life on Earth locked in a desperate struggle for survival. If the human race doesn't grow up soon enough, we'll destroy ourselves and everything around us. I happen to agree with him."

Based on past discussions, Anna knew that David would also agree. "But how does establishing a permanent base on Mars change anything?"

Evelyn said, "Ollie was right to fear us. A thriving outpost on Mars changes everything. What he called chaos, we call opportunity. Once humanity is a multi-planet species, the door will be wide open, never to be controlled or slammed shut again by a few shortsighted or greedy individuals. Greed of a different kind will take over. It won't happen overnight, but eventually, private enterprise will thrive."

"Think railroads, as an example of what's possible," said Mo. "Railroads opened the American West to development, creating a great nation in the process. Private industry built the railroads, reaping enormous profits. The U.S. government merely cleared away the red tape and served as an anchor customer. At the time, many politicians opposed the massive cost, scope, and ethics of the project. Without a real need, an existing, vocal market at the destination, the railroads might never have been built."

"And you plan to be that market."

He nodded. "We're building the infrastructure to support a small research base. As support staff are added, commercial interests will follow, and new bases will be built. New ideas will flourish. The cost of transport, as well as the risk, will drop dramatically. Humanity will explode into the cosmos."

"Now who's the visionary?" Anna scoffed again. "Or the hopeless optimist? And what about those other problems we'll invent along the way? You might be opening Pandora's Box."

"We might indeed," agreed Evelyn. "We don't know what will happen. That's the nature of chaos. The only certainty is that nothing will happen by itself. Unless some sort of aggressive action is taken, humanity will soon deplete its energy reserves, wither, and die, probably taking all other life on Earth with it."

"And Ollie's plan? It sounds like his people want the same thing you do."

Mo nodded again. "But apparently, they intend to control it all. Control is a two-edged sword. The ability to control something implies the ability to destroy it. Don't you see? That's where the real danger is. We can't place our children's future at the whimsical mercy of a few individuals, even if they truly have our best interests in mind, which I strongly doubt."

His voice had adopted a pleading tone, and Anna found her stubborn pessimism crumbling. The past 40 years of stagnation in the space program bore strong evidence in support of his arguments. Politicians and special interest groups had even obstructed NASA's latest, carefully mapped plans for lunar exploration. She agreed with Evelyn that aggressive tactics were required to smash the status quo.

"And if Ollie's friends try to stop you?" she asked.

Evelyn admitted their precarious position. "We know the snakes are out there, lurking in the shadows, and now we've glimpsed their power. They could still stop us if they learn about what we're doing before we're ready. To become self-sufficient, the new base will need a steady stream of food, equipment, and spare parts for years. Most of all, we'll need settlers we can trust with skills we can use."

"And what about Ollie? He'll try to stop you, too."

They lapsed into silence again. Anna didn't need her question answered. Their base would urgently require a second habitat in case the first one failed. Once Ollie learned of their intentions, he wouldn't leave the *Perseus* willingly, even if he had somewhere else to go.

After another half-hour of driving, Mo slowed the rover to a crawl. "We're home! Welcome to *Pegasus Base!*" he warmly announced.

Anna recalled her Greek mythology studies. Pegasus was a mighty winged horse, born from the blood of the slain Gorgon Medusa. It seemed an appropriate, romantic name for her future home.

Anna strained her neck to catch her first glimpse of the base on the flat plains before her. The site was less than inspiring. Pieces of mining equipment and several arrays of solar panels were scattered about the landscape, seemingly at random locations.

"Where's the *Pegasus* habitat?" she asked.

"Underground," said Mo. "I told you about our excavations." He pointed toward a round opening in the cliff face. The cave grew larger as the rover approached. She spotted other equipment nearby, like a communications relay and some mostly-buried fuel tanks.

They climbed a slope, and Mo drove the rover carefully into the cave. The deepest part of the interior had metallic walls that looked vaguely familiar, like something she recalled from a boring training session on garage construction.

That's it! We're inside a garage!

She now recognized the back part of the cave as the shell of a cargo vehicle. Mo's team had tipped it over and buried it deeply into the side of the cliff.

The rover pivoted until it faced the cave entrance. They waited for Wendy to park her rover nearby and hike up the incline. When she was inside the garage, Mo typed an instruction on his dashboard console. An iris doorway closed, sealing the garage from the plains outside. Darkness swallowed them completely until Mo turned the rover's headlights on.

Anna heard some scrapes and thumps on the roof. In a moment of panic, her mind flashed back to several nights ago when Ollie had performed his sabotage. The others were watching her closely, so she forced herself to appear as calm as they were.

"I'm inside," announced Wendy, over the intercom. "All clear."

Mo typed another instruction, and the rover began to vibrate. Then Anna got one of the biggest shocks in her life.

It's raining. Oh my God. It's raining on Mars!

A torrential downpour scoured the rover. Water streamed down the windshield from above. Anna sat with her mouth gaping open. As she heard soft laughter around her, she realized why her companions had been watching her so closely.

"I thought you would get a kick out of our car wash," chuckled Mo. "It gets me every time, too, right here." He thumped his chest proudly to illustrate his point.

"But how much water does this use?" Anna asked incredulously.

Mo confirmed a lot of water was pumped each time, but he didn't sound concerned. "Filtering and recycling most of the water is slow, but simple. We send it outside to an unpressurized holding tank. Normal daytime temperatures boil and evaporate the water. As vapor pressure builds, condensation is captured and routed back to a pressurized holding tank. We even generate some energy from the steam during the process, though not quite enough to run the pumps."

"A steam engine on Mars." Anna shook her head in amazement. "But why bother to clean the rovers at all?"

"We usually don't, unless we need to do some maintenance on them," said Mo. "I just wanted to impress you."

"Consider me thoroughly impressed. But I'm also quite concerned about every drop of wasted water."

Mo laughed. "We're swimming in water, as you'll soon see. We've tapped into some lateral subsurface ice deposits. The ice-to-rock ratio is poor so far, but it improves with every meter we mine. Excess heat from the *Pegasus* slowly melts the ice, thereby solving two of our biggest problems at the same time."

Anna found this revelation alarming. "But what about the risk of contamination? The ice might contain dormant life forms! Or we might contaminate the subsurface with our own Earthly microbes!"

Mo sought to allay her fears, though he agreed they urgently needed her advice in these important matters. His crew had been drinking filtered Mars water for almost a year with no ill side effects. Thus far, no native organisms had ever been detected, but they lacked the equipment for a thorough screening. To minimize their own contamination of Mars, they irradiated all solid and liquid waste products on the surface.

She continued to ask more questions while they waited. Soon, the cleansing flood stopped. Mo moved to the back of the rover and grabbed a space suit bubble helmet from a shelf. He asked the others to put their suits on.

"Ours don't work," said Evelyn. "Ollie sabotaged them."

"Oh yeah, I forgot." Mo paused, and then shook his head. "You shouldn't need them. The garage is pressurized with pure oxygen, just like the rover. Wearing space suits inside the garage is a safety precaution that we can waive this one time. Follow me, but be quick."

He opened the back door of the rover and stepped through. Anna followed, carrying her nonfunctional suit. As she stepped to the ground and darted toward the inviting hatch of an airlock a few feet away, Evelyn closed the rover door behind them.

Once they were inside the airlock with the outer door closed, Mo increased the air pressure by adding nitrogen as a buffer gas. Anna's ears popped several times. The inner door opened, and they stepped through.

She was in a small, dimly lit cave about five meters high and ten meters long. The walls and ceiling were made of featureless red rock. Her feet sank an inch into red gravel on the floor. The far end of the cave tapered down to a sandbag-filled point.

"I thought the cave would be bigger," said Anna. "And where's the *Pegasus*?"

"Through here." Mo crossed the cave and disappeared behind a wall of sandbags. In the poor lighting, Anna had failed to notice the opening. She and Evelyn followed Mo into a much larger cavern.

"Oh my."

Anna hadn't realized she had spoken aloud until Evelyn answered, "Oh my, indeed."

The huge cavernous expanse before them was also dimly lit. Its red walls were featureless again. Several terraced landings led down to a floor about twenty feet below their current level. The *Pegasus* sat innocuously off to one side of the lower level.

Several smaller caves branched off from this main cavern in every direction. Each appeared to be only about two meters across. A flash of reflected light near one of them immediately caught Anna's attention. A steady stream of water was trickling from it, accumulating in a pool near the base of the *Pegasus*.

"A swimming hole?" she asked.

"It could be used for that," chuckled Mo, "though its real purpose is merely to stabilize the temperature inside the cave. Fed by the River of Pegasus, the pool is part of our homegrown system to provide humidity and get rid of our excess heat.

Anna recalled another detail from the myth of Pegasus. Wherever the hooves of the mighty horse touched the soil, water gushed forth to form a life-giving spring.

"And the other side tunnels?"

"Your new classrooms," said Mo, winking. "We don't have any greenhouse pods, so we set aside volume for growing crops."

Anna shook her head. This would never work. Crops required sunlight in order to grow. The amount of solar energy needed to grow a tonne of vegetables was staggering.

On the other hand, underground crops were safe from solar flares and depressurization accidents. The environment could be closely monitored and controlled. She could also work amongst the plants without wearing a space suit as long as the carbon dioxide levels were low enough.

"We have a good supply of full spectrum greenhouse lights," said Mo. "However, we've lacked the energy to use them until now."

"Until now? Oh, the backup ERV."

Anna had discovered the ultimate fate of the second ERV. It was never needed for travel back to Earth or fuel generation. Via its solar panels, the ERV's real function was to provide excess energy for growing crops. Rather than storing an awesome amount of chemical energy in rocket fuel and releasing it in one explosive outburst, the energy would be released slowly over time, keeping them alive and helping them to establish a tenuous foothold on this new world.

"Wow, wait 'til David hears about all this!" Her friend would be overjoyed to learn the details of the new base. His happiest dreams had already come true, and he didn't even know it yet.

"No," said Evelyn firmly. "You can't tell him anything."

Mo agreed. "We're all dead, remember? Until we're ready to reveal the existence of this base to the public, he can't be contacted. If he's still alive, he's too exposed."

"But..." Anna couldn't think of any good "but" clause. They were right. Given the realities of Ollie's betrayal and their need for continued support from Earth, they couldn't risk the information getting into the wrong hands.

Yet, if David is still alive and he thinks I'm dead...

Fontaine will be free to seduce him. And there's nothing I can do about it.

Somehow, the thought of this unhappy prospect more than offset her joy at the wonders she had just seen. An instant cloud of depression settled over her. She would give up almost anything to share her new, miracle-filled life with David. Yet it was clearly impossible.

At least, for now. Perhaps David can change the situation back on Earth. That seems to be our only hope of ever being together.

CHAPTER 36
HORIZON

MarsDay 274, 5:03 p.m.
(August 29, 2:00 p.m.)

"When are you coming back to me, David?" asked Skye, as she rested her head upon his right shoulder.

Under different circumstances, the afternoon would have been perfect. They sat on a shaded park bench beside Boulder Creek on the campus of the University of Colorado. The sky was free of clouds, winds were calm, and the temperature hovered near 90 degrees Fahrenheit.

With school recently back in session, dozens of college students sunbathed, jogged, and rafted nearby. Had he not been with the most beautiful woman he could imagine, more than one young coed might have caught David's well-trained bachelor eye. Perhaps that was even Skye's motivation for bringing him here today. If so, she failed, as all other attempts had failed. Very little had captured his interest for the past three weeks.

David sighed as he stroked her long, dark locks of hair. "I'm trying to be here with you," he said softly, "but part of me is trapped on Mars. I need to know how Anna died. I need that closure."

"Are you still having the dreams?" she asked.

"Worse than ever."

Since Anna's death, David's dreams had been nightmares filled with horrible images. Most often, he imagined Anna walking about the surface of Mars, desperately trying to locate the backup habitat until she ran out of oxygen. Her gentle face was twisted in gruesome agony as she struggled to breathe. Other times, she ran out of daylight first and groped about in the dark, always searching and fighting, until she froze to death or fell off a cliff.

He wondered whether her body could be recovered. Would he ever know what really happened during her final hours?

"David, she was trapped in the rover with no hope of escape," said Skye, gently. "Her space suit was sabotaged, and she couldn't have reached safety even if Ben had done what you wanted. You need to trust that her last hours were peaceful ones."

He fought down his usual surge of anger. They had repeated this conversation several times over the past week, almost word for word. Nothing had changed.

As a down payment on Skye's future silence, Ben had sent her a video confession containing Ollie's image and voice. In the confession, Ollie claimed to have removed the oxygen flow regulator from Anna's space suit. He also admitted to other unlikely acts of sabotage, like dumping anti-bacterial soap down the drain to damage the waste recycling system.

The message was obviously fake because there was no way Ben could have received it. David's Mission Support technicians verified a message was sent from the *Perseus* to the pressurized rover just before all contact was lost, but the buffered copy of the message was totally corrupted. If Ollie had sabotaged the rover, which David firmly believed, he had covered his tracks well.

Ben was obviously trying to hide his own complicity in Anna's death. Had he restored the locational beacon on the backup habitat, Anna and the commander might still be alive now.

Part of his anger was directed at Skye for going along with Ben's deceit. David had immediately warned her that the video confession was a forgery, but that hadn't stopped her from airing it on her network news program several times.

The story of sabotage spread throughout the media like wildfire. Ollie's claims of innocence were drowned out everywhere except on USNN, which blamed faulty hardware. The antagonistic nature of USNN's Mars coverage had never been so starkly visible to the masses before. A backlash of public anger began to descend upon the network.

After the media battle had played out for several days, Skye unleashed an atomic bomb. Somehow, she persuaded Ben to record a partial confession of his own, with a voice and video filter temporarily preserving his anonymity.

Ben confirmed Skye's earlier story about the sabotage of the three vehicles at the Medusae landing site, another fact that David knew to be false based on Ben's earlier admissions. He also admitted JPL's involvement in the off-course landing of the *Perseus*, sabotage that was purchased by USNN. The clincher was when she included the video segments from USNN's own programs as evidence, zooming in upon the bribery transaction in the background.

The SEA steering committee had quickly jumped onto the bandwagon as well. Despite David's recommendation to strongly deny the authenticity of Ollie's confession, they issued a press release stating they couldn't confirm or deny the recording. Their ambiguous response fueled the flames of controversy.

Coverage of the scandal continued to grow every day. Several top USNN executives were under pressure from advertisers to resign. Congress demanded a full investigation by the FBI. Political candidates like Jillian Greene claimed a share of the media coverage by attacking both sides of the issue as only politicians could do.

While David applauded the inevitable shakeup at USNN, he loathed the means by which it had come about. The whole media circus was based upon a lie. Ironically, though the original USNN story about faulty hardware was a lie, too, it was closer to the truth than the hype on the other networks.

Perhaps a better-designed rover might have saved Anna's life.
But probably not.

At least he had been able to keep his own hands clean, thus far. He had sent several messages to the entire support team emphasizing their need to concentrate on keeping the remaining crew member alive and returning him to Earth safely. If Beta had any hidden eyes and ears at Mission Support, he wanted them to know he was still "doing his job."

He considered Skye's words again, looking for some new way to express his feelings. She already knew of his decision to banish Ben from his life. He still wanted to see Cassie again, and he approved of her decision to return to her husband and give him a second chance, but David couldn't do the same. Ben's refusal to lift even a finger to help Anna find the backup habitat had hurt David deeply.

"I'll never trust Ben again," he said neutrally.

"I know," said Skye. "That's a shame. The two of you are on the same side of the issues."

David no longer believed the truth of her statement. Ben was working toward some other goal. Eventually, David would figure out what it was.

But Ben wasn't his greatest concern at the moment. Since he had been suspicious of USNN for so long, he couldn't believe how quickly their little empire had fallen apart.

"Skye, does it seem odd to you that USNN hasn't struck back a lot harder? At you, Ben, or the mission planners?"

Her head shot off his shoulder, and she looked at him with eyes aflame. He had struck a nerve. "What I've done recently hasn't been easy. They've fought me every step of the way. And I've been watching my back, very closely, as should you."

David shook his head and sought to placate her. "That's not what I meant. Let me phrase it this way. When Thomas offered me a $10 million bribe, he said it was almost an insult to the people funding his efforts. How many people at USNN earn $10 million for two years of work?"

She shrugged. "The CEO, certainly, and some of the directors. Maybe ten people, I'd guess."

"That's what I thought. For everyone else at USNN, $10 million is a lot of money."

"Well, sure. It's a lot more than I used to earn there," she said.

David held her gaze and waited for her to see his point. When she didn't respond, he stated, "USNN is a fall guy. They're being hung out on the line to dry. They're taking the heat for someone else, some other entity we still know almost nothing about."

Skye looked skeptical. "You're basing that conclusion solely on Thomas's single remark about money?"

"It takes cannon fodder to recognize cannon fodder," he chuckled, pinching her shoulder as he placed his arm around her again. "There are other reasons I'm suspicious, too. I can't find any motive for USNN's actions unless some other, far more powerful organization is involved."

"I thought their motive was to embarrass the other networks, claim prophecy rights, and generate advertising revenue. Wasn't that your original theory?" she asked.

"Yes, but how did they come up with the idea? Did a bunch of executives sit around a conference room three years ago and say, 'There's this Mars mission coming up soon. Let's sabotage it for ratings points.' No, it's far more likely someone else approached them with the idea. The mission was already going to be sabotaged before USNN got involved. They simply knew about it and took advantage of their inside knowledge, as any good executives would."

"So now you're saying USNN acted ethically?" She lightly pushed him away to show her disbelief before resting her head on his shoulder again.

"I wouldn't go that far. And I wouldn't presume to lecture you about media ethics. I only got a single crash course a few months ago from one of USNN's biggest advertisers. It would explain a lot, though. It would even fit what Ollie said in his video confession."

"I thought you didn't believe that confession."

"I don't. But Ben knew about Thomas's bribery comment, too, from listening to the playback on your bug. Perhaps that's where he got the idea. He wants people to believe there's a bigger enemy out there. Ben is devious, and he thinks ten moves ahead. Don't trust him, Skye."

She said, "So now you don't believe in another, bigger Beta organization? Which way is it going to be? Do they exist? Or don't they?"

"They exist," he stated firmly, "but Ben might be leading you in the wrong direction. When he faked Ollie's confession, he could point his finger at anyone he wanted. Notice he didn't include any traceable details to make the search too easy."

"So what are you saying, exactly?"

He paused. What was he saying, exactly? "Look, it's easy to believe that some powerful, faceless energy cartel would have the finances and the strong motive to sabotage the mission, but I'm not yet convinced it's true. The other evil spirit haunting my dreams has been the voice of the woman who was interrogating me. I know I've heard it before. Until I know her identity, motives, and ties to Beta, I'm going to be very skeptical of anything I hear from you, Ben, or USNN."

Skye nodded, and after a few moments, shrugged her shoulders again. "It's out of our hands now. I've given the FBI all of the information I've gathered thus far, including the other audio and video recordings I was holding back. They've talked to Ben, too. Allow them to do their job, and let's get back to living our own lives."

"Live with you in the today?"

"Yes," she pleaded. "Yesterday and tomorrow carry too much pain."

Smiling, he kissed her firmly on the lips. Never before had he longed so much for elusive closure with Anna's death. Perhaps Skye would help him to heal.

A tiny, persistent voice inside his head was still playing detective, however. Digesting her remarks about the FBI was difficult. He had become so suspicious of everyone and everything over the past year that he couldn't simply turn off his jaded sense of mistrust like a light switch.

What if the FBI is in league with Beta? Various politicians have opposed space exploration over the years. Most have been pretty quiet throughout the Mars mission.

Some might even want an excuse to embarrass a network or an energy cartel.

He sighed at the futility of his speculations and kissed Skye again, even as his inner voice continued to whisper.

MarsDay 285, 8:00 a.m.
(September 9, 11:58 a.m.)

"There you are, Anna. I knew you would be outside with your green friends," said the commander as she approached Anna in a large side cavern dedicated to growing crops. Or rather, Evelyn approached. Anna kept having to remind herself that Mo was the commander of this base.

Evelyn wore a space suit bubble helmet and thin counter-pressure suit, as did Anna. This side cavern was maintained at the same pressure as the main cavern, but the oxygen content in the air had been replaced with carbon dioxide. The greenhouse cavern was sealed from the larger oxygen-nitrogen cavern by a low-tech sheet of plastic with a zipper.

"Sh! Nobody's awake yet. My babies are still sleeping."

Yesterday, Anna had planted her first trays of vegetables in several side alcoves branching off from the main greenhouse cavern. Her experiments had shown no signs of growth yet because they lacked adequate sunlight. She planned to vary the amount of light and duration of "day" in each alcove. Each tray contained a variety of plants, soils, and nutrient mixes.

While setting up the lighting to meet her specifications, Zen Honda had thoroughly entertained her with his jokes, puns, and impersonations. Her new Japanese-American crewmate was a master of one-liners, as Evelyn had previously warned. He apparently relished having a new person around who hadn't heard any of his material yet.

Hopefully her plants had absorbed some of her laughter. They needed every advantage they could get. Other than special varieties of mushrooms that should thrive underground, the rest of her vegetables would have been much happier on the surface. She anticipated a long struggle to learn what environment-plant combinations would succeed the best.

Compared to her first attempts at growing vegetables back at the *Perseus*, her supply of nutrients was meager and her seed stocks were several years older. She also lacked the daily supervision of her army of botanical experts back on Earth. At least she had plenty of water and soil samples with greater potential than what she was trying to use before.

"It's eight o'clock," said Evelyn. "Zen is ready when you are."

Finally. Let there be light!

For the past several weeks, Evelyn and Wendy had labored on the surface to tow each component of the second ERV back to the base. They had successfully constructed a second grid of solar cells, doubling the energy resources of the base.

Meanwhile, Zen and Mo had wired Anna's cavern for electricity and established a steady water supply. Equipment was added to regulate the humidity and adjust the mix of gasses in the air. They also engineered what they hoped would be a good heat dissipation system. Though the high performance greenhouse lights output very little excess heat, temperature control was still Anna's greatest long-term concern.

After she contacted Zen with her suit communicator, daylight flooded the alcove. Anna was momentarily blinded until her eyes adjusted. She turned off her portable flashlight and inspected the greenhouse cavern in greater detail. It was far more vast than she had realized. She would have no shortage of floor space for growing crops, and her robotic helpers would be able to navigate quite easily. She planned to use a Robonaut for routine gardening, thus saving time and wear on her space suit.

"Is there anything else you need?" asked Evelyn. "Mo has placed me at your disposal."

With Evelyn's help, she moved some of the trays so they caught the available light better. After she was convinced each alcove was exactly as she wanted it to be, she signaled her approval to Evelyn, and the two of them left the greenhouse cavern.

In the main cavern, the lighting level was dimmer. Anna's eyes required a few moments to adjust again. While she waited, she removed her bubble helmet.

"What's next?" asked Evelyn, after removing her helmet too.

"Control systems. I've already configured some of the software. With your help, I could probably finish the job in half the time."

Evelyn promised to assist, and they walked back to the *Pegasus*. As they neared the pool, Anna stopped and turned to Evelyn. "There's something else I need. Something I've been wondering about for the past month. I guess...did you see the news dump this morning?"

Each morning, they had been tapping into the news transmissions from Earth. Evelyn confirmed she had seen the latest news, though she was puzzled by the reason for Anna's question. Yesterday had been a slow news day.

"Gil Bates died in a plane crash. Did you see that story?" Anna asked.

"Yes." Evelyn's look of confusion remained. "So what?"

Anna sat on a rock by the pool next to the *Pegasus*. "Do you realize that only a few years ago, he was one of the richest and most powerful people in the world?"

"In that other world," Evelyn corrected. "What does he have to do with us?"

"You told me about Cat's wonderful dreams for the future of humanity, but you didn't tell me who he is." Anna sought the right words to ask her questions. "Is he some rich or powerful person like Gil Bates used to be? And whoever he is, how has he been able to construct a mission to Mars when so many others couldn't even conceive it as being possible?"

Chuckling, Evelyn found her own rock to sit on. "I can try to explain, but it will take a while."

"My plants can wait for a few minutes. They aren't going anywhere." Anna had waited far too long to know the identity of the mission sponsors.

Evelyn's eyes glassed over as she entered "lecture" mode. "Gil Bates is irrelevant. He lived, died, and I certainly won't miss him. What lasting good did he do in his life? The wealthy elite back on Earth often define immortality based on what they have, rather than what they could achieve. This Mars mission is all about realizing humanity's unlimited potential. Compared to the infinite amount of wealth available to future generations, even the richest person alive today is a pauper."

"And what about Cat? Is he wealthy, too?"

Evelyn looked down at her feet and studied the ground. "No. But like Bates, Cat is a businessman too, first and foremost."

Anna was mildly surprised. She had never sensed much of a business mentality within the inner workings of the Mars mission. Other than recording virtual reality tours of Mars for consumption back on Earth, corporate demands had rarely intruded upon their mission.

"Cat," continued Evelyn, "saw a short-term, golden business opportunity for his company to corner the market on large-payload space launches. He convinced his colleagues to round out their product portfolio by pumping a few billion dollars into a partnership with a highly successful rocket manufacturer. The business model for the development of their RSX-1 rocket was driven by normal factors like market size, time to market, and anticipated market share."

"The RSX-1. The rocket we used to reach Mars."

Evelyn nodded. "That rocket was the real economic driver. I understand that NASA, the U.S. military, and various governments have already purchased twice as much in guaranteed launch contracts than it cost to research and build the rocket. If they can ever get the RSX-2 off the ground, the sales trend will skyrocket, no pun intended."

"They have no competition yet."

"Right. The profit margins for each launch are enormous. However, in order to jumpstart the juggernaut, they needed a showcase event."

"What do you mean by a showcase event?" asked Anna suspiciously.

"Our mission to Mars," confirmed Evelyn. "Think of it merely as a cheap publicity stunt, though it means so much more to Cat. It's how he sold the idea, at least. He got his company to secretly donate the launch costs. In doing so, they skirted several legalities."

The "cheap publicity stunt" remark didn't sit well with Anna. Frowning, she asked, "Won't shareholders eventually learn the truth?"

"Yes, and there will be hell to pay. Since their rocket program has been so successful, hopefully Cat's past, minor indiscretions will be viewed as 'effective leadership' and swept under the rug. Had the program failed, Cat and others in his company would have ended up in jail, probably in the same cell block as former Enron and MCI executives."

Connecting the dots, Anna came to two inescapable conclusions. She voiced the first one. "Cat must run the Raytronics Corporation!"

"No," said Evelyn. "Think smaller. He's only a middle manager in one of many internal divisions of that company. Hundreds of people in a dozen companies could have done what he did, had they only taken action. Remember, the tangible, immediate profit was in the rockets. Cat merely developed the idea and sold it to his superiors. Once they made the initial investment, the rest took care of itself. In fact, Cat's systems integration division did most of the work to develop our other equipment."

Anna's second conclusion fit nicely with Evelyn's last statement. "So that's why the media couldn't follow any paper trail of major expenses and transactions!"

"It was a classic case of the right hand paying the left hand, and the stupid media never figured it out," chuckled Evelyn. "Many reporters believed their own propaganda, blindly assuming that a human exploration mission to Mars was incredibly expensive. In their eyes, only a powerful, elite organization could afford it. They kept looking for external transactions from governments, major corporate cartels, or rich tycoons like Bates."

"Still, the initial investment must have been a huge sum of money," Anna speculated.

"Not really. Only a few billion dollars to develop the rocket, and a few billion more for systems research. Try to avoid a common mistake. Upfront R&D costs are one-time events, spread amongst many products and applications. Corporations make similar investments all the time, seeking a competitive advantage. Sometimes it works, and sometimes the cost is just written off. Regardless, most upfront costs shouldn't be included directly in the cost of our mission. Yet NASA, politicians, and the media often make that mistake, and it vastly inflates the numbers."

"I guess a few billion dollars of basic investment isn't much, to a large corporation," said Anna. "But what about the cost of all our equipment?"

"Look around you." Evelyn gestured toward the walls of the cave in which they sat. "Do you see a lot of money? I see a quarter-billion dollar habitat sitting over there, some mining equipment, two fancy rovers, and a bunch of miscellaneous systems and supplies. The total cost couldn't have topped a billion dollars. It was probably a lot less."

Anna got up from her rock and stretched. As she thought about Evelyn's disclosures, she guessed at some of the simple logic behind Cat's plan. He had used the non-profit SEA as a front, while keeping most of the money and control inside his own company. No doubt, the SEA would raise the cost of future missions, including launch costs. Cat's company had created a paying customer—one of many in a lucrative new market.

She scratched at her real hair. Her wigs had been banished to a drawer in her new quarters aboard the *Pegasus*. With no water restrictions at the new base and no media appearances in the near future, she was free to dress and groom herself any way she wanted.

"Thanks for sharing all this with me," she finally said. "It really helps me to accept my role here. I'm also more willing to believe Cat has some good incentives to hide for a while. Until the time is right, that jail cell awaits."

Evelyn agreed that Cat and his inner circle of collaborators had a lengthy list of their own concerns. They would continue to assist the Mars colony in any way possible, but they held no real power. They needed to work through others. "Their only place of real power," Evelyn added, "is within the virtual support center. Cat's systems division created it, and they run it, despite what Shepherd might think."

"Is David's job just another layer of deception?" asked Anna incredulously.

"Not entirely. But consider that Mo's team made it to Mars just fine and set up their base, all without any assistance from Shepherd or the official Mission Support team."

Anna sat again, puzzled. She asked, "How did they do it? Surely Mo needed some support along the way."

Evelyn's thin smile broke into a wide grin. "The real Mission Support team is concealed in a layer atop Shepherd's visible support center. We call the hidden layer 'Wonderland.' In the software world, this type of object inheritance hierarchy is quite common."

"Wonderland. Cute." Anna cracked a thin smile of her own.

"Cat's team did a good job of keeping Wonderland separate from the rest of the virtual world, but they made a few mistakes. For example, Shepherd found a shut telescope command and used it to enter one of our private meetings."

"Actually, I found that command and told him about it," Anna clarified.

"I see," said Evelyn, showing visible surprise and alarm. "Did you tell Ollie about it?"

"No. Only David. We were just poking around, trying to figure out how you were able to enter Conference Room 4."

Evelyn seemed greatly relieved. "Well, no matter, then. The function of the shut telescope command is to replace a base avatar with a derived avatar. It's a very powerful command. Consider it a bridge to Wonderland, or a rabbit hole, if you want to continue the illusion. Once you've run the command, there's a whole new support center for you to explore. Did you move around after you telescoped?"

"I only tried warping into Conference Room 4, and I failed because I didn't possess a key. I don't know if David tried anything else."

"We need to remove or restrict that command before he does," said Evelyn. "The security team might have forgotten about that loose end. And before you ask, yes, the entire security team is composed of trusted Wonderlanders."

"That figures," muttered Anna, shaking her head again. Thinking about the virtual world brought back many happy memories of interactions with David. "I wish I could access the support center again," she mused.

"Too dangerous," was Evelyn's immediate reply. "Mo maintains an occasional connection through his 'White Rabbit' avatar, but we need to be careful. We don't want our transmissions to be detected by any prying eyes. One of the top NASA-JPL telemetry technicians is a Wonderlander known as Chicken Little. In addition to his other talents like redirecting landers and retiring orbiters, he's managed to hide occasional connection sessions for us. Mo has met with Cat's team many times since their launch from Earth."

"And they meet in Conference Room 4, I assume?"

Evelyn nodded. "We were actually very lucky the first time Shepherd burst into our meeting there. I was already present. Mo was supposed to attend, too, but an issue here at the base delayed him. If David had seen a second ghostly avatar in the meeting, one he had never seen before, I wonder what he would have thought?"

Though Anna shared Evelyn's mirth, part of her also felt like crying. She wanted to tell David so many important things. Once again, she recalled their lengthy talks, schemes, and trading of ideas. She really missed him. Her sublime Martian sky contained only two gloomy storm clouds: David and Ollie.

Evelyn asked how Anna was adapting to life underground. The other four inhabitants of the *Pegasus Base* were couples who had known each other for years. Evelyn was quite concerned that Anna might feel like a "fifth wheel."

Anna shrugged off this concern. More than anything else, she now felt like she was part of an extended family. She had never been a very social person. Though she missed David fiercely, she would adapt, while continuing to work toward the day when somehow they could be together.

"I imagined you would be disappointed about other things, too, though," said Evelyn. "Like our lack of science equipment. Until the base is better established and equipped, the only research we'll be doing is related to crop growth. The hunt for Mars bugs and geological treasures will have to wait for awhile."

A splash in the pool made Anna jump. She heard soft laughter and turned to see Zen and Wendy standing nearby. They had snuck up from behind to pull their little prank.

"What's this talk about no treasure hunts?" asked Zen. He twisted his face into an exaggerated frown. "I want my ticket refunded!"

"It's a little late for that, dear husband," drawled Wendy. "But don't worry. I'm sure she wasn't talking about our alternative energy research. Just keep reciting your mantra. Necessity is the mother of all invention."

Wendy liked to project a "southern belle" image in her casual speech, though Anna wasn't fooled for a moment. Her voice lost all trace of its accent whenever she was seriously discussing an important matter.

Over the past month, Wendy had taken Anna under her wing. Her new friend had undertaken a personal mission to make sure Anna was as comfortable and happy as possible in her new home. They had shared a lot of "girl time," even though Wendy was many years her senior.

On several evenings, after the men had gone to sleep, Wendy and Evelyn had stayed up late to visit with Anna. As they drank tea and chatted about Navy life, Anna recalled similar discussions of exotic destinations with Ollie. These women had traveled extensively and were eager to share their memories with her.

Yes, life is good here. Challenging, but good. I like my new family.

Zen and Wendy launched into an impromptu comedy routine about energy research. They speculated Mars would soon be exporting advanced hydrothermal and fusion technology back to Earth in exchange for wood to burn in campfires. They also speculated about poor Ollie, trapped in the *Perseus*—an agent of a powerful energy cartel destined to go insane because he was stranded on a planet with no fossil fuels. Before long, Anna was laughing so hard she thought she might rip her space suit liner.

Soon, the discussion turned to more serious matters, and the group became more subdued. Wendy revealed that some of her medicines were aging and would soon need to be replaced. The engineers compared their notes about various technical problems aboard the *Pegasus*, which was also showing its age, as well as its more primitive design. Their space suits were wearing out, and the added strain of supporting two new people worsened other, similar concerns.

"We're going to need the supplies at the *Perseus*," Zen summarized gravely. "And that's the biggest problem of all."

As he spoke, a Robonaut approached, and Mo's voice greeted them. He was obviously controlling the machine from the *Pegasus*.

The first-generation Robonauts were far more primitive than the ones Anna had used during her first three months on Mars. They lacked feet, legs, and torso stabilizers. Rather than walking, they rolled about on treads. Fewer automated tasks were preprogrammed, and breakdowns were more frequent. The controller equipment was also less advanced, so the movements of the robots were sometimes jerky and uncoordinated.

"Get back to work, you lazy deckhands!" Mo gibed.

"We are working," said Evelyn in response. "Working up to a daring plan. I propose we organize a little raiding party and pay Ollie a visit."

"I'll consider that," Mo said, "if you can come up with a way to approach the *Perseus* and enter invisibly, move about inside without his knowing, and retreat without leaving any traces."

"I hear a challenge!" Zen uttered, gleefully.

The engineers immediately launched into an animated discussion, trading the craziest of ideas.

Anna left the group to work on her greenhouse control programs. She had every confidence that these amazing people would solve the impossible task, and all other challenges to come their way. Their solutions would be uniquely Martian ones.

To be continued...

Printed in the United States
26421LVS00003B/73